SOLOMON'S BLUES

JOSEPHINE GARNER

Copyright © 2011 Josephine Garner
All Rights Reserved.

ISBN: 1461106311
ISBN-13: 9781461106319

Acknowledgements

I am grateful to the friends and family who guided, informed, and encouraged this book, most especially: David Johnson, Daniel Fernando, Dorotha Hall, Rose Marshall, and Lumbé Davis. I am also thankful for my grandmother, Robbie Hardeman, and my aunt, Katie Garner, and my own *Grampa*, Sam Slaughter, who blessed me with their lives and inspired this story. And as always promised: to God, and to Rosie.

*For now we see through a glass, darkly;
but then face to face: now I know in part;
but then shall I know even as also I am known.*

1st Corinthians 13:12

PART ONE

I

I took out the tube of Aunt Grace's lipstick and quickly applied a coat to my lips. Although it was dark and I could barely see my reflection in Mandy's compact mirror, I knew I needed to spruce-up my plain brown face. It was Saturday night, and the thump-thump-thump of the music could be heard and felt all the way outside. The crowd was in both places too, outside and in, standing around in the yard, dotting the porch, crowding the dance floor. There was almost as much laughter as music. Ray's was jumpin'. Vehicles in various shapes and sizes were haphazardly parked all around. Mandy eased her father's old Ford into a tight parking space behind somebody's new pick-up truck while I concentrated on how I looked.

"Is my lipstick okay?" I asked her.

"You got some on your teeth," Mandy said peering at me. "Why didn't you put it on in the house where you could see?"

"Because Grampa could see it too. You know how he is."

"You's a grown woman, Esther Fay. Don't act like a chile."

"I'll always be one to him."

"That's left up to you. Put a little powder on. I can see yo' face shinin' like new money even in the dark."

I did as I was told and fussed with my hair too. Having done my best to dress up, I still felt like sackcloth compared to Mandy's satin, but I had pressed and curled my hair for tonight like it was Easter Sunday anyway, and in a way it was kind of a resurrection. This was my first night out on the town since coming home more than year ago. Mama had been dead for almost six months and in the time since her death all I had done was go to church and see after Grampa. Everybody said it was time for me to have fun again; even Grampa said it, although he didn't think I should be going to Ray's to do it.

Ray's was a colored juke-joint, situated just across the boundary line of McConnell County where it was legal to sell liquor, so it was not a respectable place for good Baptists. During the week the establishment was a place to get delicious barbeque, and even the good Christians often came in to buy it, the white folks too, although none of them would eat it at one of Ray's rickety tables, even outside. On Saturday nights, Ray Davis, the owner and proprietor, kept barbequing, but the pool table was carried out to the shed so that there was plenty of room for dancing. Some nights, like tonight, there might even be a band, but always there was the giant jukebox full of records for the steady flow of nickels and dimes the shameless patrons supplied. Everybody said that if you wanted a better time you had to go clear to Dallas, more than fifty miles west on Route 80.

I closed Mandy's compact mirror and put it back into her pocketbook. In any case, Mandy would see to it that I got to dance too. She had enough suitors so eager to please her that she could share them with me. It was the way it had always been for us, my brief time in the land of urban sophistication notwithstanding. I was once more a loyal lady-in-waiting to a princess, a faithful protégée as a 19th Century novelist might have put it, fortunate to bask in a best-friend's brightness.

Mandy's brightness hadn't paled at all, despite her having four children and a determined fidelity to a husband who had abandoned her. She had lost none of her allure. She still swung her hips when she walked, and some man's eye was always gazing at her. And here I was again, watching her manage male attentions like she managed her life, simply and smartly, letting nothing defeat her, even that which hurt her deeply. I admired her for it.

But Grampa felt about Mandy like he felt about me wearing lipstick. In his eyes she wasn't *fallen* exactly, but she had been *left*, cast-off, children and all; and Grampa, like a lot of people, blamed Mandy for it, even though it was Willie Gaines who had done the leaving, going to California in search of a better life, and swearing to send for his family once he had found it.

There was nothing especially strange about a poor man leaving a country town to look for better prospects. During the Depression many people had done it, colored and white. Uncle Eddie and Aunt Grace had left, and later Grampa and Mama had sent Jimmy, my brother, to live with them. Grampa might have gone himself if he had not been blessed with a job as a railroad porter, and even still he had been rarely home while his children were growing up.

Willie did call, and he wrote a few letters, even wired a little money sometimes, but his family was waiting. There was talk that Mandy had been divorced, and some folks resumed the gossip that she was loose, but I knew better. There was no way

Mandy was ready to let go of being *Mrs. Willie Gaines*. She was patiently waiting on her husband to come back for her and their children. She just wasn't going to be sad while she did it. And at least Willie could come back.

Mandy worked hard and she had a happy home. Her children called me, *Aunt Esther*, and I was proud of it. I took them to church on Sundays and helped them with their lessons. Mandy put flesh on Grampa's way of thinking about hard times, how they could be a blessing to make you stronger; if they didn't kill you first, as they had done to Mama. Maybe someday I would have Mandy's grace. In the meantime, since my return to McConnell County, I shared her lot, and I counted it my good fortune that we were still as close as sisters.

Once upon a time in my childhood imaginings of the perfect world, my cousin Nathaniel had been Mandy's husband, making her a part of our family officially, inscribing her name forever in Grampa's big Bible next to Nathaniel's, enshrining her pretty face upon Grampa's front room wall. But that was all a long time ago. Day-dreams had been overcome by reality.

"You sure I look all right?" I asked Mandy as we got out of the car.

"You look fine," she replied. "This ain't the Savoy, you know."

Picture it, Esther. Me and you, at the Savoy! We'll show 'em how it's done!

But Jimmy would never take me to the Savoy. The war had seen to that. Instead I had had to beg Aunt Grace and Uncle Eddie to introduce me to the sparkling glamour and fabulous orchestras that Jimmy had talked about as he had detailed his plans for a life for us in the Promise Land that was supposed to be Harlem.

Uncle Eddie and Aunt Grace would only take me to the Savoy the one time, because even though they had become AME since moving up North, and could respectably take a little wine or champagne from time to time, they still had their limits. Jimmy had been a young man, expected to be a little wild until he finally settled down with *a good woman*, the kind of woman I was expected to be. *Good women* did not go to nightclubs. All that twisting, and swinging and sweating, all those *happy feet* that the Savoy was so famous for, wasn't dignified enough for my aunt and uncle's social set. Yet Jimmy had wanted it for me, and so I had wanted it. It was as if by seeking after every footstep that he had made I could somehow keep close behind him. Uncle Eddie had enlisted one of the young men who worked for him at the post office to escort me that one time; but all evening I had tried to absorb the scene through my brother's eyes *picturing* him as he must have been, so very fine-looking, and charming all the beautiful women with his irresistible style.

"Wait for me, Mandy," I called, walking after my friend as best I could, balancing on the balls of my feet so my heels wouldn't sink into the ground.

Even in colored Harlem there were concrete sidewalks.

"Well hurry up then," she tossed over her shoulder.

She made it look so easy. The way she strutted in her high heels you'd never know that she had been on her feet all day keeping another woman's house. Now that Mama was dead, I had started to do a little day-work too. Like Mandy, I was a domestic, a maid, wearing Mama's black dresses for my uniforms, and turning into just another *Beulah*, while Mandy always carried herself like Suzette Harbin in the *Foxes of Harrow*. I was sure even her white mistress was a little in awe of her.

Grampa hated that I was taking work in white people's houses. He had forbidden Ernestine, his wife and our grandmother, to do so no matter how hard times were. Maid-work was beneath his plans for me and contrary to Jimmy's legacy, and he didn't trust white people. But Grampa was the one who had made me come back to a place where I couldn't do any better.

> ...Doctor Mitchell say yo mama got the canser. It done gone to far for him to help her. She need you. Come home. Not nothin left to do but the waitin...

Not nothin' left to do but the waitin'.

And keeping a white woman's house was much easier than keeping Mama's sickroom. I didn't care about strangers. I didn't expect them to care about me. If they didn't eat what I cooked and rejected me it didn't matter. The worse they could do was fire me with a harsh word and a bad reference. Grampa had a pension. Aunt Grace and Uncle Eddie wanted me to come back. In a white woman's house I had some kind of say about being there. Not like in Mama's sickroom.

As Mandy and I came up the brick-paved path leading to Ray's open door, the crowd collected outside seemed to part for us—for Mandy anyway. There were glimpses of envy in the women's faces. The men were all smiling.

"Hey, Mis' Mandy, *you sho' lookin' good tonight.*"

"*When you gon' let me come see you?*"

"*You better save me a dance Mis' Lady.*"

"Y'all 'member Esther Allen, don't you?" Mandy replied to them all, catching my hand, pulling me in front of her, pushing me up the wooden steps onto the porch and into smoky light.

"You Nathaniel Green's first cousin, ain't you?" someone asked.

I nodded.

"That boy sho' can fix cars," someone else said.

"That's right," Mandy said behind me. "And if you want to do some real dancin' you best get with her. She been stompin' at the Savoy in New York City. Which one of you country boys can say that?"

My face was hot with embarrassment and I looked down. I barely knew the latest dances, and it was Mandy herself who taught them to me in her front room to music from the radio, the way Grampa and Jimmy had done when I was little girl.

"I can say it," announced another male voice.

When I looked up Danny Simmons was standing in front of me. My first thought was that Mandy had not done him justice when she had described him to me. He was dashing in his crisp khaki uniform, so tall and straight that he looked out of place with a barbeque juke-joint for a back-drop. I had never seen Jimmy in person wearing his uniform, and now there was only the regulation dress photograph hanging in Grampa's front room next to the one of Ernestine, and I hated it.

"Ain't nobody studyin' 'bout you, Danny Simmons," Mandy said next to me.

"Well now, Cousin Mandy, you did pose the question," he returned in a smooth baritone that Sister Wright would have prized in her choir.

"Esther," said Mandy dismissively. "This here my big talkin' cousin Danny Simmons. Danny, this Esther."

"Corporal Danny Simmons, ma'am," the war-bond-poster figure said gravely. "At your service."

Bowing slightly he brought my hand to his lips, kissing it. A woman in the crowd went *Oooh-wee,* while somebody else laughed. This hand had changed Mama's soiled diapers I thought as I felt his warm lips brush against my skin. Now it scrubbed white women's floors. Fortunately I had slathered on plenty of Jergens lotion before getting dressed for the evening.

"Pleased to meet you," I said shyly smiling, embarrassed by the gesture.

"Me too," Danny said, deftly pulling me closer and hooking his arm with mine. "My cousin didn't say how pretty you was."

"She didn't say you were a corporal either," I replied self-consciously.

"That's not how you fix-up a blind date, Cousin," Danny said to Mandy as he led me inside to a table, with Mandy following us.

"Who said I was fixin' you up?" Mandy shot back. "I just said you was in town and that we was comin' here tonight."

Mandy scooted into one side of the booth and I started to slide in next to her, but Danny stopped me.

"Y'all not fixin' to court martial me are you?" he asked.

"You just be sho' not to give us a reason to," Mandy answered. "He wants you to sit on the other side, Esther, so he can sit next to you."

Giggling a little I complied. Johnny Samples walked up to the table.

"Can I get that dance now, Mis' Mandy, 'fo' you get tired-out?" he asked respectfully.

"I don't know what you talkin' about Johnny Samples," Mandy replied getting out of the booth. "I don't get tired-out."

"That's right, please give her something to do so a man can have some peace," teased Danny.

"What kind of soldier lookin' for peace?" Mandy quipped as she fell into the rhythm of the blues being played by the band.

"The smart one," I said darkly.

Danny slid into the booth next to me. I scooted over closer to the wall.

"Who you pinin' for, Miss Esther?" Danny asked looking into my face.

I shook my head and smiled again.

"Mandy did say that you can be too smart for your own good," I changed the subject.

"What else she say about me?" asked Danny.

I laughed.

He had a neatly trimmed mustache above his pleasing pink lips, and his black hair was wavy-smooth, curling at the nape of his neck, reminding me of Jimmy. Grampa might have had the same kind of hair once too, but for as far back as I could remember he had been bald, with just a little incomplete rim of gray around his head that he kept cut close.

"Wouldn't you like to know?" I asked.

"Gonna work on you tellin' me too," he replied suavely.

And so he did. Every chance he got. For the little while we were together. Danny was on his way to San Antonio, to Fort Sam Houston, and expecting to end up in Korea. Things—I couldn't call it a courtship—moved quickly.

McConnell County was not the place for him Danny said. What had happened to George Dorsey and Roger Malcolm and their wives in '46, in Georgia, made the South *enemy territory* to him. I was surprised that the story was still so fresh in his mind. Maybe it was because he had lived in Chicago since he was a boy and wasn't use to this kind of trouble. Maybe it was because George Dorsey had been a veteran.

"A Negro man's better off shootin' at gooks than bein' shot at by crackers," Danny said.

Jimmy had shot at Germans and Italians, having joined-up in '41, right after Pearl Harbor, like all the other American men eager for revenge.

"You can get away from Jim Crow overseas," Danny explained as we sat together on Grampa's front porch swing one summer night.

As it had become clear that Jimmy was too smart for McConnell County's cotton fields and too self-confident for McConnell County's colored place, Grampa, with Mama's blessing, had sent him live with Aunt Grace and Uncle Eddie in 1939. Our uncle and aunt had done well for themselves *up North*, and Uncle Eddie's position as a supervisor, at one of the Harlem post offices, made possible their middle-class Harlem address and rising social status. Their immaculately-kept brownstone was far away from Grampa's tiny three bedroom house that even in 1950 still didn't have an indoor bathroom. You might never know that Aunt Grace was the daughter of a railroad porter. Poor Uncle Eddie had to sneak away to the Blue Bell Café on Lennox Avenue to get himself a mess of chitlins when he craved them, because Aunt Grace wouldn't cook them for him for fear that their smell would cling to her satin drapes and plush upholstery.

Jimmy was the one who was supposed to go to college, because Grampa, who was usually disdainful of men with *desk-man's hands*, as he put it, had decided that Jimmy should be a teacher. "He could be one of them head-men at a colored college," Grampa had affirmed. "I seen 'em on the trains," he had said. "They carry theyself like a white man. In a coat and tie ev'ry day."

> *"I promise you, Baby Sister," Jimmy declared as I watched him pack his valise for the trip to Harlem. "As soon as I get settled I'm sending for you. You ought to go to college too. Who knows? Maybe we can come back down here and open us up a school of our own. Yeah, I can see that," he said thoughtfully. "Be a real fine school too. I bet the white folks'll want to come to it."*
>
> *"We can do without them," I replied.*
>
> *Jimmy laughed, buckling the suitcase closed.*
>
> *"You soundin' more and more like Grampa every day," he teased. "I gotta hurry up and get you away from here."*
>
> *"Grampa's right about a lot of things, Jimmy."*
>
> *"Think for yo'self, Baby Sister," he replied, using his thumb to smooth out a frown on my forehead. "Every tub's gotta sit on its own bottom."*

But Jimmy had never needed a piece of paper to give him confidence. He had always carried himself with obvious self-assurance, as if it never occurred to him that anyone could consider him second-class. Such deportment might be fine in the sanctuary that was Harlem or even the anonymity that was the rest of New York, but it was dangerous in McConnell County. *Up North*, according to everyone, Jimmy could have the chance that his talents deserved. "The way ol' Roosevelt's been openin' things up for colored folk," Uncle Eddie had assured us, "A colored man can go far." But the war came.

"You talk like my brother," I replied to Danny as the crickets chirped in the hot darkness.

"I'm sorry he didn't make it back," Danny said.

The Secretary of War deeply regrets...

Everybody was sorry, full of regret and grief, but it didn't make a difference.

"They left him France," I said. "So much for all that *Double-V* talk."

"He's buried with his comrades, Esther."

"His mama and daddy are buried here. They are his people."

"Those other men were his people too."

"America's sons one and all, that what you sayin'?"

"Somethin' like that."

> ...It'll be nice to get home again, but what we're doing is really important, Baby Sister. I wish you could have seen the way they cheered for us in France. All of us Esther, the Negro soldiers too. We're changing the world. Things will be different once this is over...

"You really believe in all of that, Danny? I know they made you swear to it, but you don't really believe it, do you?"

"Things are better, Esther," Danny said, easing his arm around my shoulders. "We not there yet. We got a long way to go," he smiled a little. "But we did get us Jackie Robinson."

"You think that's what Rube Foster wanted? Coloreds and whites playing ball together, just so somebody as great as Satchel Paige could be a rookie for the Cleveland Indians?"

"What you know about Rube Foster?" Danny grinned.

"I know plenty," I answered him.

"I just bet you do."

"I'm serious, Corporal Simmons," I said sternly.

Unexpectedly he kissed me on the lips. Gasping I pushed him away.

"Danny!" I cried softly. "My grandfather'll be watchin'!"

But I was smiling too.

Because Danny made me think of love, of love not lost but possible, of love alive. His smoky way of looking at me stirred up the butterflies in my stomach, even if he was just passing through, as Mandy felt obliged to keep reminding me, as if I would forget it, as if Grampa would let me.

"Seem like to me all that smooth talkin' he puttin' down done turned yo' head," Grampa had already warned. "But he don't mean nothin' by it. I bet he got a woman in ev'ry town from here to Chicago. Prob'ly done left one or two of 'em with a big belly too."

"We're just friends, Grampa. That's all," I had replied. "We're just havin' a good time."

"Don't let that good time take yo' good name and leave you with bad trouble."

And if it did, I knew Grampa would be right there for the both of us, just as he had been for us when Daddy died. He would fuss and fume, but all the while he would be cradling that great-grandchild tenderly in the same strong arms that had cradled me.

"Don't worry," I had told him.

"Got to," he had replied. "All that learnin' in college you done ain't taught you nothin' 'bout a man."

> *"Mandy's gettin' married," I announced over supper.*
>
> *"Well, well," said Mama, spooning collards into Jimmy's plate before passing it to him. "Willie Gaines gon' do right by her after all, tell me somethin'."*
>
> *"'Bout time too," added Grampa, breaking up a piece of cornbread into his greens. "She's a hot lil' thing."*
>
> *"Willie loves her," I said defensively for my friend's sake. "He's lucky she'll have him."*
>
> *"All young gals is hot," pronounced Mama. "Ain't got sense enough not to be."*
>
> *"Esther's pretty cool though," said Jimmy grinning at me. "You ain't got to worry 'bout her. A man'll never have her whole heart."*
>
> *"Humph," replied Grampa. "Ain't seen a woman yet who couldn't have her head turned."*

"I'm not a child, Grampa."

"Bein' old don't make you wise, Esther Fay."

But experience did. And I had had my share of it. Try as he might, Grampa had not been able to protect me from everything, or maybe even most things, but he had done his best. "A colored girl's got a hard row to hoe," Grampa had once told Mama about me when I was growing up. "She better be strong." Hard times made you that way.

And I was supposed to think for myself, Jimmy had said. And that meant thinking about Danny. About how his breath was warm and pleasurable in my face, smelling of peppermint candy, and whiskey sometimes when we went to Ray's. On the dance floor he would press his manhood against me, as the music filled my head, and I could feel myself awakening and wanting him in a way that felt like nature. His voice, murmuring into my ear, ran through me like electricity in my blood. My dark brown body conformed to his embrace as if it were destined to, because in his smoldering eyes it was desirable.

Yet I wasn't forgetting myself. With Jimmy gone, Grampa had decided that I should be the teacher. Jimmy and I wouldn't be having our school but I had inherited his legacy. So after the war, I had been sent to live with Aunt Grace and Uncle Eddie.

I had done pretty well for myself too, enrolling in City College and earning good enough grades to impress the professors and satisfy my family. The same day that Grampa's letter had arrived about Mama being sick, Dean Bloom had offered me a tutorage in the English Department.

Now that Mama was dead, everyone expected me to just start living again, to pick-up where Jimmy had left off. *Thinking for myself*, maybe Danny was the way to start doing that. To start living. He was decent, and as the end of our time together approached, desires loomed larger and larger, weighing down our afternoons and evenings with hesitancy and anticipation. He was *just passing through* on his way to places even he didn't know, and I expected nothing from him, knowing I would probably never see him again. But my body protested being kept down and denied for the sake of a *good name*. I liked him, and what if no one ever wanted me this urgently again? I was getting older, passing my prime, and with little to show for myself but inherited incomplete aspirations, sickrooms, and sadness. What if waiting was a waste?

On the evening before Danny was to leave for San Antonio, he borrowed Mandy's father's old Ford and we went for a long drive to nowhere in particular. Feelings filled up the car and we hardly talked. Somewhere along the road Danny pulled off and parked the car in a clump of trees. He turned off the engine, turned to me, and pulled me into his arms. I didn't resist as he covered my mouth with his and I tasted the familiar welcomed sweetness of peppermint.

"Ain't gonna be easy for me to leave tomorrow," Danny said, holding me tightly. "You make it pretty hard."

I thought about what Grampa had said about him having a woman in every town and wondered if he had said the same things to them. It didn't matter if he had, the words sounded nice.

"You make a fine soldier, Danny Simmons," I said, pulling back to look at him. "Just take care of yourself doin' it. Don't die for this country."

He smiled.

"When you goin' back to New York?" he asked.

It was the question that everybody asked me, and it made me anxious because I couldn't give the right answer, the one that showed my life was back on the track that had been laid before me. Ambivalent, I told myself, and others, although never Grampa, that I was staying because I did not want to leave Grampa alone. He had been through so much I explained. Losing a child was not the natural order of things, and seeing that child suffer the way Mama had done, made it that much harder to bear. I was staying because I wanted to look after him for a while, I said. He deserved that.

"I was thinking about next year," I told Danny now. "When the fall semester starts."

"That's a long time," he replied. "What you waitin' on?"

"School costs money, Danny. I'm working to save up."

"Your uncle doin' pretty good. They can help you like before."

"I want to do it on my own this time. They'll let me live with them. That's help enough."

Danny smiled again.

"That's what I like about you, Esther Fay Allen. You're your own woman."

"Every tub has to sit on its own bottom my grandfather always says," I told him, once again wrapped in his arms.

"That's true," agreed Danny. "'Course in the army, a man learns to depend on his buddies. You can get yourself killed pretty fast goin' it on your own."

"You look at everything that way, Danny? Like it's war?"

"Pretty much," he smiled a little ironically. "Guess that's why the Army suits me." He kissed me. "But then you suit me too."

It was better to marry than to burn the Bible said. My family would not be pleased that Danny could make me no promises; that he was *just passing through*. But the *burning* felt alive and it was good remembering that I was. As we lay together in the backseat of the car, Danny told me I was beautiful, and I let him undress me.

"I want to get close to you, Esther," he whispered through his kisses. "You gon' let me?"

Yes. But my head wasn't *turned*. My heart wasn't his. It wasn't a Jane Austen novel, but then *we* didn't show-up in *their* stories. *Front-rooms* were not drawing rooms. And Ray's had no ballroom, just a well-worn wooden dance floor, smoothed down by a people who still knew how to have *happy feet* even in the backwoods of McConnell County.

I danced with Danny because he was real. He was living and here. His body was hard and strong and hungry for mine. He was *just passing through,* like a train in the night, but he reminded me that there were other places to go. A dying mother had forced me to back to *Egypt-land*, but I might get away again. I might find some other place to sit my tub, a place where it might not matter so much that it wasn't made of porcelain.

And besides, Danny Simmons was another colored soldier who could end up buried far away, leaving his people with only a memory to mourn over. He ought to have what he wanted. For the sake of all the colored soldiers who had died fighting for the dream of America, I ought to give it to him.

Some time long past midnight Danny brought me home. Grampa was waiting up for me as he usually did, sitting in his rocking chair.

"You got the smell of a man on you," he said as if he instantly knew what had happened.

"Yes-sir, I do," I replied honestly. "But I am a woman."

By late September the summer was winding down. I settled myself on a church pew next to an open window, and laid aside the dust-rag that smelled of the linseed oil that I had been using to polish the wood in the sanctuary. The heat was beginning its inevitable departure, carried away on the cooling breezes that now drifted across my face. Already I anticipated cold winter evenings warmed up by the wood burning in Grampa's ancient stove. Aunt Betty and Uncle Perry continued to insist that Grampa get a gas heater, but he refused, and truth be told I liked the way the burning wood smelled even if it did yellow the wallpaper.

But it wasn't winter yet, and the work-scarf tied around my head was damp with perspiration. As usual, I was fulfilling my weekly obligations to the Lord, and to Sister Callie, by cleaning up the church house. I had been doing this since I was a child, as a helper to Sister Callie. After Mama died I had had time on my hands so I had returned to being Sister Callie's helper. "You always was one of de fait'ful ones," she had welcomed me back to our Saturday vocation, her few remaining snuff-stained teeth showing in a big smile.

When Sister Callie had suddenly died too, the Sweet Water congregation had paid for her plain pine box and placed her between her husband and her son, something we had not been able to do for Mama with Jimmy left behind in Epinal, France. There had not been money enough to buy Sister Callie a headstone, but as it turned out nature had looked after her anyway, and her resting place was now smooth and green with lush grass, and Indian Paint Brushes grew of their own volition over her head. The task of cleaning the church had become mine alone, and I preferred it this way.

If there had been a headstone it should have read, *Sister Callie not mad with nobody* because people had always said that about her. Stripped of all her family, and living in a house with a leaky roof and a sagging front porch, she had faithfully visited the sick, kept a bird feeder in her front yard, and given motherly love and teacakes to anyone stopping by. "Work with willin' hands, Esther Fay," she had often told me. "That's the Bible." A broken heart could not kill her. She had been a strong woman long before there were *Rosie the Riveter* posters to encourage us. Never in the church house, even to clean it, with her head uncovered, Sister Callie had worn her head-rag as if it were a crown, all the time humming blues songs like they were the gospels too. I liked to think of her here, looking down on me with satisfaction. Of course I'd get back to Jimmy's legacy one day, but for now at least I was keeping faithful to hers.

Like most Saturdays, Pastor Wright was gone before noon, and I now had the church all to myself. I liked being alone, or to myself anyway, keeping company with ghosts who were no less dear to me just because I couldn't see them anymore. After all, you couldn't see the Lord either and we loved Him. The *evidence of things not seen* could be clear if you waited. Sometimes there was nothing better to do than the waiting. The Bible said that to everything there was a season, including a time to be still.

I often thought about Danny although I didn't miss him. He had sent me a couple of post-cards, and I knew where to write to him, but my letters were almost as short as his post-cards. What was there to say beyond wishing each other well? The war in Korea was brutal but successful according to the newspapers and newsreels. Since Danny didn't write about it, I didn't either. Nathaniel said that a man couldn't always put his trouble into words, and Nathaniel still didn't talk too much about the last war. Sometimes, suddenly, like when a cloud moved across the face of the sun on an otherwise bright day, some memory of it would appear in his eyes, and if Connie, his wife, was there, she might touch him gently or make some comment, and the sun would shine clearly again. I might have been able to do that for Jimmy if he had needed it, and the war had not made him memory for which there was no comfort.

Of course if he had lived, Jimmy might have written a book about it, about the war and what it meant. He had always been a prolific letter writer starting back when he had first moved to Harlem. His war-time letters had been pages of descriptive prose filled with funny stories about his buddies, his brooding introspection, or his optimism about the future.

"Don't he write good," Mama had gushed.

"Ought to," Grampa had replied. "He a educated man, ain't he."

I was educated too, but you also had to have something to say, and I didn't really. Mostly when I wrote back to Danny, the single pages contained news about McConnell County and reports on Mandy's children.

"Hey in here!" a booming voice disturbed the private tranquility of the empty church. "Wake-up!" Laughing Nathaniel strode up the church-house center aisle. "Thought you was s'pose to be workin'."

"I am!" I answered, having jumped to my feet.

As always I was pleased to see him.

"Yeah, yeah. Look to me like you playin' Peter in the Garden and gettin' yo 'self a little nap."

"Don't be so smart!" I laughed over a tiny pang of guilt.

Nathaniel grinned. Such expressions came easily and richly to him, war or no war. And he did have a lot to smile about. He was thriving in McConnell County. His ambitions were simple. A family. A home. A living. He wasn't trying to change the world, but he seemed capable of doing it anyway, one person at a time.

By his own hands, Nathaniel was making himself. His were the kind of hands that Grampa understood best and respected most. As soon as he had come home from the war Nathaniel had begun turning a shade-tree mechanic operation into a successful business. Now, with Uncle Perry, his father, Grampa's only son, working with him, they owned and operated Green's Garage. Nathaniel was an esteemed business man and a church deacon, even if he did smell of motor oil and gasoline.

The Greens had accomplished much, considering where we had started. Grampa's father had been born a slave and had raised his family on a sharecropper's living. But Grampa had been Pullman Car porter, and now he was retired with a pension. Nathaniel his only surviving grandson had his own business. Two centuries later the Declaration of Independence was beginning to make sense to us.

Nathaniel and Uncle Perry could keep almost any vehicle performing like new. Even white people brought their cars, trucks, and tractors to them, and when the circumstances called for it, Nathaniel would go to them, so that you might see his old rusty pick-up truck parked at any prominent address. He wasn't *mad with nobody* either. He put people at ease, the colored ones as well as the white ones, without posing a threat or sacrificing his self-respect. The world was drawn to him, which he attributed to Jesus. Grampa was sure the Lord had His hand on him. "B'lieve to my soul," he would often say. "That boy gon' preach." To me he already did. The best sermons didn't always come from a pulpit.

If it had ever occurred to Grampa and Uncle Perry to send Nathaniel to Harlem, then wisely they had not done it. New York City did not suit him. The crowded narrow streets would have cramped and confined him with too much concrete and not enough sky.

"So did you want somethin', Nathaniel?" I demanded now, my hands on my hips. "Or did you just come in here to be in the way?"

Nathaniel dropped down on the front church pew on the left side of the sanctuary. The old wood creaked but received him. He had inherited a physique from Ernestine's side of the family, as I had. Grampa said that I reminded him of Ernestine, his wife and our grandmother. He said that I had her strong sturdy build. "A man can lean on you, Esther Fay," he would almost affectionately , meaning it as a compliment. After all he couldn't say that I was pretty because it wouldn't be true. I was tall for a woman, and my shoulders were too broad, my legs too muscular. When I was little, people had predicted that I was going to make a handsome woman someday, but of course women were supposed to be beautiful.

"I guess you do have it lookin' pretty good in here," Nathaniel was willing to say, while I fretted that the heels of his work boots would mar my meticulously mopped floor.

"Well thank-you very much," I replied.

He leaned back, leisurely folding his brawny arms behind his head.

"'Course since you been here all day, it should," he added, grinning again.

"Like I said," smiling back, "Do you want somethin'?"

"Don't sass' me, gal. You know I'm right. Hangin' 'round this church-house like you was one of them Cath'lic sisters or somethin'."

"And you got a problem with that?"

"Naw, I don't, but yo' grampa sho' do. Ain't you s'pose to be cookin' his supper?"

"Oh," I said chastened. "What time is it? Oh well. There's plenty of time."

"Um-hmm," Nathaniel took his pleasure in being right.

"You don't have to be so smug about it," I said.

"You just better be glad the ol' man sent me and didn't come hisself. You ain't too grown for a peach-tree switch you know."

I laughed.

"Well you better not ever try it!" I warned.

"You jokin'?" Nathaniel laughed too. "I figger that'd be 'bout like takin' on Joe Louis."

I laughed again, because he was right and maybe it was a compliment. Although the world wasn't asking women to be strong anymore. *Rosie the Riveter* had gone home to her husband and children. The movie screens and glamour magazines instructed us to be delicate to be desirable, to have little feet and soft hands, and soprano voices that spoke softly and sung sweetly.

"Are you tryin' to hurt my feelin's?" I pretended to be offended by Nathaniel's Joe Louis comment.

"What I'm tellin' you is that the ol' man says for you to get home," replied Nathaniel.

"All right. All right. Just give me a few more minutes to wipe down the back pews, and I'll be ready to go. I suppose you can wait for me, huh? Or would you make this heavy-weight contender ride her bicycle home?"

"The back pews?" protested Nathaniel. "Girl, them sinners' seats don't need no polish."

"'And the last shall be first,' Deacon Green," I reminded him, marching to the back of the church, rag and polish in hand. "That's the Bible."

Sweet Water was not a very large church, but it had prospered and had a good-sized congregation. On special Sundays, such as *Mother's Day* and *Easter*, the sanctuary could be packed to overflowing with the faithful and the familiar. By 1950 the deacons were debating the merits of putting in an indoor baptismal tank behind the choir stand, although I didn't want to see us give up the rituals associated with gathering at the edge of Johnson Creek to praise another soul's Christian redemption. There was something sacred about the sunlight in your eyes as the water flowed over you and ultimately washed your sins away to the ocean. However, according to other more influential members, Aunt Betty, Nathaniel's mother and Uncle Perry's wife, among them, and perhaps leading them too, outdoor baptisms were backwards. In Johnson Creek, they argued, people could take the pneumonia when it was cold, and in the summer there was the danger of snakes and polio. Aunt Betty's side saw an indoor tank as an outward sign of grace, a means of testifying to what God had done for us, and a symbol of success. We might have had the tank already were it not for Grampa, who as a senior member of the deacon board, was leading the resistance to progress.

Aunt Betty's *high-tone* tastes irritated Grampa, and privately he had complained to Mama that his son had made a mistake by marrying a *yella woman*. "She keep her hands in his britches' pockets," Grampa had fussed on more than one occasion. Aunt Betty did like to buy things, subscribing to fashion magazines and keeping up with the latest trends in her home and her wardrobe, but she wasn't selfish. She bought for others too, and she and Uncle Perry always paid their tithes. They even sponsored Christian missionaries in Africa. It was Aunt Betty who wanted Uncle Perry to have a hot-water heater installed in Grampa's house, so that we could finally get rid of the ritual of boiling and hauling water, and have a real bathroom, complete with a modern toilet too. But Grampa was content to do as we had always done, boiling bathwater on the stove, and carrying the chamber pot to the outhouse at the back of his land. Aunt Betty could have been as black as an iron skillet and she wouldn't have changed his mind. Besides Grampa was *yella* too, practically white. Poor Uncle Perry was haplessly caught between them.

"I think you need a real job," Nathaniel grumbled as he watched me complete my church-house chores.

"You get one for me and I'll do that too," I told him.

"You right sho' now?" Nathaniel wanted to know as I kept working. "You ready to put up some worldly treasure instead of all this heavenly gold?"

"I'm not changin' tires, if that's what you mean." I snapped. "I don't care how big and burly you think I am."

"What about keepin' house?"

"I can get my own day-work. Mandy's always-- "

"I'm talkin' 'bout somethin' steady. And pays good too."

I hesitated from the polishing and looked up at him.

"Who for?" I asked.

"Taylor Payne."

"Who's that?"

"Oh so you is interested, huh?"

"Nathaniel, are you bein' serious or what?"

"'Course I'm serious. If you want to be a maid, you might as well do it for some good money."

I resumed polishing the wood.

"As opposed to the glory of God, I suppose," I replied.

"You can cut Him in on the profits," Nathaniel joked. "About ten percent they tell me. I bet the good reverend would 'preciate it too. Prob'ly even more than you keepin' his pulpit waxed and shiny. No matter how good it looks."

Sister Callie had been pleased with me, and I hoped God was too. I wanted to be His *workman not ashamed* and didn't mind scrubbing and dusting, and washing the bright plastic flowers we used to decorate the elevated pulpit area where the preachers sat. I left no streaks on the windowpanes and no cobwebs in the corners. I kept the pastor's study neat, and the indoor toilet smelling of Lysol. On Sunday mornings I was just another voice in the choir, and a tenor at that, singing out from among the men, and an aesthetic nuisance to Sister Wright, the pastor's wife, church musician and choir director, but on Saturday afternoons I was the keeper of the temple. What if I was one of those Catholic sisters like Nathaniel said. It might not be so bad. Dark-skinned Cinderellas so seldom got a prince. Unless he was *just passing through*.

"Okay," I said to Nathaniel, "Leave Reverend Wright out of this, and tell me more about this job you got for me."

"In the truck," Nathaniel said firmly. "Grampa sent me over here to bring you home, and you know how he is. Ain't gon' have him hot with me too. You hurry up."

On the way home Nathaniel told me more about the man whose house I could keep clean for wages instead of grace. The man was a lawyer, who had lived in McConnell County when he was boy, until his mother and father were killed in a car wreck, and he and his little sister had moved back to Massachusetts to live with their uncle.

"Maybe you heard of 'em," Nathaniel continued as we rode along.

I shook my head.

"Well he moved back and he's lookin' for a housekeeper," continued Nathaniel. "Must-a done some askin' 'round for hisself and Doc Mitchell mentioned you to him. He says he gave you a good report."

We trusted Doctor Mitchell. He was a good doctor, who worked diligently for his patients, the colored ones too. He was the only white doctor in the county who would come to colored houses. That spoke to us of his compassion and made us loyal to him. He had done his best for Mama. Maybe the hospitals in New York City were better, but their doctors couldn't be. According to Nathaniel, Doctor Mitchell's opinion carried weight with the lawyer. It carried weight with me too.

"Anyway he asked me 'bout you again this mornin' when I was workin' on his car," Nathaniel was explaining. "Got a nice car too," he added. "One of them new sporty-lookin' Chevrolets. Drove it down here all by hisself, all the way from New York City. I told 'im you used to live Harlem. He say that's part of New York City too."

It was. The colored part. Even in Uncle Eddie and Aunt Grace's elegant house.

"He said you was to come and see 'im as soon as you can. If you interested that is," said Nathaniel.

It could be a good job. Nathaniel hadn't said anything about there being children which made it all the more promising. Cleaning up after grown folks was easier, and if it was steady I could finally save some money. I needed to finish school. And if this Mr. Payne was okay to work for, then maybe Mandy would want the job after me.

"I am," I answered Nathaniel. "You think they would be all right to work for?"

"Ain't no 'they'," replied Nathaniel. "It's just him. He a bachelor."

"Oh Lord," I sighed. "A contrary old bachelor that no woman can put up with, is that it? Sounds like Grampa."

"Then that makes you perfect for the job," replied Nathaniel.

We laughed.

"Maybe. I think your Mr. Payne needs himself a *Rochester* more than he does a *Beulah*. You know, a valet."

A *George* I thought, and imagined my proud grandfather enduring all those years on the trains.

"I think what he most wants is a good cook," said Nathaniel. "So you just make 'im some of those biscuits of yours and that'll get you a raise from the git-go."

I smiled at Nathaniel. My biscuit recipe was Grampa's, and the truth be told Grampa could make his own supper tonight. He didn't need me for that. When Mama was sick he had done almost all of the cooking. He just didn't like to anymore. Perhaps it was all those years of preparing meals for strangers, years of making their beds and shining their shoes, pressing their suits and carrying their bags, years of being called

George when his name was Isaac. He wanted to be cared for, and it was time for it, and I was glad to do it.

"So you think he'll be okay to work for?" I repeated my question.

"He treats me and Daddy right," replied Nathaniel. "I guess you could say I got a good feelin' 'bout 'im."

"Oh you have a good feeling about everybody, Nathaniel Green."

"Not everybody," Nathaniel said soberly. "I don't too much care for them hot-heads that come 'round the shop yesterday. I tell you a man that'll drink in the middle of the day ain't nothin' but a mess."

"Who are they?" I asked, reading my cousin's somber expression.

"Aw, just some nobodies. But I might mention it to the Sherriff though. I don't want no trouble." He smiled again.

"'Course you go to work for this here lawyer, we be in pretty good shape. He's one of them gov'ment lawyers, you know the ones that put folks away."

"Let's hope he's an honest one and not crooked," I said.

"I don't think we have to worry 'bout that," replied Nathaniel.

"Because you got a good feelin'?"

"That's right."

But Grampa didn't.

"He's all right, Grampa," Nathaniel was soon countering Grampa's arguments once the employment opportunity had been introduced.

Now Grampa, who had started supper without me, was standing with his back to us at the cook-stove tending to a pot of boiling cabbage. Nathaniel had taken a seat at the kitchen table, and I was sitting across from him.

"He's real friendly to colored folks," Nathaniel went on. "I think maybe 'cause he was raised up in Massachusetts. The white folks can be different up there. You know like when Esther was goin' to that college. They was in the same schools and everything. He won't mistreat her."

I often thought about City College, the lecture halls, my classmates. Sometimes *they* would even invite *us* to go for coffee after class, the Marxists mostly. They didn't believe in God but they were looking for heaven just like the rest of us, only they called it utopia, *a worker's paradise*, where all men were brothers regardless of their race. They saw themselves as creators of this paradise and were convinced that it could be real, while our notion of heaven was only a fairytale for them.

Still things had been different; better even. Although you could never forget that colored was still colored, and white was still white, even in the Promise Land. There weren't any demarcating signs to speak of, but most everyone knew their places. It just seemed like the colored places had a little more room in them with *Jim Crow* not standing guard at the gates.

"I don't care nothin' 'bout him bein' 'different' as you say," Grampa replied closing the lid on the pot of cabbage a little too hard so that the metal on metal made a loud clanging sound.

Nathaniel and I looked at each other.

"We ain't sent Esther Fay to that college so that she could end up keepin' house for a white man," said Grampa with his back still to us.

I swallowed a reply aimed at reminding him that a few college classes didn't amount to all that much, because it was after all more than anybody else in the family had accomplished, and I didn't want to sound ungrateful or sorry for myself.

"It ain't like she givin' up on that, Grampa," Nathaniel offered.

"It's steady work," I said quietly.

"That all you fit for?" snapped Grampa, turning to look at us at last. "*Steady work* as you call it?"

"It's not forever, Grampa," I tried. "Just a little while."

"Yeah," contributed Nathaniel. "Just 'til she get back on her feet that's all."

"That's right. Just 'til the spring, the summer at the latest. I can save some money--"

"Filthy lucre," spat Grampa.

"Maybe so, Grampa," replied Nathaniel. "But it does take money to live. Ain't nothin' wrong with Esther workin' for a livin'."

"Would you let Connie do it?" Grampa asked Nathaniel. "Would you let her work in a white man's house by herself?"

Nathaniel and I glanced at each other again as the ghosts of Matilda and Albert floated around the small kitchen.

"That was a long time ago, Grampa," Nathaniel said. "Things change. I don't believe he's that kind of man."

"Don't fool yo'self," Grampa said. "A man ain't nothin' but a man."

Grampa would want cornbread with the cabbage. I got up from the table and went to the cupboard for the ingredients to make it. He was imagining the worst because he could not forget it. And he could not forgive it. I had worked in white houses before. Opportunities were limited for Negro women in McConnell County. You learned to do what you had to do. You were just careful, watchful, wary. I would rather work for an old white man than see after a house full of *their* brats. And it was just for a little while. Me being a domestic wasn't beneath us. Jimmy had been the one destined to have *deskman hands*. That I might have them some day was a horrible tragedy of war that I would have gladly traded to have my brother back. I mixed the cornbread, cracking the eggs into the big bowl, and beating the batter.

Nathaniel stood up. "Well, y'all, I better get on home," he said. "Connie be waitin' supper for me." It wasn't really his fight in the first place, and I was grateful for the help that he had tried to give me. It was my tub after all.

Grampa had more in common with Aunt Betty than color. Being so close to the edge of prosperity seemed to create in them both a similar kind of insecurity about being able to hold onto it. They needed constant tangible signs that it was real because they feared too much that it wasn't, like maybe it was a dream that would fade from memory in the morning. Every setback was to them potentially fatal.

Job feared a fear and it came upon him. But perhaps fear had its place. Maybe it served a purpose. Maybe it made us prudent and kept us safe. If it got in the way sometimes, maybe that was the reasonable price you had to pay for its protection.

Nathaniel went to Grampa and affectionately placed a hand on the older man's shoulder. "Good night, ol' man," he said warmly. "You worry too much. No sense in borrowin' trouble. Let Esther take this job." He grinned mischievously. "She can buy you that hot-water heater, and I'll hook it up for you myself."

Still there were times when fear should be overcome or at least ignored. Grampa frowned.

"Don't you sass me boy," he warned.

But Nathaniel had a way with him too. Sensing something anointed in his grandson, Grampa was obliged to hear him. I smiled.

"What you grinnin' at?" demanded Grampa, erasing it.

Nathaniel winked at me.

"You know what, Grampa," he said. "Sometime a job ain't nothin' but a job."

When the cornbread was baked and our supper was ready, Grampa and I sat sullenly at the table, the meal growing cold on the plates between us.

"Why you gon' settle for bein' a maid when you was trainin' to be a teacher?" asked Grampa after a time.

I sighed.

"I didn't finish that training, Grampa," I reminded him.

"But you will. I don't b'lieve in goin' backwards, Esther Fay."

He didn't always believe in going forward either.

"Sometimes you might have to, Grampa. Or maybe you just have to stop for awhile. Stay in one place until you get your bearings."

"Is that what you want? To stay in yo' place?"

"Grampa--"

"I'm tryin' to look after you," he said earnestly. "Since yo' mama died--"

And before that too. Since Daddy had died of the pneumonia. Grampa had always been there for us, for Jimmy and me, the way he must have wished he could have been for Mama, Uncle Perry, and Aunt Grace. It had cost him, all that time away from them to provide for them. But he had bought this land and built this house, with its cardinal red trim around the windows and front door, its front yard chopped clean of grass and kept swept and neat. We still had Ernestine's red rosebushes and purple irises around the front porch. It was Grampa's Taj Mahal built for his beloved black Ernestine and their brown-skinned babies even though it had meant that he had mostly missed seeing them grow up.

"Grampa," I gently interrupted him now, "I love you, and I know you want what's best for me, but, Grampa--"

"You grown," he finished my sentence.

"Yes-sir."

I was. I meant him no disrespect but since the truth set you free I might as well use it now, as I had done before with the taste of peppermint candy in my mouth. Still it saddened me to see Grampa's shoulders round as he sighed.

"It ain't what I want for you," he said. "We been cleanin' they houses and raisin' they chirren since they took us from Africa. My mama and papa was slaves, and they folks befo' 'em."

Matilda and Albert returned to the kitchen. There were no pictures of Matilda only the stories of her goodness and beauty. There was one picture of Albert, taken when he was a young man, during Reconstruction. He hardly looked like he could belong to us, but then Grampa almost didn't either.

"And then we was sharecroppers," Grampa continued. "Which ain't nothin' but slavery too. I got work with the railroad, but what'd I do but end up totin' they slop jars and ironin' they shirts? Don't you think it's 'bout time this family stop bein' servants?"

"Uncle Perry and Nathaniel aren't servants," I reminded Grampa. "Neither is Aunt Grace."

"You ain't s'pose to be one neither, Esther Fay. You s'pose to claim what's yours, what you entitled to. What b'longs to all of us even if some of us can't never get it. You didn't get to go to that college right off, but you understand that. We not rich, and Jimmy was the oldest. And the South ain't a good place for an educated colored man. He had to get away from here. When the Lord seen fit to call him home, Grace and Eddie wanted to help you. It was a blessin'."

Jimmy blowing up in the snow was not a blessing, and he was very far from home. I had prayed day after day, night after night, but Mr. Sommers had come with the telegram anyway because sometimes God said no.

"Grampa, it's not forever," I reassured him. "Just until something better comes along."

"Don't bury yo'self with yo' mama, Esther Fay," Grampa continued. "Young people is s'pose to be restless and wantin' somethin' to happen. Not just sittin' and waitin'."

I put down my fork. Surviving was *our* history, and Grampa had placed his hope in me. He wanted to see a different kind of tomorrow in me, a new beginning for our family. He was as dreamy as Jimmy in his own way. Nathaniel's success wasn't enough. He wanted mine too.

"I'm not giving up, Grampa," I told him. "You don't have to be afraid of that. After all," and now he was blurry through the tears filling my eyes. "You raised me."

I waited a week before going to see Nathaniel's *Mr. Payne*. Grampa needed time to get used to the idea, and I did too. Grampa, a man of few words by nature, and not one to waste them arguing, went mostly silent about it, and I almost wished he wouldn't. If this lawyer hired me then I would be a maid. *Day-work* was one thing, but asking to hire-on, to become a servant in a household had a sense of permanence about it that depressed me. Grampa's protest could be like having the Apostle Paul's thorn in my side, a persistent reminder not to resign myself to this.

For the interview I selected a gray cotton dress and starched and ironed it. I polished my black work shoes and pulled my hair back into a tight knot at the base of my head. The woman in the mirror before me was sufficiently nondescript. As I was going out the door, Grampa reminded me, "You change yo' mind, you turn around and come home. We'll make out fine." For this I gratefully went back and kissed him on top of his bald head. I could always come home.

"I know, Grampa," I said smiling at him. "Thank-you."

I rode my bicycle over to Nathaniel and Uncle Perry's garage. Nathaniel was lending me his truck to drive myself to Mr. Payne's house. I would have preferred to take my bicycle but it was still warm enough to make me sweat, and I needed to be fresh for the first impression. Much to Aunt Betty's dismay, I usually rode my bicycle around town and with pleasure, the wind blowing beneath my skirts, when I wasn't wearing a pair of Jimmy's old trousers. However, it seemed that what had been acceptable for me to do as a child was no longer acceptable now that I was a woman. It ought to be that becoming an adult was liberating but mostly it seemed to result in more restrictions.

You were expected to carry yourself, to be yourself, in a prescribed way. So if I went to work for Nathaniel's Mr. Payne, I'd be taking the bus like all the other domestics, since there was ample bus service between the two sides of town because the city fathers wanted to make sure that the colored maids could readily get to and from their white homes.

"I want my Saturday afternoons off and all day Sunday too," I said to Nathaniel, who was working underneath a Buick. "I have to keep my commitments to the church."

"Tell 'im that," replied Nathaniel. "He'll be all right with it."

"And I want to get home in time to have supper with Grampa. I don't want him to have to eat alone."

"Well now you gon' have to fix the man's supper, Esther Fay," said my cousin. "That's the main reason he wants somebody, to cook for 'im. A man shouldn't be eatin' all his suppers in a diner neither."

"Well maybe if I can just get home by eight o'clock then," I said.

"Let 'im know. He's reasonable."

"What y'all gabbin' 'bout out here?" interjected Uncle Perry, who joined us, as he lit a cigarette. "You's out mighty early, Esther Fay."

"Good morning, Uncle Perry," I greeted him.

"She goin' to see Payne 'bout workin' for 'im."

"Taylor Payne?" asked Uncle Perry.

"That be the one," Nathaniel confirmed. "She takin' my truck."

"Daddy lettin' you hire-out?" asked Uncle Perry skeptically.

"Why not?" asked Nathaniel. "It's a good job."

"That may be, but--"

Nathaniel emerged from underneath the car and looked up at us.

"Ain't no buts to it, Daddy," he said. "Esther can make some good money and get on back to New York and finish that school."

"Harlem," I corrected Nathaniel.

Uncle Perry took a draw of his cigarette and nodded.

"Ain't that in New York City?" asked Nathaniel, scooting back beneath the Buick.

Yes and no I thought but did not say. It seemed his Mr. Payne had convinced him otherwise.

"He know she ain't here to stay," Nathaniel continued. "But it's a good job and Esther come with a good report. It's 'tween them two now."

This was what my life had come to, I thought as I drove through town, remembering the Promise Land like it was a dream. I wondered what people would say about me, about all my *high-tone* education that had only fitted me for washing a white man's drawers. But Nathaniel said the pay would be good. So maybe this really would get me back to where I belonged, to the place where I could make good on Jimmy's promise, and make Grampa proud. And in the meantime I would be able to buy nice Christmas presents for Grampa and Little Evie, and Mandy's children. Perhaps by December, if this man paid as well as Nathaniel suggested, I might even buy a car of my own, and drive myself back to Harlem. Maybe Grampa would come with me for a visit. He should see for himself how well Aunt Grace and Uncle Eddie were doing.

I wondered if Nathaniel's *Mr. Payne* was going to like me and if I could tolerate him. Even if he was ugly, a man with a good living was still a good catch, so I wondered why he didn't have a wife. Something must be wrong with him. I imagined a house with dirty dishes in the sink and coats of dust covering everything. There would probably be mold on the bathroom walls. I would have to work hard, at least at first, but twenty dollars a week was unheard of in McConnell County, and as good as a white woman's wages. I wondered why he hadn't hired somebody else—one of his own kind. Maybe they wouldn't work for him. Maybe Nathaniel was just too nice to everybody—him and his *good feelings*.

Arriving at the house, I turned off the road onto a long graveled driveway. The house, a simple two-story building with many windows and a large front porch, sat back off the road, so that the front yard was large and dotted here and there with the occasional tree or shrub. Uncle Eddie and Aunt Grace's brownstone was finer, and I wondered what would make this Mr. Payne come back to a country town with no family living here to speak of?

It certainly wasn't *Tara* even if I was about to become a *Mammie*. Suddenly I hated the idea of all of this with a fierceness that nearly made me put Nathaniel's truck in reverse. Grampa would have been relieved, but Nathaniel had told him I was coming. I just wouldn't do this for long. I would go back to Aunt Grace and Uncle Eddie's house and get on with life. Mama was dead. I had done my best for her. It just hadn't been enough.

When I stopped at the end of the driveway in front of the house, a big German shepherd dog appeared, charging towards the truck and barking loudly. A white man, who had been perched on a ladder painting the house, jumped down and hurried after the dog, shouting, "Herman! Herman! Down boy!" The dog obeyed and stood looking up at me. I had turned off the engine but I stayed in the truck. "Don't worry," the man said. I glanced at him but immediately went back to watching the dog. "It's just his way of saying hello. He won't bite." The painter reached to open the truck's door but I resisted, holding it closed. He smiled. "It's okay," he man assured me. "Trust me. You must be Esther."

Reluctantly I moved my eyes off the dog and to the painter's white face that had been bronzed by the sun. He had smeared brown paint on his left jaw. The black hair on his head was damp and matted. He wore a sleeveless undershirt and sweat shone on his bare arms. Grudgingly I let go of the truck door handle, and the painter opened it, offering me his dirty hand which I pretended not to see, looking at the dog instead.

Once I was standing next to the truck, the man wiped his hand on his paint-stained dungarees and extended it to me again. We both might be working here I thought to myself so I shook it quickly and withdrew. After all he seemed to be my only defense against the big dog. "I'm here to see Mr. Payne," I said.

It was a good sign that Mr. Payne could afford to hire a white painter. A white hired-hand was proof that he was well-to-do. The twenty dollars could be very possible, and I wondered again why he hadn't hired one of his own to keep house for him. There were poor whites in McConnell County too. This hired-hand probably even had a sister.

The house was being painted brown, nut-colored like a pecan. The front door and the trim around the windows were being painted green. The grounds looked all right, and I guessed the laborer took care of the yard. I supposed I'd be cooking for him too. He looked like he could stand to eat a decent meal or two. Some whites didn't have as much as *we* did, and only their complexions made them our betters. With so many of *us* looking like Grampa, it was no wonder that *they* were threatened by *our* advancements. Someday *they* might have no advantage at all.

It would be uncomfortable having the hired-hand in the kitchen, but I could get used to it. The good wages would make it worth it.

"He sent word by my cousin that I should come today to see about working here," I informed the hired-hand. "Is he home?"

"Who?" the man asked.

"Mr. Payne," I answered.

"Oh," the man laughed. "Forgive me, I should have introduced myself. I'm Taylor Payne."

I stared at him, and reading the astonishment on my face the man looked down at his clothes, grinning broadly.

"I guess I don't much resemble a lord of the manor, do I?" he said.

I had to remember to close my mouth.

"Sorry," he went on, "I wasn't exactly sure when to expect you."

I looked down at the graveled driveway.

"Why don't we go inside?" he added.

Mortified, I followed after him, and Herman, the dog, followed after me. Once upon a time there had been a rose garden along the front of the house, but it looked neglected now. I worked to regain my composure. Mama had fussed over Ernestine's rose bushes, but to Grampa gardens were for vegetables. He had been a *victory gardener* long before the war had made it patriotic.

The *hired-hand*—turned into Nathaniel's *Mr. Payne*—held the front screen door open for me to pass through. It was courteous and it mattered. There wasn't a Depression anymore, and I didn't have children to feed. Domestics were expected to put up with a lot and they—*we*—did, but I wasn't desperate. I expected to be respected. Once in the foyer of the house, I stole a quick glance around while Herman trotted in after me, followed by his master—his, not mine.

"I made some lemonade," Taylor Payne said. "Somehow a cold beer seems a little decadent in the morning," he smiled again.

His smile was nice. I understood Nathaniel's *good feeling*.

"Of course this is the land of mint juleps, right?" he joked.

"Yes-sir," I said dropping my head again.

I knew nothing about mint juleps. I had never had one and didn't know what else was in them besides the mint. East Texas was the land of *home-brew* and *white-lightening*. You couldn't legally buy bottled liquor in McConnell County. Some folks drove all the way to Dallas for their spirits or bought them from a reputable boot-legger.

"Please," Mr. Payne gestured towards the front parlor, "Have a seat, and I'll get us a drink."

I nodded and complied. He hadn't led me to the kitchen. He didn't seem to know how to interview a maid. This was not a social call. He didn't need to be a southern gentleman to me.

"Come on Herman," Mr. Payne spoke to the dog. "I think you make Esther nervous."

"No," I hastened to correct his impression, not wanting it to work against me. "It's all right. I like dogs."

They were known to love their animals, treating them like children. At least Herman wasn't a hound dog, the kind they used to chase runaways, first from plantations and then from chain-gangs, the kind that tracked down desperate human beings through the woods like prey. Sometimes when he heard the deep sonorous bark of a hound, carrying on the night from afar, Grampa would shake his head and wonder aloud what poor creature was about to be *found*. Grampa didn't like dogs. He had never allowed us to have pets. In the leanest years he had said that he didn't want another mouth to feed. By the time things were better Jimmy was gone to Harlem, and I couldn't miss what I had never had.

"Hear that, Herman?" Mr. Payne said affectionately rubbing the dog's head. "At least *you've* made a good first impression. Stay, boy."

I perched stiffly on the edge of the parlor sofa to wait. Aunt Grace's parlor was nicer, and Aunt Betty's was more decorated. Herman looked like one of the dogs I had seen in the newsreels. The Nazis had used them. But maybe hunting to capture or kill didn't come naturally to dogs, and maybe he hadn't been trained that way. He sat looking up at me now wearing an affable expression. Already I was getting used to him, and if I were willing to judge him on his own merits I might even like him for real. As his large brown eyes began to win me over, I called him to me, patting him a little cautiously at first and then stroking him outright, as I had seen his master do. Placing his big front paws in my lap, the dog tried to lick my face which I resisted but actually enjoyed. "Now you sit," I ordered him pushing his paws off my lap. "Sit."

Smoothing my dress I sat up erectly again. What furnishings there were in the room appeared to be new. Besides the sofa there were matching Queen Anne chairs, a coffee table, and two end-tables with lamps. A portrait of an attractive couple, dressed in what appeared to be their wedding clothes, hung above the fireplace. It was the only picture in the room, and the couple might have looked lost in all that empty wall space except that they looked so happy. The groom was wearing a fancy long cut-away coat and striped trousers. The bride was in white lace. Mama and Daddy had taken a wedding a picture too, but their clothes had only been Sunday-best not formal. Mama had not had a fancy gown, but I had buried her in the saved dress regardless, and I liked to imagine Daddy meeting her and being pleased.

Herman lay down on the rug near my feet. A dog in the house would be unimaginable to either of my aunts. Aunt Betty used her parlor, or living room, for show. She always ushered both family and friends to the den, where the old furniture was used. When Aunt Betty had insisted that Uncle Perry, with Nathaniel's help, build the den room onto their house, Grampa had fussed that it didn't make any sense, building a new room when it was just the two of them in the house. "A new room for old furniture," he had grumbled. "That woman don't know what to do with good money." From the looks of things, Taylor Payne must have a den too because there was no sign of living in his living room either.

Presently the master of the house returned, bearing a tray with a pitcher of iced lemonade and two glasses. He had changed his shirt and now wore a white one, opened at the collar and with the sleeves rolled up to his elbows. When he leaned down to set the tray on the coffee table between us, there was the familiar scent of bergamot. Jimmy had worn it. Mr. Payne hadn't shaved but it looked like he had washed-up, and combed his hair too. All to make the *second* impression, I thought. But who was seeking approval here?

He poured lemonade into a glass and handed it to me. Thanking him I accepted the glass. Although he had washed his hands, traces of the paint remained, but his nails were trimmed. He filled his own glass, and then drew one of the Queen Anne chairs closer to the coffee table and sat down. Boyhood had long since passed from his face, but life had not been hard on him. Nathaniel had said that he was a veteran too, but I imagined that he had been an officer with the privileges of rank. He wore the countenance of a composed and confident man. He took a drink from his glass. I held mine on my lap. After a time his scrutiny made me anxious, and I had to look down at the coffee table feeling suddenly modest. I was the one who needed the approval after all.

"So tell me about yourself, Esther," my prospective employer requested.

I looked up at him again, and was ready to admire his composure, until I remembered that it was his by privilege, and therefore less remarkable. In my brother, as in Nathaniel, confidence, composure, these traits were evidence of their triumph. I relaxed a little. His parents may be dead just like mine, but he hadn't lost one opportunity for it, not one benefit. And yes he had gone to live with an uncle too, but his uncle was rich, and now he was educated, and hiring himself a maid.

"I've worked for a number of families in McConnell Coun--" I began.

"Between Mitch and Nathaniel," he interrupted me, "I think I have all the references I need about your work. I was asking about you, who you are, not so much what you do."

Who I was? What did that have to do with anything? I was a colored woman who wanted to be a colored maid. What else did he need to know?

"Maybe I should start with myself," he offered. "I'll tell you my story and you tell me yours."

I looked at him dumbly.

"Let's see," he started. "There's not much to tell. As Nathaniel would have told you, I was born here. When our parents died my sister and I went to live with my mother's brother in Cambridge. I was about twelve." He took a drink from his glass. "I suppose that makes me a emigrant it's just not clear from where to where." He paused. "Let's see, what else? Followed in the family trade so to speak and studied law. Got a little side-tracked by the war. Nathaniel and I were both in the Philippines around the same time. Did he mention that?"

He smiled but it was different this time. The mirth was missing, as if one of Nathaniel's war clouds was passing in front of the sun. I shook my head. Nathaniel didn't talk about the war.

"I practiced in New York for a time," Mr. Payne continued. "But I decided it was time to come home. You know, back to my roots. I guess that makes me a country boy at heart and answers the migration question." He paused again. "Don't you like lemonade, Esther?" he asked.

The years in Massachusetts had done away with the East Texas in his accent, or maybe it was a blend of many places: McConnell County, Cambridge, New York, and wherever he may have been during the war. Danny's accent was hard to place too. And even Nathaniel sometimes used words that we had never heard before.

"Uh-uh, yes, yes-sir," I stammered and I took a small sip from my glass.

The lemonade was sweet and sour, and cold on my lips. It had to squeeze down my tight throat. This wasn't a social call I thought again. The windows were open and there was still a morning breeze but I felt hot.

"My father built this house," Mr. Payne said glancing around the room. "My inheritance," he smiled again and pleasure returned briefly before fading. "That's their picture," he added. "Above the mantle."

I glanced up at the wedding portrait again. I could see a resemblance. He was tall and broad-shouldered like his father. His mother was classically small and delicate.

"My sister prefers Cambridge," Mr. Payne continued. "Our uncle thought we should sell the place, but I'm glad we kept it in the family. It feels good to live here again. It was in pretty good condition despite being closed up for so long. I've got a few renovations to do, some repairs. But don't worry. Nothing's too broken. At least I haven't discovered it yet. You should let me know, though, if you find something."

Was he hiring me? He glanced down at the glass I was holding and I quickly brought it back to my lips and took another sip.

"Taste okay?" he asked and waited for my response.

I nodded slightly. The lemonade was good, and I tried to take comfort in the cold hard glass I held in my hands.

"Nathaniel tells me you're an excellent cook," Mr. Payne said. "I suspect he's a good judge. I wouldn't think he misses many meals."

This new direction of the one-sided conversation helped me relax a little. Cooking was finally a topic that made sense. I smiled faintly, and not missing it, Mr. Payne did too.

"So you are then?" he asked.

I nodded again.

"People say that I am," I replied.

"What do you say?" he asked again.

He was a lawyer after all.

"Yes-sir. I can cook."

"Well?"

His eyes were a deep dark brown, really almost black.

"Yes-sir. Very well," I answered.

He smiled again, and little lines reached out and upward from his eyes warmly.

"Good," he said as if the matter was settled. "Nathaniel also tells me that you lived in New York for a time," he moved on.

"Harlem," I replied.

"You were going to college, but you came home to take care of your mother."

"Yes-sir."

"She died recently I understand."

What could he understand about it, I reacted in my head until I recalled that he had been twelve years old when his own mother and father died. That made him an orphan too.

"Yes," I said.

"I'm sorry for your loss."

"Thank-you."

"Nathaniel said you also lost your brother in the war."

"I did."

I supposed he *understood* that too. He might have seen men die. He might have ordered them to it. But it wasn't the same for him as it had been for Jimmy and Nathaniel, or Danny. They were willing to die for a cause of which they could only have a little part. He couldn't know what that was like. To have so little and then lose it all anyway.

Jimmy's captain had personally written to tell Mama what a brave soldier Jimmy had been. Grampa had made me write back to the captain, and Jimmy's other comrades too, on behalf of Mama and all of us, because it was the decent thing to do. Out of respect for Jimmy if nothing else, Grampa had wanted them all to know what kind of people Jimmy had come from. In letter after letter I had obediently written all the right things, about how Jimmy had loved his country and believed in democracy. Dutifully I had included everything I was supposed to when what I believed was that honor was no consolation, and being brave wasn't better than being alive.

"I'm sorry," Mr. Payne was saying to me again. "You might think that this last one would have been enough to make us finally beat the swords into something more useful. But maybe not."

That was from the *Book of Isaiah*. And no. Nuclear annihilation loomed. Men made war so much, they must love it. Maybe Danny would die too. Another Negro man dead for Democracy. The white captain had written, "You can be proud." As if his approval could have any effect on our pride. Mr. Payne was quiet. Herman stretched and repositioned himself on the rug. If Connie were here she might have said something. She might have even touched him kindly. Like her husband, Connie was generous that way.

"Yes-sir," I said because it was as close as I could come to being Connie.

"So you were studying to be a teacher?" resumed Mr. Payne in a different place.

Nathaniel must have been bragging.

"Yes-sir," I replied.

"I hope you'll be able to complete your studies."

"I will."

He didn't need to remind me to finish my education; I had a family for that and myself too.

"Good," he said. "Set-backs happen, don't they? But they can be overcome. They don't have to defeat us."

Set-backs? What about *kept-backs?* Could they be *overcome* too?

"One must earn a living," I said.

"But one should never sell herself short," he added.

We were not the ones setting the prices. I wanted him to change the subject again.

"It's noble of you, Esther," he said. "To put your own life on hold for your mother's sake. Many people I know wouldn't have done that."

Then he didn't know the right people. It was what families did. But what did this have to do with working for him anyway? Nathaniel had told him that this was only going to be temporary and still he had sent for me, so he must be all right with it. I had no use for his sympathy. He didn't have to be nice to me. He just had to pay me and treat me with respect. That was all. I didn't need or want his polite conversation.

History had taught *us* how to deflect and defend against *their* determined niceties, effectively keeping *them* out. We knew how to clean their houses and leave their consciences just like we found them. After all, thieves should not be allowed to feel comfortable with their ill-gotten gains. Consequence ought to always haunt them the way grievance haunted us. I sat before him, with the glass of lemonade poised primly on my lap, and waited for his concession to the distance between us that polite conversation could not bridge.

"Well," Mr. Payne finally announced. "Maybe you would like to see the house."

He was charming, just not to me. He rose from his chair. He was tall, I decided looking up at him for an instant.

"Yes-sir," I agreed, returning the nearly full glass back to the tray and standing up.

For a woman, I was tall too, having taken after Ernestine.

It was a decent house, with high ceilings and hardwood floors that he'd be expecting me to keep polished. These floors wouldn't be sacred to me like the old pews at Sweet Water but I'd work with willing hands regardless. He'd get his money's worth although we hadn't talked about that subject yet.

As Mr. Payne led me through the house he talked about his parents. They had met while Andrew Payne, his father, was studying law on a scholarship at Harvard. "My father was an impressive man," Mr. Payne said, "Humble circumstances notwithstanding. I suppose Mother was rather extraordinary herself. She always followed her own mind, the rest of the world be damned." She had followed it, and her heart, to McConnell County, I surmised, where Mr. Payne and his younger sister, Felicia, were born. Their parents had been killed in an automobile crash in the the same year that the influenza had killed Daddy. The Payne children had gone to live with their bachelor uncle. Mama had taken us to live with Grampa.

The McConnell National Bank had managed the Payne property, renting it out for a time. Upstairs there were three bedrooms, one of which was a master suite, which Mr. Payne now occupied. Located on the front of the house, the master suite had an adjoining bathroom and the renovations in this room were almost complete, and Aunt Betty would have been impressed. The dark cherry wood bedroom furnishings were plain and simple. Not surprisingly the bed was unmade. Books and newspapers spilled off the bedside table into messy piles on the floor.

Maybe now that I was going to be earning a steady living, I could buy Grampa a nice bed just like this one and then he could throw out, or more than likely give away, the ancient iron one, which had chipped paint and rust after all these years. Of course he would protest. Old and worn were not sufficient enough reasons for Grampa to change.

The second bathroom upstairs, located at the end of the hall, still had its original fixtures. The oval tub with claw feet sat on what looked to be the original tile. My employer would be expecting me to get down on my knees and scrub that tile until the floor gleamed like new because that was what *they* all wanted, for things to be kept new, as if for two-dollars a day you should make miracles. Although maybe being a man, he didn't really care too much about the condition of the grout. Grampa liked his house kept decent and in order, but it didn't have to be a showplace. Maybe Taylor Payne had similar expectations. It might be good to work in a house without a mistress. My housekeeping had rarely satisfied Mama.

The other two bedrooms were mostly empty, except for the occasional odds and ends, like a table someone had left behind or a discarded bureau.

"I'm afraid I haven't done much with the upstairs," confessed Mr. Payne. "But I was rather hoping that you'd be willing to help me with choosing furnishings and the like."

I looked at him.

"I'm not very good with these kinds of things," he added. "Wrong sensibility I suppose. But the old house does deserve better. My mother used to have things very nice. Simple, comfortable, but nice. I'm a little worried that left on my own, I could have this place looking like a hunting lodge." He grinned. "If you'd be willing to take this on, Esther, to take me on actually, I could get you a few decorating magazines for ideas. And then of course there's always the ol' Sears Roebuck Catalog."

"Don't you want a real decorator for that kind of work, Mr. Payne?" I asked, not knowing who that would be in McConnell County, since he probably wouldn't want to hire Aunt Betty for the job.

"A professional decorator, Esther?" He smiled again. "This is McConnell County after all, not Manhattan. Besides you look like you've got a good head on your shoulders. And good taste is not necessarily a professional attribute and perhaps a more intrinsic one. What do you think? Will you help me?"

Didn't he have any women friends? There had to be some Aunt Betty-types among them. There must be plenty of young ladies from good families who would jump at the chance to fix-up a big house for which they might one day be mistress. It might be taxing to take orders from one of them, but maybe he wouldn't let them boss me around too much. I liked his smile, the way it twinkled in his dark eyes. Besides I wouldn't be here that long.

"I suppose we're getting ahead of ourselves," he said. "We should first establish that you are taking the job, right?"

I didn't know what to think of him, but I told him I would do my best.

"Good!" he said. "On all counts."

If it didn't work out Grampa had said we would be fine regardless.

"Nothing fancy," my new employer instructed as we started downstairs again. "Reasonable cost and comfort. Practical, but you know, with that touch of feminine sensibility, so that when my sister comes to visit she won't think I'm a Neanderthal."

Aunt Grace and Uncle Eddie rarely visited. They came only for funerals, and then she and Uncle Eddie were back on the train the next day and gone again. "Eddie can't miss work at the Post Office," Aunt Grace would tell us. Having lived with them I knew that Uncle Eddie took vacations. He just never took them in McConnell County.

"We have to show them that we're not all cowboys and Indians, right?" my employer was saying.

The only good injun is a dead injun, so went the cowboy dictum. According to the movies, the Indians must be mostly slaughtered by now, and by white hands obsessed with *winning the West*. Or at the least taking it. Roped, robbed, and raped. Who among us could count ourselves fortunate to for encountering the men who called themselves *cowboys*?

Yet Nathaniel had his good feelings about this one, and maybe I did too; but I gathered my thoughts and focused on what was important, like how much my wages would be. It was stupid to take a job without knowing the wages, even if Nathaniel had said that he would be generous. It might be interesting to fix-up his house, to pick out nice things that he would pay for. It would only be for a little while—whatever happened anyway. Until I could get back to New York—to Harlem—and college, and Jimmy's legacy.

Mr. Payne guided me through the rest of the house, with Herman in tow. Across from the living room was the study. "This is where I spend most of my time when I'm home," he explained. The room was paneled in dark wood. Rows of shelves along three of the walls reached up to the room's ceiling. Most of them were empty. There was a large imposing desk, with a banker's lamp surrounded by books and papers. A pair of eyeglasses sat atop a stack of files on the desk. His dark brown eyes were not perfect after all. The scent of pipe tobacco hung in the air. Grampa smoked a pipe, and the scent made the study feel familiar, welcoming. Behind the desk was a big leather chair. I pictured my employer seated in the chair, working at the desk, doing whatever it was that lawyers did. I hoped he was fair. The only other furniture in the room was a black leather couch. There were things missing but I liked this room. It was a place set aside for books, and being here made me think of the public libraries in New York where I had been welcomed.

"I'll need your help to organize my library," my employer said. "You'll need to unpack the rest of the crates. Everything's labeled and should be self-explanatory. I'd like them organized alphabetically and according to category. Shouldn't be too hard."

The thought of handling so many books appealed to me. There was only the one library in McConnell County and colored people were not allowed to borrow its books. I wondered what else my employer read besides the law books and the newspapers. You could tell a lot about person by what they read, if they read, and since his house was so bare his reading habits might be the only way I'd get to know him.

"Do you read much, Esther?" he was asking.

My jaw tightened. Did he doubt that I was literate enough to shelve his books? My professors could have told him, my classmates too. I might be in a position to teach his children someday if the Constitution stood for something.

"When I have time," I answered coolly.

"Well feel free to borrow what you like from here," he said smiling in the warm way again. "And don't worry, they aren't all law books. You'll find a nice set of some of the classics. You know Shakespeare, Austen. Mother liked the Bronte Sisters. I also have a few titles by W. E .B. DuBois and Richard Wright," he listed. "Some books of poetry by Hughes. You like Langston Hughes?"

Of course he would have an integrated library. DuBois and Wright were intellectually fashionable. Gwendolyn Brooks had won the Pulitzer Prize. *Put the Negro books on this shelf, Esther*, I imagined him instructing me. He would have to say Negro, because he had been raised and educated in Massachusetts, and he was friendly with Nathaniel. Yet it must always be *separate but equal*. Up north it was usually the principle of it, but down here it was the law. The Founding Fathers had not intended for us to live together. *Happiness* was to be pursued on separate terms. I would unpack his books and read them too. It would almost be like being in a library, and I would take advantage of every opportunity when he wasn't around.

"Thank you, Mr. Payne," I said.

From the living room we passed through to the dining room, also newly furnished, and concluded the tour in the kitchen, where I would spend most of my time. There were dishes in the sink but otherwise it was clean for a man who lived by himself. There was a new hot-water heater in the far corner, and there was a gas cooking stove and one of the new new-style electric refrigerators. Aunt Betty and Connie also had new refrigerators in their kitchens, but in Grampa's house we still depended on the iceman, and the milk was always going bad. If Taylor Payne paid as good as Nathaniel said, then I would save up and buy a refrigerator for Grampa. How could he argue? It was a waste to be constantly throwing out the milk.

On the back porch there was a modern washing machine. "I think that will make your work easier," my employer said just a little too benevolently, since it would be his laundry that I washed. On the opposite end of the porch there was an old wringer washing machine like the one we had. Mama had taken in washing when money was tight, and getting the wringer washing machine had been a blessing to us, sending the scrub-board at long last to hang on a big rusty nail on the wall forever. Mama's knuckles and mine too had finally been spared.

"I should have that thing hauled off," he said of it now, "Perhaps you know someone who could use it. It works fine."

I did not say anything, but I was thinking of Mandy, of how she could use it if I could make myself ask him for it for her.

"I like my shirts done with heavy starch," he was explaining as I realized that I would never ask him for charity; not even for my best friend. "In the summer," he continued. "The courtrooms can be stifling but judges demand a fresh appearance."

"Yes-sir," was all I said.

When we were back in the kitchen, my employer leaned easily against the counter, his arms folded across his broad chest. I stood in the middle of the room.

"I'm an early riser," he said. "But I won't require you to be here before seven-thirty. I'd like you to prepare breakfast and dinner. Would you be able to stay until seven o'clock in the evenings?"

I nodded, relieved to be able to have supper with Grampa at a decent hour.

"I don't expect to entertain much but on the occasions when I do, would you be able to stay later?" he asked. "I'd compensate you accordingly of course."

I nodded again, picturing myself serving one of his pretty companions. It was only for a little while.

"Yes-sir," I said.

"Good. Some nights I probably won't make it home before seven, but I won't expect you to stay later. I'll call when I'm going to be late. On those occasions, you can just leave my dinner in the oven."

I nodded. McConnell County wasn't Manhattan, and not even Dallas, but it was thriving. Since the war, the paper said that *they* had improved their country club and upgraded the golf course. *Their* downtown no longer closed with sunset. My employer had the look of a man who was popular. He had the kind of manner that came from being esteemed in your world. Did he play golf? During the summers, Mandy's oldest boy, Spencer, worked there. Sometimes he caddied, but mostly he ran errands and did other odd jobs as they came up for tips. I would tell Spencer to watch out for Mr. Payne. I had a feeling his tips would be good.

"For the most part, I'm not hard to please," my employer explained. "But I am particular about what I eat. It has to taste good. And please, no entrails. That's one part of the Southern cuisine I can do without."

Entrails. Chitlins, you mean, I thought. Or maybe he was referring to pigs-feet, which were not entrails at all, but scraps. In either case it was not likely that this kitchen had ever seen such fare. Unless it was during the Depression, and some poor white tenant, struggling to keep up genteel appearances, had been forced to feed his children slave food. Aunt Grace didn't call it *cuisine*.

"Yes-sir," I said.

"And I don't like liver," he admitted.

Me neither, although I had eaten it often enough. Smothered in brown gravy and onions the awful taste and texture always came as a nasty surprise. But sometimes, as Uncle Perry often said, a full wasn't nothing but a full.

"If you run out of ideas," my employer continued. "I believe there might be one or two of my mother's cookbooks in one of those crates in the study."

I nodded again.

"Well, Esther," he concluded, bringing the strange interview to its end. "What do you think? I'm afraid that I'm not much of housekeeper, so I suppose the house is in a bad state of affairs. But once you get it into shape, the work shouldn't be hard. How does twenty dollars a week sound?"

Like a miracle, I thought, immediately dreaming about the kind of car I would buy. It could be a used one that Nathaniel and Uncle Perry could fix-up. And Grampa could get a new icebox—a refrigerator. I nodded slightly to indicate my acceptance of the offer. Mr. Payne smiled but crookedly.

"I hope you don't get cheated in the bargain," he said.

I didn't have to tell him that it was more than fair and better than decent. He must know that. This was not New York City. Maybe they paid that way in Cambridge. Or maybe he just didn't know how to hire a maid. It was after all women's work.

Once Grampa had hired-on as a valet, a gentleman's gentleman for an older white man, who, according to Grampa, was one of those *carpetbaggers* from the North. Grampa said that the man had paid him well too. Grampa might have stayed on with him if being a valet had not reminded him more of slavery than the porter job did. In the end, he said, it just felt better being beholding to a company as opposed to one man. Maybe white men, the good ones felt obliged to compensate *us*, to make up a little for all their unjust advantages. Taylor Payne was also one of the good ones, but I agreed with Grampa about servitude. I didn't want to be *beholding* to this man either.

"Maybe you'll find time during the day to catch up on your reading," my new employer suggested. "Independent study is a good way to continue your education. Naturally you can take the books home if you'd like."

Naturally. And there would be left-overs from his kitchen too that I could take home. And the old wringer washing machine if I would just ask for it. Perhaps he had some old clothes to give me. Uncle Perry might be able to wear his discarded shirts. They would be too small for Nathaniel. I could have brought them home to Jimmy if he were alive. But he wasn't. And neither was Mama. And I was a maid. And Jimmy wouldn't have worn them anyway. He had been a particular dresser. Even for New York City my brother had been stylish. Some day when the world was right, men like Jimmy would have valets too, a gentleman's gentleman for a gentleman.

"You can usually leave early on Saturdays, as long as you leave me a meal I can warm up later, but Sunday will be your regular day off."

At least I would still get to go to church with Grampa and have my Sunday dinners with him and suppers too. Many domestics didn't get that. Mandy didn't. I wondered what time I would be able to leave on Saturdays and if there would be enough time to keep up my custodian duties at Sweet Water. I would give up the choir. I should insist on early Saturdays, but I was silent except for the obligatory *yes-sir*. The Lord would work it out.

"You attend church, don't you, Esther?" asked Mr. Payne as if he were reading my mind.

I met his eyes again. My moral standing had nothing to do with how well I pushed a mop. He wasn't hiring me to raise his children. But then again asking me this made more sense than wanting to know about my taste in furniture and curtains. He wanted a character reference, and I had come prepared.

"Yes-sir," I said opening my pocketbook to bring out the letter that Reverend Wright had written for me. "I have this letter from my pastor."

I offered it to him. He laughed and didn't take it.

"That won't be necessary, Esther. I'm sure your character is flawless."

Then what was he asking? Grampa always said that white folks had funny ways. I put my eyes on the letter still in my hand.

"I don't know," he mused. "I suppose not being much of a believer myself, I'm just curious about what others think. You know, just in case...so I don't offend you somehow."

Did he worship the Devil in this house? Short of that, what did I care? That was between him and God. But surprising myself I asked him a question.

"If you don't believe in God, then what do you believe in, Mr. Payne?"

He smiled again, the real smile that filled his face, reaching out from his eyes.

"Fair question," he answered. "The Law, Esther. I believe in the Law."

Like Nathaniel, he was comfortable with himself, another man sure that he could make life happen by his plans, on his terms. However, Nathaniel had the greater Source for his confidence. He had the *blessed assurance.* But then again he was the colored man and so he needed it. Taylor Payne could afford to put his faith in the Law. It belonged to him. The Bible said that Jesus had delivered the rest of us from it. That even though it could betray and brutalize us, hunt us down in the dark woods with barking hounds, the Law could never defeat us. *Jesus seen to that* the preachers taught us.

It was my Christian obligation to tell Taylor Payne this gospel, this good news, but in that moment, when I could have witnessed to him, I deliberately chose not to, deciding as Jonah had done in the first place, that that was someone else's work. Besides Taylor Payne had everything already; I didn't want to present him with yet another advantage.

"What's the matter, Esther?" he asked me. "Not the right answer?"

He was toying with me and playing with God. Even if I gave him a testimony he wouldn't know what to do with it.

"I have no quarrel with the Law, Mr. Payne," I said.

"No," he said thoughtfully. "I don't imagine you would."

Only in its application, I thought, but I did not say this either, since that would in fact be an act of witnessing to him. He had such dark eyes, almost black, and they looked at me as though we were equals; reminding me of the debates at the integrated coffee houses in Greenwich Village, when I might have been a tutor. But this was East Texas. It was best to drink your coffee at home and keep your opinions to yourself.

After another pause, my employer followed, "I think you'll get along fine here."

"You will be satisfied with my work," I said.

"I don't doubt that, Esther. But I do hope this is temporary for you, like Nathaniel said. You really should pursue your education."

I tried to look past him and out one of the kitchen windows this time. He was just being interested, polite even, but I had come here seeking to clean and cook for him, to prove yet again that Jimmy and thousands of other Negro soldiers had simply died in vain one more time in one more war. Even though Jackie Robinson was playing for the Brooklyn Dodgers, and Gwendolyn Brooks was winning Pulitzer Prizes. Whether it was a *set-back* or a *kept-back*, in the end I was still going to be putting heavy starch in his fine white shirts and pressing his suits. I was going to be unpacking his books and polishing his silver and leaving his meals to keep warm in his oven.

I was incapable of appreciating his charity, incapable of showing him gratitude. I would be earning every dollar he would pay me anyway, waxing his hardwood floors and washing his linens. In fact it had already been earned. More than he would ever pay. And more than I would ever receive. And if he did speak politely to me, and serve me lemonade, make friends with Nathaniel, and commend Negro ambition, what could it mean to me? I knew his place. I knew mine. Grampa said we did not need what *they* gave away.

The interview was over. We had accepted each other. The terms and conditions were spelled out and agreed to. It was time to go, and I told him so by asking when he would like me to start.

"Monday morning, Esther," he said. "Seven-thirty, sharp."

I drove back to the garage to return Nathaniel's truck.

"So you all set?" Nathaniel wanted to know.

"Yes," I replied.

My cousin eyed me closely.

"So what you think of 'im?" he asked.

That he wasn't what I had expected. That he was like Jimmy and Nathaniel, and reminded me of Danny. That he worked out in the sun and wanted to pay me well. That he didn't like liver either. Or war. And that he had his doubts about God. That a smile could fill his face and shine in his eyes. That I could understand why Nathaniel had a *good feeling* about him.

"He seems nice," I said. "And I'll get home in time for supper with Grampa."

"Good," replied Nathaniel.

It was good; even if Grampa couldn't see it that way.

IV

In the mornings when the Clinton Avenue bus driver stopped for passengers, he would switch on the interior light if it was still dark outside. From the bus window I would watch the passengers get on and off, seeing my own my reflection in the window glass and in their faces. *We* all dropped our coins into the fare box and moved to the back of the bus, and New York seemed like another universe. I boarded the cross-town, cross-class, cross-color bus like everybody else. But it was only for a little while.

Mandy and I usually made the trip together, passing the time talking, chatting in hushed voices. Because we were among the earlier riders we were able to get seats. The later colored riders often did not. The *Whites* sign reserved more than half the bus interior for *them* whether they were there to use the seats or not. A colored man was expected to stand up to give his seat to a colored woman, especially if she was old enough to be Sister Callie, but *we* were all expected to give up our seats if *they* required them. It was better being on the bus very early because that way the only white person you typically had to concern yourself with was the driver.

"Pick out his wallpaper?" Mandy said as we rode along this morning. "Don't that beat all?" she chuckled softly.

"I'm leavin' it to Aunt Betty," I replied. "My grampa says she's good at spendin' a man's money. I'm sure it don't matter what man. She comes over when he goes to work, and you ought to see her. Loves it. She's learned a lot from those magazines she buys all the time."

"You think that's right?" asked Mandy.

"What? Lettin' her come to his house? It doesn't hurt anything."

A woman, also wearing the uniform of the domestic—black dress with a white collar—underneath her cloth coat, reached up and pulled the bell cord. At the next corner the driver stopped. Keeping Mama's collection of black dresses packed away in the cedar chest in her bedroom had proven to be more practical than sentimental. With her dresses I now had a sufficient wardrobe for work just by letting the dresses out in the bust.

"Yeah but he asked you to do it," Mandy replied. "Not yo' Aunt Betty."

We watched the woman get off the bus.

"What difference does it make?" I asked.

"It might make some to him," answered Mandy.

"He doesn't care," I said dismissively. "And what he doesn't know won't hurt him anyway. He just needs to make up his mind. Every time I show him something he tells me he needs time to think about it."

"Maybe he don't want to spend all that money you be talkin' 'bout," pondered Mandy.

Maybe. But my employer wasn't cheap. Living around my aunts I was able to recognize quality. He had spent good money on the new appliances and the few pieces of furnishings he had already purchased. And he paid me well. He wasn't lazy either. On Saturday mornings by the time I arrived for work, he was normally already busy with his various repair and renovation projects. With so much going on I wondered when he slept, although he seemed to enjoy being busy. He didn't seem to mind getting his *desk-hands* dirty, and according to Nathaniel he even wanted to learn how to work on his own car. "Sometimes I get the feelin' he lets me change the oil just so he can hang around the garage," Nathaniel had said. Yet I agreed with Mandy nevertheless.

"Some men hate to part with their money," I said implicitly.

"Not like yo' Uncle Perry," chuckled Mandy.

My wages felt extravagant knowing that Mandy was getting half as much for doing many times more the work, seeing after children while I was watching Aunt Betty pick out curtains and wallpaper from a catalog. But I couldn't bring myself to say anything about the available wringer washing machine, even though Mandy would have been glad for it with four children of her own to wash for. I reasoned that my employer could give it to her himself once she came to work for him. Nathaniel could haul it home for her while I was taking the *A-Train* downtown to finish becoming a teacher. In the meantime, to give her a part in the bounty from the house on Webster Road, I had recommended that my employer hire Spencer to do odd jobs around the house after school and on Saturdays, and he had agreed.

"You thought anymore 'bout movin' to Dallas?" Mandy asked after a time. "Maybe you could get a job teachin' there. They must have a lot of colored schools."

"I have to finish college first," I replied.

"Don't they have no colored colleges 'round here you could go to?"

There were, but none were close enough to let me live with Grampa and keep my well-paying job.

"I'd rather finish where I started," I said.

"Well just so long as you finish," Mandy said.

Sometimes it was wearisome, this thorn in my side about finishing college that everybody picked at.

"Your cousin Norma moved to Dallas, didn't she?" I asked, changing the subject.

"That's right," said Mandy.

"So how she doin'?"

"Real good. Workin' at a bakery. They pay pretty good 'cept that she got to be at work at four o'clock in the mornin'." I doubted that they paid better than Taylor Payne, and Mandy would only have to be at work by seven-thirty. She would think that she had died and gone to heaven. With the good money she'd be able to fix up her own *cabin* right here on earth.

"You ever think you'd move there?" I asked.

"Sometimes," said Mandy. "But I guess I'm just partial to home."

"Where your roots are," I replied thinking about my employer.

Mandy nodded.

"Guess so," she agreed.

"Not like your cousin Danny," I added. "He don't seem to have deep roots."

Mandy frowned.

"I hope you don't blame me for what happened 'tween you and him," she said. "I never thought y'all'd get that close."

We hadn't gotten *that close*. Not really. But I didn't want to explain it to her. Although maybe she knew anyway. Willie Gaines had been gone a long time.

"Oh Mandy, stop worryin'," I reassured her instead. "I'm glad we did."

"Well you bein' a church woman and all."

"What?" I asked lowering my voice further. "Church women don't have feelin's? I'm not a nun you know."

"He sends them post-cards sometimes, but you ain't said he wants to marry you. And every time I see Mr. Isaac I be thinkin' he gon' take a strop to me for corruptin' you."

"Who says I want to marry him?" I said leaving a puzzled look on Mandy's face.

Why did the worth of a woman always have to involve a husband?

"He never lied to me, Mandy," I continued. "That's what counts. My eyes were open. The whole time. Well," I grinned coyly, lowering my voice still further until it was barely a whisper. "Except for that one part."

"Girl!" cried Mandy loud enough to draw attention. "You's a funny woman, Esther Fay Allen. What Bible you be readin'?"

"Same one the preachers do," I answered. "I just read it for myself. You ever read the *Song of Solomon*, now that'll tell you 'xactly what to do' too!" I said matching the cadence and rhythm of the Baptist Training Union motto we recited on Sunday evenings.

This drew more attention and even the bus driver looked up.

"You know you got a hot mouth!" Mandy laughed.

I laughed with her, earning us disapproving glances. Someone was always willing to tell us about the parts of the Bible that they wanted us to know in order to ensure that we did no more than they wanted us to do. Biblical words could be used to help or hinder. To justify or judge.

The bus came to Mandy's stop.

"Well, Lord," she sighed reaching up to pull the bell-cord. "Help me remember there ain't nothin' gon' happen today that You and me can't handle together."

I knew the prayer. Sister Callie used to say it. Maybe my friend wasn't a church woman but she did trust in God; which was better than *the Law*.

"Have a good day," I said.

"Thanks. You too," she replied.

The bus-line ended a little piece from Webster Road, which in those days was still pretty much a country lane that was paved over like the streets where *we* lived, with black tar and gravel. There were no sidewalks, just worn paths along the side where walkers got out of the way of cars. Soon, however, prosperity would be making Webster Road like every other prosperous street in greater white McConnell, and no doubt they would extend the bus-service. No one could predict when *our* roads and streets would be paved. There was always the ranking of things, of neighborhoods, and of people; and *our* needs were only as important as the impact on *their* convenience. Maybe by this time next year Mandy would have a shorter walk to the house than I currently did and that would be good. When the bus came to my stop, the last one on the line, I got off and walked beside the beaten path, where there was grass. I preferred the morning dew to the dust.

As I made my way up the graveled driveway, I could see a light shining from the window off the study of the house. The house being off the road provided for some privacy, but all of the windows stood naked to the world. It was a reminder that a mistress was missing because she would have corrected the situation immediately. As a man my employer didn't seem to appreciate the oversight, and focused on other things.

By the Saturday of my first week here, he had finished painting the exterior. Once done, he had stood in the front yard admiring the results. Believing that he might be thirsty I had brought him a bottle of beer.

"Why thank-you, Esther," he had said, taking the bottle and raising it first to me and then to his house. "Not bad, huh?" he had asked, approving his own work.

"It looks nice, Mr. Payne," I had agreed.

"Appreciate the compliment," he had replied sardonically. "Even if I did have to fish for it."

I had looked at him and he had smiled. What did he expect from me? It was his house, not mine.

I opened the front door and Herman, who was now my companion too, met me for what had become his obligatory petting. The aroma of brewed coffee, keeping hot on the kitchen stove, wafted through the house also greeting me. I hung up my coat and pocketbook in the foyer closet.

"Good morning, Mr. Payne," I said pausing for a moment in front of the open door to the study.

"Good morning, Esther," he returned lowering his newspaper to speak to me. "Coffee's on the stove."

I would have to make a fresh pot to go with his breakfast. My employer liked his coffee, drinking it black. I always had my first cup at home with Grampa, who had to have sugar with his coffee, and plenty of evaporated milk. For my employer the only essential ingredient was a newspaper. The *McConnell County Dispatch* and the *Dallas Times Herald* were delivered daily. The Sunday edition of the *New York Times* arrived in the mail weekly. How many reports of world happenings did one man require, I would think to myself as I collected discarded pages from all over the house. He liked books too. The shelves were filled with various titles, including works by Shakespeare bound in leather with gold lettering; and copies of *The Confessions of Saint Augustine* and *The Pilgrim's Progress*, both of which seemed out of place in the library of a man who was not a believer.

"Yes-sir," I replied standing at the study door. "Can I bring you some more?"

"No, I'll have it with breakfast."

"Yes-sir," I said and promptly departed for the kitchen.

As October moved towards November, it was easy to see how the routine might alarm Grampa. Maybe it alarmed me too. What if this did turn out to be my life? This going back and forth across town and worlds was kind of like going around in a circle, a repetition of a history that *we* had not escaped after all. Maybe working for Taylor Payne was not hard enough. The ritual of our interactions consisted primarily of his agreeable comments and my respectful responses. It wasn't really remarkable, I reminded myself, just normal. If he made the coffee in the morning it was for his own convenience. And yes, I often got to go home early because he didn't come home for dinner, but that was because he had decided to work late or socialize. Our situation was strictly on his terms, and it didn't have anything to do with him being cordial to me. Besides situations could always change.

So I picked at the thorn myself. There was more to life than having decent wages. I took advantage of my employer's books but I wanted to talk about them too. And I missed the Broadway shows that Aunt Grace had taken me to, and the symphony. In many ways my employer was another bitter reminder of the life that should have been Jimmy's and perhaps even mine were it not for war and race. The thorn hurt, but pain was good. I would not forget that I wanted more, and like Grampa had said, was owed more.

During the week I saw my employer only briefly. Once I got passed serving him his breakfast, he would be gone within the hour. When he did come home for supper, once I put the meal on the dining room table and poured his first glass of wine, then I could go back to the sanctuary of the kitchen, where I could read a magazine or one of his books, while I waited to clean up when he had finished. After that I was out the front door and back to the back of the bus. Saturdays, however, it was a trickier to stay out of his way, as he often wanted to make conversation with me in much the same way I imagined that he liked doing with Nathaniel.

Except it couldn't be the same, and Grampa complained that my working in a household without a woman being there would make people talk.

"A man ain't nothin' but a man, Esther Fay," he said.

"That may be, Grampa," I replied. "But the maid ain't nothin' but the maid."

My employer did not lack for female company. Far from being the old contrary bachelor I had imagined him to be, Taylor Payne would be considered a good a matrimonial prize even in New York City, which must make him a prince charming in McConnell County. What was surprising was that he wasn't already married, or at least spoken for, but I supposed some men didn't like being tied down. As long as they could have their pick they didn't have to be in a hurry to make a selection. I pictured my employer at parties, with the women all eagerly hoping that he would ask them to dance. He was a man, yes, but as a woman I was invisible to him.

I made his household function smoothly, comfortably, and so was no different than the new refrigerator and the washing machine, valuable the way the new plumbing in his master bath was. He had hired me for the same reasons that he hired other workmen, because the skills he wanted were beyond his own. As our employer he was within his rights to amuse himself by interacting with Spencer and me when he was so inclined. He could even have his maid play interior decorator, although that wasn't progressing very well, as I was better at making biscuits and washing windows.

Aunt Betty had enjoyed strolling through my employer's house, making recommendations about how it should look. I had followed her around, carefully writing down what she had said he should do, trusting her tastes to be more fashionable than my own. I had left the notes taped to the corresponding pages of the Sears Catalog and the ladies magazines, and now I was waiting for my employer's directions about how to proceed. Weeks were passing but he wouldn't decide, and I was frustrated. I wanted to earn the wages he was paying me, and with this assignment I wasn't. The holidays were coming, and maybe his sister and her family would come for a visit. At the very least he would want to host a party, and the house simply wasn't ready. Aunt Betty wondered what was taking so long too. "Maybe he ain't as well-off as you and Nathaniel think," she decided.

By the first of November I decided that my employer couldn't afford to wait any longer, at least about the curtains and drapes for God's sake. He must be parading around in his bedroom naked for the world to see and that wasn't right.

"Mr. Payne," I began one morning standing beside the dining room table where I had served his breakfast, "May I talk to you for a moment?"

"Of course, Esther," he said although he didn't look up from his paper. "What is it?"

I refilled his coffee cup.

"You ought to know that if you plan to order anything from the Sears Roebuck Catalog, it might be getting kind of late with Christmas coming. Things get very slow with them around this time."

"Well I don't know, Esther," he replied now looking up at me. "What do you think?"

What I thought had been thoroughly documented and left on his desk. The coffee pot was heavy in my hand, as we made up a scene was as old as America. All that was missing was the cotton kerchief on my head to match the white apron around my waist. I was not Mandy, and Sister Callie had been a saint.

"I wrote things down, Mr. Payne," I said with a mouth as dry as the dust I wiped off his furniture. "If you're still thinking that your sister and her family might visit at Thanksgiving, you should make arrangements for things now. I'll need time to get the house ready."

He wiped his mouth and laid the napkin on top of the newspaper.

"Yes, I've read your notes, Esther," he replied, removing his glasses. "But to tell you the truth—and I don't mean to hurt your feelings—your recommendations, well, they aren't exactly what I had in mind. I'm actually surprised really. You strike me as someone with more practical tastes."

"Yes-sir," I said.

My tastes didn't have anything to do with it. It wasn't my house. It wasn't my place. He took a drink from his coffee cup, while I stood rigidly beside the table.

"Perhaps we should take a Saturday and drive into Dallas and see what we find," my employer suggested. "Sometimes it's better to see things for yourself rather than pictures."

Think for yo'self, Baby Sister.

"I think the choices might be somewhat limited in McConnell," he added.

They were. What had made him come back to the smallness of McConnell County in the first place? Could he love a house so much?

"Mr. Payne, I told you I don't really know about these things," I said defensively.

For moment, seated there at the head of his table, he appraised me, obviously, objectively, as though I might be on trial. Or perhaps standing on an auction block. Standing straighter I met his eyes directly. I did not need this job. Aunt Grace and Uncle Eddie had written that I should come back to them in the spring. I could find a job in New York. I had choices too.

"You did," he agreed. "But tell me, Esther, you really like canopy beds? All those frilly ruffles like so much pink foam?"

My firm grip on the coffee pot handle moistened. No. I had tried to tell Aunt Betty that the walnut sleigh bed was better, and more in keeping with his conservative tastes; but she had said that it was heavy and dull, and something an old man like Grampa would like. To me, the bed seemed sturdy and solid, and I liked it, and besides it was similar to the bed in the master suite. However, Aunt Betty was the expert, so in the end I had marked the picture of the canopy bed as she had told me to do.

"No-sir," I now admitted.

He smiled as if satisfied and turned his attention back to the food on his plate.

"Good," he said finishing his breakfast. "I thought we might have more in common. I'll try to get home early tonight and we can go over things together. As they say, the truth is probably somewhere in the middle."

What truth? What was he talking about? Did he know about Aunt Betty? Nathaniel must have said something.

That evening, true to his word, my employer arrived home closer to five o'clock. Herman, as usual alerted me to his master's car coming up the driveway, and I hurried to turn off the radio in the kitchen. After he had had his dinner, and I had removed the dishes, my employer invited me to sit down at the dining room table with him, where he had laid out the catalogs and the copies of the decorating magazines, with all of Aunt Betty's recommendations. We—well he—talked for a long time, pouring over the glossy pages, and then he once again had us walk through the house together to plan for its furnishings. He drew out my thoughts, and as I agreed with his ideas much of Aunt Betty's notions were not surviving the process. Of course she would never see the results, and it was his house after all. If he wondered why there was such a difference in what I thought now compared to what I had presented before, he never said so. Maybe he attributed the change simply to my deference to him. Maybe he thought that I just didn't care. I couldn't decide which possibility mattered most or at all, but in either case, since he didn't question me there was no obligation to explain.

By the time we were back at the dining room table, he had formed a plan for finishing the furnishings, including the curtains. It was almost nine o'clock, and I was tired and bothered about missing my bus.

"I should get home, Mr. Payne," I said. "My grandfather will be worried."

"Esther, forgive me," he quickly replied. "I lost track of time. Why didn't you say something?"

"It's fine, Mr. Payne."

"Go call your grandfather," he told me. "Then I'll drive you home."

"I can catch the bus."

"Nonsense. I'll drive you."

"The buses run late, Mr. Payne."

"Esther," he said firmly. "Call your grandfather, and Herman and I will wait for you in the car." The matter settled in his mind, he turned his attention to the dog.

"Want to go for a ride, boy?"

"We don't have a telephone," I informed him.

"Oh," he said looking at me again. "Then we better get going."

He was naïve, if he thought the world was his kingdom alone. Even if it did seem like it was, it wasn't. He had to answer to somebody too, just like the rest of us. Accomplished me always seemed to get this wrong. They believed that the rest of us should just go along with where they would take us. Jimmy was going to make a life for us in New York, and then bring us back to McConnell County to open a school that white folks would have coveted. He was going to take me to the Savoy and show me Paris. Easily I had been carried away, riding on his dreams, until reality had reclaimed its precedence.

I followed my employer into his foyer, where he proceeded to take my coat from the closet and hold it for me. I compliantly slipped my arms into the sleeves, knowing what it would mean to folks seeing a colored woman riding in the car with a white man at this hour of the night. Amicably my employer patted my shoulders, but he was not going get me into trouble. Not with Grampa, or anybody else. Maybe in Paris it was different. I had read about Josephine Baker thriving there, but this was McConnell County. Buttoning up my coat I turned to face my employer, who was now getting my pocketbook from the closet.

"Mr. Payne," I said, taking my pocketbook from him as I spoke, in a voice just as firm as his, "You can't take me home."

"Don't be silly, Esther," he dismissed my declaration. "It's late and it's getting cold. Why shouldn't I--"

"You just can't," I interrupted him.

"Why not? I don't understand."

"I think you do. But even if you don't, I do." I paused before going on. "And I can't be going to Dallas with you either. It's not the way--"

"What *way*?" he queried, mockery in his voice. "You're not going to tell me that they do things differently in the South, are you?"

I was silent because I didn't need to tell him.

"We are *they*, Esther," he said. "You and I."

No, only you are, I said in my head. The *they* to which I belonged did not make the rules. Not in the South. Not in this country. Not even in New York.

"I have to go, Mr. Payne," I replied but didn't move.

He studied me. Maybe he thought I was unreasonable and ridiculous, but very sure of myself I met his gaze patiently, as though he were the one being absurd because he was. Yet I liked his face, his square jaw, his brilliant eyes. His smile could be as inviting as Nathaniel's. If he had grown up here and the world had been right, they might have been playmates. He was good to Spencer. I would have liked him as a boy.

"Good night, Mr. Payne," I said more resolutely.

His right brow lifted slightly.

"Good night, Esther," he replied, a drier smile lifting one corner of his mouth.

The November night was chilly. The trees were dropping their leaves. Electrically lit houses dotted the landscape. My shoes crunched on the gravel as I strode to the end of the drive.

We are they. You and I.

I should buy a new winter hat I told myself. The nights would only be getting colder. I hurried to the bus stop, watchful of the world around me. After a time the bus came. Boarding, I dropped my coins in the slot, and as the driver pulled away, I made my way to the colored section and sat down. You didn't waste your time arguing about the absurd.

Except that maybe *absurdity* was subjective. The NAACP said that we should go to the same schools, that it was absurd that we didn't, that *separate* couldn't be *equal*. But *we* had been arguing about that for a long time, and mostly all *we* had to show for it was the *waitin'*. There were victories true enough, and as the song went, each one of them helped us *some other to win*. Such consolations gave *us* hope, but after so many years *we* were tired too. Waiting was not always a passive thing.

I sat at my employer's kitchen table, the next evening, waiting for him to finish his dinner so I could clear his table, clean his kitchen, and go home. To pass the time, I was reading my latest edition of *The Crisis*. Maybe it was a consolation that the wages he paid me paid for my membership in the NAACP. In Harlem I had gone to the meetings. In McConnell County at least I had the magazine and so didn't have to feel so cut-off.

"May I join you?"

I looked up from the journal page to see my employer standing in the doorway carrying his dinner plate and wine glass, and jumped to my feet.

"I'm-I'm sorry," I apologized. "Do-do you need something, Mr. Payne?"

"Yes," he replied setting his plate and glass down on the kitchen table. "A little dinner conversation." He pulled out a chair across from me. "Please, sit down," he instructed. "What are you reading?"

Hastily I closed the journal and stuffed it into my apron pocket.

"Not the *Ladies Home Journal*, I guess," he said.

He might be nice but he was nobody's radical.

"Well will you at least sit down with me?" he asked.

For *a little dinner conversation?* With *me?*

"Please," he repeated the request, pointing to the chair. "My dinner's getting cold."

When I sat down, he did too, and he began to eat.

"You're a good cook, Esther," he said.

"Thank-you, sir," I replied.

"Is there enough for seconds?"

"Oh-uh, yes-sir."

Taking his plate, I hurried to replenish it with meat and vegetables and brought it back to him.

"The *Crisis*," he said as I placed his plate on the table before him.

"Sir?"

"What you're reading," he said. "In your pocket there. Sit down and tell me, what 's the news."

I was embarrassed and annoyed at the same time. He had caught me reading on the job, but the kitchen was my place. His was in the dining room. Must entertaining him also come with the job? Reluctantly I sat back down, mumbling something about the letters to the editor debating the NAACP's current legal strategy.

"Marshall's right," said my employer. "The Constitution is the way to approach it. It's the law of the land. From sea to shining sea so the song goes." He looked at me, "And I believe that also includes the South, since we resolved the question of States' Rights about a hundred years ago."

"The Constitution is only as good as the men who enforce it," I said before thinking.

But at least it would put an end to this whimsical attempt at *dinner conversation.*

"I would have to disagree with you there, Esther. I believe it's better."

Casually he was cutting into the meat on his plate.

"Because it is blind?" I went further, nearly mocking the famous blind-folded lady with the scales.

"That's justice, Esther," he replied like a teacher to a student. "The Constitution may reflect the clearest vision man has ever had."

White men, anyway. And for white men. My employer made his living arguing cases, and I could be no match for him, but I did have one more point to make, knowing that I might have to find other work for doing it.

"From where you sit," I said. "That may be easier for you to say."

He looked up from his plate at me.

"You may be right, Esther," he agreed after a moment. "We don't have the same vantage point, do we?"

"No, we don't," I answered. "As I understand it, the original authors ignored women and discounted Negroes by about two-fifths. That tends to affect my opinion of your Constitution for at least two reasons."

The palms of my hands were cold and damp, but since they were tucked away under the table my employer didn't see this.

"It is *our* Constitution," he countered. "However, I do see your point." He took a drink. "Tell me more."

"About what, Mr. Payne?"

He wasn't my teacher. I wasn't his student.

"About your vantage point," he said simply. "How you see things."

"Why?" I asked.

If he were that interested, then he could read about it for himself, in one of his Negro books maybe. But what was the point of knowing? He hardly had to think about *us* at all. *We* worked in his world, but we lived apart, *separately*.

"Because," he said still meeting my eyes, "At least in this house, the way we do things will be different."

It was easy for him to talk like this in his kitchen, as if he considered us equals, but he was just being nice. It made *them* feel better about themselves. He was also wrong. The Civil War had not resolved the *Negro Problem*. It had barely changed the debate.

"You know, Esther," continued my employer. "If you're willing to die for something, then I think you ought to be willing to live for it too."

...All of us, Esther, the Negro soldiers too...

I thought of Jimmy, another bastard son dying for founding fathers who would not value him as a man but only as property, as I looked across the kitchen table into the face of a white man who wanted me to think that he was *different*, that he might want to live for what Jimmy had died for. And in that moment I was tempted to believe them both, except I couldn't afford to be naïve too. I couldn't forget all of the promises that had been made, all of the lies that had been told. Pretty lies made for pretty songs and thrilling speeches. Yet all of the *self-evident truths* were ignored. The contradictions tumbled around in my head and stumbled around in my heart, until I was confused, while this peculiar son of the South waited.

"You think maybe we could try that for a time?" asked my employer.

What if I did owe it to Jimmy not to deny the possibility? Maybe I owed it to every Negro soldier since Crispus Attucks. Yet even if I wanted to try, the customs that had been dictating our interactions for more than two hundred years were not too be dismissed. Taylor Payne thought he had a choice. I knew that I didn't.

"I work for you, Mr. Payne," I eventually said.

"Yes, but I can't hire your mind, Esther, now can I? That you'd have to be willing to share."

He drained the wine from his glass. The bottle was on the dining room table. It was my job to get up and go get it. He put the glass down again. DuBois must have left a mark upon them at Harvard, I thought. My employer did seem to be *different*. I didn't know how much, or for even how long, but he was different. Nathaniel had his good feeling about him. And Spencer liked him too. It wasn't really what Jimmy had died for, but it was worth something.

From the window over the kitchen sink you could get a full view of the backyard. I often watched through the window as Spencer played with Herman. Sometimes it seemed like keeping Herman company was Spencer's primary chore, although you couldn't call it a chore. Boys needed to have dogs. Spencer was getting four dollars a week from our employer, which he gave to his mother. He was also getting attention. Boys needed fathers too, and I was thankful that Jimmy had had Grampa and Uncle Perry.

Growing up Taylor Payne had had his uncle, although according to him their relationship had not been warm, and when he spoke about his uncle, my employer's smile often dimmed or disappeared all together. "People say I look like my father," he had explained. "I guess that's why my uncle doesn't care for me much. I'm a reminder of the man who took his little sister away. The old man never knew what to do with or make of me."

Maybe Mama had never known *what to do or make of me* either, but I looked like her mother, so she must have done her best to love me anyway. The uncle must be closer to Grampa in age and temperament, and so probably a loving man just not affectionate. Grampa could be as hard as the oak tree in my employer's front yard yet sheltering all the same.

Besides there was much to admire about Taylor Payne, so I refused to believe that his uncle or anyone else would dislike him. He was interesting and kind. I was getting used to our interactions, which mostly involved me listening and him talking. I was good at this, growing up with Jimmy and living with Grampa. As white as he was, my employer really was very much like them both. A man wasn't nothing but a man, Grampa said, and they all wanted an audience. I didn't mind providing it.

The years immediately following the deaths of their parents had been harder for his sister, Felicia, my employer told me. Since he was older, he said, he was able to handle it better. "I didn't need my uncle as much as she did," he had explained. I imagined him at twelve years old, the same age as Spencer was now, at that age when a man's swagger began to appear and they started to believe in being brave. I imagined him and his little sister burying their mother and father in the cemetery adjacent to the First Presbyterian Church in downtown McConnell. I could see him holding himself and his little sister's hand a little too courageously, as the dirt separated them from their parents too soon and forever. "That eventually made them closer," my employer had shared. "They came to rely on each other."

Leaving him out I had thought to myself. It was cruel to leave a child alone to do his mourning even if he pushed you away. After Daddy died there had been so many nights when I had fallen asleep snuggled in Grampa's lap, the rocking chair gently going back and forth until I didn't feel the movement anymore and would wake up the next morning in the bed beside Jimmy. Jimmy was gone now too, and so was Mama, and I was a grown woman who thought for herself, but I was not by myself. I had never been alone.

"She's an exact replica of our mother," my employer had described his sister affectionately. "When you meet her you'll see. Just like the portrait above the mantle. Uncle Jason adores her. She's the apple of his eye, as they say."

"And you were the beam," I had said sympathetically.

"I'm sorry?" he had replied not understanding the reference.

"It's in the Bible," I had explained. "A beam is a bad thing to have in your eye."

"Yes, then, I guess I'm a beam." He had laughed more genuinely. "Perhaps to a number of people. It's a charming way to put it, Esther, I must say."

He seemed to like talking to me, and it was what colored women did. Me, Mandy. And colored men too. Grampa had heard his share of midnight confessions on the trains. We listened, as paid companions and confidants. *We* knew *their* shames and kept *their* secrets. *They* relied on *us*, and because of the economic conditions of our common culture we—together—sustained the relationships. The *peculiar institution* persisted, adapting to the passage of time. I was here to keep his house and cook his food. That was the contract between us. I was a hireling. He knew that. The listening was extra, like the time I took to read his books.

"But family is family, Mr. Payne," I had said. "We have to work things out with each other."

"Your family seems to be very close, Esther," he had replied. "That's not always the case. Family for the most part is happenstance, and there are circumstances when it's better to be on your own."

I couldn't think of any but I didn't argue.

"Friends are the result of deliberate decisions," he had asserted.

To my mind both were blessings, and maybe he was holding himself apart a little too much. Jimmy had been like that sometimes, so sure of himself that the rest of us were a little dispensable. He had not consulted us before joining the Army, and maybe he would have been drafted anyway, but it hadn't mattered to him what we thought about it. Men like my brother made me think of Biblical men, of Old Testament prophets and New Testament martyrs; men who had been destined to be alone in order to accomplish *the work*. Paul and Peter. John the Baptist and the brooding Isaiah. I didn't know what kind of work my employer had been *called* to do. Besides how could God get through to him anyway, when he said that God was a *useful concept* if it helped a man to be forthright. He didn't think he needed such a concept. He must not think he needed family either. Or anyone.

"To each his own, Mr. Payne," I had replied to his comment about friends.

"Yes," he had smiled crookedly. "I suppose that is *the way*, isn't it?"

As I watched out the window now, our employer was standing with Spencer and they were talking. I couldn't hear their words but I saw them laugh, and Herman, who was with them, wagged his tail happily. Our employer reached down and picked up a small stick and threw it. Herman went running after it. When the dog brought it back, it was Spencer who took it from him and in turn threw it again for Herman to fetch. The two of them laughed again, and our employer draped his arm around Spencer's shoulders, as Herman trotted back with the stick in his mouth. Except for the colors it was like a Norman Rockwell painting. Perhaps our employer was making one of his *deliberate decisions* about Spencer. But *to each his own*, and I moved away from the window.

When lunch was ready I set a place at the dining room table for our employer and a place at the kitchen table for Spencer. On Saturdays I made sure that Spencer got his lunch here, and through the week I always provided a hearty snack for him when he came after school. I walked out on the back porch to call them both in, but the man who delivered wood for the fireplace had come, and our employer was helping to unload the wood. The delivery man, a colored man with gray hair and a beard was standing on the back of the pick-up truck, which looked to be older than Nathaniel's. As he dragged the pieces of wood forward, our employer picked them up and tossed them into a pile.

"You throw that wood like you know a lil' somethin' 'bout it," observed the delivery man grinning approvingly. "But I hear tell up north folks uses oil."

I had seen our employer swing an axe as well as Jimmy or Grampa, but he wore work gloves to do it which protected his hands, his *desk-man hands*.

"They burn wood too," replied our employer.

"That so?" said the older man.

"Yes."

"Bet you didn't never have to chop it though."

"I've chopped plenty."

Not for real, I thought. In this house the fireplace was for decoration. There was gas heat.

"Seems to me a man just likes to show off when a good-lookin' woman's around," the old man said. "What you think young fella?" he asked Spencer. "You showin' off for the ladies yet?"

The old man couldn't mean me but I hastily retreated back into the kitchen where I busied myself. After awhile the screen door slammed, and Mr. Payne came into the kitchen.

"Lunch is ready," I announced over my shoulder.

"Good," he replied. "Let me pay Leon and we'll be in."

A little while later I heard the truck engine start up, and Spencer and our employer came into the house, with Herman as always in tow. The dog lay down in front of the stove where a chicken was baking in the oven among carrots and potatoes for his master's dinner. Spencer and our employer took turns washing up at the kitchen sink, our employer letting Spencer go first.

"So, Spence, which one of us gets to eat in the kitchen where it's warm?" asked our employer, drying his own hands on the same cup-towel that Spencer had used.

Spencer appeared confused by the question.

"Do you think your Aunt Esther means to banish me to the isolation of the dining room while everybody else stays in here where it's nice and cozy?"

Spencer looked at me. Our employer tossed the towel onto the counter.

"Uh-uh... no-sir," the boy stammered an answer.

"Then you're with me then? I should be allowed to sit with you?" our employer continued, taking a seat at the kitchen table and gesturing that Spencer should do the same. "That makes it two-to-one. Thank-you for your vote, my good man."

Spencer looked to me again and then dropped his head.

"Uh-uh...you welcome?" the boy said awkwardly.

"Well, Esther," our employer spoke to me now. "I do believe majority rules."

At least in this house, the way we do things will be different.

"Mostly," I replied.

The audience of the courtroom must give him great pleasure, and now he had Spencer and me as well. And we were all enchanted. Power was such a bright and shiny, seductive thing. I brought my employer's food back to the kitchen and set it before him.

"Looks good," he observed reaching to pick up the sandwich I had made from left-over roast beef.

"Spencer," I said as our employer was poised to take a bite. "Say your blessing."

At this, our employer stopped and respectfully returned his sandwich to the plate.

"Jesus wept," Spencer closed his eyes and quickly mumbled.

Our employer looked up at me.

"Amen," he said.

Some days later as I was ironing lace curtain panels in preparation for hanging them in the room that had once been Felicia's, I thought about how life played with us, as if there were an audience of angels or somebody, watching, amused by our confusions. We never knew what to expect except that our expectations often didn't go like we planned. I supposed women learned this lesson sooner than men, because we had to be better at making concessions. Eating the *fruit of the Tree* first, we had been forced to see our nakedness first and reconcile ourselves to our vulnerabilities. Perhaps it was our only advantage over men. We understood weakness, our own, and that of others. Yet this understanding didn't keep us from wanting it to be different too, from wanting things to be better, right as we saw it. Aunt Grace, Aunt Betty, Connie, Mandy, Sister Callie, maybe even Mama in her own wretched way, and Ernestine too, all of us had tried to manage, maneuver, or at least mitigate what was wrong as we understood it. I also wanted to do things *differently*.

But instead for now I was settling for putting a white man's house in order. The delicate curtain fabric smoothed out perfectly with the iron set to barely warm. The white lace would look nice at the window of the room that I referred to as the *buttercup room* because that was the color of paint that my employer had used for the walls. Aunt Betty would have liked the color; even if the room would be dominated by the new walnut sleigh bed scheduled to be delivered tomorrow. My employer had gone to Dallas without me but he had taken the notes we had made together. Everything was going to be nice. Maybe, if she ever saw the outcome, Aunt Betty wouldn't be too displeased, and Felicia would like it too.

As I was threading the fabric along the rod, I was thinking that the frilliness was forgivable as this was intended to be a woman's room or maybe a nursery when that time came, although if it was to be boy's room his father would have to repaint it. The curtain hardware was already installed and my employer had left the ladder in the room for me. It sat on an old blanket to keep it from scarring the hardwood floor, which I had polished to a glow. As I repositioned the ladder closer to the window, Herman, hearing his master's car, charged downstairs to greet him. I continued with the curtains, eventually mounting the ladder to attach the rod, reaching to snap one end of it into place.

"Nice," I heard my employer's voice behind me.

Happy that he was pleased with the curtains too I smiled without turning around to look at him. His house couldn't be mistaken for a hunting lodge anymore.

"Good evening, Mr. Payne," I said stretching to attach the second rod end. "They are nice," I agreed as I worked to keep my balance. "They're just right for--"

The touch of his hands firmly around my waist stopped me short. When I looked down into his face a queer sensation set free in my stomach.

"Aren't you going to attach the rod?" he asked, as I wondered what it was I saw in the brilliant dark brownness looking up at me. Bewildered by the feeling of his strong hands through the folds of my mother's dress I could not look away. He didn't let go. "I won't let you fall," he said.

Making myself turn back to the window, I attached the other end of the rod. As soon as both my own hands were securely on the ladder again, he took his away.

"Very nice," he repeated.

I remained frozen on the ladder above him.

"I've always liked this room," he said glancing around once more before leaving.

"Yes-sir," I croaked to his departing back. "It's a nice room."

But this year Felicia was not going to see it because she was not coming. Their uncle wasn't well enough to travel, so Felicia and her family were staying in Cambridge to be with him instead. I wondered if my employer had even invited his uncle and doubted that he had. If he had made his sister choose, she had not chosen him.

Despite the fact that I had been dreading the week of cooking and cleaning for a family suddenly grown to six in number with the addition of Felicia, her husband, and their three young sons, I was sorry for Mr. Payne that they weren't going to be here. He was stoic but he must be disappointed. "Felicia doesn't think it's right to leave him alone," he had explained, and I could understand that. I wouldn't want Grampa to be alone on a holiday either. The Bible said to honor our fathers and mothers, and it didn't matter if sometimes those fathers and mothers were our grandfathers and uncles. Felicia had done the right thing.

So I was relieved for his sake when my employer announced that he had decided to go to Cambridge. It was what families did. They stayed together. Privately I was proud of him. He ought to make-up with his uncle. It was a last minute decision but it was for the best.

On the Saturday before he was to leave, I packed for him while he hovered around his bedroom supervising what I included.

"You want me to come by and see after Herman?" I volunteered as I was folding one of his white shirts to put in the suitcase.

"No, I'll drop him off at the Mitchells," he said. "That way he'll have company. A week's a long time to leave him by himself. Unless you'd like to stay here while I'm away."

"No-sir," I declined the invitation to stay with Herman. "I can't."

"No, of course not," he said.

"It being the holiday and all," I offered as if I needed to justify my answer.

It was his sister who had disappointed him. I smoothed my hand over the packed clothes in the valise and closed it.

"I'll have your lunch ready in a little bit," I said and then went downstairs back to the kitchen.

When it was time for Spencer and me to leave for the day, I appeared at the door to the study to say that we were going home. Our employer was working, books and papers re-scattered about on his desk. I was forever going behind him, gathering and straightening things. Sometimes I secretly read his papers and wondered about the people and the circumstances that had brought them to his prosecutorial attention. My employer never discussed his work with me, but from reading his files, I knew the *Dispatch* did not report all the details.

Now surveying the mess that was his desk again, I speculated that the envelopes with Spencer and my week's wages were somewhere in the piles. Usually he left the envelopes on the kitchen counter for us on Saturdays, so the upcoming trip must have disrupted his routine. I hoped he hadn't forgotten it all together so that I would be forced to ask him for what was due to us. This unexpected Thanksgiving vacation was fine, he should see his people, but the maid was counting on all her wages this close to Christmas, and no doubt so was the hired-hand.

"Mr. Payne, we're leaving now," I announced. "And I just wanted to wish you a safe trip and a Happy Thanksgiving."

He put down his pen and stood up, removing his glasses. The glasses suited his face making him bookish and boyish at the same time? Maybe Jimmy would have taken up pipe smoking too. Like Grampa. I wanted to picture my brother in one of those fancy satin smoking jackets, but his being dead made that hard and silly. I couldn't even picture his grave. That was where I would go someday, not to Paris but to Epinal where the Army had left him. I could buy Grampa a satin smoking jacket for Christmas if my employer would just pay me.

"And the same to you, Esther," my employer replied as I waited for the wages.

The right smile filled his face. The one that I liked, the one that drew yours out to meet his, no matter how you tried to carry yourself. Every day I felt myself slipping further into state of congeniality with him. Handsome men were especially appealing when they were good. Even if I was the *Mammie* to his *Mr. Rhett*.

"Thank you, sir," I said.

"Where's Spencer?" he asked coming from behind his desk and leaning against it.

"Outside with Herman of course."

He smiled again.

"I told Mitch to expect him to come by while I'm away."

"We don't want to bother Doctor Mitchell."

"It's no bother. It'll be a relief. You really see old Mitch running Herman in the mornings?"

"Like you do?" I smiled. "Before sunrise? No-sir."

He laughed cheerfully. He was a fine man. Surely his uncle had to see that.

"So what are your plans for the holiday, with your little vacation as it were?" he asked.

"We're having dinner at Uncle Perry's house."

It was Uncle Perry, who needed a smoking jacket. The smoke from his Pall Malls burned your eyes if you got caught in a closed place with him. Most of the time Connie insisted that he go out on the porch to smoke when he came to their house. He didn't like to, but he would do it, especially now that she was pregnant again and moody.

"It'll be grand I'm sure," my employer predicted. "Please wish them all a happy Thanksgiving for me."

"Yes-sir," I said.

By now I was making myself stare at the second button down on his white shirt.

"So, what's on the menu?" he asked me, folding his arms across his chest, just below my safe second button.

Inside I sighed. Did he never get tired of asking me questions?

"Sir?" I replied to stall the inquiry.

"What are you having for your holiday dinner?" he repeated his question.

"What everybody has, Mr. Payne," I said, looking up to his face again. "We're not any different."

"We aren't, are we?" he smiled as if he were pleased.

I was thinking about the bus schedule, where it was, and what I had to do. Sweet Water was waiting. And Saturday nights I cooked supper for Grampa.

"Uh--I better get going...to...uh...catch my bus," I said, hoping that this was clue enough about our wages.

It was and he went back to his desk, presumably—hopefully—for the envelopes. With relief, I watched him retrieve two white envelopes from a drawer in his desk.

"I prefer sweet potato to pumpkin pie," he said bringing the envelopes to me. "Which do you like?"

"Sweet potato," I answered, taking the envelopes.

"So another thing we have in common," he smiled again. "I guess that's the Texan in us."

He had written our names on the envelopes and sealed them. He had an even script. The teachers had always praised Jimmy's penmanship too.

"Thank you, sir," I said first, then followed with, "I've never had pumpkin pie."

In *my* McConnell County, pumpkins were for Halloween, not pies.

"Perhaps you'll save me piece of your sweet potato pie then," he said. "Since I'm bound to get pumpkin for my Thanksgiving dinner."

Maybe it was the same in *his* McConnell County too.

"It'd be spoiled by then, Mr. Payne. But when you get back I can make you one if you'd like me to."

"I'll hold you to that."

Macy's had a big Thanksgiving Day parade in New York. In my other life I had gone to the parades with Aunt Grace and Uncle Eddie. I missed it—this *other* life. When I had stood at the top the Empire State Building with whole world below me, and visited Liberty Island where the cool harbor winds had blown in my face. I had felt a kind of sympathy for the solitary lady with her torch and her promise. A woman alone on an island, eternally hoping for the best out of men, and so therefore believing in miracles. Did her arm ever get tired?

"Well... happy Thanksgiving, Mr. Payne," I said and turned to leave.

"I'll walk out with you," he said following me. "Just in case Herman doesn't want to relinquish Spence."

At last on the way home, with Spencer sitting beside me, I watched a Negro woman board the bus with her charge, a small white girl with pigtails and ribbons. The woman moved to the back, guiding the child before her, and we nodded a commensurate greeting to each other. The two sat down across from Spencer and me. The little girl immediately stood in the seat so she could see out the window. The driver, watching up at them in his rearview mirror, frowned disapprovingly. The woman tugged the little girl back into a sitting position and the bus pulled off. I gave the woman a sympathetic look. She shook her head. Raising *their* children put a colored woman in a precarious place. You had the responsibility, but the authority came only by permission, permission subject to being withdrawn abruptly without cause or warning. One day when I finally became a teacher, I would have clear, undisputed authority. I was going to teach the children—*our* children— to be strong. I would teach them to challenge everything. *We* had been passive long enough.

We reached downtown McConnell, and I decided to get off and shop a little while. Grampa needed some pipe tobacco, and maybe I would buy some lavender-scented bath soap for Connie and myself. Having steady money in your pocket was inspiring.

"You go straight home, Spencer," I said as I stood up to leave the bus. "And tell your mother I'll be by tomorrow after church."

"Yes ma'am," he replied.

There wasn't much time because I really needed to get to Sweet Water to fulfill my vocation, but I liked the idea of bringing a little something home for Grampa on payday. It reminded me of the stories that Mama used to tell about when he would come home from the railroad bearing gifts for each of them. The McConnell County Woolworths was no Macy's or Marshall Fields. It wasn't even an HL Green. But there were enough pretty things to see and buy to feed a little day-dreaming. When it came time for me to go back to Harlem, I would ask Mandy to go with me to Dallas to buy new clothes. It would almost be like putting together a trousseau, and perhaps as close as I would ever come.

In the Woolworths there were plenty of shoppers and the clerks were busy. I walked around among the ladies' dresses. *We* couldn't try them on, but it was permissible to touch them. They were cotton mostly but now that the war was over there were some silk ones too. After awhile I moved to the hats. *We* couldn't try them on either. It took Aunt Betty to pick a hat with flair, and she wore them with a style that actually bested Aunt Grace. It could be terrible to sit behind her in some assemblies because her crowns often amounted to very decorative partitions that frequently came with feathers.

"Why Taylor Payne!" a white woman exclaimed.

Surprised I looked up to see that my employer had come into the store. I tried to hide myself. I didn't know why but I was embarrassed, and furious at myself for feeling this way. I had every right to be here too. The color of money counted for something.

"Miss Spalding," said my employer as the woman made her way over to him, "Hello."

The woman extended her gloved hand to my employer who took it and kissed it. Danny had kissed my hand.

"Laura," she corrected my employer's formality.

"It's nice to see you, Laura," he said.

"Oh--I don't believe that!" the woman pouted. "Not for one minute, Taylor Andrew Payne. I haven't heard a peep from you in weeks," she chided him in that affected, instilled voice of the finest proper debutante. "Why haven't you called? Daddy would love to see you. Does that maid of yours ever give you your messages?"

I was a maid. She was very pretty, polished, and perfect. Her hair cascaded to her shoulders in thick golden waves. Mine did not do that even when I pressed it. Her lips parted in a splendid smile but her red lipstick could not work on me because there was no cream in my complexion. People said that I had good teeth. Grampa said that I had Ernestine's teeth, straight, white, and healthy. "When yo' grandmama died she still had all of hers," he had bragged more than once. "Her smile lit up a room."

"I've been keeping pretty busy," my employer said as I listened to their conversation.

"Pish-posh," the Laura dismissed his explanation. "I see you have time enough to shop at our little Woolworths. What are you buying anyway?"

"I'm going home for the holiday. I thought I'd pick up something for my nephews."

So he liked to bring gifts too. But from the Woolworths when surely he could do better?

"I thought *this* was your home, Mr. Payne," Laura replied. "You don't claim to be one of us anymore?"

"Perhaps I'm just a man without a country," he replied.

"An exile?" she asked, laughing merrily, tossing her beautiful hair. "Oh Taylor, please! Shall I feel sorry for you now?"

"I'd never asked you to," answered my employer smiling. "I don't think you're capable."

Laura gasped as if she had been wounded.

"Where are your manners, sir?! And to me, when all I want to be is your friend. Now apologize before I think you mean it."

My employer laughed.

"Now who's seeking sympathy?" he asked.

Still he would have *deliberately decided* on her.

"Not sympathy," Laura corrected him with a pretty pout. "Common courtesy. To which I'm entitled."

Yes, she was *entitled*. But he was polite to everybody. Even to the *help*.

"Please forgive this miserable cad," he said seriously, taking her hand and bowing low over it.

She giggled as I cringed and wished that I could slip out a backdoor, to which I was *entitled*.

"If you promise to behave," replied Laura.

"On my honor such that it is," said my employer solemnly.

He released her hand. He was as smooth as Danny. Chivalrous, and charming, and captivating. A woman in either of their sights would inevitably be conquered, going along willingly, with a song in her heart, even if it turned out to be the Blues. The wise ones didn't expect anything from them more substantive than diversion, maybe a dance or two.

"All right," said Laura looking as if she was determining his penance. "Then you can start by coming to our house for supper."

"It's a date," he agreed. "As soon as I get back."

"I don't know if I want to wait."

"I believe you'll have to."

She made the pouty face again.

"Besides, I can't imagine that a beautiful woman like you would have a single Saturday night free," he said smiling at her.

She giggled again. I was cooking supper for Grampa.

"Are you day-dreaming or what, girl?" a clerk, coming up from behind, startled me.

"Uh--no ma'am," I stammered. "I want to buy these."

I held up a bunch ribbons for her to see.

"What's the matter? Don't you have enough money to pay for them?"

"Yes ma'am."

"Well buy them then, and stop standing around here gawking at the customers."

Humiliated I went to the counter quickly and paid for the ribbons. Walking as fast as I could without running I escaped from the store and headed towards the bus stop.

"Esther!" I heard someone calling my name as I fled.

It was my employer. As if I had not heard him, I walked on quickly making my way around the slower, less desperate pedestrians.

"Esther!" he called after me again. "Wait!"

I had no choice but to stop, so I did, and turned around to see him striding towards me. People would think I had stolen something.

"I thought that was you," my employer said when he reached me. "What—that money burning a hole in your pocket?"

"It's my money," I said tightly, clutching the straps of my pocketbook along with the rolled up small brown sack containing Little Evie's ribbons. "I earned it."

The smile disappeared from his face.

"It was a joke, Esther," he said gravely.

I looked down at the pavement. He must have seen the clerk in the store reprimanding me. This wasn't his kitchen.

"Mr. Payne...I-I have to go," I said. "I-I don't want to miss my bus."

"That's right, your bus," he replied. "Far be it for me to keep you from your bus schedule."

I looked up at him now and felt bad about myself again. But it wasn't acceptable for us to talk in the street like we were neighbors, or I was just another *Laura* with every entitlement. I was the colored maid who took her telephone messages.

"I hope you have a nice trip, Mr. Payne," I said.

A smile came back to his face but it was crooked and not true.

"And you have a good week," he returned.

I lowered my head, staring at the pavement again.

"Well you better go," he added. "Before your bus comes."

I nodded and hurried away.

When I was at last back on the bus, I reminded myself that this was a temporary situation. I would be leaving soon, maybe in the spring but surely by the summer. Mandy would like working for him. Everything would be fine.

The driver made another stop, and a young white couple boarded. The girl was all shy smiles and the boy looked earnest. The bus moved through McConnell. The young couple got off in front of the movie theater. I didn't like to go to the movies in McConnell.

In the segregated theater, Negroes sat in the balcony. Danny had taken me to Dallas to see a movie in the colored part of town, where all the seats were open to *us* because it was *our* theater. In Dallas, they were better at achieving the *equal* to go with the *separate*.

At Sweet Water more buckets and brooms waited for me. The linseed oil was running low, and I made a mental note to ask Uncle Perry for money to restock the church's cleaning supplies. Fortunately my Christian vocation and my secular employment permitted me the same uniform. Reverend Wright's car was parked next to the church, I observed with regret. I would not have my private time today. The church side door was open.

"Hello Reverend," I called to him as I came into the building.

"That you, Sister Esther?" he called back to me.

"Yes-sir."

The reverend emerged from the pastor's study.

"Hello, Sister," he greeted me. "I 'spected to see you 'fo' now."

"My employer is leaving town and I had to pack for him. The day got away from me," I explained, leaving out the part about Woolworths.

"I know how that can be," replied Reverend Wright. "You won't need to do too much 'round here. You keep things in pretty good shape."

"I have the time, Pastor," I said passing by the compliment.

"Great is thy faithfulness," he ministered to me with another compliment.

"Just workin' out my salvation," I replied

"The Lord'll bless you, Sister."

Yes, I had the *blessed assurance*. Jesus was mine. What else could I need?

"Already has, Pastor Wright," I said. "Already has."

"Amen. Sister Esther. It's a inspiration to talk to a virtuous woman."

Maybe that was what had brought my employer into his kitchen, the inspiration of virtue. I did have something to offer even if it wasn't golden waves of hair and perfect red lips. Jimmy had been right, men liked to have someone to talk to. Respectfully I extracted myself from what threatened to be a preview of Sunday's sermon and got to work looking after the Lord's house.

For supper that night I made Grampa a small peach cobbler from some of the peaches we had put-up during the summer. Full and content when supper was over, he left me in the kitchen and went to the front room to listen to his radio shows. Many nights he dozed more than he listened, and by the time I would finish washing the dishes I would find him fast asleep, feet propped up on a stool, chin resting on his chest.

We had made a good life for ourselves my grandfather and I. I was glad to be here to take care of him. He had done so much for the rest of us. The day would come when I would have to leave him again, but he would be sending me away, and he would be pleased with where I was going.

When I finished cleaning the kitchen, I set up the ironing board and pressed our clothes for church. Grampa was also fussy about the way he dressed. Perhaps it mainly came from his days of being a valet, but he was vain in his own right. He wanted collar stays in his shirts too. When he went to town, even his overalls had to be starched and ironed. I hung his suit in his bedroom and returned to the front room. Kissing him on top of his head I woke him up from his nap.

"Go to bed, Grampa," I told him.

"What?" he grumbled. "I ain't sleepy. Too early to go to bed."

I chuckled.

"All right now, don't let me have to come back in here and take you to bed like a baby."

"Don't you get smart, gal."

I kissed him again, this time goodnight, and went to my own room. It was still Jimmy's room, and it was smaller than Mama's but I wasn't ready to move into her room yet. Perhaps I would never have to. I was going back to Harlem, and if I came back here then I might settle in Dallas. Mandy and I could buy a house together, and I could help her raise her children.

I sat down on the side of the bed to open up the envelope that contained my wages. The wages that I had *earned*.

It was a joke, Esther.

Maybe I had been too sensitive about it. I just didn't want him to think that he could speak to me any kind of way even if I did work for him. What I did on my time was my business.

And you have a good week.

Maybe I would but I would also be short a week's wages just because he had decided to go see his people. *We* were always at *their* mercy. They could change their minds and change the world, or at least mess up *our* Christmas plans. I opened the envelope. It contained forty dollars, two week's worth of wages. My little *vacation* was a paid one. The envelope also included a note.

> Your cooking I will miss; but our conversations more.
> Enjoy your holiday.
> Taylor Payne.

I laid the envelope with the money on the bed and held the note in my hand. I reread the script in the soft yellow light of the lamp by the bed. The words were as concise as if Grampa had written them, and only the T and the P in his signature were clearly legible.

Eventually looking up from the monogrammed stationery page, I glimpsed my reflection in the dresser mirror. Leaving the note on the bed with the envelope, I went over to the dresser.

But our conversations more.

> "How come you get to go to Ray's?" I asked Jimmy as he stood in front of the mirror, smoothing tonic through his soft black hair.
> "Ain't no place for a lady, Baby Sister," he replied.
> "Then who you gon' dance with?" I wanted to know.
> "Well now," Jimmy laughed. "You know how it is."
> "That's the problem, I don't," I snapped.
> "Don't be in such a hurry," Jimmy quickly kissed me consolingly on the cheek. "Your time'll come."
> "Not if I'm some ol' stick-in-the-mud like Mama," I peevishly replied pushing him away. "No man'll want me."
> "You good to talk to, Esther," Jimmy said. "That's better than dancin'. A man can talk about himself with you. You gon' keep plenty-a company, I promise you."

I picked up Jimmy's photograph, the one taken of him in the summer of '41 before the war. In it he leaned against Uncle Eddie's gleaming new car, wearing a fedora cocked coolly to the side. He looked all uptown and debonair, as though the world was his. No wonder Grampa had believed in him. No wonder we all had. So much might have been achieved had Jimmy not boldly traded it all away for stars and stripes, and French ladies tossing flowers.

I brought the picture back to the bedside to look at it in a better light. Jimmy might have been a lawyer too. As an attorney for the NAACP, he might have forced *them* to acknowledge him, *their* misbegotten son. He might have done all these things were he not wasted for a country that refused to be considered his own. I wouldn't forget that. Even if one of *them* did like to talk with me while he ate his dinner. *Supper*. It was supper. And not some classroom on his Harvard campus. Yet I hoped in my heart that Jimmy was right, that he and the other soldiers had really changed the world. I folded up the note and hid it in my Bible.

The next morning I told Grampa about the extra wages.

"The Lord is good," he said.

"Maybe Mr. Payne is too," I ventured.

"He just know good help when he see it."

VI

With a week off from work I had more than enough time to help Aunt Betty prepare the Thanksgiving dinner. She had planned big things for the holiday meal, and with Connie almost eight months pregnant, and carrying the baby so low, I was my aunt's most able assistant. She took me grocery shopping with her and we drove all the way to Tyler for some items on her scrupulously prepared list.

"Aunt Betty, you might not want to get too fancy," I had attempted to warn her. "Folks like what they're used to."

"A little change is good, Esther Fay," she had replied. "Don't never be afraid to try somethin' different."

Grampa, who could cook as well as any woman, complained that he was uncomfortable in Aunt Betty's kitchen. "With all them modern contraptions I can't tell what I'm doin'," he had grumbled. He was not one for trying something *different*.

However, truth be told, for Grampa it wasn't so much that the cooking of the Thanksgiving dinner was in Aunt Betty's kitchen, as it was the eating of that dinner at Uncle Perry's table. To Grampa the center of the Green family universe was supposed to be in his house. He deemed it his right, and Aunt Betty was disputing that right by deciding that Uncle Perry should host the gathering this year. You were supposed to *come home* for the holidays, and *home* was Grampa's house, as long as he was living.

While the rest of us rarely dared to argue with Grampa, Aunt Betty did so constantly. This time she had pronounced that Grampa's dining room—dining area of the front room really—was just too small to accommodate all of us comfortably, and his kitchen was just too ill-equipped for her to cook in. Uncle Perry had gone along with her, the same way he had ultimately done about the baptismal tank. The *majority* had ruled again, and we were doing things *differently*.

At least some things, such as the desserts for which I was responsible, were staying the same. In addition to making the sweet potato pies, I was also baking Mama's butter-cream cake. It had been Jimmy's favorite, and in the middle of the Depression, when we had had so little, Mama had always managed to have it there for us, for him, on Christmas Day, sitting in the middle of the table like it was a decoration, its rich vanilla aroma still hanging in the air.

It had been more than five years now but Jimmy's grave remained fresh to us. The only tangible symbol we had of his absence was the gold star now kept in the cedar chest with Mama's Bible and her wedding ring. After her death, I had blamed myself for forgetting to bury Mama with the ring on her finger, but there had been so much to remember, and no matter how it came, death was always shocking and confusing somehow. In spite of its inevitability it was never expected, and the smaller details like wedding rings got away from you. I wondered who had made the arrangements for Taylor Payne's parents, as he would have been too young to do it.

As the symbols of her two Jimmys, the gold star said as much about Mama as the gold ring. I had Ernestine's handsome frame and her pretty white teeth. Perhaps I symbolized her for Grampa. It was important to have things to remember by. I was saving all of Danny's postcards. I wondered what kind of Thanksgiving he would be having in Korea.

I was glad to be in the middle of a crowded family life. I was happy to be home. Even in Uncle Perry's house. I felt secure surrounded by my people.

I'm going home for the holiday.

You don't claim to be one of us anymore?

I felt blessed, as I admired Aunt Betty's beautiful roast turkey and the yeast rolls turning a golden brown in her very modern double oven. Gladly I fretted over whether or not to frost the cake and how well the sharp creases I had pressed into Grampa's dress khaki pants were holding up. Mama had never frosted the butter-cream cake when she had baked it, and I decided not to too. Grampa would prefer it that way.

Dinner was going to be a sumptuous banquet for our family, in a season of generous fortunes. There was cornbread dressing with sage, green beans with almonds and little pearl onions, and mashed potatoes with gravy. My sweet potato pies were bright orange and faultless in their deep-dish pans. Everyone was happy. Everyone laughed, even Grampa, who had seemingly put away his hard feelings towards Aunt Betty today.

It was enough for the old man to have us around him. He looked upon our faces as if we were affirmations that his life was fruitful and good. His children, and his children's children, Little Evie too, and all of the others that each of us brought into his circle, he regarded as rewards for his faithfulness, as if he were Job in a state of restoration. "The Lord'll make it up to you, Esther Fay," Grampa was in the habit of saying, and on a day like today I believed him.

Around eleven o'clock on Thanksgiving morning, Aunt Grace and Uncle Eddie called from Harlem. We passed the black telephone receiver around among us so everyone could talk. Although Grampa protested that it was a waste of money to call when no one was sick or dead, he talked too, shouting his words into the receiver because he was still not used to the marvels of modern communications.

"Papa, you ain't got to shout loud enough to be heard up in Harlem," Uncle Perry tried to explain. "Talk regular. They can hear you."

"Yo' big brother wantin' me to get off this here telephone, Gracie," Grampa said. "Here, talk to Esther Fay."

"That ain't what I said," protested Uncle Perry.

"Come on, Esther Fay, talk to your anie," Grampa ignored him.

As soon as I said hello, before the *Happy Thanksgivings*, Aunt Grace was letting me know that my room was still waiting, picking at the ever present thorn.

"Whenever you're ready to come back," she said.

"Thank-you, Aunt Grace," I replied.

"Don't you put it off too long now."

"No ma'am, I won't."

"Your uncle wants to speak to you."

"Yes ma'am."

Uncle Eddie repeated a similar admonition about waiting too long to finish school. Did they really think I might choose servitude for the rest of my life?

"Don't worry, I won't," I said when Uncle Eddie told me not to waste my talents.

"Hard times come to teach us somethin' we needin' to learn," counseled Uncle Eddie. "They make you stronger that's all."

"Yes-sir. Uncle Eddie," I cut him off before he was into a full fatherly lecture, "Nathaniel wants to talk to you."

Nathaniel made a face at me but accepted the telephone receiver. I sheepishly grinned at him.

When the call was over Aunt Betty instructed Nathaniel to bring the turkey to the table, while she and I carried in the side dishes. It was a picture-perfect table of family and food, and Aunt Betty had even set it with candles which she lit with much ceremony. Connie shook her head slightly, and we smiled furtively at each other. Uncle Perry brought out the Kodak brownie camera also at his wife's instructions. However, honoring him as the master of this house and head of this table, I volunteered to take the picture. Through the camera's tiny eye I saw clearly the grandeur of my world.

The wholeness of our *us*. There were gaps, yes, but we were complete too. And like Grampa, I was also affirmed. God really was good.

As Uncle Perry gave the thanks in a solemn and reverent voice, Grampa murmured his *Yes, Lord*, and Aunt Betty faintly hummed her deep accord. Little Evie obliviously banged her spoon against the tray of her high chair. For a moment I let myself imagine my employer's uncle's Thanksgiving table. I pictured fine china and crystal wine glasses, and vegetable dishes I had only read about in his mother's cookbooks. What kind of thanks did you say when you only credited the Law? If he bowed his head to pray at all, what did my employer pray for? Clearly his family had had their disagreements. What family didn't? But surely they must love each other too, just like we did. Maybe Felicia would come for a visit at Christmas. Maybe his uncle too. Aunt Betty could show me how to cook for them.

When the meal was over, Grampa, Uncle Perry, and Nathaniel gathered around Uncle Perry's new RCA radio in the den to listen to a football game. The women were left to clear the table and put away what was left of the food. Connie and I, signaling to each other, contrived to convince Aunt Betty to leave washing the dishes, and so the kitchen, to us.

"If you'll just see after Evie for me, Mama Betty," bargained Connie.

"You just leave that sweet baby to me," Aunt Betty gladly agreed. "Come on, honey-lamb, you come with grandma," she cooed lifting the toddler from her high chair.

I smiled at them together.

"I think she wet," Aunt Betty announced frowning.

"Take her to her daddy then," Connie replied.

"I never seen the like, the way you young women be passin' off yo' responsibilities to the man," observed the mother-in-law. "In my day we didn't ask men folks to change a baby's diaper."

"That's yo' own fault, Mama Betty," replied Connie.

"Humph!" was Aunt Betty's response as she carried a damp Little Evie to the den.

"Girl," I admonished Connie, "Now you know that ain't no way to talk to your mother-in-law. And Nathaniel's her only child too. Colored women are very particular about their sons."

Connie just laughed, turning her face as bright as her husband's could be. In as much as Nathaniel was more a brother than a cousin to me, Connie was also like a sister. She was as good as Mandy in her own right, plus she had the spiritual piety that made her a *good woman* in the community, a fitting wife for a young church deacon. She would make a fine Sister Callie by the time Little Evie's children had children. *As it is written, the eye hath not seen, nor ear heard, neither have entered into the heart of man the things which God hath prepared for them that love him.* And I had certainly gotten it wrong putting Nathaniel with Mandy. He and Connie were perfect, *equally yoked*, and set upon a common course. Nathaniel wouldn't object to changing Little Evie's diaper at all even though I knew Aunt Betty would do it herself.

I began running hot water into the sink for the dishes.

"And why you takin' her side anyway?" Connie wanted to know. "Ain't you one of them modern women? You don't even have time for a man, much less a baby."

"Me?" I asked. "I'm in service to the Lord."

"The Apostle Paul said it's better to marry than to burn."

And some preachers said that that was his thorn, making it seem like he had chosen it.

"Now how you know I even got a fire?" I asked.

"Girl, you's a Green, ain't you?"

We laughed.

"Nathaniel ain't a only child for lack-a tryin', I know that," said Connie.

"You's a hussy," I chuckled. "Talkin' 'bout the good deacon and his wife like that."

"Why not? Can't be no shame in it," she said, bringing me a stack of plates from which she had scraped the food. "The Lord Himself done said be fruitful and multiply. You need to try it some time."

"And what makes you think I haven't?"

"Oh yeah!" Connie hollered. "I told Nathaniel you wasn't no nun!"

I thought I was supposed to be ashamed of what I had done with Danny, but I wasn't. Sometimes you could do all that waiting and have nothing to show for it but wasted time.

"What I want to know is why y'all been talkin' 'bout me that way?" I feigned outrage. "Don't you have yo' own business?"

Connie knew I was playing.

"Yes, Lord," she replied, arching her back to push out her protruding abdomen further. "You see this big belly stickin' out all over the place, don't you?"

"Oh you know you love it," I told her. "You got that maternal glow."

"And piles to boot," she added.

This time when we laughed Nathaniel called to us from the den that we were having too much fun.

I washed and Connie dried, and together we worked our way through the dishes to the pots and pans. After a time we settled down and discussed more dignified things, like how Aunt Betty was determined to re-do the nursery for the new baby soon to come. When Jimmy and I were babies we had slept in bureau drawers, padded with Mama's homemade quilts. Nathaniel had not had much better, but for his children, it was going to be different. It was going to be better. Aunt Betty was seeing to that herself.

"I hope it's a boy this time," Connie said about the baby resting so low on her small frame.

"Is that what Nathaniel wants?" I asked.

"Oh, you know him. He don't care either way. But I think a man ought to have a son to carry his name. Girls can't do that for a family."

I passed her a clean pot to dry.

"Then I guess you see why I'm holdin' on to the Allen name."

Even though it meant that it would die with me. Connie's face turned sad.

"You still miss him bad, don't you," she said.

"Yes," I said knowing who she meant by *him*.

It was as if in death loved ones transcended the human label of a name. Even the name *James Jerome Allen Junior*.

"I didn't really know him that well," Connie said. "But I know he was somebody special. Nathaniel misses him too."

"He was...special," I said scrubbing hard at the turkey roaster and hating the word *was*. "James Jerome Allen Junior," I repeated. "Nobody even says Jimmy much anymore. Once upon a time there were two James Jerome Allens. Now there's none."

"Maybe if it's a boy, we'll name him after Jimmy," offered Connie.

I shook my head vehemently.

"You've already done that for Mama with Little Evie, Connie," I said. "That's Nathaniel's boy inside of you, if you name him after anybody it better be after his father."

"It must be hard on you, Esther, with everybody gone."

I shrugged.

"Not *everybody* is. I'm a Green too, remember? And hard times are meant to teach us something we need to learn, at least that's what Uncle Eddie says."

"Sometimes hard times just hard times," disagreed Connie. "There ain't always some great and good reason for them."

"Sister Green, you not fixin' to blaspheme, are you?" I asked teasing her to lighten the mood we had suddenly settled in. "The Bible says count it all joy."

"I don't mean no disrespect," she said seriously. "But sometimes it makes me tired, the way folks always want to make out like everything bad that happens to us is some kind of way our own fault but everything good is just a blessin'. I was reading in this magazine about how all those Jewish people was burned up in those ovens. Millions of people just wiped out. Nothing but smoke and ashes. Now you tell me, what lesson did a whole race of people need to learn? How they bring *that* on themselves? And what about us? In slavery all them years. What's the reason for that? What we need to learn so bad that the Lord have to let them bring us here to teach it to us?"

I was rinsing out the sink now and wiping down the faucets.

"I don't know," I said. "I guess it's just one of those mysteries. You know, somethin' that we aren't supposed to understand."

"It's just evil that's all," declared Connie flatly. "The Devil bein' busy just 'cause he can. There don't have to be a purpose for it. Some things can't make sense."

"Maybe how we deal with evil is where the sense comes in," I suggested. "Maybe it's in how we go through it."

"Maybe."

"Oh Connie, how did we get on such a depressing subject anyway?" I tugged at the tone again. "I think they may be right when they say a woman gets too moody when she's goin' to have a baby."

She finally smiled again.

"Well get with one, and find out," she said.

"You mind if I get with a husband first?" I laughed.

"Now that'll sho' 'nough mess with yo' mood. Let me tell you."

We laughed again.

"I said y'all was havin' too much fun in here," said Nathaniel, appearing at the kitchen door to interrupt our banter.

"Poor baby, and you not?" Connie teased him.

"Too many grand-daddies and mamas in one room for me," he groaned, walking over to her and lovingly placing one of his large hands on her bulging belly.

Connie smiled at him, her face as beatific as every picture I had seen of the Virgin Mary.

"And you left my child in there to fend for herself?" she replied.

"Hey," Nathaniel countered, "The Baby Jesus ain't had that much attention when He was born."

"You know they spoilin' her rotten," lamented Connie.

"Let 'em." I said.

"That's easy for you to say now," Connie reminded me. "But you just wait 'til it's yo' child they doin' it to. Then see what you say."

"I done told you now, I'm in service."

"What y'all talkin' 'bout?" asked Nathaniel.

"Woman's talk, honey," his wife told him with a playful slap on his butt.

"Say!" he exclaimed.

"Look at 'im Esther," Connie laughed. "He ain't nothin' but a big baby hisself."

"If y'all need some privacy, I can go sit with the old folks," I volunteered.

"All I need is another piece of cake," replied Nathaniel.

"Boy, can't you see we cleanin' up in here?" Connie scolded him. "This kitchen is closed."

"All right, if that's how you wanna do me," he sulked, "Maybe I'll just go ask my mama. She'll treat me right."

"She got you spoiled too," fussed Connie. "What am I gon' do with 'im?" she asked me. "Why y'all all cater to the men in this family so much?"

But even as she fussed Connie was at the kitchen table slicing her husband another piece of cake. Nathaniel sat down at the table. I stood watching and admiring their happiness. As her wedding present to them, Mama had baked their wedding cake, four layers high with white and pink roses made of frosting. She and I had gone to the wedding despite being in mourning. The whole family had been in mourning and yet in celebration. Nathaniel had been so handsome in his brand new blue suit, looking so joyful and nervous at the same time. Connie had been angelic in her white dress with a veil, coming down the aisle on the arm of Mr. Billy, her father. I had worn blue, but as always Mama had been in her black.

"Wives submit to your husbands," I reminded Connie of the Scripture as she placed the cake in front of Nathaniel.

"Amen," agreed Nathaniel.

"All right, Esther Fay. Like I said, you just wait and see on that part too. I'll get to tell you 'bout all that submittin' one day."

"Ain't no man gon' tame, Esther," said Nathaniel as he chewed contentedly.

"You sayin' I'm tamed?" his wife shot back with her hands on her hips.

"Like an ol' house cat," replied her husband. "Just good for sittin' in yo' lap."

I dried my hands on the kitchen towel and folded it to leave on the counter.

"Nathaniel, you go too far," I warned.

"Aw, you'll look out for me," he said.

"Oh no," I resisted. "I ain't in this."

And I wasn't. Because it was *their* circle. The smallest space. The intimacy of lovers. I could only observe. I could appreciate the music but not sing the song. It was theirs alone. There for the rest of us to see, but completely private.

Connie ran her hand over her husband's coarse dark hair and drifted into stroking the back of his strong neck and shoulders. He closed his eyes. The roundness of her belly was almost concealed by the broadness of his back. When she looked up at me again, she was smiling, but her Virgin Mary expression had blossomed into something more sensual, as Nathaniel relaxed into her caresses. I smiled at them both, thinking how nice it must be to be a pet sometimes. How nice it must be to know that there was always a saucer of sweet milk for you, for no reason other than that you were cherished. Their contentment nourished them both like a feast. It was as rich as any cake and as sweet as any pie.

VII

The year's first blue norther troubled the skies over McConnell County the first Sunday in December. I stood outside staring up at the changing sky, as the wind rose in the late afternoon. A thick bank of clouds was moving in. Behind the forward ridge of the storm clouds, the sky was a dull gray. Rain drops fell, seemingly one at a time, splashing my face. In New York the change of seasons was more gradual, and I had missed the East Texas blue northers having grown up with winter blustering in across the prairie as if it were tardy and anxious.

The screen door leading to Grampa's back porch creaked open behind me, and soon Grampa joined me in the yard.

"Looks like we gon' get some winter tonight," he said standing next to me.

"Yes-sir," I agreed as I continued to study the sky. "It's striking though, don't you think? You remember that movie, *Cabin in the Sky*? You think it's true? That we each get a cabin in the sky?"

"You sho' can talk crazy sometimes, gal," replied Grampa. "I'm thinkin' 'bout my rheumatism and this cold. I ain't studyin' 'bout no cabins."

He had been complaining about his *rheumatism* for as long as I could remember, but I had never seen any infirmity in him. The Greens were of hearty stock.

"I was just thinking," I mused anyway, "If Jesus said He has mansions for us, why would we be looking forward to cabins?"

"As long as I'm in Heaven, a shack'd be just fine with me," replied Grampa.

I slipped my arm around his waist and he stiffened slightly as I pulled in close, but he relaxed and I felt sheltered.

"You know, Grampa, you really should let Uncle Perry put in the hot-water heater. Just think, when your joints started to ache you could take yourself a long hot soak."

"And catch my death of pneumonia," he said.

As if a pneumonia germ had any chance at all with him. Maybe by the time he was a hundred years old and willing to die. Before then, sickness need not call. It was Daddy, an Allen by birth, who had died of pneumonia, because, the way Doctor Mitchell had explained it, the influenza had caused him to drown in his own mucous. Daddy, a handsome, happy man, who had had pockets full of rock candy and a penchant for toting me around on his shoulders, had only been sick a week, and then he was gone.

In the rising wind the leaves were tumbling down from the cottonwood trees. Spencer would have plenty of raking to do next week.

"Grampa, some day you know it's gonna happen," I went on about the hot-water heater.

"What me gettin' the pneumonia?"

"No-sir," I smiled. "You gettin' a hot-water heater and a new bathroom too. You can't stop progress."

"Ain't a thing wrong with boilin' water on the stove. Kill all the bugs too while you at it."

A few years ago a group of deacons from some of the Negro churches along with a few other prominent men from our part of town had organized and hired a man to dig a common well and install a pump for our community. This had made it possible for us to have the extraordinary convenience of kitchen faucets and bathroom plumbing. Every connected household paid one dollar a month for the privilege of turning on a tap. Running water had led to flushing toilets and septic tanks, and although we still had our privy due to Grampa's unyielding commitment to self-reliance even when it came to his own neighbors, at long last the outhouses were starting to disappear.

The community well was located behind the Mount Zion Methodist Church, and it was a source of colored civic pride. It demonstrated our independence. What we had not been provided despite our tax dollars, we had managed to buy for ourselves anyway. In the summertime it was a struggle for the pump to meet our demands, and the water from the faucets would run muddy and had to be strained through a cloth for drinking, cooking, or washing, but it was evidence of our collective determination. *They* didn't have to give *us* anything. *We* could get it for ourselves. *We* couldn't vote, but *we* could dig a well.

In a gesture of truce, I rested my head on Grampa's shoulder. The bathroom plumbing battle didn't have to be decided today. Time was on my side.

"We better go inside," I told him.

Back in the kitchen, Grampa switched on the ceiling light and poured evaporated milk into a small pot to heat on the stove. Once upon a time, gas had been a hard sell to him too, but ultimately he had agreed to it. Even mountains gave way. Time would inevitably turn the sharp, rugged Rockies into the more gentle slopes of the Smokies. If time could do all that in nature, albeit in thousands of years, it could soften Grampa too.

I sat down at the table and watched him making the season's first batch of cocoa. Soon he was pouring me a cup, and eagerly I accepted the hot drink, feeling like a child again. When we were children, while Mama would be in the front room with him looking over his school work, Grampa and I would be in the kitchen. Jimmy's marks had been more consequential than mine. The family, the race, did not depend so much upon what kind of wife and mother I would be. It was Jimmy who had carried all our hopes and dreams. Now my marks mattered too, but I was being a maid.

Winter gathered outside, but inside the kitchen was comfortable.

Do you think your Aunt Esther means to banish me to the isolation of the dining room...

The afterglow of Thanksgiving lingered with me. Perhaps it was the promise of the season; the reassurance of the Nativity; the *good tidings of great joy*. A Christmas carol hummed around in my head impatient to be sung. I looked forward to the bounty of fat peppermint candy canes and brown paper sacks of oranges, apples, and nuts. In another year perhaps Little Evie would be able to recite a short verse in the Christmas pageant. I could rehearse it with her when I came home for the holiday. Nathaniel would be very proud. She was already talking, although her best words were *mine* and *no*. Given that she was about to share her world with a new sibling, this was probably good. I wondered what Jimmy had thought about my birth. I wondered when girls learned to think *yours* and *yes*.

"You take my umbe'rella with you to work tomorrow," said Grampa, adding a teaspoon of vanilla to my brimming cup of cocoa. "Prob'ly be rainin' in the mornin'."

"Yes-sir," I said. "If you're sure you won't need it."

"Where I got to go on a cold rainy day? Got me a pension."

He sat down at the table across from me, and we blew into our cups to cool the cocoa enough to sip it. The extra touch of vanilla rode upwards in the steam from my cup, smelling sweetly, while the wind worried the window panes.

"Well now, Grampa," I reminded him, "You aren't exactly a gentleman of leisure, you know."

"Maybe. But it's my own house I got to see after. Nobody tellin' me when to come and go. I can stay put when I want to, thank the Lord."

I did. Grampa had worked all his life. From cotton fields to hotel lobbies, and finally to the railroad. He had done what he had needed to do without complaint. It was good for him to know that he had something to show for it.

"You're braggin' Grampa," I teased him, smiling at him adoringly.

"Get you a pension job, you can brag too," he replied. "Now teachers, they get good retirement."

There it was again, the thorn. Never forgotten. Although it didn't hurt so much anymore. Sometimes it felt more like a splinter that was working its way out and healing. I figured I'd be back in Harlem by summertime.

"Grampa," I sighed his name softly, in a lazy attempt to discourage the topic and sipped from my cup.

"Why you got to be at his house every day anyhow," he pressed on. "Him a single man, and no chirren. It's a 'stravagance you ask me."

Of course I didn't dare *ask,* I just tried to explain.

"I'm a cook too, Grampa," I said. "Even single men eat every day."

"When yo' grandmama passed away, I seen after myself. I learned how to cook my own supper."

He had learned to cook long before then, and he had always had us for company. He had never been alone. Even before Mama had moved us in to live with him, I remembered that we had always been around. His house had always been the center of the universe, just the way he required it.

"Why ain't he married?" asked Grampa. "Somethin' wrong with 'im? A man like that should get hisself a wife to see after 'im if he need that much caretakin'. Ol' as he is what he waitin' on?"

I wondered the same thing sometimes. He had been engaged once, my employer had shared. *Almost married,* he had said, to a woman named Sylvia. She was from New York. Manhattan. He had described her as beautiful and smart, and I imagined her having all the sophistication and style of the fashion models in Aunt Betty's magazines, more so than even the Laura I had seen him with at the Woolworths. I pictured her soft white hand adorned with a glittering diamond like in the movies or like what Aunt Grace wore when she dressed up for special occasions. All that had been left to do was to win the war and come home to her, the way Nathaniel had come home to Connie. There had been so many weddings right after the war that I used to think that they would run out of white lace. However, by the time my employer had returned, his Sylvia was married to somebody else.

"Better offer," he had summed up Sylvia's reasons objectively, as if it were a business transaction gone awry.

"Did you know him?" I had asked, seemingly more bothered by the story than he was.

"We're friends," he had replied lightly, the crooked smile showing faintly on his thin lips. "I suppose I could have been his best man, if I had made it back in time."

"And he wasn't marrying your girl," I had reminded him.

"By then she wasn't mine, now was she?"

Maybe Sylvia had not wanted to live in McConnell County. As a New Yorker, she must have thought East Texas was a backwards place too, and giving up glamorous 5th

Avenue for a country town *Main Street* must have been too much to ask. I didn't think I could blame her. Yet she had hurt my employer even if he didn't show it, and I did blame her for that. He was a nice man, not deserving of that kind of treatment. Like Grampa, Taylor Payne could be impassive, but he wasn't invincible. Her *Dear John* would have broken his heart, and it wasn't right to do that to a man in the middle of a war, even if you did love somebody else. Maybe that was why he was content to be alone. Perhaps he still loved her.

"He will someday," I said to Grampa now, thinking of the pretty Laura in Woolworths, and of all the Saturday afternoons he had sent me to Sweet Water early because he was *dining out*. One of them would make him forget about Sylvia, or at least render her as trivial as his portrayals would imply. "But until that time comes--"

"Until you go back to school," Grampa corrected me immediately.

"Until I go back to school," I continued. "He pays well and the work is easy. I can't complain."

"You wouldn't if you could," said Grampa.

The whine of the north wind was melancholy. I took a larger swallow of the cocoa.

"I get to spend time readin' his books," I offered olive branch of sorts to Grampa. "He has so many books."

I seldom took the time to read a whole book from his collection, only bits and pieces, from law to love, sampling everything. A little history today. A little philosophy tomorrow. Court cases and poetry. In no particular order. Simply following my fancy and carefully returning the texts exactly as I had found them. Sometimes I would sit perched on the side of my employer's bed, skimming through whatever it was he was reading too, wondering what he went to sleep thinking about. His tastes weren't very predictable either. Everything was possible, from obscure existentialist writers whose prose was as dry as a desert to the detailed histories of the royal houses of Europe, and various books about life in America.

"What man gon' pay you to sit around and read?" argued Grampa. "He ain't too smart, is he?"

I did feel a little guilty for spending time in the work day this way. Maybe I ought to return some part of the twenty dollars a week when it wasn't always *earned*. But if I owed anything at all, then it should be paid to Mandy. She was the one being robbed, but then of course she would never begrudge me a single bookish moment.

When Spencer came after school we often went over his lessons while I cooked our employer's dinner. I wanted to make Spencer read on Saturdays too, but our employer was usually around the house, and they were always together. Maybe our employer could tutor him. Spencer was a bright child, and our employer was in favor of Negro education, he might as well help provide it. "In the north," he had said, "the schools are beginning to integrate. It's a good thing." As I had once reminded Jimmy, *good* did not have to be synonymous with *integration*. Having our fair share shouldn't have to mean going where we were not wanted. But then again in America, maybe there was no other way.

"That's what the NAACP says too," I had replied to our employer.

"And what do you say, Esther?" he had asked me.

You could always count on a follow-up question with him.

"If we can live together we ought to be able to learn together," I had answered.

"And can we?"

"Can we what, Mr. Payne?"

"Live together?"

I looked at Grampa now and smiled, but it was sad around the edges. The answer to my employer's question was no. Plenty of *us* didn't want *them* around either.

"Maybe he's just being nice, Grampa." I said aloud as we sat in the kitchen. "As long as I get my work done, that's all that matters to him."

Grampa looked dubious.

"He not one of them communists, is he?"

"Sir?"

"A communist. That's what Perry said. They go for the colored people. All that talk 'bout freedom and rights and goin' on. Perry said that might be it, the reason why he so partial to Nathaniel. And since he practically givin' his money away to you every week---"

At times my employer did remind me of my Marxist classmates at City College, but no, he was not a communist. He loved this country too much. He was suspicious of the Russians, and the Chinese were fighting us in Korea. The way he talked about *the Law* and the Constitution, was like Nathaniel talking about the Bible. It was his Holy Scripture. He was every bit the son of those 18th Century white men of property, in their velvet coats and ruffled collars, waxing eloquent about liberty and the rights of man. It all made perfect sense to him. "We've just failed to live up to it," he had said to me. He believed human intelligence could always transcend human nature. Maybe it could, but nature came more easily, instinctively, and intelligence required discipline and work.

"Grampa, I do work."

"That's right, you cook for 'im too," Grampa said a little too derisively, as if he didn't believe it.

I wanted to change the subject. Nothing I could say was going to be sufficient to smooth out the furrows in Grampa's beige-skin brow. About the only common sense he ever trusted was his own, and maybe Ernestine's based on how he talked about her to us. He was a wary man, but perhaps wisely so. He had done his utmost for us to have better, which made him protective of us, so logically he was suspicious of everybody, and particularly strangers. Danny had been a stranger. Now there was a new one, Taylor Andrew Payne, in whose employment my virtue was safe although my reputation might be at risk. Forced by circumstances to entrust the family dreams to me, Grampa was just being vigilant. I was all that he had, at least until the next generation when Nathaniel and Connie's children could assume the mantle.

"I thought you started out concerned about me havin' to go to work tomorrow in the rain," I said now. "But it's startin' to sound like you think I'm cheatin' the boss-man."

"Well he ain't no Jew," Grampa said. "Nathaniel told me that. So if he ain't a communist, then he might be a carpet-bagger."

Like his gentleman, I supposed, whose generosity had nevertheless felt like slavery to Grampa.

"Oh Grampa," I laughed at the old-fashioned term. "Please. Nobody talks like that anymore. This is not '*Gone with the Wind*'."

"You know the kind, I'm speakin' of," Grampa persisted. "Comin' down here and makin' trouble. Stirrin' up colored folks and spookin' the white ones so much that they get nervous and have to lynch somebody just to show who's runnin' things. Yo' great grand-daddy talked about the way they did after the freedom come."

Albert Green, our great-grandfather, had been born a slave in South Carolina, growing up a pale little pickaninny, with his Confederate father's hazel eyes and Roman nose. White men in blue uniforms, way off in Vicksburg, Mississippi, had achieved a measure of retribution upon Albert's father for the drunken violence of Albert's conception, and so the Rebel Army officer never saw the last son he made. Appomattox at last meant some measure of justice could be applied to Albert's legal status and to that of his mother, Matilda. Of course it was only a measure, and a small one at that. Nevertheless once the *Freedom* came, Matilda had been able to take her only child, and walk off the ruins of the South Carolina plantation, where she too had been born and then bred, winding up in Tennessee, and never looking back.

In Tennessee, Matilda had met and married a man, named Jacob Green, who had been able to forgive her the sins that had been perpetrated upon her and embrace her boy as if he had been his own, giving him his own last name, which he himself had taken from a former slave master. Our real family name we could not know, and in Grampa's family tree there was no Confederate branch. Jacob was his *Abraham*. It was from Jacob that Grampa's sense of family came even if Grampa's complexion did not.

It was Jacob Green who had given our family dignity, guiding Albert's growing up in the years following the Civil War, in a time when although there had been official surrender, there had been very little peace and hardly any healing. Abraham Lincoln had been a dreamer too.

It was Jacob who had led the family through the brief strange years of false hope called *Reconstruction*, and nurtured them through the hard but more familiar decades that came after. Feeding his family on faith and forbearance, so that no matter what life brought to meet them, they could be strong enough to withstand it, Jacob had ensured that we would prevail. It was Jacob's name that was in Grampa's Bible as the father of us all. But unlike Matilda, Grampa looked back often. I supposed looking back was necessary to understand everything. Just having the recent pieces of the picture could be misleading. You might want to think that it was all clear and simple, when in fact it really rarely was.

"He's not a carpetbagger or an agitator, Grampa," I said about Taylor Payne as we were finishing the cocoa. "He's from here, remember? He was twelve years old when he went to live with his uncle in Massachusetts. I think that makes him a son of the South," I said. "McConnell County can claim him as its own."

Perhaps I'm just a man without a country.

"And I promise you his suitcases are leather," I added playing with Grampa a little, hoping to lighten the mood.

"I still say he's a strange white man that's all," Grampa concluded.

"Yes-sir, perhaps," I agreed swishing the last sweet swallow of cocoa around in my cup. "But in a nice way, I think, Grampa."

His hazel eyes narrowed.

"Esther Fay, you not forgettin' yo'self, is you?" he asked.

A different but old kind of anxiety cast a shadow across Grampa's face, giving it a look that might have belonged to Matilda's father a long time ago, if he had been with her. Of course Matilda had been a beautiful woman, Grampa had told us. Her father would have had cause to be alarmed. Desirability could be a dangerous asset when it could not be protected.

"No-sir," I reassured him quickly, firmly, knowing what he meant, and meaning what I said.

I was keeping the Thanksgiving note hidden in my Bible because of Jimmy, because he had believed that the world could change. I looked down into my cup again at the chocolate grit, which was all that was left. Besides what was the harm in it? To like someone who liked you first? According to the Scripture there was nothing remarkable about it. It required no spiritual gift. It was only natural.

"'Cause I don't care how nice they is they ain't never gon' be *that* nice," said Grampa. "They might treat you all right when nobody's lookin', but that don't last with the daylight."

My employer had left his Laura standing in the Woolworths to come after me. In the broad open *daylight* when anybody could see, he had pursued me to make conversation like a neighbor. But of course he had only done so to see if I had spent all of the money that he had paid me—the extra too. And of course Grampa was right. Grampa was wise. I could not refute him. Still there was a funny feeling inside of me worrying over whether or not I wanted more than I should. The past acted upon the present like an impediment, like a palsy.

Grampa was only looking out for me as he always had. From the first day that we had moved into his house, he had protected us. He had been as much a parent to us and a partner to Mama as any man could have been. Even if Mama had been lonely, she had never been alone. None of us were. Grampa had made all of our lives easier simply by living his.

And yet inevitably, Isaac Samuel Green could speak only from what he had known. Holding onto the past, he could not fully predict that which was to come. History didn't really repeat itself—not exactly. For each of us there were new stories that had to be told; stories that would surely be changed by those of us who had yet to live them out.

The next morning as I rode the bus to work with Mandy, I couldn't help but see myself as fortunate, as fortunate as a colored maid could see herself. My todays were not so bad, my tomorrows had better prospects, and I even had a little money in the bank. I could afford the hope of a soul who had seen meaner times and withstood them until the times grew kinder again. Perhaps it was just the learned collective composure of a people who simply refused to let current circumstances deny them some hope in tomorrow. I bid Mandy a good day, knowing that we were both durable.

This knowledge gave me a warm feeling on the cold December morning. Grampa's prediction about rain had proven to be wrong, and I had left the house without his umbrella. There was only the biting wind still blowing out of the north. The people were rousing, their houses brightening with the new day. I rose to pull the bell cord to alert the white driver that he had brought me to my destination, and we acknowledged each other in the way that was the fashion of our time and circumstance.

I got off the bus and it pulled away. I walked along briskly. Although I wasn't ready to buy a car, with my new wages I had bought myself a good winter coat and hat. I was singing a Christmas carol to myself and the rising sun that nudged against the clouds. Suddenly strong hands grabbed me roughly by the shoulders. In the instant terror a little scream froze in my throat as I remembered Matilda. When the strong hands spun me around I was staring up into a laughing white face.

"Mr. Payne!" I gasped once recognition let me breathe again.

The panic he must have seen in my face only made him laugh more. Herman was with him, his tail wagging excitedly.

"Did you think I was the bogey man?" my employer continued to laugh. "I didn't mean to scare you."

"You grabbed me from behind," I accused him, snatching myself away. "What do you think?"

"Come on, Esther, don't be angry," he said now more apologetic, "I just wanted to surprise you that's all."

His gray athletic clothes were stained with perspiration even on this cold morning. Across his chest was the word *Harvard*.

"What are you doing out here anyway?" I demanded, fussing with my coat and straightening my hat.

"Our morning run, what else," he replied, grinning. "Isn't that right, boy," he looked down at Herman, and the dog barked as if he understood.

"In the dark?" I demanded.

"It's not so dark. Morning's breaking." He slapped his chest in the stock gesture of the athlete. "Feels good to have the cold air in your lungs."

"Well I guess you've got nothing better to do than to scare a poor woman to death," I complained, walking away to conceal a smile that was squeezing onto my face. "It's too cold out here for foolishness, if you ask me."

My employer fell into pace beside me and slipped his arm through mine. More foolishness. Dangerous foolishness. Jimmy used to walk with me this way, and I had been so proud that he was showing the world that I was special, that I was his. But Taylor Payne was not my brother.

"Well if you must know, it's your own fault," he was saying while I wrestled with the dilemma he had created.

"What did I do?" I asked, trying to hide my confusion.

The world might be watching, but I didn't want to pull away from him again.

"Cook the best meals in the world that's all," he declared. "Turning me into a cream puff."

"Humph," I replied, covering up my distress.

His stomach was as flat as it had been in September. Like Jimmy, it was his trait to be lean. Herman trotted along in front of us, amusing himself by sniffing at various spots of shrubbery and grass.

"I'm very sorry," I said coolly as we came to his driveway.

"No you're not," my employer returned.

"Maybe you shouldn't eat so much."

"Okay," he shot back. "Since I want your outstanding biscuits this morning, come on!"

In a burst he broke into a sprint up the drive, clutching my hand tightly in his, so that I had to run with him, or at least after him.

"Mr. Payne!" I cried out, holding onto my hat, my pocketbook flying like a flag.

He did not let go of my hand until he had towed me up the porch steps and both of us stood gasping for breath at the front door. Herman, enjoying the fun, barked and jumped up and down. His master flung open the door and we burst inside, both of us laughing like children.

"That wasn't fair," I protested breathlessly. "I'm wearing street shoes."

"Yes, far be it for you to wear high heels, Miss Allen. I'd be willing to bet that you can run a mile in those dreadful things on your feet."

I looked down at my shoes and was immediately embarrassed by the dull black leather and laces. Yet shiny, sleek pumps were for Sundays and the Lord's house. You did not dress up to clean toilets and wash windows, or bake biscuits.

"It's a good thing I'm wearing this kind," I replied. "Since you've got me running like a horse."

"Black Beauty," he said looking at me.

How readily he compared me to a beast. Strong. For riding. For working. Absorbing the blow silently, I turned away from him, taking off my hat. I deserved it, for *forgetting*, if for just a little while, the separateness between the places to which we had been born. For walking with him arm in arm, when Grampa's grandmother had been raped. And Jimmy was required to fight for a country that did not want him to vote for its president. I placed my hat on a wooden peg inside the closet.

Taking me by the arm, my employer turned me back to face him again. He was still smiling, although his expression was different now. Brilliant dark brown eyes, as dark as the coffee he preferred in his cup, studied me. I was not Matilda. He could not hurt me. I took my eyes back to the *Harvard* across his chest, but then lifting my chin he brought my eyes back up to his. His fingers, still cool from the outside, were tender on my skin. I had seen this expression before. On Danny's face. On the summer nights when the jukebox music had been slow, and he had held me tightly against him. But I was not Laura either.

"Why Miss Allen," my employer quietly affected a Texas accent as he moved his fingers to my face. "I do believe there are roses in your cheeks."

He opened his strong hand, covering the side of my face softly. Because he stood too close to me, I was breathing in the scent of his fresh sweat. For a moment we held there in each other's gaze. The color of his face deepening as he drew closer. My heart beat so hard that it pounded in my ears. In the sky over McConnell County, the sun was making its certain way to the new day. And I was waiting.

Until history abruptly pushed my eyes back down to my ugly shoes, and he took his hand away.

"You-you hang up your coat," he said in an odd, husky voice that no longer sounded of Texas. "I'll start the coffee." Pivoting, he went quickly to the kitchen, and Herman trotted after him.

I waited for a moment longer before taking off my coat. When I eventually did, my fingers trembled with the buttons. I hung my coat and closed the closet door. On my way to the kitchen, I caught a glimpse of myself in the mirror that hung over the credenza in the foyer, and stopped. The face that looked back at me was pretty, as if the fine electric light fixture overhead was bathing it in the enchanting light of a candle.

VIII

Early in December, Mr. Leon delivered a Christmas tree to my employer's house. It was a large dark green pine that filled the air with the festive scent of the holiday. From the attic, my employer had brought down the tree stand, boxes of ornaments, and strings of lights, but he was at work when the tree arrived, so it was left up to Mr. Leon and me to decide where to place it.

"Now lots-a folks want they trees to show in the front window," advised Mr. Leon. "'Course now his mama used to have it over there on that wall," He explained pointing to the wall opposite the entryway to the living room. "That way when he was workin' at his desk, Mr. Andrew could see it, and Mr. Taylor got his desk in the same place."

"You knew Mr. Payne's mother and father?" I asked.

"I did," the old man replied.

"So you knew him and his sister when they were children?"

"That's right."

"They must have been a nice family."

"That they was."

"It was sad about his parents."

"One of the saddest things you ever wanted to see."

"He told me it happened on a rainy night," I contributed.

"Back then the roads 'round here wasn't that good," added Mr. Leon. "Now, where you want me to put this here tree?"

It was appealing to think of my employer being able to see the tree when he was sitting at his desk as his father had done. He often worked late. In the mornings when

I came behind him to straighten up his desk, I would find more than one dirty coffee cup or cocktail tumbler left from the night before. And having the tree against the wall opposite the study was in keeping with his mother's tradition.

"Let's put it over there," I said pointing to the wall Mr. Leon had directed me to.

He nodded approvingly, and I hurried to set-up the tree stand.

"What were they like?" I asked as Mr. Leon was fitting the tree into the stand.

"Who?" he asked. "The Paynes?"

"Mr. Andrew and his wife," I clarified.

"Like that picture there," said Mr. Leon nodding towards the wedding portrait over the fireplace.

I looked up at the portrait again. The coupled looked like they were in love and happy. I couldn't imagine a single reason why my employer's uncle would have been against their being together. If any man had put that kind of look on my face then Jimmy would have thanked him for it and been happy for me. Yet after all, it was a wedding picture, and everybody looked happy in their wedding pictures. Perhaps my employer's uncle had known something else, something not visible in the young bride's blissful face.

"I know what you gon' say," said Mr. Leon. "Everybody looks sweet on they weddin' day. But they was like that all the time. The chilluns too. Guess a good nature just runs in a family. Wouldn't you say Mr. Taylor got a good nature?"

My cheeks burned suddenly.

"He does," I agreed, oddly embarrassed.

Mr. Leon looked at me, smiling broadly.

"Can I get you a cold drink," I offered. "There are coca-colas in the icebox."

"No'm, I b'lieve I'll be gittin' on down the road. You have yo'self a Merry Christmas."

I followed him to the front door.

"Won't you be back before then?" I asked, surprisingly reluctant to see him go.

"I'm always 'round when you need me," he replied, leaving me and Herman on the porch.

"Merry Christmas!" I called as he climbed up into his truck.

"Happy New Year!" he called back waving to me as he drove away.

By the time our employer came home that night the Christmas tree had taken shape. When Spencer had arrived after school he had helped me string the lights on the branches. He had wanted to put on the ornaments too, but since I couldn't be certain that Mr. Payne would approve of where we had placed the tree I had informed Spencer that it was best to wait.

"But you said his mama used to put it over here," Spencer had protested. "He gotta like it."

"Yes, I know," I had agreed. "But it's not for us to say. We have to wait. It's his house not ours."

"Aww," Spencer had whined. "He like everything you do."

"Well I don't know about that," I had quickly countered, feeling embarrassed again. "Besides, maybe he wants to hang his own ornaments. Wouldn't you?"

"Yes ma'am, I guess so," Spencer had conceded ruefully.

We had never had a real Christmas tree at Grampa's house. When we were little there had been an artificial one that Mama had ordered from the Sears Roebuck catalog. We had used it for years, bringing it out of the shed-house in the backyard each year and dousing it with buckets of warm soapy water to clean away the dust and cobwebs, and any bugs that might have made their homes in it. After Jimmy was killed we had stopped putting up a tree. There had been barely any Christmas at all in Grampa's house. And after Mama got sick all of the holidays, even *Easter* and *Mothers' Day*, had become just dreary days in the wretched weeks and miserable months.

Nathaniel was thinking of getting a real tree for Little Evie this year, but with Connie so big and weary with the pregnancy, he didn't want to make any extra work for her. Maybe Mandy could buy a real one for her children. I could ask Mr. Payne to get in touch with Mr. Leon. I could even pay for it if it cost too much. Spencer's sweet face had been so disappointed about the ornaments. Maybe he could stay later tomorrow and go home with me, and that way help our employer finish decorating the tree, although what would be best was for Mandy's children to have their own tree. Mr. Leon would surely give us a discount, maybe on one of the trees that nobody wanted. Mr. Leon had a *good nature* too.

It was after six o'clock when Herman perked-up hearing his master's car. I turned off the kitchen radio. Maybe I would ask Mandy to let Spencer have a dog. Mr. Payne could help us find him a puppy. The rest of Mandy's children would like having a dog too. I heard the front door open, followed by my employer's voice as he greeted Herman. Tonight, eager to see what he thought about the Christmas tree, I went looking for him too.

"Good evening, Mr. Payne," I said to him when I was standing in the open doorway to the study.

He was already seated at his desk going through the mail.

"Hello, Esther," he returned as he opened an envelope. "How was your day?"

"Fine. How was yours?"

"No complaints. Something smells good as usual."

"It's steak and rice."

He nodded.

"I'm hungry," he said absently as he was reading the letter in his hand.

"Mr. Payne?"

"Uhm-hmm."

"Mr. Leon brought the Christmas tree today."

"Was it all right?"

"Yes-sir," I replied, moving aside to give him an unobstructed view across the foyer into the living room. "I wanted to see if we had put it in the right place. Spencer and I hung the lights, but I told him we should wait on the ornaments in case you wanted to move it. Or maybe you'd want to do that part yourself."

When I looked back at him, my employer had removed his glasses and he was staring across at the tree. I smiled proudly. The tree was already pretty with just the colorful lights. The ornaments would make it beautiful. Growing up we had used popcorn on our tree; and maybe popcorn was homier, but in this instance I preferred aiming for elegance. Aunt Grace would have been pleased, Aunt Betty too.

"Mr. Leon said this was where your mother used to put it," I explained admiring what Spencer and I had accomplished. "And this way you can enjoy it while you're working at your desk."

I turned back to my employer. The expression on his face was blank. He put down the letter he had been reading and stood up. Perhaps there was something bad in the letter I thought, remembering the War Department telegram. And here I was talking about Christmas trees.

"Leon remembered?" my employer asked.

Perhaps whatever was troubling him had to do with the Christmas tree. Sometimes people didn't want to remember things. Sometimes it hurt too much. If you remembered what was good and it had been lost forever then all you were left with was the grief. But hadn't he come back here to remember? He kept his parents' wedding portrait over the mantelpiece. How much harm could it be to have the Christmas tree in that space? It looked good there.

"Maybe you'd prefer to have it in front of the window," I hastily suggested not wanting to get Mr. Leon in trouble. "Mr. Leon said most people do. I was the one who said to put it over there. He just did what I ask."

He met my eyes, but I couldn't tell what he was thinking.

"You wanted it there?" he asked.

"Yes-yes-sir. But we can move it. When Spencer comes tomorrow I'll get him to help--"

"It stays where it is," my employer said. "It's perfect."

He like everything you do.

"Spencer wants to help with the ornaments," I told him.

Sitting down again, he put on his glasses and returned his attention to the mail.

"Good idea," he said. "It'll be fun for him."

"Maybe he can stay later tomorrow night," I suggested. "That way he can help you after sup- I mean dinner."

"You two better go ahead without me," he said.

But it was his Christmas tree, not ours.

"You're going to be home late tomorrow, Mr. Payne?" I ventured.

"No," he answered. "But I think you're going to be busy the next couple of days." He looked up at me again. "I've invited the Mitchells and the Spaldings for dinner Saturday night. We'll be six."

The Laura in the Woolworths last name was Spalding. She was the *entitled* one.

"Hope that's not a problem," he added.

Why should it be? I could ask Nathaniel to make sure that the trash cans were emptied before service at Sweet Water. It would mean that Grampa would have his supper alone, but this was my job. The thorn moved, but the prick was slight.

"No-sir," I replied. "I'll put together a menu for you to look at tomorrow."

"Good," he said, opening another envelope. "It's the first time I'll have guests. We want to make a good impression."

"Yes-sir."

Impressions were important to him, but *I* was not in his *we*. No matter though, I would make sure that *they* were very impressed.

By Saturday afternoon, it wasn't just the placement of the Christmas tree that was *perfect,* the entire house was. The hardwood floors were polished to a glow and the carpets were vacuumed spotlessly clean. The wood parts of the furniture shone as brightly as the pews at Sweet Water and the fabric parts were brushed and immaculate. Cushions were as plump as new. Books were on their proper shelves. Newspapers had been reassembled and stacked alphabetically in chronological order along with the magazines. The front porch was swept and the windows were washed. Even Herman had been brushed and groomed. Poor Spencer had never worked so hard, and I was reminded of the times when I had gone to work with Mama to help her for some important event like an anniversary party or a wedding. Undoubtedly such a big event would be coming soon, but then I would be leaving soon, and Mandy would be here, so this was good practice for Spencer. Besides he did get to decorate the Christmas tree.

For the menu I had researched my employer's mother's cookbooks, but they were from the 1920's, and while some dishes were classic, it seemed appropriate that he should serve his guests something contemporary too. For that I had consulted with Aunt Betty again, who had been only too happy to advise me. The menu that she had recommended, and to which my employer had given his approval, would come in four courses, and the entrée would be crown roast of lamb.

His guests were expected at seven, and I was instructed to serve dinner about an hour later. Before the meal, there were to be cocktails and hors d'oeuvres. The bar cart was stocked for martinis. My employer would tend to it because he was sure that my Baptist upbringing had left me ill-prepared to mix drinks. I didn't bother to tell him that living with Aunt Grace and Uncle Eddie had given me experience with distilled spirits. He wouldn't know what the AME Church was, and if he thought I was too ignorant to tend his bar then that was simply one less thing for me to do.

Around six-thirty, with almost everything ready, and the lamb roasting in the oven, I went upstairs to change into a fresh dress that I had brought with me in the morning. Once I had finished pressing my employer's dinner clothes, I had starched and ironed the second dress so that my uniform was impeccable. The apron I had borrowed from Mandy, for the occasion, was trimmed in stiff ruffles. I had borrowed Mandy's maid's cap too, and I had shined my shoes just as I had shined my employer's.

I was determined to see to every detail and ensure that my employer would have his *good impression*. Laura Spalding would be pleased, and I imagined her telling him that she wanted to keep me on after they were married, but of course by then I would be in New York, having my martinis with Marxists.

Coming out of the bathroom where I had changed my clothes, I met my employer as he came out of his bedroom. He had dressed for dinner, and tonight there could be no mistaking him for a laborer. He was striking in his dark navy double-breasted suit and white shirt. The gold and red striped silk tie was in keeping with the holiday season. Gold cufflinks shone at his wrists and his silk pocket square was gold.

"You've changed your clothes," observed my employer surprised.

"Yes-sir," I replied, focusing on his polished shoes.

"And your look," he added. "The apron. And that cap."

The disapproval I heard in his voice drew my eyes up to his face. The morning in the foyer seemed a long time ago, and it was never discussed.

"I know you don't much care for ruffles, Mr. Payne," I replied. "But you said you wanted to make a good impression."

"You don't dress like this," he said continuing to look me over. "In-in this uniform kind of thing."

What did he think my mother's black dresses were? There was a knock at the front door, but he acted as if he did not hear it, although even Herman, who was being kept in the master suite for tonight, barked. There was another knock.

"It wasn't necessary for you to--"

"Mr. Payne, your guests are here," I interrupted him, heading towards the stairs.

"I'll get that," he grumbled, roughly pushing passed me on the staircase to reach the front door first.

"But it's customary for the maid to answer the door," I protested following behind him.

Did Laura Spalding really mean so much to him that he wanted to personally open the door to her?

"To hell with custom," my employer sneered under his breath.

"But Mr. Payne," I insisted at the foot of the stairs. "Your company will be expecting--"

"Check on the lamb, Esther."

Dismissed, I went to the kitchen. The lamb was fine, but I was frustrated. How long should I wait before I brought out the hors d'oeuvres? If my employer had allowed me to do my job then I would be taking coats by now and that way have a better sense of timing. Now the rhythm was all off. You were supposed to give people time to settle. I looked up at the kitchen clock. Should I come in at five minutes or ten? Standing at the closed kitchen door I strained to hear the voices. Was that Laura Spalding's laughter?

There was another knock at the front door. Good. With my employer and his guests in the living room, this was my chance to make things right. I rushed to answer the door and arrived there at the same time as my employer. He looked at me opaquely. "Serve the hors d'oeuvres," he instructed before opening the door. The cold night came in. I defiantly remained, standing behind him, waiting. It was my job to take their coats.

"Mr. and Mrs. Spalding, Laura, welcome," my employer warmly greeted the family on his threshold.

"Hello, Taylor!" Mrs. Spalding returned, kissing him on the cheek. "Merry Christmas!"

"Good to see you, my boy!" followed her husband as the two men shook hands.

When it was Laura's turn, my employer took her hand into his again, and they smiled at each other.

"You're looking beautiful as always," he complimented her.

There are roses in your cheeks.

Mr. and Mrs. Spalding exchanged approving looks, as Mr. Spalding handed me their coats and his hat.

"Why thank-you, Taylor," Laura replied sweetly.

He helped her take off her wrap, which was a bright red satin stole. Her dress was made of deep green velvet, revealing her creamy white shoulders and flattering her tiny waist. A single strand of pearls adorned her slim neck. The roses in her cheeks shone more brilliantly. I went to the foyer closet to put away her parents' things. As I was hanging the coats, my employer moved to pass me Laura's wrap, coming so close that I could smell his cologne. When I turned to take the wrap from him I met his eyes and our hands touched. Hastily I turned away, draping Laura's satin wrap over a wooden hanger.

Being back in the kitchen once more felt like being in a safe place. I peeked in at the lamb and its fragrant aroma bolstered me. I collected myself and the tray of stuffed mushrooms and headed to the living room.

I had read somewhere that in English estate houses it was the obligation of the servant to be invisible, as if a tray of stuffed mushrooms could magically appear, floating on air around a room to pause before company. And in any case servants could not become invisible by their own power, they had to be rendered that way; and the house on Webster Road was not an English estate. It wasn't even sufficiently Southern, or typically American. Nevertheless I moved around the room offering the tray of appetizers, and I tried not to see *them* at least.

"These are excellent, Taylor," Mrs. Spalding said about the mushrooms.

"Esther's a great cook," my employer said.

"Well aren't you the lucky one?" replied Mrs. Spalding. "CoraLee just fries everything."

"You have to train her," Mrs. Mitchell suggested as she was taking an appetizer. "I imagine Esther learned how to cook when she was in New York."

Harlem, I wanted to correct her.

"Don't tell me you brought your own cook with you," laughed Mr. Spalding. "Don't you care for our Southern fare?"

"You forget I was in the Pacific," my employer said. "I can eat whatever's in front of me."

"Well now to hear you young fellas tell it," replied Mr. Spalding. "War wasn't even invented until 1941."

"Please don't get him started reminiscing about the war, Taylor," Laura said, daintily taking one mushroom.

"Trench warfare, now that's combat," declared Mr. Spalding.

Negro soldiers had died in that war too. At least the French could recognize it and appreciate them. To them Negroes could be heroes too.

"Nice to see you, Esther," Doctor Mitchell spoke to me when I came to him with the tray of mushrooms.

"Good evening, Doctor Mitchell," I politely replied. "Care for a stuffed mushroom?"

"Believe I will," he said taking two. "They look delicious. How's Isaac?"

"Very well. Thank-you for asking."

"Connie keeping off her feet?"

"Yes-sir."

I moved to Mr. Spalding next, who took a stuffed mushroom and popped it into his mouth, nodding as he chewed.

"Very good, very good," he said, immediately taking two more. "What's in them, some kind of cheese?"

"I don't imagine anybody could teach CoraLee anything," complained Laura.

"She can be as stubborn as an old mule," agreed Mr. Spalding, as he took another mushroom.

"But Mother won't let her go," added Laura.

"CoraLee's been with our family for years," Mrs. Spalding explained defensively. "It wouldn't be right. She's practically in her dotage."

"Oh, Mother," sighed Laura.

By now I was standing in front of my employer who stood beside the fireplace, where a piece of Mr. Leon's wood was burning brightly. Declining to take an appetizer, he directed me to leave the tray on the coffee table, but Mr. Spalding intervened.

"Bring that tray back over here!" he said.

"Now Franklin," cautioned Mrs. Spalding. "Don't fill up on hors d'oeuvres before dinner. You know how you are with your stomach. Tell him, Doctor."

"If it was left up to my Helen we'd be running a Marshal Plan for the coloreds right here in McConnell County."

"Say what you will," concluded Mrs. Spalding. "All I know is that if it hadn't been for CoraLee when my mother was sick, I don't know what I would have done. She was as good as gold. Wasn't she, Doctor Mitchell?"

I placed the tray with the few remaining mushrooms on the coffee table.

"She was indeed," agreed Doctor Mitchell.

"When you find yourself a good one," Mrs. Spalding said. "You really have yourself something."

"But Mother, sometimes you have to get yourself a newer model," Laura replied as I was leaving the room. There was laughter. "You have to change with the times," she added.

Minutes before eight o'clock I lit the tall white candles on the dining room table. It was a fine table. He used them as his everyday-dishes, but my employer had purchased a nice set of china, as well as silverware and glassware. In the middle of the table I had placed a centerpiece that Aunt Betty had artfully put together using holly and bright red berries based on a picture in one of her magazines. When I brought out the tureen containing the tomato soup, Mrs. Mitchell complimented me on how lovely the table looked.

"Did you work in many fine homes while you were in New York, dear?" she asked.

The thorn hurt again, but I made sure that the tomato soup didn't splash as I ladled it into their bowls.

"Esther was a student, Mrs. Mitchell," my employer answered.

"That's right, Dottie," said Doctor Mitchell. "I told you about that."

"Oh," said Mrs. Spalding. "You're taking up a trade, Esther?"

"She's studying to be a teacher," my employer answered again.

When I brought out the roasted lamb, adorned with the traditional frilly white caps to cover the bones, Mr. Spalding warned my employer that he would do everything he could to steal me away and have me work for them.

"CoraLee can be your lady's maid, Helen," he declared. "I want this girl in our kitchen."

"I'm afraid she won't be staying in McConnell County," my employer replied. "We must enjoy her while we can."

"Don't let her go, man!" exclaimed Mr. Spalding spooning more potatoes onto his plate. "What's he paying you, Esther? By-god, I'll double it! Twenty dollars a week. How does that sound? You won't find wages like that up north, I guarantee you."

"Esther will be going back to school," said Doctor Mitchell.

"Yes, she's only working for Taylor temporarily," added Laura.

"Well Esther," Mrs. Spalding said. "You are quite talented."

"Thank-you, ma'am," I finally got to say.

"Yes, Esther, everything's just delicious," agreed Mrs. Mitchell.

After dinner the party took dessert, a coconut cake with coffee, back in the living room, and I began clearing the dining room table.

"So Taylor, what do you Harvard folks think about your boy, Bunche?" I overheard Mr. Spalding ask.

To me, at his kitchen table, my employer had been impressed by Bunche, proud even, a little self-congratulatory. Ralph Bunche was a Harvard graduate and one of its professors. The son of a barber, Bunche had risen to be an advisor to presidents. Now he was a diplomat. He was also a Negro. A Negro who had won the Nobel Peace Prize. I waited for my employer's answer. It was one thing to admire a Negro to me and to Spencer and another thing all together to do it to his polite company.

"It's damn fantastic," answered my employer.

I resumed stacking the dirty plates.

"Well I can't believe it," declared Laura.

"I know," agreed her mother. "A colored man. Whoever heard of such?"

"Maybe old buck-tooth Eleanor had something to do with it," Mr. Spalding speculated. "She's always been partial to the niggers."

"He does speak very well," remarked Mrs. Mitchell.

"I guess so," said Mrs. Spalding.

"I suppose he learned something at Harvard," Laura added.

"Did you take classes with them, Taylor, with coloreds?" asked Mrs. Spalding.

"Yes," replied my employer.

"I guess maybe yours are different," said Mrs. Spalding.

"In any case it is extraordinary," said Doctor Mitchell.

"Do you know him, Taylor?" Mrs. Mitchell asked as I returned to the kitchen.

By the time I brought the party a second pot of coffee, the fire in the fireplace was burning down, as was the conversation. Returning to the kitchen, I looked up at the clock. It was almost ten. I had been here since seven-thirty in the morning and it had been a long day. At least Nathaniel had agreed to come pick me up, and I was to call him when I was ready to go. As I scrubbed the roasting pan, I hoped to be able to leave by eleven. I had earned the twenty-dollars in my pocketbook this week. I might be the *Mammie* to my employer's *Mr. Rhett*, serving coffee and cake to his blond-haired *Miss Scarlet* and her family, but I had done it with as much dignity as Hattie McDaniel had demonstrated accepting the Oscar, or even Ralph Bunche accepting his prize. Mandy would have been proud.

You are quite talented.

Someday I would have a house like this, with a husband to sit at the head of the table. I sighed with the satisfaction of knowing this to be true.

"Tired?" my employer asked behind me.

"No sir, I'm fine," I replied swiftly drying my hands on a towel. "Can I get you something?"

"Wax paper. Spalding wants to take a piece of your cake home."

"Yes-sir," I said smiling pleasantly.

Mr. Spalding was a greedy man. No doubt he gobbled up everything CoraLee cooked too, fried or not.

"I believe that's the first time I've seen you do that all evening, in days to be exact," observed my employer.

"Sir?" I asked cutting a generous slice of coconut layer cake.

"Smile," he said. "You'd think with so many compliments tonight you might have had reason to, but not you."

You're looking beautiful as always.

Briefly I looked up at him, and then returned my attention to wrapping the cake.

"I once asked you if you were a good cook," my employer continued. "Do you remember what you said?"

"'People say that I am.'"

"That's right. And tonight was no exception. Quite the performance. Straight out of Central Casting."

"Sir?"

"Your presentation. And your...uh...costume."

"You wanted to make a good impression," I reminded him.

"Yes," he said dryly. "I wanted that, didn't I? Tell me something, Esther, are you always so... shall we say... compliant? Or only when it suits you?"

What did he have to be angry about? By *their* standards it had been a perfect evening.

"Mr. Spalding must be waiting for his cake," I said, replacing the lid over the cake-plate.

"Answer the question, Esther."

Ralph Bunche who had sat with kings could not sit at my employer's table, and neither could I, except in his kitchen.

"There are rules, Mr. Payne," I said, folding the hand towel.

"We make them," he replied.

"No," I corrected him, now meeting his eyes. "You make them. As it *suits* you."

"Taylor," said Doctor Mitchell coming into the kitchen. "Spalding's asking about his cake and insisting that Esther give Helen the recipe."

"It came from one of Mrs. Payne's cookbooks," I said evenly.

"Oh good," replied Doctor Mitchell. "You can write it down for her later. He doesn't need it tomorrow. He had two pieces tonight, not counting the one he's going to eat later. And he wonders why he has stomach trouble."

"The man enjoys his food," said my employer.

"Too much so," pronounced Doctor Mitchell. "Esther, do you need a ride home? The buses must have stopped running by now."

"Thank-you, Doctor Mitchell, but Nathaniel's coming for me."

"At this hour?" Doctor Mitchell replied. "They must be in bed. No sense in disturbing them. Connie needs her rest. We'll take you home."

"Esther doesn't accept rides from strangers, Mitch," my employer said looking at me.

"Strangers?" Doctor Mitchell laughed. "I've known this child since she was born. In fact, didn't I deliver you, Esther?"

"No-sir," I said, carrying the cake knife to the sink.

"Well I could have," Doctor Mitchell responded. "*Strangers*. Ha! You better get some sleep, Taylor. You might have had too much to drink. Esther, are you about finished? Surely you can let her go and give her tomorrow off too given the feast she prepared for us tonight."

"Sunday *is* her day off," my employer said. "She leaves me on my own. That's the rule, so to speak."

Our eyes met again but I quickly looked away.

"I'm sure you're no worse for the wear, old boy," Doctor Mitchell replied. "Come along, Esther, get your coat."

"Uh—can you give us just a minute, Mitch?" my employer asked.

"All right," the doctor agreed reluctantly. "A minute. It's late. And your other guests are waiting to say goodnight."

The swinging door between the kitchen and dining room came to a full stop before my employer spoke again.

"Since you believe I make the rules," he began. "I'm making another one now."

I faced him once more, waiting.

"I never want to see that cap on your head in this house again," he said. "Do I make myself clear?"

No, I thought. And yes.

"Yes-sir," I said. "In your house we do things differently."

PART TWO

As was the tradition at Sweet Water Baptist Church, 1951 was prayed and sung into the present by a congregation of devout adults and sleepy children, many of whom were bearing small white candles wrapped in white paper to catch the dripping wax. It was time to witness, to proclaim our gratitude for the goodness of the Lord; a lord whose Michelangelo-inspired face gazed down upon us from behind the new baptismal tank. We were as sure of Him as if He had been a descendent of Ham too. Once in a small gallery in Harlem I had seen Him painted as a Negro. He had had a face like mine, but with brilliant brown eyes as dark as black coffee.

As the clock approached midnight, Reverend Wright signaled for us to stand for the hymn, *This Little Light of Mine*. Little Evie was asleep on my lap, so I was permitted to keep my seat, along with Connie, who was sitting next to me, and due any day now. I sang out strongly and clearly, with conviction, because the idea of a diminutive light being something to sing about appealed to me. It appealed to others too. Aunt Betty was smiling and swaying gently to the rhythm of the singing. Grampa, who stood with Uncle Perry and Nathaniel in the deacon's section, also nodded his head from side to side as he sang. Nineteen-fifty-one had come to a small but sacred place where an assembly of tiny and flickering flames shone a bright belief in tomorrow.

♪*Let it shine, let it shine, let it shine.*

New Year's Eve was an important time of prayer and reflection, and not to be taken lightly or frivolously. It should not be a time for fireworks and champagne, or dancing in the street in Times Square, as I pictured my employer doing, on this his second trip in as many months up North. The day before Christmas Eve, he had announced that he would be spending the holidays with friends in New York City, thus gifting me with another unexpected *paid* vacation; in addition to a new blue silk scarf in its Niemen Marcus gift box. How could I help but feel fortunate, relieved nearly, to have an employer who was so generous? Generosity was part of his nature. Spencer had received a Christmas present from him too, a very fine looking baseball glove.

I could only imagine what he had given Laura Spalding; although she must have been crushed that he was spending *Christmas* and *New Year's* in Manhattan and not with her. No doubt she had been counting on his strong arm and gallant attentions as her escort to the rounds of holiday parties and dances. But she would soon have him with her always.

Sometimes taking a little time away was the right thing to do. Sometimes that was all it took to put things back in order. His Thanksgiving in Cambridge must have gone well enough. Now he was with his friends in New York. Laura Spalding would have to get used to his friends, his world. He would want to travel north often. Perhaps his experiment in McConnell County was coming to an end. If he was right about not fitting in anywhere then a city the size of New York had room enough for him to be *different*.

Being away for two weeks would give time for things to settle down. Something unspoken, and unwelcomed, had come into his home with the winter winds, riding in on a bank of clouds, and hiding in the branches of the Christmas tree. Something natural and disconcerting sat at his kitchen table during breakfast and dinner, waiting to be addressed; often making words awkward between us, sometimes even for him. And now that it was January I needed to start making my own plans to leave anyway. Things would be normal again.

At midnight, Reverend Wright gave the order that all the lights in the sanctuary be turned on and suddenly everything was bright. All the celebratory commotion awakened at least one baby who cried mightily. But now it was time to make a joyful noise, time to proclaim our *New Year's Day* testimonies. Sister Johns began for us by celebrating the birth of her niece in Detroit, Michigan.

"The doctors said my sister wasn't gon' have no chirren," she told us. "But I told her, Bernice, they don't know the power of Jesus!" She clapped her hands together triumphantly. "They may got they scientific medicine, but we got the blood of the Lamb! And I want to thank Him tonight, y'all!"

Amen!

What a wonder about you Jesus!

"I want to thank the Lord for providin' for me and my family," Brother Jackson rose up from the deacon's pew to say. "He done brought us from a mighty long way!

Chirrens, I seen the time when we didn't even now know where our next meal was comin' from. Times so hard, 'bout break a man's heart. Puttin' his babies to bed hongry."

What you talkin' bout!

"But the Lord seen fit to bless me and mine," Brother Jackson testified. "This past year we didn't have to want for nothin'. I gots to praise him! Brothers and sisters, I gots to!"

Bless the Lord!

Praise him!

Connie was using the back of the pew in front of us to pull herself up.

Let all His people praise him!

"First givin' honor to God, Pastor Wright, pulpit guests, Christian friends," began Connie, "I just want to thank the Lord for my family and for this little one 'bout to come. He blessed us all this past year! And we gon' trust Him in the new one!"

Aunt Betty nodded proudly and added her amens. I smiled and wondered what would happen if Aunt Betty stood up to give thanks for her brand new bedroom suite. It, too, was an extravagance, but that was also a part of the sacred promise, that we would have an *abundant life*, a life beyond our needs that included such frills and ruffles *like so much pink foam*, and not just on aprons and maids' caps.

When Connie sat down again I squeezed her hand affectionately. Perhaps I should rise and testify too, testify to my family's health and prosperity, say something about how God had *brought us through*. But the *through* also carried with it an *away*. Away from the days when more of my *us* occupied these treasured pews. It was hard to be thankful for that. Hard to count it *all* joy. Besides I had Little Evie sound asleep on my lap, and little ones could be fussy when they were awakened. I made my testimonies in private, during the precious solitude of the Saturday afternoons at Sweet Water, when no one could hear me but God.

Mary Wells was asking the church to pray for her father, who lived in Louisiana. He had heart trouble and he was failing. He might not live to see another Christmas.

Put your trust in Jesus, child!

God is able!

God was. And maybe this was the most mysterious thing about Him. The thing that inspired faith. And without faith we could not please Him. By faith the Red Sea parted and the Jericho walls had come tumbling down. But it was also a thing that inspired fear too. He was able and yet so many times He didn't do.

Please don't let him die.

Yes, of course it was a war and the Bible warned us that there would always be wars, and people must die because that was what happened. People died all the time. It was the only way to Paradise. Enduring inevitable loss was the only way to obtain eternal victory. Families had to be torn apart. Hearts had to be broken. It was like the song said, trouble was in our way and we had to cry sometimes. But yes, God was able.

So when Johnny Madison said that his cousin's little girl had contracted the polio, we took comfort in Job's story, and in Sarah's barren years, and in Gethsemane itself. A disease that crippled children was a bitter thing. It wasn't even the summer yet, and I wondered where the little girl lived that she would have access to a swimming pool.

"Doctors say she gon' be a cripple," Johnny told us. "But my Bible tells me that Jesus heals the lame and makes the blind man see."

That's right! That's right!

"He in the miracle business," testified the young man, who would soon be ordained another deacon in our church. "I want y'all to thank the Lord with me for what He gon' do for her!"

Thank Him! Thank Him!

Miracles. We all believed in miracles. To our graves we went trusting.

Amen!

It was Ben Thompson who was standing now to make his own request for prayer. He said he wanted to grow stronger in the Lord and do better by his mother.

"Y'all know I ain't always lived right," said Ben, choking back his contrite tears. "But I'm here tonight to rededicate my life to Jesus."

"Thank You, Lord!" cried out Sister Thompson, his mother. "Thank You!"

She was sitting beside Aunt Betty, who fanned her and patted her on the back comfortingly.

"I want His will to be done in my life," finished Ben.

Confess your sins, son. Jesus' forgives.

Sister Thompson started singing, *I love the, Lord, He Heard My Cry*, and the congregation followed her lead. She dragged the song out too mournfully for it to be a *joyful* noise, but it was coming from her relieved heart. Her oldest boy wanted to get right with God. It was every mother's prayer. As we sang along with Sister Thompson now, some of us clapped our hands as the Holy Ghost moved us. Others of us waved our hands to say how true the words of the song were.

♪*He pitied every groan*

Every groan. All those painful days and nights when Mama's suffering had forced her to admit it out loud. So many groans until at times I seemed to hear them now. When she was too weak to groan there had been the tears on her face. Maybe God did pity every groan. But maybe it was also the least He could do.

Ben, his face now broken and wet with tears, came to his mother and knelt before her. She was weeping too, as she put her arms around him and rocked him back and forth as if he would always be her baby.

♪*Long as I live where troubles lie*

Reverend Wright came down from the pulpit to put his hands on the pair, while he petitioned for Ben's salvation.

♪*I'll hasten to His throne*

"We thank you, Lord, because you do not forsake none of your sheep," prayed the preacher. "You are the Good Shepherd! You call the lost to be found. You wait on us, Lord. You make a way for us all to come home."

Where was *home*? And was Jimmy really there? With Mama and Daddy, and Grampa's Ernestine? Were they really all there and not simply in the cold, dark earth vainly trusting in the Resurrection?

Thank you Jesus!

Yes, thank you, Lord!

I was hopeful for Ben and happy for his mother, and I guessed that the *rededication* was going to interfere with Ben playing guitar at Ray's Café on Saturday nights. He played very well, and Nancy Davis liked him to accompany her when she sang. He was a good dancer too. He would be much missed if he gave up his *worldly* life for a *sanctified* one. Our tradition decreed the two incompatible. Living in the Spirit was supposed to mean living without the jukebox, and the laughter of a good time where people also drank and danced.

But Mandy said that a *joyful noise* could be made anywhere, and besides the good colored Christians of McConnell County were willing to buy Ray's barbeque. They just wouldn't eat it there. They wanted to get it *passing through*. "It ain't for decent folks," Aunt Betty had declared about Ray's. "And I don't see why yo' grandpa puts up with you hangin' 'round there."

He barely did. But he believed in me and trusted that someday I would wear my righteousness more consistently. After all I had been raised to be good, and the Lord must have his hand on me too. He could afford to let me to answer the call of my youth. It wouldn't last much longer. Time was on the Lord's side.

Long ago I had decided against telling Grampa that I believed that the Blues came from God as much as the Scriptures had. Truth was truth no matter how it was told. Mandy was right about making joyful noises. But if I told Grampa all of that he would hear it as sacrilege and it would be hurtful to him. For the same reasons, I also didn't tell him that at Christmastime I sipped spiked eggnog with Mandy after her children had gone to bed. Prohibition was not a Biblical concept. After all, even Jesus had turned water into wine not Welch's. We each had to know God for ourselves.

Reverend Wright expanded his supplications to cover all the young men in the world, and by doing so made me think of Danny. The war was going badly again. The Americans had been driven back in retreat. I was fearful for him. Did he really intend to make war his life?

Danny had been thinking of me too. He had sent me a Christmas card. "Chicago got nothing on the cold here," the card read. He wanted my arms around him. He said he thought about what had happened between us in the secluded clump of trees all the time. As I sat stroking Little Evie's back, keeping my head bowed in the prayer with the congregation, I thought about it too. It would be nice to see him again. It would be nice to be in love; to smile some set of secrets across a room the way Connie and Nathaniel did.

Some of us good Christian folk wanted to make that part of life sinful too, to reduce the *Song of Solomon* to a parable about God and man, instead of leaving it a love story between a man and a woman. Like the Apostle Paul some of us believed that we had to punish this flesh that the Father had fashioned from clay, in His own image. We regretted our passions and hated our needs. Except this most natural and essential truth was not to be denied. We had to heed its request and submit to it too. Otherwise, how else could we hope to be fruitful? Even sweet old Sister Callie, long before I had become her acolyte, had made her peace with this part of life. And for it she had reserved for herself a place between a husband and a son. She had loved, been loved, and made love. It was not a thorn in her side. Maybe it was her balm in Gilead.

Danny was my only lover, yet I had hardly considered myself virginal that night in the back of the Ford. I had come close enough to glimpse over to the other side plenty of times. I had been pulled on and urged forward, coaxed and cajoled, by urgent, clever boys at first and then by charming, seductive men. Jimmy's friends. Nathaniel's friends. Men that Uncle Eddie knew. Men who came from good families and who might make decent husbands and loving fathers. Yet I had remained modest enough to and stay elusive, until I was now nearly too old to have eager suitors. Time had been narrowing my field of play, setting and sealing my fate, and I had just let it, until Danny had come along. Maybe it was because I had been so weary of all the dying that I had found myself craving the life of the flesh. Healthy, vital flesh. Sweating and smelling of aftershave. And peppermint.

What if I fell in love with him? How would that be? It didn't seem prudent to. To love another soldier too much. Men died in wars. Yes, we had our Nathaniel back. But the odds weren't that good. And Danny was planning on making the Army his life's work. But still what if he came back to McConnell County and drove me to Dallas to see a movie? What if we came upon another clump of trees and shared ourselves? What if I paid honor one more time to the woman in me and the soldier in him? I could surely risk that much. It was the love that consecrated it, not the license, and I could learn to love him.

♪*Jesus gave it to me, I'm gonna let it shine.*
Let it shine, let it shine, let it shine.

The day after *New Year's* was a Tuesday. With most of a vacation week still in front of me, I decided to make quilt-tops. It had been Mama's custom to stitch together quilt tops in the winter, in preparation for the actual quilting, which she had done in the summer, as Ernestine had taught her, and then as she had taught me. We still had a decent set of quilts, and they seemed durable enough to last forever, but putting together the quilt tops reminded me of her and it reminded Grampa of Ernestine, and so it was a good way to be busy. Grampa helped me bring Mama's old Singer sewing machine from her room and we set it up in the front room by the window.

Late in the afternoon I needed electric light and rose to turn on a lamp. Looking out the window, I saw Nathaniel's truck pulling up to the house. My first thought was that something had happened with Connie, because he had opened the garage today and it was too early for him to leave work for any other reason. Concerns quickly vanished, however, as soon as I could see that his face was unworried as Nathaniel came into the yard.

"Hey!" I greeted him when he came into the house. "What you doin' here? Is everything all right? Connie okay?"

"Hey yourself," he replied, going over to the wood heater to warm his hands. "Where's the ol' man?"

"Out back. Stackin' wood, I think."

Mama's sewing machine hummed as I resumed stitching my cloth squares together.

"What you cookin'?" asked Nathaniel.

"Butter beans."

"Can I get a cup of coffee?"

He opened the heater to stir up the coals and toss in a new piece of wood.

"We're not exactly runnin' a café around here," I teased, concentrating on my seams.

"Well that sho' is cold. A workin' man can't even get a cup of coffee in his own granddaddy's house."

"Can't that workin' man see I'm busy?" I pretended to complain even as I got up to go to the kitchen to make the coffee. "Why you not home botherin' your wife anyway?"

"You don't mess with a woman in her condition," replied Nathaniel now rocking easily in Grampa's chair. "I wish she'd come on with it."

"Don't you be rushin' that boy," I called back from the kitchen. "He'll come when he's good and ready."

"How you know it's a boy?"

"I got a feelin' that's all. And she's carryin' low, and you know what the ol' folks say."

I put the coffee on to brew and then stirred the big pot of beans cooking slowly at the back of the stove. The steam pungent with white onions and pork tickled my nose. I replaced the lid and stole a glimpse out the window over the sink to check on Grampa. Sometimes he wanted to work too hard, as if he were his grandson's age. The old man could still swing a chop axe very effectively, rheumatism or not, and he didn't wear gloves. The calluses on his hands had been worn down to a smoothness like the original skin only tougher, so that an axe handle could rub no more blisters into his palms. For Grampa chopping wood was a necessary act, not one of vanity.

"The coffee'll be ready in a minute," I said when I sat back down at the sewing machine.

Nathaniel nodded, watching me. I looked back at him and smiled. He was physically confident too, I thought. The South had never bent his back.

"You ought to go see if you can help your grampa," I suggested over the machine's hum. "He's been out there a while."

"I'm doin' fine, me myself," said Nathaniel.

"Well I guess you are," I smiled again. "But I wasn't exactly askin' about you. But I am surprised you not at that garage. Time is money as you say."

"Bidness a little slow today. It'll pick up," explained Nathaniel. "Might as well as take it easy while I can."

We chatted for awhile about nothing in particular. I sewed, Nathaniel looked on, and the coffee brewed. When I assumed that the coffee was ready I went to get him a cup.

"You do that right nicely," my cousin complimented me when I handed him his cup sitting in a saucer. "I guess it's all that practice you be gettin'."

"Um-hmm," I said rolling my eyes at him. "And since Connie won't wait on you, I guess somebody has to."

"Kinda sweet though," Nathaniel said after he had taken a sip.

"Like I said, this is not a diner," I returned, going back to my quilting squares. "The pot's on the stove."

"That how you talk to yo' boss-man?"

"I get paid to wait on him."

"I'll say."

We looked at each other and laughed together. I resumed sewing.

"Speakin' of work," said Nathaniel after a time, "He come by the garage today."

I stopped, looking up at him again.

"Who did?" I asked.

"Yo' boss-man," replied Nathaniel.

"He's not due back yet."

"Must-a changed his mind. 'Cause it sho' was him 'less he got a twin."

"It takes at least two days to get here from New York. He wouldn't travel on New Year's Day."

Unless Laura Spalding had begged him to. Maybe there was about to be an engagement notice in the *Dispatch*.

"Maybe he flew one of them airplanes," said Nathaniel. "I don't know. But I do know he's back in town."

The sewing machine hummed again.

"He must have an important trial coming up," I replied lightly. "What's wrong with his car?"

"Nothin'," said Nathaniel.

"Hmm. Just brought it in for an oil change then. You got 'em all trained, don't you, Nathaniel, I must say."

"Maybe. But I think he just come by to kill some time."

"Why you say that?" I asked concentrating on keeping the seams straight.

"'Cause he didn't want nothin'. I didn't even look under the hood." There was a small pause. "He asked about you though."

Again the machine was quiet.

"Does he want me to come back to work this week?" I asked.

"Naw, he didn't say nothin' 'bout that." Nathaniel sipped his coffee. "Just asked me how you was doin' that's all. You know," he looked at me carefully, "Like you was weighin' on his mind or somethin'."

"Well I'm glad he didn't say for me to come back to work," I brushed off Nathaniel's interpretation and started to sew again. "I'm enjoyin' the time off. I've been needin' to get some things done around here. Grampa doesn't make a fuss, but you know he takes some lookin' after too. Sometimes I worry about him, Nathaniel. He'll go all day without eating when he gets too busy. He just forgets--"

"That'd be you," Nathaniel mused cutting me off. "Always lookin' after folks."

"That's right," I agreed, turning the fabric to follow the edges of the square.

"Connie say that you heard from that boy, Danny Simmons," Nathaniel said after another time.

"I did," I replied as I worked.

"What he have to say for himself?"

"Oh the usual. You know how you soldier boys can be," I chuckled.

"Depends."

"Depends on what?"

"Who we writin' to."

I held up the expanding quilt top to examine my work in the light. I hadn't replied to Danny's Christmas card letter. Every time I tried to write to the blank page intimidated me. We had never made promises to each other before, and that was the easier plan. Just let life take us where it would. But in Danny's last letter there were implicit questions floating around the margins and squeezing between the lines, declarations and solicitations looking for a response from me.

"Well?" asked Nathaniel.

"Well what?" I asked back.

"Who he writin' to?"

I didn't have an answer.

"You know, Nathaniel, it feels to me like you're snoopin'," I said. "That's not like you."

He stopped rocking in the chair.

"Feels to me like you hidin' somethin' and that's not like you," he replied. "Not from me anyway."

I put down the quilt top. The light from the lamp shone on his face, and he looked darkly handsome and too discerning.

"I don't have anything to hide, Nathaniel. I got no secrets. Danny wrote to me, yes. And he's talking about coming here for another visit. If he does, then maybe I'll have something to tell you. But trust me, there's nothing else to say about it."

Nathaniel began rocking again, the chair creaking in the quiet room.

"Esther, I'm not tryin' to take Jimmy's place or nothin'," he said gazing at the wood heater. "But you and me always been close in our own right. Like brother and sister too. And since I'm older than you that kind-a makes me your big brother." Now he looked at me. "So if you ever need to talk, you know, if you need some advice about somethin' that you don't want to talk to the ol' man about, you can come to me. You don't never have to hide nothin' from me."

"I know," I replied. "And thank you for saying that, Nathaniel. But whatever's botherin' you, don't let it. Just concentrate on that baby that's on his way."

"You right sho' it's a boy."

"I got a feeling."

"Esther, I want you to be happy," Nathaniel returned to his other point. "If schoolin' is what you want, then I want it for you. 'Cause all I really want is for you to be all right. To be happy." He stopped rocking again and studied me. "A man can make you promises, Esther. He can even mean them, but you have to be careful. Real careful. This world can make it hard for a colored woman. You understandin' me?"

Hearing Grampa coming in from the woodpile, we both looked towards the back of the house.

"I understand, Nathaniel," I said quietly turning back to him.

He wanted to protect me too. Men thought that they had to do that. To look out for what and who was theirs, however it was that we belonged to them. They must guard us from whatever and whomever would threaten harm. Nathaniel had suspicions, but they were as unnamed as the thing that waited around the rooms of my employer's house. And I intended to keep it all unnamed and unacknowledged until it died from neglect. My employer might have New York. But I had silence. And time. And eventually New York too, only it would be Harlem. I could manage this. I wasn't Matilda. And Taylor Payne was not a Confederate soldier. Besides I already had my own Jacob, in the person of Danny.

Nathaniel would like Danny. They had things in common. They could talk about the army and Asia. Nathaniel agreed with Danny that the army offered a decent living for a Negro man. Some day Danny might show me Paris on military orders. Some day he might show me the world. A big wide world that saluted his uniform. What if I just ran away with Danny and made a life with him far from this place? What if it were up to Little Evie to be the first college-educated member of our family? What if I just passed the legacies and the dreams onto her?

Grampa came into the front room, changing the conversation. But enough had been said. Later that week Connie went into labor, and by Friday morning Nathaniel James Green was born to us, and that was all that any of us could talk about.

My first day back at work, excitedly I reported the birth of my new "nephew".

"That's excellent!" said my employer upon hearing the news. "Nathaniel must be thrilled."

"Everybody is," I replied from my usual place at the door of the study. "He's a beautiful baby!"

My employer was smiling. The trip had done him some good. He seemed at ease with himself again. Everything was fine.

"Well, you're very much the proud aunt, aren't you?" he remarked.

"No more than I am of Little Evie," I asserted immediately.

"I look forward to meeting them both."

There had been momentary lapses in judgment, but they were corrected, and now standing in the doorway to his study, I imagined benevolent white planters visiting the *quarters* to see the newborn *coloreds*, bringing with them baskets of decent food for the mothers and pretty little white shirts for the babies. Maybe Laura Spalding would come with him and that way make the scene complete. I painted on a courteous smile.

"I'm sure Nathaniel would be proud to have you stop by," I told him.

The Christmas tree in my employer's living room was dead, and there was a mess of needles for me to sweep up. Once the holiday was done Christmas trees were without much cheer. The first days of the new year worked against them, turning them into large, green, aggravating signs of finished festivities, like the uneasy sensations you got after you had consumed a feast, and you were reminded that you had been a little bit foolish, and you felt a little bit exhausted. As I was taking off the ornaments from the tree, more needles fell to the floor, and when my employer carried the tree to the back yard to turn it into firewood, still more dropped off, leaving an annoying trail from the living room through the kitchen. The roar of the vacuum cleaner was not as musical to me as the hum of my mother's sewing machine.

There was washing and ironing to be done, meals to cook. Keeping very busy I carefully ignored that the *something* still lingered silently in the house, like a phantom. I dismissed it, pushing it away from my mind, even in those moments when I sensed my employer's dark eyes watching me too intently. I was only there to clean and cook. If a maid's cap offended him then of course I would never wear it in his house again. I worked for him.

Eventually I managed to put the right words on paper and responded to Danny's Christmas card. Writing just enough to suggest possibilities circumspectly tempered by prudent caution, I met his sentiments levelly and wondered if he would even write back. It was not a love letter. I wondered if he would up the ante more directly next time, and I wondered if I really wanted him to.

One evening late in the month, my employer announced that he was going to see Nathaniel's new baby, and that he would be taking me home, because, as he informed me, it made no sense for me to take the bus when it would be on his way. He had been waiting for me in the foyer, already wearing his coat, my coat draped over his arm.

"So be advised, Esther," he said. "I will not take no for an answer. If you require some kind of justification then you may tell yourself that you'll merely be showing me the way to Nathaniel's house. That should satisfy the propriety police I think."

By now he was holding my coat for me again, certain that this time he would prevail in the disagreement. "Well?" he said, either expecting me to slip my arms into the coat sleeves or confirm my submission, or both.

Of course I could quit. Right here and now. And maybe I should. But what sense would that make? The money was too good and I didn't want to risk offending him so much so that he fired Spencer too or didn't hire Mandy when I left. It was after all just one car ride. It was the night-time. No one would see. Nathaniel could give me a ride home from his house or I could just walk. What Grampa didn't know wouldn't worry him. I slipped my arms into the sleeves of the coat.

"Just let me put on my hat, Mr. Payne," I said, wishing that the hat had a veil.

Once outside at his car, my employer opened the passenger-side door for me. On the back seat was a brightly wrapped gift for Baby Nate. He must have shopped for it himself, or maybe Laura Spalding had helped him. Would Laura have lowered herself to shop for a colored baby? Would he have told her it was for a colored baby? I pulled the front seat forward in order to crawl into the back, but placing a hand firmly on my shoulder my employer stopped me.

"No," he said, pushing the seat back in place. "I'm not a chauffeur."

But I was a maid.

When I got in the car, he closed the door, and I scooted up against it, where I sat rigidly with my hands folded tightly, resting on my pocketbook. Obviously he knew where he was going and did not require directions. And yes it was reasonable for him to bring me to Nathaniel's house. Reasonable and kind. But this was neither a reasonable nor kind world. He might not care. But I had to.

"It seems I've offended you in some way, Esther," my employer said after a time, breaking the silence.

I stiffened more. Being lord of the manor did not make you king of the world. Maybe that was why he couldn't get along with his uncle. They were too busy fighting over the top. Grampa was undeniably the head of our family, and when it came time, Uncle Perry would be, and then Nathaniel. There was an order to things. To everything. White men did not drive their colored maids home, with them sitting in the front seat like passengers.

"I want us to be friends," my employer went on. "And please, don't tell me that you work for me, or give me some antebellum drivel about the way things are done."

By the light of the street lamps we passed, I glimpsed the profile of his face, the narrow slope of his nose, the thinness of his lips. Grampa grieved the dilution that these features had done to the Africa in his own face, grieved the violence and the violation that had made him and his family Americans. He had given his allegiance, and sacrificed his grandson, but the Confederate soldier was not forgiven for the physical form left in my grandfather's face, the paleness of my grandfather's complexion. His beloved Ernestine had blackened and softened the bodily scars of slavery, but the *ol' times* were not forgotten.

My employer took his eyes off the road and shrewdly smiled at me.

"I dare say it would be very un-Christian of you, Esther, to refuse my friendship," he said before looking back to the road once more. "Isn't there some kind of Scriptural admonition that you should love your enemies? Surely you think more of me than that."

He was ever self-assured and self-possessed, self-righteous even, as much as a non-believer could be. Perhaps he had read something else besides his precious books of Law. Maybe Presbyterian children also went to Sunday School. What must it be like to know that you owned the whole world, in addition to your soul?

I looked at the road ahead too. We bumped over the railroad tracks. The nicer ones always wanted to read more into agreeable associations than was either real or necessary. They gave us Christmas presents and visited our babies. They looked after our old ones in their *dotage,* and when we died, they favored us with their presence at our funerals. They were just so many irregular shapes of white in the black patchwork patterns of our lives.

"You do, don't you?" he pressed.

It was easy for him. He was the *entitled* one. More so than even Laura Spalding. He could pick and choose his life. He didn't have to wait for it to happen to him. Everything was on his terms. Why should he care what I thought, about him, or anything else?

"It wouldn't do to have enmity in your house, Mr. Payne," I replied.

I wasn't sure what I meant exactly, but I liked the way I had said it, as a confident, educated equal. He smiled again.

"All right," he said. "So may I assume that we're friends then?"

I remembered walking with him, and the *roses* in my cheeks. He was good to Spencer.

"Yes-sir," I answered.

And I also remembered that Laura Spalding was beautiful, the approving glances between her mother and father. His Manhattan world must glitter, and Laura would shimmer there.

"Good," replied my employer.

Friend was a broad concept, a term into which you could fit many meanings. Deep and shallow. Long and short. I could give him that much.

We did not talk the rest of the way to Nathaniel's house. When we arrived Nathaniel's porch light was on, shining invitingly. Nathaniel's mother-in-law, Mis' Inez looked out the window and watched us walk up to the porch. Nathaniel came out to meet us.

"How y'all doin'?" he greeted us.

"Just fine, Nathaniel," my employer said reaching out to shake Nathaniel's hand. "But surely not as well as you."

"No-sir, I bet not! Y'all come on in."

Nathaniel held the door open for us, and I passed through first. Connie, with Baby Nate in her arms, was sitting in a kind of royal maternal state, in Nathaniel's easy chair, which had been moved closer to the Dearborn heater. She beamed and cooed at the same time. Mis' Inez stood next to her, wearing an impenetrable expression.

"Esther!" exclaimed Connie happily. "You come too."

"Hello, Connie," I said soberly and then spoke to Mis' Inez.

"Esther," the older woman sternly returned, barely nodding her head.

"Girl, you ought to see this big boy," bragged Connie. "I think he might be smilin' at me already."

Mis' Inez looked down at her daughter.

"Milk done soured on his stomach and give 'im gas," she said.

"Mama, Connie," Nathaniel was saying, "This here's Mr. Taylor Payne."

My employer had removed his hat. I took mine off too. Mandy would be standing at the stop to wait for the bus tonight like every other night.

"Good evening, ladies," my employer spoke. "Nathaniel, a little something for your son," he added, presenting the wrapped package.

"Oh that's real nice of you, Mr. Payne," Connie responded. "We're happy to meet you! Nathaniel talks about you all the time."

Mis' Inez raised an eyebrow.

"Thank you, sir," said Nathaniel, accepting the gift.

"Yes, thank you, Mr. Payne," chimed Connie again.

"Can I take yo' hat and coat, Mr. Payne?" asked Nathaniel.

Mr. Payne this and *thank-you, sir* that. Even in *our* houses the *antebellum drivel* applied. Everywhere was his domain, including Nathaniel's hard-earned living room.

"Yes, thank-you," said my employer, passing his hat to Nathaniel and removing his coat.

Then he moved to help me with mine, and Mis' Inez made a rough sound in the back of her throat. Nathaniel waited, finally looking slightly awkward. Connie was absorbed by her son.

"Thank you, Mr. Payne," I said softly, electing to let him help me so that both the moment and Mis' Inez's scrutiny would pass more quickly.

Still there was time enough for him to read her face for a reminder of the way things were done in McConnell County, even in the colored section. Yet apparently undaunted my employer passed our coats and hats to Nathaniel and crossed the room to the mother and child.

"Please, may I see this beautiful baby, I've heard so much about?" he requested.

What could the disapproval of an old Negro woman mean to him anyway, if it registered at all?

"Nathaniel, I hope you not boastin' all over town," chided Connie, as she made sure to uncover Baby Nate enough so that his candy brown beauty could be fully appreciated.

"It's his aunt who sings his praises," my employer said bending down for a closer view.

"Oh what Esther know?" prattled Connie. "You just better judge for yo'self."

"Esther showed him the way here," Nathaniel was explaining.

"And we glad she did, ain't we, Nate?" Connie cooed to her little boy. "His Aunt Esther just wantin' to show him off. But can you blame her? What you think, Mr. Payne?"

"You don't mind taking me home, do you Nathaniel?" I quietly asked, desperately looking at my cousin while my employer looked at the baby.

Nathaniel nodded quickly.

"He's everything she says," Mr. Payne praised the baby to the exquisite delight of the mother.

Mis' Inez had taken a seat next to Connie and was looking impatiently at the white man standing over her daughter and grandson as if she was barely able to endure it. But he had brought a present. A sudden sense of advocacy surprised me.

"Tell the truth now, have you ever seen a sweeter child than him?" asked Connie shamelessly.

Some other child might have his January birthday crammed into *Christmas* and *New Year's*. But Nate was Connie's baby. She would always set aside the day to remember. Boy children were important. But then again Connie was the same over Little Evie too. Her children enchanted her.

"No, never," my employer replied kindly earnest.

He was indulging Connie completely, and if it were not for Mis' Inez's unyielding affect, I might have smiled too. The older woman was thoroughly unimpressed by his generosity. Because she knew, and served to inform us, that no matter what he was saying to us now, in the world, *his* world, our beloved Nate could never be as beautiful as the blonde-haired, blue-eyed cherubs that decorated Christmas cards. The world would not treasure him. Like Thurgood Marshall argued, his school books would be inadequate in number and outdated in content. He would sit in the balconies of movie theaters and ride at the back of buses.

"Please, y'all sit down," urged Nathaniel, who was still holding the hats and coats. As if suddenly remembering them he hung our things on the coat rack by the front door.

"Why impose upon Nathaniel?" my employer turned to me and asked directly. "I can take you home."

In his eyes I saw that the change I had maneuvered mattered, and in that moment it was as if I was as unkind as Mis' Inez.

"It's no trouble, Mr. Payne," Nathaniel attempted to intervene. "I was plannin' to get by there anyway."

"Where's Little Evie?" I asked looking around the room for a distraction.

"Just gone to bed," answered Connie innocently.

"Don't wake her up," instructed Mis' Inez.

Now chastened, for a variety of reasons, I dejectedly sat down on the sofa. My employer sat down next to me, and then Nathaniel took a seat. He declared again how happy we were to have Mr. Payne visiting and thanked him once more for the baby's present. My employer sat back against the sofa cushions comfortably and crossed his legs with his ordinary ease, as I watched Mis' Inez, who under normal circumstances was a friendly woman.

At least the mother, the child, and the guest—the stranger—were content. The gift sat unopened on the coffee table, appearing as out of place in the room as its giver. Alternately I felt disrespectful and unkind, although I ceased to be clear as to whom and about what. Surely this was not what DuBois had had in mind when he had argued for integration. My head hurt. How impolite would it be to leave the room for an aspirin? Couldn't I just walk home from here? Grampa was waiting supper for me.

The ever resilient Nathaniel eventually found his own way, despite his mother-in-law's countenance and his cousin's tension, and the two men fell into conversations about the garage and automobiles. While Mis' Inez continued her unrelenting resentful examination of the white man and the colored woman who had brought him here, the men, perhaps both accustomed to the battlefield, attained for themselves a common *at-ease*, as the mother and child dwelled in their private paradise, and Little Evie had escaped all together to her undisturbed dreams.

Emerging just long enough to do so, Connie offered coffee to the guest, who politely declined. The conflict in the room began to seem silly even if it was intractable. I wished someone would open the present. I needed to see something other than Mis' Inez's eyes if I looked up or my employer's large well groomed hand if I looked down. It was a strong hand, but it was a *desk-man's hand*. Without a single callous. But it had taken me by the waist through my mother's widow's dress. It had lifted my chin and cupped my face. Snatching my eyes away I only ended up in the eyes of Mis' Inez once more, and she seemed to know that I had wanted the hand to touch me, that his breaking the rules had *suited* me too.

After some time the spoken conversation returned to the new baby, and Connie asked my employer if he would like to hold Nate. "Yes, thank you," he said eagerly, rising from the sofa and going to them. He bent down and Connie lovingly placed the small blanketed bundle into his waiting arms. He gazed at the child, while the rest of us watched them together.

He would be a good father some day. They could move the sleigh bed and make the buttercup room a nursery again. A new born baby was like a new day, full of promise and potential. Jimmy would have been a good father. But then we did have Nate. And little Evie.

An eternal kind of tenderness further softened my employer's features, disarming me. "The only beam you'll ever be is one of light," he cooed to Nate, whom he cradled in the crook of one arm. With his other hand he played gently with the infant's tiny fingers. Nate, making adorable baby sounds, wriggled free of his blanket, and his tiny brown hand grasped the strong adult finger, clutching it tightly.

Beam was a broad concept too with more than one meaning. I liked the way he used it now and perhaps so did Nate. He was looking up at the white man who cradled him, with eyes too young to see through a filter of history.

"Say, hello, to Mr. Payne, Nate," Nathaniel said from across the room. "He come to see you and brought you a present."

I thought of the three Wise Men and the Baby Jesus. I thought of the way Mary looked on, in every depiction of the Nativity, unafraid and open to the strangers who admired her child. Open even to *us*, in the person of Balthazar bearing the myrrh. They called it the Epiphany and I had learned about it living with Aunt Grace and Uncle Eddie.

My employer looked up from Nate's small face to my own. There the brilliant dark brown eyes met an authentic smile that was no longer blocked by an old woman's reckoning.

>♪ *I'm gonna let it shine.*
>*Let it shine.*
>*Let it shine.*
>*Let it shine.*

II

The winter began giving way to spring in the middle of February. Hard-frost mornings warmed up rapidly, and in the afternoons it could be warm. Tiny green buds spotted the branches of trees and hardy little green shoots pushed up through Grampa's rich dark garden dirt.

The Scripture said *He made His sun to rise on the evil and on the good and sent rain on the just and unjust*, including the house on Webster Road. Not that my employer was either or all. What he was was unbelieving. It wasn't my business. As the unsettling aura of the December morning further receded, it was replaced by the more fitting fellowship of the January night in Nathaniel's front room. Once I decided that I didn't have to be afraid of the *something* anymore, it became easier in the house for both the master and the maid. We became as though we could be friends.

With the coming of spring Saturdays Mr. Payne worked outside, with Spencer at his side, and Herman never far. Spencer was having such a good time that I tried not to dwell on the sad irony of it. If things were as different as my employer said they could be in McConnell County and in America, in fact if they were what they should have been from the start, and at least since all of the wars *we* had died in for *them*, then Willie Gaines would have been here to teach his own son and show him how to do things. How much then was the white man's benevolence only the complicated result of what was also his injustice? So much for the Law and the Constitution. For the Bill of Rights and all the ratified Amendments. For all of the victory campaigns and political promises. Another generation was being held in contempt.

But at our employer's kitchen table, while his dinner cooked, I often helped Spencer with his school work, and sometimes on Saturdays, Mr. Payne would join in, at times making games of it for Spencer so that it was fun for them both. Mr. Payne challenged Spencer, pushing him harder than the class assignments required.

"He's a bright, kid, Esther," he had said. "He's going far."

Then it would certainly have to be farther than McConnell County I had thought darkly.

"Maybe his father will send for him to come to California," I had replied.

"'Go west, young man', is that it?" our employer had asked.

"You never hear anybody say 'Go South'."

"And yet we did just that."

"For different reasons, Mr. Payne."

"Same outcome. We're here."

"But I'm not staying."

"No. You're not, are you?"

For his birthday Mr. Payne gave Spencer a world atlas. It was a big book of maps, with illustrations and descriptions of the different countries and their peoples. Spencer loved it. He took it to school and brought it with him when he came on Saturdays, and he and Mr. Payne would study the pages together. Over time I couldn't tell to whom these Saturday afternoons mattered most, the boy or the man, and soon the relationship that flourished between them did not depend upon me to be. According to my gardening grandfather, we planted the seeds but God granted the increase. And so He had. The boy valued the man, and the man was good to the boy. I tried not to think of it as something that time and circumstance would work against.

"Aunt Esther, I want to be a lawyer," Spencer said to me one day as we were on our way to the bus stop and home. The grass was greening along the roadside beneath our feet. Maybe he was becoming too fond of our employer, I thought, but I had to smile at the earnestness in Spencer's voice. Every generation brought forth its own promise, like the blossoms on Grampa's peach tree. Somewhere along the way the promise had been successfully planted in the child who walked with me. It was exciting to watch it taking root and reaching for the sun, regardless of who nurtured it.

Mandy did not have any willing well-to-do relatives, who could send for Spencer, and I didn't really hold out much hope for Willie Gains to do the right thing, but there might be other opportunities, other means for Spencer. Wasn't that the meaning of spring? A fundamental proof of tomorrow? Of regeneration? There were scholarships to be had for a bright young man with potential even if he was colored. *We* could go to Harvard too, and Ralph Bunche had won the Nobel Peace Prize. It was years away yet, but when the time came Mandy could ask Mr. Payne to write a letter of reference for him. He would remember Spencer, and I was certain that Harvard would remember him. Our employer would want to help Spencer. To everything there was a season, a purpose under heaven.

Spencer was full of potential, the way Jimmy had been. If no wars came along to take him, then why couldn't he be a lawyer too? Thurgood Marshall was one, and people said that Howard University was as good as Harvard. Separate *and* equal. If Taylor Payne could help Spencer accomplish his dreams, then at least it was some small down payment on all that Spencer was *entitled* to.

"You can be anything you want to be," I told Spencer as we reached the bus stop, hoping it wasn't a lie.

Later that evening, as we sat together in Mandy's front room, I told Mandy about the conversation with Spencer, about his aspirations, and his growing affection for our employer.

"Well I think it's nice of him the way he treat Spencer," she said.

"They can all be nice sometimes," I replied. "I just don't want Spencer to get hurt."

"You know, Esther, holdin' him responsible for bein' born white seems just the same as holdin' us back for bein' born colored."

"If things were fair in this world," I argued, "Willie could have found decent work right here, and been with you and his children to this day."

"Plenty-a colored men didn't run off," said Mandy thoughtfully, sipping leisurely from a cup of coffee. "I love that man and ain't shame to admit it, and I ain't blamin' him neither for his choices, but I am sayin' that they was his to make. Yo' boss-man didn't make 'im to go to California."

"But Mandy Gaines, you know how hard it is for our men to find decent work. Us too, for that matter."

In the next room, when they should have been sleeping, Mandy's three youngest children were squabbling as they played.

"You a bucket-head!" we heard Mildred exclaim.

"Who you callin' bucket-head?" Nancy demanded.

"You is!" Mildred fired back.

"Bucket-head, bucket-head, Nancy is a bucket-head," John Henry was singing.

"If y'all don't settle down in there," their mother called out. "I'm comin' in there and somebody gon' be kickin' the bucket."

Instantly the children quieted, and Mandy and I grinned at each other. I called good-night to them.

"Good night, Aunt Esther," came the chorus reply. "Good night, Mama."

Maybe Mandy was right. Everything had its price. It cost to go. It cost to stay. It even cost to come back. I only wished it was as simple as black and white. But maybe there was also such a thing as being too stoic, too reconciled. Too *compliant*. They counted on that about *us*, counted on our endurance, on our forbearance. To make a better world by tomorrow, *we* were going to have to fight in the one we lived in today. There was so much to be done. What if we really were *they*? Co-conspirators in our own oppression because of our long-suffering resolve to wait upon the Lord?

"What's a colored man to do in this county?" I asked forlornly.

"Maybe I don't know," Mandy answered, reaching for the pot to refill her cup. "But why don't you ask Nathaniel? Or yo' Uncle Perry. Yo' grand-daddy too. And my daddy stayed. Maybe one of them know."

"All right, Mandy," I gave in. "Just don't be so indebted to Taylor Payne, that's all. Spencer works hard for him, you know."

"You do too," she added. "It's what you got against him that I don't see."

"I got nothing against him," I replied.

"That's what I know," she said smiling. "And that's what I mean."

Our employer, with Spencer's help, planted new rosebushes along the front of house and planted other assorted flowering plants in pots on the front porch. His potted garden reminded me of Aunt Grace's windowsill flowers. I was a fickle gardener at best.

"My mother used to have flowers all along this porch," he reminisced as I stood over him watching him pat down the dirt around a large pot of zinnias. "Water these in the morning, Esther. That's the best time."

"Yes-sir," I said accepting my new assignment.

It was nice the way he continued to bring things back to the way his parents had had them. I could tell that he loved them deeply. When he spoke of them it was with a tenderness that he did not often show. In a way they were becoming important to me too.

"What do you think?" he asked, finished with the pot and surveying his work.

"Your mother would be proud," I said dragging the large pot towards another spot where I thought it would look better.

Picking up the planter, he laughed.

"Here?" he asked.

I deliberated a moment.

"No," I told him as he held the pot. "There," I pointed.

He carried the pot to the new place.

"Your mother was a good gardener?" I asked.

"Yes, she was," he said.

"Did she raise vegetables too?"

"Herbs for cooking mostly."

"It's a lot of work to keep a garden, you know," I said, moving the pot again, pulling it just a few inches to the right.

"Yes," he said, chuckling again. "So I see."

"I like wild flowers myself," I informed him. "The kind that grow where they want to."

"And here I was thinking there was no room in you for natural sentiment," he grinned.

"I'm a country girl, Mr. Payne," I reminded him.

"And I'm a country boy," he returned.

Of course he wasn't. Cambridge wasn't exactly country living, but I didn't argue with him.

"Your parents must have been very happy here," I said in order to change the subject.

"Yes, Esther, they were," he replied. "We all were."

Guess a good nature just runs in a family.

Is that why he had come back then? Because he had been happy here? The black soil covered his hands and filled in under his fingernails, but this was a hobby, a sentimental act, and his hands would be washed clean in just a little while. His desk-man hands. They were not like Nathaniel's. And Jimmy's were gone.

"I'm glad that they died together," my employer said.

I stared at him astounded by the remark.

"Neither one of them would have been much good without the other," he explained.

The casual sound of the words coming out of his mouth contradicted the expression on his face. A cloud was passing in front of the sun. Connie might have put her hand on his arm if she had been there, but there was only me and it still wasn't my place.

It was a ridiculous, romantic notion, I thought, the idea of dying together, like Romeo and Juliette. Andrew and Jessica had left children behind. What about the fragile daughter and the abandoned son? Mama had stayed with us to raise us in spite of losing Daddy. In the end losing Jimmy had proven too much for her, but still she had not given up, not right away. And Grampa, working all those years away from the woman he loved, only to retire in time to lay her in the ground, had gone on for us too. It was not always more sacrificial to die for love. Sometimes the real sacrifice was in living for it.

"Your mother and father couldn't have wanted it that way, Mr. Payne," I said after a moment. "Not to leave you and your sister on your own like that."

"Maybe," he replied, cleaning the dirt from under his nails. "It's just a theory." He looked at me again. The cloud had passed. "Life's full of tough choices, Esther. Maybe it was one of your blessings that neither of them had to make that one."

A *blessing*? Connie was right, some things couldn't make sense.

"The blessing was that you and your sister got through it," I objected.

He was a strong man regardless of his *desk-man* hands, but none of us were born strong, we were trained into it. We became so out of necessity. When we had to be. For ourselves. Or for those we loved.

Easter was coming, and because she usually had to work, for the last couple of years Mandy had let me take her children to Easter Service at Sweet Water. Afterwards the children would stay with us from the Easter Egg Hunt to the Easter Dinner, and even Grampa enjoyed them, buying them chocolate bunnies and jelly beans.

My employer made it a point of explaining to me how the original Church had deliberately chosen this time of the year to commemorate the resurrection of Jesus, in order to coincide with the pagan rites of spring.

"Celebrating it in this season allowed them to capitalize on traditions already long-standing," he had educated me. "No one knows exactly when the crucifixion and this alleged victory over the grave occurred."

Alleged.

That was the way he thought of it. Like it was something that needed to be argued about in a courtroom. I had smiled, feeling no threat from the prosecution. My sagacious, self-assured, socialist classmates had already introduced me to these arguments. Religion anesthetized the people they had said, turning us into docile sheep and taking away our sense of personal responsibility. In other words, it made us surrender, and the master classes had used it as a weapon against the rest of us for centuries, so that all of that hoping for heaven had rendered us mostly at peace with hell. I had heard it all before.

"Or *if* it did," I had said about the *alleged* victory.

"Well, yes, there's that general debate too, of course," my employer had replied, a little taken aback.

I liked to remind him on occasion that I was not as provincial as he might think. I, too, read books other than the Bible, and not just in his study.

"Which makes it a matter of faith," I had continued, smiling. "And so by definition, it doesn't have to be proved, just believed. As a mystery it doesn't have to be explained, Mr. Payne. It's supposed to be beyond our understanding."

"Touché, Miss Allen," he had conceded, smiling too. "I might have known not to challenge you in matters of religion."

"In matters of faith, Mr. Payne," I had corrected him. "There is a difference."

At Easter-time, and all the time, I delighted in the Savior's triumph. Every knee would bow, and every tongue would confess, I was thinking to myself, including that of the Roman Centurion.

On *Easter* morning the Sweet Water congregation, including Mandy's children, was vividly decked out in celebration. Every life needed a little ornamentation. After all it was the springtime. The song birds and the sunshine were inspiring. All the children were in crisp new outfits, the little girls smoothing their skirts, the little boys tugging at their collars. The women held their heads high showing off their fine hats, and the men walked proudly in their best Sunday suits.

My new dress was a floral print on a light green background, and I wore new dark green pumps that Mandy had convinced me to buy, along with a new matching hat and pocketbook. I missed singing in the choir, but on this day I was happy not to be under a robe. The shoes pinched my toes a little, but vanity did have its price. "You put me in mind of yo' grandmama the way you look in that dress," Grampa had complimented me before we left the house; and as we had walked to church together, with Mandy's children in front of us, Grampa and I had done so arm in arm, as if he was escorting me.

There wouldn't be many more Sunday mornings such as this. I would be back in Harlem by late summer, in less than four months. I had written to City College to inquire about readmission in the fall. The dean of women had written back to me personally. "Nothing would please us more than to welcome you back, Miss Allen," her letter had said. I had *promises to keep,* as Robert Frost had written in his poem about a snowy wood. It was time to finish what had been started, and I felt ready. Once upon a time it had been a privilege to be in Jimmy's shadow. It was the same to follow in his footsteps. I wanted to take on his mantle, to pick up where he had left off. In a way it was like Mr. Payne restoring his parents' house. Despite the years away, he had come back to finish what they had started here.

Following in the family trade so to speak.

I would be doing the same. To everything there was a season and a purpose.

And after all, I missed the academy, the excitement of discovering new ideas and the stimulation of revisiting old ones. All the encounters and interactions around my employer's kitchen table and throughout his house tested and confirmed my intelligence, raising my expectations, urging me back to something beyond the havens of Sweet Water and home.

The dean's letter had pleased Grampa too. He talked about the life I was going to lead and had circled a set of matching luggage in the Sears and Roebuck Catalog. "You gon' go far, Esther Fay," he kept saying. Me and Spencer, both going *far*. Far away. And for the journey Grampa wanted me to have nice suitcases. I did have nicer clothes to pack in them.

I wished that I had known Ernestine, this woman that my grandfather cherished even today after so many years without her. I wondered what people must have said about him choosing her, when she was so black and he was so not. If he had surrendered to what the advertisements, even those aimed at us, told us, then he could not have wanted her. But he had loved her and loved her now, so much so that Mis' Janey, the widow who lived across the street from him, pined for Grampa hopelessly.

It was the dark Ernestine who had put the ebony back in our complexions, so that Jimmy had been the beautiful, red brown of cinnamon, and Little Evie, who looked adorable today in her yellow dress and white Easter bonnet, could be her rich shade of mahogany. In my own face the red highlights of vitality had finally returned, blending with my own dark brown, so that the light green and floral print suited my face and my bare arms and legs.

Many Negroes hated our blackness, detesting the *Dark Continent* that persisted in our complexions in spite of the bleaching creams and the hair straighteners. But Grampa said differently. The darkness in our faces, the coarseness in our hair, he had taught us to value. Being light-skinned might be important everywhere else, might define beauty for everybody else, but in the center of the Green family universe, it was an insult, an impurity. When we women pressed our hair, smoking up the kitchen with our hot-combs and Royal Crown hair grease, Grampa objected severely. Ernestine had never used a hot-comb, he preached, and I had been sixteen years old before I had stopped wearing plaits and started straightening my own hair. "It ain't na'tral," Grampa had complained vehemently, and even though I now regularly straightened my hair anyway I loved him for it.

Were it not for Ernestine, for the Africa preserved in her body, we could not have been the people that we were. We would have been denied Nathaniel's triumphant smile flashing white against his own black skin, or Nate's sweet candy brown. So many of *us* sought out the higher tones and lighter colors. It was as though if we couldn't be white we at least wanted to be closer to it, so that even in our own communities light color had its privileges. Just not in Grampa's house. In his house beauty was the color of black.

Black beauty.

I do believe there are roses in your cheeks.

Buoyed by revitalized plans for my future, I decided to remind my employer that I would be leaving by the end of the summer. He had gotten used to having me around, so I felt I owed him this, and I wanted to make way for Mandy. One night soon after *Easter*, while he was having his dinner—at the kitchen table—I broached the topic. I was getting used to him too, even learning to sit politely with him while he ate, although I always saved my own suppertime for my grandfather.

When I made my announcement about leaving my employer's response was positive and supportive, as if I were Spencer.

"You're going to make a wonderful teacher, Esther," he declared.

"I can help you find someone to keep house," I offered.

"Thank you, but let's not rush the goodbyes. I'm in New York all the time. I could look you up."

My mind flashed to some future scene in Uncle Eddie and Aunt Grace's house. Maybe they would call him by his first name, but among their friends I knew there would be the *Mis' Inez's*, the *Grampas* too. Harlem was separate from New York no matter what my employer said.

"Spencer's mother, Mandy," I said. "She does really good work."

I wanted Mandy to have this job, to have the easier time finally. She should not have to come home worn out at the end of every day. I wondered if my employer would want to be her friend too. Would he want to sit in his kitchen with her and learn how she viewed the world? He would enjoy Mandy. She would be able to talk with him generously, without hesitations and nagging reservations. She would be willing to pardon him. Or to *acquit* him as the case may be.

"I'm sure," he replied. "But I'd rather not think about your leaving right now."

Maybe she would even use his library too. She was literate, just too busy. And as for Spencer's siblings, I could see my employer helping all of them with their homework. It might be paternalistic, but it really was almost fatherly too. It was not the worst substitute. It might even be some compensation. It was kind. Until a Miss Laura-type ultimately came along and changed things, or put a stop to them. Including his trips to New York.

I hoped he would look out for Mandy, and shield her from some nervous, uncertain bride obsessed with trying to overcome her inexperience at running a household. It was hard to work for those types. They could be critical and demanding, ignorant and mean, all in such a sugary sweet way that it could be missed by all but the persecuted. Soft voices growled too. Pretty smiles bared teeth. If he were in love, my employer might not see what was happening. As perceptive as he was, as analyzing, love could make fools of men, even him.

"I can speak to her, and ask her to come by," I pressed on. "So you can meet her. You'll see. She's the reason why Spencer is such a wonderful child."

"Esther," my employer spoke my name firmly. "There'll be time for that later."

Recognizing the tone, I fell silent. I had forgotten my place again. It was his decision, his kitchen, his house. He took a drink from his wine glass, and I rose from the table and carried my cup and saucer to the sink.

"I'm sure Spencer's mother is a fine woman," he said to my back. "But I'll miss you, Esther."

...But our conversations more.

My heart beat faster. The Thanksgiving note was still in my Bible, saved like Danny's post cards. I didn't turn around to look at him for fear that the *something* had abruptly set upon us once more; for fear that it might not be easy to say good-bye to him either; and for fear that it mattered to me too much. We were not really friends, I repeated in my head. He just wasn't my adversary. And Mandy was right about that, he never had been.

Sometimes I found myself wondering if our paths had ever crossed before last September; wondering if we had seen each other when we were children, or passed by each other in a busy subway train station. It was pointless. We had nothing in common. Living in the same town here or there was not the same as living in the same world. Up until now. Yet if we were companions, it was only because we shared this house, his house. I was a servant. His servant.

But we were here together now, in this place. He always spoke more words than I did, but I often felt just as revealed. In the light of his sincerity, my precious mask seemed transparent. Perhaps he was my friend, this man for whom I cooked and cleaned, and from whom I took wages. As much of a friend as he could be anyway. He had been right about not being able to hire my mind. I had eventually given it to him of my own free will, thinking for myself. Yes, he might miss me.

"I will miss you too," I confessed to the soap bubbles rising in the hot water, the steam on my face.

For a time the only sound in the room came from the faucet, so when I shut it off, there was silence.

"Ever been to Atlantic City?" he asked after a while, although it was still to my back.

"Once," I answered, placing my cup and saucer into the sudsy water that was almost too hot for my hands.

I heard him push his chair back from the table. Then he was standing at the sink too, and there was the faint familiar scent of bergamot.

"It's a great place," my employer said.

If I turned around I would be looking into his face. I would see his eyes as they were seeing me, and seeing too much. Frantically I yearned to shrink myself into something small and hard and tight, so I could leap over the hot sudsy water onto the windowsill, away from him. And at the same time I longed to expand myself into something voluminous and floating so that I could fill up the whole kitchen, every cabinet and every corner, and that way be all around him. Neither was possible. Nothing was possible. All I could be was the size that I was, experiencing his body too close to me, feeling his words prickle the back of my ear.

"You do have to go," he said quietly standing behind me.

I didn't move. Starched cotton cloth brushed against my bare arm as he drew closer, placing his dinner plate in the hot dishwater. For a moment his hand was submerged below the suds with mine. I tried not to tremble.

"And I'm certain Spencer's mother is a fine a woman," he continued.

By now his deep voice competed with my pounding heart. The sink was solidly in front of me and he was the one who seemed to be everywhere else, even in the dishwater; his arm starkly white in the bright light shining down from above the sink.

Sleeve and skin and suds, there was so little difference. All was whiteness. And under the soap suds my dark brown hands lacked resolve. Grampa was right too, but it wasn't Grampa's face that I saw reflected in the kitchen window glass. If he took my hand now the dishwater would conceal it, as had all the backrooms and dark nights from our shared, shame-filled past. How sweet the apple must have tasted to Eve. Had it been golden, glistening at her in Eden's sunshine?

My employer took his hand out of the water, resting it on the porcelain lip of the sink. Blue veins were visible beneath the wet skin. The nails were trimmed and clean. Only the scraped knuckles suggested manual labor. I had seen this hand wielding hammers and setting fence posts in the ground, but it was a *desk-man's* hand. It put scholarly words on paper and led dazzling women onto glossy dance floors as orchestras played, but it had also wrapped a gift for Baby Nate, and rested on Spencer's shoulder.

"But I must confess, Esther," his voice still tingled my ear. "Goodbyes don't suit me, and I have been known to postpone them as long as I can."

I had seen this hand taking Nathaniel's hand with respect. This hand now wet with dishwater had touched *roses* in my cheek. I could not move, and I had to go.

"Sometimes," my employer added while I fixed my eyes on his hand, "I manage to avoid them all together."

The black hairs on his bare arm now brushed against my damp brown skin.

"I like Atlantic City," he continued.

I was rigid in place—and time.

"Do you swim, Esther?" he asked.

The Hebrew children couldn't swim. That was why God had parted the Red Sea, so that they could escape. The Egyptians had not been invited to the Promise Land.

"No-sir," I almost whispered as the soap bubbles continued popping and disappearing.

"Well it's great place to take a walk too," he offered. "Great beaches."

"Separate ones," I said quietly.

III

If Mandy came to work in the house on Webster Road everything could be almost the same. Everything that should be anyway, so while my employer ignored the need for making the necessary arrangements, I kept talking about it to Mandy.

"I don't know if I want to try to take your place," she said on another Sunday afternoon when I brought up the subject yet again to her.

"The work's easy," I assured her. "It'll feel almost like a vacation to you."

"It's not the cleanin' and the cookin' I'm speakin' of."

"That's all there is," I said.

"For you maybe," she replied.

Which was why I had to leave soon; before a *something* happened that everyone would be sorry for. Another *antebellum* outrage. And maybe another little pale pickaninny in need of a new Ernestine to color the shame.

Fortunately my employer's interactions with me were mainly confined to the house on Webster Road. Grampa imagined things. Nathaniel wondered. Mandy even suspected. And Mis' Inez disapproved. But none of them had any proof. And the absurdity of it was my best defense. A man like Taylor Payne could have his pick of the most eligible women in the county, so why would he ever pick me? "Because it won't be the first time his kind used our women so he can respect his own," Grampa had warned when I had dismissed his worries. "You know that."

A man ain't nothin' but a man.

I did; and it would not come to *that*.

Other than Spencer, few persons saw us together, a workman who wouldn't notice, or a delivery man who didn't care. Occasionally Doctor Mitchell would stop by on a Saturday afternoon while Spencer and I were still there, but the men would have their conversations apart from the maid and the houseboy, and so there was little opportunity for the *something* to embarrass anybody. It could go on like this forever, but I wasn't going to let it. I was leaving.

Fortunately there also continued to be evenings when my employer did not come home before it was time for me to go. I was grateful for the distance these absences put between us. We both had reputations to protect. The dinners, and dances, and the kind of women who decorated these events were good for him, right for him. I understood this even if I did like to read the novels that must have been his mother's, or perhaps his sister's, stories which argued for different outcomes.

One such night when he was late coming home, I decided to wait until my seven-thirty-time in his study. I sat on the leather couch reading last Sunday's *New York Times*, with Herman dozing at my feet. If my employer had done the right thing and called to say that he wasn't coming home for dinner I could have been home by now, so the idle time on my hands was by his own making.

Suddenly Herman raised his head and a moment later I heard the car too as it pulled around to the back of the house. Quickly I folded the newspaper, and as I was placing it back on the coffee table, someone was knocking urgently at the backdoor. Herman growled. It definitely wasn't the master of the house, and I was a little afraid. What if it was Nathaniel with some kind of bad news? I hurried to backdoor door and flipped on the porch light. Standing at the door was a well-dressed white woman. Herman was barking loudly and the woman looked down at him fearfully. Hastily I hushed him.

"Is-is Mr. Payne home?" asked the woman.

Panic was in her voice and in her face.

"No ma'am," I said.

Hearing my answer she covered her face with her gloved hands and looked as though she might faint.

"You want to come in?" I offered holding the door open for her and leading her in.

I didn't know who she was but she was in trouble, and having her collapse on my employer's back porch seemed to be among the worst options.

"When do you expect him?" she wanted to know standing in the kitchen now.

"I-I don't know, " I replied. "He works late sometimes."

"He's not at his office. I went there. I have to talk to him. Will it be all right if I wait for him here?"

"Is-is he expecting you?"

"No. But I have to speak with him tonight. I can't go back there!"

Back *where*, I wondered still not knowing what to do. She was white but she was a stranger to me and to Herman too. Clearly my employer didn't know that she was coming, and I had let her into his house and now she wanted to stay. I didn't even know her name. What kind of trouble was she in that would make her come to his backdoor? Was it his trouble too? She had been crying. Her eyes were red and puffy.

"You can wait in the front parlor," I said helplessly.

"Thank-you," she replied.

In the living room she dropped down on the sofa. I switched on a table lamp and rushed to draw the drapes. When she removed her gloves, I saw her wedding ring. Where was her husband and why was she here alone to see my employer? She opened her pocketbook and took out a silver cigarette case. Lighting a cigarette, she drew in the smoke and this seemed to relax her a little. Her stiletto pumps matched her pocketbook and gloves. All were sky-blue. My employer preferred women in high heels. None of the women in my family smoked. And none of us showed up unannounced and unescorted at a single man's backdoor.

"What's your name?" the woman asked me.

"Esther," I answered.

"You're the housekeeper."

"Yes ma'am."

"I'm Cordelia Collier."

The Colliers were one of the richest families in McConnell County. No wonder she was dressed so well. A beautiful white silk scarf was tied around her neck. I had a beautiful silk scarf too. I moved an ashtray from one of the end-tables and set it down in front of her on the coffee table.

"Can I get you a cup of tea," I offered, hoping that there was tea in the house. My employer was not a big tea drinker.

"Something stronger would be better," she said. "But yes, a cup of tea would be fine."

My employer kept a decanter of scotch in his study, and there was wine in the pantry, but I decided that she was better off with tea.

I went to the kitchen taking Herman with me. By the kitchen clock it was almost half-past seven. I began preparing a tray with a single cup and saucer, and cream and sugar, while the water heated. What if it got later and later and she wouldn't leave? It was even less my place to make her go than it was for me to have let her in. My employer could be out right now with one of his other *Lauras*, while his *Cordelia Collier* was sitting in his living room weeping.

Maybe they were having an affair, like in *Madame Bovary* or *Anna Karenina*. Maybe they had met at one of the country club dances and he had swept her off her fashionable heels. Maybe her husband had found out about them and she had come to my employer for protection. Here he was taking a rich man's wife, and Grampa worried that he might want me. A man might not be nothing but a man, but Taylor Payne still had his standards. Even if she was another man's wife. So would he keep her like *Count Vronsky* and make me work for an adulteress? I wouldn't do it. Mandy might be able to look over it, but I couldn't.

The kettle finally whistled and I brought the woman her tea. By this time she was smoking another cigarette and a little gray cloud of smoke hovered around her head. "Thank you, Esther," she said when I placed the tray in front of her. She put her cigarette in the ashtray, and while I stood before her, my hands clasped in front of me, waiting, she added sugar to her tea, stirred it, and took a sip. "This is good," she said breathing deeply. What time is it?" she wanted to know.

"Going on eight o'clock," I exaggerated, hoping she would leave soon.

She took another sip of tea.

"It was foolish of me to come here I know," she said setting the cup and saucer back on the tray. "But he's the only one who believes me."

"Yes ma'am," I said by rote.

"Everyone else just says things will get better. Even my own mama," she continued staring into the distance. "But they don't know what it's like." Her recently regained but fragile composure began to fray again. She lit another cigarette. "They don't know him."

Know *who*, I wondered. My employer? But that didn't make sense, not if she had come here for his help.

"Let me go warm up your tea," I suggested reaching for the cup and saucer.

She looked at me again as if she just remembered that I was there.

"No," she said. "It's fine. Sit with me."

Sit with her? What was it about this house that always made *them* want to keep company with Negroes? Still I did as I was told and perched myself on the same chair that my employer had used when I had sat where Mrs. Collier now did, and the drink had been lemonade.

"Are you married, Esther?" asked Mrs. Collier.

"No ma'am," I replied.

"Do you have any children?" she followed, taking another drink from her cup.

Did she expect me to? Just because I was a poor colored maid? She would never guess that I was going back to college in the fall. That I had something better to look forward to than cleaning a white man's house for the rest of my life. One day I would probably have a better education than she did. And I would be married too, and faithful.

"No ma'am," I said to her bowed head.

She looked up at me again.

"Then don't marry for love, Esther."

Her blue eyes shone with unshed tears.

"Ma'am?"

"You'll be so happy at first," she continued. "You'll think you're the luckiest woman in the world, because he can't live without you. But be afraid of that, Esther." She took another sip of tea and held the cup and saucer in her lap. "Because he'll have to own you and when he can't, it'll do something to his mind. And at some point when love is too strong, it turns into hate."

They were having an affair I decided. She was unhappy in her marriage and my employer had been kind to her, no doubt kissing her hand, and seducing her.

"Yes ma'am," I repeated.

He was better looking than Fredric March. Now that the affair had been discovered, guilt-ridden and terrified of the consequences, this lovely Greta Garbo was trying to make it her husband's fault. *Such is the way of an adulterous woman; she eateth, and wipeth her mouth, and saith, I have done no wickedness.* Did she really think that she was some kind of *Anna Karenina* with me here for a comfort like a Russian serf, someone to speak when spoken to, but otherwise invisible? Those days were over too.

"Do you believe me?" Mrs. Collier asked.

"I believe you are very unhappy, ma'am." I granted.

She smiled sadly and a tear spilled down her cheek.

"Yes, I am," she said.

Wherever it was that was a woman's place, on a pedestal or in a kitchen, in a sweet secret rendezvous or in a terrible violent rape, her lot was too dependent upon a man. Maybe it was all our fault from the beginning, because Eve had known better first and tricked the gullible Adam. But it was the serpent who had seduced her, and wasn't he a male? I began to feel sorry for her.

"You have to pray and ask God, Mrs. Collier," I advised, *not Taylor Payne* I wanted to add but didn't. "There's no trouble He can't see you through."

"What do I say to Him?" she replied dismally. "I don't know what to ask for. I don't want to lose my children."

"Then pray for that," I advised earnestly. "The Lord will lead you. Marriage is a sacred vow." "And what is this?" she said abruptly removing the silk scarf to reveal ugly purple bruises covering her slender neck.

I gasped.

"Is this sacred too?" she asked.

Had her husband done this to her because of the affair? No wonder she was frightened. Adultery was a sin, yes, and in the Bible they had stoned women to death for it, but those days were also over. She didn't deserve to die for love. She put her scarf on again, hiding the bruises, and then she put on her gloves.

"I better go. It's late," she said.

I stood up and she did too. But now I didn't want to send her back *there*.

"Is there somewhere you can go?" I asked.

She seemed to be no safer than Matilda despite all of her *privileges* and *entitlements*.

"Please tell Mr. Payne I came to see him. But don't tell him about this." She touched her neck. He'll worry. I'll see him in his office tomorrow."

I could only hope so. Herman trotted towards the front door. There was another car outside. Mrs. Collier's eyes widened, and for a moment I was scared too. But when Herman just stood at the front door expectantly I knew we were safe.

"That must be him," I said and followed the dog to the door.

My employer had gotten this woman into this trouble. He must take responsibility for it and help her.

"Mr. Payne," I began as soon as he was inside the house. "Mrs. Collier is here to see you."

His first expression was one of surprise, then concern. Then a kind of curtain came down showing nothing.

"You can go now, Esther," was all he had to say, as he handed me his hat and briefcase before going into the living room. I hung up his hat in the closet and carried his briefcase to his desk.

The next morning I was back at my place, putting his breakfast on his kitchen table. I was relieved that Mrs. Collier wasn't here, but I still hoped she was safe. I didn't ask, however, and my employer didn't say. Maybe he had put her up in a hotel. He must have taken her to Tyler at least. Otherwise people would talk. Maybe that was where they had been meeting all along. The Colliers were too prominent in McConnell County. People would know her.

As was his custom my employer appeared in the kitchen doorway at eight o'clock. The scrambled eggs were waiting along with the two slices of bacon, the two pieces of toast, and the small glass of orange juice—freshly squeezed. Aunt Grace and Uncle Eddie had fresh squeezed orange juice every morning too. In Grampa's house we just ate the oranges whole when we had them. Grampa even liked to eat the peel. Aunt Betty couldn't convince Uncle Perry to drink orange juice because he said it wasn't sweet enough. My employer took his seat. He had not brought his newspaper. I poured his coffee. Green men didn't dishonor their women either.

"Thank you," my employer said.

But what did I care if he was having an affair? As long as he was discrete and kept it away from his house, it didn't involve me; and pretty soon I would be gone and not a part of it no matter what. I worried about Spencer though. I didn't want him to see anything. Mandy wasn't a *nun* either, and Willie Gaines had been gone a long time, but she was always careful to respect her children. It was our obligation to do so, all of us, including my employer. Children had to grow up soon enough and see sin in the world. We should spare them as long as we could.

"Esther," said my employer.

"Yes-sir," I answered as I busied myself at the kitchen stove.

"I'd like to talk with you about last night."

"Yes-sir."

"Not to your back, Esther," he said. "You think you could sit for a minute."

I didn't want to hear any confessions. The less I knew about it the better. Yet obediently I came to the table and sat down.

"What you saw last night," my employer began, "What Mrs. Collier said to you, it should go no further than this house."

Where he did things *differently*. I supposed the *Ten Commandments* didn't carry much weight with him either. After all, God was just a useful *concept*.

"I'm not a gossip, Mr. Payne," I told him.

"I didn't say that you were," he replied. "I just want you to understand the sensitivity of the case."

The case? Everything was the Law to him. Well maybe it was. Too bad it wasn't against the law to sleep with another man's wife.

"It's none of my business, Mr. Payne," I said.

"To some extent it could be," he explained. "Mrs. Collier may have made you a material witness last night."

"But I didn't see anything. She didn't say anything about the two of--"

"You saw evidence of the assault," he continued. "If there are criminal charges, you could be called to testify."

"*Criminal* charges? Isn't she just going to get a divorce?"

"Nothing is certain at this point. Mrs. Collier has a good deal to consider. It's hard to say what she'll do."

"But last night—"

"Last night she was desperate and afraid. You were a comfort to her, Esther. Thank you for that. You made her feel welcomed. That means a lot to me. However it's important for you to understand this is not something she wants talked about. Discretion is--"

"You don't want it talked about either," I interrupted him.

"That's right. It's a matter of client--"

"I mean, I-I never would," I hastily assured him. "What goes on in your house stays in your house. It's your business, Mr. Payne."

His eyes narrowed as he looked at me.

"What do you mean my business?" he asked.

"I-I mean it's your right... to live any kind of way you want to."

"What are you saying, Esther?"

I dropped my head at the rise in his voice.

"Do you think there's something between me and Mrs. Collier?" he asked.

I shook my bowed head.

"Mr. Payne, it's not my place—"

"You're damn right, it's not!" he cut me off.

Stunned by an anger I had never expected him to show, I looked up.

"Are you suggesting…I-I don't know what to say."

"You-you don't have to say anything."

"I think I'd better," he retorted, roughly pushing back from the table and standing up. "At least for Mrs. Collier's sake."

I met his eyes. I was fired, but it didn't matter. I could just go back to New York earlier than I had planned. Hopefully he would still hire Mandy. Grampa would be relieved.

"Mrs. Collier is my client," he said icily. "A legal client. Or should be anyway, as she is the victim of a crime against her person, and the perpetrator happens to be her husband. Who just so happens to be one of your fine Southern gentlemen," he added scornfully. "From a highly regarded family, whose women do not send their husbands to jail for attacking them. As you would say, 'it's not the way'." Throwing his napkin on the table he stormed out.

The rest of the day I spent zealously cleaning his house; dusting every nook and cranny, polishing every piece of wood, shining every object of silver. I changed the linens on all the beds and replaced the towels in both bathrooms. I made certain that every comb, hairbrush, toothbrush, and razor was clean and lined up in perfect order. I starched and ironed shirts and thoroughly brushed suits. I waxed the floors and vacuumed the rugs, and when Spencer arrived after school I put him to work sweeping out the garage.

"Is somebody comin'?" he wanted to know.

No. Somebody was leaving. And I wanted whoever was to come to behind me to find a perfectly kept house. Spencer would take it all right, and especially if it was his own mother who came to work here.

"No, we're just doin' spring cleanin'," I told him. "That's all."

Mandy would be a much better fit. The three of them, Mandy, Spencer, and my employer would get along well together. And there'd be no *something* coming up between them to cloud and confuse things. Mandy was much too sensible for that.

In the first place, I had had no right to comment on how he lived his life, or who he lived it with. But it was his fault too, for encouraging me to think that what I thought about him might matter to him. If I had forgotten my place at all it was because he had dragged me out of it time and time again. When he got home tonight I intended for him to see that I had come back to it, to my *place,* and he could send the wages due to me by Nathaniel or Spencer. And the *something* that now smugly haunted this house, making me feel ridiculous, would trouble me no more.

It was getting late, I needed to make a decision about dinner. Maybe he wouldn't come home tonight, but I should fix his dinner. I owed him that much. I could leave it in the oven, and a letter of resignation on the table. And with it perhaps an apology. *Judge not, that ye be not judged.* Because what had I seen last night? A frightened woman seeking his protection. Why wouldn't she turn to him? He was a lawyer, and he must be good. Sometimes he made it where I couldn't think straight.

With the chicken cooking I stood at the counter snapping green beans. The radio blared with more chirpy messages to buy things than music. Hearing the back screen-door slam shut I sighed and got ready to scold Spencer again about letting it do that. Boys. How many times did I have to remind him? Oh well. Hopefully soon his mother would be here to correct him. It wasn't my concern anymore. I turned on the faucet and rinsed the beans under the stream of cold water.

"If you want a Coca-Cola, there's some in the icebox," I spoke over the running water.

"Sounds like a good idea," my employer said.

I whipped around. He set his briefcase on the table and draped his suit-coat over the back of a chair. Spencer stood next to him, grinning. I looked up at the clock on the wall to see if I had somehow lost track of the time, but it was just passed four.

"How's about it, Spence," our employer asked. "Could you use a cold drink?"

"Yes-sir!" Spencer eagerly replied.

Our employer went to the refrigerator and took out two bottles of coca-cola, and retrieving the bottle opener from a drawer, opened them. He passed one bottle to Spencer, and the two of them tapped their bottles together in a friendly salute before drinking.

"The garage looks great, Spence," our employer said following a swallow that generated a small burp.

"Thank-you for helpin' me, Mr. Payne," Spencer replied.

How long had he been home? I remembered to shut off the faucet.

"Sure thing," said our employer. "It was a lot to do for an after-school job."

When Spencer burped too he covered his mouth, looking at me sheepishly.

"Yes-sir," he agreed with our employer. "Aunt Esther made me."

"Well I'm sure she had her reasons," our employer smiled crookedly. "Tell you what, why don't you go give ol' Herman a little run for his money and then head on home."

He reached into his pocket and offered Spencer money for bus-fare.

"Aunt Esther always give me my fare, Mr. Payne," explained Spencer.

Gives me, I thought wanting to correct his English.

"Let's break with tradition this one time," the man said pressing coins into the boy's hand.

"I can ride the bus a whole bunch of times for this!" exclaimed Spencer before he looked at me to be sure it was all right to accept the money.

I nodded.

"Buy your little sisters some candy on the way home," our employer suggested.

"Yes-sir!" exclaimed Spencer and scampered out of the kitchen.

I moved to turn off the radio.

"Something smells good," my employer said leaning back against the counter. "What am I having for dinner?"

"Chicken," I answered.

"And green beans?" he asked glancing over into the sink where the beans floated in a bowl of water.

"Yes-sir," I nodded. "And potatoes."

"White wine with poultry," he reminded me matter-of-factly and took another drink from his bottle of cola.

"Yes-sir. I know."

Just say it, I thought. Tell me I'm fired. And then you can get your own supper and have any kind of wine you want. But instead he just stood there, swirling the remainder of the cola around in its bottle, studying it like he was a chemist. Did firing a maid make him uncomfortable, even if she was a disrespectful one? Or was he concerned about how things would be between him and Nathaniel after this? They were friends now, and Nathaniel was not like that. Connie wasn't either. And Mis' Inez would simply say it was about time before *something* worse had a chance to happen.

I didn't need his letter of reference. I had a college letter of acceptance, of affirmation, of proof. But I didn't want what I had done—or said—to hurt Mandy's chances. She was not like me. She wouldn't forget her place. His meals would be just as good, his house just as clean, and his shirts just as starched. They would even talk together and her good-natured tales and gossip would amuse him, but everything, everything would stay *decent and in order.*

"Remind me again," my employer requested. "When are you leaving for New York?"

Here it was; the end, or at least the beginning of it.

"The end of the summer," I answered.

Perhaps sooner if he fired me. Grampa would be pleased, Aunt Grace and Uncle Eddie too. All things worked for good according to the Bible.

He was quiet again, seemingly in thought. I watched him play with the cola in the bottle. In spite of the morning runs he wasn't as thin as he had been. All his clothes still fit and no doubt they always would, but good food and hard work tended to put muscles on a man, and he was proving to be no different. My time here had served him well.

"So you anticipate some date in August then?" he eventually asked, still examining the contents of the soda bottle.

"Yes-sir," I replied.

Did he still want me to work for him until then? I could do that. It wasn't long, less than four months, and that way Mandy would have plenty of time to give notice.

"Mr. Payne," I pushed towards a conclusion so I could get to the potatoes. "I understand if—"

When he looked at me the words along with my poise went away.

"What Esther?" he asked. "What do you understand?"

He must still be angry. I smoothed the palms of my hands down the front of my apron.

"That you are...uh-upset with me."

"You understand that, do you?" he asked.

I might not have been fair in my judgment of him and Mrs. Collier, but now he was toying with me, like he was a cat with some poor prey that could neither get away or die. I hated it when he did this, when his self-assurance bordered on arrogance. If he treated Felicia this way, no wonder they couldn't get along. Perhaps that was why Sylvia had left him too. They weren't subject to him for wages.

I looked down at the tops of my shoes. Anybody would have thought the same thing. A desperate married woman showing up unannounced at a single man's house, asking to wait for him because she has to talk to him and won't *go back there.* What else would you think?

"This morning," I said forging ahead anyway because I was doing it for Mandy. "I-I spoke out of turn."

"You accused me of adultery," he said. "Not to mention Mrs. Collier."

"Yes-sir."

"A baseless charge."

Except for the *circumstantial evidence,* which he had taught me was not based on observation, and therein was its weakness for him.

"Yes-sir," I said.

But all of life was a subjective experience. Open to interpretations that differed by perspectives, by *vantage points.* He had his interpretations too. We all did.

"Is that the kind of man you think I am, Esther?" he asked as though it did matter to him what I thought.

No, I thought, looking up at him. He had such dark intense eyes, darker than the cola in the bottle. Desirable eyes. Eyes that melted you and caused you to forget yourself and perhaps rushed your judgment. His tie was missing and his shirt sleeves were rolled up. Smudges of dirt, from helping Spencer no doubt, spotted the white cotton fabric. Mrs. Collier was a beautiful woman. Rules didn't seem to matter to him, and she was vulnerable. It was possible. With some men it was likely. Such things happened all the time. Married or not, a woman wasn't nothing but a woman too.

"No," I answered him honestly.

"I deserve an apology," he said.

"Yes," I agreed quietly. "I'm sorry."

He came towards me, diminishing the distance between us, before setting the bottle down on the counter. I felt for the freshly waxed floor beneath me. The chicken sizzled in the oven and the clock ticked on the wall. I could not look away from his eyes.

"So," he began after a time. "You think Spencer's mother is a better judge of character?"

"Sir?" I struggled to make sense of the question.

He smiled a little.

"I'd like to meet her," he said. "Perhaps you should arrange it."

I struggled to focus my thoughts. He was talking about Mandy now.

"Oh--oh yes-sir," I replied. "I can-I can ask her to come on Sunday afternoon. That's when she's off. If-if that's all right with you."

"It doesn't have to be right away, does it?" he asked. "We have until August, right?"

August. The end of the summer, and the start of the fall. The return to Jimmy's dream. Although maybe I would also dream of coffee-colored eyes and black hair, of strong white hands pressing coins into Spencer's hand to buy candy for his little sisters. Could we choose our dreams?

"Yes-sir," I agreed relieved, trying to concentrate on how much he would like Mandy. "I'll just let her know," I told him. "You won't be sorry, Mr. Payne, I promise."

He picked up the bottle, drinking the last of its contents, before returning it to the counter.

"Call me when dinner's ready," my employer said. "I'll be in the study."

Turning back to the sink to resume washing the beans, I was thankful for the cool water running over my hands.

IV

A hot April predicted a scorching May. With my employer's dinner ready, I went out the back door to escape the kitchen heat. Summer was in a hurry this year. Already I was adding extra starch to my employer's shirts to ensure his particular appearance. I was used to the vanity of men, Grampa's, Jimmy's, and now Taylor Payne's. Perhaps if I were beautiful I might be more preoccupied with my own appearance, but since I was not, at least I could take pleasure in my contributions to theirs.

I sat on the back porch steps watching the sun set. The sky was a soothing mixture of blues, and oranges, and purples. Herman got up from under his favorite tree and came to sit beside me. I rubbed his head and stroked his coat, wondering how furry animals put up with the heat, when even a cotton dress felt like a coat of wool. Germany was farther north than East Texas, so it must have a colder climate. I supposed dogs could have proper places to be too.

I hoped Grampa would come to my graduation because it meant so much to him. Maybe Nathaniel could drive him to Harlem, since he adamantly refused to ride on trains any more.

"Being a passenger is not the same as being a porter, you know," I had reminded him once.

"Maybe so," Grampa had replied. "But ain't nothin' more lonesome to me than a train whistlin' in the middle of the night. It reminds me of things."

Of being away from Ernestine, I thought. He had hated it Mama used to tell us, being apart from her, from them, but he had done it for her, for them, and ultimately for us. I would miss him too when I was gone. We had always been close, and I didn't like to think of Grampa by himself in Ernestine's Taj Mahal, getting his own supper, ironing his own clothes. I wanted to take care of him, but I supposed fulfilling Jimmy's dream was the most important way to do that. It would be a long drive to New York, and Harlem, but the *Green Book* would guide them to decent places to eat and sleep along the way. I would send them one as soon as I got back to Harlem.

Since it was such a nice evening, maybe my employer would enjoy having his meal on the back porch, the way Grampa and I sometimes did on summer nights. At least he ought to want to eat in his dining room again. If he wanted me to, I could sit with him in there too. In all the time that I had worked here I had only sat at the dining room table once, when we were going over his decorating plans. He had been so strange to me then, odd, different. He still was. Only now it wasn't what was wrong with him but rather what was right.

Mandy would be happy here. They would do well together. The two of them had yet to meet but they would soon because I would see to it. Maybe I could borrow Nathaniel's truck after church this Sunday and bring her here, or she could borrow her father's car, the old Ford.

I kept up with the war in Korea, relying mostly on what I read in my employer's newspapers. Things were improving for the American side, although Danny's intermittent letters never talked about his combat experiences. He wasn't as good a writer as Jimmy had been. He didn't write about the philosophy of war, or freedom, or life. There were no explorations of the human spirit or deliberations of destiny in Danny's correspondence. Mostly he just wrote about the bad food and the awful weather, and of wanting to see me again.

Soon Danny would have to come to Harlem to do that. He could take me to the Savoy. I would buy a new dress for him, something with chiffon, or maybe sequins. I would wear lipstick openly. Danny would be handsome in his uniform, and safe. Me and Danny together on the Savoy dance floor—now that would be *jumpin'*.

Herman's ears perked up. It must be his master's car approaching the house. By the time I heard it too, the dog was on his feet, wagging his tail excitedly. "Go get 'im boy!" I released him, and off he went, charging around the side of the house. I stood up too and brushed off the back of my dress before going back inside the house. The single place-setting was ready on the kitchen table. I went to the pantry for a bottle of red wine to go with tonight's pot roast. Maybe some night I would have a glass with him. What covenant could not tolerate a little compromise?

"Esther!" my employer called to me from the front of the house.

He knew where to find me.

"Coming," I called back, quickly putting a pan of yeast rolls into the warm oven.

In the study I found him sitting at his desk. He looked tired tonight, a little flushed. Maybe he was coming down with a summer cold. He hadn't had much of an appetite for breakfast.

"Your dinner is ready, Mr. Payne, but for the bread," I announced as I came into the study.

"Hello, Esther," he returned crossly, as he loosened and removed his tie.

He picked up the stack of mail and looked through it. I picked up his suit-coat which he had tossed on the couch.

"How was your day?" I inquired politely.

"Long," he replied. "I think I have a cold."

I nodded.

"You don't look very good," I agreed. "A summer cold's the worst. Would you like me to make you a cup of tea?"

"Well thank you, Esther," he said dropping the bunch of letters back on the desk. "Good to know I look as bad as I feel."

I looked down at the floor, suppressing a giggle.

"Why don't you go to bed early tonight," I suggested. "I can make you some tea and bring it upstairs."

"And some chicken soup too, I suppose," he said dryly.

"Well no, I wouldn't have time to make it for you tonight, Mr. Payne."

"Then I guess I'll just have to eat what you have prepared. Unless you mean to send me to bed without my supper."

"No-sir, I wouldn't think of it," I said smiling again before excusing myself to go upstairs to hang up his coat.

When my employer came into the kitchen, I brought his dinner to the table.

"I think I will have that tea," he said sitting down. "I've got a chill."

On a warm night like this, I contemplated, as I put the kettle on the stove. At least his mood seemed better. I opened the wine.

"No wine tonight," he said, massaging his temples. "I feel a little queasy."

He wasn't eating his dinner either. I re-corked the wine bottle and carried it back to the pantry. Puttering at the counter, I waited for the kettle to boil. When it finally did, I filled a teapot and brought it to the table.

"You do look feverish, Mr. Payne," I said. "I think you should go straight to bed tonight."

"Feed a cold, starve a fever," he quoted the old wives' tale.

"I don't know about all that, but I do know you could use some rest."

"If you'll tuck me in," he bartered, grinning.

"You must have been a triflin' child," I mumbled on my way to the cupboard for cup and saucer for his tea.

"What's that you called me, a beam?"

"Yes. In somebody's eye," I replied back at the table pouring his tea. "And a little devil too, I bet."

"A little more compassion for the sick, Miss Allen," he admonished me.

He picked up the cup and I saw his right hand shake. Colds didn't do that. I took my seat across from him. He sipped the tea slowly and never touched his food.

"I'm sorry, Esther," he ultimately apologized. "It looks good. I guess I'm not very hungry."

"Yes-sir," I said, rising to remove the plate of food.

Since he didn't seem ready to get up from the table himself, I returned and sat down with him again. While he drank the rest of the tea, I made chit-chat about what should be ordered from the A&P, and about Sweet Water's annual Sunday School rally coming in June.

"I hope we can count on a donation from you," I prattled. "It's a very worthy cause. We're hoping to buy new robes for the children's choir with what we raise."

In June August would only be two months away. Eight weeks. But it was only April now. The goodbyes did not have to be *rushed*.

"Choir robes," he smiled, "How could I refuse? God might get me for that."

To bring the cup to lips he was using both hands. I should tell him to call Doctor Mitchell, but he was a grown man, after all, he should know when he needed to see a doctor. Besides everybody caught colds, even invincible men like him. He finished the tea and announced that he was going to bed. It was early for him, and I was satisfied. He got up slowly from the table, stretching his back like Grampa did when his alleged rheumatism bothered him.

"It might be the flu," my employer speculated. "I've got the worst backache. Maybe I'm just getting old."

"I think it's just a bad cold that's all," I disagreed almost urgently.

Daddy had died from the influenza, and I had learned to worry about everything.

"Well, at any rate, I'm heeding your advice and hittin' the sack," he said. "Let Herman out for me please, and lock-up when you leave. Good night, Esther."

"Yes-sir," I replied, watching him. "Good night."

Leaving the kitchen, he stumbled, steadying himself against the wall to regain his balance.

"Mr. Payne," I said rushing to him. "Are you all right?"

"Just a little dizzy," he grinned again. "But keep your distance. It wouldn't do for you to catch something. Who'd look after me?"

"You want me to call Doctor Mitchell?" I ventured at last, letting my concern show.

"Oh, Esther, for what? So he can tell me to go to bed too? Same advice prettier source."

"You must have a fever," I said.

"Now why is that?" he teased. "Because I said you're pretty."

"Because you look like you do. And you're talkin' foolishness."

He laughed.

"Mr. Payne, I'm serious. I think you ought to call Doctor Mitchell."

"Don't be such an alarmist," he replied, standing straight once more. "There's nothing wrong with me that a couple of aspirin won't fix. Don't worry so much. And learn to take a compliment."

I let Herman go outside while I finished cleaning the kitchen. People seldom said I was pretty. Danny had called me beautiful that night among the trees, but that had been in the rise of his nature, when a man was all sweet words and compliments. People said I was handsome, good, dependable, but not *pretty*. "What do you say?" my employer had asked me once, but that had been about my cooking. Grampa wouldn't like him calling me pretty, but it was nice to hear. I let Herman in, and he went over to his dish for a drink of water then disappeared, presumably going upstairs.

Later I went upstairs too to let my employer know that I was leaving. I knocked softly on his bedroom door, but there was no response. The door was ajar, and I pushed it open further, poking my my head inside. He had lay down on his bed still wearing his clothes and appeared to be asleep. He must be really sick. I should call the doctor. Quietly I went to the linen closet in the hall and took down a blanket from the shelf. This was not just a cold. I was sure of it. He was more than tired. What if it was the influenza? But people didn't die of the influenza anymore. They had better medicines.

I brought the blanket back to his room and nimbly spread it over him. Herman, who had settled on the rug next to the bed, raised his head and looked at me. As careful as I was trying to be, I disturbed my employer, and he opened his eyes, smiling up at me drowsily.

"So you are tucking me in," he said.

"Go back to sleep," I told him softly as I began to unlace his shoes to remove them. "I'll see you in the morning."

As I was putting his shoes in the closet, he called me.

"Yes-sir?" I replied going back to the bed.

"I could really use a couple of those aspirin we talked about. Do you mind--"

"Oh, yes-sir," I said hurrying to the bathroom to get them.

I returned with two tablets in my hand and a glass of water. It seemed to be difficult for him to sit up, and instinctively I helped him, placing my hand against his back to support him, while steadying the glass of water as he drank from it. Now I was certain that I should call Doctor Mitchell. When he lay down again, I smoothed the blanket over him.

"Florence Nightingale would be proud," he said.

"Mr. Payne, are you sure you don't want me to call the doctor?" I asked.

"In the morning, if I'm still alive and no better, then you can call him. And if I'm not, then I suppose you can call the mortician," he joked.

"Hush that kind of talk!" I scolded him in a whisper.

"So you're superstitious too," he grinned.

"Job feared a fear and it came upon him," I told him.

"What does that mean?" he asked.

"Nothing. Just don't talk about dying that's all."

"Because you'd miss me?"

"You have a bad cold that's all."

"Be sure to bury me in the blue suit and the red tie."

"Hush now , I told you."

He laughed and raised a hand to salute me.

"Yes ma'am."

I finally smiled too in spite of myself.

"Go to sleep," I said more kindly. "And I'll see you in the morning."

When I turned off the lamp, the room was lit only by the light from the hall.

"I think it's customary to kiss the child, even a trifling one, good night," he said.

My own face, concealed by the darkness, was hot with embarrassment.

"You might be contagious, remember," I replied hoping I sounded casual as I backed away from the bed. "Goodnight."

Later that night at Grampa's kitchen table, whatever it was that had stolen my employer's appetite did away with mine too.

"You feel all right, gal?" Grampa asked looking down at the food sitting on my plate.

"Yes-sir," I assured him.

"Why you so quiet? What's on yo' mind?"

The influenza. And Daddy. And what Mama might have thought when Daddy had come home complaining of a chill. Men did not always choose wisely. I should have called Doctor Mitchell. By the time they had sent for him for Daddy it had been too late.

"Oh nothin', Grampa." I lied. "I'm just quiet tonight that's all."

Perhaps I should have stayed. His fever could get worse. I could ride my bicycle down to Uncle Perry's house right now and call Doctor Mitchell. There was a spare key under the pot of zinnias. He could let himself in. Maybe he even had his own key. They were good friends.

"Might as well get used to the quiet again," Grampa was saying. "Since you 'bout to be leavin' me."

Grampa took out his pipe and filled and lit it. Nathaniel would drive me back to my employer's house if I asked him. It was late. My employer was a strong man. I would get back there early in the morning. He would be all right. Everything was going to be fine.

"Yes-sir," I agreed with Grampa absently and began clearing the table.

"Hope you don't forget 'bout yo' ol' grampa when you get back up there with all them fancy city folks," said Grampa. "I'll be lonely for you, gal."

But I'll miss you, Esther.

I started to wash the dishes as Grampa enjoyed his pipe and his visions of tomorrow. By the time I finished the dishes, the flesh on my fingers was all puckered and wrinkled and desperate for a dollop of Jergens Lotion. I had strong hands like Mama. I had good hands, *willin' hands,* like Sister Callie used to say.

I went to bed early as well, but for hours I lay in the dark. From the front room, Grampa's radio broadcasts accompanied by his occasional laughter reproached my fretful imaginings. I couldn't help it. If the worst happened enough, you started to expect it, and when everything was going along fine that was when you expected it the most.

And everything was fine. I even had money in the bank. When I went back to Harlem I would be doing it in style, wearing nice new clothes fashionable enough to impress Aunt Grace. Mandy would come to work for Mr. Payne, and he would continue to help Spencer with his school work. Everything was good, which meant troubles were due.

Don't be such an alarmist.

Grampa, Sister Callie, and even Mandy all said the same thing about me. They just used different words to say it. It was *corroboration* to use one of my employer's legal terms.

The next morning I was up and dressed before Grampa had even stirred.

"What you doin' up so early?" he wanted to know when he came into the kitchen.

"Mr. Payne went to bed with a fever last night," I explained. "I want to go see about him."

"Don't make no sense you gettin' to work 'fo the crack of dawn," Grampa griped as I poured him a cup of coffee. "Just 'cause yo' boss-man done took a cold."

"It might be serious, Grampa," I said, adding evaporated milk to his cup until his black coffee was practically white. "He looked pretty bad last night. It could be the influenza. You know, like Daddy had."

"Ain't yo' problem if it is less'n you catch it from 'im."

"Grampa--"

"Just sayin'," he sipped his coffee. "A man need a wife to see after 'im. Cookin' and cleanin' don't make it yo' place?"

"I'll try to get home early tonight," I said pecking him affectionately on his bald head. "We'll have supper together."

"Don't we always?"

"Yes-sir," I smiled. "Tonight you just won't have to wait so long. I promise."

"Don't bring no sickness back here with you," he said.

PART THREE

From the bus stop I hurried until I was almost running up the graveled driveway. At the porch steps I paused to collect myself so my employer wouldn't see my foolishness. I climbed the steps slowly, normally, pacing myself like it was just another workday morning. The front door was still locked and it never was by the time I arrived. Retrieving the key from my pocketbook, I unlocked it. No doubt he was just sleeping late. The rest would do him good.

That the house was silent wasn't unusual, but this morning it was dark too. There was no light coming from the study and there was no light on in the kitchen, no smell of brewing coffee. Inside the foyer I switched on the light that shined down over the credenza. Something was wrong. I felt it. I had felt it all night.

There was only Herman, trotting down the stairs to greet me. I set my pocketbook down on the credenza and checked my appearance in the mirror, removing my head scarf and making sure my hair was in place. As I smoothed the front of my dress, Herman barked, demanding attention. "No morning run for you, huh, boy?" I asked him in a cheerful voice that sounded false clashing with the quiet, as I patted his head and looked up the empty staircase. "Looks like you're on your own this time," I said, returning to the front door to let him out.

"Jimmy, what's the matter?" I wanted to know. "Why Mama cryin'?"

"Hush, Esther," he said solemnly. "Daddy sick."

"Bad sick?"

Jimmy didn't answer. I tugged on his arm.

"Is he dyin'?" I asked.

"Hush now," he told me. "We have to be quiet."

I started up the stairs. In the old days it had been left up to *us* to bathe and dress *them* that final time before the eternity of the coffin.

...*Then you can call the mortician.*

There would be no need for me prepare him the way we had done for Daddy. There would be insurance and undertakers. Doctor Mitchell would blame me for not calling him last night. Maybe Mandy would let Spencer have Herman. Aunt Betty had come to help Mama dress Daddy, while I had watched. Grampa had said it was good for me to learn. It was woman's work to prepare a soul to meet God.

...*Bury me in the blue suit and the red tie.*

Mama had barely been able to let Aunt Betty help. In life Daddy had had love enough to cover us all, but in death Mama still could not bring herself to share him.

By the time Mama died there had been enough money for mortuary services. As her only surviving child it had been left up to me to choose her burial dress. I had selected the dress she had worn the day she had married Daddy. She must have wanted it that way. After all, she had saved it all those years. From the cancer she had lost so much weight the dress had been more than big enough.

Felicia would have to come. Doctor Mitchell would send her a telegram.

The Secretary of War deeply regrets...

She would have to choose his burial clothes. He looked good in all of his suits, good enough to be in the movies, like he was too important to be living in this little town. At least he could be buried next to his mother and father. Not like Jimmy left behind in France. I could tell Felicia about the blue suit and the red tie. Family was family no matter what. I wouldn't want to be Felicia between my employer and their uncle. Proud men were not easy men. There was usually only room for one cock of the walk.

I kept climbing the stairs and telling myself that I was being ridiculous. Job feared a fear and it came upon him, Sister Callie used to say. People didn't have to die of the influenza anymore, and people took the pneumonia in the wintertime. It wasn't like he was in the war, and cancer didn't kill you suddenly. Besides I wouldn't be the one losing this time—if it came to that.

Because you'd miss me.

Yes. I would miss him. We all would.

His bedroom door was still open as I had left it last night. I pushed it wider and went in without knocking. The room, like downstairs, was cast in the gray light of early morning. He was in bed as I had left him too; still wearing his suit slacks and the white dress shirt and covered by the blanket I had spread over him.

"Mr. Payne," I called his name softly.

He didn't stir. I switched on the lamp on the bedside table. His face was pale and beads of perspiration glistened on his forehead. I was almost relieved. Dead men didn't sweat.

"Mr. Payne," I thankfully called his name again, this time touching him on the arm. "It's me, Esther."

He opened his eyes.

"Esther," he said groggily. "What time is it?"

"About seven o'clock," I replied.

He started to sit up, but wincing he fell back.

"Damn," he muttered. "I feel horrible."

"Maybe I better call the doctor," I urged again, watching him massage his back and then his temples.

"It's just the flu, Esther," he replied as he stiffly moved to sit on the side of the bed. "I don't think we need to call in the Red Cross just yet."

He rubbed his face.

"Mr. Payne, my father died of the influenza."

He looked up at me.

"I'm sorry," he said. "Bad joke. But don't be so quick to panic."

He offered me the crooked smile.

"Mr. Payne, please."

"Okay, okay," he conceded. "I'll stay home today. Consider yourself warned, however, I can be a terrible patient."

"Then I better make you some peppermint tea with a lot of whiskey," I quipped. "And put you right out."

"Hmm," he chuckled. "I like the sound of that. But doesn't that break one of your Baptist rules?"

"It's fine for medicinal purposes," I said smartly.

"So that's how you--"

Standing up, he wobbled so severely that he was forced to sit back down. The humor disappeared. A moment passed.

"Looks like I'm a little woozy already," he observed.

"It's the fever," I told him.

"Right."

I should be calling Doctor Mitchell, I was thinking.

"You want to put on your pajamas?" I asked instead, quickly going to the bureau to get him a pair.

"Good idea."

Turning back to him I saw him lose his balance again, and I managed to reach him in time to keep him from falling to the floor.

"I'm all right," he assured me, even as he was steadying himself by holding onto me. "Just a little stiff that's all."

If the influenza could kill you then it could also make you too weak to walk, I thought waiting outside the closed bathroom door. I wished he would let me call the doctor. He must be very feverish. Everybody got sick from time to time, but then they got better. The Bible said that all sickness was not unto death. My imagination was getting away with me.

When my employer finally emerged from the bathroom, dressed now in the pajamas, he looked worse, paler, and exhausted. It didn't seem right that I should be seeing him in his pajamas, when I had never even seen Grampa in his union suit. Still I stood guardedly watching him slowly make his way across the room, because it was as if the fibers of the rug were grabbing at his feet and holding them down.

By the time he was seated on the bed again, a stream of sweat was running down the side of his face. With some effort he labored to get back into bed, pulling his right leg up onto the mattress by hand. Reaching for the covers he pulled them over himself as he lay back against the pillows catching his breath. I waited for him to tell me what to do.

"Call my office at eight-thirty," he instructed. "Let them know I won't be in today."

"Yes-sir," I replied, relieved at last to have a task. "What should I tell them?"

"Tell them what I said," he said. "I won't be in today."

Back downstairs Herman was whimpering at the front door and I let him in. He followed me into the kitchen where I put his food in his dish and refreshed the water in his bowl.

Doctors say she gon' be a cripple.

But it wasn't summertime. And besides the only child I ever saw him around was Spencer and Spencer was fine. It must be a very bad of case of the flu. He had been working too hard that was all, and he had run himself down. Rest was all he needed. He would sleep today, and tomorrow he would be better; and if not, then Doctor Mitchell would come, and if it turned into pneumonia then they would take him to the hospital in an ambulance. He would be fine. There would be no morticians. His handsome blue suit would not be his shroud.

At the kitchen sink I washed my hands vigorously with soap and hot water. To be safe I would send Spencer home when he came today. All Mandy needed was a house full of sick children. Soon the aroma of brewing coffee was filling the kitchen like it should, but before it was ready I had decided that it was a mistake, and I put on a kettle to boil water for more hot tea instead. Tea was better. It had soothed Cordelia Collier that night and she had looked terrible too. I walked down to the end of the driveway for my employer's newspapers. He would want to read them when he felt better this afternoon. At eight-thirty sharp, I called his office. The clerk answered.

"Mr. Payne asked me to let you know that he has come down with the influenza," I said departing from my employer's instructions because it was just the influenza, and they might as well know it so they wouldn't have to worry. "He won't come in today," I told the clerk.

"Sorry to hear that," replied the clerk. "You make him up some peppermint tea with a shot of whisky and he'll be just fine," he advised.

"Yes-sir."

Home remedies were common between us too.

"Call us if he needs anything," the clerk said.

My Bible tells me that Jesus heals the lame and makes the blind man see.

"Yes-sir."

I hung up the telephone. I could send Spencer to the Woolworths for the peppermint candy when he came after school. Of course peppermint was a Christmas candy, and it was spring; and still too cold for swimming in Johnson Creek. The country club had a swimming pool.

He would feel better if he ate I decided and I made him oatmeal. I prepared a wooden tray with his breakfast, and squeezing both the *Herald* and the *Dispatch* onto the tray, I carried everything upstairs to his room. "You don't exactly have the right kind of tray for the bed," I chattered standing in the room with the tray. "But if you feel like it, maybe you can hold it on your lap or just sit up for a little while on the side of the bed--"

"Leave it on the table, Esther," my employer said.

I set the tray down. He didn't move to sit up.

"I made you oatmeal and hot tea instead of coffee," I continued. "I hope that's all right. You don't have any lemons, but I put it on the list. If you want me to I can send Spencer to the store to get some when he comes today. Or I could go this morn--"

"Spencer shouldn't come today," my employer said.

I was quiet.

"No-sir," I agreed.

Then there was silence again.

"Mr. Payne, you don't want your food to get cold," I reminded him.

Please, Mama, you have to eat.

"You didn't eat your dinner last night," I added. "You really should eat. Do you want me to fix you something else? What do you have a taste for? I'll make some chicken soup. I can have it ready for your lunch. Just take a little oatmeal this morning. I put in raisins like you like."

"It's fine, Esther, thank you," he replied. "That'll be all."

"Yes-sir," I said, and accepting the dismissal I left his room, quietly closing the door behind me.

You's a good child, Esther. Eva's blessed to have you.

Everybody had praised me for being a good daughter, even Grampa, who could be stingy with praise. From Mama there had been nothing. She was her father's child, so as a rule most of her praise and thanksgiving was reserved for the Lord; or Jimmy as long as he wasn't around to hear it. Yet her silence in her last days had felt like a rebuke to all of my efforts to care for and comfort her. I had felt useless no matter what anybody else said. I couldn't fix it. I couldn't make it up to her. Jimmy could have. He had been her consolation after Daddy died. He had been like that to all of us, carrying Daddy's name and all of our devotion.

Back in the kitchen again I put a chicken on to boil. There were plenty of onions, carrots, and celery in the refrigerator and I took some out, leaving them on the counter. I poured myself a cup of the coffee and added milk. My employer was all the time chiding me about the beige concoction that passed for coffee in my cup. Maybe he was right about it, but I liked my coffee the way Grampa liked his, full of milk and sugar, and not black the way my employer drank his. Only this morning he was not here to complain about it. I sat at his kitchen table alone, watching the clock over the door. It was after nine, and dread was coming into the room like sunlight through the sparkling windows.

II

The morning dragged. There was nothing to do but the waiting. The remainder of the sweet milky coffee turned cold in my cup, and I went to the sink and drank a glass of water to rinse the taste of it out of my mouth. I should go upstairs and collect the breakfast tray but I was afraid to.

Grampa was right. How much better off my employer would be if he had had himself an *Ernestine* instead of the *Sylvia*? An *Ernestine* would have waited for him, and followed him too; the way Jessica had done for his father. Soon he would have himself a *Laura*, for whom McConnell County, or at the least East Texas would be home in the first place. And I would be back in Harlem. And Grampa would be relieved. And Mandy could hold her own with any mistress of the house.

Ultimately I had to collect the breakfast tray, and I had to see if he needed anything too, so I knocked on my employer's bedroom again. As soon as I saw him I knew that his condition had worsened. I went to him and placed my palm against his forehead. He was hot. He opened his eyes.

"Esther," he said weakly. "I'm sick."

"Yes-sir," I tried to say calmly. "I'm going to call Doctor Mitchell."

He grabbed my wrist.

"I'm very sick," he told me again, his voice sounding desperate. "Don't leave me."

"No-no, I won't," I reassured him. "I'm-I'm just going to call the doctor. You need a doctor."

"Something's wrong with me. I can't get up."

"You're going to be fine, Mr. Payne. Don't worry. The doctor--"

"Help me, Esther," he pleaded, clutching my wrist tightly.

"Yes-yes I will," I replied even as I pried his fingers from my wrist. "But I have to call the doctor."

"You're leaving me," he said, his hand falling away. "You're leaving me."

I ran downstairs to the telephone on the credenza and dialed the operator. Maybe it was too late. Maybe there was only the *waitin'*. When Doctor Mitchell at last said hello, I shouted at him.

"I should have called you last night, Doctor Mitchell!" I cried. "But Mr. Payne didn't want me to. But he's worse now. Please Doctor, please hurry!"

"I'm on my way," Doctor Mitchell said and hung up the telephone.

In the kitchen I frantically filled a pan with ice and took it back upstairs. In his bathroom I covered the ice with water and grabbed a washcloth. As I washed his face my employer opened his eyes again.

"Esther," he said hoarsely.

"Everything's going to be fine," I insisted to us both and folded the cloth, placing it on his forehead. "Doctor Mitchell's coming."

"Don't leave me," he repeated.

"I won't."

I got another towel from the bathroom and soaked it in the cold water too. Opening his pajama shirt, I wrung out the towel and placed it against his chest.

"I'm sick, Esther," he repeated. "I'm very sick."

"Everything's going to be fine," I assured him again.

According to Brother Pete, who was a janitor there, the hospital in McConnell wasn't good. *They* didn't take *us* as patients at the hospital, but Brother Pete claimed we were no worse off for it. "Me," he had said, "I rather die with my loved ones 'round me. Not in one of them cold, sad places." Aunt Grace had wanted us to bring Mama to New York but it had been too late and too hopeless. Was my employer going to end up dying in a little backwards town too, far from the help he needed, too far from his own loved ones? Dying young, like his mother and father, when their car had crashed on a rainy night? He should never have come back here.

I sat on the edge of my employer's bed, bathing him with cold water, as the minutes seemed longer than hours. I listened for a siren convinced that Doctor Mitchell would send an ambulance. There was time to get him to Dallas.

After a time my employer opened his eyes again.

"Don't leave me," he mumbled feebly.

Please don't leave me, Mama.

But she had had to. She had wanted to. I had come back for her but it had not been enough. She had needed Jimmy to come back. Now she was gone to him.

"I won't, Mr. Payne," I said, immersing the washcloth in the basin of ice water to wipe his face again. He closed his eyes. "You just don't leave me," I whispered.

If my people, which are called by my name, shall humble themselves, and pray, and seek my face, and turn from their wicked ways; then will I hear from heaven, and will forgive their sin, and will heal their land. But my employer didn't go to church, or profess any faith in anything but the Law. Yet he was one of God's people too. He was kind and generous. Such a bad thing could not happen to him. But Daddy had died, when he and Mama were still in love and his children were little and vulnerable. And Jimmy had not come home from the war and he had been the best.

Please don't let him die.

And then Mama. Bad things happened to good people, to good men. And good women wept inconsolably.

Doctor Mitchell came, and I was left to wait with Herman, standing fixed outside my employer's closed bedroom door. When we heard him cry out, Herman whimpered and scratched insistently at the door. I moved away from it. I didn't pray anymore because it was giving form to fears, and Job had made his fears come upon him.

At last Doctor Mitchell came out of the room, and seeing his face, I knew. Before he could say it, I knew, by the white mask covering his face and the grim expression he then revealed behind it. He closed the bedroom door. I had suspected it even last night, and more so this morning, when my employer had barely been able to walk to the bathroom. Like the *Buy Bonds* campaigns during the War, the *March of Dimes* campaigns were constant, reaching us all with dire warnings to be careful and urgent exhortations to give.

In the summertime no child was safe. Polio crippled or killed indiscriminately. It was contagious, passing mysteriously between people, implicating swimming pools and water fountains, movie theaters and church sanctuaries, leaving victims in iron lungs and wheelchairs. What if Spencer was infected? What would Mandy do? He was her first-born, the little man in her house. Did I have it? What if I had given it to Grampa? Maybe I had exposed Little Evie and Nate. I struggled to tamp down my terrors and hear what Doctor Mitchell was saying.

"I think there might be some paralysis but he's breathing all right on his own," the doctor was explaining in a hushed voice. "We can't predict what will happen. We'll have to watch him--"

"You have to get him to the hospital!" I cried, wondering why he wasn't calling for the ambulance right now.

"Keep your voice down, Esther," he ordered, grabbing me by the arm to pull me away from the door. "We can take care of him here."

McConnell County's hospital may not be much of a hospital, but at least it was a hospital. They must have medicines. And those terrible iron lungs.

"But he's too sick, Doctor Mitchell!" I whispered anxiously. "He has to go to the hospital!"

"It's polio, Esther," he replied. "People are afraid. We'd have to take him to Dallas. The trip would be very hard on him and there's no guarantee that they'd take him either."

"But why...I-I don't understand. What are your hospitals for?"

"We can take care of him here," Doctor Mitchell said again. "His legs are affected, but his breathing is good. It could be a mild case. We'll just have to see. If we can get his fever down--"

"Please, Doctor Mitchell! You have to call an ambulance! People die from--"

"Esther! Get hold of yourself. You have to be calm. I'm going to need your help."

"Doctor Mitchell--"

"Try to understand. People are afraid of this. And when people are afraid...well it makes them do things to others. It's not right...But that's the way it is...sometimes."

"You have to do something," I shook my head. "He's so sick. If-if he gets worse--"

"Be calm, Esther. You have to stay calm. I need your help."

Don't leave me.

I looked at the bedroom door again. I wanted to go inside, but I was afraid too. I thought about all the ways I had touched him in the last few hours, taking off his shoes, washing his face, holding his hand. I had had no mask. It must be too late for me. But there had been no one else. No sister, no lover, just his maid. If it was your job, your obligation to do it, then you did it. How could people working in a hospital be permitted to turn away the sick for fear of the sickness? *Their* world made no sense.

"Does he know?" I asked, staring at the closed bedroom door.

"No," replied Doctor Mitchell. "The fever. He's delirious."

I nodded, almost relieved for him. He would have seen the posters and read the pamphlets too. And Roosevelt.

"He's crippled," I said, hating the word as it had formed in my mind.

How could he be? He couldn't. It simply could not happen to him.

"We can't be sure at this stage," answered Doctor Mitchell. "Not in the beginning. The most devastating cases can turn around in a few weeks, a few days. I've seen people get up from their sick beds like nothing happened. We have to wait and see."

There was always the *waitin'*.

Yet being crippled was better than being dead. How many times had I wished that Jimmy had come home to us, without his arms, without his legs, without his eyes, missing anything but a beating heart? I would have taken care of him, devoted my life to whatever it was he could have needed from me, and thanked God for the blessing. But I wasn't *his* family. *They* could no longer demand that of *us*. *We* could turn away too.

"Am I going to catch it?" I asked the other question finally.

"Esther," began Doctor Mitchell carefully. "I can't guarantee that you won't. That any of us won't for that matter. We don't really know how Taylor contracted it. You may have both been exposed to the same source. Spencer could have brought it home from school. It's a-a peculiar disease. Some people will get sick and others won't." He paused, clearing his throat. "One theory is that it may be more dangerous to those of us who are…are better off," he said. "With…uh… advantages…that would prevent exposure. One needs to be exposed to the germ to develop immunity."

"Mr. Payne was exposed and he doesn't have the immunity. He has the sickness."

Doctor Mitchell cleared his throat again.

"I'll have to quarantine the house," he said. "You will…you will have to remain here in any case."

"You mean I can't go home?" I asked.

"Well, not—not for a few days, at least, or so, Esther. We have to be careful. In case you are carrying it. It's the law."

I looked again at the closed bedroom door. *The Law.* His faith was in the Law. Only now he needed God and was too sick to ask for Him. What would Grampa say? I would have to call Nathaniel.

"What about my people, Doctor Mitchell?" I wanted to know. "Mr. Payne was sick last night. What if I've already carried it home? And Spencer, what about him? Is he in danger?"

Spencer shouldn't come today.

I looked back to the bedroom door. Perhaps he did know.

"We just have to see, Esther," Doctor Mitchell was saying. "I wish I could tell you something more certain, but I just don't know. What I do know is that Taylor needs us. And you're strong. You come from hearty stock. I believe you'll be fine. We have to think of him right now. He needs our help."

"Mr. Payne is strong too," I said as much to myself as to Doctor Mitchell, who looked worried despite his hopeful words. "I'll go call Nathaniel."

Doctor Mitchell frowned.

"Esther, we don't want to start a panic," he said. "There's already been two cases in the county and it's not even summertime yet. This disease can make people behave irrationally. We have to be careful."

I just want you to understand the sensitivity of the case.

All right. People were afraid, but it wasn't a scandal to be sick. It wasn't his fault.

"What do you want me to do, Doctor Mitchell, lie?"

The older man sighed wearily.

"Be discreet, Esther," he said. "That's all. We can't have this whole town in some kind of an uproar."

The pamphlets described the miracles of water therapy and research, and hoped for cures; and *we* had also given our dimes in the same spirit as *we* had purchased the war bonds. Like Hitler and Hirohito, Polio was *our* enemy too. My employer had survived the war, returning home like Nathaniel, triumphant, if betrayed. And yet now a little germ may have done to him what the bullets and bombs had not. It was an injustice, almost as awful as Jimmy not coming home at all.

Uncle Perry answered the telephone at the garage. I stood at the credenza in the foyer, the palms of my shaking hands cold and damp. I couldn't make up my mind what to say or how much to tell.

"Hello...Uncle Perry, can-can I speak to—to Nathaniel?"

"Esther? What's the matter?" my uncle asked. "You sound funny."

"Everything's all right, Uncle Perry. I just want to give Nathaniel a message... from, uh, from Mr. Payne," I stammered.

"He pretty busy right now. Can it wait? Or tell me and I'll tell 'im."

"Uh...No-no sir," I struggled. "It would be easier for me to explain it."

"Well, all right then. You gon' have to hold on a minute."

Uncle Perry put down the telephone receiver. What would Doctor Mitchell tell the people at Mr. Payne's office? How would he tell my employer's sister? Would he hang a big sign on the front door like it was the blood of a lamb, although it would only protect those on the outside of the house? Would he be as matter-of-fact with the fragile Felicia as Grampa had been with me about Mama?

Nathaniel would have to be the one to tell Grampa that I was being confined in the house where he had never approved of my working. Cooking and cleaning did not make it my place. Felicia would come just as I had done, dropping her life and the hard feelings between them to get on the next train. Maybe she would fly on one of the airplanes. Sisters were like daughters and she was all that he had.

"Yeah, Esther, what you want?" Nathaniel's voice came through the receiver.

I wanted him to come and get me. But for now I was sealed inside with the plague, and Pharaoh's son.

"Mr. Payne caught polio, Nathaniel," I blurted out.

"What?!" my cousin cried. "When?!"

"Please Nathaniel, don't say anything," I pleaded, regretting that I had confessed it. "Doctor Mitchell is here. He's with him--"

"You get outta that house right now! I'm on my way to get you!"

But he couldn't. I couldn't.

"What's the matter?" I could hear Uncle Perry demanding in the background.

"I can't," I tried to say calmly. "I can't go."

Don't leave me.

"What you mean?" demanded Nathaniel. "You not sick, is you?!"

"Esther's sick?" I could hear Uncle Perry asking. "I knowed she sounded funny."

"No. No, Nathaniel I'm not sick. I'm fine. I'm really fine."

"What's the matter with her?" Uncle Perry was asking.

"Doctor Mitchell said that he has to quarantine the house," I explained. "But please--"

"Lord Jesus, Esther!" Nathaniel cut me off. "Quarantine? That means you could catch it too."

"Catch what?" demanded Uncle Perry. "Boy, if you don't tell me--"

"Don't say anything, Nathaniel! Please," I begged. "Doctor Mitchell doesn't want it talked about. You can't tell anybody. It-it scares people too much."

"You can't stay there," argued Nathaniel.

"I have to. I'm fine. And it's just for a little while. It's the law."

"How you know you fine? Doctor Mitchell tell you that?"

"Doctor Mitchell?" Uncle Perry was saying. "Boy, give me that telephone!"

"Please Nathaniel," I repeated. "Don't tell anybody."

"It's okay, Daddy," Nathaniel said to Uncle Perry, seeming to conspire with me. "Everything's all right."

"Thank you, Nathaniel," I spoke into the telephone receiver.

"What's all this talk about sickness and Doc Mitchell?" Uncle Perry was asking. "What's the matter?"

"It's Mr. Payne, Daddy. He took sick. Doctor Mitchell's there. Esther's all right."

"Don't say anything about the polio, Nathaniel," I implored again. "Just find Spencer and let him know not to come here."

"Esther, people gon' find out about it," Nathaniel warned. "You can't hide it. What you think Grampa gon' say?"

"Find out about what?" demanded Uncle Perry. "What about Papa?"

"Mr. Payne got the polio, Daddy," Nathaniel announced to him at last.

Hearing Uncle Perry's reaction I better understood why Doctor Mitchell didn't want anyone to know. I imagined them telling Grampa.

"I'll be home as soon as I can," I said to Nathaniel who was busy trying to manage Uncle Perry, who was again ordering Nathaniel to give him the telephone. "Tell Grampa not to worry," I added and hung up.

I went into the kitchen and washed my hands with soap and hot water again. They would come for me. I was sure of it and they were right to do so. I drifted out onto the back porch where it was still a beautiful day. The early afternoon sun shone like all was right in the world. The grass in the yard was at its freshest green. Along the side of the house the shrubs were adorned in bright pink and white blooms. Around the front porch the rose bushes were starting to thrive again. The birds were singing from the branches of the trees. Soon to come was the dry hotness of an East Texas summer, but for now it was the best of the season, when nature was mature and sure of herself, strutting and strolling, before the heat dulled her colors and exhausted her songbirds.

Doctor Mitchell called me from the kitchen and I hurried back inside the house. I should have thought to ask Nathaniel to bring me some clothes. He could leave a suitcase in the yard and drive away. There was Little Evie and Baby Nate to think about.

"I want you sit with him while I'm gone," Doctor Mitchell said. "I'll be back as soon as I can but I have to see other patients."

"What about the quarantine law?" I asked, confused. "Won't you be exposing people?"

"That's a fair question, Esther, and a little hard to explain. But it doesn't apply to me."

"The Law is funny that way, isn't it, Doctor Mitchell," I said bleakly. "It doesn't treat us the same, does it?"

He looked at me but offered no answer.

"What should I do if he gets worse?" I asked more calmly than I felt. "If he can't... can't breathe?"

"Call my house. My wife will know where to find me."

Were the undertakers afraid of polio too?

"Is there anything that I should be doing for him?"

"Just stay with him, Esther."

"Yes-sir."

When it was safe again, no doubt Laura Spalding would want to do this for him. Or Mrs. Collier. I followed the doctor to the front of the house. And by then Felicia would be here.

"You need to wear one of these," Doctor Mitchell said reaching into his black bag to retrieve one of the white masks. "For the time being you must cover your face and wash your hands all the time."

"Isn't it too late for that?" I asked.

"I don't know. But we must take precautions."

I nodded and took the mask.

"Your presence will be a comfort to him, Esther," Doctor Mitchell added, putting on his hat. "He's been calling for you." He paused a moment. "He wants you," he said.

"It's the fever," I replied. "He's out of his head."

"Just stay with him," replied Doctor Mitchell. "And don't let him go."

III

And don't let him go.
 Maybe this time the vigil would make a difference. Maybe this time I was holding on to someone who was not pushing me away. His sister would be here soon; and in the meantime if my employer called my name, I was here to answer, and when he opened his eyes he would see me, because he wanted me to stay.

He wants you.

I drew my chair closer to the side of the bed. Every now and then Herman raised his head to look up at me with doleful eyes as if he also knew how bad things were. With nothing encouraging to say to him I kept silent, and he would lower his head again, breathing out in a sigh.

My employer seemed to sleep, but he didn't rest. His brow was deeply furrowed and damp with perspiration. I kept applying the cool compresses to his forehead, and now that the fear had been realized anyway I could pray for him again. "Our extremity is God's opportunity," Grampa told us when things were at their worst.

Filling my head were pictures of little white children in the big machines that looked like coffins, except that their heads were always left sticking out. Unfinished coffins for incomplete deaths. Watching him now I could not imagine my employer trapped like that, looking up at the world from a mirror and no longer even a reflection of himself. He would not want to live. And yet I would hold onto him until his sister was here. She would not want him to die either.

We just have to wait and see.

There was always the waiting. And the hoping. Until life had no hope. What did it take to convince you to live? If you lost yourself, could that make you want to die? I freshened the washcloth in the cool water and returned it to my employer's forehead.

The most devastating cases can turn around in a few weeks, a few days.

Recoveries happened all the time. My employer was strong. He took care of himself, constantly fretting about getting soft around the middle from my cooking, running in the morning before the rest of us even got up. He had Nathaniel's constitution. God could intervene.

Tears welled in my eyes, but I refused to let them fall. It wasn't my place. He didn't belong to me. What must it have been like for the Hebrew children to hear the Egyptians shrieking in the throes of God's wrath? Even if you were spared the plague, sometimes you still endured the pain, witnessing the misery as you prayed for mercy, for everybody.

I went into the bathroom and gathered my employer's dirty clothes for the laundry. The clothes smelled of him, of the cologne he wore. Staying with him last night would have made no difference. By then it was already too late. By the time I was making small talk about Sunday School rallies and choir robes, the germ had been inside of him wreaking its havoc. I heard him call my name, and I dropped the clothes, rushing back to his bed.

"Yes, Mr. Payne," I answered coming close. "I'm here."

He peered at me as though he did not recognize me.

"Where am I?" he asked.

I pulled down the face mask I was wearing revealing my face.

"You're at home, Mr. Payne," I said. "Would you like a little drink of water?"

Quickly I poured water into a glass, but he shook his head when I offered it to him.

"It's bad," he said.

How much did he understand what *it* was? What would I say if he asked me? Mama had never asked that question, not of me anyway. By the time I had come home she had hardly been speaking at all.

"Yes-sir," I could not lie to the glazed dark eyes.

"What's wrong with me?"

I put down the glass and wrung the cool water out of the washcloth again, gently placing back on his forehead.

"You're going to be fine," I told him because I hoped it was the truth. "Doctor Mitchell will be back soon. Just rest now." My smile was false but came with good intentions.

"You're staying with me," he said.

I nodded.

"Yes-sir, I am."

He closed his eyes.

"Keep talking," he told me.

"I…What-what do you want me to say?" I asked wanting to oblige him as best I could short of the truth.

Opening his eyes again he looked up at me.

"My name, Esther. Say my name."

"Mr. Payne," I obeyed.

"No," he corrected me. "Say my name."

Why I wondered. How could it help?

"Taylor," I said.

He closed his eyes again.

"Don't leave me, Esther."

Did he think he was dying? Perhaps he was. If he stopped breathing they would never get him to Dallas in time.

"I won't, Mister—Taylor. I won't."

When I took my seat again next to his bed, I didn't replace the mask.

There are roses in your cheeks.

He had offered us friendship when we worked for his money. If he was going to open his eyes again, I didn't want him to see a mask where my face should be. If he was asking me to wait with him as I had done with Mama, then I would do it and be uncovered. It could be the last thing I ever did for him. That, and saying his name.

Once his sister came, the promise I had made to stay would be forgotten like a dream. He was after all delirious and would never remember it. When she came it would be like we had never talked this way. It wasn't real. It was the fever. And if it turned out to be the end, then all it would be was a sad memory that would be mine alone; as were so many memories that I carried of Mama from the last days when there was no one in the room but the two of us, and death. Such memories I didn't even tell Grampa about because they could never be his no matter what I said.

A man can lean on you, Esther Fay.

Could Felicia be strong? You never knew what you were made of until you were tested. A sickroom proved you like a fiery furnace. Of course they would hire a nurse. And they would have me at least until August, and then Mandy after that. And he would be recovering not dying. His sister only needed to be here. She could make pretty bouquets from the rose bushes around the porch for his sick room, and sit with him, and read to him. Spencer could do that too. I hoped she would let him. Spencer adored him. It wouldn't matter to him if he was crippled.

The telephone rang, but I didn't go to it. It might bring a question that I wouldn't be able to answer. Soon enough the house would be filled with concerned and well-meaning visitors, once the scare of contagion had passed. A house of strangers telling me what to do and upsetting the rhythm that we had made. I couldn't look forward to the prospects of it. Whatever the *differences* we had managed to create together in this house would be gone in the company of others. But they would be his friends and he would want them around him. It was *their* place.

His sister would probably bring her children, especially if it took a long time for him to recover, if the days turned into the weeks, and then the weeks turned into months. The bride and groom over the fireplace would have both their children at home again, but it would not be a happy reunion.

Yet if anyone could overcome such a disaster then Taylor Payne could. Unless he stopped breathing. How long did it take to suffocate? All sickness did not have to be unto death. And there was Warm Springs in Georgia, where the patients laughed and played in the swimming pools. Some of their bodies did recover. It might only take time. There might only be the waiting.

Maybe his sister would want to take him home. To *her* home. In Cambridge. She should. There must be better hospitals there. Harvard had a medical school. I could close up the house, the house he had worked so hard to make a nice home. I would be sorry to see him have to leave it, but when I went back to Harlem I could take the train to visit him. We wouldn't be able to share a walk on the beach, but then that had been a fantasy anyway.

I hoped Felicia would not take him back to his uncle's house. Surely she wouldn't abandon him in a house where he had never felt wanted. Surely not. If that were the case, then I would take care of him myself. Or Mandy would. Or he could just hire somebody—a nurse. No. He had to be in his own house. He would do better here. This was his home. The place he had loved enough to come back to when the war was over.

I stood and for an instant marveled at being able to. We took such things for granted until a day came when we could not. I inspected the amount of ice in the water. My employer was sleeping. I hoped the fever was going down. I wished I could get him to take a drink of water. His lips were dry and cracked.

Herman stood at attention just before I heard the car too. Assuming it was Doctor Mitchell returning at last, I was relieved. Herman bolted out of the room. Going after him, I was shocked to see Grampa and Uncle Perry at the foot of the stairs. They stopped short seeing the barking dog. "Hush, Herman! Hush!" I said, grabbing the dog by his collar, fearful that he would charge them.

"Esther Fay, get yo' things," Grampa ordered, watching the dog.

"You can't be here!" I said frantically. "It's against the law. The house is quarantined!"

"We takin' you home!"

"That's right!" confirmed Uncle Perry, standing behind Grampa. "You can't stay here, Esther Fay. Let's go."

Grampa started up the stairs. Herman, straining against my grasp on his collar, was barking fiercely.

"Herman! Stay!" I commanded the dog. "Sit! Sit! Grampa, please. Please, you can't be here!"

"Come on I said," ordered Grampa, continuing up the stairs. "We goin'--"

"I can't, Grampa," I said desperately, backing away, pulling Herman with me. "I can't leave."

"It's too dangerous. We not leavin' you here," insisted Uncle Perry, following Grampa. "You could catch it too."

"It *is* dangerous. You're not supposed to be here." I pleaded. "Doctor Mitchell says—"

"He ain't got no say over you," rejoined Grampa. "They can't make you stay."

"Grampa, please," I begged. "You can't be here. Please, you have to go."

"Esther," I heard my employer calling me from his bed. "Esther, where are you?"

I turned to go to him, pulling Herman with me.

"You not goin' back in there!" shouted Grampa, reaching to stop me.

For this Herman charged at him, rearing up so that it took all my strength to hold him back.

"This what it come to?!" demanded Grampa. "You gon' put a dog on me?!"

"Esther," my employer called again. "What is it?"

"Grampa, please," I entreated. "I have to go to him."

Pulling Herman with me, I shut the bedroom door behind us and returned to my employer's bedside. "What is it?" he asked as he struggled to sit up. "What's wrong?"

"Nothing. Nothing's wrong, Mr. Payne," I tried to assure him, placing one hand on his shoulder to get him to lie still again. "Everything's fine."

"Who is it?" he insisted. "Who's here? Something...something's wrong...Herman--"

"Shhh, hush now. Herman's right here. Everything's all right."

"I can't get up...What-what's wrong with me?"

"It's all right," I repeated soothingly. "Just Rest. Everything's fine. Don't worry. Herman," I called to the dog. "Come!" Leaving the door, the dog came to me. "See, Mr. Payne, here's Herman. Right here. Everything's all right. Sit, boy," I said to the dog and he obeyed. "Good dog," I said and then smiled at his master. "See, everything's fine."

My employer was still again, and refreshing the water in the glass, I sat on the edge of the bed, cradling him in one arm, and bringing the glass to his lips. "Take a little drink," I said.

Don't you like lemonade, Esther?

He accepted the drink, his brown eyes watching me. Once upon a time I had mistaken him for the hired-hand. Yes, I liked lemonade very much.

"Now isn't that better," I said, gently easing him back down to the pillow.

"Don't leave me," he murmured, closing his eyes.

"I won't," I said.

"I need you, Esther."

"Rest now. Everything's all right."

Herman, on his feet again, was growling. Grampa stood in the open door, his face dark and blank.

I got up from the bed and again commanded Herman to stay. Then withdrawing from the room, I carefully closed the door behind me, moving away from it before speaking.

"Please, Grampa," I pleaded once more but in a calmer voice. "You cannot be here. The house is quarantined. You could get sick."

"You can too!" he snapped in a voice that remained indifferent to the sickroom. "You touchin' him like that? What kind-a hol' he got on you, gal? You done los' yo' mind?"

I moved further away from the door.

"It's too late for me," I said.

"That what Mitchell tell you?" demanded Grampa.

"You just work for him, Esther Fay," argued Uncle Perry who had come no closer than the top of the stairs. "This don't concern us."

I need you, Esther.

"I'll be all right," I replied. "You don't have to worry."

"I know I don't," said Grampa. "'Cause you comin' home."

He reached for me again but again I stepped back.

"No, Grampa," I said. "I can't leave."

"What's the matter with you?" he asked studying me closely. "You fool enough to wanna stay?"

Yes.

"Uncle Perry, please," I said looking passed Grampa's face. "Make him understand. It's a quarantine. I-I have to. It's the law."

"Ain't no cure for it, Esther Fay," warned Uncle Perry. "What if you get it? We can't let you take that kind-a chance. Let 'em take care of they own."

But his *own* wasn't here. I had to stay until he wasn't alone.

"It's just for a few days," I continued to plead. "Until the quarantine is over and his sister can get here."

"The girl is right, Isaac," Doctor Mitchell said.

He had come back and was now mounting the stairs. Uncle Perry stepped aside so that he could pass.

"This house is quarantined," Doctor Mitchell repeated. "You cannot be here. It's against the law."

"Now we don't mean you no disrespect, Doc Mitchell," Uncle Perry began. "But the law can't make my niece be in danger. That ain't right."

"I can't let her leave here," replied Doctor Mitchell, passing Grampa to stand beside me. "Not now."

"He ain't got no claim on her," Grampa spoke again looking at me. "This not our concern."

"You don't want to put your whole family at risk, Isaac. You've got little ones to think about. We can't take the chance of having this disease spreading through the county."

"She come home last night," argued Uncle Perry.

"And that was dangerous enough," said Doctor Mitchell. "Don't make me call the sheriff. I will. I got the rest of this county to think about. Your people too."

"I want to stay, Grampa," I confessed.

"What you think you owe this man?" retorted Grampa. "You's a hirelin' that's all you is to him."

"It's not right to leave him like this, Grampa."

"You're Christian men," Doctor Mitchell followed. "He needs her. I expect it's Providence that she found him when she did. He might have died."

Grampa didn't see providence. He only saw disobedience. He was Moses and I was his Hebrew daughter choosing to stay behind in *Egypt-land*. But it was my choice to make. Like being with Danny. I was just thinking for myself, only it was in his face this time. In my whole life I had never disobeyed my grandfather to his face, and I dropped my eyes to the floor because I was sorry for it.

"I don't know about this, Esther Fay," Uncle Perry was saying. "I just don't know."

"It's the right thing, Perry," advised Doctor Mitchell.

I still didn't look up, because I had to stay and I could not be sure that I would if I looked into Grampa's eyes again. When the Red Sea crashed in over the Egyptians, someone among the emancipated Israelites must have wanted to help the drowning men. *Love ye therefore the stranger: for ye were strangers in the land of Egypt.*

"She has to stay, Isaac," I heard Doctor Mitchell tell Grampa. "I won't let her leave. Not now."

And when my grandfather and uncle left the house, I stood with Doctor Mitchell outside my employer's door. The back screen-door slammed as my people left without me. Doctor Mitchell went into my employer's bedroom, but I remained where I was, listening to the motor in Uncle Perry's truck turn over, hearing the gravel crunching beneath the tires. I belonged with them but he needed me. I was between two places, only one of which was mine. I was separate and alone, between Egypt and Exodus.

"Esther," my employer was calling me again. "Esther, where are you." I returned to his bedside where I had decided to be. For now. Until the quarantine was lifted and his sister came. Doctor Mitchell walked over to the window. Dipping the cloth back into the cool water I placed it on his forehead again. He looked up at me.

"You're here," he said weakly.

"Yes, Taylor," I replied, squeezing his hand. "I'm here."

"Don't leave me."

"I won't."

This time it was Doctor Mitchell watching us. Now there were two witnesses. The contract was binding.

The hours passed. Doctor Mitchell, Herman, and I sat in my employer's room, keeping the watch, lest the disease, that wracked his body, steal his breath and therefore his life away from us. Doctor Mitchell was concerned that I would not wear the mask.

"We have to be careful, Esther," he cautioned.

"I think it scares him," I said.

When we weren't attending to him, Doctor Mitchell sat in a chair by the window or went downstairs to smoke, Herman lay on the rug, and I sat in the chair next to my employer's bed. Occasionally he would stir a little, almost awakening, mumbling incoherently. I wondered if he could be praying. I had always believed that the Roman Centurion's knee would bow; I just never expected it to be like this.

Months of caring for Mama had prepared me to be a capable assistant to Doctor Mitchell. I knew illness and suffering. Still seeing my employer this way was unsettling. Doctor Mitchell had taken off his pajamas leaving him wearing only his white cotton drawers, and the first time the doctor had uncovered him in front of me to examine him I had had to look away. But I had quickly collected myself. You didn't blush or cower when a naked body was sick and helpless. You took care of it. You ministered to it. I had refrained from doing what was my Christian obligation towards this man, keeping silent about the Gospel's good news in the face of his disbelief, determined that he should not have all of the advantages. Now I prayed for him like he was my brother because he was.

"We need to make up his bed, Esther," Doctor Mitchell said later in the day. "With a rubber sheet in case...uh in case..."

He couldn't bring himself to finish the sentence, and I didn't want him to, in case my employer could hear and understand that Doctor Mitchell was trying to say that he might not be able to control his bowels and bladder anymore.

"Yes-sir," I said.

The doctor passed me a pair of medical gloves.

"I want you to wear these," he told me. "Go ahead now. Put them on."

I had never worn gloves to take care of Mama and I pulled them on reluctantly.

"He's contagious, Esther," Doctor Mitchell reminded me. "We have to minimize the risk..."

I nodded to show I understood this too.

"You remember how to do it?" asked Doctor Mitchell. "How to make up his bed? I mean as you did for your mother?"

I nodded again.

"We'll do our best to be gentle but...well you remember how it was."

"Yes-sir."

As we lifted and turned him to put the rubber sheet in place and re-make the bed around him, my employer writhed and moaned. When we had him settled again, Doctor Mitchell positioned his feet against something he called a footboard. "The board is for support, Esther," Doctor Mitchell explained. "We want to prevent foot-drop."

I didn't know what *foot-drop* was, but this must be the beginning. Everything would truly be different now. In time I had learned to relate to Mama's body as something simply to be kept clean, and, in any way possible, made comfortable. Eventually it had ceased to be her really; circumstances redefining the relationship between us. Sickness could change everything. My employer could be left with a body that none of us knew anymore, including him. It could be some strange thing over which he had no control, no longer the body of the man who made short work of Mr. Leon's woodpiles, painted houses, and batted baseballs to Spencer. It could be left a patient's body, a body to be placed on bedpans and sat in wheelchairs.

Still it would be a living body and not a dying one. And a wheelchair was better than a gravestone. I took off the gloves, and refreshing the towel in the pan of ice-water I put it to his face again. He opened his eyes. He could still open his eyes.

"What's wrong with me?" my employer feebly repeated the question I didn't want to answer.

"Hush now," I replied and smiled for him as I applied a little dab of Vaseline to his parched lips. "It's all right. You're going to be fine."

Throughout the night Doctor Mitchell monitored my employer's temperature and his breathing, and sometimes he would gently move his legs and massage his heels, explaining that we would have to do this for him until my employer was stronger and could move on his own.

"We'll be watching for bedsores, Esther," Doctor Mitchell said. "You remember how it was with your mother."

I did. I watched and learned, and remembered. This would be my place until his sister came.

Sometime before dawn, a weary Doctor Mitchell decided that I should practice doing the range of motion exercises. "Put on your gloves, Esther," he said. But I didn't want to for fear that the barrier they provided would make me too rough with him. Mama's skin had become like tissue paper towards the end, so that no matter how careful I was there had always been tears and bruises.

"Please, Doctor Mitchell," I replied. "I can't tell what I'm doing with them on. I don't mind."

"All right," the doctor relented. "It's okay for this. But if…I mean…when we have to clean--"

"Yes-sir," I said stopping him again. "I understand."

"It is best, Esther."

Nothing could be *best* about this except a miracle. Jesus arriving to make him whole. I hadn't really asked for that for Mama. For Jesus to come. Because she had wanted to go to Him. To Jimmy and to Daddy. They were waiting for her. I had not been enough to make her stay.

Doctor Mitchell guided me as I carried my employer's legs through the movements. Although we didn't do anything strenuous, the small movements hurt my employer, and I could hardly bear to do them. Mama had suffered at my hands too. "It's the infection," Doctor Mitchell tried to reassure me. "It makes his muscles sensitive to touch, but we have to do it." He had said the same things to me about Mama. There were just things that had to be done. Why must there be no way to alleviate misery or at least avoid being a cause of it?

When I completed the exercises, I covered my employer again and walked away from the bed, fighting back tears. Doctor Mitchell followed me and placed his hand on my shoulder.

"You're tired, Esther," he said kindly. "You should get some rest."

Doctor Mitchell was tired too. Neither of us had slept and there were dark circles under his eyes. A nurse should come soon. Doctor Mitchell could hire her on behalf of Felicia. Then he could take a break and go home. The quarantine didn't apply to him; and besides he always wore the mask and the gloves.

"I'm all right," I said, reaching into my pocket for a handkerchief to wipe my eyes.

"His fever will break soon, Esther, I'm sure of it," said Doctor Mitchell. "And then we will have some idea of what we're facing. That's when the real work begins. He'll recover. He's strong, Esther, you know that."

"His sister will need to hire a nurse," I said. "Do you know of someone? Someone good?"

I didn't want to think of him in the hands of someone who was brutally efficient and coldly professional. His sister must get here quickly. She must look after him.

"Yes," replied Doctor Mitchell. "I think I do."

"Good," I replied wiping my nose and returning the handkerchief to my pocket. "I can make-up the bed in the room down the hall for her. The room across the hall would be better, but that used to be his sister's room when they were children. She'll want to stay there when she comes. Mama had a bell she could ring for me if she needed something. Grampa's house is smaller, but you could probably still hear it if he rang it. You should get him one."

"That's a good idea, Esther."

"When will his sister get here?"

"I don't know."

"But she must be on her way."

Doctor Mitchell sighed deeply.

"That's going to have to be settled between them," he said.

"I don't understand," I replied.

"I mean...we-we just have to wait until the fever breaks, and then we can talk about it."

Wasn't Felicia on a train at this very moment rushing to her brother's side? Did she know how sick he was? Maybe she was afraid, but the quarantine would be over soon. And regardless my employer needed her.

Felicia would come then I could go home. To Grampa. I tried not to think about what had happened between us. Because it wasn't really *between* us. It was simply the law. And it made sense. Doctor Mitchell had to protect the community, all of it, *our* people too. Grampa had only been trying to protect me. They were both right. Grampa would come to see that. And whatever he imagined that he was seeing between me and my employer, I would help him understand that too, help him realize that human compassion, not to mention the Lord Jesus Christ, required no less of us.

"I want to be a help, Doctor Mitchell," I offered. "As long as I'm here."

"Yes," the doctor nodded. "I'm going to need your help. But you have to pace yourself. It could be a long race."

But it wasn't *my* race, and I could only be here until August anyway. Mandy would help them take care of him. She was strong. They would be able to rely on her. Everything could be all right. Once his fever broke, everything could be fine. The most devastating cases could turn around in a few days. Doctor Mitchell had said so. Outside the sky was lighting to gray with the coming sunrise. Herman would need to go out to relieve himself. I called softly to Herman and he came to me. "I'll let the dog out and make us some coffee," I told Doctor Mitchell.

The second day went very much like the first, with us keeping the watch, moving my employer's limbs, and fighting his fever. In the middle of the day, I left the sickroom and went to the kitchen to make us something to eat. Doctor Mitchell was not a young man and I worried about how he was holding up. I had always known that the two men were friends. Like Mr. Leon, Doctor Mitchell had known my employer since he was a little boy. Perhaps Taylor Payne really had come home.

I was sorry that his uncle had been unkind to him, *unkind* being my word not his. He never charged anybody with anything, *charged* being his word not mine. He told his stories too objectively, like he was merely a narrator of his life and not really experiencing it. His uncle had rejected him but he seemed to understand why. Sylvia had taken a *better offer* who just happened to be his best friend. He even saw the value of his parents dying together and leaving him and his sister orphans. Perhaps this was how it was to have a legal mind. You saw both sides of a case impartially so that you were able to argue it either way. It must be nice not to ever be angry or hurt, to be free of grudges and resentments, but it was cold too, detached, maybe even indifferent.

But he wasn't like that. Not really. He cared about things. His mother's rose bushes. Spencer. Herman. Laura Spalding. Even Baby Nate. Things mattered to him. His work. The Constitution. Even what his maid thought. Watching Doctor Mitchell caring for him the way he did was reassuring. The two men had a bond, and that meant that Mr. Payne was loved. I hoped that Felicia would understand this and not take him away from his home. I wished that I could see Mr. Leon.

I'm always 'round when you need me.

But this was not the season to burn wood or decorate Christmas trees. It was still spring. It wasn't even summer yet.

Over into the second night fatigue forced Doctor Mitchell to sleep. I listened as the older man snored softly in his chair by the window. My employer seemed to rest too, and when I placed my hand on his forehead it seemed cooler. Maybe the worst was over. Eventually the snoring of one and the more even breathing of the other worked with weariness to lull me to sleep too.

When I awoke with a start it was morning. I was panicked that I hadn't kept the watch, but when I looked at my employer he was looking back at me.

"Good morning, Esther," he said, even managing a smile.

Jumping up I placed my hand on his forehead again. It was still too warm, but it wasn't hot. The fever had broken. Putting my hand over my mouth I suppressed a happy cry of relief, which seemed to amuse him and he smiled again.

"That bad, huh?" he asked.

His voice was hoarse, but he was making sense. My eyes watered.

"I guess so," he concluded.

"Oh Mr. Payne," I murmured. "Thank the Lord!"

"Taylor," he corrected me. "I like the way you say it."

Embarrassed I started to go awaken Doctor Mitchell, who was still sleeping.

"Don't go," my employer said, catching my hand.

His own hands must be good. And he could breathe on his own. We wouldn't have to bury him in an iron lung.

"I should get Doctor Mitchell," I told him.

"Let him sleep for awhile," he replied letting go of my hand. "From the looks of things I must have given you two quite a time." He paused to breathe deeply before continuing. "Was I thrashing around so bad that you had to tie me down? What is this thing you've strapped me to anyway?" he asked, pointing to the footboard. "I can't move."

He didn't know. And he would have to. But I couldn't tell him.

"Can I get you anything?" I heard myself asking.

"Some water if you don't mind," he replied. "I don't think I can reach it."

I hurried to pour him a glass. Struggling to sit up, he discovered that he couldn't, which left him both surprised and spent.

"I think you're going to have to help me," he said.

As I supported him, I kept telling myself what Doctor Mitchell had said, that it was too soon to tell, and that the worst cases could make complete recoveries. It could be like that for him. All sickness was not unto death, but for the glory of God, that Jesus might be glorified. *Please Jesus.*

"Guess I'm pretty worn out," my employer observed when he was resting again on the pillow. "My legs feel like lead. Maybe you should wake Mitch. I'd like to get this thing off of me."

It wasn't my place to tell him, and I wished I was wearing the mask again because I could see in his face that mine was giving my feelings away.

"It is the flu, isn't it, Esther?" he probed.

"Everything's going to be all right, Mr. Payne," I said.

"What is it?" he now pressed. "Why can't I move my legs? What's wrong with me?"

I kept silent. He closed his eyes.

"Wake him," he told me.

"**Y**ou're going to be fine," Doctor Mitchell assured him as I listened. "I'm certain of --"

"Just tell me what it is, Mitch" replied my employer, cutting him off. "Say it."

"Polio, son," the doctor finally admitted. "You have polio."

Hearing it again was like hearing it for the first time, but worse, because now I saw him hear it too.

"But it doesn't have to mean what you're thinking, Taylor," insisted Doctor Mitchell quickly. "I've seen very serious cases recover. People, children, who couldn't breathe on their own at first, completely well. It's-it's really too soon to tell the extent...You're just very weak right now. You'll be amazed at what a few days of rest will do."

"I'm crippled," my employer seemed to say more to himself than to us.

"You're going to get stronger, Taylor," Doctor Mitchell resolutely promised him. "You've got a good constitution. Your fever just broke, and you're still very weak. Things will get better."

"Uncover me."

"Taylor...Son...Don't--"

"Take the goddamn covers off of me."

Doctor Mitchell pulled back the linens, holding them up like a curtain. My employer straining to raise himself, managed to do so only briefly and collapsed. He laid there, his face blank as stone.

"It's too soon to tell what we're facing," Doctor Mitchell said again.

My employer turned his face away.

"You're going to be fine," the doctor kept trying. "You'll see. I know it's hard right now to comprehend all of this, but...Esther, why-why don't you get us some breakfast?"

I looked at him, resisting being sent away when I should have been glad for it. There was nothing I could do to help him now. The bedroom was a terrible place.

"Mr. Payne, I'll freshen up Mis' Felicia's old room for her," I offered.

The comment drew his eyes back to me.

"Esther, we should talk about that late--" began Doctor Mitchell.

"No," my employer said before the doctor could finish.

No? He needed her.

"But-but she'll want to come," I persisted. "To help you."

It was what families did.

"I said no," my employer repeated.

"Well now, Taylor," intervened Doctor Mitchell reluctantly, "She does make a good point. Felicia is your fam--"

"I said no!" he shouted, trying again to sit up but failing. "I can manage this," he said breathing hard. "I can manage this."

"All right, all right, son," Doctor Mitchell placated him. "Take it easy. Esther, please, go make us some coffee."

Dismissed once again, I did as I was told this time and went to the kitchen. Why wouldn't he want her to come I brooded while trying to figure out what to cook. Mama had had no appetite. He wanted to *manage* it. He would have to have a nurse and Felicia should be here to oversee his household. Without a mistress in the house the nurse would run things, or maybe worse Laura Spalding would. Maybe I should make him oatmeal again.

I can manage this.

But he couldn't sit up. He couldn't hold a glass of water. Doctor Mitchell would have to feed him the way I had had to feed Mama the rare times when she would eat. He needed his family.

I need you, Esther.

But Felicia should come. I filled a pot with water to boil for oatmeal, but then I poured it out, not wanting to cook it again. I should call her anyway; speak to her woman to woman. *Mrs. Richmond, you don't know me, but....* She probably knew that her brother had a maid. It was Doctor Mitchell's place to call her on my employer's behalf, but hearing from me would not be out of the realm of possibility. Her telephone number must be in the address book in his desk somewhere. If he fired me for disobeying him then I could just go home and get ready for August. Grampa would be relieved. I had saved up enough money. It wouldn't be a problem. Mandy would come. It would be the same as me.

I made scrambled eggs and toast. I brewed coffee too but also made another pot of tea. I thought of Mrs. Collier, her beautiful neck swathed in silk hiding the brutality of her husband. All men were not good. But my employer was, good and decent, and kind. And crippled. *No.* Doctor Mitchell said that he was just weak. He could recover his strength. It might be a *long race*, as Doctor Mitchell had said, but it was also one that he could win. He just needed his sister to help him.

Balancing the heavy tray, I knocked on his bedroom door and entered. Doctor Mitchell was standing by the window once again smoking a cigarette. The room wore a shroud. "Mr. Payne, I made scrambled eggs," I tried once more to say cheerfully, but the words, falling off my lips awkwardly, had no effect on the gloom. I sounded silly.

Aunt Betty used to bring her *Ladies Home Journal* custards to Mama, determined to entice her dying sister-in-law to eat. More often than not it had been left to Grampa and me to consume the custards, with their caramel or fruit tops. The custards had been good. Perhaps I could resurrect those old recipes now that I would be cooking for another invalid. *Invalid. In-valid.* Why were the two words spelled the same? One did not make the other true.

"Leave it there, Esther," said Doctor Mitchell gesturing towards the dresser.

"You don't want the eggs to get cold," I said looking at my employer who stared straight ahead although it was as if he saw nothing.

"That's fine, Esther," Doctor Mitchell replied.

"Can I get you anything else?" I asked to either of the men, hoping that my employer would answer.

"No, that'll be all," answered the doctor.

Back downstairs, I retreated to the study. I sat on the familiar leather couch, and the faint scent of pipe tobacco and the mild chaos of my employer's desk almost made it seem as though nothing had changed. The fever had broken. I thanked God for that. I should call Nathaniel. Everybody would be worried. I went to his desk to find the address book because his sister ought to be worried too.

...There are circumstances when it's better to be on your own.

This was not one of them. I found the address book and turned the pages until I found his sister's name in the Rs. Underneath the address and telephone number was a list of birthdays. I was pleased to see the notations, to see that he remembered all of their birthdays; that his sister had named one of her children after their father. He had even included Felicia's wedding anniversary date. This proved that he loved his family. He seldom talked about them, but he must be very fond of his nephews. He liked children. He was so good with Spencer, and I remembered the way he had held Baby

Nate. He had shopped for his nephews at the Woolworths and perhaps for Baby Nate too. Why should he face all of this alone?

I flipped through the rest of the pages of the book looking for evidence of other connections. In the G-section he had recorded Spencer's birthday. I didn't know Mr. Leon's last name, and I didn't find him listed in the L's. I turned more pages. The Mitchells were there, their birthdays and their wedding anniversary too. Marriages mattered to him. Sylvia's rejection must have wounded him. In the front of the book in the A's I read my name and my birthday. This surprised me. I sat down in his desk chair. He must have asked Nathaniel when it was. I would be gone before it came again. Out of Egypt. Making my home and future in New York City, where he might have stayed and been safe, or at least properly cared for in a decent hospital.

It would make sense to take him back to Massachusetts. Compared to Cambridge, or New York, or even Dallas, this was a primitive and backwards place, just like his uncle had said. Maybe compromise had its place. Maybe *the way* worked better when it was a collection of all *our ways*. Maybe my employer had had *his way* too much. What if to have your way you had to forfeit everything and everybody else?

On a piece of his monogrammed writing paper, I copied down Felicia's telephone number. My employer wasn't thinking clearly now. His brilliant mind was overwhelmed by what had happened to his poor body. Mama had not wanted me either; yet it had been my duty to take care of her. It was woman's work after all, and I was her daughter. Just like Felicia was my employer's sister. Maybe family was *happenstance* as he called it, but his circumstances had changed. His relationships had to too. It was Felicia's responsibility to look after him. It was what families did.

Someone knocked on the front door. I put away the address book and hurried to the door. Had Doctor Mitchell hung an ugly quarantine sign outside? What would I say? I opened the door. It was Mrs. Baxter, one of my employer's neighbors.

"Oh Esther, there you are," the woman said coming into the house.

There must not be a sign.

"We noticed Doctor Mitchell's car over here so early this morning. Is Mr. Payne all right?"

I had no idea what to tell her. Doctor Mitchell didn't want anyone to know. Polio made people panic he said, and the Baxters had small children.

"Yes ma'am," I said. "He's doin' some better."

I should tell her not to come in, but that might alarm her and she would want to know why.

"Oh," she replied. "Well, is he very sick?"

"Just a nasty infection," replied Doctor Mitchell coming down the stairs. "I don't want it to spread."

"No, of course not," agreed Mrs. Baxter.

"I'll tell him you stopped by, Florence, but I don't want him to have any visitors for awhile. We want to nip this thing in the bud."

"Well, all right, Doctor," said Mrs. Baxter turning back to the door. "Let us know if he needs anything."

Once Mrs. Baxter was gone, Doctor Mitchell went to the front door and locked it.

"Don't let anyone in, Esther, until I tell you it's all right," he instructed.

"Yes-sir," I replied. "But what do I tell people? Are you going to put a sign on the door?"

Doctor Mitchell sighed.

"It is the law," he said wearily.

People were going to find out about it, but why should there be shame? It was a germ. It could happen to anybody.

The morning dragged into the afternoon. Doctor Mitchell mostly remained upstairs with my employer. They did not need me, so I moved aimlessly around downstairs for awhile, fussing in the kitchen, anxiously waiting to be summoned. Felicia's telephone number was in my pocket. I wondered what kind of nurse Doctor Mitchell would get to take care of him. If everyone was so afraid of polio, who would be willing to work here? Mandy couldn't, not right now. She had her children to think about. I would be needed at least until a nurse was hired, so it wouldn't do for me to give my employer cause to fire me today. Maybe I would just give the telephone number to Doctor Mitchell. He should make the call. My employer would not send him away for disobedience.

In time I went back upstairs and stripped and remade the beds in the other two bedrooms preparing for Felicia and the nurse to come. I brought all the old sheets and pillow cases back downstairs and started the washing machine. I was hanging sheets on the line when Nathaniel drove up. I had forgotten to call him, but now here he was, and it was like seeing an angel. I almost ran to him to hug him, but I remembered the quarantine and how I hadn't worn the mask or the gloves.

"How's he doin'?" asked Nathaniel as he walked over to the clothes line.

"The fever broke," I replied, bending to pick up another sheet from the wicker laundry basket.

"Can he walk?"

"I don't think so, Nathaniel." My throat abruptly tightened. "Not right now, but Doctor Mitchell says it's too soon to tell," I continued. "He said his legs felt like lead." My eyes were stinging. "It's not a good sign. But it's just too soon to tell."

"He's a strong man," Nathaniel said. "If anybody can beat it--"

"He can," I finished for him, but the tears in my eyes argued that I didn't believe it.

"Yeah," said Nathaniel, ramming his hands deep into the pockets of his denim overalls.

Neither of us spoke for a time. I dried my eyes with the corner of the sheet in my hand and then hung it over the line.

"I brought you some clothes," Nathaniel said, looking down at the grass. "Guess you won't be needin' 'em. You can come on home now."

I can manage this.

But of course he couldn't and I couldn't. Doctor Mitchell was worn out. I needed to stay until the nurse came; and besides there was still the quarantine. And Felicia wasn't here yet.

"I don't know, Nathaniel. The quarantine. And I think I might have to stay for a little while. At least until Doctor Mitchell gets a nurse."

"Grampa's not gon' like that, Esther Fay. I don't like it myself."

"You have to make him understand," I insisted. "You all do."

"I think the ol' man's right about it. They can't make you stay. You done enough. I'm sorry for him, but--"

"You mean just leave him?" I cut Nathaniel off.

"To his own," said Nathaniel reading my face intently. "Yeah."

"I don't think I can do that, Nathaniel," I said. "His own isn't here yet, and I-I can't leave him by himself."

"Esther," Nathaniel began carefully like he was looking for his words, "A while back… I-I told you… you can talk to me about anything…If there's somethin', somethin' I don't know, but you need--"

"He is my friend, Nathaniel," I interrupted him again. "Yours too for that matter."

"You his maid, Esther Fay," Nathaniel said grimly.

I took a pillowcase from the basket and hung it on the line.

"It's not your place," he continued.

What if *place* had a broader meaning too? The same way *friend* did.

"For now it's where I am," I told Nathaniel.

"What about Grampa?" Nathaniel asked. "You know how he is."

Think for yo'self, Baby Sister.

"He's in trouble, Nathaniel. I have to stay."

"No you don't," Nathaniel corrected me. "You want to."

Nathaniel left the small suitcase he had brought to me on the back porch steps, along with a haunting feeling of being at cross-purposes, with people and events, and *the way* things were done. I carried the wicker basket back to the porch and set it down next to the washing machine and went back for the suitcase. It was Grampa's old valise. He had used it during his days as a porter. It had seen many hard miles, but it was durable. I couldn't imagine what Grampa would have packed for me but the suitcase was light. Perhaps Aunt Betty or Connie had done the packing. Maybe Grampa had not been willing to. Maybe he would have to forgive me first.

My employer's house did not have a backroom where *the help* could stay, and it would be strange to be naked in a house where I earned a living. I could not have come to work for him if he had wanted a *live-in* housekeeper. With no wife in the house, reputations could not have borne it. He might have been better off with a *CoraLee* or a *Sister Callie* in the first place. I could make a bed for myself on the sofa in his study, and be surrounded by his books. I thought about the walnut sleigh bed, in the buttercup room, closest to his, with the white lace curtains. I thought about his hands on my waist.

I won't let you fall.

It made more sense for the nurse to sleep in the buttercup room, although maybe she would want to have a cot in his room. I had had a pallet on the floor in Mama's room at the end, laying there night after night waiting for her to call me, listening for her breathing as it had become weaker and weaker. No one rested in a sick room.

Doctor Mitchell called to me from the kitchen.

"Yes-sir," I acknowledged him, and he followed my voice out onto the back porch.

"There you are," he said.

"Yes-sir?"

He paused and looked at the old wringer washing machine.

"Does that thing work?" he asked.

"Yes-sir, Mr. Payne says it does."

"Good," he said.

Sick-beds could generate a large amount of soiled linens. After a time even the bedpan did not help because the patient stopped knowing when to ask for it. I had barely been able to keep up with the wash and take care of Mama too. We had cut up old sheets to make diapers for her. The easy work I had hoped to pass on to Mandy had become arduous overnight. Maybe Mandy should keep her job with the exacting mistress and the demanding children.

"Did you need something, Doctor Mitchell?" I asked. "Is Mr. Payne all right?"

"He's fine. I want to talk to you."

"Yes-sir?"

"Come," he directed me, "Let's sit down."

I followed him back into the kitchen where we sat down at the table. He did not begin right away, and I wondered what it was that was so difficult for him to say. Was the paralysis worse? Wasn't it too soon to tell? Maybe he was just very tired. I waited, thinking of how much I respected Doctor Mitchell, remembering how good he had been to Mama, and the compassion in his face as he had told us that it would be *any time now.* I was thankful that he was my employer's friend.

Colored McConnell County trusted Doctor Charles Mitchell and considered ourselves fortunate to have him. His commitment to us no doubt cost him some white patients, but he seemed to pay little attention to that. Once he had been the only doctor that *we* could go to, but now there was also Doctor Bookman over in Tyler, who was a colored doctor from Washington D.C. Doctor Bookman was trying to recruit other Negro physicians to the area, and *we* were happy for that, but it didn't take away from *our* loyalty to Doctor Mitchell. He was white but we knew him, and that was the most important thing.

"Esther, have you ever heard of Sister Elizabeth Kenny?" Doctor Mitchell finally spoke.

"I read about her in the newspaper," I said. "She's a polio nurse."

"Well, she's a bit more than that," he said. "She's a very smart woman. A good therapist. She developed a new way, a better way to treat infantile paralysis."

"Are you going to get her to take care of Mr. Payne?"

Doctor Mitchell smiled.

"Well now, Esther, I don't think we can actually get the good sister herself," he replied. "But what we can get are her methods."

I waited.

"What I mean to say," he continued, "Is that we can get someone who is trained in her methods."

"You think he is going to stay paralyzed, don't you?" I asked forlornly.

"It may take a while for him to recover, from what I can tell, yes, Esther."

I sighed. On the counter, Doctor Mitchell had set the breakfast tray. The food was untouched. Through the kitchen window I could see the sheets caught up in the breeze, brightly white in the sunshine.

"But it is too soon to be sure," I reminded him. "You said he's just very weak right now. The fever was so terrible. He didn't eat. That could be the worst of it."

"Maybe, Esther. But we have to be prepared. It won't be easy."

"There is somebody trained like that, like Sister Kenny, in McConnell County that you can get?"

"Well, yes and no, Esther," he said, studying me. "Really good nurses are a little hard to come by. But I could train someone, someone who was willing. Sister Kenny's methods are just common sense if you think about it. She calls it *re-educating* the affected muscles. You see, it's as if Taylor's muscles have forgotten what they are supposed to do. Think of a patient being sick with something else, or had an operation, maybe a broken leg. As soon as you can, you want to get the patient up on his feet again. We have to get the mind and body working together. If the patient just lies there, then the mind can start to forget too. And the patient becomes an invalid.

"We used to treat the paralysis with plaster casts and splints to immobilize the affected limbs," he continued. "We thought that the strong muscles pulled against the weaker ones, and caused the contractions. You know, twisted the limbs. That's usually the worst of it really, what cripples the patient, the contractions. But now we're using Sister Kenny's methods. So as soon as he's up to it, we have to start exercising Taylor's legs. The re-education starts right away. The sooner the better. While he still knows what they are supposed to do. He can't move them right now, so we move them for him."

"But if he's paralyzed, Doctor Mitchell," I said. "The nerves are dead. I don't see how--"

"Not always, Esther," Doctor Mitchell interrupted me. "With polio the nerves aren't actually dead, just damaged. He can feel his legs, Esther, he just can't move them. That's why I say it's easier to understand if you just think of him as being very weak. And it's up to us to help him regain his strength."

"Are you going to tell his sister to come?" I asked, reaching into my pocket for the folded paper. "I wrote down her number."

"No, Esther. He doesn't want us to do that."

"But he needs his sister right now. It's what families do."

"Not all families are the same."

"Well who's going to take care of him? I know you're going to hire a nurse, but someone has to look after him. What if the nurse mistreats him or something? He won't know her. No, Doctor Mitchell, he needs his sister. Maybe he doesn't realize it, but he does."

"He has friends."

You his maid, Esther Fay.

Of course he had friends. We all did. When people died, they came with covered dishes of food and sympathetic words. Then they went away after the funeral, and left you alone in a house that was empty and desolate. And when the dying took too long to complete, the friendly visits ceased even while you still needed them, ending long before life did. Who would be there daily waiting for my employer's strength to come back, for his legs to *remember*? Mrs. Baxter? Doctor Mitchell? Laura Spalding? Mrs. Collier couldn't. If it took later than August then even I would be gone. Felicia must come.

"It's a lot to ask of friends, Doctor Mitchell," I said. "And you can't be here all the time to see after him. And Mandy, she's very good, but he doesn't know her--"

"Mandy?" asked Doctor Mitchell.

"Yes-sir. Spencer's mother. She's going to come to work for him when I leave. But they've never met. He needs somebody he knows, somebody he can trust."

"You're right, Esther. He does need somebody he can trust."

I need you, Esther.

"So you're going to call Mis' Felicia then?"

"No."

"But I don't understand. Who--"

"Taylor needs the right person to look after him," said Doctor Mitchell. "Someone who knows how to nurse the body, and the soul. He won't make a good patient, Esther. This will be hard for him. It would be for anybody, but you know how he is. On his own, always doing things his way. He won't be able to do that now. He won't like it. Whoever it is has to understand that. And he will have to know he can trust them. That's not Felicia."

"Maybe you can find a good nurse in Dallas," I conceded. "Someone that's trained."

"I could train you."

I stared at him.

You his maid, Esther Fay.

"I'm not a nurse," I said and got up from the table.

At the counter I began taking the dishes off the tray.

"Yes, you are, Esther," Doctor Mitchell disagreed. "A very good one. And he needs you."

Don't leave me.

How easily Doctor Mitchell said it. He sat at the table calmly, expectantly, as if he were entitled to ask this of me, as if he might have been my grandfather requiring me to come home for Mama. As if it made perfect sense. Perhaps to him it did. It was in keeping with *the way* things were done. The docile, dedicated slave then servant, depended upon and dutiful. CoraLee had done it for Mrs. Spalding's mother. I used to wonder why there were any Negroes still living in the South at all. In America for that matter. Much like Danny, I wondered why my ancestors had not simply deserted this place when the *Freedom* came. Why had so many been willing to wait for the return of the beaten Rebel warriors just to help *them* rebuild what they even today could not bring themselves to share with *us*? Why would anyone stay in *Egypt-land*?

Perhaps it was because it was *our* home too, even back then, when some of *us* could still remember Africa. Perhaps it was because it was as much *our* place as it was *theirs*, even if only *we* knew it. Perhaps some of *us* just tried to live the Scriptures too literally, and Jesus was a very demanding example. Maybe Karl Marx was right. Religion had pacified us and made us too patient.

But Doctor Mitchell was asking too much. I had done my time in sickrooms, around sick-beds. I was going back to school. I was going to be a teacher. I didn't want to spend the rest of my life wearing aprons and toting trays. I was sorry for my employer. I cared about him. But I had already given up Jimmy and Mama too. I barely remembered Daddy and I had never known Ernestine. Was I now supposed to surrender Grampa's dream?

I need you, Esther.

"But I'm not trained," I said scraping the rejected food into the kitchen trash pail.

"I saw you take care of your mother, Esther," said Doctor Mitchell. "I know how good you are. And I've watched you with him. The rest, the specific methods, I can teach you."

"His sister might want to take him back to Massachusetts," I said desperately.

"It's not my place to discuss their family," Doctor Mitchell replied. "But I think we shouldn't count on that."

So even Doctor Mitchell had a *place* and yet did not hesitate to ask me out of mine.

"But there must be places where he can go," I argued. "Hospitals that will help him. There's Warm Springs in Georgia. I read about it."

"Would you have him sent to some kind of home, Esther?" Doctor Mitchell asked. "Where they can teach him *how* to be crippled?"

I hated that word. It could not be true, not for him.

"It's not left up to me, Doctor Mitchell."

I turned on the faucet and began to rinse the dishes.

"I was with those children when their parents died in the hospital," Doctor Mitchell talked over the running water. "I was the one who had to tell them, explain to them that they were orphans. My wife and I had to help Taylor, a boy mind you, make the funeral arrangements. And it was left up to me and Mrs. Mitchell to put those children on the train to Cambridge. Jason Morgan wouldn't even come get them."

The old man never knew what to do with or make of me.

"He was twelve years old, Esther," Doctor Mitchell re-told the story I had heard before although this time it came with sadness instead of irony. "He was strong, even then. Taking care of his sister and facing everything on his own. Don't you think it's about time somebody took care of him?"

I turned and looked at Doctor Mitchell. Jimmy and I had had Mama and Grampa. Uncle Perry and Aunt Betty. Aunt Grace and Uncle Eddie. We had family. It was what families did. Why each of us needed each other. Families had to stay together. You couldn't just choose to cut yourself off from your people.

"That is why you have to call his sister," I said from the counter. "People need their families at a time like this."

"People need people who care about them," replied Doctor Mitchell. "Will you help me, Esther? Will you help me help him?"

Don't leave me.

"Did he ask you to ask me?"

"No."

"Then how do you know he would want me? He has to want the best, somebody trained. He doesn't want his maid to--"

"Quite frankly, Esther," interrupted Doctor Mitchell. "He doesn't want anybody. He wants it to be a nightmare, a bad dream, but it's not. He's in trouble. And I see how you are with him, how he calls for you. And...and I've seen other things too."

"Doctor Mitchell--"

"It happens, Esther," he interrupted me. "There's an attachment between you. He trusts you." Doctor Mitchell cleared his throat. "I don't know what all has gone on in this house, and I don't need to know. I just want to use it."

Grampa said that I was a *hireling*. The Bible warned about hirelings.

"Why won't you call his sister?" I asked despairingly. "Here," I said, reaching into my pocket and taking out the piece of paper with the telephone number. "I found the number for you. I'm sure she will come."

"He doesn't want her to come," Doctor Mitchell repeated.

"But she's his sister. I came back for Mama."

Maybe why I had come back for Mama was why some of us had stayed here in the first place. Maybe being needed was as good as being wanted. Or at least as compelling. Nobody talked about it. Not really. But the *something*, sometimes good, confined mostly in the shadows, creeping around the quarters and in the kitchens, the *something* had made some of us stay when the *Freedom* came.

"Yes, you did," Doctor Mitchell said. "And that's what he needs from you. Your kind of commitment, Esther. I'm counting on that to help me get him back on his feet."

"I'm going back to New York in August," I faltered. "I can't stay."

Canaan was waiting across the Red Sea. The waters would not stay parted forever. If I did not get away from this place, I might not ever leave it.

"We can accomplish a great deal in what-- four, five months," Doctor Mitchell said quickly, seizing on the wavering he detected. "I'm counting on him too, Esther. Like I said, he's strong, determined. He's a fighter. Stubborn. You know it. With your help, I believe everything can be all right. And if we can only have your help for a little while, I believe it may be enough to work miracles."

It could only be until August.

"Miracles are God's business, Doctor Mitchell," I reminded him.

"Yes, and you are His servant, Esther Allen."

Yes, I was. *A workman not ashamed.*

VI

This not our concern.

It wasn't. The Bible said a man reaped what he sowed, and we had no part in Taylor Payne's terrible harvest. As a hireling I had a right to flee now that there was trouble. Yet I had agreed to stay, choosing Doctor Mitchell's part, and thereby my employer's, over my grandfather's and thereby my own. But I was thinking for myself. I might actually owe it to him for all those afternoons when all I had done was read his books. There would be little time for that now. By August I would have paid in full any untoward advantage I had taken of his generosity.

And if August came and there were no miracles? Then, after all, it was his fate not mine. Jimmy's future had been full of promise too, but he was dead. And for *their* victories. Tragedies happened all the time. *He that sitteth in the heavens shall laugh: the Lord shall have them in derision.* Sometimes I did wonder if the good Lord laughed at us, amused by our pitiful plans, knowing all along that each of us in our own way must meet Him on a road to Damascus.

Late in the day Mrs. Mitchell called and wanted to know if her husband would be coming home tonight. I went upstairs and rapped softly on the closed bedroom door.

"Come in, Esther," said Doctor Mitchell.

When I was in the room, with nothing to offer him, and frightened by all that he needed from me, I did not look at my employer, opting to stare at the floor instead.

"Yes, what is it?" asked the doctor from his seat next to the bed, where I had sat for hours scared that my employer would die.

"It's Mis' Mitchell, Doctor," I said. "On the telephone."

Doctor Mitchell went to answer the call, and I followed him but then I stopped and returned to my employer's room. Of course I had something to offer him. I had faced catastrophe before. Standing in for the sister that should have been on her way to his side, I would be his sister in the Lord. He didn't have to be a believer in order for *my* prayers to be answered. Maybe God did laugh, but He was merciful too.

"Mr. Payne," I asked standing at the door, "Can I get you anything?"

"No," he said.

Sooner or later Doctor Mitchell would have to go, and then I would be all that he had. At least until August. Doctor Mitchell's strategy must work.

"I know it's hard, Mr. Payne," I encouraged. "But you'll get through it."

And I'll help you, I was thinking.

Wearing my grandfather's face as it had been on the day the telegram had come about Jimmy, a face that was empty, with eyes beyond the relief of tears, my employer did not reply. Mama had wailed and wept on that terrible day and for many days, but not Grampa. I had held and rocked her until her whimpering went away because she slept from exhaustion. No one had held Grampa. He had been beyond our reach. All that dreadful day he had barely spoken a word, had hardly made a sound, had never even smoked his pipe. My employer was like that now. Silent. Separate from the rest of us. Was this the way of all strong men in devastating circumstances?

"Everything's going to be all right," I added, even though I might as well have been standing at the foot of Mama's bed again, inadequate once more.

"Esther," my employer began without looking at me. "What Mitch, what he asked you to do…it's… too much. I can manage this…You don't --"

Don't leave me.

I won't.

"I don't mind, Mr. Payne," I replied before he could finish.

Maybe this time it really could be all right. With his determination and my willing hands. Doctor Mitchell was a very good doctor. He said that Sister Kenny's methods were amazing. He wouldn't offer false hope, and if he said so, maybe I really could be adequate this time.

"I can't ask you to…to--"

But you already did, I was thinking. And I already promised. And Grampa heard us. And then Doctor Mitchell. You were delirious, but I wasn't.

"Mr. Payne, you're going to be fine," I interrupted him earnestly, speaking around a clod of sadness in my throat that threatened to choke me like clay. "You're just very weak. Doctor Mitchell says that the most terrible cases get completely well. You just need time." I came closer to the bed, willing him to look at me. And you need me, I thought. You said so yourself, I wanted to tell him. "He says time is the healer."

"This is not your concern," he said.

This not our concern.

Uncle Perry, Grampa, Nathaniel, and now him, all of them wanted to say what was *my concern*. None of them trusted me to choose for myself, except for Doctor Mitchell, who had at least asked me. Perhaps they were right, and Doctor Mitchell wasn't thinking of me, but it didn't matter anymore. This *concern* was mine because I had taken it.

"Don't be discouraged," I consoled my employer. "If anyone can beat this you can. You're a very strong man, Mr. Payne. You'll see."

"Esther, please," he replied as if I exasperated him. "I am grateful for your kindness, but--"

"Well!" announced Doctor Mitchell bustling back into the room. "Esther, shall we go over Taylor's care? Apparently Mrs. Mitchell misses her husband. And after thirty years too. Imagine that. Women are a mystery, don't you think, Taylor?"

Going to the bed, Doctor Mitchell pulled back the sheet, uncovering my employer. In the hours just passed I had looked upon his nakedness, seen his weaknesses many times, but now it was different again, because he was seeing me see him. I felt like a daughter of Ham bringing humiliation simply by looking. Yet I looked anyway, and calmly. This broken body was barely his anymore and mostly my responsibility—for now.

"Come over here, Esther," Doctor Mitchell was saying. "I just want to show her how to massage your legs and back, Taylor, to keep the blood flowing. That's all we want to do for right now. Light massage. Nothing too strenuous at first. Just a little range of motion exercises which should help with the spasms."

The doctor began to manipulate my employer's left upper thigh, working down the limb gently, and finishing with rubbing his heel.

"Now you do the right one," Doctor Mitchell said.

"No," said my employer.

I hesitated, meeting his eyes, but then I looked down and placed my hands on his thigh. He caught my arm.

"You're not my nurse," he told me.

You his maid, Esther Fay.

My heart beat rapidly and I kept my hands from shaking by gripping his paralyzed leg.

"Gently now," Doctor Mitchell cautioned. "You don't want to cause him too much pain. The muscles are sore."

My hands tenderly squeezed the flaccid limb.

Work with willin' hands, Esther Fay. That's the Bible.

He let go of my arm. I didn't look up.

"Not like this," I heard him say quietly.

"No, son, she's doing right," replied Doctor Mitchell as I moved down my employer's leg. "Good job, Esther! Now bend the knee a little."

My employer caught his breath, but still I didn't look up.

"I know it's a little uncomfortable, but it'll get better," said Doctor Mitchell. "She's doing it perfectly. I told you. It comes naturally to her. In the beginning, Esther, until he's better able to move on his own, you'll need to do this for him every couple of hours or so. All this laying in one place too long can make the pain worse. And we have to watch the condition of the skin. Taylor, when you're not comfortable you have to let her know."

At the end Mama had said nothing, and nothing I could do had helped anyway. But this time could be different. I could feel his stoney eyes on me, but it was not necessary to venture to his face again so I didn't. It was enough knowing that he didn't want to die.

"Now we want to turn him on his side and do similarly for his back," Doctor Mitchell instructed. "At first, Esther, you'll have to do much of the work, but Taylor, you must help her as much as you can. It's good exercise for you to try, and it will get easier."

Following Doctor Mitchell's directions, I rolled my employer onto his side and rubbed his back as he clung to the side of the mattress struggling to maintain his balance. His skin was smooth and warm and I remembered again the first time I had seen him, wearing a stained sleeveless t-shirt, looking more like Nathaniel than Pastor Wright. Now the powerful *lord of the manor* was the prisoner of his own bed, and dependent upon the hands of his maid.

"Do this routinely, Esther," said Doctor Mitchell as my hands moved in a slow circular motion over the broad, stricken back.

Was the polio was still inside of him, still working its way up his spine? Doctor Mitchell was preparing to leave. In the middle of the night could the muscles in my employer's chest fail too? I'd never rest in this house for fear of losing him.

"You have to do this for him even when he tells you not to," the doctor was telling me.

Satisfied with my efforts, Doctor Mitchell said that I should help my employer to rest on his back again. My employer strove to straighten himself in the bed on his own, but failing, he was forced to submit to my help.

I can manage this.

I risked meeting his eyes again, but now nothing was there. He was gone, the way Grampa was the day the War Department telegram had come, the way Mama was by the time I had come home from Harlem. Perhaps it was better this way. The two of us separated, connected only by need and work. Perhaps this was how it was supposed to be. The way it must have been between CoraLee and Mrs. Spalding's mother.

Doctor Mitchell was re-rolling the towels to place under my employer's ankles to keep his heels from resting on the sheet.

"Taylor, liked we talked about," he continued. "You have to try to keep your feet flat against the board. Esther, you watch out for that too."

I nodded.

"There's one more thing we need to go over," said Doctor Mitchell methodically, as if we were in a classroom, and my employer was some kind of academic assignment. "That's your bowel and bladder care."

I already knew what to do with the bedpan, so Doctor Mitchell only needed to explain how to use the bottle which was designed to make it neater for male patients to pee. He said that I would have to place my employer's penis into the mouth of the bottle, until such time that he could do this for himself.

"We might also have to give him an enema if the situation requires it. Different muscles can be affected," the doctor said. "And sometimes it's simply due to being bedfast. You remember how it was with Eva."

You're not my nurse.

You his maid, Esther Fay.

We had been sitting by *their* sick beds since slavery. Disposing of their wastes. Holding their hands and wiping their brows. It was what *we* did. Proximity did not make us intimates. Even if Doctor Mitchell believed I was his friend, friend was a broad concept with many meanings.

"We're fortunate the weakness seems to be so low," said Doctor Mitchell. "If you continue to hold your own, Taylor, we probably won't have to concern ourselves with enemas very often. And as soon as you are able to get out of bed, we'll get you a commode and throw out the pan all together."

We're fortunate...

We must have many meanings too. My employer didn't seem to hear Doctor Mitchell. And my own throat was still tight with the miserable clay.

It was nearly nine o'clock by the time I was standing at the front door, watching the red taillights of Doctor Mitchell's car disappear from view as he turned onto Webster Road. Tomorrow, he had said, he would bring me one of Sister Kenny's manuals.

"It might even make you reconsider your profession," he had suggested.

I was a maid. It was not a *profession*.

"I'm going to be a teacher, Doctor Mitchell," I had reminded him.

"It's worth thinking about," he had insisted. "You have a gift."

I closed the door. Herman stood in the foyer looking up at me expectantly. He had had both his dinner and his outside time. Now he was just in search of company. I looked upstairs at the closed bedroom door. *He* had had his dinner too, but he didn't eat it. I would surely be turning to Aunt Betty for help again. Perhaps this time her tastes would be more acceptable to him. I could learn to make the custards. If he would eat it, I would make him chicken soup every day. I was willing to do anything to bring about the miracles in time.

Glancing at the telephone, I debated whether or not to call Nathaniel. I ought to let him know that I was all right, and I wanted to hear a word of encouragement. Unsure of the second objective, I elected not to aim for the first. My resolution was too fresh and fragile. I should pray some more. Taylor Payne was no Christian, but that didn't seem to matter anyway. The hedges failed all of us at times, leaving us exposed to tragedy. This world had no sanctuary for anyone.

But at least my employer was resting now according to Doctor Mitchell, so I took some time to take a bath. It had been days, and I had a change of clothes now. In the buttercup room, I opened up the small suitcase. In it there were some under garments, a nightgown and a robe, and another one of Mama's dresses. I sighed. Nurses wore white not black. And caps.

I never want to see that cap on your head in this house again.

I placed the few clothes in a single bureau drawer.

In the second bathroom, I filled the old oval tub with the claw feet and sank down to my chin in the warm water. I was thirteen years old when I was baptized, because Grampa said that children should wait until they were old enough to understand the responsibilities of salvation. For him it was a privilege, the one privilege, the one *advantage* that no one could deny even *us*. Salvation was yours with the baptism, and nothing could take it away from you, not life or death or time. Grampa's edict had meant that Jimmy, Nathaniel, and I were the last among our peers in the Sweet Water congregation to be baptized, practically making us outcasts among our own, but his rules were not to be compromised. Isaac Green's grandchildren could not be like everybody else. For so many Sundays I had sat humbly in my state of *Original Sin*, while the *Bread of Life* and the *Cup of Salvation* had passed me by. The first lesson of salvation seemed to be realizing your unworthiness and knowing how apart from God you were because of it. When Reverend Wright had finally carried me down under the cold flowing water at Johnson Creek to bring me back up again in the spring of my 13th year, at long last I belonged to God and He belonged to me. *Fear thou not; for I am with thee: be not dismayed; for I am thy God: I will strengthen thee; yea, I will help thee; yea, I will uphold thee with the right hand of my righteousness.* This was the first promise that things could be different.

In the tub the liquid warmth washed over me, melting the tight lump trapped in my throat, releasing its streaming sobs. All day long, for days in fact, I had wanted to cry, now I could, burying my face in a warm wet towel, so that hopefully even Herman could not hear me weeping.

After awhile the water began to cool, and I was calm. The conflicting responsibilities and obligations, the contradictory expectations and loyalties, God would work these things out. For now I just let myself be at rest in the quietness.

♫*Blessed quietness*
Holy quietness
What assurance in my soul
On that stormy sea, Jesus speaks to me,
How the billows seems to roll

August would come, and when I left it could be with a clean conscience, having done my best to please God. The days would be hard, but they would be hardest for him. Surely I could wait with him just a little while. And no matter what happened, I could still walk away.

I dressed in the cotton nightgown and robe and felt immodest in my employer's house. At least I wasn't going to be sleeping in the sleigh bed tonight. It would put me too far away from him, and besides the bed was intended for Felicia. She still might come, and she wouldn't want to sleep where a Negro had lain. Grampa had forgotten to pack a pair of house slippers for me, but then again I never wore them at home, preferring to go barefoot summer and winter. But I had never been barefoot in this house. Here was not my home. I carried my dirty clothes downstairs to the washing machine and made myself a cup of tea while my clothes washed. When they were done I hung them around the back porch to dry.

Doctor Mitchell had said that he would order a special machine for the hot-packs that were the key to Sister Kenny's methods. In the meantime, we were going to use the old wringer washing machine because the wool strips we needed to use had to be very hot to work. "We can use wool blankets, cut into strips," Doctor Mitchell had explained. "The wool holds the heat very well. The wringer on the washing machine will spare our hands because we'll be using boiling water so that the packs will stay hot longer. Having the machine in his room will make it easier to manage."

I can manage this.

In better days, my employer had wanted to give away the old washing machine, but I had been unwilling to accept his charity for the sake of anyone I knew. Maybe all things did work together for good according to God's purpose. At least I hoped so. Even though I did not understand His purpose I hoped so. Maybe Mandy would be using the machine anyway, and when he was well again he could give it to her himself.

It was getting late, and I was drained. I climbed the stairs slowly, with Herman following behind me. I took down another blanket from the linen closet, this time for me. I knocked on Mr. Payne's bedroom door. There was no response and I had not expected one. I went in anyway. Without looking at him, I crossed the room and left the blanket on the larger chair that was by the window, where Doctor Mitchell had slept. Now it was my sleeping place when I would be sleeping at all. The vigil was not done. Maybe it never would be. At least not until August.

Returning to the side of my employer's bed, I told him it was time to move him. He said nothing, staring blankly. He didn't have to talk to me, I just needed to do what had to be done, adhering to Doctor Mitchell's instructions. Meticulously I rubbed his flesh from his shoulders down to his heels and tucked pillows around him to support him in a different position in the bed.

"Would you like me to get the...the bottle?" I asked him once I had him settled again.

Tomorrow I would be bathing him, seeing him naked, and he would be conscious and know it, so tonight I might as well get used to touching his manhood. It wouldn't be like Danny's which I had felt more than seen in the backseat of the Ford. It would be like Baby Nate's because everything was different now, changed into urine bottles, and wringer washing machines, and footboards, and helplessness.

"No," he answered.

"Is there anything I can I get you?"

"No."

"Shall I leave the lamp on?"

"No."

Herman lay down on his place on the rug and rested his head on his paws.

"Good night, Mr. Payne," I said, switching off the lamp.

Again he said nothing. I didn't blame him. He couldn't see anything *good*. But what else did you say? I returned to the chair by the window and sat down, covering myself with the blanket. I wasn't cold. My robe was warm enough. But I didn't know what else to do either.

There was a bright moon tonight, and it glowed serenely. The world outside was silver. As if nothing had happened.

"You don't need to stay here," my employer said after a time.

Stay with him, Esther.

"I'm fine, Mr. Payne. Good night."

....There is a train. I am boarding it. Grampa is a porter, and he reaches down from the train to help me up the steps. I hand him the small suitcase I am carrying instead, and I mount the steps on my own.

"You gon' need more clothes than this thing can hold," Grampa says.

"I'm going to the beach," I tell him.

The Atlantic Ocean strokes the shore. I sit on the sand wearing a black cotton dress, a white cotton apron around my waist. The water reaches to my feet. I take a piece of crumpled paper out of my pocket. There are numbers written on it. I let a wave take the piece of paper out to sea. The sun is warming my face....

The sun was warming my face, pouring in through the window, passing through my closed eyelids. It was the next morning I realized with a start. I had slept through the night. I rushed to my employer's bedside. "Mr. Payne, I'm sorry," I said. "Are you all right? I didn't mean to sleep...I-I was tired. Why didn't you wake me? Doctor Mitchell said you have to tell me." I pulled back the covers. "Let me--" The scent of urine shocked me. The bed was wet. For a moment I stood there looking down at him, at the soiled linens and wet drawers. Protectively I wanted to cover him up again, to hide his shame and also my failure.

"I'm sorry," I whispered again, meeting his eyes. "Why didn't you...why didn't you wake me?"

"You're not my nurse," he said impassively.

It wasn't like taking care of Mama. It was too sudden. Too different. Too difficult. I couldn't do it. But I began to anyway. Competently, silently, I cleaned him and changed the bed linens. The rubber sheet was a blessing.

"You have to tell me when you need something, Mr. Payne," I said when at last I was smoothing the new top sheet over him.

"You're not my nurse," he told me again in the same empty voice.

"I'm here to help you."

"I can manage."

Once again it didn't make sense to argue with the absurd. There wasn't any point. I gathered up the soiled things to take downstairs to the washing machine.

"Just please tell me when you need a little help," I replied. "There's no reason to wet...I mean, that's what I'm here for."

"To change my diapers, is that it?" he asked now bitterly.

Straining he raised himself up, resting on his elbows.

"Mr. Payne," I said, surprised and encouraged by this return of strength so soon. "You're better."

"Am I?" he demanded, breathing hard.

The pungent smell of urine was burning my nose.

"Are you praying for me, Esther?" he taunted me. "Intercession. Do I get that in the bargain too? Maid. Missionary. Nurse. I must say you're quite a... a-a package."

I lowered the malodorous bundle as far away from my face as I could without putting it down. Mama had been cruel too, saying mean words to me, when it was not my fault, when I was only trying to help. Learning how to bend then had saved me from breaking, and I had become as pliable as the willow trees along the edges of Johnson Creek. I would take care of him anyway. And yes, I would pray for him too. God would use me to help him.

"I...I suppose if you...you're going to lay your hands on me," he said sadistically. "You have to make it mean something. Isn't that what you people do?"

...You people...

Hot tears spilled out of my eyes and down my cheeks. With my arms full of his dirty linens and wet drawers I could not wipe them away. If I threw them down on the floor and ran out of this room and away from him, nobody would blame me. He wasn't mine. I wasn't his. But I stood there, with no recourse to hide my wretchedness.

"Are you...are you praying now?" he shouted at me although his strength was waning.

"Te-tell me. Say it. Out loud. I want to hear it."

I looked at him. I owed him absolutely nothing. The Samaritan had only paid for the arrangements and then gone on his way, and we called him good. The tears had stopped and were drying on their own. Weakening, he clutched at the mattress trying to support himself.

"Say it," he said again.

Say my name.

"Pray...pray for," he struggled as he was collapsing. "I said..."

He fainted, slumping over to the side. Dropping the linens I went to him and dipped my hand into the pitcher of water on the night stand to sprinkle on his face. He regained consciousness, but he was limp and unresponsive as I worked to resettle him in the bed.

"You...you're not my nurse," he mumbled again as I was placing his feet against the footboard.

I wasn't his *missionary* either. I was his maid. *It's God's will*, someone was always saying about whatever happened, good or bad, or impossible. Maybe it was. But sometimes, sometimes, it was also our own. Our own choices, like Mandy said. The consequence of thinking for yourself.

"Hush now," I admonished my employer quietly as I covered him again. "You've worn yourself out with all of that. You need to rest." He was looking up at me, and I mustered a smile. "Doctor Mitchell's gonna be proud though," I said. "You sat up all by yourself and so soon too. It's a good sign. But that's enough for now. You take a nap while I make you a little breakfast."

I carried the dirty clothes downstairs and turned on the washing machine. I was shaking. I had forgotten to wear the gloves again and maybe he was still contagious. Maybe I could still catch it. But he had raised himself up. At least he wasn't getting weaker.

...You people...

If rage gave him the strength, the will, then so be it. He could rage at me all he wanted as long as he got well. After all, Jesus had forgiven the crucifixion, loving us all anyway, and leaving us an example to follow.

Maybe this time it wouldn't be hopeless. Maybe this time I could do more than *wait*. Maybe this time I could make a difference. My faith had works to show for itself, and I wanted my place with the biblical *Esther* and *Ruth*, and with Sister Callie. Heavenly crowns didn't have to be earned but they did have to be honored. I wanted to be a workman not ashamed. This time I would *make it mean something.*

Doctor Mitchell brought me the book, *The Kenny Treatment for Infantile Paralysis.* I moved into the buttercup room proper, leaving both bedroom doors open at night so that I could hear if my employer should call me, which he didn't. As with Mama, I learned how to sleep in naps again, waking up almost instinctively to turn my employer and attend to whatever else he might need. Whenever I had a free moment I studied the treatment manual. In the beginning we made the hot-packs with the wringer washing machine and foot-tubs of boiling water, and by the time the hot-pack machine arrived I was skilled at making and applying them to my employer's legs, and I had completely incorporated the sister's instructions about muscle *re-education.* Reviewing the pictures of the human body in Doctor Mitchell's anatomy book, I was determined to know my employer's body better than I knew my own, in order to coax and cajole it back to its former wholeness.

In those first weeks, I met my employer's physical needs, although his eyes, if he looked at me at all, accused and condemned me with every act. He refused to talk to me but his aggrieved silence was no match for my unrelenting determination. It was enough to be needed. I did not have to be wanted. Mama had never written but I had come home anyway. For her sake. If once again, I was another ram in the bush for someone else who couldn't be grateful for me either, if once again I was God's unwelcomed providence in the face of calamity, the blessing that you had instead of what you wanted, then fine, I was used to it.

If ever there had been a friendship between me and my employer, an *attachment* as Doctor Mitchell had called it, there no longer was. The only *attachment* we shared now was to his body. It was my mission. My employer could disappear into himself, but his body, his legs, remained in my hands. Were it not for Doctor Mitchell, who came every day, and usually twice a day, my employer would never eat or drink since he would accept neither from me. I supposed this was all he could do, his only means of defiance, this and not speaking or looking at me. All the rest I controlled, learning to manage his body and see to its functions as though it were mine. If he would not ask for the bedpan or the urine bottle then he did not have to. I attended to these matters on a schedule so that he was rendered a passive participant in his own miserable existence. It was probably better this way anyway. His bedroom became a sterile efficient place and the detachment, the wall he built around himself, protected me too.

The therapy sessions went better when Doctor Mitchell was with us, whether he was conducting them himself or just overseeing me. However during the times when the doctor was not there the sessions still had to be completed, and thoroughly. August was coming. There was no time to spare. I could not leave my employer so undone; and so I pushed him even if he would only lay there as alienated from me as Sister

Kenny's manual said the muscles in his legs were from his mind. I was resolute all the while preaching Sister Kenny's counsel constantly as he stared vacantly. No matter. He wasn't deaf. He had to be hearing me. It had to be working.

Because there was improvement. By the time the quarantine was lifted, my employer could flex and push his left his foot against the pressure of Doctor Mitchell's hand, and he could bend his left knee. The right leg wasn't progressing as well and Doctor Mitchell decided put it in a splint to prevent the contractures. Because this seemed to be in conflict with Sister Kenny's methods, I protested.

"Sometimes we have to combine our approaches, Esther," the doctor counseled me as we stood in the hall outside my employer's room. "We don't have to be so strict."

But I had become a disciple and was unwilling to compromise.

"But you said that her methods are the best," I argued.

"And I believe that," Doctor Mitchell replied emphatically. "Look at the progress he's made."

"I think you should hire a real nurse," I said sullenly. "The quarantine is over. You ought to be able to find someone now."

Frowning, Doctor Mitchell pulled me away from my employer's closed bedroom door.

"You mustn't get discouraged, Esther," he said. "I know it's hard, but you're doing very well."

"He doesn't want me here, Doctor Mitchell. He says so all the time."

"What does he say?"

"That I'm not his nurse. If he speaks to me at all."

"This is a terrible ordeal for him, Esther," Doctor Mitchell explained urgently. "A man like Taylor, you know how he has lived his life. On his own terms. To find himself helpless and dependent, he doesn't know how to be this way. He's afraid, that's why he lashes out. We have to be patient with him. He needs time to reconcile himself to it. We must be understanding."

"Sister Kenny says the person must be determined if the treatment is going to be successful," I insisted. "He has to try. When you're not here he just lays there, Doctor Mitchell. I don't know what to do when he doesn't try."

"He does try, Esther," maintained Doctor Mitchell.

"If you say so, Doctor," I said unconvinced. "But a real nurse would know what to do better than me. A real nurse would know how to keep him encouraged, how to make him determined."

"Esther," Doctor Mitchell said, "Believe me. He is trying. But in his mind he-he only fails. He doesn't want you to see that. Yes, of course it's a matter of pride. And all right, foolish pride if you will. But no man wants to be a burden. Maybe what he's trying to do most of all, shield you in…in some small way from the full measure of his…his predicament. You're a wise woman, Esther. I'm surprised you can't see that."

But I was the maid. Not some delicate flower of southern womanhood, fanning and fainting, and subject to the vapors. I didn't expect any kind of *shielding*, and especially not from him.

"That doesn't make sense, Doctor Mitchell," I said.

Men could be ridiculous, valiant creatures, and the Bible said a man's pride could bring him low. What could my employer hide from me? I was here every day, in that bedroom, with the uneaten meals and the despair, here because I was called to be, and wanted to be. We did not have time for his pride. August was coming.

"In some ways, Esther," said Doctor Mitchell soberly. "That might be the worst of it. You seeing him like this. It's what I'm counting on. He'll fight for you, Esther."

You his maid, Esther Fay.

Doctor Mitchell was ridiculous too.

"Be patient with him," he pleaded. "It is after all his affliction not ours. We have to give him time to cope with it in his own way. Don't give up on him, Esther. I'm counting on you." Doctor Mitchell smiled encouragingly. "And I believe in his own way, Taylor is too."

VII

The Lord must be a mystery. The creatures, no matter who we were, could never fully comprehend the Creator. I had to walk by faith, not by sight. Even if that faith wasn't shared by the man who needed it most. Or the family who loved me. Once the quarantine was officially over, Nathaniel returned. Seeing his truck pulling up outside late in the afternoon, I was jubilant, running out the backdoor and practically leaping off the porch steps into his strong embrace.

"Hey there, Little Sister!" my cousin said as he wrapped his powerful arms around me.

"Oh Nathaniel!" I exclaimed happily, burying my face in his overalls, soaking in the familiar scent of his work, his person, feeling finally secure and comforted.

"I come to take you home," he said.

Joy fading, I let go of him, and stepped back.

"I can't go now, Nathaniel," I had to say.

"Why not?" he frowned. "The house ain't quarantined no more."

"I'm taking care of him."

"You done enough."

"He needs more."

"So you b'lieve you can just stay here?" Nathaniel demanded. "Livin' with 'im?"

"There's no other way," I replied.

"Yeah there is. He got money. He can hire somebody. If he don't want his own sister to come, he needs to get himself a nurse."

"He hired me."

"Not for this," Nathaniel insisted.

"Who knows?" I asked. "Things happen for a reason, Nathaniel. Maybe I'm supposed to be here."

"Sometimes things just happen, Esther Fay," returned Nathaniel shaking his head. "Bad things. Sad things. Don't mistake his will for the Lord's."

"It's not his will, Nathaniel," I said. "Mr. Payne's, I mean. Can you stay for a little while? Come in the house. Have somethin' cool to drink."

"What you mean it's not his will?" asked Nathaniel.

"How's Grampa?" I asked instead of answering him.

I brooded about Grampa all the time, about how he must be making his own coffee, and ironing his own Sunday clothes. I had abandoned him for a *concern* that was not ours, just mine. The war had not been *ours* either. But Jimmy had taken it for *his*. Men might get to choose their battles, but women were expected to just accept the ones handed to them. Grampa, himself, had bought the war bonds. Mama and I had never had any say.

"Doc Mitchell ain't got no right--" began Nathaniel.

"It's just 'til August, Nathaniel," I interrupted him, pulling him towards the house. "Or until he gets well."

"And what if he gets well and still can't walk? Then what? What about New York, Esther Fay?"

I couldn't allow myself to think like that. I had to believe it would be different. I had to believe in him, even if he didn't believe in anything.

"I gave my word, Nathaniel," I said.

"To him?" asked Nathaniel.

Yes. And there were witnesses. Grampa and Doctor Mitchell. And God.

Other people began coming to the house too: Henry Adams, the courthouse clerk, Mr. Walton, the district attorney, other men in suits, and even a group of elders from the First Presbyterian Church to which my employer formally belonged although seldom attended. My employer would see none of them, not even Mr. Walton for whom he worked. Their flowers wilted and died throughout the house because he wouldn't have them in his room. Their expressions of concern meant nothing to him. I had no choice but to turn them all away, as politely as I could and as steadfastly as I dared.

It was the same when Laura Spalding and her mother came to visit. She had called many times, and each time I had dutifully delivered her messages to my employer, sometimes even hopefully, still wanting to reach him somehow. He had never responded. Even she seemed to be nothing to him.

Nevertheless, Laura Spalding wanted to see him. I could understand that. She was entitled to. So the day when I opened the front door to her and her mother, Mrs.

Spalding, I was not surprised. Sooner or later Laura Spalding would be here and I would be gone. If the *sooner* came before August, it would relieve everybody.

"I'm sorry, Mis' Laura," I still had to say, using my body to block them from the stairs as they stood in the foyer. "Doctor Mitchell says he's not s'pose to have visitors."

"That's ridiculous!" Laura dismissed the prohibition as she was removing her gloves.

"Well, dear," her mother hesitated, handing me a colorful bouquet of flowers. "If Doctor Mitchell says--"

"Mother, he must be better by now. I want to talk to his nurse. Get her down here," she ordered me.

"I'm lookin' after him, ma'am," I said.

"You are?!" she exclaimed. "You're not a nurse."

You his maid, Esther Fay.

And his *missionary* too, I had accepted. Neither of which required me to have silky hair or ruby lips. Just willing hands that were no prettier than Sister Callie's.

"Doctor Mitchell trained me," I explained.

"I've never heard of such thing!" snapped Laura. "What could Doctor Mitchell be thinking?"

That there was an *attachment.*

"I'm sure it must be all right," suggested Mrs. Spalding. "You remember how good CoraLee was with your granny."

We people were always looking after *them.*

"You'd think he had the black plague," Laura complained. "All this secrecy. Doctor Mitchell won't tell me a thing."

"I think it must be serious," Mrs. Spalding speculated. "Your father said he heard it was contagious."

"You must know something," Laura turned on me. "What is it? Is it tuberculosis? I wouldn't be a bit surprised. He's always down there in that dreadful, dirty jail, with the worst kind of people. Who knows what he picked up in that nasty place?"

Or in the swimming pool of your country club, I thought. The painted roses in her cheeks were redder, flushed with irritation. How long could Doctor Mitchell keep everyone from knowing? There must be rumors. But it wasn't a shame. It was a tragedy.

"Answer me, girl," Laura ordered. "Don't just stand there with that stupid look on your face."

My employer's bedroom door was open as usual, so he could probably hear us. He must know Laura was here. I looked at her lovely face, expecting at last to hear the ring of the bell summoning me, to have me bring her to him. I even almost hoped so.

McConnell County was not Manhattan. Secrets got out eventually and then moved quickly across both sides of town. Everyone would ultimately know. I was surprised that the Spaldings didn't know already. Someone was going to tell someone else. Bad news rushed around on winged feet.

"I think we should go, dear," Mrs. Spalding was saying. "Clearly Esther has her instructions. We don't want to get her in trouble."

"No!" declared Laura. "I want to see him. Go up stairs right now and tell--"

"Laura, dear," intervened Mrs. Spalding, placing a soothing hand on her daughter's arm. "We don't want to make a scene. Taylor is ill--"

"I know, Mother," insisted Laura. "I'm worried about him. All this time. He must want to see me."

"Mis' Laura," I appealed in my most placating voice. "I have strict orders from Doctor Mitchell. He can't have no visitors yet. I'm sure just as soon as he's up to it, you'll be the first person he asks me to call."

Even as I was deliberately lying to flatter and soothe her ego enough to persuade her to go away, I knew that it was more her place to be here than it was mine. She should be the one bathing him and applying the hot-packs, rubbing his heels, and massaging his back. Maybe he would eat for her, take a drink if she offered it to him. If Doctor Mitchell thought he would fight for me, then how much more would he fight for her? Maybe I should let them go upstairs. What if I was blocking a blessing?

"That's right, sweetheart," added Mrs. Spalding. "As soon as he's up to it, he'll send for you. Come," she urged. "Your father will talk to Doctor Mitchell and get a report. Esther, put those flowers in fresh water right away. And you take good care of Mr. Payne, you hear. Don't let us down."

"No ma'am," I said. "I won't."

"It makes no sense," Laura grumbled but she was pulling on her gloves. "Keeping that man a prisoner in his own house."

It was the polio that had done that, I thought as I quickly moved to hold the door open for them to leave. A thing too tiny to see had taken him away from us all. Ambivalently I watched the Spalding car depart down the graveled drive, and then shut and locked the front door. Jesus' disciples had rolled the stone in front of the tomb too; the difference was that I was burying myself as well.

The melancholy days were consumed with the scalding hot strips of wool, and work, and sweat, and silence. I didn't even turn on the radio anymore. In the movie, *Home of the Brave,* the white doctor had shouted at the Negro soldier, calling him a nigger to make him angry enough to come back from the place he had retreated to. Jesus had shouted at Lazarus. But I was neither a savior nor a doctor, so my voice grew rusty from disuse.

Aunt Betty brought over a larger a suitcase, which she had gone to Grampa's house to pack for me.

"If this what you determined to do," my aunt said. "Then ain't no sense in you doin' it without yo' clothes."

"How is Grampa, Aunt Betty?" I asked.

She had parked at the back of the house, and now stood beside Uncle Perry's car, still fearful of coming too close. I stood on the back porch steps. Briefly I remembered her other visits and was glad that she did not want to come inside the house. She would have been disappointed with the choices that my employer had made.

"You know him," Aunt Betty replied.

"Why won't he call me?" I asked glumly.

"Now you know how Papa Isaac is about telephones."

"I worry about him."

"I think you got yo'self plenty to worry 'bout right here 'thout lookin' for more."

"You understand, don't you Aunt Betty?" I implored.

"Nathaniel say you b'lieve you called to do it," she said. "It ain't up to me to understand it."

I looked down at my shoes. The laces were graying and fraying with wear, but they would do until August. The shoes that came with leg braces must not be stylish either. They would not become the suits that were pressed and ready in anticipation that faith was indeed the evidence of things not seen.

"Oh," Aunt Betty said reaching into her pocketbook and bringing out a letter. "Yo' grandpa said this come for you the other day."

I stared at my name written on the envelope. It was from Danny.

"It's from that boy in Korea, ain't it?" my aunt asked.

"Yes ma'am," I told her.

"Well, life does go on."

It always did. No matter what. I stared at the letter.

"Ain't you gon' open it?" Aunt Betty asked.

"I don't have time to read it right now," I said. "I'll save it for later."

"Don't wait too much later," Aunt Betty advised. "You look up and life be done passed you by."

VIII

Summer finally arrived almost vindictively, as if it had something to prove to the spring. This was East Texas. The hot wool tortured my employer, tortured us all, but nevertheless I was dogged, as was Doctor Mitchell. The left leg grew stronger and inspired us. The right one remained barely responsive, and despite our efforts Doctor Mitchell admitted to me privately that the limb was wasting.

"I suppose a bad limp is not the worst way for this to turn out," the doctor wavered one day at the end of one of his visits.

Picturing the man my employer had once been now dragging his right leg only fueled my resolve. It was a compromise I could not accept. Half-healed could not be God's plan. We just needed to work harder.

"You can't give up on him, Doctor Mitchell," I said firmly. "The Lord is able."

Although he looked worried, the old man mustered a smile.

"And so is Taylor," he added.

Now I smiled too.

"Yes he is," I replied with conviction. "Yes he is."

But it was time for a wheelchair. I didn't like the prospect of it, the compromise it suggested, but it was practical. Now that he was stronger, with Doctor Mitchell's help, my employer could transfer from his bed to the Queen Anne chair that Doctor Mitchell and I had carried upstairs for him. He could sit up for short periods, which made it easier to change his sheets and make his bed, and with the ability to transfer from the bed he had even graduated to a bedside commode. He still required the bedpan and urine bottle for the times when Doctor Mitchell wasn't here, because the transfers only happened with Doctor Mitchell's help. This was best, because besides the fact that there was a *cold war* between us, my employer was still a large man despite having lost weight. If he fell I couldn't be sure that I could get him up. And since he still refused to let Spencer come to the house, there would be no one to help me.

Moreover a wheelchair would give my employer some mobility, and according to Doctor Mitchell some sense of independence too. I came around to the idea of it and was able to share in Doctor Mitchell's positivity about it. Unfortunately the morning that Doctor Mitchell pushed the wheelchair into his room, our mutual positivity met my employer's fury and was erased. Our well-intended plans exploded in our faces. The patient did not share our *vantage point*.

"Take it away!" my employer shouted.

"Taylor--" began Doctor Mitchell.

"Get it out of here!"

"It's just temporary, son."

"Goddamn you!" he railed, hurling a coffee cup towards the wheelchair and Doctor Mitchell. "I said get it out of here!"

Luckily the throw went wild and the cup shattered against the wall. I stood by dumbly, feeling a little afraid but mostly sorry for Doctor Mitchell.

"Esther," the doctor said, visibly shaken. "Put the chair away. Perhaps it's too soon."

"Yes-sir," I obeyed, quickly taking the chair from him to push it away. "You meant well, Doctor Mitchell," I attempted to console him. "We have to be patient," I repeated the doctor's own words to me.

"Patience is a virtue, is that it?" said my employer sarcastically.

Doctor Mitchell and I looked at him.

"You needn't feel obligated to expend so much of it for my sake," he continued cuttingly. "I'm sure there's someone else out there willing to empty a bedpan for the right price."

"Taylor!" said Doctor Mitchell. "No."

> *"What you come back for?" Mama asked her voice weak but clear. "Ain't nothin' for you in this place."*
>
> *"You're here, Mama," I said.*
>
> *"I didn't ask you to come. Papa ain't had no right to."*
>
> *"But I wanted to come. I want to help you."*
>
> *"You can't help me."*

Grampa had said that Mama didn't mean it, the harsh things she had said to me. My employer didn't mean them either. He would never hurt Doctor Mitchell. It wasn't really his fault. It wasn't him. Not anymore. It was the sickness, the suffering.

"Esther," the doctor turned back to me. "I'm sorry. He's just upset. He doesn't mean it."

"Don't talk about me as if I weren't here," said my employer angrily.

But he wasn't here. Not the Taylor Payne we knew him to be. I looked down at the wheelchair. It was shiny and new. They were making them smaller since the war. They were more wieldy and convenient. You could fold them up and put them away when you didn't need them. But then when was that? Would God grant a heathen a miracle?

"Taylor, we—we didn't mean to imply anything," Doctor Mitchell now tried to apologize to him.

"You think it's hopeless, don't you?" my employer said coldly. "You think I'll never walk again."

I pushed the chair out of the room to avoid hearing the answer.

Later when Doctor Mitchell was leaving, I followed him out onto the front porch. He lit a cigarette and inhaled the tobacco deeply.

"It's contrary to Sister Kenny's philosophy," the doctor said. "But braces could work. He's got good strength in his hips. We could teach him how to propel himself well enough."

And leave him like Roosevelt. Not well, just *well enough*. In The Crisis someone was always willing to say that things were *well enough*. Someone was always arguing that it was unwise to expect too much, to want too much. The problem was that the *too much* to some wasn't even *enough* for others. After all we had the Constitution. We had miracles. It was all in how you looked at it. It was all in your *vantage point*.

"It's too soon to predict," I took my turn at boosting our mutual morale.

Doctor Mitchell sighed deeply.

"Yes, maybe you're right, Esther. But that didn't go well, did it?"

I shook my head.

"I think maybe he's hoping for more than *well enough*," I said. "You can't expect him to accept it."

"But the chair's only temporary, Esther. Just until he gets stronger."

"I-I think sometimes it has to be all or nothing with him. Like the Bible says, hot or cold. Maybe the wheelchair is what you could call lukewarm. He expects the best out of himself, remember? And that chair's not it."

"Sometimes you have to learn to accept things for what they are. A wise man comes to terms with things."

"He'll do what he has to do, Doctor Mitchell. He just needs time. You said it yourself."

Doctor Mitchell took another long drag from his cigarette and tossed the butt onto the graveled drive.

"What happened in there, this morning, him throwing things, that hasn't happened before, has it?" he asked.

"No-sir, never," I replied.

"He has a temper, I know. But he's never tried to hurt you?"

"No-sir, Doctor Mitchell."

The doctor sighed again. I thought about Cordelia Collier. My employer had never been one of those *fine Southern gentlemen*.

"Because if he ever did--" began Doctor Mitchell.

"He never would," I cut him off.

"I never thought I'd see him throw something at me."

"It wasn't at you, Doctor Mitchell."

"All right, at the chair then."

"Maybe he was just fighting back, like you said. The only way he knew how."

"Nevertheless, you be careful, Esther. Don't provoke him."

I smiled again, amused.

"Provoke him? Doctor Mitchell, most of the time he doesn't even know I'm here. I'm invisible to him."

"No you're not, Esther," Doctor Mitchell replied. "You never were."

He headed down the steps to his car.

"I'll be back in the morning," he called back. "You call me if he needs anything."

You never were.

In her last letter Aunt Grace said that her minister had asked about me. "Maybe you could teach Sunday School," she had written. "It will be good practice." I was going to be a teacher, but I wanted my employer to be able to walk on the beach again even if it was segregated.

Herman whimpered at the front door, and I let him out. For awhile I watched him explore the front yard. The lawn needed cutting. Sometimes when she got a moment Mandy would call. In snippets I disclosed my miseries to her sympathetic ear. She told me that Spencer was worrying her to death about coming back to work. He wouldn't be able to see our employer, but at least if he was around the house again Herman would have a companion, and me too. I could pay him out of the household money that I used to buy groceries, or just pay him out of my own wages which had been doubled by Doctor Mitchell. I wouldn't wait for Mandy to call again. I would send word by Nathaniel to tell Spencer to come. It was time to put some normalcy back in this house.

So before the end of the week Spencer was back. Herman was ecstatic if a dog could be that way. It was a joy to me too to see them playing together, romping around in the grass, like nothing was changed. Although everything was. And Spencer's feelings were hurt that he couldn't see our employer, his tutor, benefactor, and friend. I tried to explain to him about the consequences of sickness.

"But why he changed?" Spencer had asked.

"Don't leave out the verb," I had replied.

"Why *is* he changed?" Spencer had dutifully corrected himself. "Why don't he like us no more?"

"*Doesn't* and *anymore*."

"Why doesn't he like us anymore?"

Because he has to be angry at someone, I had thought the reply, and he doesn't believe in God.

As the days passed I was weary at one moment and energized at another. I was determined and depressed. Faithful and fearful. It was harder to be patient without certainty. With Mama the outcome had been known. There were no questions about the future because there hadn't been one. My employer's progress was slow, at times seemingly stalled; and I was constantly reminding myself that we were still only talking in terms of weeks not months.

Patience is a virtue, is that it?

Yes, it was. And the Bible said that the prayers of a righteous man availed much. I hoped that *righteousness* was a broad concept too.

I wrote a letter to Danny, telling him all about my plans for August but nothing about my life now. Because it wasn't *my* life now—not really. In a way I had given it over to this work, to this task of seeing this man get back on his feet again. I felt like Doctor Mitchell, not wanting to talk about my employer's plight, because it was his, and not something to be looked at and examined by strangers. It was a private thing, his pain, and I wanted to protect him. Danny would feel sorry for him and somehow the thought of that was just too wrong. Danny could not know him as I had known him. Danny could not understand.

Another week passed and with it another Sunday. I missed going to church, especially with Grampa. Devotedly reading my Bible by myself, I came to appreciate more why the Lord would have us assemble together. Where two or three of us were gathered together in His name, He had promised to be in the midst of us. Two of us were here, and often times even three or four, but there was no shared worship, and the instances of fellowship left me wanting. Mostly I just felt alone.

Harlem was farther away than Webster Road in miles but not in distance. Grampa was only across town but the Red Sea rolled between us. Nathaniel could not convince him to come here again.

"He said you sicced the dog on 'im," Nathaniel had told me.

"You know that's not true!" I had protested.

"Yeah, I know," my cousin had agreed. "But you might as well-a done it. You takin' Doc Mitchell's side over his felt like the same thing."

"The house was quarantined, Nathaniel."

"It ain't quarantined now."

No, it wasn't, but I was bound here. At least until August.

Let's not rush the goodbyes.

There was never a letter from Felicia either, and I wondered how she could be so distant from her brother. Couldn't she sense what was happening? Didn't she love him at all? Every single day that Jimmy was in the war I had thought about him and prayed for him. If he had suffered long surely I would have sensed it, felt it in my soul. But he had blown up in an instant to be taken to Paradise. He had had no pain. That was all ours. I missed him. We could have been in New York by now. Maybe *stompin'* at the Savoy.

I decided to bake teacakes. Spencer could take a batch home with him. Mandy's little ones would love that. Maybe they might even tempt my employer's appetite. Maybe the sweet buttery aroma could get through to him. I felt gloomy. The teacakes would do me good too.

I was taking butter from the refrigerator when I heard a car in the driveway. I assumed that Doctor Mitchell had forgotten something. Or maybe it was another one of my employer's friends that I would have to turn away. By the time I reached the front door, Reverend Wright was getting out of his car. I came out onto the porch as the reverend went around to open the door for his wife.

I'm not a chauffeur.

I was genuinely glad to see them. They were company, and I was amazed by their visit. Dressed in their Sunday clothes, they looked very nice. The reverend was wearing a coat and tie in this heat. Sister Wright wore a pretty peach cotton dress and a fine hat trimmed with lace. My mother's black dress and the white apron made me feel humble and unworthy. They must be expecting to also see Mr. Payne. They would be offended when I was forced to tell them that their Christian kindness would be rejected. Hopefully they would understand that it wasn't disrespectful because it wasn't. He refused everyone.

"Hello, Sister Allen," my pastor greeted me warmly.

Although the *Sister Allen* was more formal than I was used to. Most of my life I had just been *Esther* to him, only earning the church title of *Sister* after I had come back from New York.

"Afternoon, Reverend, Sister Wright," I returned pleasantly.

"Hello, Esther," greeted Sister Wright as the couple mounted the steps to stand on the porch.

With his social status the pastor could come to the front door. He wouldn't know that my employer would have welcomed him here regardless—if he could only welcome somebody.

"We've missed you," said Sister Wright, extending a gloved hand to me.

"It's nice of you to come see me," I said shaking first her hand, and then her husband's.

"We hope we didn't come at a bad time," said Reverend Wright.

"No-sir," I assured him. "Please come in."

I held the front door for them to enter. It was not my house, but for now I lived here. At least until August. I showed them into the living room, where they took seats next to each other on the sofa. Sister Wright made note of the handsome couple over the fireplace, and I explained that they were my employer's parents.

"I think I remember seein' them around town," Sister Wright said.

"They died in 1926," I told her.

"Oh, how sad," she said.

"Yes, it's too bad," agreed her husband. "But he does have a sister, ain't that right?"

"She lives in Cambridge. Can I get you a cool drink?" I asked. "Some lemonade maybe?"

That first lemonade was a very long time ago too, I thought. When my employer laughed easily, and painted his own house. Perhaps I could tempt him with some tonight. Left to his own devices, he might just as well dry up and blow away.

"No, Esther, dear," answered Sister Wright for them both. "We don't want you to go to any trouble."

"It's no trouble," I said.

"Why don't you sit down?" she recommended kindly. "You must be worn out these days. You look very tired. And so thin. Are you eatin' dear?"

More than my employer. But there was something vaguely unsympathetic in Sister Wright's voice. I sat down stiffly in a chair across from the sofa, beginning to feel a little uneasy.

"It's nice of you to come," I said again to put something in the silence. "The quarantine kept most folks away."

"But that's over now, isn't it?" asked Sister Wright.

"Yes, ma'am."

"Then he must have many visitors."

"Yes ma'am."

"And how is the patient?" asked Reverend Wright.

"He's doing well," I lied protectively.

"Oh," replied Sister Wright, "We heard that he's crippled."

I hated the word, and Doctor Mitchell and I never used it.

"He's still very weak," I said. "For now."

"I see," she looked down at her hands and took off her gloves.

They were white gloves with single pearl button closures at the wrists. Sister Wright always made such an elegant presentation, determined as it were to set a standard for the young colored women in McConnell County. Reverenced Wright was very proud of her.

"Makes you wonder what he did to reap such a bitter harvest," Sister Wright said.

There it was. The judgment. She set a standard for that too. No wonder Doctor Mitchell wanted the diagnosis kept secret.

"It was a virus," I said defensively. "A contagious disease. Like a cold."

"That you didn't get-- thank the Lord," said the reverend in a paternal way.

They were, after all, my elders; even if Sister Wright hated admitting it. They were leaders in our community by virtue of position and tradition. Their status was without question, and they had come all this way to see me. I would treat them respectfully.

"But you have taken it upon yourself to take care of him?" asked Sister Wright. "All by yourself?"

It wasn't really a question because she knew the answer.

"Doctor Mitchell comes every day," I said.

"But you're the one who sees after all of… of his needs?" clarified Sister Wright.

"Yes ma'am."

"That must be very hard on you," she said shaking her head slightly.

Her words were sympathetic, but I felt the way I used to whenever I did not reach the right note in choir practice. Her words had sounded sympathetic then too, *poor Esther with a man's voice*, but they had left me yearning for the comfort of Sister Callie's mops and brooms.

"We manage very well," I said.

I can manage this.

She looked at me with eyes rounded by charitable concern.

"Don't you think a nurse would be more proper, Esther?" asked Reverend Wright. "You not trained to be doin' this kind of work. You went to school to teach, ain't that right?"

"Doctor Mitchell trained me," I said looking to him and away from his wife's fretful inspection.

The couple glanced at each other. I wanted them to leave.

"It's very Christian of you to be so compassionate towards him," granted Sister Wright.

"I'm very good at it," I added. "I took care of Mama."

"But that's not the same thing, dear," Sister Wright said. "It's what families do, especially daughters, but…" Her voice trailed off as if she were embarrassed. "But for you to be seein' after a grown man like that," she continued. "Well…"

Reverend Wright cleared his throat.

"To tell the truth, Sister Allen," he now resumed. "This isn't purely a social call."

"No Esther, dear," his wife chimed in. "Your granddaddy came to see your pastor and ask him to come talk to you. Pastor, thought it best for me to come with him, for somethin' like this."

The Bible said if you found your brother in a fault it was your duty to confront him and correct him. Obviously I had fallen short of the glory of God again, but did Grampa really believe that my soul was in trouble?

"About what, Pastor?" I asked looking away from Sister Wright again.

You sent the shepherd for lost sheep. Even the black ones. But when had my grandfather ever needed help to control his family?

"What is the *this* you're speakin' of?" I continued.

"Well about you livin' here... alone," confirmed Reverend Wright.

"I work here," I said flatly.

"Well...it's the kind of work you doin', Esther, dear," Sister Wright said carefully. "We can understand that you feel sorry for him and all, we all do. But it's not...not respectable."

"He's sick," I said. "I'm taking care of him."

"You not a nurse," Reverend Wright repeated the charge that everyone, except Doctor Mitchell, used to put me in my place.

"You're not trained," added his wife.

"I'm very trained," I told them both. "Doctor Mitchell is very good, and I've learned a lot from him." "Sister Allen...Est-Esther, chile. After all you's a young woman," counseled my pastor. "People might get the wrong understandin' 'bout you livin' here all by yourself with a young man." He cleared his throat again, as if the matter were strangling him, the words, knowing themselves to be wrong, not wanting to come out. "You know... bathin' him and everything," he went on. "That's uh-uh real personal. Something a mother or uh–uh wife would do for a man. And if there's no family, then at least somebody who has been trained properly. I must tell you, Deacon Green is very worried about you."

"Everybody is, Esther, dear," interjected Sister Wright. "People want to know why his sister doesn't come to see about him."

That was between them. Nobody else had the right to ask that question.

"Yes," asserted Reverenced Wright more confidently. "That does make more sense. It's the way it should be. I mean, you could be here to help her. But-but the way it is now...well...it just don't look right. It's not the way we do things."

At least in this house, the way we do things will be different.

Had I sounded like that, like a Pharisee preaching the laws of tradition? Grampa was so certain of the world and our places in it. He never imagined that anything could be different.

"It's the way it's always been done," I told the minister and his wife, CoraLee fresh in my mind.

"Sister Allen," the minister began more sternly. "The Scripture says a good name is better than great riches. And a colored woman has to pay special attention to hers. They don't treat our women with respect, you know that. A woman, a colored woman, livin' alone in the house with a white man, by herself, well..." He cleared his throat again, "I don't have to tell you, sister, people will talk. You a single woman... Even- even if he was colored..."

People would talk. Mis' Inez would talk. Perhaps she did already. Connie just never let on. Reverend Wright and Sister Wright were frowning in unison.

"It just doesn't look right," the reverend was saying.

"Reverend Wright," I said evenly. "He's paralyzed. From the waist down. He can't turn over in the bed by himself. I don't think that the church needs to worry about him laying on top of me."

"Esther Fay Allen!" cried Sister Wright, covering her own mouth with her hand as if she herself had said this most obscene thing.

"Sister, now," her husband added hastily. "There's no need for indecent talk."

The indecency was coming from them. In the moment I pictured the pastor on top of his wife. I wondered if theirs had ever been as natural as Danny's and mine had been. What was a preacher's wife like without her hat and gloves? Without her choir robe and the congregation's sanctified respect? Did the preacher call for Jesus when he reached his climax? Or did he say her own, such that it sounded like a royal title? I thought of Connie and Nathaniel making love and making Little Evie and Nate. I thought of the absurdity of thinking that holding a man's penis so that he could pee was somehow as sexual as having his manhood alive and hard and pushing into you deeply.

"No-sir, you're right, Pastor," I said standing up. "We don't have to speak indecently. I know you wouldn't be suggesting that I abandon somebody who needs my help just to get a drink of water, not for the sake of my reputation because people *talk*. That couldn't be what you mean," I continued. "You, being a servant of the Lord and a preacher of the Gospel. Reverend Wright, Sister Wright, I do appreciate this visit, but you can understand, I better go see to him now."

They looked at each other.

"Sister Esther, there's no need to get yo'self upset," Reverend Wright said more soothingly. "As yo' pastor, it is my responsibility to look out for yo' welfare. You's a member of my flock."

"You've got your work, Pastor Wright," I said. "And I've got mine."

Sister Wright stood and her husband did too.

"I hope you know what you're doin'," Sister Wright warned. "Deacon Green is worried enough to send us to see about you. He ought to be. If you want to teach school in this town someday, your name can't have a mark or a question. Folks can have long memories."

"Yes they can," I agreed, remembering the first time I had come into this living room, how he had tried to make me feel welcomed, washing up for me and bringing me lemonade. We didn't have the scent of bergamot in the house anymore. Doctor Mitchell could barely get him to shave at all. In his own kind of wilderness my employer resembled how I pictured John the Baptist, harsh and unkempt, but without hope of a heavenly dove. All he had was me, a ram that had been entangled in the bush. Well at least I was here to wash his broken body as best I could. How dare they accuse me of anything else? I walked towards the front door, forcing the righteous couple to follow me.

"You be careful, Esther," cautioned Reverend Wright, as I held the front door open for them, bidding them—still respectfully—to leave my employer's house. "Sometimes we think we hear the Lord, but it's really our own minds."

Think for yo'self, Baby Sister.

"Or the Adversary," added Sister Wright, passing through the door first.

Or a friend.

I need you, Esther.

Sister Wright was wearing White Shoulders perfume. I missed the scent of bergamot.

"Yes, pastor," I said as they passed. "Thank you."

"We gon' keep prayin' fo' you," Reverend Wright added as he helped his wife into the car.

"Pray for Mr. Payne too," I replied.

When they were gone, I went back to the kitchen and began to make the teacakes for Mandy's children. What about my reputation? Conviction was its own kind of consolation. Besides, as long as I could remember I had kept my good name, and I was a maid anyway. I would wax the kitchen floor. Spencer could help me when he arrived after school.

In time my employer would want to see the boy. When he was stronger, he might be up to helping Spencer with his studies again. He used to enjoy that. We could move everything upstairs; away from the kitchen table where it must have begun, this *attachment* that Doctor Mitchell spoke of, this *something* that kept me in this house, with him, in spite of everything *people* thought I was putting at risk. Things could be—would be—better. The butter and sugar began to cream together smoothly in the bowl. On my way to the refrigerator for eggs, I heard the sound of a crash from upstairs, and I ran after it.

At the bedroom door the first thing I saw was that my employer's bed was empty except for the right leg splint and the footboard. The trapeze bar was still. Rushing around the bed I found my employer in a heap. The bedside table was over-turned as was the Queen Anne chair. The water pitcher and glass were broken and scattered on the floor.

"Mr. Payne!" I cried, dropping down beside him on my knees. "Are you all right?! What happened?! Are you hurt?!"

I reached out to help him.

"Leave me!" he shouted, shoving me away with a force that knocked me over, stunning me for a moment. "I can—I can manage this," he said, vainly trying to pull himself up using the over-turned chair.

I was still while my mind raced on its own. If I had to wrestle against him I would never get him back into his bed. I needed a plan. I got up from the floor, leaving him there, struggling. Quickly I went downstairs to get a broom and dust-pan to clean up the broken glass, giving us both some time. On my way I organized my plan, talking to myself. Why had he tried to get up in the first place? He had the bell to call for me. I kept it within his reach. He refused to use it. Why couldn't he ask for help? It made things so much harder for him, for us. If I failed to anticipate his needs, didn't ask him soon enough, then he would just lay there, hurting, starving, thirsting, or soiling the bed, punishing us both for his pride's sake. Now there was broken glass everywhere. If he were crawling around in it he could cut himself. Spencer would not be here for hours yet. I couldn't leave him on the floor. What if he had broken his leg? He would never walk again and he had to. He had to stop fighting me.

By the time I came back upstairs, my employer had worked himself into a sitting position against the side of the bed, and all the energy had drained from him. His hands were still, his shoulders slumped, and his eyes blank. Most of the bed clothes were in a pile on the floor beside him. Carefully I stepped around him, sweeping up the broken glass as best I could, without saying a word. If he could get up by himself then he must be stronger, so if I gave him a little time to rest, while I cleaned up and straightened the furniture he might be able to help me. I emptied the shards of glass into the bathroom wastebasket. I just had to figure out how he could. I leaned the broom and dust-pan against a far wall. He would simply have to try. Using a towel I mopped up the spilled water. We could use the bed for support. Continuing to work around him I righted the bedside table and the chair, and I returned the linens to the bed. If he could push up using the bed rail, then I might be strong enough to lift him up the rest of the way.

At last I knelt down beside him again.

"Mr. Payne, let me help you," my voice squeezed out passed another enormous ball of sadness and frustration that had swollen up in my throat.

It was time for me to be finished with crying, time for me to be finished with feeling sorry for him and for myself.

"I'm crippled," he said.

There it was again, that terrible word. I never wanted to hear it in this room, in this house, or at all.

"We'll have to work together," I ignored his statement.

Taking his right hand I placed it behind him on the solid wood of the bed frame.

"You feel this?" I asked. "The frame? I want you to push down against the frame and try to lift yourself as I lift you."

"I thought if I could just stand up…" he said letting his hand drop from the rail. "I thought my legs…my legs would work." He shook his head. "All I wanted to do was stand up."

Maybe he was listening to me when I tenaciously talked to him about Sister Kenny's methods of *re-education*, when I said we had to make his legs remember what they were supposed to do.

"Listen to me," I said to him now, grasping his shoulder and forcing him to meet my eyes. "We have to do this together."

His dark brown eyes might as well have been Mama's eyes. They were as lifeless. But he was not going to leave me. Firmly I put his right hand back on the rail and held it there, while I placed his left hand on the rail too.

"You push down and I'll pull up," I told him. "We can do this."

I can manage this.

He couldn't but *we* could.

"It's useless," he said.

"Mr. Payne," I insisted. "We have to get you back in the bed. Are you ready?"

"Leave me," he replied dismally, letting go of the bed rail again. "Leave me alone."

"Stop it!" I said, gripping him by his arms, arms that still seemed to be strong in spite of his self-imposed famine. "You have to help me, do you hear me? You have to help me. I can't lift you by myself. You have to help me."

I returned his hands to the bed rail and held them there.

"On the count of three," I instructed. "You will push down and raise yourself while I lift you."

I straddled him and squatted down, readying myself.

"I'm crippled," he said again.

"No!" I rejoined. "You're just weak that's all. You're getting stronger."

"I can't walk."

I locked my arms around him. His clothes were damp with perspiration or maybe from the spilled water. We were close enough that I felt his breath on my face. He had lost so much weight that his own face was almost gaunt. The black stubble on his cheeks was stark against the ashen gray of his complexion.

"Well right now you don't have to," I said. "Your arms are good enough."

"It's useless."

"Concentrate," I ordered. "You have to help me. I can't do this by myself. We have to work together."

I never forgot every single time he had come close to me, only now it could not possibly matter. Not in that way. My breasts touched him now and I felt the warmth of his body in my arms, as I searched his face for any remnant of the man I had known before. Any trace of the man who had sat at his kitchen table, discussing politics, and law, and social sciences and history with his maid. The man who would have missed me when I was gone. Where was he now? Was he really lost to us? To me? I had promised not to leave him. But we were apart anyway. As close as we were in this moment, we were both alone. A wall of his own construction separated us. A wall he had built when all he had ever talked about was a world without walls. "You have to help me," I repeated, desperation rising in my voice. "I can't do this by myself. Oh, Taylor, please try." I needed him back, the man who had taken a gift to Baby Nate and defended an abused wife. "Please. Please try."

Our eyes held fast. The muscles in his arms hardened as he established a stronger grip on the rail of the bed. I closed my embrace more securely around him. "Now," I said with growing confidence. "On the count of three. One...Two...Three." As he came off the floor I felt first the fullness of his weight and then the release as he landed on the side of the bed. Producing one more burst of effort I pushed him to a more secure position on the mattress, collapsing for an instant on top of him. In that instant with our hearts beating against each other, our eyes met again, but I sprang up swiftly and righted him fully on the bed.

"Are you hurt?" I asked again, catching my breath.

He did not respond and anxiously I examined his legs, then his arms and hands. Satisfied that he was fine, only then could I be upset. I sat down on the edge of the bed.

"Promise me you'll never try that again unless I'm with you," I said, clasping my shaking hands together in my lap as I stared at the floor, collecting myself.

Still he said nothing.

"Promise me!" I insisted, turning to face him.

Resting against his pillows again, he was also catching his breath.

"I want you to swear it!" I said in a trembling voice. "Right now. Say that you will never try that again. Not without me."

"You're not my nurse," he at last replied.

"And for God's sake stop saying that to me!" I snapped hotly. "I'm sick to death of hearing it. From you, and from everybody. What difference does it make? I'm here. And I'm taking care of you. Just promise me that you'll never try to do that again. Not without me. I've got to have some peace of mind in this house, Taylor Andrew Payne, and you're goin' to give it to me. I won't live on pins and needles worried to death that you might fall and break your neck. I just won't do it, do you hear me?"

"Nobody's asking you to," he said. "I didn't hire you to nurse me."

"Well we're doing things *differently*, aren't we?"

"I can manage this," he said yet again.

I closed my eyes and sighed.

"And stop saying that too," I said sharply when I looked at him again. "It's nonsense. You cannot *manage* it. You need help. And I'm tryin' to help you."

"That's exceptionally noble of you," he replied coldly.

"Why are you so hateful?" I asked. "What's wrong with you?"

"I think that's obvious. Perhaps you should use some of that saintly compassion of yours to forgive my disposition."

It was the first time in weeks that he had said more than two consecutive sentences to me. As sarcastic as they were I wanted them. I hungered to hear his voice.

"I know this is hard, Mr. Payne, but--"

"I said forgiveness," he cut me off. "Not sympathy. You know nothing about this."

"You think *I* don't know what it feels like to be afraid?" I angrily demanded. "Weren't you listening to me all this time? Didn't you hear what I had to say? All that talk, about *vantage points* and *perspectives*? What was all that for? Did you learn anything? Or was it all just for show, Mr. Payne? Was I just puttin' on some kind of minstrel show to amuse you as you ate your peas and carrots and drank your fancy wine?"

"That has nothing to do with it," he replied. "This is different."

"There you go again with that word," I charged. "I'm startin' to think it's just for your convenience. When you want things to go your way. You think all you gotta say is that it's going to be different and everybody's just suppose to go along with it. Well I'm the one sayin' it now. It *is* going to be *different* around here. If you want to call it sympathy, then fine, call it that. If you want to think I'm noble, then all right I'm noble. But any way you look at it, you get this one thing straight, I'm taking care of you, and you're going to treat me better than this. It's not my fault what's happened to you. You can't blame me for it, so you've got no right to punish me for it."

I hadn't volunteered for the army or bought the war bonds either, and yet I had had to make up for it. And still Mama had died. At least if I was going to do the *making-up* for things this time, I wanted the record to be straight.

"Is that what you think?" my employer asked. "That I'm punishing you?"

"It's what I know," I said. "Maybe you can't help it. You have to be mad at somebody, and you won't let your sister come."

"I told you before," he replied. "I can't ask you--"

"Yes you can," I said, now cutting him off. "You did. And what did I say? Can you remember that?"

"You're leaving in August," he answered.

That was what he remembered?

"I won't leave you, Mr. Payne," I told him. "Not like this."

The revelation surprised him far more than it did me, since I had felt it coming for so long that I was used to the idea of it.

"Because you're such a Good Samaritan," he mocked. "And I'm some wretch you've found along the road?"

Well-well, he must have read the Bible at least once, although he did not have the right story. I was his Ananias and the road was to Damascus. I almost smiled, but I was too irritated by his foolishness, and I didn't have my promise from him yet.

"You might want to think twice about it, Esther," he continued. "As it could cost you more than a night's lodging, and I might have very well gotten what I deserve."

"You don't believe that," I said.

Somebody might think so, I thought, but he'd never make me believe it either.

For what seemed like a long time the room was quiet. He reached up and caught the trapeze bar to pull himself up into a sitting position. I moved to help him.

"No," he said declining my aid. "I think I can at least *manage* to sit up on my own."

He may be making fun of me, but that was all right. It was what he did, or what he used to do, when he would talk to me.

"So tell me," he queried. "What else don't I believe?"

"Anything you can't understand with your head," I said immediately.

"Damn the intellectuals, I suppose?"

"Well you know how *you people* are," I said as I put his right leg back in its splint.

I could feel his eyes on me while I rolled up the towels again and carefully rested his ankles on them.

"I do have a heart, Esther," he said as I repositioned the footboard against his feet.

I knew that. It was wounded too. No doubt more times than he wanted to recognize.

"We're counting on that, Mr. Payne," I assured him as I straightened the bedding. "Me and Doctor Mitchell. It's how you're going to get better. It's part of the *package* as you might say."

He smiled crookedly.

"I guess I've been a jerk," he finally admitted.

"Worse," I said, meeting his eyes. "But it's understandable. Doctor Mitchell says you have every right to be."

"But not to you."

"That's right."

"Yet you're still here."

With my whole family and my church in an uproar about it. Maybe the Lord would come to Grampa in a dream, as he had done with *Joseph*, and straighten everything out. Poor *Mary*. It would have been so much easier if the Lord had simply declared his intentions broadly.

"Afraid so," I replied more coolly than I actually felt. "Unless you fire me of course. It is your call. But if you do, for the sake of the next one to come, and somebody does have to come, please know this one thing: at some point in this life we all need a little charity, a little kindness. Even educated white men who believe they rule the world."

The crooked smile appeared again.

"Is that what you think of me?" he asked.

Is that the kind of man you think I am, Esther?

"It is who you are," I replied. "You're not used to being down on your luck, and I hope you never are again, but right now that's the way it is. The sooner you come to terms with that the better. You'll get well. But it won't be easy. So in the meantime, you just have to learn a little humility like all the rest of us. And learn how to accept a little help. Now you won't find that in your law books probably," I went on, standing at the foot of his bed. "And I'm pretty sure it's not in the Constitution. But, Mr. Payne, even the Lord Jesus Christ had to humble Himself. And I don't care what you say about His resurrection date, the important thing is that He rose again. You will too."

"I don't believe in miracles, Esther," my employer said.

Of course not. He couldn't. It would mean recognizing mysterious powers that he could neither define nor control, powers not subject to human statutes, no matter how enlightened.

"I don't care if you don't," I replied easily. "I do. And if you just believe in yourself, the rest will come."

"Maybe you're the one who's just a little too sure of herself," he said.

"I don't think so, Mr. Payne. I might not have a college degree, but I do have credentials. And by the way, Sister Kenny didn't go to nursing school either."

The smile came back, but this time it was real and it reminded me of better times.

"You do argue a good case, Miss Allen."

"For a maid you mean?"

"For a teacher."

"Well that's good to know. Maybe all that dinnertime conversation was worth something after all," I finally smiled too. "I guess I might have had a decent tutor."

He almost smiled again and his face was softer.

"The defense rests," he said.

"You're a prosecutor," I reminded him.

"Then I withdraw the charge."

"It's about time," I said in a voice that quivered slightly.

"I feel the need to make restitution," he added after a moment. "Is there something I can do to make it up to you? For being such a son-of-a-bitch?"

"Don't talk bad about your mother," I chided him.

"All right then. What would you call me?"

"I plead the fifth amendment."

He actually laughed.

"You are a good student," he declared.

"Teacher beware," I said mildly triumphant.

"That can work both ways, you know."

"Then you had better make your peace with me."

"As I recall, that was my original intent," he replied.

"Not really," I countered.

"I'm not talking about just now."

"Well in any case, I hope we're on one accord."

"I suppose that remains to be seen."

And I would show him.

"As you are not a man of faith, right?" I asked, collecting the broom and dust-pan.

"It is a bit suspect if you ask me," he answered. "But now," he continued, "Back to the issue of restitution. Is that all you want, peace?"

Don't you think it's about time somebody took care of him?

"No," I said. "Promise me you won't try anything foolish anymore. Not without me."

"It couldn't be foolish with you, now could it?" he replied. "You wouldn't lead me astray."

"I don't imagine that I could lead you at all."

"Then perhaps you're the one who's foolish."

I smiled a little.

"So do I have your word?" I asked.

"Yes," he said.

"And one more thing."

"All right."

"I take care of you, you take care of me, and everything else we let take care of itself."

I set the broom and dust-pan down again and returned to the side of the bed, extending my right hand to him.

"Agreed?" I asked.

He studied my hand for a moment. Chipped nails, chapped skin, it was a working woman's hand, more like Nathaniel's than it was like Laura Spalding's. Someday it might be finer, softer, prettier, wearing gloves like Sister Wright, but today all it needed to be was willing, and I refused to wear gloves when I touched him.

"Is that really fair?" my employer asked.

"Yes," I said. "I think so. You don't?"

"I was thinking that perhaps you're entitled to a good deal more."

Than my now forty dollars a week, I wondered. He needn't concern himself. The rest was between me and the Lord.

"It'll do for now," I replied. "So what do you say? Do you agree?"

"Almost," he replied, taking my hand into his. "Although the defendant usually doesn't have much of a say in the settlement, I would like one concession."

"This is not a court of law, Mr. Payne."

"No," he said holding my hand. "It isn't, is it?"

Warmth from his hand coursed up my arm, reaching all the way into some place deep inside of me.

"What do you want?" I asked.

"If you are so determined to perform your Christian charity in this house, then you must at least call me by my Christian name."

Say my name.

"I will," I consented with my hand still in his. "In this house," I qualified.

He smiled, and this time it was the best one, the one that reached out from the lines around his eyes to fill his face.

"I suppose that's enough for now," he said. "As you say, the rest will come."

He was dear to me, and I was a daughter of the Hebrews, discovering herself to be content in the land of the Pharaohs.

"Case closed," I said.

Then this prince of Egypt raised my dark brown hand to his lips and kissed it softly. Someone among the Jews must have chosen to remain behind. If only for a little while. Until August.

"Perhaps we've just opened it," he said, lowering my hand from his lips although keeping it in his.

My face was warm in a blush. Surely the roses had returned.

"Well...I-I don't think it would do for us to agree on too much," I whispered timorously. "You do like a good fight."

"When the prize is worthy," he said.

PART FOUR

The *prize* was recovery, and restoration, and the return to his former self and his real life. It wasn't a great and grand good we were working for. It wasn't to change the whole wide world. It was just to overcome the crisis that had befallen his. We would get his world back, and then, if he still wanted to take on everything—everyone—else then he could, and *on his own terms* again.

The change in Taylor, and in me, was immediate, as if we had raised a window shade or switched on a light, or perhaps rolled away a stone. All the tasks were the same but the tension was gone. I still pushed him just as hard, all the more determined to have the miracle, but now he strove to meet me. We were equally yoked. Lazarus had come forth.

The very next morning when Doctor Mitchell returned, the mood in the house was different because my employer was. A few days later when my employer asked for the wheelchair, Doctor Mitchell was speechless.

"They say you have to crawl before you walk," explained Taylor. "But maybe I can start with the chair."

I was rolling up the wool strips and placing them back in the pan to wait for the next session. Taylor and I smiled at each other. Perplexed, Doctor Mitchell looked first at him and then at me. Then a smile broke on his face too.

"Sure, son," he said. "Esther, bring us the chair."

"Yes, doctor," I replied.

At the end of his visit, as Doctor Mitchell was preparing to leave, we stood at the foot of the stairs.

"He certainly seems to be doing much better," he observed.

"Yes-sir," I agreed.

"What happened?"

Many things, I thought. The right things. But private things too, and it was not my place to explain.

"He's feeling better, I guess," I offered.

"Well whatever you did seems to have worked."

I was quiet.

"As I knew it would," Doctor Mitchell added.

"What would?" I asked wanting to know what he was thinking.

The old man nodded his head thoughtfully and headed towards the door.

"I'll stop by later to help you get him back into bed," he said. "We don't want him to get tired."

It was almost June. Soon it would be August. If I didn't go back to New York, Grampa would never forgive me.

"You know how he is," said Nathaniel one evening days later as we sat together on Taylor's back porch.

"It wouldn't hurt him to come with you sometime," I complained. "He knows I can't leave here, Nathaniel. Who would look after Tay—Mr. Payne?"

"So you callin' him by his first name now?" asked Nathaniel.

"We're friends, Nathaniel," I replied. "If we were in New York I'd call him by his first name."

"But you not in New York," my cousin reminded me.

"Things can change. Even in McConnell County."

"Maybe. I sho' hope so. But don't fool yo'self, Esther. They ain't changed yet. And some folks gon' put up a hard fight to keep things the way they always was."

"I know he can be stubborn, but I never thought that Grampa could hate someone," I said sadly.

"Maybe hate's not what it is, Esther," countered Nathaniel. "Maybe the Lord don't require us to forgive everything. 'Specially that what ain't been repented for."

"I'm livin' in the present, Nathaniel," I defiantly claimed.

"We all is," said Nathaniel. "But it ain't like we don't have fresh memories."

Mine were just different now. Lemonade and birthdays remembered. A kiss's caress on the brown skin of my hand. These too were *fresh memories*, and more compelling than the segregationist signs that deferred *our* dreams, even if the signs weren't memories at all but features of now. Except in this house. Where we kept trying to do things *differently*.

Taylor and I worked together, and Doctor Mitchell, with rejuvenated optimism, coached and applauded us both. Taylor submitted to the crusade patiently, keeping the faith as it were. As we pressed against the wall of paralysis it began to give way. His left leg grew stronger. Encouraged we increased the frequency of the hot-packs and arduous rounds of therapy. I called my employer's muscles by their proper names, *quadriceps, tibialis anterior, gastrocnemius, soleus,* the new words rolling off my tongue, easier than his Christian name. Sister Kenny would have been proud. Sister Callie too. And as for Taylor, he seemed to value me, obediently following my instructions to the best of his abilities.

"That was perfect, Esther," Doctor Mitchell observed one typical morning, as I finished carrying Taylor's legs through the range of motion exercises. "How do you feel, Taylor? Up to pushing the right leg a bit more?"

Taylor, his forehead damp with perspiration, was catching his breath.

"Come on, Mr. Payne" I urged. "You can do it."

He looked at me, a wry grin filling his face. I never called him by his first name in front of others, not in front of Doctor Mitchell or even Spencer.

"What's in it for me?" he joked.

"Breakfast," I smiled back.

"Waffles?" he asked.

I nodded.

"Waffles," I agreed.

"Shall we give it a go?" asked Doctor Mitchell.

We.

But it was Taylor who prepared himself, the smile vanishing, his hands becoming fists. Then at last we saw him draw his right knee upwards without our hands to help.

"Look at that!" Doctor Mitchell exclaimed under his breath.

"Come on leg, move," said Taylor, straining to raise the right knee higher. "I hate oatmeal."

I smiled at him, as he pulled the heel of his right foot a few more victorious inches, until he nearly flattened his right sole against the white bed sheet.

"Ha!" Doctor Mitchell cheered out loud. "I told you we could do it!"

We.

Taylor held the knee in the bent position briefly before the leg collapsed, quivering. The effort had exhausted him, but his dark eyes were bright and he looked pleased with himself.

"Lots of butter and syrup," he said, breathing deeply.

"Whatever you want," I beamed.

"I'm going to hold you to that," he grinned.

"I hope so," I replied.

"Taylor," interjected Doctor Mitchell. "That was fantastic! You'll be back on your feet in no time!"

Doctor Mitchell must measure time like the Lord, I thought, mysteriously. Still my employer was stronger, better somehow for his fall. He accepted my hands, my back, my will, maybe even my faith, as his own resources. He had even relented to ringing the bell to call me when he needed me. He was able to tolerate the wheelchair for longer stretches of time during the day and this did increase his independence. His vitality returned. The bedpan was put away for good, and he took care of his own urine bottle. I gave him his baths and helped him to dress, but indeed he was learning how to *manage*. Doctor Mitchell even arranged for a barber to come to the house to cut his hair, but then again Doctor Mitchell had always *arranged* for everything. After all I was here too.

I tried not to think about August and did not dwell on what I had promised him about staying. The Lord would have to work it all out. What was supposed to be would be. Nobody could block it. I wrote to Danny and to Aunt Grace and Uncle Eddie, sending my letters to the post office by Spencer. My employer would not always require my hands. One day he was going to return to his life as it had been. To his office and to his work. To his country club dances and dinner parties. I wanted this for him, prayed for it in fact, and constantly, convinced that God would grant it. And when He did I would have to have somewhere, someone, to go back to too.

With his continued progress, it seemed to me that my Taylor should stop wearing the clothes of an invalid. His pajamas and robes, as nice as they were, said that he was still sick, and he wasn't. He was recovering. And Roosevelt had worn suits and ties, and become our president. I broached the subject that he should dress one afternoon while I was in his room putting away his laundry.

"You're not ill anymore," I reasoned. "You ought to dress to meet the public."

He was sitting by the window reading the *New York Times*. It might have been before April except that his chair had wheels. He did have a *public* in a way, made up of all of us, me too. We were a constellation of the concerned, the compassionate, and yes maybe the curious; all of whom Taylor kept at various distances, physically and emotionally.

"This chair doesn't work so well on a staircase," he said as read his paper. "And I won't be carried."

"And if your public wants to come to you?" I pushed.

Although Doctor Mitchell was still telling me to say that my employer was not yet strong enough for social calls, a few visitors were permitted, Mr. Walton, Mrs. Mitchell, Reverend Scott, the Presbyterian minister.

"What are you getting at, Esther?" asked Taylor lowering the newspaper.

"Nothing," I replied, needlessly rearranging the clothes in the bureau drawer. "I was just thinking that maybe you might be missing your friends. Wouldn't you like to see them sometimes?"

Was I actually advocating for the likes of a Laura Spalding? Did I really want her here? If it helped him to recover, then my guess was that the answer had to be yes. It didn't matter what she thought about me or how I felt about her. "People call," I continued. "Send messages, flowers. You should reply. People would like to see you, Taylor. They would understand."

"What?" he asked, removing his reading glasses now. "What would they understand, Esther? That I'm crippled?"

I could never accept that word for him, and I fidgeted with the buttons on a shirt in the drawer rather than look at him.

"You want them to come and pay their respects, is that it?" he continued. "I'm afraid this chair isn't much of a throne either. Perhaps you think I should be more open to their sympathies, their condolences as it were, regarding my misfortune."

I sighed and regretted bringing the dark cloud that blocked an otherwise brighter day.

"It won't be like that, Taylor," I said and closed the bureau drawer softly. "People just want to wish you well."

"I am well, as you say."

But he was weary too sometimes, and frustrated, perhaps even still frightened. I had to be patient, I reminded myself. We hadn't reached the *happy ending* yet. He was ashamed of his body, of his long legs that had become too thin and too still. He was embarrassed by the wheelchair and bothered by the bell. Sometimes it was as if he did blame himself. As if Reverend and Sister Wright could be right, that he had brought this upon himself. But it was a germ. It could happen to anybody. It did happen to anybody. It was not his fault. I finally faced him.

"They are your friends," I said.

"Friendship is a complex concept with many meanings," he replied rather casually. "In large part having more to do with diversion."

Friendship was a broad concept, but he seemed to speak unfairly about his friends, I thought, when he was helping to make them that way himself. Everybody wasn't like Sylvia or the friend who had married her while he fought a war in the Philippines. Some of them—of us—were loyal. I didn't like having to turn people away from the house.

He wanted to keep people at a distance; and now when he was in trouble all he had was his maid. His hireling. It was not right that he should be so dependent upon me. It was not right that he should make himself so alone. He couldn't even reach out to his own sister. If he kept his friends–and family—away until he was healed, and he didn't heal, then what would become of him? How could I be all that he had when he could not have me?

A breeze carried Spencer's laughter upwards and through the open window. I walked over and looked down to see him playing with Herman on the front lawn. He would soon be covered in dirt and grass stains, which meant more work for Mandy, but he and the dog were having a good time. What was my employer going to do when August came? There had to be others. I couldn't stay here forever. I had made other promises too.

"But some of it must also have to do with devotion," I responded to his strange comment about friendship, as I watched the boy and the dog playing.

"He's good with Herman, isn't he?" Taylor observed looking out the window too.

"Yes," I agreed.

"A boy and his dog."

"A boy and *your* dog. Spencer can't take your place with Herman, Taylor. No one can take your place."

"What is my place, Esther?"

I looked at him. Perhaps he really didn't know anymore.

"Nothing's changed, Taylor," I said earnestly.

"I think this maybe another one of those point-of-view conflicts we always seem to have," he replied.

He was right of course; and all I wanted to do was make it like it was. I couldn't bring Jimmy back. I couldn't even bring him home, but maybe I could return Taylor Payne to his former self.

"How did he do this last term?" Taylor asked mercifully changing the subject as he looked out the window again.

"Very well," I replied, glad to hear him ask about Spencer. "He was head of his class again," I went on. "But if things come too easy for him, he might get lazy, you know, rest on his laurels. He can't afford to do that."

"You're continuing to tutor him, aren't you?"

"No, I'm not."

"Because you have your hands full with me I suppose."

I looked at him again.

"No. That's not why," I said, and mostly it was the truth.

My hands were full, but they were willing.

"The best part of it for Spencer," I explained. "Was studying with you. You're kind of his hero. It hurts his feeling that you won't let him come see you. He misses you."

Doctor Mitchell and I had brought up a small table under which Taylor could fit his wheelchair. He had his meals at the table, and it served as a desk too. He had finally written a letter to his sister. Only one letter, in all this time, and after all that had happened, but at least he had written. I wondered what he had told her—if he had told her. Maybe she was making plans to come to him right now. And I liked the buttercup room. He could work with Spencer at the little table. It would be good for them both.

"Maybe that's how it is for others too," I ventured. "They miss you."

I will miss you too.

Felicia should come. He should have his family with him, but I had given up asking about it.

"Are you about to tell me what kind of jerk I am again?" asked Taylor.

"I never said that," I replied defensively. "But-but maybe you are being a little hard on people."

"Why? Because I don't feel like being the life of the party?" he asked sharply. "I'm not like you, Esther. I'm not so concerned with polite society. I don't have to be. As an educated white man, I rule the world, remember?"

"You've been through a lot," I said, embarrassed by the return of my own words. "No one could blame you for--"

"For what?" he asked. "What don't you blame me for?"

"For-for not wanting to see people right away," I faltered.

"But you do blame me for it," he said. "You think I'm a coward, don't you?"

Having lost control of the conversation, I was floundering.

"No," I denied quickly. "No, of course not."

He was entitled to his seclusion. Doctor Mitchell said that he needed time to get used to what had happened. Everybody needed a mourning period. We all hid ourselves sometimes. I hadn't gone back to New York after Mama died. Rushing right back into life after death, whether it was the death of a brother, a mother, or a self-image, wasn't easy and not even always wise, even if people were always telling you to just get on with it. Everyone was impatient with everyone else. Yet there was a time, a season for everything, a time to weep and to mourn, and to refrain from embracing.

"I'm sorry," I said. "I didn't mean it to sound like--"

"Like what?" Taylor asked.

"Like I was criticizing you."

He seemed amused for a moment, and putting on his glasses again he returned his attention to the newspaper.

"I'll dress, Esther," he said, as if this finished the matter. "With your help of course."

"Taylor," I started. "You know that I don't think--"

"You win, Esther," he interrupted me. "I do need to get on with it. You didn't sign on forever. I realize that. But perhaps we can dispense with the ties, what do you think?"

Let's not rush the goodbyes.

It didn't feel like a win. But maybe it was. For us both. He was right I didn't *sign on forever*. City College was waiting. Aunt Grace and Uncle Eddie too. They wanted to repaint my room. I couldn't stay here. No matter how accustomed I was becoming to this house on Webster Road and yes, *attached* to the man who lived in it. This was not *my* place. The center of the Green family universe was the house on Spring Street, where the front-yard was without grass, and I had to heat water on top of the stove.

"You can tell Spencer to come see me," Taylor said. "After all, no one gets to rest on his laurels in this house."

The third weekend in June of 1951 promised to be two days of celebration for colored McConnell County, Sweet Water Baptist Church, and the Green family. Colored McConnell County would be celebrating *Juneteenth*, Sweet Water would be having its *Pastor Appreciation Day*, and the Green family would be honoring *Fathers Day*. On such a weekend there would be something happy for everyone—every *colored* one. With Taylor doing so well, I wanted to have my part in the festivities too. I didn't mind giving up the Saturday speeches, the barbeque and the peach ice-cream. I could miss seeing Nathaniel risk life and limb to steal third base, and it was all right to forfeit the Blues guitars, but I wanted to be with my family on *Father's Day*. I wanted to be with Grampa. In spite of everything I had shopped for Grampa, Uncle Perry, and Nathaniel using the Sears Roebuck Catalog. Connie was keeping their presents for me, and I wanted to be there to give them to them, after the big Sunday dinner that we always had at Grampa's house. The Greens were patriarchal. We were a *king's* dynasty. Some day it would be at Uncle Perry's table, then Nathaniel's, and so on, one proud generation after another.

So much celebrating and commemorating made it seem like having a *Fourth of July-Christmas* all in the middle of June. *They* could only watch from a drive-by distance and ponder how we could make so merry about the Lord, Negro fathers, and some bit of delayed news about freedom. It was *our* secret. We didn't have to tell anyone. After all Negroes were a *happy people*, singing and dancing all the time anyway, without a care in the world. Or so *they* believed.

I had decided to ask Doctor Mitchell's permission to take the Sunday off, because for me to do so meant that he would have to spend the day with Taylor. I believed it would be all right because the Mitchells were childless, and Doctor Mitchell treated Taylor like a son. Spencer had eagerly volunteered for the assignment, now that he could worship his hero again in person, but I was too anxious to entrust the man to the boy's care. Having thus far kept Taylor out of the McConnell County Hospital, I was unwilling to take that kind of chance now. We took care of him at home.

I waited until I was seeing Doctor Mitchell to the door after one of his visits to make my request, explaining that I wanted to go to church with my grandfather.

"But I can't leave Mr. Payne by himself," I said.

"Well of course, Esther," Doctor Mitchell immediately agreed. "I think that's a fine idea. You're due a day off. You've certainly earned it."

"It's Father's Day and Pastor Appreciation Day," I further explained. "We'll be in service all day."

"All day!" exclaimed Doctor Mitchell. "You people certainly take your worshipping seriously."

We people knew where our help came from, but I supposed Doctor Mitchell was another one of those educated men too smart for faith in the Lord. No matter. Just as long as I got my day with Grampa and my family.

The special Sunday came. Nathaniel was coming to get me in time for the eleven o'clock service at Sweet Water. In the buttercup room I examined myself one final time in front of the dresser mirror. I was wearing a pink cotton dress with a white eyelet collar and capped sleeves. I had on a little white hat too, and I was wearing my hair down again having curled it so that it framed my face. I had put on the faintest hint of lipstick, and I smiled now, thinking of my aunts. Hopefully Grampa wouldn't notice it, and in any case it would be faded by the time church was over. I pulled on my white gloves. I looked like it was *Easter* and I felt like it was. Perhaps it didn't really matter what the date was. Resurrection could come any time. For the lord of the manor too. Nathaniel would be on time, so quickly I went to check on Taylor and Doctor Mitchell.

"I'm leaving now," I said brightly when I came into the room. "Do you need anything before I go?" The two men were playing chess at the small table. Taylor was teaching Spencer how to play chess, and it was something they could still do together. But why must we always study war? Even the Bible must be a *sword*, promising us *wars and rumors of wars*. Men must need battles. They must need to act upon the world. Maybe that was all right. Jackie Robinson was a decorated veteran, after all, and he had made the cover of *Life Magazine*.

"We're fine," said Doctor Mitchell replying to my interruption. "Have a nice time. Well-well," he boasted to Taylor, who had pushed back from the table. "I've got your queen, my boy. Call me MacArthur himself."

Truman had fired MacArthur. "The cause of world peace is more important than any individual," he had said on the radio, giving me one more reason to like the bespectacled little man from Missouri. I would have voted for him too if I had not been back in McConnell County by the fall of '48. Both Danny and Nathaniel admired MacArthur. Taylor, however, had been noncommittal. "Truman out ranks him," was all he had said. And still the war went on. Men were killing each other for inches of ground that couldn't possibly matter.

Elatedly Doctor Mitchell claimed one of the black chess pieces, but Taylor crossed the room to where I stood.

"I left a casserole in the refrigerator for-for your lunch," I reminded them both, but primarily Doctor Mitchell. "All-all you have to do is put it in the oven...for about forty-five--"

With Taylor's eyes fixed on me I was suddenly very self-conscious.

"Mr. Payne?" I ventured hesitantly. "Is-is something the matter?"

The white shirt opened at the collar flattered him the way it had on the first day we had met. Doctor Mitchell had brought him a set of dumbbells so that he could train for the crutches he would surely soon graduate to. With us on either side of him for support, he could stand for a few minutes at a time. His trousers with my perfectly ironed creases and his shoes with my perfectly applied polish almost concealed the paralysis, except that his right leg leaned against the side of the chair and did not move.

"Forgive me, Esther," he replied surveying me. "It's just that I don't think I've ever seen you in anything other than black. You look rather wonderful."

"Mr. Payne," I blushed.

"You do," he said. "Very nice."

Very nice.

I remembered his hands around my waist again and I cast a discomfited glance towards Doctor Mitchell, who fortunately remained too involved in the game to notice.

"Thank you, Mr. Payne," I said dropping my head.

"Head up, Esther," he directed me. "So that we can see your face. The roses too."

When I raised my eyes again I met his smile. It was my favorite one. Did he really remember that morning in foyer?

Herman got to his feet, and a moment later we all heard Nathaniel's car as it went around to the back of the house.

"Nathaniel's here, I believe," announced Doctor Mitchell from somewhere outside of us.

"I better go," I said hastily.

"I'll wait up for you," said my employer as I was leaving the room.

Looking back at him, I smiled happily.

"I'll bring you back some pie," I promised.

Nathaniel was driving his car instead of the pick-up truck, and when I came out of the back door, Connie was getting out of the front seat carrying Nate on her hip. I rushed down the porch steps, ecstatic to see her, and we managed to somehow embrace without crushing the baby.

"Girl!" Connie exclaimed. "I done almost forgot what you look like!"

"Well you're still your gorgeous self!" I said joyfully. "And look at Nate! He's 'bout big enough to carry you," I declared.

"He gon' be a big man just like his daddy," Connie proudly agreed with my appraisal.

Looking into the car, I saw Little Evie peering at me from the backseat. Throwing open the rear door, I scooped her up into my arms. Her initial hesitation melted into jubilant giggles as I hugged her and covered her faces with kisses.

"Y'all better come on," fussed Nathaniel. "We gon' be late. Get in the car."

Connie rolled her eyes playfully.

"Just like a man," she told me. "He know good and well Sweet Water ain't never started nothin' on time. How we gon' be late?"

"He just wants to lead the Devotion," I said as we climbed into the car. "And if he don't get there in time and Mr. Eddie starts out--"

"We'll be 'til twelve o'clock before the choir march in," finished Connie.

The two of us were laughing.

"And four o'clock before we get to dinner," I said.

"Now that's what really got 'im so worried!" laughed Connie.

"I thought today was Father's Day," Nathaniel complained, as we were pulling out onto Webster Road. "Can't a colored man get no respect even from his own women?"

"Little Evie," Connie turned and looked back at their daughter, who was sitting in my lap. "You respect yo' daddy, don't you, baby?"

"Say yes, sweetie," I told her.

"Yeah," she said innocently.

"Well now, Happy Father's Day to you!" proclaimed Connie.

"I'll say," grumbled her husband.

As we drove across town, Connie fretted that Little Evie sitting in my lap was wrinkling my dress, but I would not let her go and she did not want to get down and sit on the seat. Nathaniel said that Ben Thompson was going to be ordained as a deacon in July. I talked about how much he would be missed down at Ray's, because he would certainly have to give up the Blues and play his guitar for the Lord. Connie said that maybe Sister Wright would let Ben play his guitar with the choir, which made us all laugh again because of course that was absolutely impossible. Sinners and saints were supposed to live in separate worlds, and according to Sister Wright's music training harps, not guitars, were the stringed instruments of heaven.

Sweet Water sat in the center of a grassy place with trees to shade it, so that Sunday summer afternoons were bearable as long as we had our hand-held, mortuary fans, with their bright pictures of happy, Christian, colored families, all dressed immaculately. Just below the pictures were the addresses and telephone number of the funeral homes that had paid for their printing. Everyone died. The sinners and the saints and competition could be fierce among the morticians.

Sweet Water's parking lot was unpaved so there was only the gravel, which did more to wear out the heels of the ladies' shoes than it did to protect us from the mud on rainy days. The brethren had mowed the grass and touched up the building with fresh paint. The church sparkled. I helped little Evie out of the car and paused to smooth the front of my dress.

"See," said Connie with a frown, "I tried to tell you about holdin' that child in yo' lap."

"Like the Lord cares about a few wrinkles," I waved away her admonishment.

Nathaniel was crossing the lot ahead of us, but he turned to look back.

"Come on now," he said. "We late."

"Go on, honey," replied Connie. "We comin'."

"I hope it wasn't too much trouble to come for me," I said apologetically as we took our time, as Nathaniel hurried through the double doors.

"Girl, hush," Connie assured me. "It wasn't nothin'. I'm just glad you could get out of that house for while and be with us. Grampa Isaac gon' be so surprised. We didn't tell 'im a thing."

"Why?" I asked surprised by the revelation.

"Mainly 'cause we wanted to surprise 'im," she replied as she pulled open one of the big church doors. "And if something happened, you know, so that you couldn't get away, then we didn't want 'im to be disappointed neither."

"It still bothers him that much that I'm workin' there?"

"Yeah," she whispered now that we were standing inside the church vestibule. "But you doin' what's right, so I wouldn't worry about it."

"You do understand then?" I asked, encouraged.

Connie smiled.

"Don't have to," she said. "I know you, Esther."

Little Evie's hand was in mine. To our left was the choir room. The door to the small room was open, and I could see the choir robes of gold and white hanging neatly on the rack. Would Sister Wright accept me back in the choir now that I had willingly looked upon a white man's nakedness?

"And don't worry 'bout that either," said Connie knowingly with another reassuring smile. "Yours is still there waitin' on you."

"Sister Wright would probably dispute that," I sighed.

"This yo' church home, Esther. And home is where you always welcomed."

Connie opened the door into the sanctuary. The congregation was in the middle of singing *Search Me Lord* accompanied by Sister Wright on the piano. Sister Maxine Bailey was ushering at the door. She nodded her head in time with the music and beamed at us warmly as she and handed us fans. Nathaniel, Connie, Little Evie, and Nate could have been pictured on the fans. They were perfect. I was thankful again that Nathaniel had brought Connie into our *us*.

♪*I wanna be right. I wanna be saved. Lord, I wanna be whole.*

Nathaniel was already at the front of the church singing, seated at what was now the Devotion table, the same table would later become the Offering table. Today's offering would be especially fruitful. We raised money all year long for *Pastor*

Appreciation Day, through sacrifice, bake sales, and handmade crafts. The church sisters always raised the most money.

Three church members, in good standing, always led the Devotion. Today Nathaniel was leading it, along with Sonny Lewis and Ben Thompson. Sonny Lewis was a deacon too. They made an impressive trio, these young devout men of our church.

♪ *Search me, search me Lord.*
Turn the light from heaven on my soul.

The elder deacons occupied the front pew on the right side of the church. Uncle Perry was nodding his head with the music. Seeing Grampa excited butterflies in my stomach. I wanted to run up to him and be wrapped in his stern embrace, but Connie was leading the way to the second row pew on the left side of the church, where Aunt Betty was sitting. It would not be right to make a scene. There would be time for embracing later.

The sanctuary appeared no worse for my absence. Someone was seeing after the church building just fine while I tended to my new vocation. A kind of throne-like place had been prepared for Reverend Wright and Sister Wright. Two handsome high-back chairs from the pastor's study had been brought into the sanctuary and were placed on either side of a tiny table which was draped with a pretty white table cloth. Aunt Betty's best crystal vase sat on the table filled with a bouquet of fresh flowers. The bouquet on the little table was cheerful not charitable.

Connie was waiting for me to go in first, and I did leading Little Evie in front of me. Connie came after carrying Nate. Aunt Betty's satisfied smile met me as she sang, and when I sat down I kissed her on her powdered cheek. She smelled discretely of Chanel. Maybe I ought to wear perfume. I smelled too much of Watkins Liniment and Lysol. We settled in our seats, and Sister Gates, who sat on the front pew, turned around and patted me enthusiastically on the leg.

"We been missin' you," she mouthed.

"It's good to be here," I leaned forward and whispered back.

"'Bout time they let you out of that house," said Aunt Betty under her breath.

It was *about time*, but I hoped he would be all right without me. And I hoped his *freedom day* would come soon too. Connie raised her own melodic voice.

♪ *You know where I go*
Know where I belong
You know all I do
You know my secrets too
Lord, search me, touch me, cleanse me through and through.

Nathaniel stood to read the Scripture and the rest of us faded into a hum of the hymn before we became quiet to hear the Word.

"'I am the good shepherd: the good shepherd giveth his life for the sheep,'" he read. "'But he that is a hireling, and not the shepherd, whose own the sheep are not, seeth the wolf comin', and leaveth the sheep and fleeth: and the wolf catcheth them, and scattereth the sheep.'"

Reverent amens called back from throughout the church.

"'The hireling fleeth, because he is a hireling, and careth not for the sheep,'" continued Nathaniel. "I am the good shepherd, and know my sheep, and am known of mine. As the Father knoweth me, even so know I the Father: and I lay down my life for the sheep.'"

Nathaniel paused.

"Thank you, Jesus!" more than one congregant shouted out.

"'And *other* sheep I have,'" my cousin's deep voice carried on, emphasizing the word *other*. "'Which are not of this fold: them *also* must I bring, and they shall hear my voice; and there will be *one* fold and one shepherd.'" He closed the Bible and looked directly at me. "I have read to you Saint John, Chapter ten," he told us. "Verses eleven through sixteen. May the Lord add a blessing to the reading of His Word."

Amen!

The Lord is good the Good Shepherd!

Amen!

Someone began the hymn, *What a Friend We have in Jesus*, and we all joined in. Sister Wright followed on the piano.

> ♪*All our sins and grief to bear*
> *What a privilege to carry*
> *Everything to God in prayer*
> *O what peace we often forfeit,*
> *O what needless pain we bear,*
> *All because we do not carry*
> *Everything to God in prayer.*

I thought about Nathaniel's Scripture selection, and how we had our own churches, our own families, and our own places, but yet there was only the One Shepherd. One Good Shepherd who had never failed us. Any of us, as the old folks said, having *brought us from a mighty long way*. My eyes filled. Connie reached over and squeezed my hand. Sonny Lewis was kneeling to pray. The plaintive singing softened and became a low, stirring moan as Sonny began.

"Heavenly Father," prayed the young deacon. "We come here today, thankin' You for this here church. For our homes and our families, Lord. For all Yo' 'bundant and tender mercies..."

> ♪ *Can we find a friend so faithful*
> *Who will all our sorrows share?*
> *Jesus knows our every weakness;*
> *Take it to the Lord in prayer.*

"...Lord, if justice had-a been done, who among us would be able to stand?" asked Sonny.

I might have gotten what I deserve.

"We ain't worthy of you, Jesus. But Lord," Sonny continued. "You been so slow to anger with us. And Yo' mercy is great. We know that it's Yo' grace that done brought us safe thus far. And Father, we come here askin' for yo' continued blessin's on this congregation and this community. Stir up yo' fire in us Lord. Make us fit for yo' service. We ask all this in Jesus' name. Amen!"

Amen!

Amen!

As the service proceeded, Sister Wright played for the Sweet Water choir to march in and directed them through their A and B selections. Then she moved from the piano to sit in the place of honor with her husband. The guest preacher today was Reverend Eli Carson, who had come all the way from Dallas. He was on the faculty at Bishop College. Young and fiery, he gave an inspired and exciting sermon that tightly wove fatherhood and leadership together, bringing us from Abraham's frantic faith to the Lord's most desperate moments in the Garden. He was seminary-trained, perfectly calling out the nouns and in complete control of the verbs, and the congregation enthusiastically responded to him. I was reminded of going to church with Aunt Grace and Uncle Eddie, where too much whooping and hollering wouldn't do.

In summary, Reverend Carson told us, it all came down to obedience. Obedience was how we honored our fathers, natural and spiritual. Obedience was how we honored God. "Behold!" he preached, "To obey *is* better than sacrifice, and to hearken is better than the fat of rams!" My mind returned to my last encounter with Reverend Wright, and then to the scene between Grampa and Doctor Mitchell outside of Taylor's room, when he was still *Mr. Payne,* and I had turned into a disobedient ram.

It wasn't supposed to be a revival, but somebody was bound to have an encounter with the Holy Spirit today. Maybe it would be me. Maybe I would be the one to rush up to the altar and repent. Maybe I needed to repent for wanting to be in the house on Webster Road.

At the end of the long service, Sister Wright returned to her post at the piano. The choir started to sing their last selection and began to descend from the stand to march out.

> ♪ *How I got over, how I got over*
> *How I got over, how I got over*
> *My soul looks back in wonder how I got over*

I must have been watching them too longingly, because Aunt Betty said softly under the music, "Ain't been no job requirin' you day and night, seven days a week, since slavery." She meant it to be a sympathetic and supportive comment, but it made me feel sad and apprehensive. I should have told her that it was not so much a job to me anymore, that sometimes it felt like it wasn't work at all. Not for wages anyway. That sometimes when I was holding onto him and he was holding on to me, I wanted to move in closer and linger there.

Grampa clapped his hands as he sang with the choir. It was already good to see him, no matter how the day turned out.

> ♪ *Thank Him for the Holy Bible*
> —Oh yes!
> *Thank Him for good ol' revival*
> —Oh yes!
> *Thank Him for heavenly vision*
> —Oh yes!
> *Thank him for the old time religion*
> —Oh yes!

Little Evie was clapping her hands too, although she was too little to accomplish the rhythm or understand the words.

It was late and I hoped that Taylor was resting now. Sitting up too long left him tired although he wouldn't admit it. If I were not careful for him, then the hard set of his jaw, the color draining out of his face would catch me by surprise. Sometimes he was too determined, just like Doctor Mitchell had tried to tell me. For all their protection, the walls must almost close in on him sometimes.

By now Reverend Wright had also left the special place of honor and was mounting the step to the pulpit. He wore a broad, proud smile. We had had good church.

♪*Gonna view the host in white*
Who traveled both day and night
Coming out from every nation
On their way to the great coronation
Coming from north, south, east, and west
On their way to the land of rest
Well I'm Going to join the heavenly choir
Gonna sing and never get tired

    Reverend Wright looked out over Sweet Water benevolently. We were all his children. Old ones and young ones alike. His flock. Me too. He thanked us for thanking him, and then asked the Lord to bless us and the ones we loved in the coming week and always. Normally we finished with the hymn, *Blessed Be the Ties That Bind*, but today Sister Wright wasn't her staid self, and she finished with the recessional hymn. She made the ivory keys dance in the Spirit, in the splendor of certified salvation and the exuberance of reaffirmed faith, we all joined in.

♪*How I got over! How I got over!*
How I got over! How I got over!
My soul looks back and wonders how I got over!

II

When the service was over, a group of deacons, Nathaniel and Uncle Perry among them, disappeared into the back of the building to count the tithes and offerings. Grampa engaged Reverend Carson in a lively conversation. I watched as the young preacher soaked up Grampa's praise for his performance while at the same time dispensing his own praise for how fine our church was. Today's impromptu, although to be expected, *love offering* was fine too, and proof that we were indeed a prosperous congregation. Reverend Carson would have a pleasant drive home.

Grampa had not seen me, since he was the kind of church member who seldom turned to look behind him to see who else would approach the altar of God. If you did not come boldly—or humbly—all the way down to the front, then he was not likely to witness your supplication. The Green women, who included me, and children filed out with the other church members for the ritual of community in front of the church that followed the service.

Set free from the confines of worship the little children played boisterously on the church-house grounds, Little Evie among them. It had barely been three months, but she had grown up so much. The more dignified members of the congregation exchanged our greetings and compliments in a merry cacophony of conversation accented with laughter, as we confirmed to each other that we were each in our own way *wonderfully blessed*. In a rainbow of complexions and *Sunday-best*, we flourished in our separate part of the world. *Juneteenth* really was our own *Fourth of July*, even if this did make *Independence Day* a *separate* affair.

Sister Wright was vivaciously accepting her own praise for both her piano proficiency and the talented choir she directed, but I could see that she was making her way over to where I stood with Aunt Betty and Connie catching up on neighborhood news with Sister Miller, the colored grocer's wife.

"Well-well, Esther Allen," the minister's wife greeted me perfectly. "What a blessin' to see you out today! Deacon Green must be relieved to have you home again."

"Hello, Sister Wright," I said, reaching out to shake her gloved hand with my own. In an English court I might have curtsied. She was after all the queen of our church. "The choir was wonderful," I settled for complimenting her instead.

"Yes," agreed Aunt Betty. "You sholey blessed my soul today!"

As a deacon's wife Aunt Betty was nobility too, as was Connie. But me, I was just a poor relation, educated, but destined to be nothing more than a governess at best.

"Didn't they!" exulted Connie.

"And how is your patient today?" Sister Wright asked.

He had a name, I thought behind my gracious smile. And he wasn't really my patient. Not anymore. In the mornings he got up and dressed like the rest of us.

"Oh fine, Sister Wright," I replied as genuinely as she had asked. "Just fine."

"Must be, thank the Lord," she said. "If he let you away from his side this long. Does this mean that things are back to normal? Can I count on your lovely tenor voice to be with us again on Sunday mornings?"

Normal? When had she ever considered my voice to be *lovely*? I hadn't sung with the choir since September.

Can't you just try to sing alto, Esther? Lord, I just don't know what to do with you.

"No, ma'am," I said.

"Oh. So you still workin'--" began the pastor's wife.

"Oh now, Sister Wright," Connie interceded. "This the Lord's day, we don't want to be talkin' 'bout work."

"That's right," Aunt Betty followed Connie's lead, grasping me by the arm and pulling me away from the scene. "Excuse us, Sister Wright," she said very sociably, "But if Esther don't speak to Sister Alberta over there, well then we won't never hear the end of it."

The church grounds began to empty and the Green women went to wait for our men by Uncle Perry's car. "You gon' be able to eat dinner with us?" asked Aunt Betty, opening the front door on the passenger's side so she could sit down on the car seat. Little Evie was clinging to the hemline of my dress.

"It might be gettin' a little late," I said reluctantly.

And if I did miss him, it was only to be expected. It was how I spent all of my time. It should feel strange to be away from him.

"Sholey God," Aunt Betty said, removing her gloves and putting them into her purse. "That man'll keep 'til you have some dinner."

Surely God we lived separate lives.

"He got his doctor with 'im," Connie agreed. "He'll be all right."

By now Doctor Mitchell should have warmed up the casserole. They would have had their *lunch*. I had left detailed written instructions taped on the Frigidaire just in case.

"Are we havin' sweet potato pie?" I asked.

"Lord, yes," said Aunt Betty a little puzzled by the question. "Don't we always?"

Grampa emerged through the double doors of the church and stopped a moment to put on his hat before starting across the church yard towards us.

"I think it'll be all right to stay," I allowed, focusing on Grampa. "Excuse me, y'all." I said, steering Little Evie to her grandmother. Aunt Betty and Connie turned to see whom it was I saw.

"Well Lord," I heard Aunt Betty say quietly as I left them.

Grampa stopped again when he saw me coming towards him.

"Hello, Grampa," I said solemnly. "Happy Father's Day."

"Esther," Grampa nodded.

"How are you?"

"Can't complain. You?"

"I'm fine, Grampa."

I kissed him on the side of his face and hugged him timidly. His return embrace consisted of a cool pat on my back.

"You lookin' well," he said when I stood apart from him again.

Looking up into his eyes, I dared a little smile.

"You too, Grampa."

"How's yo' patient?"

The smile faded. Grampa's shoes also had a perfect shine.

"He's much better," I said.

"Guess so," he observed. "Since I see he lettin' you out the house today."

"Doctor Mitchell is with him," I explained looking up again.

I tried to look passed his flat expression and hear beyond his cool words, remembering what was his due privilege. He was after all a king himself. And Jimmy had been a prince. I might have inherited his title, only I seemed to be squandering it by keeping to an enemy's castle. But Nathaniel's Scripture reading said that there was one flock, and we all belonged to it. I could assure Grampa once more that all of this was for just a little while, but Reverend Carson was right, the Bible said obedience was better than sacrifice. I wondered how you could reconcile paying honor to *all* of your fathers when their expectations did not agree.

Little Evie was again tugging on the tail of my dress and I reached down and picked her up.

"So when you got to be back?" asked Grampa, and perhaps his tone was kinder. "He lettin' you have dinner with yo' own people?" But still there was the recrimination.

"Yes-sir," I answered with a small dose of hope. "I arranged to have the day off."

"Humph," said Grampa, starting across the church yard again. "Mean to tell me you ain't indispensable after all."

"No-sir," I replied following behind him with his great-granddaughter on my hip. "I'm not."

I am just needed, I thought, and that can't be a bad thing.

Ours was one of the last families on the church parking lot. Aunt Betty, who was holding Nate and attempting to defend her elegant appearance against the hot day with one of the mortuary fans, looked cross. Little Evie restlessly kept moving between her mother's and my attention to entertain herself.

At the car Connie commented that Grampa was looking good enough to keep company to which he replied that he had no more use for women folks.

"Po' Mis' Janey," said Aunt Betty.

"I done had the best," Grampa said aloofly. "You young folks didn't know my Ernestine."

"I wish we did, Grampa Isaac," Connie said sincerely.

"Esther put you in mind of her," he said.

I looked at him, surprised by and grateful for the acknowledgment. I always heard a little *I love you* when he said I was like Ernestine.

"Got her face and build," Grampa added. "'Course nobody got skin like hers. Black as the sky on a fair night."

"Mis' Ernestine was a handsome woman," agreed Aunt Betty, remembering. "And good as she can be too. Everybody said so. Esther, you take after yo' grandma in that way too."

"Her skin was as smooth as velvet and she didn't need none of that face powder junk neither," said Grampa.

Aunt Betty seemed unbothered by this implicit criticism of her, accustomed as she was to his disapproval.

Finally Uncle Perry and Nathaniel appeared through the side door of the church, and the Green family of colored McConnell County was all present and accounted for. Four generations of us, the past, the present, and the future, proud, pretty and *handsome*, together, as we should be, in front of Sweet Water. Someone should have had a camera.

"All right!" announced Uncle Perry. "Let's us go eat! Esther, you comin' with us, ain't you?"

"Yes-sir," I said.

"Good!" said Uncle Perry getting into the car. "You ridin' with us or Nathaniel? Come on, Papa, let's go."

"B'lieve I feel like walkin'," said Grampa.

"Oh now, Papa Isaac," groaned Aunt Betty. "Folks ready to eat. This ain't no time for a stroll."

"Won't take long," Grampa dismissed her. "Y'all gone on to the house and get dinner ready. 'Fo' you get done I'll be home."

"I'll walk with you, Grampa," I volunteered.

He looked at me. I dared to smile at him again.

"That's a good idea!" said Connie. "Yo' kitchen's barely big enough for two women, Grampa Isaac. Lord knows what we go through with three. Come on, Nathaniel, let's go. Little Evie, get in the car, baby."

For a time Grampa and I walked along silently, the unspoken reproaches and unuttered explanations between us. He did not hurry and kept his eyes straight ahead. I waited in my heart for him and carefully set my pace to his. I might have been ten years old again, except at that age I had not disappointed him yet, and Jimmy was alive to be the hope of our family. Now Jimmy was a memory and I was a bewilderment. Or maybe he thought I was worse. I didn't know. He didn't say.

Grampa slipped off his suit coat and rolled up his shirt sleeves as we walked. He had strong arms too, made so by swinging an axe and other forms of hard labor. Grampa probably didn't even know what a dumbbell weight was. When had he ever had time for leisurely exercise? But then these days it wasn't leisure for Taylor either. I wished that Grampa would want to know him. He might see something in him to respect. To admire. Maybe even to forgive.

We turned the corner onto Benson Street. I continued to keep up with his stride, staying beside him, waiting. "Grampa," I decided to begin. "I'm sorry you thought you had to send Reverend Wright to see about me." His lips drew into a tight line across his face. He may have married dear, dark Africa back into our bloodline, but that he was the grandson of a Confederate soldier remained evidenced in his features. His lips were no fuller than Taylor's and just as capable of disappearing when he was not pleased. "It must have been embarrassing for you," I continued. "I'm just sorry you didn't think you could come to me yourself. I wanted to talk to you. You can ask Nathaniel." Grampa lifted his chin and continued to look straight ahead as we walked. Moses would not have gone back to Egypt for a lost daughter either. "I realize that you didn't want to come to the house, but you could have called, Grampa. I'm not really doin' anything wrong. It's not wrong to help somebody who needs you."

The tree tops gently brushed at the clear blue sky. Children were playing in the front yards, darting across our path and into the street. *Our* streets and roads were paved in black-top tar mixed with gravel. In the middle of the summer the tar softened and pieces of it would stick to car fenders and shoes. It wasn't real pavement, not yet, perhaps not ever, but it was an improvement over the muddy messes that most of our streets and roads used to turn into on rainy days. As we encountered our neighbors sitting on their porches and passing us along the street, we waved or briefly spoke with them. I found myself hoping to see Mr. Leon.

One of our neighbors, Mr. Henry, commented that it was good to see me and Grampa together on Father's Day. "Good chilluns a comfort in yo' ol' age," said Mr. Henry. Grampa didn't say anything, but Mr. Henry didn't notice. "You's a lucky man to have yours all 'round you, Green," he added.

Grampa shifted his coat to his other arm. We weren't all around him. Aunt Grace was in Harlem. And Mama and Jimmy were gone. And I was in a white man's house, which to Grampa might make me the farthest away.

"Happy Father's Day, Mr. Henry," I said for us both and Grampa and I walked on.

After a time Grampa spoke to me, picking up where I had left off.

"Why it's left up to you?" he wanted to know. "Where his people?"

...*his people*...

...*you people*...

...*And there will be one fold and one shepherd.*

"I don't know, Grampa," I replied. "It's just the way it is, I guess. The way it turned out."

I knew Nathaniel was right. It wasn't hate that was in Grampa's heart, just *fresh memories.* But there really was only the one world. The one flock. The One Shepherd.

At the corner Benson and Spring Street, Grampa stopped. I waited again. He looked at me.

"A man ain't nothin' but a man, Esther Fay," my grandfather said. "And a woman's a woman. No matter what color they is. You be with 'im all the time, seein' after 'im the way you do, and somethin' gon' start to happen 'tween you. Prob'ly already has. Way 'fo' that sickness come upon him. I 'spect he got feelin's for you. That' how come you think he yo' friend. But all that kind-a man'll do is use you. He might not mean to but he can't help it. It's how they do us. Don't be fool enough to think different. You's a colored woman and that's all you ever gon' be to him. Good enough to clean his house. Good enough to cook for him, and even now nurse him. But when he got no more use for you, he'll send you back where you b'long. I can't b'lieve all you wanna be is his nigga-maid."

Grampa crossed the street. History was a formidable proof of the present, and it was on Grampa's side. Slave ships and shackles. Diluted complexions, and Billie Holiday's *strange fruit* hanging from the limbs of stark trees while upstanding citizens picnicked with their children. Separate water fountains and the backs of buses. Negro men who fought and died for a Constitution that had deemed them fractions of men. The memories were fresh, bitterly fresh. Everything else was mostly ideals, denied and deferred, waiting for their justification. Declarations and Proclamations. Hopes and dreams. Just so many miracles. Waiting on God. Waiting on us.

By the time I caught up with Grampa we were almost to Mandy's house, where Spencer was growing into a man. Where Mandy had said that holding *him* responsible for being born white was no different than *them* holding *us* back for being born colored. But Grampa could not respect what Mandy had to say. She went to Ray's Café, and if she got a Sunday off she didn't spend it at church.

"Grampa," I said once I was with him again. "I'm sorry that's what you think. But it's not what I am."

"That's what I mean, baby," Grampa sighed as we reached the white picket fence that surrounded his yard. "You think it's left up to you to say."

By the time we were seated around Grampa's table, the world outside of our circle was mostly sealed off, away from our *us*. The Green circle would not be broken, and Grampa's face softened as he considered the ones all around him. Black and brown. Powdered and plain. We were his own. All of us, the proof that mattered most, living, loving proof of God's faithfulness. The Green men opened their presents to much fanfare and gratitude. It was good to be home again.

After dinner and presents I helped Connie put Little Evie and Nate down for naps in my room, Jimmy's room, and Jimmy watched the children sleep from his sporty lean against Uncle Eddie's car. They would only know him by our stories, the way I knew Ernestine. But their world was already better for him, as was mine for her.

Perhaps I really did have my grandmother's smile. I hoped so. I thought it might have been nice to have her color too. To be really black. *Black as the sky on a fair night.* But I was also made up of Grampa. And of Daddy and Mama. All of them were in me, and so I was like melted chocolate. A deep, rich brown. With red undertones on occasion. Like when I ran fast on a cold morning. Or received a compliment.

Later it was again Connie and I who cleaned up Grampa's kitchen, while the others relaxed in Grampa's front room.

"I think Daddy Perry 'bout done talked your grandpa into gettin' a hot water heater," she reported, bringing the teakettle over to the sink to add hot water to the dishwater.

"At first we had to boil the water on the stove for Taylor's hot-packs," I replied carrying a stack of plates over to the counter by the sink. "But Doctor Mitchell bought a special machine that heats the water in his room."

"*Taylor's* hot packs, huh?" Connie said, returning the kettle to the stove.

It had slipped out, this use of his Christian name outside of the house.

"He wants me to use his first name," I explained awkwardly.

"And do you?"

"When we're by ourselves."

"I don't see why you shouldn't," said Connie. "He calls you Esther. You call him Taylor. Ain't nothin' wrong with it."

"Maybe," I said, placing dishes into the sink of hot soapy water.

"Esther, a man ain't nothin' but a man."

And I was only a woman. Everybody kept saying so.

It was Nathaniel who had to ultimately ask, "Esther, don't you think it's 'bout time for you to be gettin' back?" and with that question he returned the hardness to Grampa's face.

"Guess you right, boy," Grampa said derisively. "Don't want 'em to send the paddyrollers after her."

Mr. Lincoln had seen to it that nobody had to come after to anybody anymore. Now we had *Juneteenth*. Still it was time to say good-bye, which I didn't want to do since nobody wanted me to go, and that included me. Connie tried to distract us with the children, and Aunt Betty and Uncle Perry tried to moderate as much as they could. Right before I left, while Nathaniel waited for me in the car, I went back to my room for Jimmy's photograph, wrapping it carefully in a cup-towel to take it back with me to the house on Webster Road. Then once again I kissed Grampa on his unresponsive cheek.

"Maybe you could come to the house sometime," I tried. "It would be all right. I could fix you supper."

"He gon' be in the kitchen too?" asked Grampa.

I thought about the wheelchair and the staircase.

"I hope he can be someday, Grampa. It's what we work for."

"Can't see myself at no table with a white man."

"He's a good man, Grampa."

"He's a white man, Esther Fay. The Law says I don't have to."

And it was Taylor's law, I thought ironically. Taylor's law and Grampa's justification.

Uncle Perry and Aunt Betty were taking Connie and the children home, since Nathaniel was taking me back. At the same time we were all leaving Grampa alone again in the center of the Green family universe. A sun with nothing to shine on but the framed faces on the front room wall. Yet he was the true the center of my life, and leaving him again meant that I was leaving that center, wandering off course into an unknown wilderness. It seemed to be the Lord's way, this calling you off to another place.

Sometimes we think we hear the Lord, but it's really our own minds.

And sometimes it was simply the entreaty of a good man who had asked you not to leave him.

At Moss Road Nathaniel turned the car to the right and I gave him a puzzled look. "I just want to stop at the garage for a minute," he said. Now that I was on my way back, I was increasingly remorseful for spending so much time away from my responsibilities. What kind of dinner would I be able to put together quickly? I always applied the hot-packs around eight o'clock in the evening so that Taylor could be at rest again by ten.

"On a Sunday?" I asked impatiently. "You not fixin' to work on somebody's car, are you?"

"Naw," replied Nathaniel, parking in front of the garage. "I just want to check on things."

He got out of the car. I remained inside. A large piece of Aunt Betty's sweet potato pie was wrapped up in wax paper in one of Grampa's older plates, and sitting securely on the backseat. Jimmy's portrait was in my lap. I had kept the promise about the pie, and it was a nice oblation. Nathaniel went around the building, examining locked doors and windows. Who would be messing around at the garage I wondered. It was not like him to be concerned unless something was wrong. I was restless.

"What were you lookin' for?" I asked, once he was back in the car. "Is something wrong?"

"Just some ol' white trash been hangin' 'round, lookin' for trouble," Nathaniel said lightly and we were on our way again.

"You tell Sheriff Boden?"

He grinned.

"Esther, don't look so worried. You worse than Connie."

Don't be such an alarmist.

"Be careful, Nathaniel," I said seriously. "You know what envy can do to people."

"The Lord got his eye on the sparrow. Sholey God, He not gon' miss a big ol' garage."

Or a large, strapping man with a beautiful smile.

The sun was setting by the time we reached the house on Webster Road. When I did not see Doctor Mitchell's car in front of the house, a thousand new butterflies suddenly filled my stomach to die among the remains of ham, candied sweet potatoes and collard greens. I looked up to Taylor's bedroom window and saw that a light was on in his room. Had something happened? Where was Doctor Mitchell?

"Park here," I told Nathaniel before he could drive around to the back of the house. "Park here!"

He did, and I hurried out of the car. The front door was locked and I frantically searched through my pocketbook for the key.

"What's the matter, Esther?" asked Nathaniel coming up behind me. "What's wrong?"

As soon as the door was open I was running up the stairs not knowing what I expected to find. Bursting through the bedroom door, I startled Taylor, who was sitting in the wheelchair reading. Herman barked excitedly.

"Esther?" Taylor said alarmed. "Esther, what is it?"

He put down his book and rolled towards me. Relieved to find him well I dropped down on the side of the bed to catch my breath.

"Where's Doctor Mitchell?!" I asked.

"I sent him home," Taylor replied. "It was getting to be a long day for him."

"He left you alone?"

This brought the wry expression to his face.

"I'm a big boy, Esther," he said. "So contrary to popular belief, you actually don't need to arrange for a sitter. I know my limitations."

"I'm sorry, Taylor," I offered. "I didn't mean--"

"Did you have a good time?" he halted my apologies.

"Yes, but--"

"Don't worry about it, Esther. Everything's fine."

His dark eyes, when they looked back at me as they did now, were irresistible. A smile faintly raised the corners of his mouth. I didn't deserve his confidence.

"Uh- y'all 'scuse me," said Nathaniel from the door, breaking the spell.

I jumped up, facing him.

"Is uh-everything all right?" my cousin asked.

"Hello Nathaniel," said Taylor, rolling himself forward to greet him.

Nathaniel instantly looked down at Taylor's legs, the wheels on his chair. Although he quickly returned to Taylor's face, it was not fast enough to go undetected. These were the moments that Taylor loathed, when each new pair of eyes registered again that he was changed, reminding him again, in their sympathetic reflections, that he was no longer the man he had once known himself to be.

"It's good to see you again," Taylor said amiably moving us through the moment as he reached out to shake Nathaniel's hand.

"Good to see you too, Mr. Payne," replied Nathaniel.

Taylor smiled up at him.

"You know, Nathaniel, if this is going to be a social call, then we ought to be on a first name basis. Please, call me Taylor."

Nathaniel looked to me.

"Yes-sir," he said uncomfortably. "Uh- Esther, you run out the car so fast you forgot the pie, and this here picture."

Now Taylor glanced back at me and smiled.

"She worries too much, Nathaniel," Taylor said. "Is it sweet potato?"

"Yes," I replied, much more brightly and went to take the plate and picture from Nathaniel. "Just like I promised."

"You did promise, didn't you?" Taylor said.

"Yes, I did."

Taylor invited Nathaniel to sit down, and I took Jimmy's picture to the buttercup room and the pie to the kitchen where I quickly put on coffee. Doctor Mitchell had not made a mess of the kitchen during the day, but I was angry that he had left Taylor alone. Spencer would have been more reliable.

As the coffee brewed the telephone rang and I went to the foyer to answer it. It was the errant doctor.

"Esther?" he said to me. "Good. You're back."

"Yes-sir," I answered coolly.

"Well, I was just checking on things. Taylor insisted that I go home. I didn't want to leave him, but you know how he is."

And if I weren't here how would you *check*, I thought but did not say.

"Yes-sir," I said instead.

"I hope you had a nice time with your folks."

"Yes-sir, thank you."

"Good. Esther?"

"Yes-sir."

"Did Taylor mention to you that he wants you have your Sundays off like you used to?"

"No-sir, we haven't spoken about it."

"Well he does. And I think it's a good idea too. Of course it would have to be limited to the day. I mean we would still need you at night. But I think we could manage just fine during the day. Unless I was called away for an emergency. What I'm saying is that I would come over and stay with him just like today. Some of his other friends would be willing to do so too, I'm sure. You know we might even be able to get him out of the house sometimes."

"He won't be carried, Doctor Mitchell," I said.

"Yes, he's made that clear to me too. But with the progress he's making I don't think we'll have to concern ourselves with that too much longer."

"Yes-sir."

"At any rate, we want to arrange for you to have some time off. It's important. We don't want you to wear yourself out. You're the best thing in the world for him. We have to keep you happy."

But I was happy here.

"Doctor Mitchell, excuse me, but I have to check on the coffee on the stove."

"Oh. Well, all right. I'm glad you're home."

But this was not my home.

"Yes-sir. Thank you for calling, Doctor Mitchell. I'll let Mr. Payne know that you did."

"Bye now."

"Good-bye, doctor."

Sundays off, I thought to myself when I was in the kitchen again. Every Sunday. That was something to take back to Grampa. I placed a coffee service on the large tray to take upstairs to the center of what was my other universe.

Nathaniel stayed with us for awhile, and for dinner Taylor wanted only the pie and coffee. "She keeps trying to fatten me up," he pretended to complain to Nathaniel, who laughed and looked easier with us. I sat on the side of the bed and watched the two men revisit their acquaintance and resume the journey to friendship. And I was content to be a spectator, remembering the way they had been in Nathaniel's house, and fantasizing about how they could be in the future. I was like Maid Marian or Mary Magdalene, very content in the company of men.

"Somethin' I been wantin' to ask you for the longest," said Nathaniel during the course of a conversation about working on cars. "What you be lookin' for under the hood anyway?"

"I wanted to see what you were doing," Taylor replied.

"But you ain't knowed what you was lookin' at," Nathaniel told him.

"You'd be surprised what I was learning from you, Nathaniel."

"Best leave fixin' cars to me and I'll leave the lawyerin' to you....Taylor."

Taylor smiled. It was such a little thing, using a first name, but it meant they too were doing things *differently*.

"Sounds like a plan," Taylor said. "You ever need a good attorney, you know where to find me."

"Yep," laughed Nathaniel. "Under the hood of a car."

Taylor laughed too.

"That has to be better than here, don't you think?" he said.

The laughter faded into smiles that faded away.

"God is able," Nathaniel said soberly.

"I hope I am," replied Taylor.

"That's the best part," Nathaniel told him. "It ain't all up to you."

"So I've been told," Taylor said winking at me.

It grew late. After I said good-night to Nathaniel and came back upstairs, Taylor said that we should forego the hot-packs tonight.

"It's been a long day," he said. "I'm a little tired. You must be too."

I was quiet but my face protested.

"Don't look so offended, Sister Sergeant," he said, unbuttoning his shirt. "Surely we can break the rules sometimes. What's all that stuff about forgiveness for anyway? What's the point of having it if you never use it?"

"That's strange talk for a prosecutor," I replied.

He smiled.

"That's the second time tonight that someone's reminded me that I used to practice law."

He took off his shirt and handed it to me.

"Maybe you could work on some things from home," I suggested as I turned back the covers on the bed. "You have your father's law library downstairs. And with Spencer out of school for the summer, he could run your errands. He'd love it."

"And I suppose you wouldn't mind clerking for me too."

"Who knows?" I replied. "I might learn something."

"Law and grace," he said shaking his head dubiously while rolling over to park beside the bed. He locked the wheels of the chair. "I don't think the world's ready for you yet."

"And why not?" I asked gently placing his feet on the floor.

With my arms around him for support, he used the arms of the chair to bring himself to his feet. Once he was standing, I placed my hands on his waist to steady him while he grasped my arms tightly. The standing was good for him and part of the re-education process. Bearing his weight allowed him to practice his balance even though he always shifted his weight to the left because his right leg was too weak even with someone's help.

"This is not a theocracy yet, you know," said Taylor, holding onto me.

It was a taxing exercise, and the longer he stood the more tightly he held onto my arms.

"Then what's all that 'In God We Trust' on pocket change?" I asked.

"Ever heard of hedging your bets?" he replied.

"I don't' gamble," I informed him smugly.

He laughed a little.

"No, you don't, do you?" he concurred.

Perhaps it was being away from him all day. Or maybe it was watching him with Nathaniel. Or remembering him with Nate, and thinking about him with Spencer. Perhaps it was knowing that Grampa was right about a lot of things, but wrong about him. Or perhaps it was only the depth of his dark eyes and the way he could smile at me as if he were watching me open up or turn pages. Whatever it was, on this night, I moved in closer to him, until our bodies touched, and I slipped my arms around his waist. Hesitating at this change in our routine, he stiffened slightly. But I pressed the side of my dark brown face against the soft white cotton of his under-shirt. When the strength of his arms went around me, it was as if he would pull me into him, and it was where I wanted to be.

A man ain't nothin' but a man. And a woman is a woman.

And there were those times when Nature would have her way, so that even if something was kept unspoken, it would at least be felt. There was nothing safe about this, yet inside this consecrated space, I was willing to let myself dream that it was. It still wasn't gambling. It couldn't be when you knew you couldn't win. I held my own breath and listened to the beating of his heart. After a time, he was forced to remind me, "Esther, I…my legs…I can't…" snatching me from the dream.

Embarrassed and ashamed I swiftly helped him to the bed, pulling away from him to care for him. My hands were damp and shaky, but my actions were deft and efficient. There were only sparse words between us while I helped him get into his pajamas. Necessary words, nothing immaterial to the task at hand. What he felt I did not know. My own feelings raised and roared through me but they were hidden behind a mask of care-taking.

When we were done and he was settled for the night, I straightened the room and gathered up things that needed to be taken downstairs, including myself. We said good night to each other as if nothing else had happened, but when I was at the bedroom door, he added, "I'm glad you came back." At this I stopped but did not turn around.

"Why wouldn't I, Taylor?" I asked him.

"Why did you?" he asked me.

Because I love you.

"I had to bring you your pie," I said as I left his room.

III

I loved him. Knowing it brought me a kind of peace because at least I wasn't fighting with myself anymore. With acceptance came relief. Like it was bad news that had to be heard so that you could get on with coping with it. One thing for sure I knew what to do with bad news. I began by dawdling around downstairs for hours, so that by the time I finally made my way back upstairs, Taylor's bedroom was dark, and I was getting used to the idea of it. Simply put, the *something* had a name. That was all that had changed.

In the buttercup room, I set the photograph of Jimmy on the table beside the bed where I slept. This photograph captured his real moment of glory, regardless of what the war movies said we should think. Jimmy was missing from me, from us, and nothing could bring him back. If only he had been a coward in 1941, he might have been left alive to show his bravery on another day. He might be somewhere making a place in the world for himself and for me. I might not have wandered into this house to love yet another man, whom I could not keep.

♪*Yield not to temptation*
For yielding is sin
Each victory will help you
Some other to win

So the song went, but I hadn't been looking for some other victory to win. All I had ever wanted was Jimmy and all that my life was supposed to be as his sister. But that was not what God wanted. His ways were not our ways. His thoughts were not our thoughts. Grampa said that I would have nothing to show for it. The Bible said *by this shall all men know that ye are my disciples, if ye have love one to another.* They couldn't both be right.

But of course it wasn't that kind of love either. Not the Scriptural agape for your enemies or your brethren. What it was was the *Song of Solomon*. The kind that made your breath come quickly as deep vital places became hotly poised and insistent. *Let him kiss me with the kisses of his mouth: for thy love is better than wine.* That, too, was the Bible. And when I finally fell asleep that night, it was this verse that repeated in my head and described my dreams.

But they were only dreams. Silly, selfish dreams that could matter to no one, not even me. I would make it all mean nothing; except perhaps, if need be, a brief deferment of Grampa's dream, a little postponement of Jimmy's legacy, and whatever part it played in restoring Taylor Payne to his former self.

It would be my secret. Come the next morning, the next days, the next weeks, I would make myself reconciled with it. In secret I would honor it, letting it pour out of me and onto him in every way, except candidly. It would be my private thing. And though it could not be forever, then at least it could be for now. It had a utility, a purpose. It would help him walk again. Love could work miracles.

Nathaniel's visit on Fathers' Day proved to be the necessary breach in the wall that Taylor had built around himself since the polio. I had been able to climb over it and even slip Spencer around it, professional contacts had entered the gates, but it was Nathaniel, kind, constant Nathaniel, who had finally brought it down enough to let the rest of his life back in. Soon the house on Webster was being regularly visited by the people who made up his world.

He belonged to these circles that did not include me. Work ones, social ones. The ones that he should not give up. I had my own other circles too. Big ones, little ones. The ones that I could not give up either. Our circles were not supposed to converge. They were supposed to be kept separate and the little *we* that we were now making constantly parted.

On Sunday mornings, Nathaniel came for me, and I went to church. If people talked about me, I decided that I didn't care. Immediately after every service, I would go to Grampa, forcing him, by my presence at least, to talk to me no matter how dryly his words came. I had my Sunday dinners with Connie and Nathaniel, and took comfort in playing with Little Evie and Nate. Sometimes Grampa could be persuaded to join us, but most of the time he preferred Uncle Perry's table. Late in the afternoon, Nathaniel would be ready to take me back, whether I was ready to go or not. "The man counts on you, Esther," he said one afternoon. "Ain't no need-a takin' advantage of his situation."

As if I ever could. I was far too vigilant for that. Breaking away to spend the day with my family, in my circles, was more difficult for me to accomplish than it was for Taylor to allow. Nathaniel didn't understand that, and I didn't want him to. I didn't want anyone to understand it, because no one could know it.

Not even Taylor. When I suggested that he should have a second telephone installed upstairs, he missed the point entirely.

"Telephones. Sitters," he said. "I appreciate the way you provide for me, Esther. But I suppose you do want your life back."

He had no idea what was in my heart, what was all around him in this room.

"It's you who could have yours," I said.

"This *is* my life," he replied.

"Mine too."

And it absolutely was. For my own private, personal reasons that I was not going to divulge to anyone, including him. Although Doctor Mitchell still visited every day, and stayed all day on Sundays, because Taylor and I had shown ourselves to be very adept at the therapy regimen on our own, mostly the doctor left that up to us, further tightening the little circle that was ours together, despite everyone around us.

"Because you won't leave me," he said with no inflection in his voice, although I could hear the question.

But we didn't need to talk about it. I only needed to act accordingly. He needed me in a way that I needed him to need me. It was almost like being loved. Our circle was sacred to me.

"That's right," I told him. "It just makes sense to have a telephone extension upstairs. I don't mind taking your messages, but really this is a big house. One more telephone, maybe out in the hall by the landing, would be so much more convenient."

The telephone company man came the next week and installed a new telephone upstairs and also one in the kitchen.

"For added convenience," Taylor said regarding the telephone in the kitchen.

One Saturday evening in early July Mandy came for a visit. I was thrilled to have her here and we hugged and laughed. I had missed her so much.

"I told my mis' lady that I needed to visit my friend today, and I just took off early," Mandy explained. "You got time to see me?"

"Of course!" I replied. "Have you eaten? I can fix you a plate."

"How's he doin'?" asked Mandy, pointing up to the ceiling.

"Gettin' better all the time," I was pleased to report. "Would you like to meet him?"

Mandy looked unsure.

"I don't want to bother 'im, " she said. "If he's restin' and all."

"He's still up," I said. "I think he would be pleased to meet you, Mandy. I talk about you all the time. Come on."

Tentatively she followed me upstairs.

"Can't he walk at all?" Mandy asked catching me by the arm on the way.

"No," I said. "Not yet."

With Doctor Mitchell and me on either side of him for support, Taylor tried to make steps. In the bed and in the chair he could muster so much voluntary movement. It was when he stood on his feet, unable to bear his own weight without one of us to help him, that we were forced to realize again how weak he remained. His left leg was stronger, and he could now transfer between his bed and his chair almost by his own power, by bearing weight on the left leg and pivoting. But too often the right knee buckled and threatened to pitch him forward into another fall to the floor. Doctor Mitchell considered crutches, but he didn't believe that Taylor was steady enough at this point for them on his own. So fearing the setbacks of fractures to his bones or to his spirit, Doctor Mitchell and I were his crutches.

"Maybe if he wore braces," Doctor Mitchell would waver sometimes when we were alone. "It would be better."

"Sister Kenny doesn't say that," I would never fail to argue.

"Esther, sometimes we have to compromise."

Then that would mean Roosevelt's recovery. It had to be different for Taylor.

"What you gon' do come August?" Mandy asked at the top of the stairs.

The door to Taylor's room was open and I shook my head at her.

"Not now," I whispered urgently.

I knocked on the open door and Taylor looked up from the book he was reading. The room was fragrant with the scent of his pipe tobacco.

"Don't tell me it's time for my steam bath already," he sighed, laying his pipe in the ashtray.

It had been nearly four months of the hot wet wool applications, and though we believed they continued to help, Taylor detested them.

"No," I said. "Spencer's mother is here, Mandy Gains, and she would like to meet you."

"All right," he agreed.

Stepping outside his room, I ushered Mandy forward.

"I'm glad to be able to tell you myself," Mandy said, when she was shaking Taylor's hand after I had introduced them, "How much I 'preciate the in'trest you take in my boy."

Mandy had not looked down at his legs, but straight into his face, as if she had never been taught to do otherwise. She treated him as if he were any other man to whom she was being introduced. It was like we were at Ray's.

"Spencer's a great boy," Taylor told her warmly. "You must be very proud of him, Mrs. Gaines." Mandy glanced at me, a delighted grin of surprise filling her face.

"Well he brags on you all the time too," she said. "You got 'im talkin' 'bout goin' to college, to one of them law schools. He used to want to be a soldier. I guess I don't have to tell you, bein' his mama, I'm thankful you put somethin' else on his mind."

Taylor smiled.

"He's one of the brightest kids I know," he said. "And with Sweatt's case settled unanimously," he glanced at me before continuing. "He should be able to do that closer to home."

Marshall's right. The Constitution is the way to approach it.

June 5, 1950, in the matter of *Sweatt v. Painter*, Chief Justice Frederick Moore Vinson had written:

> "With such a substantial and significant segment of society excluded, we cannot conclude that the education offered Mr. Sweatt is substantially equal to that which he would receive if admitted to the University of Texas Law school."

With that Herman Sweatt, a colored mailman, like my Uncle Eddie, was admitted to the University of Texas Law School. Thurgood Marshall and the NAACP had won. It seemed a distant victory without much impact on our daily lives in McConnell County, but Taylor reminded us that the decision might in fact have changed Spencer's life too. Even at the University of Texas they could do things *differently*.

When Mandy and I were back in the kitchen, she was still delighting in meeting her son's employer and patron. Sizing him up in her own way, she decided that she liked him.

"Humph! *Mrs. Gaines*," she declared. "Can you beat that?"

Once she came to work here she would be *Mandy* soon enough.

"Oh now Mandy," I admonished her. "Don't go on and on about it. After all you are *Mrs. Gaines*, aren't you?"

"Now look here, Esther Fay," she set me straight. "You might be used to it. But I done lived my whole life in this county and ain't never been called 'Mrs. Gaines' by no white man. Not even ol' man Sullivan show me that kind-a respect when he come to collect my money for the insurance, and I ain't never missed a payment. If I want to take note of it, then you just let me alone about it."

"All right, all right," I granted, pouring her a cup of coffee. "But you act like he's some kind of prince or somethin'. A man ain't nothin but a man."

"You right 'bout that," she agreed, generously spooning sugar into her cup. "And it sho' is good to finally meet one of *them* that don't mind actin' like he know it too."

Taylor cordially tolerated all of the well-meaning bearers of flowers, covered dishes, and encouraging words, and I courteously served plenty of iced tea, coffee and cookies. In his better days he had rarely entertained in his home, and now he was compelled to endure an assortment of persons in his own bedroom. It had to be uncomfortable for him, and sometimes when I would hear him sigh a little wearily as another well-wisher was chatting obliviously, or worse still seeking to console him about his *terrible misfortune*, I wondered if I had pressed him too hard to reengage socially in the interest of doing what was best for him, because truth be told it was also what was best for me. I could not be all that he had because I could not have him.

If any of his visitors thought that it was odd that a colored housekeeper should also be his nurse, and even his physical therapist, most of them never said this in front of me. At most someone would casually compliment me on my baking, or how well I brewed coffee, otherwise I was left to the invisible state that was my place. This was the tradition of polite society, the well-bred guest would never think of questioning the wisdom of the host.

Unless of course they were *entitled* to.

The day Laura Spalding returned to the house on Webster Road, she swept in like a lovely angel, her slender porcelain arms filled with a bouquet of red roses, that she handed to me with instructions that I was put them into a vase and bring them upstairs to *Mr. Payne's* room.

"Don't take all day," she said, pulling off her white gloves and putting them into her pocketbook.

"Yes ma'am," I replied as I watched her crisply ascend the staircase, leaving a sweet cloud of perfume behind her.

In the kitchen the rose thorns pricked my fingers as I arranged them in the large crystal vase, the only one he owned. When she was mistress here there would undoubtedly be lots of crystal vases, and he liked roses. I imagined the romantic reunion going on upstairs. Laura had been kept away for a long time. It would be awkward at first for them, for him, but she would melt the moment with her beautiful smile and he would reach for her, not as he did for me, for help, but for desire.

Fortunately, as a matter of course, she had called in the morning to announce that she would be coming for a visit that afternoon. I kept his house immaculate anyway, but with the morning's notification I had made doubly sure that everything was perfect in his room, the added fussiness amusing my employer.

"We're not expecting the Queen of Sheba," he had observed, watching me as I had wiped each windowpane and then made sure the curtains hung flawlessly.

No, that would have made Laura an Ethiopian queen.

"You don't know women," I had replied.

"Perhaps not," he had agreed.

"Trust me, it's important."

"Why?"

Laura Spalding would be a difficult mistress I had thought, thinking of Mandy. She would certainly not be calling her *Mrs. Gaines*.

"Mis' Laura is a very dear friend of yours," I had explained. "She will be concerned about your care and how I keep your house."

"But it's not her concern," Taylor had said.

I had smiled, a little amused myself. Men could be so naive.

"She will make it that way," I had told him.

When she is your wife, I had thought.

"And we don't want her to think bad about Doctor Mitchell," I had added. "Accusin' him of malpractice and what-not."

"What do you mean?" Taylor had asked frowning.

"You know, my being here instead of a real nurse."

"I'm in very capable hands, Esther."

Willing ones, I had thought.

"That may be," I had replied pulling back the bedspread to fluff his pillows again. "But I want her to be sure about it."

"I believe mine is the only opinion that counts," he had said.

Of course he did. It was after all his world. Even Laura Spalding had to know that. But she belonged in his world. I only worked here.

Now I stood outside the closed bedroom door with the vase of roses, listening to their conversation which was sprinkled now and again with the sparkles of Laura's laughter. Had she ever been in his bedroom before? Perhaps on some tender night they had come back here after a candlelight dinner or starry night drive and consummated the inevitability of their relationship. She would have had expectations because she was entitled to them. Maybe they would have been married by now were it not for the polio.

I knocked softly on the closed bedroom door. It was never closed. Laura Spalding had closed it.

"Yes, come in, Esther," my employer responded.

They were seated by the window, he in his wheelchair and she in the Queen Anne, where Spencer sat when he and my employer worked on his studies or played chess.

"I remembered how much you like roses," Laura said pleased with herself as she came to me and claimed the vase from my hands.

He was smiling.

"Thank-you, Laura," he replied. "They're lovely."

"Oh Good!" she exclaimed happily. "You do like them. Father said that you wouldn't appreciate getting flowers, but I thought after all this time cooped-up in this house a little natural color would do you good."

As if she were the only one to bring him flowers, I thought crossly. She set the vase in the center of the table-desk. I would be moving it later when it was time for his dinner.

"Esther," my employer said. "Please bring us some lemonade."

"Yes-sir," I replied and returned to the kitchen to fetch their refreshments.

Moments later I was back with a pitcher of cold lemonade, a plate of teacakes, glasses, napkins, and small individual plates for the teacakes because Mis' Laura wouldn't want to risk getting crumbs on her pretty white linen dress. I set the heavy tray on the table next to the flowers.

"Thank-you, Esther," my employer said, then added, "Oh—you're short a glass."

But there were two. I looked at him. There was a smile around his eyes.

"Not a problem," he said, rolling himself across the room. "I can use my water glass."

Confused, I glanced at his guest, who was confused too. He returned to the table with the glass in his lap and placed it next to the tray.

"Bring the other chair over, Esther," he continued as he was pouring the lemonade into the three glasses.

Laura's blue eyes were wide as she watched what was happening, and I was frozen in place, my eyes wide too.

"Mr. Payne?" I stammered. "I-I--"

"Esther makes fabulous teacakes, Laura," he said ignoring all the distress around him. "Please have one."

Laura didn't move. We looked at each other again, and I nearly apologized to her.

"Esther," Taylor reminded me. "Your chair."

Obediently, awkwardly, I crossed the room for the other chair, a simple straight back one. I brought it over by the window, placing it at some distance from the table, and even there I could only bring myself to stand next to it.

"Please sit down, Esther," Taylor had to tell me.

I searched his face as he watched me expectantly, and took my seat apprehensively, as if it were on fire, perching on the edge of the chair tensely.

"Laura," he spoke easily, offering her one of the glasses of lemonade.

As disorientated by events as I was, she accepted the glass from him as if she didn't know what else to do. Then he turned to me and offered me the second glass.

"Esther," he spoke my name, as though he had not just upended the world.

We might have been in Nathaniel's living room, or in one of the New York coffee houses in Greenwich Village. Only he wasn't a Marxist, and Laura's eyes looked at me in ways that Mis' Inez's never had.

"Ladies," said Taylor raising his own glass to Laura and then to me, "To friends."

He took a drink but neither one of us followed suit.

"I believe it's impolite not to drink after a toast," he remarked reaching for a teacake.

Laura and I looked at each other again. Her gaze was now colder and harder than the glass in my hand, but this wasn't my fault I wanted to plead. She had to know what kind of man he was, how he was determined to do things differently. I pressed the glass against my lips and let drops of lemonade seep in. Even from this distance I could hear her breathing as she watched me. I kept my eyes on the floor.

"The roses really are beautiful, Laura," said Taylor. "Did you get them in Tyler?"

"Yes," she finally spoke again. "Ogden Farms. Mother swears by them."

"I'll have to get over there," he said. "I suppose they have hearty varieties. The kind that can take this summer heat."

"Yes," she replied dryly.

"Looking at these I'm reminded of the painting by Renoir, *Roses*. Have either of you ladies seen it?"

I swallowed and kept silent. Laura Spalding said no.

"What about you, Esther?" Taylor asked.

I looked up at him.

"You and your aunt spent a lot of time visiting museums in New York," he said. "Do you like the Impressionist period?"

It was one thing to talk like this when we were by ourselves, or only Spencer was here, but we couldn't be like this in front of others, and especially Laura Spalding.

"Yes-yes-sir," I answered, feeling frantic.

"Esther used to live in New York, Laura, you recall, when she was pursuing her degree, when she wasn't roaming the art world that is." He was smiling pleasantly, as though he were introducing us to each other. "I used to spend a fair amount of time in museums myself when I was in New York. It's a wonder our paths never crossed, Esther. You like museums don't you, Laura?"

He was making polite conversation as worlds were colliding.

"Of course," Laura Spalding replied almost helplessly.

"But you've never been to the Met?" Taylor continued.

"No."

I was frightened for him, and for myself, and I wanted to be invisible.

"That's right you've never been to New York, have you?" he asked her.

"I have not," she coldly informed him as if the inquiry insulted her.

"There's no place like New York," Taylor added amiably. "Wouldn't you agree, Esther?"

My head hurt, and even sitting by the window where there was a decent breeze, I was sweltering, my mother's black cotton dress sticking to my back.

"Yes-sir," I replied.

"I like Homer too," Taylor mused, returning to the discussion of art. "Winslow, I mean. Laura, I think you have one of his prints, *Snap the Whip,* over your fireplace. What I like about Homer's work is that he painted all of American life. All of her places, and all of her people."

Stealthily I dabbed at my sweating temples. Winslow Homer had even painted Negroes, and not as cartoons of buffoonery, but with dignity and grace. Aprons and all. Cotton sacks on their backs. Maybe he had taken tea with Frederick Douglas but I doubted that he had ever done so with a maid.

"This is ridiculous!" Laura at last snapped, setting her glass down so hard that a little of the lemonade splashed out onto the table. Indignantly she stood up. I stood up too, but a glance from Taylor pushed me back down instantly.

"I'm not going to sit here and put up with this…this spectacle," she vehemently declared.

"Is that what you see, Laura," asked Taylor. "A *spectacle?*"

Calmly he reached for the pitcher of lemonade and refilled his glass.

"I most certainly do!" she retorted.

He took a drink.

"What is the meaning of this, Taylor?" she demanded. "What's going on here?"

"I believe we're having a visit," he replied.

"Like this?" she shot back. "Never in my life have I--"

"That's unfortunate," he cut her off.

Just then mercifully—at least for me—the telephone rang. I sprang to my feet a second time.

"Excuse me," I said hastily and bolted towards the door.

Closing the door behind me and still carrying the glass of lemonade, I raced by the telephone in the hall and went to the one downstairs in the foyer. The caller was Mr. Walton asking for another visit.

"You can let him know I want to talk to him about coming back to work," Mr. Walton said. "Doc Mitchell tells me he's doing pretty good, and we could use that head of his around here. I expect he'll want to work at home and that's fine, with him being confined to the wheelchair and all."

And not willing to be carried down the stairs, I thought.

"Yes-sir," I said. "I'll tell him."

"Good. When's a good time to stop by?"

"After lunchtime," I replied, looking up to the closed door.

"All right I'll be by after lunch, about two o'clock."

Mr. Walton said good-bye and there was a click as the line was closed. I returned the receiver to its cradle. This was wonderful news. Going back to work was an important part of the healing process. This too meant recovery and restoration.

And I suppose you wouldn't mind clerking for me too.

Spencer could be his courier. I took a real drink of the lemonade finally. I would give Spencer my bicycle. Deciding against delivering Mr. Walton's message while my employer still had his real company, I retreated to the kitchen instead and finished the glass of lemonade at the kitchen table.

Laura Spalding couldn't help it. She had been raised a certain way too—just like me. Like Mis' Inez, and Grampa, and even Nathaniel. She had her own *fresh memories*. There were rules and rituals that the laws simply wrapped around and codified. I didn't like her but it wasn't because she adhered to convention and expected everyone else to do the same. We lived separate lives in separate worlds even if we did share the same space and time. Our circles were not supposed to converge.

Yet Taylor Payne ignored these rules. He could, he made them, or men like him did; and what you created you controlled.

I believe mine is the only opinion that counts.

Laura Spalding, Cordelia Collier, me, even Sister Wright, we all had to live by their terms and conditions. The Bible said so. But Taylor would look after Mandy. He wouldn't let Laura Spalding abuse her. And besides maybe Laura Spalding, once she was *Laura Payne*, could learn how to behave *differently* in his house too.

He just needed to give her time to adjust. I could understand how she felt. We were all unprepared for him, for what he inexplicably expected of us. There was a process for change: introductions, resistance, then acceptance, and custom. Some people needed more time, and sometimes it seemed that things were changing too quickly. From Jackie Robinson to Herman Sweatt wasn't even five years. And now Taylor Payne wanted Laura Spalding to have lemonade with his colored maid, when *never in her life* had she expected it. I almost felt sorry for her. It would not be easy to be his wife. You would never know what to expect.

After a time I heard the sound of the bedroom door slamming and I hurried to the foyer. Laura was descending the stairs. Her face wore a strange, strained expression. I didn't know what I should say to her so I kept quiet. Briefly, she stopped to look at me, her eyes narrowing as though I were a target in her sights, but because we were in fact in Taylor's house, I met her gaze steadily.

"I don't know who you think you are," she spat contemptuously. "But I know what you are. There's a name for women like you."

Then she was gone, slamming the front door behind her too. I stayed in the foyer and listened to her car drive away. I was a dark shadow to her, of no substance and no consequence. I could not possibly matter. Except that Taylor said I did.

I believe mine is the only opinion that counts.

I looked up at his closed bedroom door. I still had the message to deliver from Mr. Walton, but I turned and went back to the kitchen.

Late in the afternoon I started dinner. When a pork roast was cooking in the oven, I made my way back upstairs to Taylor's room. Still sitting by the window he was reading one of his newspapers as an extremely excited sports announcer described plays from a baseball game on the radio.

"There you are," he said as I came in.

"Do you need anything?" I asked and began to collect the dishes on the table, placing them on the tray.

"No, I'm fine," he said.

The teacakes were gone as was most of the lemonade. I doubted that that was Laura Spalding's doing unless she had flushed it all down the toilet.

"I started dinner," I said. "But you can't be too hungry with a stomach full of teacakes."

"I told you I liked them," he smiled.

"That you did," I smiled too. "Would you like to lie down for a little while before supper?"

"Yes, I think that would be good," he said folding the newspaper before laying it on the table. "I've been in this chair for quite awhile today."

"I'm sorry," I said guiltily. "Why didn't you call me?"

He smiled crookedly, removing his glasses.

"It was not a complaint, Esther."

But it should have been. I deserved it. No matter what else happened his physical needs had to come first. He depended on me. That was the agreement between us, and why I was here in the first place. Whatever else people thought of me, I knew what I was, I took care of him. Rolling over to the bureau, he switched off the baseball game, while I went to the bed and pulled back the bedspread.

"Are you all right?" he asked coming to the bed.

The question surprised me.

"Yes. Of course," I replied.

"If she said something to you," he said. "Laura I mean--"

"It's all right," I said quickly.

"No," he replied reading my face. "It's not. And you don't have to tell me if you don't want to, since I can imagine what might have been said."

"It's nothing," I assured him.

"That's right, Esther," he said. "It is nothing."

I smiled a little.

"And what it says is more about her than you," he added.

"She's very fond of you, Taylor," I said. "I don't think having me as part of your visit was what she had in mind."

"Host's prerogative," he shrugged.

"You might have prepared us."

"That's not how it works," he grinned.

"Which one of us was on trial?" I asked.

He moved closer to the bed and parked the chair.

"As you once said, I plead the Fifth," he replied.

"So it was you then?" I said, kneeling before him to set his feet on the floor and flip the rests out of the way.

He laughed.

"And by the way Mr. Prosecutor," I continued, now standing before him. "That was Mr. Walton calling. He wants to talk to you about coming back to work. You can work at home he says."

"Is that so?" asked Taylor looking up at me.

"Yes. Just I like suggested before."

Using the arms of his wheelchair he brought himself to his feet and quickly grabbed my upper arms to steady himself while I placed my hands on his waist and watched our feet so that they would not get tangled.

"You did, didn't you?" he said.

"Yes and he wants--" I stopped talking.

Taylor's left foot had moved forward followed by the right one. He had taken a step. At first the realization broke faintly in my mind, so that it was more like a feeling than a fact, as if it would be gone instantly like a startled fantasy. But when I saw him do it again, my heart, now allied with my eyes, beat wildly. *He can walk!* The words cried inside my head. *He can walk!*

"I suppose I'm ready to earn my living again," he was saying as he attempted to turn to sit on the side of the bed. Incredibly it seemed he was unaware of what he had just done. I held onto him firmly and would not let him sit down.

"What is it? What's the matter?" he asked.

"You moved your feet," I was barely able to say. "You-you walked."

"What?" he asked impatiently.

"Couldn't you tell?" incredulity gave way to thrill, "You walked, Taylor! You did!"

He wobbled a little and gripped my arms more tightly.

"Esther, please, I have to sit down," he said.

"No!" I denied him. "Do it again first."

"I can't, Esther. You-you know I can't."

"But you just did!" I insisted. "Do it again."

He stared at me, and when I took a step a back from him, fear clouded his face.

"Do it!" I repeated.

I wished for the old arrogance that had once made him self-possessed and confident in himself, even as he had been this afternoon with Laura Spalding, but the polio had left his spirit as unsteady as his legs. He didn't really trust himself anymore.

"I can't," he said again.

But he could trust me.

"Do it," I insisted. "I've got you. I won't let you fall."

He was clutching my arms so tightly that he was hurting me.

"Please, Taylor," I encouraged him. "I just saw you do it. I know you can. Please, do it again."

He looked down at his feet.

"No," I instructed. "Don't look down. Look at me. Walk to me, Taylor."

He raised his eyes to meet mine.

"I-I can't," he said faintly.

"But you can," I said. "I saw you. Move your left foot first," I coached him. "You can, Taylor. Trust me. I know you can. Try."

Straining against the paralysis, he slowly brought his left foot forward again.

"Now the right one," I said eagerly, watching for the triumph. "You can do it!"

The right foot jerked forward. I looked up into his face again and I moved back just a little more. Tiny beads of sweat covered his brow. He was crushing my arms. I held him fast with numbing fingers.

"Again," I told him. "Do it again."

Laboring he moved his feet towards me once more. They weren't perfect steps. He didn't pick up either foot, but pushed them across the carpet in nothing more than a feeble shuffle. But it was forward motion and that was all that mattered. His legs had at last remembered that they should take him where he would go. I thought of Sister Kenny and thanked God for her, for the army blankets cut into strips, and the gallons of boiling water.

In the midst of the miracle, by now I was crying, urging him forth, in order to be sure that it was really happening. We had worked so hard and waited so long. That the walking should come when neither of us were expecting it or even trying for it, made it seem that much more divine. It had come in its own time and in its own way, with nothing left for us to do but receive it. As Sister Callie had often said, *What a wonder about you, Jesus. What a wonder about you, Lord.*

When Taylor took another full step towards me, I moved into him, and spent, he leaned into my embrace, resting in my arms.

"I did it," he said after a time, with all the amazement of a man who had both shocked and proved himself to himself.

It was his victory, and it had been such a very long time coming.

"Yes, Taylor," I celebrated with him, holding onto him tightly, burying my face against his shirt. "Yes, you did! Thank the Lord!"

"I can walk, Esther," he said. "I can walk."

With one arm he continued to hold onto me. With the other hand he touched my face, lifting it so that he could look down into my eyes, his own dark eyes shining brilliantly. A smile spread out across his face, reaching upwards to his black hair in the familiar happy lines that said he was not young anymore, but tested too. I was still crying but I smiled to meet his. To be happy with him. To be thankful to God, Himself, too, and for us both.

He lowered his dark head and I felt first the brush of his lips on my face. We had shared so much. More than many people shared in their married lifetimes. In these past months our stories had woven together as if they would be one narrative. It was not so extraordinary then that we would share this moment as if we were companions. This was our circle, and in the afterglow of faith fulfilled, proximity might blur into intimacy, might make love seem natural and all together fitting and proper.

But that was the joy of the mountain top, and where we lived was on the prairie. In East Texas. At the beginning of the Big Thicket, in the South, and America. When he moved to my lips with his own, to that place and in that way that sang of Solomon, I lowered my face from his again, hiding it against the white shirt once more.

IV

By the time Doctor Mitchell arrived in the morning, Taylor was eager and able to show him what he now could do. He had made me practice with him late into the night until he was utterly exhausted and his legs would no longer bear him even with my help. By morning, however, he was rested and more excited, as he had every right to be. It was the new day we had all hoped for. Relying on my arms again, he walked once more, doing even better, and Doctor Mitchell had tears in his eyes, excusing himself to go downstairs and smoke a cigarette. No doubt Doctor Mitchell had seen his share of defeats and unhappy endings, but this time his patience and persistence was paying off. His patient, his friend, was going to recover. I was happy for them both.

When I saw the doctor out later, he told me how grateful he was to me.

"You made it happen," he said.

"God is good," I replied sincerely. "With many wonders to perform."

The doctor looked at me and put on his hat.

"Yes, Esther, I'm sure I believe that too," he agreed. "But what I've seen is your work. I think it's safe to say neither one of them could have *performed* it as you say, without you."

"We're all working hard," I modestly reminded Doctor Mitchell. "You too."

The older man nodded his head and walked out onto the porch.

"What's that Bible verse you're always quoting? Something about faith being dead without work?"

"Yes-sir," I answered him. "'But wilt thou know, oh vain man, that faith without works is dead.'"

"That's right," Doctor Mitchell said, lighting another cigarette as he got into his car. "You're a credit to your church, Esther, and you do old Isaac proud."

The next verse in Chapter Two of the Book of James read, *Was not Abraham our father justified by works, when he had offered Isaac his son upon the altar.* Grampa was our Abraham, I was the ram in exchange for Jimmy, and these were not the *works* my grandfather dreamed of.

But it was only the middle of July. There was still time for me to be able to make it right for everybody. And maybe someday Taylor and I could meet in a museum in New York, and go to one of the coffee houses where we could discuss art and the Law. Maybe we could even go for a walk on the beach and watch Jackie Robinson play for the Brooklyn Dodgers. There might indeed be many *wonders* to be performed.

For now it was not necessary to dwell on all of that. That faith was being proved in the house on Webster Road was enough. The *Summer Plague* would pass over this house, and there would be healing. Taylor could walk. And whether or not I was a *credit to my church* I was at least a *good and faithful servant*. And *servant* like *friend* could mean many things.

In the days following his first ambulation, Taylor, determined to improve quickly, wanted to try using forearm crutches. "Now son," cautioned Doctor Mitchell. "You don't want to push yourself too hard." I completely agreed but didn't say anything. It taxed every bit of Taylor's strength just to move around the room and with our support. We always kept the wheelchair close by. His right leg remained very weak and at times the knee would suddenly buckle. Doctor Mitchell wanted to have a set of parallel bars installed, but Taylor didn't think he needed them, convinced that he could rely solely on the crutches instead.

"That's exactly what I want to do," replied Taylor, slowly pulling his right foot forward, holding tightly to my arms. "Isn't that right, Sarge?"

"Yes-sir," I said looking up to his eyes and smiling.

He wasn't healed yet, but it was impressive the way he claimed the blessing. In the evenings when we worked on his therapy exercises in bed, his leg muscles would tremble with fatigue even after the hot-packs, and before the session was finished he would fall asleep, worn out from the day. Unlike the Apostle Peter, Taylor refused to fear the wind or the water, forcing himself forward only, as if he might be called to come by the Lord. I hoped this anyway.

"Rome wasn't built in a day," Doctor Mitchell grumbled under his breath.

And the temple that was Taylor's body hadn't been raised up in three days either; still it was rising all the same. We had always believed in his strength and determination, he was simply impatient to show it again.

Later as I saw him out, Doctor Mitchell repeated his concerns.

"We have to be careful, Esther," he said. "We can't let him hurt himself."

"He wants to try, Doctor," I defended Taylor's decision about the crutches. "You can't blame him for that."

"All right," the doctor shook his head dubiously. "It's against my better judgment, but I'll get him the crutches. But I want you to promise me, Esther, somebody's always got to be with him for the time being. We can't let him fall."

"Yes, Doctor," I said. "I'll do my best."

And when Taylor fully regained his independence, achieved his liberation, then I would go. Because then there could be no other reason to stay. I did not belong here. Regardless of what a few dizzy moments tried to tell me. Once I had helped him through the worst of it, the threads of our lives must begin to come apart as necessarily as they had come together. The single narrative should become two once more and we should go back to being our *separate* selves again.

He had resumed some of his legal duties, and in the mornings by the time I brought him his first cup of coffee I would usually find him already busy with papers and law books spread out over the bed around him. I worried about him but would say nothing to discourage him. He had always enjoyed work, and now with a renewed sense of physical accomplishment he was all the better for it.

Taylor got his crutches, but one of us was always with him when he used them. Eventually Taylor and Doctor Mitchell decided that his recovery could be further assisted by leg braces, a compromise which seemed to denigrate the miracle to me, like we weren't trusting God, as good as He was. We weren't trusting Sister Kenny either, and I protested when Taylor told me about the decision.

"Her manual says that it's not good," I said. "That--"

"Perhaps you could be a little less dogmatic," Taylor interjected.

We had just completed the night's last set of exercises, and I was straightening things on the night stand next to his bed.

"Being dogmatic, as you say, is what brought you this far," I informed him a little sharply.

"Don't confuse dogmatic with dogged," he said.

"I do know the difference," I returned. "I'm not ignorant."

"Esther, please," he sighed. "Do we have to quarrel about this? I really could use a little more rigidity in my legs and perhaps --"

"A little less in your maid?" I finished for him.

Catching me by the wrist, he roughly pulled me down on the bed next to him.

"Don't do that," he said.

"Do what?" I asked haughtily.

"Put words in my mouth," he said sternly. "Particularly those kinds of words. I'm going to try the braces. My right leg's not very good. Mitch believes a brace will help. How can you fault me for wanting to try it? Do you realize how long I've been confined to this house, this room? I would think you'd support me in this."

But I was afraid he was going to be like Roosevelt. That was how it began. A compromise here. A concession there. And then we would all get used to it. To a recovery that wasn't a healing. I sighed. He let go of my wrist.

"You'll have to be fitted," I said, yielding. "You'll have to go to the hospital."

"Mitch says I can be fitted here," replied Taylor.

"I see. I was wondering what we would do about the stairs," I said darkly.

"I'd like to make that a moot point some day. The braces should help."

"They're heavy, Taylor," I reminded him earnestly. "Roosevelt said so."

"I think I'm strong enough," he smiled crookedly. "Roosevelt didn't have you to put him through the paces."

"But it's worked," I said.

"I know," he replied. "Nobody knows it better. Don't worry. This is not some kind of betrayal of your sainted Sister Kenny. I'll keep doing the therapy. You're still in charge here, but I do believe the braces will help, and I think I should have some small say in my recovery too. Wouldn't you agree?"

It was his body after all. I had only claimed it. And I must relinquish it come August.

"You'll still practice without them though?" I wanted to know. "So you don't become dependent on them."

"The way I am on you?" he asked.

"You're not dependent on me," I said.

"Of course I am, Esther. More than you know. Or perhaps more than you'll admit." His smile had lost some of its mirth. "Either way, the braces can't replace you either."

They were right about the braces. Taylor could stand longer and walk farther wearing them. What they added in weight they more than made up for with support. He couldn't pick up his right foot anyway, and now at least his right leg was more stable. With the working and the walking, even within the confines of the second floor, Taylor continued to gain confidence. Sometimes there could be strength in compromise. There could be courage in concession. Success in surrendering. Anything could happen. The good as well as the bad. We merely had to be willing to try new things, to adapt and adjust, to do things *differently*.

In their last letter, Aunt Grace and Uncle Eddie had written that they wanted me to vacation with them at Niagara Falls before fall classes began at City College. Nathaniel told me that Grampa had bought a new set of matching luggage. "He won't say nothin', but I know it's for you." The NAACP had moved on to school districts to defeat segregation. Some, including Taylor, said that they could win. Times were changing. I needed to prepare myself. I could have a good future, and I would. The bright, little, brown-skinned children would surely have me as everyone wanted, including me.

Somebody's always got to be with him for the time being. We can't let him fall.

For the *time being*. That was all. Not forever. Just for now.

August 1st 1951 fell on a Wednesday. I wrote a letter to the dean of admissions stating that for personal reasons I would not be registering for the fall classes. I was grateful for their acceptance, but illness had forced me to defer until the following spring.

The following Sunday, Aunt Betty came over to Nathaniel and Connie's house, after her Sunday dinner with Uncle Perry and Grampa, explaining that she just felt like having a visit with her grandbabies, and me.

"Grace and Eddie sho' lookin' forward to you comin' back to stay with them," my aunt eventually got around to saying.

I had also written to Aunt Grace and Uncle Eddie to tell them that I wouldn't be back in August, but I hadn't mailed the letter. It was one thing to disappoint a dean of admissions, and something else to defer a family's dreams.

Nathaniel had gone outside, taking Little Evie and Nate with him, and leaving the women in the house to talk. The three of us sat in Connie's living room with our shoes off, fanning ourselves, and sipping iced tea. It had been a picture-perfect Sunday afternoon, but Aunt Betty had brought up my going back to New York. Now I was on alert, like a creature suddenly detecting pursuit. I owed them all a report, and with it there would have to be an explanation. As long as it had not been August no one had pushed to talk about it, about my leaving, not me, not them, not Taylor, but today was August 5th.

"So when you think you gon' be leavin'?" asked Aunt Betty as she fanned herself. "Now that yo' Mr. Payne can walk."

He wasn't *mine*, I thought. Connie straightened a stack of magazines on the coffee table.

"He can't walk very well," I replied not answering her question.

"Well Nathaniel said--"

"He's not strong enough to be by himself," I added quickly. "Doctor Mitchell says that somebody still has to be with him."

"All right. But that somebody don't have to be you. I mean sholey God he can hire himself another housekeeper now. You never was goin' to stay. Didn't you say Mandy Gaines wants to work for him? I mean, he don't need a nurse no more."

You're not dependent on me.

Of course I am, Esther. More than you know. Or perhaps more than you'll admit.

"I still have to help him with his therapy," I said. "Doctor Mitchell --"

"But he can walk now," interrupted Aunt Betty. "Why he still need this here therapy?"

"He has to get stronger," I explained. "He-he still needs the hot-packs."

And the range of motion exercises I also thought but chose not to say because at that moment my aunt made me think of Sister Wright, and I didn't want her to picture me touching Taylor's body.

"And you need yo' schoolin' Esther Fay," she declared flatly. "'Less'n you intendin' to keep house all yo' life. Seem like to me you done done more than anybody can ask. And what about that boy in the army? What's his name?"

"Danny Simmons," supplied Connie.

"Yeah, him," Aunt Betty wanted to know. "What about him? What he got to say about you puttin' off yo' plans for this man? He know 'bout it?"

It had been easier to tell him too, because I had not written the entire truth. Danny thought I was just working to save more money so I wouldn't have to be a burden to Aunt Grace and Uncle Eddie. Education did cost money; and what I was earning now, I was mostly saving, given that I had not seen the inside of the Woolworths in a very long time and now had little need for new things. I wore Mama's black dresses every day except Sundays.

I would have a substantial sum of money when this was over, despite having refused the raise Taylor wanted to pay me. It was the Lord's work, I had informed him. Did he really think I would take money for it? Money could not be used to measure the value of everything.

"I see," Taylor had said to me about the raise. "You're expecting some greater reward then? A diamond in your crown, perhaps?" he had asked.

No, I thought. Diamonds are for sacrifice not desire.

"'And when the chief Shepherd shall appear, ye shall receive a crown of glory that fadeth not away,'" I had taken refuge in a Bible verse.

"Where your treasure is, there will your heart be also," he had replied.

"Now where did that come from?" I had asked surprised.

"Luke, if I remember correctly."

"I'm impressed," I had smiled.

"So am I," he had said.

And Danny thought I was thrifty, writing back that I would make a fine wife. I could imagine it being to him. Perhaps we would settle in California, or Washington, D.C. Staying in McConnell County was out of the question for him. To Danny, Willie Gains was right about leaving, just wrong in the way he had done it. According to him, Willie Gaines had responsibilities, and in particular to Spencer and John Henry who needed a father to show them how to be men. "I wouldn't mind having me a boy like

Spencer," one of his letters had said. He could see himself standing-in for Willie Gaines with Mandy's boys. There was no value in telling him that at least with Spencer Taylor had assumed that place.

Spencer was having a grand time being the trusted courier between the house and Taylor's office in town. The boy took his assignments very seriously. As I might have anticipated, Taylor had bought him a new bicycle *to expedite his duties*, he said.

"He could use my old one," I had suggested in an attempt to be sensible.

"Spencer on a girl's bicycle?" Taylor had been appalled by the suggestion. "Impossible. He's a young man."

What he was was a boy with a generous benefactor, and a brand new bicycle that Nathaniel, at Taylor's request, had taken Spencer all the way to Dallas to buy. When Nathaniel and Spencer had returned with the new bicycle it had been hard to tell who had been more delighted with the purchase Spencer or Taylor, or Nathaniel for that matter.

I wondered when exactly I had learned how to divide up the truth, how to issue it out in bits and pieces in order to keep the peace, or at least avoid the trouble. Grampa had not taught me this. At least in his house he always spoke his mind. Perhaps I had learned it from watching Mama. Perhaps it was just a woman's innate skill, like darning socks and making quilts, or caring for the sick. Some things truly were best left unsaid.

Danny assumed that Taylor was the elderly bachelor I had once assumed Taylor to be. I let Danny think this, dreading the day that Mandy would be obliged to correct his wrong assumptions. Although even she didn't know the whole story. A secret was easier to keep if you never admitted it to anyone except yourself.

"I can't leave him, Aunt Betty," I said now in Connie's living room. "He depends on me."

Taylor trusted me, and I wanted him to. Outside on the front porch, Nathaniel was teaching Little Evie how to sing *Jesus Loves Me*.

"Where's that boy's family?" asked Aunt Betty. "Where his people? You mean to tell me there ain't another soul in this whole world willin' to hand him a glass of water?"

How many times had I asked the same questions, and hearing them now asked by Aunt Betty depressed me. Sometimes when I thought about Felicia and Taylor's Uncle Jason, I would get angry at them, for failing him this way so that now I was forced to fail my own family. I didn't expect very much from his uncle, but I had hoped that his sister would do differently.

At first I had imagined myself having some kind of kinship with Felicia, both of us being the younger sisters of extraordinary men. But she and I were different in a multitude of ways. There was nothing that Jimmy could have said or done that would have ever kept me away from him. Even Grampa, Grampa who had no desire to ever ride on a train again, would have gone to him. People did not always mean no even when they said it. You had to understand that. And besides even if they did mean it, and it was ridiculous, then why would you heed it? If you loved them. I had stayed with Taylor even when I hadn't known why, when the *something* was just an un-named feeling. How could there be less than that between a brother and a sister?

"I don't know about his family, Aunt Betty," I answered drearily. "Why they're the way they are, I just know that he needs me."

Little Evie's voice was sweet floating in from the porch. The Lord loved Taylor too.

"Esther, honey," said Aunt Betty. "If yo' mama was here she'd be tellin' you, you can't...can't be--"

"I 'spect they told Ananias the same thing," Connie finally spoke again.

"Who did?" asked Aunt Betty.

"Maybe it's like we talked about, Esther," Connie explained. "Maybe the Lord had to strike him down so He could work with him, and maybe you s'pose to be there to show him the way. What if the Lord s sent you to him?"

"That's foolishness, Constance Marie!" declared Aunt Betty. "The God I serve is not the author of confusion."

"But what if there ain't no confusion?" asked Connie. "Unless other folks make it? Mr. Taylor wants her to stay, and she wants to be there. It looks to me like they got a clear understandin'...between them."

Don't leave me.

I won't.

When September came, and there could be no more fantasies of mad dramatic, dashes to the train station, the 1951 fall semester at City College began without me. At least I didn't have to think of it anymore. It was a quiet resolution, a good peace. I frequently found myself humming the way Sister Callie used to do, a little gospel, a little blues, but singing just the same. I was satisfied. It was left to others to attend the lectures and improve their minds, left to others to get themselves ready *for that great day*. I had other work to do. And no, it wasn't a burden. Far from it. As always, I was the workman not ashamed. But it wasn't work either. At first yes, but no more. For nearly a year I had given this man my hands. Now he had my heart too. Except that the heart was the unnamed present, wrapped up very carefully in a smooth lustrous secret.

"Maybe I don't wanna get married, Jimmy. The Bible says some people ain't meant for it."

"Yes, you do, Baby Sister. You not plannin' on spendin' yo' whole life lookin' after Mama and Grampa, are you?"

"I can look after you too."

He laughed, but it was kind.

"That's not how it s'pose to be, Esther. What I look like keepin' you all to myself?"

"Well if we're going to build a school together I won't have time for a family."

"Now what if Grampa thought like that? Where would we be? Not even born. Family first, Esther Fay. Save room in yo' life for love."

"I love you," I declared defiantly.

Jimmy smiled.

"I love you more, Baby Sister, 'cause I'm older than you and I been at it longer."

Grabbing me by the hand he twirled me around even though there was no music.

"But I'm still gon' keep company with Hattie Mills," he grinned.

"And any other pretty girl you see," I added giggling happily.

"That's right!" Jimmy agreed. "The Bible also says a man needs him a wife. You wait

> and see, the right boy gon' come along and turn yo' head. Just like Grampa says. And I'll have to set 'im straight right quick."
>
> "About what?"
>
> "That'll be 'tween him and me."

The coming of September meant another birthday was fast approaching for me, and like a lot of women I did not want to think about it. I didn't feel old, but I was getting to be that age when people started pity a woman or at least wonder about her. On occasion someone would make their opinions known out right.

Can't see why some fine young man ain't claimed you yet.

Ol' Green ain't chased away all your suitors, have he?

It was time, Jimmy would have said, and Danny could be a real opportunity. He was the *right boy*. I just didn't love him. Maybe I didn't have to, not at first. I could grow to love him. Women were supposed to be wives and mothers, even Negro women, who raised the children of other women, were supposed to have babies of their own. Someone had to breed the servant class. Teachers, however, were often old maids. If had I been raised a Catholic, I might have become a nun and married Jesus. Assuming that they took women who had known a man's seeking, searching touch. Perhaps it was the price a professional woman paid, the price of not belonging to a man. Perhaps it was also the price of loving the wrong man. If I wanted to have a family, Danny was my best chance for it, so I couldn't risk all of that carelessly, even if it did mean keeping secrets.

And this was why a shame whispered softly. Making its case in my head. Arguing that the secret was also a deception. Insisting that disavowing a truth, or at least taking it apart, was as much as telling a lie. And God would not conspire with me in it. But I didn't know what else to do. I would just have to see it through to its inevitable end. And once it was finished, then I would get on with being whatever it was I was supposed to be. And maybe, in time, I would understand plainly which truth it was that I had been disavowing in the first place.

God was good and a mystery too. His thoughts were not our thoughts. His ways were not our ways. He had brought me here, and He would lead me away when my work was done. It must change again and become what it had been before. I wanted it to be that way again, the way it was supposed to be. Although almost like any desire it was somehow an ambivalent aspiration. And I was ashamed of myself for not being completely delighted that in the days soon to come Taylor would only need me to be his maid again.

Danny was my future. It was better to marry than to burn, the Bible said, and Danny was a good man. I used to think that the Apostle Paul, having been redeemed from his Saul of Tarsus state, had only been speaking about the fires of hell in his admonition to the Hebrews. I had dared to dismiss his urgent warnings when Danny had taken me dancing, and we had parked among the trees. Perhaps now I better understood Paul's meaning. Perhaps now I appreciated that it could be good for a man not to touch a woman, and a woman not to touch a man. When everything else but their feelings for each other was wrong, such things complicated living, and it was already hard enough.

But that was hindsight, and life did not permit us to go back. By the time we were there again, we were different. So then it was different. The past was ever a memory. Fresh or forgotten. And the Bible said that we should not think about tomorrow. Today was all we ever had. If we remembered that, we might be able to enjoy life, to revel in it, to be glad for it, and let it just be without bother.

A few days before my birthday, Taylor invited me to a dinner party.

"It isn't fair to ask it of course," he said. "Given that you will be the one preparing it, but do you think we might have dinner together to celebrate your special day?"

After everything that had happened he still remembered that it was my birthday. Standing at the window I was enjoying the morning sunshine on my face. Now that the miserable summer was waning, the sun was a friend again. I turned to him. We had never *shared* a meal. I served him, but I usually ate over the stove, standing up, and always when he wasn't present.

"I can't offer you Broadway," Taylor added. "At least not this time. But we might make it festive." He smiled. "With a few candles on a cake, and dinner for two."

Dinner for two.

I had read about them refusing to serve Josephine Baker at the Stork Club in New York City. All that she was and it was still not enough. Even her French husband could not protect her from her blackness in America. And that was in New York—the *Promise Land*. Taylor thought of Broadway, but I remembered the Stork Club. They always kept my *us* uptown, and *his* Liberty Bell was cracked ringing discordantly.

But this was his house. The small table could be cleared and set for dinner near the window. I could fold the lace table cloth to fit it, and he only had the nice dishes. Maybe I'd have a glass of wine with him too. More than my birthday, we had his recovery to celebrate. I thought I remembered seeing a bottle of champagne among the wine bottles stored on the pantry shelf. It might be fun this one time.

I began collecting his breakfast dishes. When I thought about his lips on my face then the memory was as warm to me as the sunshine, splendid and redeeming. Yet too long in the sunshine would burn you. Even my black skin.

My black skin. His white lips. What would his friends make of it if they truly knew? His family? Laura Spalding? They would make of it what so many of mine had already made of it with their speculations, and worse. It would be something degraded when all it was was forbidden, because it had come too soon to survive the history and too late to have prevented it. Matilda's misery was real and it looked back at me from Grampa's face. We shared this truth. We had made it together. It belonged to all of us.

At the end of the day, when we had said goodnight, and I was safe in the buttercup room, then I would enjoy the finer memories we made, replaying what was past to ease the rehearsing of the future, thinking of the first days in preparation for the last ones. Try as I might, the now did not anchor me so firmly, but instead sent me spinning off to where I had been with him tenderly, as well as to where we could not go together.

Perhaps Laura Spalding would come back. It was not fair to blame her for deserting him. She had been persistent in her concern for him; and a long time ago I had run away too, from Mama's grief. Someday I might be able to tell Laura Spalding that I understood what it was like not to be up to it, up to the suffering of those you loved. Because maybe Taylor would give her a second chance, now that he was getting better. Maybe for the sake of love, he would forgive her and allow her to come back to him. Maybe she was not another Sylvia.

I reasoned that it was his pride that had sent her away. After all, I was the one who had insisted that he let his friends come to see him in the first place, when he had not been ready to do so. If, as Doctor Mitchell had said, Taylor had wanted to shield even me from his plight, then how much more must he have wanted to shield Laura? When he was whole again, he would miss her and want her, and she would want him.

And if I had fallen in love with him myself in meantime, it was maybe my price to pay for having abandoned Mama after Jimmy died. Now when I really might want to stay, I would have to go. Oh well. Moses had only led them to the Promise Land. He could not himself enter in.

I looked at Taylor and smiled, to myself, and at my secret. He was seated in the Queen Anne chair. I checked to see what remained in the coffee pot, and then refilled his cup. He was the lord of manor again, I thought to myself. The handsome chair resembled a throne. The handsome man, a prince.

At times our conversations could be irregular, as if words were missing, but there was no wall between us. There was only my secret. And it wasn't between us, but rather all around us, filling up this room, engulfing us and the work we did here together. There was some measure of safety in knowing that he could never come so far as he would have to in order to reach me. I was certain that I would never go any farther to meet him. We would keep a safe distance between us. My dignity and respect would be preserved in case I did want to teach in McConnell County someday. I would be able to make Danny a fine wife. So when I answered yes to his proposition regarding dinner, it was in the full knowledge that no lasting harm could come of it, of our playing social equals. Grampa didn't need to worry, and besides he would never know.

"That would be nice, Taylor," I said. "I like chocolate cake. Mama used to make the best. I hope I can remember her recipe. Do you like chocolate cake? Will that be okay."

Suddenly I was chattering like a school girl would do to her beau. And yet the butter-cream cake was Jimmy's cake, and I could not share it with him. It was important to keep some traditions separate for when the time came that I should have to leave this place.

"It's your birthday, Esther," Taylor smiled. "You must have whatever you like."

"And champagne too?" I asked more excitedly at the prospect. "I think there's a bottle in the pantry."

He was still smiling.

"Yes, Esther," he said again. "Whatever you like."

I would be able to tell Mandy all about it. The next time I was in Dallas I would buy a bottle of champagne for us. We could drink it on a Sunday afternoon, once I came back home. It would be cumbersome to bring everything upstairs, but it would be worth it. I would set the small table as if the universe were perfect. And perhaps it would be for the one night. In this place and in this time.

"Then it's a date," I pronounced brightly as I left with the tray.

"I hope so," he said. "I'm wearing a tie."

All of the family, including Grampa, gathered at Nathaniel and Connie's house for dinner to celebrate my birthday the Sunday before. Connie had baked me a birthday cake, a white layer cake with strawberry-flavored frosting.

"I got the recipe out of one of Mama Betty's magazines," she boasted proudly.

"It's real good, baby," Nathaniel complimented his wife as he enjoyed his first forkful.

"Sho is!" Uncle Perry agreed enthusiastically as he did the same.

"Kinda sweet though, ain't it?" Grampa observed.

"It's supposed to be, Papa Isaac," Aunt Betty replied. "It's a cake, ain't it? It ain't cornbread."

"Do you like it, Esther?" Connie asked.

"I love it!" I assured her. "And thanks for skippin' all those candles too. You understand."

Everyone, except Grampa, laughed.

"Guess you would be wantin' yo' cakes out them fancy white folks' books by now," he said.

The laughter went away.

"Well," Aunt Betty followed. "They come to my mailbox same as anybody's. Connie, you did a fine job. And Esther Fay, havin' a little fancy doin's for yo' birthday is all right. You deserve it. Nathaniel, cut yo' daddy another piece. He deserve it too."

There were presents for me. A new dress from Nathaniel, Connie, and the children. A wrist watch from Uncle Perry and Aunt Betty. And from Grampa a book of poetry by Langston Hughes, entitled *Shakespeare in Harlem*, which I had already read as it was in Taylor's library.

"Thank you, Grampa," I told him sincerely, kissing him on the cheek.

"I had Grace pick it out and send it to me," he replied gruffly. "No sense in you forgettin' you got a head for books."

The afternoon of my birthday, I was in the kitchen of the house on Webster Road making another birthday cake for myself, this time carefully following Mama's recipe as I remembered it, and adding my own touches to it as Grampa had taught me. The rich aroma of the baking chocolate soon began to fill the kitchen, and the dark chocolate frosting was turning silky in the big bowl.

Taylor's kitchen was equipped with an electric mixer, but I had grown up hand-beating cakes, so I was comfortable making the frosting this way. I supposed that was the Grampa in me, this holding on to old ways because they were familiar. I paused from whipping the frosting and dipped my finger into the creamy texture to taste it. It was good. No doubt I would be sending half of it home with Spencer when he came back tomorrow. Mandy's little ones would love it. I imagined their sweet chocolate faces covered with sweet chocolate cake. Tonight, however, I would leave the cake perfect for the candles. Left up to me, there would be none at all, but Taylor had insisted.

I wondered when his birthday was. Doctor Mitchell couldn't remember. "I seem to recall it being cold when he was born," he had said when I had asked him. "So sometime in the winter I guess." I made up my mind to ask Taylor himself. If he was going to be so conscientious about everybody else's birthday then he deserved the same. He was older than I was, I was sure of it, only I couldn't decide by how much. I guessed that he was around Nathaniel's age, although perhaps a little older as there were a few gray strands throughout his thick black hair and of course the shallow lines around his dark brown eyes, especially when he smiled.

I had the radio set to a station that played big band music, and Duke Ellington's *Mood Indigo* filled the kitchen. I liked the big bands best when they played slow music and gave you a reason to dance close. After Daddy died, Mama had rarely danced. She had stayed a somber, devout widow until the day she herself had died. Maybe now she could be a wife again. I hoped they danced in heaven. Heaven was not supposed to be like that, with souls bound by the earthly contracts and commitments, but living, dead, or resurrected, Mama could be the wife to only one man, James Jerome Allen. It was a nice thought, the two of them together. Maybe they had even met Andrew and Jessica.

It had been mainly Grampa who had taught me how to dance to Ellington, and Cab Calloway and Count Basie; in the days before he had become the perfect Baptist deacon, and he still had a little *flesh* left in him. He must have made Ernestine very happy. I expected that I would grow more appropriately ascetic with age too, but I was glad that it wasn't time for that now. I liked the way the clarinet found its way around the kitchen. Cradling the mixing bowl in the bend of my arm against my body, the way I had learned, I beat the chocolate butter frosting in time with the steady downbeat, nodding my head with the music, swinging my hips from side to side, the way Mandy did, and the way Grampa had taught me when blues music had been played in his house.

I can't offer you Broadway.

I had already had it. Aunt Grace and Uncle Eddie had seen to that, taking me to the theater, and hosting candlelight dinners at their table too. Their tony New York lifestyle had made Grampa cantankerously uncertain about their religious piety and the effect on me. "Don't you forget yo' raisin'," he had warned when I had been getting ready to go that first time. But at least I had been in the company of my own kind, and not apart from him in the house of a stranger.

Grampa and I had not talked about my failure to go back to New York in August. What was there to say about it that he hadn't already said, and Grampa did not waste words. I had obviously made my choice, thinking for myself and disobeying him, but maybe Jimmy would have been proud. Maybe there was a kinship among veterans regardless of race. I could see there was something between Nathaniel and Taylor. But this was between Grampa and me, and it was ironic that each time I had forfeited the approval of the one man who was the constant in my life it had been for men who were only *just passing through* it.

In the music there was a piano bridge. Waiting for rest of the orchestra I kept time with the wooden spoon in the bowl. *Mood Indigo* had been one of Grampa's favorites, and as he had deftly turned me around the room at arm's length to the music, he had counseled me, "You keep the boys off-a you, just like this, Esther Fay. You don't need no man sweatin' on you. Make yo' hair nappy." I laughed to myself at the memory. Back then keeping the boys off of me had been an agreeable goal. It had taken becoming a woman to change that, rendering it in some cases completely *different*. What a sentinel Grampa had been for my precious virtue, until one night a soldier on leave had overcome his watchful protection. Grampa may have been wise, but Jimmy had been right.

I often wondered how it must have been for Grampa and Ernestine. Had they waited for a preacher? Grampa didn't talk very much about their courtship, except to say that Ernestine's father had been a hard man, who suspected evil in every boy that came around. "He ain't liked nobody," according to Grampa. "I was lucky to get her away from 'im." I suspected my grandfather had seen his share of juke-joints, maybe even a few jazz clubs too, during his days on the railroad, and judging from how he talked about his beloved Ernestine, I was sure that she hadn't kept him off of her for too long.

"So this is what goes on down here."

It was Taylor's voice, so I ignored the report of my imagination. It was just the memory of the kitchen conversations again. At first I had wanted him out of my space, until he had finally made me accept that it could be *our* space. It was always his house but he had shared it with me, even from the beginning when he had had a choice. Concentrating on the music, I followed the clarinet as it made its way to the end.

"I came all this way," the imagined voice spoke to me me again. "Surely you're not just going to ignore me."

This time the spoon froze in my hand and I whipped around. Taylor was standing in the kitchen doorway. He smiled at the expression on my face, at my open, speechless mouth and disbelieving eyes.

"Surprise," he said.

"Taylor?" I stammered, "How-how... did you...I mean--"

"A little practice, a little patience," he replied. "Amazing how it pays off."

He started towards the kitchen table and I practically threw the bowl down on the counter and rushed to pull out a chair for him.

"When—" I struggled, "I mean—when did you..."

I was staring at him in wonder; as if the angels had brought him to me, having borne him upon their wings. But it was the braces that had done this. The braces that had felt like doubt to me, and compromise.

"The first time was a few weeks ago," he replied releasing the braces and dropping heavily into the chair. "By yesterday I pretty much had my sea legs so to speak."

His right leg began shaking, and resting his crutches against the edge of the table he clutched the knee to hold it still.

"So maybe you're a little impressed," he baited me.

"Oh Taylor," I whispered jubilantly. "I can't believe you didn't say anything. The stairs! You came down the stairs! All by yourself!"

"More or less," he smiled. "You're not going to scold me, are you?"

I was too thrilled to see him to be worried. The right leg rested finally.

"No," I said happily. "No!"

"Good. The more I thought about it," he said, "The less I liked the idea of you having to bring our dinner party upstairs. We've had enough of this room service business. So here I am. Meeting you halfway at least, starting tonight."

"Yes here you are!" I beamed. "Just like old times. The way it used to be. Us here in the kitchen."

I went to get him a glass of water.

"No, Esther," he said, taking the glass from me. "Not exactly like old times. I want to eat in the dining room if you don't mind." He drained the glass and set it down. "The kitchen is inappropriate for champagne."

"The dining room?" I asked.

"Yes," he replied. "It's not as good as it gets, but it'll have to do. This time anyway. And it does have a nice enough ambiance, I think. I consulted an excellent decorator."

I smiled again. His confinement was finished now. He had accomplished the staircase, and we had never carried him.

"If I had only known how this was going to turn out," I said smartly, "I would have insisted that you hire a professional."

"As I recall, you did."

"But you got your way."

"Yes, wise man that I am."

Laughing I went to turn off the radio.

"Don't turn it off," he said. "Just because I can't dance doesn't mean I don't want to watch you," he grinned. "In fact I didn't know you had so much devil in you, good sister."

I realized now that he must have been watching me for some time. Embarrassed, I attempted to mask it with an air of indignation.

"What do you mean?" I demanded with my hands on my hips.

"All that side to side action," he motioned with his hand. "Hardly the cavorting of the saints, you must admit."

"Why Mr. Payne, I'm scandalized! Just scandalized, I tell you!"

"Well, my dear Sister Sergeant, I'm merely pleased. And the cake smells marvelous too. I think I'll stay here for awhile. If you don't mind a little company."

...*A little dinner conversation*...

"Mind?" I replied. "I'll even fix you a cup of coffee."

I turned to the stove to put on the pot.

"I'd rather watch you dance," he said quietly behind me.

I smiled because I wanted to. I wanted to dance for him and with him. And today he was that much closer to being able to again.

"So what kind of frosting are we having?" he asked.

"Chocolate of course," I replied.

"Mother used to give us her mixing spoon when she made frosting," he remembered aloud.

After I started the coffee, I brought the mixing bowl and spoon over to the table. Then making sure it was coated thickly in the chocolate, I offered him the wooden spoon.

"My mother used to do the same thing," I said. "It was lovely, wasn't it?"

He looked at me for a moment, and then covering my hand with his own he brought the spoon to his mouth and tasted the chocolate.

"Yes," he answered. "It was."

His hand made mine seem smaller, almost delicate. My nails were not manicured and my skin was dry because I often forgot to use the Jergens Lotion, but he seemed not to notice, and so it was all right for me to forget. He directed the spoon back to me for me to taste from it, and I did. Then I watched as he brought it back to his own mouth again. In the world beyond these walls, by law, his law, we drank from separate water fountains, but in this place we shared the same wooden spoon. I placed the spoon back in the bowl.

"How is it?" I asked him, stirring the spoon around in the bowl, mixing our mouths here at least.

"Good," he said. "Very good."

Nice. Very nice.

A tiny spot of the dark chocolate remained at the corner of his mouth, and instinctively I reached out to wipe it away. He caught my hand again in his, and pressed my fingers to his lips, seeming to savor them like the frosting. In the background Glen Miller's *Stardust* was playing. It carried me away, to drift among the stars that shone in the dark brown eyes looking up at me. I swayed a little with the rhythm, and if I could not catch my breath then it was as if I did not need to breathe.

"You will again," I murmured words from the place of some previous thought.

"Will what?" he asked me, his words warm and soft between my fingers.

"Dance."

He lowered my hand from his lips but threaded his fingers through mine.

"Such great expectations, Esther," he replied smiling crookedly.

"You will," I repeated. "And when you do, I *expect* my name to be first on your card."

"I can't think of a better inducement."

I felt him pulling me towards him and I felt myself going willingly. The distance between us was not so far to come after all. A man wasn't nothin' but a man, and a woman was a woman. Taylor slipped his hand up my arm, drawing me closer. Only Herman's barking outside made me remember myself. Who I was really. Who he was too. I glanced up at the kitchen clock on the wall. Spencer must be coming. The music finished again. I remembered the cake. I remembered how to breathe.

"I better see about the cake," I said, withdrawing my hand and myself and from him.

He smiled, faintly, ironically around the edges.

"Yes," he agreed. "The cake. We wouldn't want it to burn."

Minutes later Spencer was bursting through the backdoor and into the kitchen, with a happy Herman on his heels. The commotion they caused overwhelmed the radio broadcast and changed the mood in the room. When he saw Taylor seated at the table, Spencer stopped short, his eyes rounded by shock.

"Mr. Payne!" he exclaimed.

"Hello, Spence!" Taylor greeted the boy, laughing heartily.

Herman had bounded over to his master and Taylor rubbed his head affectionately.

"Hello to you too, Herman," he said to the dog.

Spencer looked to me.

"Aunt Esther, you said that he couldn't...that he--"

"She was just as surprised as you are," Taylor interrupted him still petting his dog. "Always remember, Spence, women like surprises." He looked across the room at me as he spoke. "It keeps them interested and a little excited."

And here we were smiling our own secrets to each other, as if we could be like Nathaniel and Connie.

"Yes-sir," said a baffled Spencer.

"And that makes them sparkle," added Taylor.

"Yes-sir," Spencer said again, still confused.

The radio's music could be heard once more, along with the thumping of Herman's tail as it struck the table leg. I turned back to the stove and shut-off the flame under the coffee pot.

"Well," Taylor said. "Come along, Spencer, let's see how well you've maintained things around here during my confinement."

"Yes-sir!" replied Spencer eagerly, much clearer about this communication.

I was anxious at the thought of Taylor undertaking so much activity, but I decided against showing it. He wanted to feel his freedom more fully. I wanted him to feel it too. If something went terribly wrong then we would just have to deal with it. He wasn't afraid. I wouldn't be either. Spencer hurried to help Taylor to his feet, taking him by the arm. Taylor paused.

"Thanks, Spence, but I can manage," he told the boy.

This time I believed he really could, but Spencer looked hurt by the rejection of his assistance. Taylor came to his feet, leaning on his crutches.

"But," he added, "I'm counting on you, Spence, to stay close to me. This is my first big test, you know."

This assignment brightened Spencer's face.

"Yes-sir!" he declared. "I'll look out for you!"

I won't let you fall.

But sometimes it was the risk you had to take, and if you fell then that might be okay too. Standing at the kitchen counter, I watched them leave, the lord, the page, and their dog, Spencer just a step ahead, carefully making sure that there were no obstacles for Taylor to overcome, and Herman, bringing up the rear.

When the cake was done I carried it out to the back porch where it could cool more quickly. I noticed the strips of wool blanket left hanging on the wringer washing machine to dry. Now that he was expanding his domain again, I prayed that Taylor's body could keep up with his will. From the back porch, I could hear Spencer's animated voice as he described how he had kept up with the yard work. I peered at them through the screen. Spencer was very serious and Taylor was very amused. The day was coming when there would be no more pain for him, when the wool strips would be discarded, and the crutches, like the wheelchair, would be given to charity. When everything would be as it should be. And I would finally be a teacher in somebody's school. Far away from here. I loved him, and each day's passing confirmed it even as it brought it to its end. Still in this moment, watching him with Spencer and Herman, in the beauty of the September day, my heart was not troubled. I would always have these memories. I would keep them fresh. Today, at this moment in time, I seemed to want for nothing. *Happy Birthday, Esther Fay Allen. Happy birthday to you.*

VI

I set the dining room table. Taylor was right; we couldn't go back; we shouldn't want to. Lot's wife had taught us that much. Life ought to be lived in a forward progression. That love had miraculously come upon you once, should be reason enough to believe that it would come upon you again. And when it did, that next time, you would know it better, even when it was still a *something* you felt just beginning to surround you.

The lace tablecloth was the color of flax, and it dressed the polished cherry wood table perfectly. I smiled to think of the fried chicken on Taylor's fine white china. He would have had it before I was certain. It was a southern tradition shared by all the sons and daughters of the Confederacy, claimed and denied. Life could be amazing. It could be *dinner for two* when you least expected it. What would champagne taste like with fried chicken I wondered.

The table set, I wandered away from my chores and went to see what Taylor and Spencer were doing and found them on front porch, where Spencer was watering the potted plants. Taylor sat on the porch swing watching him. I came out onto the porch, and Taylor invited me to sit with him.

"He's done a good job, hasn't he?" I asked, accepting the invitation.

"I had no doubt," he replied.

"Are you all right?" it was impossible for me not to ask although I did so hiding the concern.

"I'm fine, Esther."

He had been perspiring, but the exertion seemed to have done him good. I should get him another glass of water but I liked sitting next to him on the swing.

"He was very diligent," I said going back to Spencer. "Surely there is a gardener in him."

"Among other things," said Taylor.

"You know, you're his hero."

"I'm his friend."

"That too."

"That most of all."

The swing barely moved. The heat of the day had cooled into late afternoon. The shadows were longer. A few roses still bloomed on the bushes vividly. When Spencer finished watering the plants he put away the watering can, and returned to stand before us.

"Can I go exercise Herman now?" he wanted to know.

"*Exercise?*" I laughed. "What happened to just *playing* with the dog?"

"Why don't you get your books and let's go over your homework first," said Taylor. Spencer frowned.

"Oh it won't take long," Taylor consoled him. "And we'll do it out here on the porch. So we don't get too consumed and forget the time."

It was obvious that Spencer wasn't buying it at all, but obediently he went to get his books.

"Spoken like a father," I commented as Spencer disappeared into the house.

"Do you want children, Esther?" asked Taylor.

My mind flashed back to kind-faced white women, whose homes I had cleaned and whose children I had cared for diffidently, while they had pronounced me *mother material*. That recollection bumped into an image of Taylor tenderly holding my baby in his arms as he had held Nate. Sister Alberta wanted to know when I was going to give Grampa *a little doll-baby to dote on*.

Did my life really look so barren to all of them? It didn't feel barren. And if I married Danny, I would be far away from here when I had children. My babies might be as old as Spencer when Taylor saw them for the first time. I supposed time was setting the rules even as we were sitting here on this swing. Danny was getting too old too. But then again men could make babies long after women could no longer carry them.

I imagined Taylor's children. Perhaps Laura Spalding would be their mother, if she came back. They might all come back now that the worst was over. At least I had a place on his dance card. And just where would that dance be? At Ray's Café? Such foolishness. Grampa was right. I had no place. I hoped Taylor's children would have his black hair and dark eyes. They should be tall like him too, with odd unidentifiable accents when they spoke, but that would mean that he could not raise them here.

"Yes," I responded to Taylor's question, and then asked my own, "Do you?"

"I didn't always," he replied. "But yes. Now, I think it would be nice."

Nathaniel said that war made some men think more clearly, made them get things—important things—straight. Perhaps sickness did that too. Suddenly I was melancholy or nostalgic or something, and I stood up so that Spencer could take my place on the swing.

"What is it?" asked Taylor.

"Where is that boy?" I replied. "Can't he find his books?"

"You don't like my company?"

What I did not like was talking about the children he was going to have with another woman.

"I have to finish cooking," I said. "Spencer!" I called as I went back in the house. "What are you doing? Mr. Payne is waiting."

By the time I finished frying the chicken and placed it in the oven to keep warm, Spencer's homework was finished, and he was riding his new bicycle home. Herman had found himself a nice shady place outside and was dozing, and Taylor had returned to the kitchen and was seated at the table again.

"Smells very good in here," he remarked.

"Like a proper southern kitchen," I teased, having put away the future images of children, mine and his.

"Okay," he allowed. "But I'd be willing to bet a Yankee kitchen or two has seen a fried chicken."

"Impossible!" I laughed.

"People migrate, Esther. And bring their customs and their cooking with them."

I thought of Uncle Eddie and his little escapes from Aunt Grace's fancy meals.

"Maybe," I conceded as much. "But what would you know about it?"

"More than you give me credit for, I think."

I walked to the backdoor to let the breeze blow away the heat of standing over a frying pan.

"You're about to make me think this is really your home, Mr. Payne," I said.

"It is, Esther," he replied. "I grew up here, remember?"

I came back into the kitchen.

"Is twelve years enough time to make you a son of the South? Especially when your mother was a Yankee."

"Let's see," he said laughing lightly. "To Uncle Jason I was never good enough for Cambridge, and you deem me unfit for McConnell County. I guess that really does make me one of those pilgrims you sing about in your gospel songs. A wayfaring soul with no place or people to call my own."

"You do have a sister," I reminded him.

"I suppose I do, don't I?"

Why did I seem to have more conviction about that than he did?

"You ought to call her, Taylor," I took this opportunity to tell him again. "I know she would love to hear your voice."

"You know that, do you?" he asked.

"Well why wouldn't she?" I insisted.

"Why wouldn't she indeed?" he smiled crookedly.

"What?" I asked. "Don't you think so?"

"We're not like that, Esther."

"Like what? Close? She's your sister, Taylor, your family. You keep up with their birthdays, and her wedding anniversary. I saw the dates in your address book. They must be important."

"When did you read my address book?" he asked intrigued.

"When you were sick," I said defensively. "I thought she should know."

He laughed again, dryly, but he wasn't angry though perhaps he had a right to be.

"But I didn't call her," I quickly stressed.

"Well at least you respected my wishes, if not my privacy," he said.

"I thought you needed her, Taylor, and you were being so stubborn about it."

He smiled again.

"I'm not close to Felicia, Esther," he explained patiently. "It's difficult for you to accept that, as important as your family is to you, but it is true."

"That's a very hard thing to say," I replied.

"Not really. But I don't mean it to be unkind if it does sound that way."

"If I were your sister," I argued. "I'd be hurt by what you're saying, how you're treating her."

"But then you're not my sister, are you?" He paused. "What you are is my friend. A friend of whom I've asked much. As though you were my family. But you yourself said it, I don't have much choice."

"I'm glad I was here," I told him, embarrassed by his assessment.

"*Was?*" he smiled obliquely.

"*Am,*" I corrected myself.

"Me too," he said. "And I'm pretty sure I'm not ready to fly solo yet. Even though August has come and gone."

"Taylor--" I started to assure him.

"Yes, Esther," he interrupted me, his tone now somber. "I remembered you were supposed to go. I remembered it every single day. All thirty-one of them. And into September. You might have relieved me a little, once you knew you weren't leaving. I could have used a bit of assurance. I'm not much of a man of faith as you know."

"But you did have the evidence," I reminded him, smiling a little.

"It would have been nice to have it beyond a reasonable doubt," he replied.

"I didn't want to argue about it."

"Because I wouldn't want you to go?"

"Because you would have sent me away."

"How could I?"

"You're a man. You do foolish things."

Now he smiled again too, but it was enigmatic, shadowed.

"What your family must think of me," he continued. "Keeping you here. Day after day. It's too much, whether you will ever say so or not."

"No, Taylor," I said sitting down at the table with him. "I want to be here."

"It's not like you to leave a job half-done, is it?" he replied. "And it won't be the first time I've disrupted a woman's plans."

Was he talking about Sylvia? Or maybe Laura?

"You're doing so well, Taylor," I said squeezing his wrist quickly, comfortingly. "You'll see, in no time at all--"

"I'll be as good as new," he finished.

"Yes!" I said ardently.

"Maybe," he replied, and at least the crooked smile returned. "At least I'm not lying in my own excrement anymore."

"Taylor," I said quietly, dropping my head.

"That embarrasses you, doesn't it?" he asked. "Yet you didn't falter. Not one time."

I looked up at him again. *Not one time* that I had let him see anyway.

"Felicia's not half the woman you are," he said.

But she had never needed to be, I thought. Because whatever she was, the world said she was enough, the right amount. Perfection.

"A man can count on you, Esther," Taylor said. "Even the *foolish* ones know that."

A man can lean on you, Esther Fay.

"Because I'm strong," I said, wishing for beauty instead.

"Yes," Taylor agreed, also meaning it to be a compliment.

But once again it sounded like a consolation prize, not a crown.

"I rely on your strength, Esther," he was saying.

I should be satisfied with that, honored even.

"You're strong too," I replied. "Stronger than you give yourself credit for."

"Maybe," he allowed. "But I need you."

I was quiet, and letting go of his wrist, clasped my hands together in my lap.

"When I was a boy," he said. "My father used to take me hunting. Sometimes we would use traps. You know the kind that clamp down on an animal's foot to hold it. When we came back we would find the rabbit or the fox had chewed off its own leg to get itself free. All there would be is this bloody paw left behind. Nothing else. That's what it felt like at first. Like I wanted to chew off my legs and leave them behind. Then maybe I could at least crawl. I don't know...is that strength or desperation?"

I didn't answer.

"In either case," Taylor continued. "The Sister-Sergeant wasn't having it. You make me work, Esther. You push me so hard sometimes I think you're going to tear me apart. In the beginning about a hundred times a day I wanted to tell you to get the hell out of my house. And if my useless legs meant that much to you, then you could damn well take them with you. You don't know what it's like, Esther, to loathe a part of yourself that much. To be helpless. Watching your body wither and turn grotesque."

I listened, remembering how detached he had been from the therapy in the beginning, how distant he had seemed even with his body in my hands. How he had not tried, or said thank-you, or asked for help. Maybe that was how it had been for Mama too. Maybe she had been striving to free herself while all the rest of us had been holding on, a collection of traps clamping down on her. Maybe it had not been fair, our asking her not to die. At some point life could become hopeless. And sometimes you might have to lose it to be free. Or at least surrender it.

"You weren't grotesque, Taylor," I said quietly.

He smiled faintly again.

"*Aren't,*" I quickly corrected in case he had misunderstood. "You *aren't* grotesque."

"But I am a little withered," he laughed at his own expense.

Nevertheless the humor was pleasant enough for me to relax a little.

"So that's why you didn't want Felicia to come?" I asked again after a time. "Because... you-you didn't want her to see you that way?"

"How long have you carried that question around?" he asked.

"From the beginning," I answered honestly. "I've never understood it. It's what family is supposed to do. I would have come."

"We've already established that, haven't we?" he replied. "That's the way you are. A very kind and generous missionary."

"Taylor," I said, frustrated. "Please don't patronize me. You know what I mean. Why didn't you want Felicia to know? And does she even know now? Why in heaven's name would you keep your sister away from you? I can understand about your uncle. But you love Felicia. She loves you."

"We have an understanding, my sister and I."

I didn't say anything.

"I leave her to her life," he added. "And she leaves me to mine."

"Oh Taylor, what does that mean?" I demanded. "You live here. She lives there. All right, so she doesn't like East Texas. Aunt Grace and Uncle Eddie don't like it either. But they would come if something happened to one of us. And she would have gotten over it, seeing you so sick I mean. You just never gave her a chance."

"You don't know her, Esther. She's different. I told you she was young when we went to live with our uncle. He really raised her."

"But why do you make her sound so cold, Taylor?" I asked. "Whatever happened between you can be worked out. If you don't shut her out. I *do* know what's that's like. It hurts. It hurts very much."

"Believe me, it's fine this way. All families are not the same, Esther," he said again.

I was almost ready to tell him about Mama; about how sick she had been, about how rejected and helpless she had made me feel, and about how I had always come second to Jimmy.

"Family is family," I settled for saying.

"Is it?" he asked. "Maybe not. Perhaps you're the one with the more privileged point of view in this instance."

"No, Taylor."

"Yes, Esther. Blood's not always the tie that binds best. Sometimes our choices separate us. Even from our families. You learn to accept it, and live with the consequences. You make your own way in the world."

"Even if that means being alone?"

What kind of sense did that make? We weren't made to go through this world alone. Without God. Without family. Why was he so obstinate about these things?

"Yes," he replied. "Sometimes."

"No," I insisted. "Nothing should come between you and your family. You are her brother, and this is her home too."

"At least it's *my* home anyway."

"Taylor, after all--"

"She was born here?"

"Well yes."

"Is that what makes it home? Being born in a place? Didn't you just say that twelve years was not enough to make me a son of the South?"

"I was trying to make a joke, Taylor."

"Maybe. But perhaps what you were saying is that home is a feeling. Not an address, not an event. It's the feeling we have for a place, for a person. A connection."

"And you don't think she has that kind of feeling?"

"I know she doesn't. Not to this town. Or this house. There's nothing for her here."

"You're here."

"And not to me either."

They could fix that.

"Your parents are buried here," I persisted. "She must feel connected to your mother and father."

"She blames our father for that," he replied.

"For what?" I asked.

"That they are *buried* here," he said. "That they are dead."

"I thought your people died in a car wreck. How is that your father's fault? I don't' understand."

"He brought her here. My mother, I mean. He made her live here, in this 'backward' place. According to Uncle Jason, my mother was a foolish girl, and my father exploited her naïveté."

I thought about the happy couple captured eternally in their mutual bliss over the fireplace. How could anyone have doubted their affection and devotion? It was so obvious. In all of what Taylor had ever told me about them there was this constant theme of their happiness. Even Mr. Leon had said so.

"*Foolish?*" I replied. "They loved each other."

"And you believe love is enough," said Taylor.

"Yes," I replied.

He smiled as though he appreciated the answer.

"Do you know what a Bohemian is?" he asked.

"Yes," I answered. "I know the word."

"But do you know the type?"

"Like the people who live in Greenwich Village? Yes, I attended classes with some of them."

"And went to the coffee houses too, right?"

"Sometimes, yes."

"What did you think of them?"

I remembered them being artists, and actors, musicians and Marxists, men who talked about revolution and women who did too. They were people for whom the institutions of society were cumbersome and even evil. They were daring and dangerous, and willing to be free about everything. Was that his sister? Was Felicia a Bohemian? Surely not, not if she was their uncle's favorite.

"Everybody seemed nice," I said.

"But I'd imagine a little wild for you."

I shrugged.

"What do you think your grandfather would think of them?" Taylor asked.

"He wouldn't understand them," I said.

"Uncle Jason doesn't *understand* them either."

"The ones I knew didn't much approve of going to church," I said. "My grandfather would have a hard time with that. I didn't really fit in with them either."

"What if I told you my mother was a Bohemian?" asked Taylor.

"Jessica—I mean Mrs. Payne? Not your sister?"

"Felicia?" laughed Taylor. "No, not Felicia. Never Felicia. But yes, my mother."

"But-but she's from Cambridge."

"Well it's not like New York has a monopoly on the type," he laughed again. "When she was nineteen, she ran away to New York to become an actress, and wound up in Greenwich Village for a time. My father followed her there."

"And brought her back to Cambridge?"

"No. By that time he had graduated from law school and so he married her, and brought her here, to McConnell County."

"Well he did the right thing by her, didn't he?" I said. "I mean rescuing her from her wild friends."

Taylor smiled.

"Yes, you could say it was the *right thing*. After all she hadn't taken Broadway by storm by any stretch of the imagination. Although she might have. In time. She was very talented."

She was very beautiful too, I thought, judging by the wedding portrait.

"Anyway," Taylor continued. "My father wasn't the kind of man that Uncle Jason had in mind for his little sister, even if she was a bit wild. And McConnell County wasn't the kind of address."

"People admired your father, Taylor."

"In McConnell County," he said. "It's like that old saying, a big fish in a little pond."

"Well that's just snobbery," I charged.

"Ignorance is ignorance, Esther. Call it snobbery. Call it bigotry."

"It's not the same thing."

"Of course it is."

"Taylor, your father was a good and decent man. Everybody says so, Doctor Mitchell, Mr. Leon."

This earned me another one of his crooked smiles.

"Well I see somebody's been checking my references?"

"They told me about your family, yes. What kind of people your mama and daddy were. They loved each other, and they loved you and Felicia. Mr. Leon said that you were very happy. What else could possibly matter?"

Taylor reached for his crutches.

"I better go up stairs and get dressed," he said, changing the subject. "It takes me a little longer these days."

"I still don't understand about what happened between you and your sister," I persevered. "If it's because you stood up for your father, then you are right and she is wrong."

"Because that's what the Bible says?" he smiled patiently.

"Because you loved him. And your mother loved him. That's all that matters. Your uncle had no right saying anything bad about him, to you or your sister."

"But it was his right," Taylor defended his unkind uncle. "My mother was his sister, and he believed, believes, that my father came between them. I'm not that sure I'd be any different in a similar circumstance."

Of course he would be different. He wasn't mean. I had always known that, even during his worst days, when he might have banished me or hit Doctor Mitchell in the head with a coffee cup.

"It was your mother's choice, Taylor," I argued. "She followed her heart. You said yourself that she loved this place. And her leaving Cambridge wasn't your father's doing."

"He simply sealed the deal, so to speak," replied Taylor. "So there could be no going back. That's the way it is sometimes, Esther. One heart is happy and another one breaks, all over the same thing. That's the truth about choices. It's chance. Somebody wins. Somebody loses. You always know that going in."

And sometimes somebody was betrayed I thought thinking of Sylvia and her *better offer*. Would he defend her too?

"Sometimes it turns out perfectly," I decided to say. "I'm glad your mother did what was right for herself."

Jimmy would have been proud I could have told him, but didn't.

"Otherwise we wouldn't be here, now would we?" he smiled again.

Well, I would be, I thought. His mother's choices had nothing to do with me. I just wouldn't be in this house, seated at this kitchen table, and feeling attached to the wrong man. So maybe for that much Uncle Jason had been right all along. Maybe he was my proper ally even if I didn't like his cause. If he had been better able to control his little sister then Grampa would have remained better able to control me. And if Jimmy had lived, there would have been no need for control at all. I would have been with him.

"That's right," I now said emphatically. "Thank the Lord."

For what, I could only partly be sure.

"Yes," agreed Taylor. "I suppose we should thank Him."

"I know that's just an expression to you, Taylor, but I do give thanks for people like your mother and father," I said seriously. "Your uncle had no right to talk bad about your father. That was wrong."

"No hard feelings, Esther. What's done is done."

"It can be undone too," I countered. "You're always wanting to change things, why not change that?"

"You do like your happy endings, don't you?" he teased me.

"I'm not ashamed of that," I said. "What's wrong with hoping for the best, and working for it?"

The Bible said faith without works was dead, I was thinking, but I didn't say that either. He would think that I was being too religious.

"Nothing," he answered my last question. "Maybe you can teach me a thing or two about it. I wouldn't mind being a little hopeful."

"You are going to get well, Taylor," I said, believing that he was referring to the polio. "You are. Then you can concentrate on making things right with your sister."

"One crusade at a time is that it?" he teased me again.

"Don't make so many jokes," I chided him.

"But I like to hear you laugh."

"Then make up with your family."

"I'll say this for you, you are tenacious."

"When the prize is worthy," I now smiled back at him.

"Touché, Madame," he smiled again too. "But seriously, can we change the subject? I've had enough of confession for one day, I think."

"Is that what this was? You making a confession?"

"Maybe."

A man can talk about himself with you.

"I'm a Baptist, Taylor. We believe you can talk to Jesus directly."

"I think I'd prefer to use an agent."

"An intercessor," I corrected him.

"Okay," he accepted.

"You don't need one," I said.

"But I want one."

"Well if you mean me, then you might as well know I'm not ordained."

"That's just one woman's opinion."

I laughed out loud and got up from the table.

"Aha--made you laugh!" he declared triumphantly.

"Taylor Payne, I'm gettin' away from you right now before the Lord strikes you down for blasphemy!"

"As long as you're around to pick me up, I think I'll be fine."

But I wasn't his savior. Saviors were perfect and promised to be with you always. And I wasn't perfect and I couldn't make that kind of promise. Human beings failed. We failed each other all the time. I thought I should tell him that. But then again he should be able to believe in something other than the Law. Maybe this was the real work that God had brought me here to do.

The end would surely come, but then I would always have these moments to wrap around myself and remember how it was to be close to this man. Whenever I read fairytales to children, whether they were my own children or belonged to others, I would have these days to think about, treasuring the secret of almost having one fairytale for true. A romantic fairytale. Of lords and ladies. And knights in shining armor. Who fell from their horses and reached out to women who had no titles at all, but who loved them anyway. As much as they dared. Knowing that they must let them go at an appointed time. When the story was done. But I was joyful anyway. Everything had a purpose under heaven. If my heart was troubled, then it was also excited too, and thrilled, and enchanted.

"So when are we going to have dinner?" asked Taylor. "I could use a party."

"Well, if somebody would just let me finish cooking," I replied.

"And might you wear something a little more festive?" he ventured with a charming little grin. "You know, something other than your...uh...rather dreary uniform."

I stiffened slightly.

"Not that black doesn't become you," he hastened to add. "It' just that...well--"

"Well what?" I pretended to demand an answer, hands on my hips.

"Well, I'd like to see you in a little color," he said. "I mean you do wear black very well, but--"

"Are you actually suggesting that I *dress* for dinner? For fried chicken no less?" I laughed again.

"Yes, that's precisely what I'm suggesting," he told me. "I'm going to. Like I said a tie and everything. It doesn't have to be fancy. But yes, it ought to be pretty. We're having champagne, remember?"

Yes, I remembered. I knew I would always remember.

"I don't own anything fancy or pretty!" I declared.

"Now you forget I've seen you in your Sunday best, Miss Allen."

"But it was my *Sunday* best, Mr. Payne."

"I don't think He'd mind too much if you wore it for me too," he said pointing up at the ceiling. "Just this once. And something a little less buttoned-up. Something, you know, a little more secular."

"More Saturday night as opposed to Sunday morning, is that what you mean?"

He grinned again.

"I would remind you that it is neither," I haughtily informed him.

"But you'll do it for me, won't you?" he asked, coming to his feet. "You can keep your hair up, but wear a dress with a little less collar."

Yes. For him I might try to do anything.

"Sir," I laughed. "Just who do you think you are? The lord of the manor? My gentleman caller?"

"Yes," he replied. "Tonight, I am both."

VII

When I finished cooking I went upstairs to get ready. Passing his closed bedroom door, I was tempted to see if Taylor was all right, but he had made it very clear, tonight I was not *on duty*, as he put it. Now in the second bathroom I stood in front of the mirror examining the plain black sack of a work dress that I usually wore.

> Mr. Miller's store telephone rang again, setting free bunches of butterflies in my stomach. "Esther Fay!" Mr. Miller called to me from inside the store. "Yo' call come through!" Almost before the words were out of his mouth, the big cow bell was clanging and the screen door was banging behind me.
>
> "Jimmy!" I cried happily into the mouthpiece, pressing the earpiece against my ear to hear every word he would say. "I just knew you'd call! I was waitin' all day. Grampa said you'd be too busy, but I told him you promised, and--"
>
> "Happy Birthday, Baby Sister!" came Jimmy's voice over the crackling line. "You doin' all right?"
>
> "I'm all right, Jimmy. And Mama and Grampa. But we miss you! We miss you so much! Mama would-a been here too but we didn't know what time--"
>
> "I called for you, Esther. It's yo' birthday."
>
> "Are you all right, Jimmy? Are they treatin' you all right?"
>
> "I'm fine, Baby Sister," Jimmy laughed. "Just bald-headed as Grampa that's all."
>
> "It'll grow back," I attempted to console him, and Jimmy laughed again.

> "'Course it will. What you think about yo' big brother sportin' a mustache? Might make me look like Clark Gable."
>
> "You'd look wonderful!" I exclaimed eagerly. "Grampa hung yo' army picture on the wall right next to Grandma Ernestine's. He's so proud of you, Jimmy."
>
> "Well I'm proud of you, Baby Sister."
>
> "I love you, Jimmy."
>
> "I love you too."
>
> "Nathaniel got to come home for leave. Do you think--"
>
> "Can't say right now, but we'll see... Now you know we can't talk long."
>
> "I know."
>
> "Besides, it makes lonesome for you...Say hi to everybody for me."
>
> "I will."
>
> "And make sure you have some fun today."
>
> "I will."
>
> "I'll be writin' real soon."
>
> "Be careful, Jimmy. Please be careful."
>
> "I will. Now go put on a pretty dress. It's your birthday."

I decided to wear my new dress, the one that Nathaniel and Connie had given to me. It was a dark blue dress with a matching belt and a shallow scoop neckline. I liked that my first time to wear it would be for Taylor. Nathaniel and Connie seemed to understand my being here, and Nathaniel and Taylor were even becoming friends in their own right.

Quickly I bathed in cool water and smoothed rose-scented lotion all over my body. Taylor liked roses. Back in the buttercup room, I combed my hair. Regretting that there wasn't time to curl it for the evening, I tried to soften the severe tight bun by adding a side part and combing a little more hair forward to frame my face. Men liked for women to wear their hair down in curls. Danny had run his hands through mine, sometimes grabbing a bunch of it to tilt my head back before he kissed me hotly on the mouth.

Where was Danny tonight? What was he doing? Writing me some affectionately assuming letter, while I fussed over how I looked for another man? Still it was only one night. It wouldn't last. It wouldn't change things. It couldn't make a difference. Danny would never know. No one would. Eventually I would learn to forget about it myself.

I put on a little lipstick, and when I finally zipped up the blue dress I stood examining myself in the dresser mirror. I made a decent presentation. I might indeed have *fun* tonight. It had been almost a year since I had first come to this house, so tonight was kind of an anniversary of that too. Almost twelve months of getting to know him and his ways, and his house, and his life. Twelve months of learning to care about him and then for him. And now here I was dressing for him too. It was ridiculous, but it was also just one night. It was my birthday. He was so much better. It was a night worthy of commemoration. We had this year between us.

Yet you didn't falter. Not one time.

I wished that that were true. I wished that I had never doubted, never feared, never failed. But I had almost given up many times. I had just always tried again. Sometimes that was all it took. Another chance to get it right for each time that you got it wrong. Falling down and getting up. Sometimes with help. Felicia Richmond deserved a second chance too. No matter what she had done, or hadn't done. Taylor couldn't just give up on her, on his family, or what was left of it.

His mother had been a Bohemian, an actress, who had run away to New York. A rebel, ignoring family tradition and social convention like it was nobody's business but her own. Taylor might have chosen his father's profession, but he must have his mother's spirit. Back downstairs, I went to look at the wedding portrait again. His parents must have loved each other. They must have been very happy. Like Mr. Leon said. Like Mama and Daddy. And Grampa and Ernestine. But why was it that *happily ever after* seldom seemed to last a long time? Were there no fairytales for old-age?

I set the food on the table and waited for Taylor to come down. According to what I read and to Doctor Mitchell's assessments, Taylor's recovery was progressing at a good pace. Some patients spent more than a year in the hospital and still couldn't walk. Sister Kenny's methods were excellent, but a shared commitment to hard work and perseverance, and yes even to each other, was perhaps what made these methods miraculous. Tonight marked the beginning of the end. Soon he wouldn't need me anymore. But that was the goal.

Maybe Felicia could finally come for a visit at Thanksgiving this year. Perhaps by then he might only require a cane. And if not for Thanksgiving then certainly for Christmas. They could have a family reunion. That was what we would work for. And tonight was all a part of it, marking the returning and the leaving.

When Taylor came downstairs, he was wearing a black dinner jacket with satin lapels, and at his neck was a black silk bow tie. Were it not for the crutches, you might think he was perfect. Reminded of William Powell and William Holden, I thought he was anyway.

"I see you approve," he said as I gazed at him.

"Do you?" I asked timidly, modestly twirling around in front of him.

"Absolutely," he smiled. "Absolutely."

"It's not silk or satin," I apologized. "But it's brand new. Nathaniel and Connie gave it to me for my birthday."

"I'll send them a thank-you note," he said.

As we sat down to dinner, Taylor held my chair for me. Taking my seat I looked up at him. This was all impossible.

"Thank-you," I said softly.

"Thank-you," he replied.

Enthralled I watched him pop the cork on the chilled champagne bottle and fill our glasses.

"To friendship," he repeated the theme of the last toast we had shared, the one with Laura Spalding in his bedroom. "And to birthdays," he added.

This time I raised my glass willingly and he tapped it lightly with his. Daintily I took a sip, the bubbles tickling my nose.

"Does it meet with your approval?" he asked.

"Absolutely," I replied, beaming.

The chicken however was harder to deal with. Despite all the church suppers I had attended, *never in my life* had I eaten fried chicken with a knife and fork. Or eaten dinner with a white man. I cut at the chicken awkwardly at first, regretting that I had not chosen some kind of boneless roast for these firsts as mundane and monumental as they were. Taylor seemed not to notice my struggles, as he filled the conversation between us with interesting chatter and generous compliments for the meal. Having slipped his crutches out of sight under the table, he sat comfortably as if it was the most natural thing in the world for us to be sharing this little *dinner for two*. And once I got used to leaving meat on the bones, I became comfortable too, and the eating of fried chicken in this genteel way went well enough for a country girl from the dark side of town. I would have something to show Aunt Grace when I went back to Harlem.

Besides I hardly tasted the food and the champagne anyway. It was all just something to do with my hands, between the words I replied and the time I was listening. It kept me grounded when I might have otherwise been swept away. Determined to be bright and gay, I acted out the parts in movies I had seen with Carole Lombard and Myrna Loy, ensuring that I used the right tone, the right style, the right fork, as the champagne pranced along my veins. Tonight I myself was more Suzette Harbin than Hattie McDaniel, and I was having fun.

When we finished dinner and before the cake, Taylor said that we should adjourn to the study.

"Leave the dishes," he told me as I began to clear the table.

But I needed to collect myself and so insisted that I should at least take them to the kitchen.

"I can't have people thinking that I don't take proper care of your house," I excused myself.

"Fine," he replied impatiently. "Fret about your references then, but don't take long. This party is not over yet."

"Well of course not," I said brightly. "We do have cake."

"Among other things," he said. "So don't make me come after you, because now I can you know."

"Yes-sir," I laughed.

He could indeed.

"And bring the rest of the champagne too," he instructed.

Efficient with my duties and my emotions while in the kitchen, I soon reappeared in the doorway to the study with a tray, bearing the cake and the remaining champagne. Taylor was seated on the couch, Herman near his feet. He had turned on the radio and there was orchestra music playing in the background.

"And where are the candles?" he wanted to know as I set the tray on the coffee table in front of him.

I reached into my pocket for the three candles to show him.

"You're awfully tall I think for three years old," he observed.

"It's enough," I replied.

"All right then," he smiled. "It is impolite to ask a lady her age."

"Thank you for that," I said sticking the three candles into the cake.

I went to retrieve his pipe lighter from his desk in order to light them.

"Let me," he said taking the lighter. "You come and sit down beside me."

"Do you know that I've been working for you for almost a year?" I said as he was lighting the candles.

"You better blow out your candles," he advised. "They melt faster than you do."

I looked at him.

"Blow," he directed me.

I blew out the candles easily for which he applauded me. Herman looked up.

"What did you wish for?" asked Taylor.

What did I wish for, I wondered myself.

"It won't come true if I tell you," I said.

"You want to know what I wish?" he asked.

I was sure that I already did. I wished it for him too.

"It's not your birthday," I said smiling at him.

"Oh right," he conceded. "Next year then."

When I wouldn't be here. But the crutches wouldn't be here either. And that was what I wished for. For the crutches to be gone.

"Taylor, when is your birthday anyway?" I asked.

"What? You didn't discover that with all your snooping around?" he grinned.

"Taylor--"

"I know, I know, you were on a mission."

"You know that I would never--"

"Yes, I'm certain of it," he said. "Now, before the cake, I want to give you your present."

"Present?"

"Ah, that's the secret to erasing your frown," he teased me yet again. "Mention the word present."

"You shouldn't have gotten me...a-a present," I worried.

"Too late," he said reaching into an inside coat pocket and bringing out a red velvet case.

It was a jewelry case. I looked at him. The silk scarf was still safely packed away in its original store box. It was too pretty, too precious, and now there would be something else to treasure like that. Something else too pretty and too precious to wear. He placed the case on the table next to the uncut cake.

"But first I want to make another toast," he announced, reaching for a tattered Bible that was on the table next to the sofa.

He turned to a marked page.

"Surely *you* didn't put all that wear and tear on it, did you?" I said making reference to the Bible's condition.

"As a matter of fact, no," he replied. "It belonged to my father."

It was nice to think of him having his father's Bible, nice to think of his father having a Bible in the first place. He adored his father. There was hope for him yet.

"You don't have one of your own?" I asked.

"No," he said. "Now listen. I want to get this right."

He peered at the page.

"Maybe you need your reading glasses," I suggested, taking my turn to tease.

"For the sake of the occasion I will ignore that comment," he said without taking his eyes off the page.

I smiled.

"I'm sorry," I said, and prepared to respectfully hear the Word even if it was about to come from a reader who did not revere it.

Taylor closed the Bible and returned it to the table. Then he refilled our glasses, handing mine to me before raising his own. "'Who can find a virtuous woman?'" he began reciting the familiar passage. "'For her price is far above rubies.'" His dark eyes were their most brilliant. "I have found such a woman," he answered the question. "To you, Miss Allen, a woman who dresses herself in strength and honor, and opens her mouth in wisdom and kindness. A woman worthy of praise."

When the prize is worthy.

No one had ever toasted me before. Not for my birthday, or my graduation, or my character. I was euphoric and flustered at the same time. My heart beat rapidly. My face felt hot. It was a lovely, wonderful, unimaginable thing.

"Happy Birthday," he finished, tapping his glass to mine before taking a drink.

I was still and silent, gazing at him, too amazed to do anything at all.

"You know," he said after a time, a warm smile filling his face. "I don't know what it is about southern belles, why you will refuse to drink after a toast."

Swiftly I sipped the champagne which once again I hardly tasted.

"And aren't you supposed to say amen, or something," he asked mischievously.

"Thank you, Taylor," I managed to get out.

"I suppose that'll have to do. Now open your present," he nodded towards the jewelry case.

I looked down at the velvet box and set down my glass before picking it up. Nervously I looked at him again.

"Go on," he told me. "Open it."

In the case there was an exquisite pearl necklace.

"Oh!" I heard myself cry and my first thought was to close the case again.

I couldn't have this. He couldn't give it to me.

"You like it then?" Taylor asked. "Of course they're not rubies, but I had to consider what you might actually wear. And it seems to me that pearls are dignified and subtle enough to suit you. Am I right?"

"They're--they're beautiful," I whispered.

"I'm glad you like them," he smiled.

"But Taylor," I said looking into his eyes. "I can't....I mean it's too generous. I can't--"

He put down his glass.

"Turn around," he told me taking the case from my hands.

"It's too much," I protested weakly.

"Turn around," he repeated.

I did as he said because I wanted to. I wanted to feel the pearls at least one time around my neck, and in a moment there they were, cool against my skin. Taylor's hands fastened the clasp at the back of my neck. His breath was like feathery down against my flesh. My dark brown flesh. Tingling and trembling from his touch. He turned me back to facing him.

"They're perfect against your skin," he said, slipping a finger between the glossy strand and my throat.

Gently he caressed the hollow above my sternum, as if it too were perfect. As if he should touch me at all and I should let him. When he took his hand away he sat back looking very satisfied with himself. I looked down to see the pearls but where the necklace rested I could not see it.

"It's totally proper to go find a mirror," he allowed.

So I did, hurrying to stand before the one over the credenza in the foyer. Where there had been roses in my cheeks. Now there were pearls around my neck. I touched them. They were real. They were beautiful. And they were intended for me. He had placed them around my neck as if I could keep them. But how could I? It was a gracious gift. The whole evening was. But it was just one night. And pearls lasted forever. I reached up to undo the clasp.

"You do have to come back," Taylor called from the study.

I took my hands away from the clasp and went back to him.

"I'm ready for birthday cake, what about you?" he said, slicing into the cake at last.

"I'll make some coffee," I offered.

He looked up at me and let go of the knife, leaving it to rest in the chocolate cake.

"What's wrong, Esther?" he asked.

Everything, I thought sadly. *Absolutely* everything.

"Nothing," I replied.

"I don't want any coffee," he said.

"All right."

I sat down, but it was in the chair, not on the couch. Taylor sighed deeply.

"I know this house isn't haunted," he said. "So you want to tell me what happened out there."

But the ghosts of Matilda and Albert were here because I had brought them with me. I may have sent Grampa and Uncle Perry away, but Matilda and Albert stood guard over me as Grampa's *fresh memories*. I didn't know how to politely give Taylor back the necklace. Perhaps I could just keep it with the silk scarf, and my love for him, in a secret place. Reaching up now I undid the clasp and carefully returned the pearls to their velvet case.

"I want you to wear them," he said.

He should get his money back. No one had to know that they had been purchased for me.

"Taylor," I began. "I can't. You shouldn't have--"

"Why not?" he asked.

"It's too generous. I know you appreciate my working here but--"

"It's not a bonus, Esther, if that's what you think."

I had offended him, and I didn't mean to. It wasn't my fault. It wasn't his either. It was just how it was.

"I know that," I said, wishing that it could be different, truly different.

But it was not. This was *the way* it was. He couldn't change it. I couldn't let him try.

"I don't think you do," he replied. "I'd wish that you did, but it's not my birthday."

"It's not the kind of present you give to your maid, Taylor."

"But it is what you could give to a friend. Would you grant me that?"

At that moment I would have granted him anything. *Everything.* I opened the velvet case again and took out the necklace and started to put it back around my neck.

"Let me," he said, so I moved back to the couch next to him. "I like the smell of roses," he said when the necklace was back in place.

And because instantly the other roses filled my cheeks, I was glad my back was to him.

"Do you know how a pearl is made, Esther?" he asked as he turned me to face him again. "It happens when a grain of sand or some other kind of irritant gets inside the oyster's shell, and the oyster takes that irritant, the thing that's a problem for it, and turns it into something beautiful. Something valuable. Isn't that amazing?"

And we know that all things work together for good to them that love God, to them who are the called according to his purpose. It was God Who was amazing, but he had not come to that part in the Bible yet. How else could he be so in awe of an oyster? Or charmed by his colored maid. Whom he called a friend.

For the rest of the evening I wore the pearls, wore them like they were a tribute, while we kept company in his study, the radio and records on his phonograph for our concert. We ate cake and drank champagne, and I was giddy once more, ultimately at ease again, and even open.

"I spent so much time with Jimmy and Nathaniel," I shared parts of my childhood. "That Mama used to worry that I would turn out to be some kind of *man-ish* woman."

"*Man-ish woman?*" queried Taylor.

"Yes. You see not being pretty," I explained. "If I were too much of a tom-boy, well then I wouldn't be lady-like either."

"You're not pretty?" he asked, surprised by my honest self-assessment.

"No. I'm what you call handsome."

"I'm not sure I understand the difference."

"Handsome in a woman means she is dignified and proper," I explained. "Respectable. It's what they say about women who are nice but plain."

"Is that what they say?" he asked quizzically.

"Yes. It's meant to be a compliment."

"And so you're dignified, and respectable, and proper. Just not pretty?" he asked skeptically.

"Yes. But that's fine," I said. "It's good to be handsome. My grandmother was handsome."

"And extraordinary too I'm guessing."

"Oh yes," I said eagerly. "Everybody says so, of course they don't use that word exactly, but it's what they mean. I never knew her. She died before I was born. My grandfather says I remind him of her."

"Then that confirms it."

A blush and a smile competed for my face.

"So you and your grandfather are very close?" asked Taylor, taking a drink of champagne.

"Yes," I nodded. "We are."

"He doesn't like you being here, does he?"

Glen Miller's version of *a nightingale singing in Berkeley Square* filled up the silence where my answer should have been.

"He's right you know," said Taylor.

"He worries about me that's all," I replied.

Taylor nodded.

"You must be more a daughter to him than a grandchild," he said. "Since he raised you."

Doctor Mitchell must have told him that; and I wondered what else the doctor might have said. Did he remember that Grampa had come here to take me home?

"Like your uncle did you," I redirected the discussion.

"To some extent, yes," Taylor agreed.

"We were blessed not to be orphans," I told him.

"You were, yes," he replied.

"Well your uncle--" I began.

"Does not love me like a son, Esther," he stopped me.

This made me quiet.

"So," he continued. "You haven't talked much about your mother."

The Glen Miller orchestra began the *Beguine*.

"She must have been proud of you too," he assumed.

"Jimmy was the one," it was my turn to correct him, but I was happy to. "I wish you could have known him," I said wistfully.

"Would he have accepted me?"

Accepted him?

"Of course," I answered. "You would have liked him. Sometimes you remind me of him."

"How so?"

"The way you own the world," I said.

But then I hesitated, unsure of how that sounded to him.

"Does that seem strange to you?" I asked. "To say that a Negro man can own the world?"

"No," answered Taylor. "It's good for a man, *any* man, to feel that way. It lets him feel responsible for making it better."

"Is that what you want to do?" I asked. "Make the world better?"

"Some of it at least," he smiled wryly.

"It must be something to believe that you can."

"Are you saying you don't?" he asked.

I shook my head. I just wanted to get through it, to get to my place in the sky, be it mansion or cabin. I wanted to see Jimmy again. And Daddy. And meet Ernestine finally. And tell Mama that I was beginning to understand why I had not been enough for her.

"That's not really true, Esther," Taylor said. "You may choose to take it on in little bits, perhaps so no one will notice and be on to you, but you're working on the world nonetheless. Subtlety as subterfuge is a rather classic strategy." He smiled again. "But your secret's safe with me. I won't give you up."

He took a bite of cake.

"But beware, my friend," he continued. "You're not as invisible as you'd like to think."

You never were.

"Well at least we can agree that we both had the benefit of good mothers," I said moving beyond the comment. "Women who dressed themselves 'in strength and honor.'"

"You like that passage, I see," he smiled the smile I liked best, the one that filled his face and shone in his eyes.

I took another drink from my glass, touching the pearls around my neck.

"You're not the first person to call me a virtuous woman," I educated him.

"I'm crushed," he chuckled. "Though not surprised. So tell me, who is my rival?"

No one, I thought.

"Reverend Wright used to call me that," I said.

"*Used to?*" he inquired. "Don't tell me you've changed?"

"No," I said truthfully. "Not at all."

Even if most everyone seemed to think that I had. I was the same woman I had always been. It was just that now I was the one deciding my purpose. I was thinking for myself like Jimmy had wanted. And I had these pearls.

It was after midnight by the time I was putting away the remaining food and cake, and I was still wearing the necklace. "I'll wait for you downstairs," Taylor had said when I went to take care of things in the kitchen. The late hour worried me for him.

It had been a long day. He must be tired. Yet as he had reminded me more than once tonight, I was not *on duty*.

When I returned to the study, still seated on the sofa, he was having a nightcap.

"I don't suppose you'd care to have one with me," he offered.

I shook my head.

"I think I'm still a little light-headed from the champagne," I said.

And the whole miraculous day.

"Then I guess that means the party is over," he replied.

He finished his drink and set the empty glass on the table.

"It was really wonderful, Taylor," I wanted him to know. "Thank you."

Reaching for his crutches, he labored a little to get to his feet, and I resisted the impulse to assist him. Even at the foot of the stairs, he indicated that I should go up first, and when I hesitated, he reminded me, "You're not working tonight, that includes monitoring my gait."

He escorted me to the door of the buttercup room, where I urged him to let me help him do a little of the stretching exercises. After all he had made Spencer do his homework. Routines should be respected. However, Taylor was firm, "Say goodnight to me here, Esther." But the truth was that I didn't want to say goodnight, and end the day, the evening. It just wasn't my birthday anymore.

"You'll be all right then?" I asked.

"Yes, Esther," A small enigmatic smile flickered across his lips. "I'll be fine."

Still I stood there, keeping him on his exhausted legs, as hopeless as Cinderella, without any expectation of a fairy godmother that could wave her wand and give me the desires of my heart. This prince could never be mine.

He leaned his left crutch against his body for a moment and took my hand into his.

"Happy birthday, my dear, virtuous, and *handsome* friend," he said and turned my hand to kiss the inside of my wrist. When he looked at me again I could not find my way, because the only way I knew to go was into his arms, and I could not go there.

"Thank you, Taylor," I heard my own voice speaking.

Letting go of my hand, he grasped the crutch once more.

"Good night," he said.

Resigned to the finality of his words, I felt for the doorknob behind me.

"Good night," I replied and left him to go into the buttercup room, closing the door between us.

For a long time afterwards I sat on the side of the bed, telling myself that I was waiting, in case he called me or rang the bell. But I knew he wouldn't. He would be fine without me. I would be too, although I would never be the same. I still felt his lips on the inside of my wrist, felt his fingers in the place where the pearls were, tasted the chocolate we had shared on the wooden spoon.

In the middle of the night, I got out of bed and crept across the hall and opened Taylor's bedroom door and then left the buttercup room door open too. He might need me, and I wanted to be able to hear him. When I finally fell asleep I was still wearing the necklace in the hopes that it would preserve the magic spell until morning.

PART FIVE

I

The enchantment lasted, and when Sunday came I wanted to wear the pearls with my new dress to church. The two gifts went together. The necklace was my first piece of fine jewelry. I didn't even wear earrings because Grampa objected to women piercing their ears. "If the good Lord had-a wanted more holes in your head, He'd-a put 'em there," he had said. Even Aunt Grace still only wore earbobs. He would surely think the necklace was too extravagant. But after all *Rhett Butler* had given *Mammie* a red petticoat, not for any reason other than he had valued her loyalty.

At night before I went to bed I would look at the pearls, holding them in my hands, placing them around my neck, remembering what it had been like to see such an image of myself reflected in Taylor's dark eyes. It was not an image of *Mammie*, but rather one of Mandy. This must be how my friend felt, when men admired her not for what she could do but for how she looked when she was doing it. It was flattering that Taylor could have this kind of regard for me.

Now that he was no longer trapped upstairs, Taylor and I continued to have meals together. We were like companions. It wasn't so remarkable that Spencer and I should have become fond of our employer. The pearls were no different than Spencer's new bicycle. Just another token of an employer's gratitude for a servant's loyalty. *Mammie* had been a true friend too, holding *Mr. Rhett* and *Mis' Scarlett's* world together in the face of every disaster.

So there was nothing wrong with things being convivial and pleasant between Taylor and me. It was just the circumstances that was all. I was helping him. When he was well again then we would part company. Connie had said it. I was like Ananias, called to a purpose. There was nothing wrong with being his friend.

Soon I would be back with Grampa. We wouldn't have long together, as I was supposed to be on my way back to New York, but I would make it up the time away from him somehow. There must always be change. Time ensured it, bringing us birth, and age, and death, and new experiences, new people, reunions and goodbyes. The hands on a clock went round and round and yet never covered the same space twice. No moment was exactly like the last. As soon as something was it was becoming a memory. Surely Grampa understood that.

I came downstairs Sunday morning, wearing Nathaniel and Connie's dress and Taylor's pearls. I walked into the study where Taylor was at his desk. The expression on his face said he was pleased when he looked up at me. He removed his glasses.

"Perhaps you'd like to explain to me again this meaning of handsome you've come up with," he said smiling sagaciously.

I was glad that I was wearing the pearls.

"What time is Doctor Mitchell getting here?" I changed the subject, my face flushed by his approving gaze.

"He's not," he informed me.

"Oh?" I said surprised.

Was Laura Spalding coming back; or some other stranger to me who would upset our rhythm?

"Then who'll--" I started to ask.

"No one," he interjected nonchalantly. "I'll be fine, Sister Sergeant."

"Taylor," I fretted. "You really think--"

"It's just for a few hours, right?" he cut me off again. "Until you come back."

"But... what about your lunch?"

"Take the casserole out of the fridge," he said as if by rote. "Put it in the oven. Bake for one hour." He smiled again. "I vaguely remember my way around a kitchen."

But not with crutches, I wanted to say but didn't as I tried to make my face show acceptance.

"So did you get a new watch for your birthday too?" he asked. "Come here, let me see it."

I crossed the room to stand in front of his desk and presented the wrist wearing the watch. He caught my hand and held it.

"Very nice," he commented examining the watch as he led me around the desk, bringing me closer to him.

"It's from Uncle Perry and Aunt Betty," I said evenly although my heart skipped.

"Nathaniel's mother has excellent tastes," he replied.

But not when it came to decorating his house, I remembered.

"She can be a little extravagant sometimes," I said.

"Extravagance has its place, don't you think?" he asked threading his warm fingers through mine. "We mustn't always be practical."

And there it was again, in his eyes, an image of myself more reminiscent of the Biblical *Esther* or the dark daughter of Jerusalem in the *Song of Solomon*.

"Are you sure you'll be all right today?" I asked seeking after some bit of composure. "Nathaniel can bring me back right after church."

He shook his head, and I yearned to touch his face as he had once touched mine that morning in the foyer.

"You enjoy your day with your family," he said. "I'll be fine."

"Nathaniel has a telephone," I heard myself offering almost in a faint voice. "I could call…"

A little smile lifted the one corner of his mouth as he shook his head again.

"I'll wait my turn," he said squeezing my hand. "Then you can tell me all about it over dinner."

Herman began to bark and we heard Nathaniel's car driving up outside. I looked towards the window.

"Now go," he said letting go of my hand and shooing me away cheerfully. "Your Lord and Savior awaits His most virtuous lady."

"I'll give Him your regards," I tossed over my shoulder as I hurried to get my pocketbook.

"Tell Him I said thanks," he called after me.

At this comment I stopped short and returned to the study.

"Taylor, do you mean that?" I asked very seriously.

He laughed easily, and outside Nathaniel lightly tapped the car horn.

"Go!" he dismissed me again. "Judges are particular about punctuality. It won't do to have my advocate arriving late."

Connie and Nathaniel noticed the pearls immediately, looking at each other and then back at me.

"Your necklace is nice," Connie said seeming to speak for them both.

"Thank-you," I replied gaily as Little Evie reached for me to climb into my lap. "Taylor gave it to me for my birthday."

I hugged my little niece-second-cousin tightly and pulled her long neatly plaited braids. She giggled. The expressions on her parents' faces remained somber as Nathaniel pulled out of the drive onto Webster Road.

"I told him it was too much," I explained. "But he wants me to have it. He even found this Bible verse to make a toast to me. From the book of Proverbs. It was really nice. He said that I'm his friend, so I had to accept it. And they really do go with this dress, which I just love. Thank-you again!"

"You look real nice, Esther," Connie finally inserted.

Nathaniel cast his wife another worried glance. Little Evie shyly touched the strand of pearls.

"Aren't they pretty?" I asked beaming down at her.

"Pretty," she agreed.

During the service I sat next to Connie, with Baby Nate asleep across my lap and Taylor's tribute around my neck. Nate was getting to be a big boy. He pulled up easily, and teetered on his fat baby legs, so that we knew that he was only a little while from walking. *Walking.* What a wonderful thing it was. I had never thought about it before. Now I could see a miracle in every step. The lustrous piece of jewelry around my neck had enchanted Nate too. Repeatedly he had tried to tug at the pearls with his chubby hands as I held him in my arms.

I put my hand to the pearls now, caressing them gently, and hoped that Taylor was all right on his own. Reverend Wright was preaching Paul's exhortations to Timothy, reminding us to put our confidence only in the promise of the Christian life, and this meant studying the *Word* so that we could rightly know the truth, and have no need to be ashamed. "The Word tells us to put away youthful lusts and follow righteousness!" urged the minister emphatically to the eager faithful from the elevation of the pulpit. "That you may recover yourself out of the snare of the Devil!"

Tell him I said thanks.

To Taylor the Bible was just a book of philosophy, a collection of intriguing essays and provocative letters. Just so many stories and poetic verse. Meant to make us hopeful in a world fraught with too many disappointments. Meant to make toasts. "The sentiments are nice, Esther," he had once said. "Until somebody misuses them." Jesus loved him anyway. Whether or not he ever realized it. Losing his parents and being robbed of his sister had left him to grow up alone. As an orphan. And then Sylvia had come along and betrayed him too. And Laura Spalding, where was she? I could not fathom that anyone had ever been capable of walking away from him when there was no valid reason to do so. To simply turn away from his touch, I found nearly impossible. Oh well. Laura would have the place that had been hers once again. She would have Sylvia's life. She would enable him to love again by showing him how to be loved.

But perhaps I was the one who had opened the door for him to pass through. Perhaps I had drawn him out to the rest of us. Laura Spalding ought to thank me. Or perhaps it was the polio that had done it. Perhaps she should be thankful to it too. Perhaps she could *count it all joy.* As I dared to do.

"The Lord wants us to be meek and pure in heart, teachin' all men," the reverend was saying. "*All* men! That means we got to teach them that don't want to learn. If the Lord had-a turned his back on us, then where would we be?" Reverenced Wright demanded. "We are instruments of His will on this earth. People ought to be able to see the Word in your life! You must be born again, children! Washed white as snow in the Blood of the Lamb!"

The blood of Jesus!

The blood done signed my name!

I shifted in my seat, and little Nate, sensing the movement, wiggled and turned his head towards me. He was going to be the *exact replica* of Nathaniel. How was it that white was clean and black was dirty even to *us*? Why did we accept and argue a truth that *they* had defined, a truth used to desecrate and deny *our* dignity. Why did we hold onto these images when they only justified our subjugation? Grampa didn't think that way. And neither did Taylor. The pearls were *perfect* against my skin.

"I'm telling you, brothers and sisters, you ain't no match for Satan without the Lord! The foundation of God is sure!" Reverend Wright warned us. "You better get His seal upon you! So you can be strong in His grace!" Reverend Wright took his traditional pause, Sister Wright, attending to the cue, began to play an invitational hymn. Grampa rose from his seat and solemnly set out the altar chair, and then returned to the deacon's pew to wait.

♪ *Jesus gettin' us ready for that-- great day!*
Jesus gettin' us ready for that-- great day!
Jesus gettin' us ready for that--- great day!
O—o-oh, who shall be able to stand?

I hoped that Taylor's mother and father were in heaven. The Bohemians I had known had either been opposed to religion on political grounds or opposed to it because it didn't make sense to their scientific minds. They couldn't fit such things as slavery, war, and Charles Darwin into a religious framework. What was the use of having God if He let bad things happen? Besides the *Evolution* theory made more sense to them than ribs and clay. I thought they were interesting people, my Bohemian classmates, and I liked them usually. They were so determined to save the world from itself with their enlightenment, that they couldn't see that they were no less zealous than the missionaries they held in such dismissive disdain. Some things were just mysteries that we would have to wait to understand better *by and by*. And in the meantime what if the *Origin of Species* was just another book in Bible? Surely God was still inspiring His people and revealing His truth. Besides before Saul was Paul, he had been a heretic too.

Since there were no new souls ready to answer the call to Christ, Grampa reclaimed the altar chair, and Reverend Wright assumed his seat of distinction at the right of the pulpit. Sister Wright let the piano music fade, and Grampa, along with Mr. Eddie, moved to the front to turn the devotional table into one for collecting the offering.

"Let the church say amen," said Grampa.

Amen!

"I don't know 'bout y'all but my soul been blessed," Grampa told us.

Amen! Thank you, Jesus.

"Like we was hearin' the Apostle Paul, hisself," agreed Mr. Eddie.

"Amen!" said Grampa.

The reverend smiled and nodded graciously.

"What a wonder about You, Jesus!" exclaimed Sister Thompson, the proud mother of Sweet Water's newest deacon, Ben Thompson.

"We gon' ask y'all to give like the Spirit tell you today," said Mr. Eddie.

We were already opening up our purses and wallets. I thought of Saul on the Road to Damascus. Sometimes the conversion could only come with a physical blow that hurt you and humbled you and then finally made you stronger.

"That's right! Give out of the abundance that the Lord done blessed you with," added my grandfather. "It's all His anyway. B'long to Him 'fo' it ever did you."

Amen!

It did all belong to Him. We all belonged to Him. Yet we constantly divided ourselves, and clung to *mine* and *yours*, to *theirs* and *ours*. *Separate thyself, I pray thee, from me: if thou wilt take the left hand, then I will go to the right; or if thou depart to the right hand, then I will go to the left.* Even on the same journey, it seemed we couldn't find enough agreement to go together.

Sister Wright started another gospel selection, and Sonny Lewis and Ben rose from their seats to move through the church with the wooden bowls that were our offering plates. Aunt Betty wanted Sweet Water to purchase new plates. She had set her sights on a pair of shiny gold ones that were lined with green velvet, which she had seen at the Baptist Bookstore in Tyler. She wanted us to have them. "Beautiful things inspire people," she had said. She was right, I thought, as I reached up to touch the pearls again.

Extravagance has its place, don't you think?

Beauty was inspirational. Inviting you to lie down in green pastures even though you could not stay.

When service ended, I waited outside the church-house door to greet Grampa. He could not forgive my choices but they were only temporary choices with interim conditions. I would always come home again. To my grandfather's house, the true center of my universe; even if for now I was wandering among the stars.

In these Sunday afternoon encounters Grampa never failed to initiate some inquiry about the *condition* of my *employer* to which I would resolutely report that my *employer* was doing much better every day.

"So you gon' be goin' back to day-work then?" Grampa had asked me once.

Day-work? No, not in the house on Webster Road. You couldn't go back to what had been.

"I think I might have enough money saved up, Grampa, to quit domestic work," I had replied.

"Mean to tell me, you want somethin' else out yo' life, Esther Fay?"

"I'm not a maid, Grampa. It's what I do, not who I am."

"The Lord renders to a man accordin' to his deeds, Esther Fay," Grampa had said. "Maid work gets you a maid's life."

A maid's life was not what my grandfather dreamed of for me, but it was not a life without dignity. It was not without pearls. I could always point to Mandy and the way she made her way in the world. Yet I knew that she did not want Spencer to wind up a Pullman Car porter either, even if the railroad pension was good. Spencer had the *promise*, the abilities and the will to take us into Canaan. Just like Jimmy. And perhaps I could even do something with the world too, in *little bits* at a time.

When Grampa finally came through the church doors, I went to meet him.

"Hello, Grampa," I said.

"Esther," he greeted me in his usual rigid way.

Then he saw the pearls.

"My employer gave them to me for my birthday," I offered up timidly.

Grampa's eyes narrowed and his face turned into the pale white granite.

"This what you come to?" he asked in a quiet voice that took my breath away with its contempt. "It ain't enough to clean his house, you gon' be his harlot too?"

"Grampa... it's not..." but words died on my lips.

"And you dare to come 'round here shamin' our family like a Jezebel."

Snatching the necklace from around my neck, he flung it to the ground. In the sparse grass the pearls glistened in the sunlight. I looked up into Grampa's eyes. The image I saw of myself in the angry hazel glare was worse than any reflection of Matilda. Where the pearls had been my skin was hot, stinging with their loss.

"You done los' yo' mind, gal," he said and stalked away.

Frozen where he left me, the world around me swirled and blurred.

"Come on, Esther," Connie's voice spoke softly at my side. "Let's go."

I tried to see her through the wet blur. She was bending to pick-up the pearl necklace.

"He's rememberin' the way it used to be," Connie said, placing the pearls into my shaking hand. "He ain't never known it could be different. You can understand that."

The necklace was broken.

"We can get it fixed," Connie assured me. "Nathaniel can take it to Friedman's in the mornin'."

She was leading me to their car.

"He set in his ways, Esther Fay," she kept talking, her arm protectively around my waist. "The world might be tryin' to change, but it ain't gon' be easy. You just caught up in the middle that's all. But ain't nobody to blame for it. Somebody's got to be in the middle if we gon' come together."

We waited in the car for Nathaniel to finish his Sunday finance duties. On better days, Connie and I would have filled the time with chit-chat. Today only the children were happy. Little Evie prattled about driving us to the store as she entertained herself playing with the car's steering wheel. Her baby brother gleefully bounced up and down holding tightly to the car seat, Connie's hand strategically placed behind him to catch him if he fell.

The broken necklace was still in my hand along with Grampa's bitter words in my head. He thought I was a harlot, a woman who was whore, who sold herself for a price. Matilda had had no choice. The sin had been committed against her. She was violated but innocent. But there were Taylor's words too, chosen from the Bible itself, to praise my virtues. One of them was wrong, terribly wrong.

The Scripture said that to lust in your heart was the same as the act, so yes I was guilty. When I touched him it was less and less to heal him and more and more to love him. Willing hands had turned into desiring ones, so that the exercises I helped him complete were veils for the caresses I secretly committed. But I never spoke of it. Vigilantly I hid behind caring for him and keeping his house. And if I did sow seeds of passion then it was also true that I never let myself hope for a harvest. I knew I would be gone before the tender shoots could flower. And this way there was no sin in the house on Webster Road. There was longing, but not lust. There was nothing to make me deserving of God's or Grampa's judgment.

At last Nathaniel appeared. He opened the driver-side door and scooped up Little Evie who gladly flung her arms around her father's neck.

"It's about time," fussed Connie. "What'd y'all have in there, Pharaoh's gold?"

"Men folks' b'idness, honey," replied Nathaniel good-naturedly as he handed Little Evie over the backseat to me.

I let go of the pearl necklace long enough to take the child, leaving the pearls in my lap.

"Esther give me the necklace," Connie said reaching over the seat. "Nathaniel, you gon' have to take it to Mr. Friedman."

"Why?" asked Nathaniel.

He was turning the key in the car ignition.

"It got broke," explained Connie. "You gotta get Mr. Friedman to fix it."

"Broke?" asked Nathaniel. "How'd it get broke?"

"Come on, give it to me," said Connie again.

I placed the necklace in her open palm.

"Don't make no difference 'bout how," Connie answered her husband. "It ain't too bad though," she said inspecting it. "Just look like the fastener is all. If you go by after dinner maybe he could even fix it today."

Nathaniel looked back at me.

"Was you pullin' on it?" he asked.

I dropped my head.

"What happened to it?" Nathaniel asked again.

"I told you that don't matter," Connie said. "Now let's go. These children need to eat."

"I'll take it in on Monday," said Nathaniel. "I don't feel like all that drivin'. Besides it's Sunday anyway."

"Don't see why not, you know you gon' be goin' by that garage anyhow. And Mr. Friedman does his worshippin' on Saturday. Esther, do you know if Mr. Taylor bought it from him?"

I didn't know; and I didn't want Taylor to know what had happened. Maybe Aunt Betty could take it to Tyler.

"Ol' man Friedman lives clear on the other side of town," grumbled Nathaniel.

"Then you can go when you take Esther back."

"I can catch the bus," I offered feeling like a burden.

"That's not necessary," Connie said. "Nathaniel'll take you home same as always. And Monday mornin' he'll take the necklace to the jewelry store. I bet he can fix it the same day."

It was late when Nathaniel brought me back to the house on Webster Road, which was not my *home* no matter what Connie said about it. I belonged on Spring Street, in Ernestine's Taj Mahal, with the man who loved us both. Nathaniel parked the truck. Neither of us moved.

"It was just too much for 'im, Esther," said Nathaniel with a deep, sad sigh. "You wearin' them to church and all." He looked up at the house. "You and him might got somethin' 'tween you, but this *still* McConnell County. Things not gon' change overnight. You messin' 'round with things that folks can get pretty riled up about. If things was the other way 'round, and you was the man--"

"He gave me the necklace out of friendship," I interrupted the picture Nathaniel was about to paint of Negro men swinging from tree limbs, their genitals cut off and crammed into their mouths, their bodies ablaze, while white mobs watched righteously. "He gave it to me because I stood by him when he was sick."

"You ain't got to confess," Nathaniel replied. "Not to me."

"There's nothing to confess," I said and opened the truck door to get out.

"You want me to go in with you?" he asked.

"Taylor's always happy to see you," I replied. "But you don't have to. He'd understand."

"Might as well go in and speak," decided Nathaniel, opening his door too.

We walked slowly towards the house.

"What you gon' tell him?" Nathaniel asked as we climbed the porch steps.

I stopped. I knew he was referring to the broken necklace.

"That the clasp broke," I told him. "And that you are taking it to Mr. Friedman's store tomorrow."

"What if he asks how it got broke?" Nathaniel followed.

"We can't tell him what happened, Nathaniel," I said grabbing his arm. "He wouldn't understand. Please, don't tell him."

"Esther... if the two of you gon'...I mean, you gon' have to face more than--"

"Nathaniel, please," I pleaded. "There is no *two* of us. Why won't y'all believe me?"

"Because we got eyes, Esther Fay," replied Nathaniel. "Listen to me. I ain't sayin' it's wrong, but it sho' ain't invisible neither."

You never were.

"Please, I'm begging you, Nathaniel. He just needs me a little while longer. He's getting better all the time. Just a little while. Then I'll go back to New York, and everything will be fine. I promise. You'll see. It'll all work out."

Nathaniel looked at me.

"Esther, what's s'pose to be gon' be. Can't nobody block it."

"I'm not trying to block it," I said. "I just need a little more time."

By now Herman knew Nathaniel and came into the foyer to greet us both. Maybe Nathaniel would get Nate a dog. Maybe Nathaniel and Taylor would always be friends. While I put away my pocketbook in the closet Nathaniel went on ahead of me into the study, where Taylor might have spent the whole day.

"Hello, Nathaniel," I heard Taylor say pleasantly.

"Well now would you look at you!" replied Nathaniel in his usual bright boisterous way. "Esther told me you was up and walkin' like a new man. Thank the Lord!"

I let Herman out the front door.

"Maybe like a new baby is the more apt description," Taylor said.

"Still it's good to see you gettin' 'round so well," encouraged Nathaniel undaunted. "And workin' too. 'Course now it is the Sabbath, and on the seventh day we s'pose to rest."

"To Taylor working is resting," I said, joining them.

Taylor and I smiled at each other.

"Don't let her fool you, Nathaniel," he said. "I didn't know what work was until I signed up for Esther's program."

The men laughed.

"Please, sit down," Taylor gestured towards the leather sofa.

"Naw-sir," Nathaniel shook his head. "Just wanted to come in and speak. Got my own bossy woman back at the house, so I better get on home and see what she done figgered out for me to do."

"What happened to your day of rest?" asked Taylor.

"The way she figgers, the Good Lord'll see it her way anyhow," answered Nathaniel.

They laughed again.

When I walked Nathaniel back to the front door he told me he would take the necklace to the jewelry store first thing.

"Thank-you, Nathaniel," I replied.

He continued out onto the front porch but then stopped and turned back to me.

"Esther," Nathaniel began.

Fearful of what else he might say and that Taylor would overhear him, I followed him out onto the porch, closing the front door behind me.

"We not judged by what other folks say," said Nathaniel. "The Lord looks at each of us, one at a time."

"Nathaniel, I promise you--" I started defensively.

"I'm not the one you owe a promise to, Esther," he interrupted me. "Just don't do nothin' you gon' have to be 'shamed of, that's all. Do right by yo'self. And him."

After Nathaniel left I went to the kitchen to start Taylor's dinner. As I had worried, I found the casserole left untouched in the refrigerator, and there was precious little evidence that Taylor had eaten at all, just an empty Coca-Cola bottle, a dirty knife, and a few bread crumbs. I put the casserole in the oven and marched back to the study.

"Taylor," I began sharply.

"Yes, Esther," he said looking up from the document he was writing. "What is it?"

"You didn't eat today," I scolded him.

"Yes I did."

"Not the casserole I left for you."

"I improvised," he said returning his attention to the document.

"What does that mean?" I demanded.

"I ate something else."

"You see. I didn't think you should stay alone. You do have to eat."

"So I'll make up for it at dinner."

"Taylor, you know what I mean."

He put down his fountain pen and took off his glasses.

"No, Esther," he said. "Why don't you tell me what you mean?"

I was quiet.

"I mean that if…if you're going to be on your own," I now said as if I was the one being chastened, "Then…then I'll need to leave something else for your lunch, that's all."

"Something I can handle a little better with these?" he asked glancing in the direction of the crutches leaning against his desk.

"Yes," I replied.

"Sounds like a plan," he said putting his glasses back on and picking up the pen.

"Dinner should be ready in just a little bit," I said after a moment.

"Good," he smiled dryly. "I'm hungry."

I smiled a little too and turned to leave.

"Esther," he said.

I turned back to him.

"You took off your pearls," he noted.

Of course he would notice.

"Oh," I began the lie. "The baby pulled on them too hard and broke the clasp."

He looked at me.

"Those little hands can be fierce," I went on. "Nathaniel's getting it fixed."

"I'd like to think the necklace could withstand a child's fascination," Taylor replied. "It must be defective. I should exchange it."

"No!" I said too emphatically. "I mean…It was just an accident, Taylor," I tried to sound more casual. "Nathaniel's taking care of it."

"All right," he replied.

The room was quiet enough that I could hear the katydids singing to the setting sun.

"I better…uh see about dinner," I said.

Yet I kept standing in the same place as if I wanted him to make me tell the truth.

"Did you deliver my message?" he asked.

"What message?" I asked back, breathing a little better.

"I'm guessing you didn't then."

I searched my mind for the reference he was making.

"Oh," it dawned on me. "You mean about the… I mean the giving thanks?"

"So you do recall?" he smiled obliquely.

I chuckled a little awkwardly.

"Hmm," he continued thoughtfully. "You seemed to take it much more seriously this morning."

"You know, you could thank Him yourself," I reminded him.

"I'd hardly know where to start."

II

Early in the week Nathaniel brought the pearl necklace back to me. He didn't have to come to the back of the house, but old customs died hard. Generally Nathaniel kept to the way things had always been done in the South, even if he was learning to call Taylor by his first name. I went out to meet him, holding the screen door open for him. He passed by me, carrying the pungent prosperous odor of the garage clinging to his clothes.

"Can I get you a cold drink?" I offered.

"I can't stay long," Nathaniel said standing on the porch. "I just wanted to bring you this."

He handed me a small burgundy velvet bag, tied securely at the top. I opened the bag and poured the strand of pearls into my hand.

"Mr. Friedman say wasn't much harm done," he said. "Just broke the fastener is all. He fixed it up good as new. Did you know he come over here on a Sunday so that Taylor could pick it out hisself? Kinda surprised ol' man Friedman that I was bringin' it in. He was lookin' at me all suspicious-like at first, like he was wonderin' if he should call the Law. But since you work for Taylor he just figgered I was doin' an errand for you. Which I was."

"I guess he didn't know the necklace was for me," I said, fingering the pearls.

"Guess not. Pearls ain't somethin' a man usually gives to his housekeeper."

"He does things differently," I repeated the familiar refrain.

"No doubt about it."

"Thank you, Nathaniel," I said looking up at him. "What do I owe you?"

"Nothin'."

"No," I insisted. "I want to pay for it. You shouldn't have to."

"I didn't."

"Friedman fixed it for free?"

"No, Grampa paid for it."

"Grampa?" I asked, taken aback.

"Yeah, Esther," Nathaniel said. "He thought about it and was sorry for it, for what he done. So he paid for gettin' it fixed. Simple as that. Grampa can do things *differently* too as you say."

That he had paid for the broken necklace made me a little hopeful.

"Esther!" we both heard Taylor's call.

He had come into the kitchen.

"Yes, Taylor," I called back, hurriedly slipping the pearl necklace back into its pouch before going back in the house.

"I saw Nathaniel's truck," Taylor said.

"That you did!" boomed Nathaniel from behind me. "How you doin' tonight?"

Quickly I went to the table and pulled out a chair for Taylor to sit down, as Nathaniel crossed the room to shake his hand.

"Thank you, Esther," Taylor said. Then to Nathaniel he asked as they shook hands, "Is it me, or has she always been this anxious about everything?"

"Hate to say it but she's a na'tral-born worrier," Nathaniel chuckled.

"Good," replied Taylor. "I was beginning to think that I had driven her to distraction."

"Nathaniel brought the necklace, Taylor," I reported changing the topic of their discussion. "It's good as new."

"Yes," Taylor said. "I want to reimburse you, Nathaniel. How much was it to repair it?"

"It's paid for, Taylor," Nathaniel told him.

"It was no fault of yours that it was broken," replied Taylor as if he might actually know the truth. "You shouldn't have to pay for it."

Feeling somehow found out, I felt queasy in my stomach. Had he heard that it had been Grampa's hand? Gossip was a swift if unreliable means of communication. It could move rapidly across communities no matter how *separate*. Many eyes had seen what had happened on the church grounds last Sunday. Many tongues must have wagged about it. But they couldn't have told it the right way. Ripping the pearls from around my neck only looked brutal. Grampa was a proud man. It was my fault for wearing them. My fault for accepting them in the first place.

Things not gon' change overnight.

They never would.

Just don't do nothin' you gon' have to be 'shamed of, that's all.

"Don't worry about it, Taylor," Nathaniel was saying. "Things like that just happen. It's a fine piece of jewelry you give Esther."

I'll give it back I thought, and I was sorry for taking it, I wanted to say. For a moment I was terrified that Nathaniel was going to say who had paid for repairing the necklace, and explain why, revealing Grampa's truth and exposing my lie.

"I can't manage without her, Nathaniel," Taylor spoke of me in the third-person, his face sober.

"Oh Taylor," I chided him trying to make light of such a disclosure. "Don't believe a word of it, Nathaniel," I laughed nervously. "He's getting better every day."

"People come into our lives for a reason," replied Nathaniel speaking to Taylor, matching his tone as if they were sharing one of the war clouds. "What's s'pose to be will be. Can't nobody block it."

This time the war cloud was me, and I felt awkward and guilty, as if they were having a private conversation about the trouble I had made. Ramming my hand into my pocket, I came across the smooth fabric of the small pouch. I did have the pearls again, and Grampa had paid for their return to me. Even if I had to tell the truth about what had happened, that he had paid for the mending must count for something. Taylor must understand. It was American history. It belonged to all of us. We had made it this way between us. It was nobody's fault. Not anymore. It just was.

After dinner, I did the dishes and eventually made my way to the study where Taylor was busy at his desk. He looked up at me as I came into the room.

"Can I get you anything?" I asked.

"No," he replied. "Thank-you."

The scotch decanter and glass were next to him again. I wondered what case he was working on tonight. Someone from the courthouse was at the house all the time. Mr. Walton was eager for him to come to the office too. It would not be long before he would return to the courtroom. I gathered up the day's newspapers to take to the kitchen.

"Have you thought any more about what Mr. Walton said?" I asked. "You could start out half-days," I volunteered. "Somebody could drive you."

"What's up, Esther?" asked Taylor as he continued to write. "Are you trying to get rid of me?"

"You're doing so much better, Taylor, and it's been six months. Mr. Walton needs you."

Now he looked up at me.

"I know exactly how long it's been," there was an abrupt edge in his voice.

"You told me you were a litigator," I said anyway. "I would think you missed the courtroom."

He returned his attention to the paper he was working on. I wondered what had become of Cordelia Collier. Was she divorced now? Did she have her children? Who among his colleagues had assumed *the people's case* for her?

"I miss a lot of things," he replied.

I knew what he meant. As well as he was doing, the recovery still seemed too slow—to both of us. Sometimes it frightened me to think that he might always have difficulty walking.

"The crutches would incline the jury to sympathy," he added. "Any competent defense counsel would protest."

"You'd make them forget about the crutches, Taylor," I assured him. "Once they see how brilliant you are."

"And you?" he asked. "Do you ever forget about them?"

All the time, I thought.

"Yes," I answered him, keeping the reasons to myself.

He looked up at me again.

"Perjury is a crime, Esther," he said. "And entirely unbecoming of a virtuous woman. Even for a good cause."

I had lied about the necklace, but I wasn't lying about the crutches. They did not define him. Why didn't he know that? One day he would. And one day he would not need them anymore. And I would go to the courthouse and see him at work. I would sit up in the balcony, where the Negroes sat, and watch him win for justice. But it must be when a white man was on trial, so that the sides would be fairly matched. I turned to go and leave him to his work.

"I see you don't like my company tonight" he said.

"I thought I might read for awhile," I replied, turning back to him.

"Read here. I won't disturb you."

"I don't want to bother you."

"I want you near me."

I didn't know how to respond to that. I was always close by. Except on Sundays. And that had been his idea.

"Of course you'll just be upstairs, won't you?" he added, examining another page from a file. "For the time being anyway."

I hesitated for a moment in the room, then took the newspapers to the kitchen. Sometimes I wondered if he thought about my leaving, if he considered how temporary this all was. Temporary and dependent upon his dependency upon me. But he liked Mandy very much. They would get along well together.

When I went upstairs, it was only to retrieve the Dorothy West novel that I was reading. I went back to the study. When I returned he looked up from his work again, and I smiled at him as I took my usual seat on the couch. The book was entitled *The*

Living Is Easy. I opened it. If only it were. It wasn't. Even in a novel. Living was complex, complicated. Mysterious. Unpredictable. It really was mostly a matter of faith. That was if you had someone or something that you could believe in. God help you, if you didn't have that. And if you didn't have that, then you didn't even have Him. Or at least you didn't know that you did. That was the worst blasphemy, not knowing. And whose fault was that?

Ain't nobody to blame for that.

Maybe Connie was right. Maybe that was the problem with the whole wide world. Why life was hard even when it was good. Why we just couldn't find or keep the peace that passed understanding. We were always too busy finding fault instead. What if we just stopped looking and lived? I supposed that if each victory helped you some other to win, then each defeat must improve your capacity for losing. *Yielding to temptation* this time made it easier to yield the next time.

Later in the week, Taylor announced that Doctor Mitchell was driving him into town after breakfast. I was surprised, but I was pleased too. Maybe he was going to his office. It would do him good, and it was wise to have Doctor Mitchell with him the first time back.

"Are you up to it?" I asked anyway.

This elicited one of his crooked smiles.

"What—you don't think I am?" he asked. "I thought you wanted me out of the house."

I hated it when he answered a question with a question.

"Of course you are," I replied.

"Then you'll just miss me, is that it?" he followed.

Yes. It was selfishness on my part. I felt bad about it, but I felt it.

"Yes," I told him.

A little while later Doctor Mitchell came, and they left together in Taylor's car. I was left alone in the house with Herman and my ambivalence. The time dragged, but there was always work. In the afternoon Spencer arrived. Not finding Taylor in the study, he wanted to know where he was, and I informed him that he had gone out.

"For real?" Spencer asked.

"Yes, Spencer," I said.

"That's good, ain't it, Aunt Esther?"

"*Isn't* it. And yes."

"He's going to be fine one day…*isn't* he? I mean well for real."

"Yes, Spencer."

"Then things be back right again. Like they used to be."

"Yes," I said. "Just like they used to be."

Late in the afternoon Taylor and Doctor Mitchell returned, the car horn announcing their arrival. Taylor would be tired. I hurried downstairs and went out on the front porch to meet them. Taylor was emerging from the driver's side of the car. I couldn't believe it.

"Aunt Esther! Aunt Esther!" Spencer exclaimed excitedly, swinging on the car door. "Look! Mr. Payne drove hisself!"

I had stopped on the porch steps. Herman barked.

"We had it fitted with hand controls," explained Doctor Mitchell who was by now standing in front of the car. "And he's such a quick study. He mastered it right away. Besides we'll be taking the contraption off before you know it anyhow, the way he's coming along."

Leaning against the side of the car, Taylor grinned broadly, very pleased with himself. I was very pleased too.

"It's wonderful!" I finally said myself, going to him.

"It's not so bad," Taylor agreed, smiling down into my eyes.

But he seemed to stand taller, to rely less on the crutches. I wanted to throw my arms around him, but Doctor Mitchell and Spencer were with us.

"You didn't say anything about it," I said.

"I wanted to surprise you," he replied.

"Yeah, Aunt Esther, women like surprises," affirmed Spencer astutely.

"It's pretty much a miracle what they can do these days," said Doctor Mitchell.

"We like miracles, don't we Esther?" asked Taylor.

Miracles. Could a man of no faith believe in Providence? Perhaps it didn't matter. Perhaps it was enough that one of us did.

"Yes, Mr. Payne," I replied a little huskily. "We like them very much."

It was a blessed day, I told myself as I started dinner. It was one more milestone along the road that took me away, but I was truly glad for him. I decided once and for all that my only objective was to see him have his life back before I left him.

While I cooked, Taylor and Spencer were occupied in the study with the basic elements of expository writing. For his English assignment, Spencer wanted to write an essay about famous lawyers who, in his words, had *helped colored people.*

"Like Abraham Lincoln," he had said. "Or you, Mr. Payne."

The comparison had both embarrassed and flattered Taylor. Seen through a child's eyes the world could look very straightforward. There was the good. There was the bad. Heroes were those people who helped you.

The scene had left me ruminating about Willie Gaines and all that he was missing by seeking the Promise Land of California. He had made beautiful children with Mandy. He should be raising them. To each was supposed to be his own. What was so special about California anyway? The Gold Rush was history, and it had never been much more than a fantasy in the first place.

"Why don't you write something on Thurgood Marshall instead?" Taylor had suggested. "He's doing exciting things. I think your teacher would be impressed with your grasp of current events."

It was such a conspicuous choice but Taylor's intentions were prudent. Spencer ought to have Negro heroes. It would inspire him. But would he have made the same recommendation if it had been one of Felicia's boys writing the essay? Did he so readily remark to his colleagues about the *exciting things* that Marshall was doing? What would Mr. Walton have to say about it? Even Spencer had looked skeptical.

"Is he smart like you?" the boy had wanted to know.

"Smarter," Taylor had assured him.

"And nice to people? *Colored* people?"

"The nicest," Taylor had said.

This was at least subjective, and wholly dependent upon what you were in this country. It always came down to your *vantage point*.

"Well, all right," Spencer had reluctantly agreed. "But I ain't never heard of him."

"Don't say 'ain't'," I had finally interjected.

"Yes ma'am."

"Trust me, Spence," Taylor had said. "You will. Marshall's a great American."

Like Ralph Bunche? It was too soon to tell. If he did not win, wouldn't he just be another tragic figure? One more martyr impaled upon the American dream?

"He's a lawyer too?" Spencer had asked.

"The best," Taylor had told him.

Colored men had to be better than best. And what was best was not always what was wanted.

Maybe old buck-tooth Eleanor had something to do with it. She's always been partial to the niggers, you know.

By the time Sunday morning came again, I was ready to go back to church. I had to go back.

Nathaniel was right. Not even when one of the *other folk* was my grandfather. Church had always been my refuge. My certain and true place. The Lord was there. I looked for the brightest dress I had in my small wardrobe and chose the floral print, the dress I had worn on *Easter*.

I didn't put on the pearls, but Taylor would approve of the color. Compliments came easy from him. No wonder women were enchanted. This Sunday morning was no different.

"You look lovely," he said to me when I came downstairs to wait for Nathaniel and Connie. "Or should I say handsome?"

"You don't like that word, do you?" I asked him.

"For you?" he replied laying aside the newspaper he was reading. "No."

My face felt hot. He smiled.

"Rosy seems more apropos," he teased, reaching for the crutches so he could stand.

"There's roast chicken in the icebox," I said. "And some *lovely* apples. You be sure to eat lunch."

"Yes ma'am," he grinned.

"So what will you do today?" I asked making light conversation as he came towards me.

"I don't know," he replied. "It's a nice day. Maybe I'll take Herman for a run."

His self-deprecating humor made me uncomfortable. Although he could go without the left leg brace, he always wore the right one and he still dragged his right foot. It gave him pause at the staircase and the porch steps, and made him wary of thresholds and the edges of carpets.

"Okay," he sighed with a crooked smile. "Bad joke. But please, don't take that face with you. Nathaniel won't bring you back."

Mustering a brighter expression, I went to him and covered his right hand with mine as he gripped the handle of the crutch.

"That's better," he said.

"You could always come after me," I reminded him.

"That's right," he agreed.

By the time I was climbing into Nathaniel's car I was nearly at peace, and I was certainly unrepentant. "You got the smell of a man on you," Grampa had said to me once. Last Sunday I had had his pearls. But I was a woman. It ought to be my choice. Why should I be sorry for it?

When we arrived at Sweet Water, we filed into church the usual way, with Nathaniel leading, Connie coming after him carrying Nate on her hip, and me following her holding onto Little Evie's hand. For those who had witnessed or who were simply interested, they had had a week to talk about what had happened on the church house grounds last Sunday. Sister Rosalie was ushering at the church door today, and I met her surprised expression with a friendly smile, holding my head up in the custom of our family. I was not going to be ashamed of Grampa's anger or Taylor's affection.

The congregation was singing a hymn, as Connie and I made our way to the pew where Aunt Betty was sitting. I quickly looked for the back of Grampa's head, but he wasn't in his seat. Connie indicated that I should go in before her, and I obeyed steering Little Evie in front of me. I kissed Aunt Betty and sat down next to her with Little Evie tucked in between us. Connie, holding Nate in her lap, sat on the other side of me.

Expecting to see Grampa emerge from the side door to the lead the Devotion, I was puzzled when the leaders were: Uncle Perry, Ben Thompson, and Brother Jackson.

I wondered where Grampa was. Ben Thompson stood to read the Scripture selection, when he finished Aunt Betty began a new song. The congregation joined her. Uncle Perry rose and knelt on the wooden chair and began praying. Aunt Betty closed her eyes and gently swayed. Her voice mellowed into a resonant hum, and the rest of us followed suit. Uncle Perry's prayer was short and to the point. He declared our unworthiness, asked for forgiveness, thanked God for His mercy, sought His guidance, and praised His name. Uncle Perry was, after all, Grampa's son.

When the choir was getting ready to march in, I finally leaned over to Aunt Betty and asked where Grampa was. "I guess at the house," she whispered. Except that he never missed church. Even on bad days when there was sleet and snow, or the worst days of Mama's sickness, Grampa had always been at church on Sunday's mornings. Would he actually allow a strand of pearls to keep him away from his service to the Lord? Did he honestly believe that I had shamed him this much?

For the rest of service I brooded, my morning audacity fading steadily into afternoon guilt. My grandfather was not a mean man. It was the memory of Matilda and Albert, and the thousands of other injustices and insults he must have endured that had raised his hand to me to snatch away the pearls. Nathaniel was right. The necklace was too much. Out of Christian kindness he had allowed me to stay with Taylor, to nurse him and help him, but I had gone too far.

I should have explained that to Taylor and given him back the pearls. He was an intelligent and understanding man. Yet I had been afraid to talk about it, afraid that he would only hear blaming for deeds he himself had never committed. And I didn't want to hurt him either. No wonder segregation was the Law. It was easier this way. It was simply too hard when we had to tell our stories to each other.

After church I wanted to go to Grampa's house and talk to him, but both Nathaniel and Connie disagreed.

"What you gon' tell 'im, Esther?" asked Nathaniel. "If it ain't that you comin' home, I don't know what good it'll do."

"I just want to say that I'm sorry, Nathaniel," I insisted. "I didn't mean to hurt him. I want to make things right between us."

"But then you gon' go back to Mr. Taylor," said Connie.

"I have to," I said earnestly. "He needs me."

They looked at each other.

"Then leave 'im be right now, Esther," advised Nathaniel. "Don't ask him to forgive you for somethin' you ain't sorry for."

I could have walked over to Grampa's house, but I didn't, because Nathaniel was right about this too, I wasn't repentant. I hadn't done anything wrong. A good and decent man needed me, was thankful for me, and cared for me. How could I be sorry for that? Poor *Ananias*. What had his fellow Christians said about him giving aid to *Saul of Tarsus?* He must have been scared to death. Yet what else could he do but say, *Behold I am here, Lord.* Why was God always proving us? Did He forget what He had made us of? We were clay. Even if the fiery furnaces of life baked us hard as stone, we were still only made of clay. And Connie's *middle* was the Red Sea.

As usual Nathaniel brought me back late in the day. He didn't come in this time, however, saying that he wanted to go by the garage to check on things.

"What's the matter, Nathaniel?" I asked. "You still havin' trouble with those hoodlums? Didn't you talk to the sheriff?"

"They just some hot-heads, Esther, that's all," he said. "Tell you the truth, I feel kind-a sorry for 'em. It ain't only colored folks that's got troubles."

"Be careful, Nathaniel," I warned. "You can't pray everybody into heaven."

"Listen at you," he laughed merrily. "If that ain't the pot callin' the kettle black."

"Maybe so," I said getting out of the truck. "But that don't make it not true."

Herman and the quiet melody of Debussy met me as I came into the house. The music, *Clair de Lune,* was serene and soothing. I put my pocketbook away in the foyer closet. It was *our* culture too. We did have Marian Anderson and Paul Robson.

In the study Taylor lay on the leather couch asleep, his dark head resting on one of the throw pillows I had ordered from the Sears Roebuck Catalog back in November. I stood in the open door listening to the music, watching him. His face was at this moment like a child's, a boy's face, without lines or wisdom, just peace. As if he had only just begun this life, and there had been no car crashes and family conflicts, no war in the Pacific, no lover's betrayal, no polio.

His reading glasses were on the coffee table on top of a book, next to the decanter of scotch and an empty glass. His crutches were beside the couch on the floor. As he was now, it was easy to imagine that he did not need them. He might have been the man he was just a year ago when I first came to this house. I might have been that woman. But the crutches were here and we were linked by them.

Perhaps he was a better man for them. Stronger somehow. It was easy enough to be courageous when you were perfect to the world. It was different, it required more of you, when your body failed you, and demanded that you rely on others. In some ways he was more compelling for what had happened, more virile. And I was a better woman. A proven friend in this *attachment* that had taken me to strange places where I certainly would have never gone otherwise. It had bridged chasms and reached great distances. It had drawn a broken body and a broken spirit up and supported and sustained them until they had their own power again.

You gon' be his harlot too?

No. No, I wasn't his harlot. I never could be. Prostitutes did not yearn to give their passion away. Not even for pearls. It must be for them a very cold, calculated act.

Void of soul. The places deep inside of me that filled and swelled for him had no price, were not cold, were not void.

You're not my nurse.

I wondered if I ever had been, and now I knew I wasn't because I wanted to brush my cheek against the beard darkening his jaw. I wanted to run my hands along his sinewy arms, and press myself against the muscular frame that adapted to and compensated for all of the challenges he faced. I wanted to lay with him and match the rhythm of my breathing to his own, hear his heart beat, and taste his skin. Yet it was not a desire to have, only to feel, to want. I could not be here much longer. There would be no reason to be. When he did not need me anymore, I could not stay.

As if sensing my presence Taylor opened his eyes, and seeing me, he smiled sleepily.

"How long have you been standing there?" he asked.

"Not long," I said. "Do you need anything?"

He stretched his arms over his head.

"You've just been standing there watching me?"

Among other things, I thought.

"You looked so peaceful," I explained myself. "I didn't want to bother you."

"I was dreaming," he said.

"Of what?" I asked.

"I think it had something to do with the first day you came here. And you hated my lemonade."

"That's not true," I protested. "I didn't hate it."

"Well perhaps it was just me then," he said, the crooked smile making its appearance. "As I recall you liked Herman well enough and he barked at you."

"I was taken by you both," I confessed.

"I think maybe you were *taken*, Esther," he said abruptly somber. "And you thought fixing up this old house was a lot to ask. Little did you know how much you'd end up having to, shall we say, *fix*."

"Yes," I said, sitting down in the chair across from him. "You always were a little too confident in my abilities."

"The evidence remains irrefutable."

"Your interpretation may not be without some subjectivity."

"Such is the human condition."

We smiled at each other.

"Fortunately God is our judge," I said.

"You don't think He has a bias or two?" he asked.

"I don't think I know."

"Hmm. Not the answer I was expecting," he replied. "What are they preaching at that church of yours?"

"Well you said yourself there are contradictions in the Bible."

"Yes, but then I'm a heathen."

I must remember his smile when I was gone, I was thinking. I wanted to hold on to its intelligence and integrity, to always remember how the head had a heart, and a soul. I must remember this even after the memories were dusty with time.

"What if the Devil was just some poor misunderstood soul?" I pondered.

"Really?" he baited me a little, sitting up. "Another wayfaring wanderer, you think?"

"Maybe," I said staring across the room at the collection of books that I had shelved so resentfully at first, before they had started enticing me and teaching Spencer.

"So you think God might have been a bit harsh, casting him out like that?" he queried.

"Maybe he just ran away," I said sadly. "Sometimes when it's not how we think it should be, we do that. We run away from love."

"Yes," he agreed. "Perhaps we do."

"Are you hungry?" I asked looking at him again. "I can start dinner."

"Maybe God drove him away because of that," he said thoughtfully. "Because He loved him too much."

I was uncomfortable with this talk of fallen angels, outcast or runaway. Beethoven's *Moonlight Sonata* filled the background, slow and deliberate, each note deepening. Aunt Grace's friend, Mrs. Shaw, who taught piano, once described the piece to me as sensual and seductive, as the meeting of two lovers and their ultimate submission to their passion. Having mostly been raised on gospel music that was never meant for anything but praising the Lord, I had been captivated by the romantic interpretation. Now, however, it made me melancholy.

"This is nice, isn't it?" I said about the music, remembering Aunt Grace and the symphonies, and Mrs. Shaw.

Once I returned to New York Aunt Grace and I would go to concerts again. I would look for him among the crowds. I would always be looking for him.

"Yes," Taylor agreed. "It was one of Mother's favorite pieces to play."

"She played the piano too?" I asked.

"Yes."

"Do you miss her, Taylor?" I asked after a time, softly, so not to disturb the music.

"Yes."

"Were you close to her?"

"Yes."

"Boys always are, aren't they?"

"I don't know. I thought mothers were supposed to be closer to their daughters."

I thought of Mama and Jimmy and the bond between them. Yet I had never been jealous. He had had ample love for us all. He made up the difference. He had made everybody believe that they were special. It was his way. His gift with people. We had all been equally important to him for our own unique reasons.

"Maybe at first," I replied to Taylor. "Until the daughters are women too. Then things change."

"You weren't close to your mother, Esther?" he asked.

"I was helpful to her," I answered.

"I don't think that answers the question. But then again maybe it does."

The Beethoven piece was finishing. I looked at him. He was rubbing his right thigh and squeezing the knee.

"Don't read between the lines, Taylor. There's nothing there but blank space."

"Words cast shadows, Esther."

"Is that why you don't talk to your sister?" I asked. "Because your words have shadows?"

"In part."

"But you're a lawyer. Isn't it your business to shine a light on the shadows so we can see the truth?"

"Getting to the truth doesn't necessarily get you a happy ending, Esther."

"I realize that. It just sets us free."

"And you don't think Felicia and I are free?"

Taylor and Felicia could make things right again between them. It was wrong to let an angry old man, who carried around his futile resentments like a millstone, come between them. Jesus said let the dead bury the dead. Why hold onto the past instead of claiming the present and reaching for the future? Why grant it so much power?

"I don't know her," I said. "I just know that I'm a sister and there's a not a day that goes by that I don't wish I had my brother back."

He poured himself another drink. There was another piece of music.

"Perhaps she would too if I were Jimmy," he replied. "But I'm not."

He drained the glass in one swallow.

"You shouldn't be," I said. "You're her brother. Not mine."

"In any case," he concluded. "I'm nobody's hero."

Regretting that I had brought up the subject of his sister I stood up.

"I should make dinner," I announced.

He reached for the decanter again.

"It's early," he replied. "Keep me company for awhile."

That was the problem. I wanted to keep him company all the time. And that was not why I had come to work here. It was not why he had hired me. If it was, then maybe I was a *harlot*. A companion for a price.

"Would you like me to get you some ice?" I offered because perhaps he was drinking too much.

"No."

I sat down again.

"I didn't mean to upset you," I apologized.

"You didn't," he replied. "It's probably just my condition."

Condition? He had never used that word before, and there was something odd about the way he said it, the tone almost too sardonic even for him.

"Does your leg hurt?" I asked. "Would you like some aspirin?"

"My leg's paralyzed, Esther. You really think an aspirin will help?"

He had sent the hot-pack machine the way of the wheelchair, banishing it as well from his world. I had disagreed with him about stopping the treatments, but at least he continued the exercises and massages which I gave him with a new liniment that Doctor Mitchell had prescribed.

"Don't be discouraged, Taylor," I said. "Some cases--"

"So what else is on your mind, Esther?" he cut me off.

Nothing that I could talk about. Matilda and Albert, and the Confederate soldier were my shadows, inherited from my grandfather, who had not come to church today because the beautiful pearls had shamed him in front of his neighbors and friends.

I wanted to tell him. He must be indomitable in the courtroom. Patient, gauging, until he ultimately was able to get to the truth. I would not want to see him prosecute a Negro, because when he won I would be left wondering if justice had been served. The odds would be too easy, the outcome too predictable.

A man ain't nothin' but a man.

Maybe. Except in America's halls of justice. There, as in all the world, complexions mattered. I was nervous. A radio announcer interrupted the music to sell Gladiola Flour.

"How was church?" asked Taylor.

"It was good," I replied, although I wouldn't be able to recall the sermon if he were to ask me about it. They all ended up with an invitation to accept Christ as your *Personal Savior* anyway. I would at least have that to report.

"And since we're talking about families," he went on. "How's yours?"

"Doing well," I said. "Nathaniel and Connie send their regards."

"We should have them over for dinner some evening."

Picturing Nathaniel and Connie seated at Taylor's dining room table as if they were just another *Mr. and Mrs. Spalding* ensured that my face revealed my response to the suggestion without me speaking a word.

"It does happen, Esther," said Taylor. "It's not as though the entire world subscribes to Plessey v. Ferguson. There is that truth too."

Somebody's got to be in the middle if we gon' come together.

"I'm sure they would enjoy it," I replied unconvincingly. "Speaking of which, it is getting late, I better go cook."

"Nothing on your mind then?" he asked as if he was expecting some specific answer. "Except for preparing my dinner of course."

"Well… you do have to eat," I said somewhat perplexed. "Scotch is not a meal." I tried to smile.

"That could depend on what you're hungry for," he replied bleakly.

"Maybe you'd like to lie down for a little while before dinner," I suggested. "I could give you massage with the liniment."

"Companion. Cook. Nurse. My good fortune is extraordinary. But do be careful, Esther. Aiding and abetting the enemy is treason."

Treason? He had had too much to drink and his derisive humor was not funny.

"I don't know what you mean," I said.

"Ignorance of the law, my dear Sister, is no defense," he replied.

 III

From a dream about Danny I awoke suddenly, fearfully. Sitting up in bed, I stared into the darkness, getting my bearings. Danny was not here. Nothing had changed. This was the buttercup room. The walnut sleigh bed. I could see the lace curtains billowing at the open window.

In the dream Danny had been wearing his Army uniform, and wearing a face like Jimmy's in the photograph that hung on Grampa's front room wall. A serious, somber face. Not the face I remembered from our summer time together. Not the face of the man who had held me in his arms in the clump of trees. And there had been a battle. Things blowing up. Men falling down. And in a flash of light the pearls, lustrous in the mud, and the sound of thunder.

It had started to rain, the drops beating against the roof. It had only been a dream. Danny was all right. Collecting myself I got up and closed the window. Taylor's window was open too. Silently I went across the hall and into his room. There was another ice blue flash of lightning followed seconds later by a loud clap of thunder. Herman was on alert, next to his master's bed, but his master had not stirred. Quietly I lowered the window, leaving the room noiselessly so I would not disturb him.

Taylor had been so moody tonight. I was relieved he was sleeping soundly. Everyone could have a bad day sometimes; and with men you just had to let them get through it in their own way. Even Jimmy had not always been sweetness and light. And Grampa had perfected the stern father figure, whose affection you had to see even though he refused to show it.

Hurrying I closed all the windows throughout the house to keep out the rain, and then back in the kitchen I turned on the light and sat down at the table. In Grampa's house when there were thunderstorms we didn't turn on the lights but lit coal-oil lamps instead, and kept quiet while the Lord was doing *His work*. In Taylor's house there were only candles.

Danny was fine, I told myself again. He would come home. I should write to him. Neither of us wrote very often, certainly not enough for lovers. Perhaps because we weren't. I could not answer Nathaniel's question about who he was writing to because I didn't know. Who were we to each other? Who did I want us to be? The letters between us were just short interesting notes that kept matters alive while making no promises.

Taking out a tablet from a kitchen drawer I started to write,

> Dearest Danny,
> I hope you are well and safe. All is well with me and mine. It is fall here. The weather is cooling down at last. It is so much easier to sleep at night. Grampa is already stacking wood for the winter....

I had awakened from a dream about Danny to give him a weather report? If he exploded into death somewhere were these going to be the last words he would have from me? That Grampa was already stacking wood? The mediocrity of it embarrassed me, but I had nothing else to say. I lay the letter aside.

Herman came into the kitchen. I rubbed his head, and he went for a drink from his water dish. Folding up the start of Danny's letter, I decided to come up with something to write to him tomorrow. Turning off the kitchen light, I went back upstairs.

In the sleigh bed again, I considered my own *condition,* how I was on the Egyptian shore wanting to stay and needing to go, and getting used to the ambivalence. When Jimmy was alive everything had made sense. He had put order in the world. But he was gone. And I was as much a casualty of the war as he was. Impaired by the loss of him. Like Mama. Only she had died, escaping her grief. And Grampa, who was badly wounded, was waiting for me to bring his dreams, *our* dreams, back to life. I was *his* ram in the bush. That was my first obligation. My only real duty. But I wanted to wear pearls and love a man who already owned the whole world. I wanted to belong to him too. But it was wrong, or at least pointless. All this thinking for myself, as Jimmy had wanted, wasn't easy. How long could I sail my little boat back and forth across the wide Red Sea before the waves overtook me?

But the weather continued fair enough in the early days of October. Summer tended to hold fast on the Texas prairie. This was a land of Indian summers; belated, buoyant, blooming times just before the winter winds finally reached down from the north. In the kitchen one warm afternoon I stood at the ironing board ironing Taylor's shirts. Believing that he would soon return to his office, I kept his wardrobe prepared for it, looking after his clothes with the same dedication that made me insist on his exercises diligently, *doggedly* and *dogmatically*.

The telephone rang, ringing throughout the house musically. Would I ever be able to convince Grampa that he must have one? Perhaps—if I went home to do it. I put down the iron and went to answer the telephone that hung on the kitchen wall.

"Hello," I said. "Payne residence."

"Long distance, person-to-person for Esther Allen," a woman's voice announced.

"Speaking," I answered, surprised, wondering why Aunt Grace was calling me here.

"Esther?" a man's voice spoke. "Esther, that you?"

It must be Uncle Eddie.

"Go ahead, sir," said the woman.

"Esther," repeated the voice on the other end of the telephone receiver in my hand.

It was not Uncle Eddie. The voice was very deep. Almost familiar. And it was very excited.

I want to get close to you, Esther. You gon' let me?

I could not breathe. What if Taylor had picked up an extension? What would I tell him? I composed myself. He almost never answered the phone unless he was standing right by it when it rang. Catching a ringing telephone was for the more agile.

"Esther?" the voice was saying. "Esther, can you hear me?"

"Danny?" I heard myself say.

"How you doin' girl?" the man on the other end asked happily.

"It is you," I said quietly.

"Surprise, baby!" he exclaimed. "Is it okay to call you at work?"

"Where are you?" I asked him. "Are you callin' from—from Korea?"

"Try California," he told me, laughing.

"California?"

"Yeah that's right! I'm home."

"Oh, Danny," I said shakily.

"Listen, I can be in McConnell County for Thanksgiving!"

"Thanksgiving?"

Dread filled me up and spilled into my voice.

"Yeah," he said, then followed with, "If I can wait that long. Girl, I want to see you. I want to see you bad."

"Danny...Danny I–I don't know what to say."

"Say you want to see me too," he laughed.

"I--I do. I do," I struggled.

"We got us a lot to talk about. You all I been thinkin' about, baby. Can't get you off my mind. I been readin'--"

"Danny--Danny," I said more strongly. "You—you sound good. I'm so glad you're all right. But...but is the war over? All the papers just say that they're talkin' about peace. Not—not that it's over."

Didn't I want it to be? Didn't I want there to be peace?

"Well it's over for me!" bragged Danny. "I'm goin' state-side. I don't want to study war *no* more."

"Are you—you leaving the army? You like the army."

"Well it don't have to be combat," he said. "Can you get some time off from that ol' broke-down patient of yours? Aw-hell! You can just quit. I want you to come back here with me. It's great out here, Esther. How'd you like to live in the same town where the movie stars live?"

"Danny--"

"Please deposit fifty cents," said the operator.

I heard the coins as they dropped.

"Esther," Danny said eagerly, "What do you say? You want to come to California?"

Not now, I thought. I would—just not now.

"He's–he's not broken down," I said. "He's not my patient."

"Glad to hear it," Danny said. "I'm gettin' you out of that dead ol' town, you hear me? I'll be there for Thanksgiving. We got us a lot to talk about. All this writin' back and forth is all right, but ain't nothin' like the real thing. I miss you, baby."

There was a period of silence. I knew I was supposed to fill the space. I knew it was polite and right, and still I didn't say anything.

"You miss me?" Danny finally had to ask.

I had always counted on our time together in days. Summer days and summer nights. In *slow-drag* dances around Ray's Café. And in the backseat of a Ford. I hardly knew him at all. I couldn't even remember what we had talked about. If we had talked at all.

"Esther," he was saying my name again.

I had to say something. I owed him that much. For the letters. For the time in the Ford.

"Yes, Danny, I miss you."

"Please deposit fifty cents," said the operator.

"Okay--okay, operator," Danny said and then I heard the coins drop. "Esther, I run out of change. Listen, I'll be there next month. You cook a big--"

"You can't come," I cut him off.

"What?"

There was silence.

"I mean you can," I stammered. "But I can't—I can't see you. I can't get off."

"Esther, I'm comin' cross the country, surely you can--"

"I can't. I—I promised."

Don't leave me.

I won't.

"*Promised?*"

There was more silence.

"Your time is up sir," said the operator again.

"Esther! Esther, I love you!" Danny shouted into the telephone.

"I'm—I'm glad you called, Danny," I replied. "Take care--"

We were disconnected.

"Of yourself," I finished and returned the telephone receiver to its cradle.

I went back to the ironing board. To the starch and iron. To Taylor's white shirt and its collar. He liked a lot of starch. The judges required it. He had to look crisp in the courtroom. Because he had to go back. Danny had come home. It was over. I wanted Danny to be home. I wanted what I was supposed to have, what I could have. I had to want it.

We got us a lot to talk about.

Danny and I would be planning how we were going to take on the world together, so that his best was matched with mine and doubled. We would encourage each other. I would stand beside him, and we would advance ourselves and *our* people. The way Connie stood beside Nathaniel. It was never enough just to make *our own* homes and raise *our own* families, not when *we* could be *credits to the race.* My best was not mine to give away as I pleased. It belonged to what I was in the world.

Grateful for Taylor's preoccupation with work, I didn't talk to him until lunchtime when I appeared at the study door with a tray bearing a sandwich and an apple.

"I thought you might be ready for a bite to eat," I said.

"Thank-you," he replied, closing the file he was working on.

"It's just a sandwich. You seem to be very busy," I explained setting the tray down on the desk. "I thought you might prefer to have lunch in here."

"Who called?" he asked.

"Oh, it was my Aunt Betty," I lied again.

He nodded. I had never talked about Danny to Taylor, not even when he had been telling me his Sylvia stories. That was *the way* it was done. *They* told *us* their stories, unburdened *their* hearts and minds, and *we* listened, as though we had no stories of our own. It was easier this way. Arranging my life in little boxes and bottles, I had stored everything next to each other and yet kept it all separate. The McConnell County city fathers, maybe even those *founding* ones too, would have been proud. But then they were all liars too.

"I'm expecting Sanders this afternoon," he said. "We're going over one of his briefs."

With his friends and associates coming and going from the house all the time, his study had truly become an office. There were few women among his visitors now; mostly they were men, some of whom looked at me as if they saw the harlot that Grampa had seen. Their assessments went unspoken but they could not be missed, the examining eyes, the smirking lips. I suspected what they thought. What maybe they all thought. Perhaps even Doctor Mitchell.

I know what you are. There's a name for women like you.

"I'll make sure Spencer doesn't disturb you," I said.

"I should be free around the time he comes," replied Taylor.

"All right, I was just thinking--"

"I like having the boy around, Esther. I look forward to it."

I nodded.

"Can I get you anything else?" I asked.

"No. Thanks."

I was turning to leave.

"I've decided to go back to work," Taylor announced.

I stopped and came back to his desk.

"When?" I asked.

"Monday."

So it was to be over as easy as this. Of course it must. He went back to work. I went back home. And Danny came.

"Are you sure you're ready?" I asked.

Wasn't it what I had been wanting? Urging? Asking for? Praying for? He should go back. He was talented and important. He must have his life back before I left him.

"As much as I might ever be," he replied.

"But what about the crutches?" I ventured tentatively. "And what you said about biasing the jury?"

"Walton will keep me out of the courtroom," he said as if it were already worked out in his mind. "And if need be, then I can just sit in the second chair. You know, avoid opening arguments and summations."

"The second chair? Isn't that like being second class?"

The crooked smile came to his face.

"It sounds much worse when you say it," he observed.

"Taylor, that's not you," I protested. "You're a litigator. You have to lead."

"But I don't have to be center-stage. Things change, remember? We have to learn to accept it."

"Maybe you just need a little more time," I argued, not accepting it. "We can do more therapy," I offered. "Doctor Mitchell says--"

"That I'm making great progress," he interjected, the irony still in his expression. "I know."

That we have an *attachment* was what I had wanted to say. I didn't have to go to California right away.

"But you are making progress," I insisted.

I could go to Danny in the spring. Taylor could be fully recovered by then.

"I'm crippled, Esther," Taylor said simply, without emotion. "It's about time I come to terms with what's happened."

What's s'pose to be will be. Can't nobody block it.

But we could fight it. We didn't have to give up. Old men resigned themselves and counted on their crowns in Glory, after having learned too many hard lessons, after having suffered so many disappointments. But Taylor was a young man. His whole life was in front of him, and he had no expectations of a crown, no belief in them. He had to believe in himself. He was all that he had. I couldn't believe he was giving up. He had worked so hard. I had worked so hard. He was just weary. We were going to have to start managing his activities better. It wasn't good for him to get tired. He became discouraged, depressed. Then he talked as if it would always be this way.

If I stayed with Taylor until April, it wouldn't hurt anything. I could even be a June bride just like Aunt Betty's magazines said. I would make it up to Danny. We would keep following Sister Kenny's methods. We had gotten rid of one brace; we could get rid of the other. We could put the crutches away too. I would ask Danny to wait. I would make it up to him. I didn't have to leave Taylor. Not now. My decision felt like a reprieve.

"No," I said emphatically.

"Esther--"

"No," I repeated.

"We seem to have another difference in perspective here," said Taylor. "But believe me, these are my legs. I think I know."

"I won't believe you," I said defiantly.

"Esther, please don't be kind about it," he said. "You might think it helps but it doesn't."

"No," my voice broke.

I take care of you, you take care of me, and everything else we let take care of itself.

I wasn't through taking care of him yet. It wasn't time to stop. It wasn't time to leave.

"Esther, if I'm willing to face--" he started.

"No!" I cut him off again. "You--you should go back to work. They need you. But you're not— you're not...crippled. God is able, Taylor," I told him what Nathaniel had said. "He is. Please don't give up. Please. You can't."

"All right, all right," he sighed, returning his attention to the file on his desk. "We'll do it your way."

"It's got to be your way too," I pressed.

"All right," he said wearily, not looking up.

He was just tired today. That was all. He would feel better about it all with the next milestone, the next achievement. And there would be others. I was sure of it.

"You're going to get well, Taylor," I maintained resolutely, and quoting Grampa I added, "What's supposed to be will be. Nobody can block it."

"I thought I was well."

I had looked up the word *litigator* to be sure that I understood it, how it was different than just being a lawyer. Taylor was a trial lawyer. He had a mind for details. He questioned purposely. He could turn your own words against you.

"Stronger," I hastily adjusted my argument. "You're going to get stronger."

He chuckled dryly.

"I'm sure I will."

But he was not convinced, not today. Oh well. Tomorrow then.

It was pleasing enough to think of Taylor and Spencer in the study together, I encouraged myself while later on I peeled potatoes for dinner. Spencer with his Harvard-educated tutor. Taylor with his bright, McConnell County-raised pupil. Philanthropy and gratitude, filling the room, reaching up to the ceiling, pulling down the cobwebs from the darkest corners, shining out of the windows to meet the sunshine. It wasn't a wrong thing, this mutual need to give and receive. When I went back to Grampa, before I left to join Danny, I would remind him of the Good Samaritan, and of Jonah, and of the Egyptian princess who had raised Moses as her own. The Bible was full of stories of strangers brought together to fulfill God's purpose. His ways were not our ways. His thoughts were not our thoughts. The world might be a decent place, if people would only let it be. We could still be in Eden if we had only left that one tree alone.

"Aunt Esther, Mr. Payne says to tell you that he's going to take me home," said Spencer at the kitchen doorway.

"He is?" I asked.

"Yes ma'am."

I put down the potato I was peeling and dried my hands on a kitchen towel. Should I volunteer to go with them? What if something happened on the way back and Taylor needed help? But I would not always be around to look after him, I reminded myself again.

"Well, all right, Spencer," I said reluctantly.

However, as if I needed to review the situation somehow, I returned to the study along with Spencer, where Taylor was waiting.

"This is very nice of you, Mr. Payne," I said, assuming he knew what I meant.

Spencer was busy gathering his books.

"Hardly," Taylor replied casually. "I told him that he'd be riding with a neophyte, so to speak."

"That means he's a beginner," Spencer readily explained.

I smiled at him. He was a good student.

"I'm not worried, Spencer," I said. "Mr. Payne is an experienced driver."

"Well," Taylor said coming to his feet. "On that note, you ready, Spence?"

"Yes-sir!" replied Spencer.

"You can load your bike in the trunk," said Taylor, tossing the car keys to Spencer.

"Can I start the car too?" asked Spencer eagerly.

"Okay. But wait 'til I get there."

"Yes-sir!"

Spencer sprinted out of the house ahead of us. Taylor commanded Herman to stay, and the dog whimpered pitifully. I wanted to suggest that he take him along, but the thought seemed too protective.

"Spencer, do you know the way?" I asked once Taylor and I were standing on the front porch.

"Yes, ma'am," he called back from the car and slammed the trunk closed.

"Taylor does too," Taylor said.

I glanced at him sheepishly and then spoke to Spencer.

"Tell your folks I said hello, you hear."

"Yes ma'am."

"You will be careful," I finally said to Taylor.

"Yes ma'am," he mocked me.

"Taylor--" I said seriously.

"It's all chance, Esther," he interrupted. "Everything."

It seemed that way, didn't it? Chance that we both had left this place, only to return to it, finding each other when we had needed to. But was life really as random as all that? My Bible said that everything had a season, a time, a purpose under heaven.

"Of course you needn't worry," he told me, teasing me a little. "I'm sure Spencer's got a guardian angel."

Slowly he made his way down the porch steps. I was sure he was already stronger than Roosevelt had been when he had nurtured a nation through want and war. It might not matter so much if the recovery was less than perfect, except that Taylor could not bring himself to bear the sympathetic response. To the people who didn't really know him, the crutches were a reason to pity him, and as long as he needed them, that part of him which was more proud than wise would suffer for it. No, he had to recover completely. Everyone else would just have to wait.

The sky was the burnt-orange of dusk before, keeping watch at the living room window, I saw Taylor's car returning up the drive. I took a long relieved breath and hurried back to the kitchen, so that he would not know that I had been worried. My scamper in the opposite direction made absolutely no sense to Herman, who upon hearing his master's arrival had gone straight to the front door, wagging his tail eagerly.

By the time Taylor found me, I was sitting at the kitchen table, attentively turning the pages of the latest *Crisis*. I looked up, completely disguising my relief. His face looked a little drawn. He was fatigued I was sure of it, but I made no mention of it.

"Well," I pretended to scold him, "I wondered if you were out on the town, or somethin'. Dinner's *been* ready."

"Miss me?" he asked, taking a seat at the table.

"Yes," I admitted.

He looked at me intently.

Yes, I thought, I missed you. I'll miss you for the rest of my life.

"And here I was giving you a little time off," he said.

"I'll set the table," I said, again looking down at the magazine before closing it.

Then I went to the counter to get the dinner dishes.

"You made a good suggestion," he said behind me.

"About what?" I asked.

"Let's go out," he said easily.

I turned back to him.

"I-I cooked," I replied dubiously.

I'm colored, I thought.

"So we eat it tomorrow," he said. "That's what refrigerators are for."

"Taylor, it's been a long day," I started. "Don't you think you should rest?"

"What's the matter, Esther? Afraid that others won't overlook these crutches as easily as you do?" he asked sardonically. "Are you ashamed to be seen with me?"

Caught off guard by the charge, I carefully set the plates back down on the counter before I spoke.

"How can you think something like that?" I asked. "You know it's not me. We—I mean you can't just --"

"I can do whatever I want, remember?" he said. "Well. Almost."

Did he really think that we could just dismiss a fact of life because we had suspended it in his house for a time?

"Taylor--"

"Besides, haven't we already broken most of your precious rules?" he asked. "I say the harm's already done."

My precious rules. He knew better than that too. I looked at him. As if *we* could prefer the back doors and the back seats. The rusty water fountains and the last-class status.

"But if it's your fine reputation that you're worried about," he went on, "I'm quite sure people would think you were simply being charitable. No one could mistake us for an item."

When he was tired, he could be irritable, even caustic. It was the way of people who did not feel well no matter the reason. Caregivers had to learn to understand that.

"All right," I said, patient enough to placate him, but also chafed enough too to pick up his gauntlet. "I can put the food in the icebox."

But we'll have to take my face, I was thinking. No, no one would mistake us for an *item*. They would, however, see us as a scandal. And the sooner he saw the world through that dark veil, through my eyes, and saw the way the world looked back at him when he was with me, then the better. It would help with saying good-bye. There was nothing like reality to shine on a thing and make you accept it for what it truly was.

But then the late summer evening blew so refreshingly upon my face as we drove through town that the last thing I wanted to do was teach him any kind of lesson. I only wanted to be with him for as long as I could. He felt powerful behind the wheel, taking the turns too quickly and laughing at his own recklessness and my terror. And I was laughing too, drawn as I was into his apparent vigor and vitality. I went along, for all intents and purposes happily, absorbing every detail to keep as if the evening were a trophy, although less like the beautiful pearls and more like the shiny gold star.

If we made a public spectacle, I decided to ignore it. His reputation could withstand it; and mine was going to ultimately be made somewhere else. Mandy was always telling me to stop borrowing trouble because plenty of folks would give it to you for free. So I let the evening be as if we were on our way to some beach in Atlantic City. To some place halfway between his world and mine. It was nearly enough.

"So what would you like to eat?" Taylor asked me as we drove along.

"Ray's barbeque," I replied.

He slowed the car and looked over at me.

"Who's Ray? And where do we get his barbeque?"

"On Junction Road. You never heard of it?"

"That's clear across town," he laughed. "What's wrong with one of the places right here?"

"I don't want to eat in the kitchen," I informed him. "We could have done that at home."

When he glanced at me again, his face had changed, and I was sorry for the abrupt way that I had reminded him of limitations that even applied to him. He was just so sure of it, of all the promises about *life, liberty and the pursuit of happiness*. Him and Jimmy with their high and mighty ideals. There was a danger in loving daring, determined men. They could be naive about the power of right. And they could make you cry because you foolishly, hopefully believed them, even in the face of reason. They had a way of making you *forget* yourself.

"I thought you had let go of the rules," Taylor said soberly.

"I might have, and you might have, but we didn't consult polite society regarding this revolution of yours. This is not Greenwich Village."

"It is the United States," he replied.

"It's the law, Taylor," I said.

Your law, I felt like telling him, and he had sworn to uphold it, but he looked troubled enough.

"You think I can't take care of you, don't you?" he asked. "In my condition?"

There it was again. That word *condition* and the pejorative way he had of saying it.

"That's got nothing to do with…I mean it's just the law. That's all."

"Not really," he replied. "As you once said it's the men who enforce it."

"Taylor, if you've never had Ray's barbeque," I tried to say more brightly, because I did want to love this man if only for a little while, "Then you're in for a treat. I promise."

The mood was wounded, but it could recover. I would make the moment go away, even if it were destined to come again. That was how you learned to live with these moments. You prepared for when they came and you endured them until they went. In between you laughed. And you loved. And you lived.

Taylor parked the car and shut off the engine. The delicious odor coming from Ray's enormous pit greeted us the same way it did everybody, even though the sleek Chevrolet looked out of place among the rusty pickups and boxy sedans. Stares and whispers from among the knots of people out front greeted us too. I inhaled the fragrance of good cooking and disregarded the rest. At least we would get a meal here—together. The law would not be enforced. Ray's barbeque *was* the best in the county, and everybody's money was green. It was all a part of how we made it work, these strange relationships between former slaves and former masters.

"It's such a nice night, why don't we eat outside?" I suggested sincerely, realizing too that it was another precaution. It wasn't fair for me to bring Taylor into the middle of what was *our* world without broader permission. Outside he would be on the edge, and I would be with him. "I'll go inside and order for us," I said. "You get us a table."

The picnic tables were scattered around in front of the building. Strings of glowing electric light bulbs were stretched from the roof of the main building to wooden posts in the yard, providing dim but sufficient light. As an added measure, Ray had placed candles in big glass jars on each of the tables.

After his sophisticated life in Harlem, Jimmy had renounced the *Ray's Cafés* of the world, and Taylor had never even heard of this place, but I had enjoyed myself here on many Saturday nights. In the dim light I searched Taylor's expression now, looking for something that said he couldn't do this, that we should go back to the house on Webster Road and the meal I had prepared, but there was nothing there; and I wondered who had picked up whose gauntlet.

"What do you recommend?" Taylor asked as he studied the scene.

"Everything!" I replied as enthusiastically as a hawker. "Though I'd pass on the chitlins. Knowing how you feel about 'innards' and such." I grinned mischievously. "So what'll it be? Pork, beef, or chicken?" I asked.

"What are you having?" he asked.

"The pork ribs, I think. But I must warn you, they are not for amateurs."

"I like to live dangerously," he smiled wryly.

"I'll say. But relax," I squeezed his arm affectionately. "This'll be fun. You'll see."

"Are you okay?" he asked. "Since this is probably *not* the way things are done here either."

"Let's not think about that right now." I said, casting away the bad moment again. "We're out on the town. Let's just enjoy it."

"That was my idea, remember?" he reminded me.

"Yes."

He smiled again. It was better this time.

"Though this isn't quite what I had in mind," he said.

"I know."

But this was *my* world. He should see it. And here we were safe.

"So am I suppose to sing for our supper or what?" I teased him.

"What? Oh," he said, realizing what I meant once I put my hand out to him.

He reached into his pocket and brought out his wallet and gave me a twenty-dollar bill.

"Is this enough?" he asked.

It used to be a week's worth of wages for me and I was among Ray's better paid patrons.

"This'll be the best meal you've ever had, *and* you'll get change," I replied popping out of the car. "There," I pointed to an empty table, "There's a place for us."

Walking a little defiantly pass the subtle and not-so-subtle looks, I entered the building and went up to the counter. Among the group gathered there were a few faces that I knew, and I spoke to them. Mostly the responses were cool, standoffish, as if I were strange and not to be trusted. I thought about the warning words of the Wrights, but like Taylor had said, the harm was already done. The pearls were already on the ground. Danny was going to take me away far from here, and whenever I looked back I would not be recalling the way these people wanted to shame me.

I placed our order for pork ribs and asked for potato salad and red beans as the side dishes.

"What to drink?" Judy-Jane, Ray's wife asked flatly.

"Lemonade, please," I answered her.

"That'll be three-fifty."

I placed the twenty on the counter.

"Ain't he got nothin' smaller than that?" she demanded.

It was not surprising that she knew I had a companion. The whispers always went ahead of you. Not surprising either that she knew the money was his.

"No, this is all *I* have," I said firmly.

And *I* was the one who was standing in front of her.

"Take all my change," Judy-Jane grumbled, but she took the bill.

That, too, was not surprising.

"Sorry for the inconvenience," I offered falsely.

A young woman behind the counter was putting our meal into a brown paper sack.

"We'll eat it here," I said.

"Now look here, Esther Allen, I ain't havin' no trouble 'round my place. What y'all do up there in his house is y'all's b'idness. But we run a respectable place."

You run a juke-joint was what I said in my head.

"We'll eat outside at one of the picnic tables. Or maybe you want us to eat in the kitchen."

She glared at me but I did not blink.

"Put it on a tray," she barked at the poor girl, who looked nervous.

When the food was brought back to the counter with no room on the tray for the drinks, I realized I was short two hands.

"Can someone help me carry it to the table?" I asked.

"You know we don't wait tables," Judy-Jane told me smugly. "People get they own food. Everybody does. That's the rules. No exceptions."

The sheriff and his deputies didn't have to. Ray brought them their food himself.

"I'll give you a hand, Esther," a man said behind me.

I turned around to see Johnny Samples. His sweetness was all for Mandy, but I was her friend.

"Hi Johnny," I said eagerly, glad for a friend in what had become a hot and stifling space.

"How you doin'?" he asked.

"Good. You?"

"Just fine."

"You holdin' up the line," complained Judy-Jane, and Johnny shot her a dirty look.

"The man crippled, Judy-Jane," he said to her while he passed me the drinks. "I know you was raised better 'an that."

"Humph!" was Judy-Jane's unmoved reply to his reproach. "Should-a left it in the paper sack, and made 'em take it away from here."

"Don't mind her," Johnny said to me as we carried the food and lemonade outside. "You come here for Ray's cooking, now you see where his salt come from."

When Johnny and I reached the table where Taylor was waiting, I introduced the two men to each other. They were congenial but awkward. Johnny asked me about Mandy and then blushed as I teased him about being infatuated with her, which helped all three of us to relax a little.

"I'll tell her I saw you tonight," I said pleasantly. "And that you weren't with another woman."

"That's right now, Esther Fay," replied Johnny. "You give me a good report."

"You know I will."

Give me one too, Johnny, I thought, because I couldn't help but to wonder what people were going to say, what they might tell Danny when he came to town. How much did he believe in me? Human beings failed each other all the time.

"Well," Johnny said, anxious to make his exit from us. "Y'all enjoy."

"Thank you, Johnny," I said again, almost wishing he would stay, and thereby add some legitimacy to our picnic table.

"Yes, thanks," echoed Taylor.

"Nice to meet you, Mr. Payne."

"Taylor," Taylor corrected him.

"Mr. Taylor," said Johnny.

"He seems nice," Taylor commented once Johnny was far enough away that he could not hear us. "Have you known him long?"

"A while," I said. "I met him when I used to come here with Mandy."

"So he's one of Mandy's beaus then?"

"No, not really," I explained. "Not if you let her tell it. She doesn't take any man too seriously. Keeps them all guessin'."

"Pursue at your own risk," he said.

"She's kind-a choicy," I said lightly.

"I believe the word is choosy," he said.

"When in Rome," I returned.

"I wish I could."

I smiled.

"Mandy still considers herself married," I redirected the conversation. "She wears her wedding ring."

"A woman of unwavering commitment," he said.

She was I wanted to tell him. She was better than I was. More worthy of tribute than I could ever be. Maybe he was thinking about his own broken engagement to Sylvia. I was convinced that she hadn't meant to hurt him. It had just happened. One day someone else had had her by the heart. And Willie Gains had just wanted a better life for himself. Maybe he was thinking of Laura Spalding, or of some other pretty McConnell maiden. They would all rediscover him soon enough. And I wanted this for him. He should not be alone. He might never speak of love, but he knew too well how to hold a woman, how to make her feel beautiful and treasured.

"Aren't you going to pray over the food or something?" Taylor asked as he explored the potato salad with his fork.

I bowed my head.

"We thank you, Lord, for the gifts we are about to receive," I recited.

Seated at some elegant table draped in fine white linen, sipping champagne from a crystal glass, with the woman who would be his wife gazing at him, would he remember this place? And think of me?

I raised my head and looked at him.

"And for friendship," I added.

In his eyes at that moment, by Ray's candlelight, I saw the answer that I wanted. Mixed-in with the memories of the spicy sweet, savory taste of Ray's homemade sauce and the sourness of the yellow mustard potato salad, the sugary tartness of the lemonade, would be my face.

"Yes, we are very thankful for that," he agreed smiling genially.

The food was good. It was soothing too, and distracting. After a time we seemed capable of fashioning our own private world even here. Someone was always putting nickels into Ray's jukebox so it was singing nonstop through the building's open windows and doors. I bobbed my head slightly to the beat, and occasionally glanced back over my shoulder to see if I could see someone on the dance floor inside.

"So is this where you come for a good time?" asked Taylor.

"Yes," I replied. "Even if my grandfather can't stand it."

"I can't imagine that he would approve. A bit too strict for that I think. So does that make you a rebel in your own right?"

I laughed.

"Sometimes you have to be," I replied.

"Yes," agreed Taylor. "Depending on the cause."

Or when the prize was worthy.

"My grandfather's just a little old fashioned," I said.

"Tradition has its place," replied Taylor.

"So does change."

He smiled and took a drink of lemonade.

"Somewhat radical talk for a woman concerned about polite society."

"You don't agree?" I asked.

"I think I may have corrupted you."

"I do have my own mind, Taylor," I said.

I could think for myself, I wanted to say.

"I've been counting on it," he replied.

But Grampa was entitled to his reservations, his resentments. Maybe Taylor could afford to ignore his people, put them out of his mind and out of his life because he didn't agree with them, but I couldn't. And I wouldn't. At least not for always. Sometimes the understanding, the loving, was hard. Sometimes it hurt. But whatever wounds it made eventually healed. They smoothed over. And could even be forgotten. Grampa would get over what I had done. I was going to get over it too. Thanksgiving was going to come. And then there would be Christmas. Then someday soon, California.

My neighbors were clapping their hands and snapping their fingers. The lyrics might be anguished but the melodies always had an irresistible beat. *We* knew how to have a good time singing about our broken hearts.

"I bet you're something on a dance floor," Taylor mused aloud.

"We don't all sing and dance, you know," I said. "That minstrel stuff is mostly a myth."

"I wish the chip on your shoulder was."

"I'm sorry, Taylor," I had to apologize.

"I'm not like that, Esther."

"I know."

"I hope you do."

"Sometimes I forget that's all."

"The past dies hard, doesn't it?" he said quietly. "Even if it's not exactly your own."

But it was my own. His own too. It belonged to the both of us undeniably. It held on fast. Even when you wanted to let it go, put it down, and leave it behind. Because you couldn't let it go. Because it would mean letting go of yourself. And unless you lost your mind, that could not be done. You were always the you that you had been born into and lived through.

"We must be close to the county line. Does this place have a license?" Taylor asked after another quiet time.

It was my turn to react defensively.

"Now, Taylor, don't do that."

"Do what?"

"Get all official and everything."

"I just wanted to know if I could get something a little stronger than lemonade."

"Oh."

"Well, can I?" he asked.

"Well yes. Do you want something else?"

"Well yes."

"I don't think they have wine."

"I was thinking more along the lines of something on tap."

"Beer?"

"Yes, Esther, beer."

"Well yes, of course. I mean I think so. Bottles though."

"I suppose you're too much of a lady to do so, but perhaps I could get your friend, Mr. Samples, to buy it for me since I see I'm not allowed to go inside."

"You needn't be sarcastic, Mr. Payne. I'll get it for you."

"I wouldn't want to embarrass you."

I rolled my eyes at him, and this made him laugh again finally.

Shortly I returned to the table with two bottles of beer.

"One would have been enough," said Taylor.

"One's for me," I replied lightly, handing him his bottle.

"For you?"

"That's right."

I sat down at the table again.

"Beware, madam. Such public displays of cavalier behavior could cost you your virtuous reputation."

"And if I'm not as virtuous as people think?" I asked coolly.

"Your secret will be safe with me," he answered, raising the bottle to his lips.

"Wait!" I stopped him.

He lowered the bottle.

"What is it?"

"*I* want to make a toast."

"Okay," he smiled. "Go ahead."

"To change," I declared emphatically, valiantly.

He looked thoughtful for a moment.

"To change," he agreed. "And the will to accept it."

At least the faith. But I kept silent. He reached across the table and tapped his bottle against mine. We both took a drink. Grimacing immediately I set my bottle down on the table.

"You're right," Taylor laughed. "It's not the best."

My first taste of beer was like eating wet unsweetened cornflakes. Mandy's rich creamy eggnog and even Taylor's un-sweet wines were better. Beer was awful, although Taylor leisurely drank again from his bottle, as if he savored it. I looked down at my own bottle feeling as though I had wasted his money.

"Like everything, Esther," he counseled. "Beer takes some getting used to. It's an acquired taste."

"Why would you want to?" I sounded like a child.

He smiled again.

"Why indeed?" he asked. "I suppose therein lies the mystery."

I returned to the glass that had held my lemonade. There were only chips of ice left, but the residual sweetness clinging to the ice took away the bitter taste on my tongue.

IV

The following Saturday afternoon, as I was taking in the laundry from the clothesline, Mandy strode nonchalantly into the backyard, swinging her pocketbook in her hand and completely surprising me with an unexpected visit.

"Hey Girl!" she greeted me easily.

Although I automatically lit up to see her, it was nevertheless the middle of the day, so my first thought had to be that something was wrong. Had she come to get Spencer? She was too cheerful for there to have been a death or some other trouble.

"Mandy," I said a little warily. "Hey. What you doin' here? Is something the matter?"

"Well I'll say—what kind-a greetin' is that?" she replied huffily. "Why somethin' got to be wrong?"

"Well you're here in the middle of the day," I answered.

"It ain't so middle. And besides you not the only one with a tolerable employer. Mis' Lady is all right when she wants to be. Where that boy o' mine?"

"In the house with Taylor. They're working on his lessons. How'd you get away?"

"I just told Mis' Lady I was takin' the afternoon off," said Mandy. "She ain't gon' fire me. Don't nobody else want to see after them bad-butt chirren of hers."

Mandy set her pocketbook down on the back porch steps and began helping me take down the clothes.

"You ought-a have Mr. Payne buy you one of them 'lectric clothes dryers," she suggested, tossing a wooden clothespin into the basket.

"Instead of pearls you mean?" I asked dryly.

"I seen 'em in the Sears Roebuck book," Mandy continued, popping a big towel before folding it to put in the basket. "Just think—when the weather be bad you wouldn't be havin' to string up clothes on the back porch. Lord knows they take forever to dry that way."

"You can suggest it when you come to work here," I said and then felt immediately morose about the impending change, as if I resented it.

"Winter's comin'," Mandy noted matter-of-factly. "I say do it now."

It was the middle of October. If I went back to New York after Christmas I could enroll for the spring semester—except that I wanted to stay until April which was just six months away.

With Mandy's help taking in the clothes went quickly. As we emptied the lines and filled the basket I worked on my mood. When I smoothed them over his mattress to make Taylor's bed, the sheets smelled of fresh air and sunshine. An electric dryer couldn't do that.

"We'll see," I said.

At home Aunt Betty and Connie were taking turns doing Grampa's washing and ironing. Maybe I should go home and just come back here every day, like a normal domestic, the same way Mandy did and would do. Taylor could be fine on his own if I left everything easily manageable for him. But then again how would I make sure that he did his exercises? He needed me. I needed to be here with him.

By April he would be completely recovered. Then I could go home, back to Grampa's house, or to Harlem, or to California, or to wherever I was supposed to go. I hardly knew where that was anymore—where I belonged.

"You gon' fool around here and let them wrinkles get stuck on yo' face," warned Mandy.

"What?" I replied. "Oh." I laughed a little. "I was just thinkin' is all."

"Broodin's mo' like it," she declared. "I come over here for some comp'ny, wantin' to have me a nice visit with my friend, and you ain't got a sociable word for me."

"I'm sorry," I quickly apologized. "Let's go in the house. I made teacakes yesterday. I'll put on a pot of coffee, and we'll have us a good time."

"Now that's better," said Mandy.

I picked up the basket of freshly folded linens, she grabbed her pocketbook, and we went inside. On the back porch I left the basket of laundry on the new washing machine.

"Do you know anybody who could use this?" I asked Mandy about the old wringer machine.

Mandy looked thoughtful.

"Do it work?" she asked.

"Yes."

"I'll ask around. Must be somebody we know usin' a washboard and prayin' for a blessin'."

"It's just a washing machine," I reminded Mandy.

"It'd be a blessin' to somebody that's got less."

By the time the coffee was brewing, Mandy and I were fully occupied by the happenings in colored McConnell County. It was gossiping of course, but it wasn't mean-spirited, and we excused ourselves as we amused ourselves. Besides it was really hard to tell the difference between neighborhood news and what the proper folks called *idle gossip*. So when Mandy got around to letting me know that I was part of the *neighborhood news*, I really didn't have the right to feel persecuted or even offended.

"So folks are talking about it?" I asked resignedly.

"Some. Yeah," replied Mandy.

"We were just having dinner."

"Well it ain't every day that a white man takes his colored woman out on the town, even if it is only to Ray's."

I thought about Josephine Baker and the Stork Club. She had finally given up on America all together and moved to France. Lena Horne was living with her white husband in California, where Danny wanted to take me. I went to the counter for the porcelain jar of teacakes and brought it back to the table.

"And what about your mis' lady?" I ventured sitting down again. "Does she talk about it?"

"Not to me," Mandy said reaching inside the jar. "But I guess there's talk 'mongst them too. He ain't trash, you know. He get off them crutches, and they'll all be back around, swarmin' like flies after honey."

I thought of Laura Spalding.

"That's what we're working for," I told Mandy.

"What—to have a house-full of white women aggravatin' you to death?" she asked.

"For him not to need the crutches anymore."

"Humph. Tell me somethin'," Mandy bit into a teacake and nodded approvingly. "I was fin' to say, that sho' ain't what he workin' for."

"We're just friends, Mandy," I offered the obligatory declaration.

"That's what you say, but that's not what folks see."

"And what do you see, Mandy?" I asked. "You think I'm doing something wrong by being here?"

"If I did, do you think I'd let my boy be here?"

I got up from the table to pour our coffee.

"To tell you the truth," Mandy continued. "I like what he seein' by bein' 'round y'all. The way Mr. Payne is with him too, ain't that the way the world's s'pose to be? At least that's how I always figerred it."

I brought the coffee to the table and returned to the refrigerator for milk.

"Nobody else figures it that way," I said sadly.

"Some folks do," Mandy said reaching into the porcelain jar for another teacake. "And a lot more say they do. But you right. Just as soon as somebody gets the nerve up to do it, then somebody else just as quick to get theyselves in a uproar."

"So what do people say, Mandy?" I asked sitting down at the table again.

"You know."

"No, tell me. I want to hear it."

"'Bout like what yo' granddaddy said."

I sighed.

"Why is it always the woman who has to be degraded?" I asked.

"Don't ask me," replied Mandy. "Ask yo' pastor. Adam ate the apple too but all the preachers wanna talk about is how Eve got tricked by the snake and then tricked her po' husband. Seem like to me the woman always gets blamed."

There's a name for women like you.

"Well whatever they say," I said. "The truth is we are just friends. Good friends."

"Ain't nothin' wrong with that either," replied Mandy as she continued to munch on the teacake. "That's the way it's s'pose to be 'tween a man and woman. If me and Willie had-a been--"

"Aunt Esther," Spencer appeared at the kitchen door. "Mr. Payne—Mama!" he exclaimed. "I didn't know you was here!"

"Hey baby," Mandy switched topics and tone effortlessly to greet her son. "I come for my own visit with Aunt Esther. Do Mr. Payne need somethin'?"

"Oh," remembered Spencer. "He smelled the coffee and asked me to bring 'im some."

I was already up pouring another cup.

"Here you go, Spencer. And you might as well take some teacakes too," I said, placing a few on a small plate. "You want a glass of milk?"

"Mama, come speak," requested Spencer as he carefully took the cup from me.

"I don't want to disturb him," Mandy replied.

"It's all right. We was just doin' arithmetic."

"Oh is it now?" she glanced at me and grinned. "Anything to keep from them books."

"Mama," groaned Spencer.

Mandy got up from the table to follow her son, picking up the plate. I handed her the glass of milk.

"Gone boy, 'fo' the man's coffee gets cold," Mandy instructed. "I'm right behind you. You comin', Esther?"

I shook my head.

"Y'all go 'head," I said.

Come April this was the way it would be, the three of them in this house together. The way it was *supposed* to be.

I didn't really have to go so far away to become a teacher, did I? We had Negro colleges in East Texas too. I could be just as unknown in Dallas as anywhere else. I could make a good living for myself and stay in visiting distance of McConnell County. I could remain close enough to spend the rest of Grampa's life making it up to him, for all these months, and all these feelings. Mandy was always saying that there was plenty of work in Dallas. It was a big city. Even Jimmy had liked it. It might be a good place. There must be plenty of Negro children in Dallas, plenty of schools where I could teach. I could join a new church and find another missionary society. I could find myself a new choir where I could sing tenor, and find another set of pews that I could polish. Canaan could be anywhere.

By the time Mandy returned to the kitchen I had finished my own cup of coffee.

"Y'all must have had a nice visit," I remarked.

"He's a nice man," replied Mandy going to the stove to refill her cup before sitting down at the table again. "Spencer's plumb crazy 'bout 'im."

"Yes, but if you and Willie had been friends," I said picking up the thread of the former conversation. "He could be raising Spencer himself."

"True enough," Mandy agreed. "But I ain't done so bad with him on my own, now have I?"

"No, he's a wonderful boy," I said.

"And now with Taylor to show him what it means to be a man--"

"*Taylor?* I noted.

"That's right," replied Mandy. "He asked me to get used to it, to using his first name."

"For when you come to work here?"

Mandy would get used to it faster than I had done. She was freer than I was. She had always thought for herself.

"I'm not comin' to work here, Esther," Mandy said.

"But you have to," I insisted. "He needs someone--"

"He needs you."

I need you, Esther.

I looked at her.

"And not me or anybody else can take yo' place," she said.

"It's not my place," I replied.

"What it's *not* is all up to you to decide that. It's just left up to you what you gon' do 'bout it."

I got up from the table and went to the counter. In one of Jessica's cookbooks I had tucked away a letter to Danny. Retrieving it now, I brought it back to the table.

"Mandy, can you mail this for me?"

I handed her the letter. She took it and read the name and address.

"You tell 'im yet?" Mandy asked pointedly.

For an instant I wasn't sure who she meant.

"Tell him what?" I asked back although I knew the *what* already in either case.

"You my best friend, Esther Allen, but Danny's blood-kin. I gotta think about him too. He gotta right to know where he stands."

"Danny knows I work here."

"Esther--"

"We're friends," I sighed. "There's no law against it."

Of course there were *laws*. I knew them and broke them anyway. Still it was my secret. I didn't have to tell anyone. I could keep it in this house and give no account. When all was said and done some people would think I was good for having done it. When all was said and done my reasons would make sense to somebody.

"That's not what I'm speakin' of," Mandy replied.

"That's all there is," I said firmly. "Friendship."

"Then how come you can't mail it then?" she asked.

"I don't get into town much."

"You know what I mean."

In the letter I had asked Danny not to come for Thanksgiving, not to see me. By the spring I would be ready to go with him, I had promised. If Mandy wouldn't mail it for me, then I could just give it to Nathaniel. I reached to take the letter from her.

"I'll mail it, Esther," Mandy said, putting the letter into her pocketbook. "If this is what you wanna do."

"It's a friendship," I declared again.

"You tryin' to play it safe, Esther Fay," she said shaking her head. "And I guess I can't much blame you neither. But you know what else? You playin' one of them too. And sooner or later you gon' have to do what's right. You gon' have to decide which one of them you playin' for keeps."

Yes, *sooner or later* would surely come. I just intended to make it later.

The next morning I announced that I was not going to church, when I brought Taylor his first cup of coffee in the morning.

"We don't have to be in a rush this morning," I said.

"Why aren't you going?" he asked.

"I just feel like staying in today, that's all."

"What about your time with your family?" he continued. "Will you see them later?"

"That's a funny question coming from you."

"I think that was meant to be unkind," he replied and sipped his coffee. "And in any case we are talking about you."

"I'm sorry," I said.

"You want to tell me what happened?" he asked.

"When?" I asked. "I mean—nothing happened. I just feel like not going today that's all. If that's all right with you."

"Whatever you want, Esther."

But that was not possible. I couldn't have whatever I wanted because I wanted to be with him, and Grampa to accept it, and the rest of the world too. I wanted him to be well, and his family put back together. And for Jimmy not to be dead.

It was a strange Sunday with both church and family missing, and I was glad when Monday morning finally came with its promise of a fresh start. It was Taylor's first day to go back to work, and I bounced out of bed myself, before five o'clock in the morning, with a reinvigorated sense of achievement. He was recovering, I could say to myself even if he didn't want to hear it. This time I was not failing.

"So Miss Allen, what will you do with so much time to yourself?" Taylor asked me that first new morning, while we stood in the foyer together.

"Pine," I instantly replied.

In the mirror over the credenza were our reflections. He was straightening his tie. I was watching him. At times, by shifting his weight to the left leg, he could stand for short periods without leaning on the crutches. He smiled at me in the mirror. I smoothed a wrinkle I saw in his coat and brushed away a strand of Herman's hair from his trousers. It was delightful to see him in a suit again. It had been a very long time. But *time was not as long as it had been* Grampa always said.

"Yes, but for whom?" Taylor asked, turning away from the mirror to face me.

For you, I thought.

"Now don't you be practicin' your techniques on me, Mr. Payne. You can just save all of that cross-examination for the courtroom."

"No courtrooms, remember," he reminded me, reaching for the right crutch.

He looked very well, handsome and capable. I was sending him back to the world almost as good as new. *Almost.* Like the war *almost* being over and Jimmy *almost* surviving it. However, this time the *almost* would not be all that there ever would be. This time the *almost* was full of the promise that it would be completed. I was sure he would not stay in a *second chair* for long. He would put that away too, like wheelchair and the left leg brace. He just needed time. *We* just needed time. And time I was going to take. Until April.

"Have a good day, Taylor," I said, impulsively slipping my arms around him, pressing the side of my face against the light gray wool of his coat.

He was strong. The world would see. I had been good for him. He put his arm around me, but I let go and stepped back quickly, without meeting his eyes, and picked up his briefcase. It was new and equipped with a strap, which I slipped over his shoulder.

"Rather like dressing me for battle, is it not, my lady?" he teased.

I smiled, stroking the soft leather of the strap.

"And where are your colors?" he asked.

I looked up at him. What did I have to give him? The black of my mother's dress? The white of my apron? Yet I liked the way he had said *my lady*. What if I was of noble birth? What if Ernestine connected me to one line of royal blood and Grampa connected me to the other? Many people traced their historical origins, but *ours* had been left to disappear into dark unknowns. What was my heritage? Who had *we* been before we were slaves?

"You better go, my lord," I said, handing him his hat with a smile. "Your court awaits."

Initially Taylor planned to work only half-days in the office, but that plan lasted no longer than the first day. He was too glad to be back. In the mornings after he left, I would sit at his desk reading his newspapers. From Manhattan to McConnell, they all seemed hopeful for peace in Korea. But war was easier to achieve than peace. Jesus had warned us. He knew us. We knew conflict. We understood it better. We carried ourselves best in the midst of it. We knew how to be afraid. How to struggle. How to grieve. But being happy, that was the hard part.

I went through the hours that Taylor was away, and before Spencer came, thinking too much about everything, swinging like a pendulum between hope and despair, between conviction and doubt. Between now and April. Taylor was making wonderful progress but his right leg remained too weak to free him of the crutches. Grampa had paid for repairing the necklace but in a rage he had snatched it from my neck in the first place. Laura Spalding did not come to the house anymore but she believed I was a whore. Nathaniel and Connie understood why I was here but they warned me that the rest of the world did not. Mandy supported me too but she thought I was lying to Danny. Danny offered me a future but it was in a place far away from all that I loved. Taylor wanted me near him but I could not stay.

As the first week passed I constantly considered catching the bus and going to see Grampa, but I kept reconsidering what Nathaniel had said about how I wasn't going to give him what he most wanted and so going to see him seemed futile at best and selfish at worst. The prospect of another Sunday coming with things so wrong between us was depressing. I was a woman and yet a still a child under him. But what if something happened while I was away from the house and Taylor needed me. He wouldn't know where to find me. Ultimately I chose to put off seeing Grampa because *sooner or later*

I was going to be with him forever. Until I went to be with Danny in California. Or went back to New York to finish what Jimmy had started. Or moved to Dallas to figure out my own life.

Grampa would learn that my *employer* was well enough to go back to work. Someone was going to tell him. "What you gonna do?" Connie had asked me when she had learned. *When you comin' home?* was what I had heard behind her question. Stripped of no more righteous reasons for Christian compassion, if Grampa were to come for me, I would have to go with him. Or maybe I would simply have to admit to him why it was that I stayed. And that I could barely admit to myself. Living this strange life, in a perpetual state of ambivalence, left me feeling like I was listening for Gabriel's trumpet to announce the end of the world I had made for myself with the man in this house.

The days passed, including another somber Sunday when I did not go to church. Fall was coming. Nature had begun confessing what the calendar confirmed. The leaves were losing their green and dropping, pulled down by winds that drifted down from the north whispering persistently. Flocks of birds began their journeys farther south, moving through the sky in strong, tight formations, the way the planes had flown over Europe. Where Jimmy was.

The days grew shorter, and the nights were cooler. Spencer wanted to chop the wood for the coming winter, but I forbid it for fear that he might just chop himself in the process, and like last year, Taylor arranged for Mr. Leon to deliver a load already cut to fit the fireplace. Very happy to see him again after all this time, I brought Mr. Leon a big glass of ice water and stood in the backyard keeping him company while he stacked the cords of wood.

"You-all been through a lot I hear tell," Mr. Leon said.

"Yes-sir," I agreed. "Mr. Payne caught polio."

"That's what he said. But he doin' pretty good. Done gone back to work."

"Yes-sir. But we're hoping for a complete recovery."

Mr. Leon nodded.

"He wonderfully blessed to have you to see after 'im," he said. "God is good."

"Anybody would have done the same," I replied modestly.

"That may be true. But the Good Lord seen fit for it to be you."

Mr. Leon laughed a little but I didn't understand the joke.

"I was thinkin' about last fall," he explained. "When I brought the wood. I could tell he was kind-a partial to you. It tickled me to see 'im slingin' that wood like Samson."

Even then, I thought, the *something* had been between us. Mr. Leon paused a moment from unloading the wood and pulled out a large blue kerchief to wipe the sweat from his face. Then he took another drink from the glass of water I had brought to him, setting the glass down on the tailgate of his truck.

"Handsome home you got here," he told me looking around.

"I don't live here," I replied.

"Say you don't?" Mr. Leon asked, stuffing the kerchief back into his pocket.

"No-sir," I said. "I work here."

He returned to the wood.

"Well how long you been workin' here?" he asked.

"A little over a year now," I answered.

"And mean to tell me in all that time, you ain't done no livin' here at'-all?"

It was a curious comment, and smiling I decided that Mr. Leon had a sense of humor for himself.

"Well, yes-sir, I guess I have done some livin' here too."

He nodded his head as if he approved of the answer, and it was in fact true.

"This good-a place as any," said Mr. Leon. "To do yo' livin' in, that is. They didn't have much back then, just this house and the land, but they was good people. Wasn't nobody who could say different. It was a terrible sad thing when the mister and missus got killed. I 'member I come to the house that day with a load of firewood just like today, and I found that boy out here swingin' an axe like a man. Had wood chips just-a flyin'. Pret' near come close to knockin' hisself out or choppin' hisself up. 'Bout broke my own heart. I took that axe away from 'im 'fo' he be done killed hisself with it.

"I says, 'Mr. Taylor, what you choppin' wood for, son? I bring all you need.' He says his mama and daddy died, and he got to look out for his baby sister. He don't want her to catch her death o' cold. There won't be nobody left, he told me. It wasn't even cold. To this day, I just think he had to work out his terrible grief.

"Men be like that, Mis' Esther," Mr. Leon continued. "Even when we boys. When somethin' hurts us, we have to do somethin'. We have to work out grief. Guess the Good Lord made us better at sweatin' than weepin'. 'Member, He even now told Adam in the sweat of thy face shalt thou eat bread. Now you take women folks, y'all can just sit and cry 'til y'all get all yo' troubles out. You know how y'all do. A-rockin' and a-weepin'. Then after while y'all be all right again. But men folks, we need to work it out." He laughed cheerfully. "Sometimes I wonder just how many ditches got dug and how many houses been built behind a man's broken heart. If a man can't do somethin' then he don't see hisself as a man. He gets all confused and maybe end up doin' the wrong things, unnecessary things, but he just gotta be doin' somethin'. You think the Good Lord was troubled, Mis' Esther, when He made the world? Him bein' God and all, He must-a knowed how we was gonna turn out." He laughed again. 'Course now, His ways not our ways and His thoughts not our thoughts." He shook his head. "Guess some things just a mystery. What you think?"

That maybe Mr. Leon was right. And I thought of Taylor. Of him as young as Spencer, with only Mr. Leon to protect him from the axe. I thought of Grampa and his years on the trains away from us and for us. Of Jimmy and his plans for me with him. Of

Nathaniel and Uncle Perry and the garage. And the way Uncle Eddie provided for Aunt Grace. Danny wanted to do the same for me in California. The way Taylor's father had done for his mother, rescuing her from her Bohemian life and building her this house.

"So you knew the first Mr. Payne." I said. "What was he like?" I asked.

"Well, for one thing," replied Mr. Leon. "He wasn't the first. We all come from somebody else, Mis' Esther. You go back far enough, they tell me, then we all come from the same somebodies."

Adam and Eve, I thought. But who were those people in the *Land of Nod*? Who had been living in the place east of Eden? *Separately*.

Mr. Leon was building neat stacks of wood. It would be easy to reach and not likely to tumble down as the pieces were removed. Taylor had telephones all over the house. He could drive his car. He had gone back to work. I could leave him now. The mission was done. It was time to go home. I felt suddenly sad.

"You do that very well, Mr. Leon," I told the older man about his work.

"Work with willin' hands," Mr. Leon said.

"That's the Bible," I said as if on cue, and now remembering Sister Callie.

Mr. Leon kept stacking the wood. A broad smile filled his face.

"The price of a virtuous woman is far above rubies," he said.

"And pearls," I murmured.

Mr. Leon smiled again.

"She do a man good," he went on. "And not evil, all the days of her life."

I thought of Sister Callie faithfully keeping house for the Lord while she sang her Ma' Rainey's blues like they were spirituals. She hadn't been good enough to sing in Sister Wright's choir either, but she had loved, and lost, and gone right on living as if life were truly good. Perhaps it was. But I could never really be like her. Or like Mandy for that matter, who had so much dignity and grace that she could make a maid's life honorable. "You always was one of the faithful ones," Sister Callie used to say. I just needed to figure out to whom.

Everyone would have been so glad to set a place for Danny at our next Thanksgiving table. So glad and so relieved. They would have shaken his hand and patted him on the back, and assured him that I had been here in this house only out of Christian kindness. Danny would have probably believed them too. Grampa would have been so pleased that he would not have cared at whose table we sat. They would all get their chance. It would just be next year.

"You know the Word," acknowledged Mr. Leon as he worked.

"Knowing it doesn't make me virtuous," I confessed.

"No," he stopped to look at me. "You right about that, Mis' Lady. It's what you do with it that counts."

"Faith without works is dead," I repeated the Scripture.

"That's the Bible," declared Mr. Leon, his warm grin granting a kind of absolution that I received gratefully. "Funny thing 'bout the Lord," he continued. "He will makes us work for our rewards. Even the Hebrew chillun had to fight for Canaan. Seems like none of us can just stroll into paradise, even though He be the one leadin' us to it. Guess if it was easy, it wouldn't be worth it. Ain't that right?" He laughed brightly again. "Work's a good thing, Mis' Esther, don't you forget it. You can have yo' time to cry 'bout things, but faith moves mountains. And the way I figger it, yeah, the Good Lord could do it for us, and be quick about it too, but He wants us to do it, even if that means one shovel-full at a time. Take this here wood pile, you build it up and take it down one piece at a time."

By the time Mr. Leon left, a serene feeling had come over me, as though he had brought me good news. When Spencer came I asked him to mow the front lawn. It wouldn't be much longer before the grass would go dormant for the season. Following a quick snack, Spencer, with Herman in tow, went out the backdoor to get the push mower from the garage, but when I happened to come out on the back porch I spotted him just sitting on the chopping block. Herman sat on the ground next to him.

"Spencer?" I said coming outside. "What's the matter?"

He looked up at me gloomily.

"I wish Mr. Payne could-a chopped his own wood," the boy said. "He likes doin' it."

I put my hand on his shoulder comfortingly.

"I know," I said. "This time next year he'll be able to do it again," I reassured him.

"It's not fair, Aunt Esther. I don't want him to be crippled."

I would always hate that word.

"He won't be, Spencer. You'll see. It hasn't been that long, and he's gettin' better all the time. He can drive now, and he went back to work at his office."

"But he can't walk without his crutches. And Mis' Nelson said Roosevelt had polio and never got over it. I collected a whole bunch a dimes, but--"

"Your teacher's right, Spencer. But that didn't stop Roosevelt, now did it? He still got to be the president. And one day nobody will get polio anymore."

"But is Jesus goin' to heal him?"

"I don't know," I said. "Maybe He has healed him just in a different way."

"I want Mr. Payne to be like he was before he got sick. I want us to be able to play ball like we used to. He was goin' to teach me how to fly a kite."

"He'll do those things with you, Spencer," I said sincerely. "Just give it a little more time. We have to have faith."

"In God?"

"Yes. And in Mr. Payne too."

V

Taylor came home from work early that afternoon, surprising me, and I was glad to see him. I waited on the front porch as he got out of the car. Spencer, leaving the mower in the middle of the yard, had also run over to greet him, and Herman was with them wagging his tail happily. This must be was how it was at Nathaniel's house every day. It was good for a man to be welcomed home.

"Get my bag for me, Spence," Taylor said.

"Yes-sir!" replied Spencer. "Mr. Payne, I got my essay back from Mis' Nelson today!"

"You did?" Taylor smiled down at him.

"Yes-sir," Spencer said grabbing Taylor's briefcase. "I did real good too. Wanna see?"

"Yes, I'd like that, Spence."

"You're home early," I said pleasantly as Taylor was climbing the porch steps.

"Hope that's all right with you," he replied.

Immediately I recognized that something was wrong by both his face and his tone with me, however I forced myself not to ask what the matter was. If he wanted to, he would tell me in due time. I stepped aside to let him pass through the front door first, but, as usual he stopped and waited for me. In the foyer I took his hat from him and hung it in the closet. Spencer carried his briefcase into the study. Taylor followed and sat down at his desk. Absently, he loosened and removed his tie.

"Spencer, be a good boy and get Mr. Payne some ice water," I said to send the child on an errand and out of the room.

"Yes ma'am," he complied.

"Wash your hands," I called after him as I went to Taylor to help him remove his suit jacket.

"Could you fix me a drink," he asked me as I took his coat.

"Sure," I replied.

Draping the suit coat and tie on the arm of the sofa, I went to pour him a drink. When I handed him a tumbler with little more than a dash of scotch covering the bottom the glass, Taylor looked up at me and smiled crookedly.

"Leave the decanter on the desk," he said.

"Wouldn't you like some ice?" I suggested.

"I'd like to be left alone," he said.

"All right," I said turning to leave.

Spencer was back bearing a pitcher of ice water, and I took it from him.

"You get to go home early today, Spencer," I said. "You can finish mowing tomorrow."

He looked around me to see Taylor, his young face shadowed with disappointment.

"I want to show Mr. Payne my marks," replied Spencer.

"Tomorrow," I told him. "Mr. Payne's got a lot of work to do this afternoon. You can show him tomorrow. Now run along. Take Herman outside with you."

Spencer was not happy but he was obedient.

"Okay," he said, and looking around me again, added, "Good night, Mr. Payne. I'll see ya' tomorrow."

"Good night, Spence," Taylor said.

I watched the boy and the dog go out the front door before bringing the pitcher of ice water to the desk. Using the dishtowel I had been carrying for a coaster to protect the desk's finish, I set the pitcher down.

"I'll just leave this here," I said.

"Don't suppose you'll have a drink with me," he suggested. "It's not supposed to be good to drink alone."

"I'm cooking," I replied.

"I'm not asking you to get drunk," he curtly rejoined, raising the tumbler to his lips.

"Is everything all right?" I ventured gently.

"As well as can be expected," he said.

He needed more time to adjust to the physical demands of his new schedule. In any case I had learned not to press comforting on him.

"Mr. Leon did a nice job with the wood," I reported, changing the subject. "He left a perfect stack by the back steps."

"To Mr. Leon," Taylor raised his glass then took another drink.

I was silent for the moment, having run out of things I thought I could say.

"And how was your day, Esther?" he asked looking at me.

"Oh good," I replied eagerly. "Mr. Leon and I had a nice visit."

"Yes, Mr. Leon and the firewood."

"How was yours?" I returned politely.

"You already ask me that."

His voice was hard in the quiet room.

"Did something happen today?" I asked uneasily.

"Something happens every day, Esther."

"Maybe you'd like to lie down for a little bit," I finally risked suggesting. "I'll go get you a pillow--"

"You're not my nurse."

I hadn't heard those words in a long time and they sounded as they always had when he said them to me. He picked up the decanter and refilled his glass.

"Taylor, if you're tired--" I said.

"Don't take it out on you?" he replied.

"Dinner won't be ready for a little while, but I could fix you something, a little snack," I offered.

A humorless smile again lifted one corner of his mouth.

"This will do just fine," he said and took another sip from the tumbler.

"Taylor...maybe...maybe you shouldn't have so much to drink," I suggested.

"And certainly you are not my mother," he replied sarcastically.

"No," I said. "I am your maid."

He closed his eyes as if I had struck him, and I felt instantly guilty.

"I'm sorry, Esther," he replied running his hand through his hair. He looked at me again. "Forgive me."

"For what?" I asked. "You didn't say anything wrong."

"I am...I am very tired," he explained. "I just think I need to be alone for awhile."

"Maybe you should lie down," I suggested again.

"Yes, maybe I should," he said more to himself than to me. "Maybe that's the best way. Lie down. Play dead. Be done with it."

"Taylor, I'm sure you've just had a hard day," I truly sought to encourage him. "It'll get better, easier. It will."

"Esther, please," he held up his hand to stop me. "No Norman Vincent Peale. Not today."

I nodded and turned to leave again. When you loved somebody and they were in pain, for whatever reason, you just took it. I slid the pocket-doors closed and left Taylor to his decanter and his troubles. You learned to understand it was the sickness. Sometimes it was all you could do, the only comfort you had to offer, just understanding, and soaking up some of the hurt and rage that came with it. Taking the blame because they couldn't put it anywhere else. In the end for Mama even that little bit of comfort had become impossible too. I had had to watch her turn in on herself, consume herself, and die. But by next fall Taylor would be able to chop his own wood again. And Mandy or Laura or somebody would be here to watch and worry, although none of them would love him like I did.

In the kitchen I finished cooking his dinner because this was the reason I was here, the foundation of whatever it was that was between us. I turned on the radio again to keep me company and took the fish out of the refrigerator. We were having baked flounder tonight.

I smiled to myself. It had been months since I had had catfish coated in yellow cornmeal and fried to a golden brown. In *our* houses fish was almost always catfish, occasionally there was carp or perch, but the staple was the dark gray whiskered creatures that filled the creeks, served with fried potatoes, dill pickles. Tonight the flounder would be coming to Taylor's table with broccoli, carrots, and the rice. In Taylor's kitchen I prepared the rice so that it would cook up loose and fluffy. Grampa liked his thick and sticky, with sugar on top, so that it was sweet with the savory meat and gravy. I wondered what Danny was used to now. Oriental people ate rice all the time. Danny said they steamed it. He'd have to teach me how to do that. I had never had rice with fish until coming here, but now I liked it; the flounder with lemon juice, the fluffy rice with mixed vegetables.

"What's for dinner?" asked Taylor.

I looked around from the sink.

"Fish," I replied amicably, harboring no hard feelings from earlier.

He looked a little better. I shut off the tap and dried my hands, and went to turn off the radio.

"Why do you always do that?" he asked me when the music was gone.

I turned the radio back on but lowered its volume.

"So that we can talk, Taylor," I explained. "That's all."

He sat down at the table.

"What else?" he asked.

"No other reason, really," I insisted.

"I meant what else are we having for dinner?"

"Oh," I said. "Uh, rice and vegetables, broccoli and carrots."

I went back to the fish.

"I think you got a very good deal with Mr. Leon," I chatted as I was arranging the pieces of flounder in a shallow baking pan. "You should go see the stack he delivered. And he's an old man too, but just as strong as an ox. And very wise, Taylor. We had a nice talk."

"I'm not, in either case, so if you don't mind, I'll just sit for a while," he said.

I turned to look at him.

"All right, Taylor," I replied. "Can I get you anything?"

"No."

I turned back to the counter. Satisfied with the fish in the pan, I went over to the sink and washed its smell off my hands.

"Esther... about the way I behaved before, I am sorry," he said.

I opened the oven door and stuck the pan in.

"No harm done." I replied casually, but with my head in the oven I breathed my relief.

"It's not like that between us," he added.

"I know, Taylor."

I went to the refrigerator to get the vegetables.

"I hope you do," he said.

His apology was embarrassing me.

"You had a difficult day that's all," I said, smiling at him. "You're tired. Like you said."

"It was difficult," he admitted. "But my mood is not your fault."

"It's nobody's fault," I said.

He sighed deeply. I peeled carrots.

"You must have better," he told me.

My hands became still but I didn't turn around. The *better* meant leaving him.

"You deserve it," he added.

I *deserved* what I wanted, but I couldn't have that.

"I have it pretty good, Mr. Payne," I said in a voice that concealed my sorrow and resumed peeling the carrots.

"You don't believe that, Esther," he replied.

"Vantage point, Taylor," I reminded him casually. "We do have different ones, remember?"

"Even now."

"Even now."

Keeping my back to him I finished peeling the carrots and chopped them, and soon I had both carrots and broccoli in a small pot with just enough water to mostly steam them. According to his mother's cookbooks the object was seldom to boil a vegetable.

"So what did you and Leon talk about that impressed you so much?" Taylor asked.

"He is very wise," I replied, peeping in on the flounder. "But you know him. He talked about your father. He really liked him."

"What do you think of him?"

"I think he's very romantic."

"Leon? Or my father?"

I thought for a moment.

"Both," I answered.

"Leon's been around a long time," said Taylor.

"Seems like it. But I'd never met him before. He must not be from McConnell County."

"The world's bigger than McConnell County, Esther."

My world wasn't. Not really. I didn't think I could count New York. It seemed I had just been *passing through* it. One day there would be California. I wondered what segregation was like out west. *If* it was out west. Maybe it would be like living up north. Not by law just by custom. Was there no place that I could feel fully free? What was life like for Lena Horne? Perhaps you had to be very beautiful for such allowances to be made. Very beautiful, not just *handsome*.

"Well I'm glad I met him," I said. "I like him very much. He's quite the philosopher."

Calling him a philosopher in this instance seemed more prudent than saying he was a Christian. Taylor's mood was improved, and like Mama used to say, everything didn't have to be talked about.

"Besides enjoying the company of old men, what else did you do today?" Taylor asked.

"Oh the usual," I said, turning the fish. "Whatever it is I always do. Cleaned here, waxed there. Ironed."

Acted as though I was the woman of this house, I thought. As if I did *live* here. The rice was ready and I turned off the flame. At last I turned to face him.

"Read your newspapers too," I smiled. "That was while I was on my coffee break of course."

"I thought I was forgiven," he said sullenly.

I smiled again.

"You are," I replied. "I'm just teasing you."

"Then come here and shake my hand on it," he said, holding out his right hand to me.

I put my hands to my nose and smelled them.

"I better not," I said turning up my nose. "I don't think the fish is off of them."

"I'll take my chances," he said. "Give me your hand."

I did as he asked, and he squeezed it tightly before kissing it again.

"Oh!" I gushed playfully. "You are so chivalrous, sir!"

"I would do anything for you, Esther," he said.

You must have better.

I love you, Taylor, my heart said deep in the confines of my chest.

"Then just let me see about your supper," I said, pulling my hand away.

"So what did Leon have to say about world events?" he asked as I retreated to the kitchen counter.

"We didn't exactly discuss dispatches from the Associated Press, Mr. Payne."

I shut off the heat under the vegetables and took the flounder out of the oven.

"What did you talk about?" he asked.

"Oh about workin' and livin'. That kind of thing. And some about religion."

"You miss that, don't you? Talking about religion. I guess I'm not much of a believer, am I?"

I had forgotten my own warning, but we were here now.

"Not in God anyway," I said as lightly as I could as I came back to the table.

Not yet, I added in my head. I loved him so much, I couldn't possibly see his soul surrendered to Satan, and God loved him more.

"Yet oddly enough here you are," replied Taylor. "Living in this den of iniquity. What kind of missionary are you, Sister?"

"*Den of iniquity?*" I laughed.

"I take it you don't agree with the assessment."

"Oh Taylor Andrew Payne," I shook my head. "Of course not. And it's time for dinner."

Taylor Andrew Payne. I would never tire of saying his whole name completely. Of rolling each of the letters off my tongue and listening to the sound they made. Like music. Like what everyone believed about the name of their champion. But I never forgot that he wasn't *my* champion. This hero belonged to somebody else. I could not be living as if I could be the beautiful heroine in a romantic novel. Cinderella's shoes did not fit my feet. My hero was in California, making a place for me, where the movie stars lived.

Mindful of Taylor's weariness, I suggested that we eat dinner in the kitchen tonight. Since my birthday he had become rather strict about us having dinner together in the dining room, but this time he agreed.

I wondered where Danny would want to have his meals. Would our house be big enough to have a dining room? I pictured him at the head of his table, our sons and daughters with bright faces and promising futures all around us. Maybe futures free of segregationist signs and laws to hold them back. Maybe by the time they were learning American history, there would be glory in the story for them too.

You must have better.

And my children must have best.

"Engaged in some private contemplation?" inquired Taylor as we shared dinner.

"Oh. No," I said, "I was just thinking."

"A contemplative soul is a brooding one," he said.

I watched him refill his wine glass. He should eat more I thought, but kept this to myself too, and only smiled at him.

"Not always, Taylor. Is the flounder okay?"

"It's fine."

"Someday I'm going to make you catfish, fried, but you'll like it."

"I've had it before."

"When? I can't imagine you'd find it in Cambridge or New York."

"I'm from McConnell County, remember? Or do you forget that too?"

I smiled again indulgently.

"Yes, Taylor, I suppose, I do sometimes. But anyway, I'll fix it for you the way my grandfather taught me. I don't think you've had *his* recipe. Do you like dill pickles?"

"Probably," he said, taking a drink of the Chablis.

"When I was little I used to eat dill pickles with peppermint candy canes stuck down in the center," I related.

"Sweet and sour."

"Yes," I chuckled. "And minty."

He finally smiled.

"I remember."

"*You* do?"

"Yes."

"Oh Taylor, please!" I shook my head and ate my fish. "When did you ever have pickles and peppermint?"

"You don't believe me?"

"No," I laughed.

"Why not?" he asked sharply.

Conversations were not going to be easy with him tonight. Neither the scotch nor the wine had been sufficient. Down every discourse a skirmish seemed to be waiting. The edge in his voice remained, and I kept bumping into it, nicking myself. The full days were too much to start with. There must be a difficult case. Laura Spalding or someone else had done something to upset him. He would get around to telling me all about it when he was ready, when he could be matter-of-fact, when it was not a *fresh memory*.

Maybe he had had peppermint and pickles. It was a small world. And try as we might we could not keep it truly *separate*. Mr. Leon said we all came from the *same somebodies*. Even if we didn't, we at least intersected with each other along the way. Encountering each other, forging improbable bonds, since the hellish merchant ships had brought their human cargo to these shores. Perhaps we really had become Nathaniel's *one flock*. Perhaps Taylor was just a ram and I was just an ewe, one of which happened to be white and the other one black. If enough of us eventually held fast to that, then there might be a peace that passed understanding.

"I guess I just can't picture you at that age," I smiled hoping he would too. "Eating candy canes."

It wasn't true. I pictured him all the time as a boy. When he must have been happy before his parents died and left him to the coldness of his uncle.

"It was a long time ago," Taylor said dryly, taking another drink from his wine glass.

"I didn't mean that the way it sounded."

"It's all right. 'The truth sets you free.'"

"Careful, Taylor," I teased. "You're coming awfully close to quoting the Scriptures again."

He looked at me.

"You don't think I know anything about sound doctrine?"

I didn't even know he knew the term.

"Well, it's a little more than a doctrine," I replied.

"Ah yes, faith," he said. "Believing in the impossible."

"Nothing's too hard for God. That's in the Bible too."

"Are you so sure about that, Esther?"

"Yes, Taylor, I am."

I ate some rice.

"It's easy for you, isn't it?" he said. "That's really how we're different. You're the wheat and I'm the chaff."

By law I was the *chaff*. I focused on the food on my plate. It was *his* side that claimed the difference. *His* side that said that the one world, the one small little world, had to be divided up into endless pieces, until the spaces were too cramped to avoid contamination and conflict. And companionship too. I looked up at him. Even in the conflict there was inevitable companionship. Even though it was his Law that threshed us apart, casting off the chaff with the straw in the field.

"I wonder how pickles and peppermint led us to social analysis," I said.

"Everything is social analysis with you," replied Taylor. "You refuse to let life just be."

With my fork I moved the broccoli around on my plate.

"You made the rules," I at last reminded him.

"You play by them," he replied.

Again I looked up from the food and into his eyes.

"Not in this house," I said.

VI

When I finished washing the dishes, I stayed in the kitchen to stay out of argument's way, flipping through the pages of a *Life* magazine at the table. I considered filling the aluminum foot-tub with water and setting it on the stove to boil later to make the hot-packs. His right leg still bothered him, and throughout the evening he had repeatedly rubbed the right thigh and knee which usually meant the leg ached. The hot-pack machine was gone, but I had stored the wool strips just in case. I could squeeze them through the wringer of the old washing machine and carry them upstairs in a covered dishpan the way we had done in the beginning.

Perhaps we should continue the hot-packs at least until he was strong enough to require only a cane. A cane didn't have to be an object of pity. It wouldn't necessarily bias a jury. Indeed walking sticks were fashionable in some circles. Fred Astaire danced with a walking stick.

The pain explained the strain between us tonight. The alcohol had only exacerbated it. Like Nathaniel said, alcohol could make you mean. I made myself a cup of tea, and thought about Cordelia Collier. What was it like to love a violent man? Taylor was not like that. If he was really willing to do anything for me then he should agree to the hot-packs. Sometimes a woman needed to have something to do to work out her feelings too.

Herman standing in the kitchen doorway, barked at me. "What is it, boy?" I asked. "You need to go out?" Did he hear somebody outside? He didn't come towards me or go towards the back door either. Instead he trotted back a short distance towards the front of the house, stopped and looked back at me, as if he wondered why I did not follow. When he barked again, I got up from the table and went after him.

He led me to into the foyer where his master was crawling along the floor towards the staircase.

"Taylor!" I cried, dropping down beside him to help him. "What happened?"

"Don't!" he shouted at me.

I recoiled, having learned my lesson from before, and watched him drag himself to the staircase railing. Once he could grasp it, he used it to pull himself into a sitting position on the bottom stair.

"Are you hurt?" I dared. "Is there something I can do?"

"Just get me the damn crutches," he replied through clenched teeth.

Swiftly I collected them and brought them to him.

"What happened?" I asked again.

"I fell," he said. "Cripples are known to do that from time to time."

"Well if you're going to drink you have to eat," I scolded him, ignoring the word I hated so much. "It's no wonder you--"

"I can hold my liquor, madam!" he retorted, snatching one of the crutches away from me. "It's your goddamned waxed floors that put me on my ass."

I looked down at the polished hardwood, glossy in the foyer light.

"Yes, I know," he said mordantly. "You forget that I'm crippled."

"I'm–I'm sorry," I apologized. "I didn't realize--"

"There's so much you don't realize."

"I'm sorry, Taylor," I repeated.

"For what?" he asked coldly. "In some ways you're as much a victim of the circumstance as I am. Two for one," he continued, using the crutch and the banister railing to bring himself to his feet. "My punishment and your penance."

He reached down to secure the right leg brace.

"Don't talk like that," I said quietly.

"It's the truth, Esther," he replied taking the other crutch from me now. "That's why you're really here. Fulfilling some kind of penance. Although for what I can't imagine. Guess you're right after all, I can't understand how you people think."

You people.

"I tried to," he continued, turning to climb the stairs. "But it seems to me life is already hard enough. Why would you make it a sin too?"

"It's not a sin," I said to his back.

"It doesn't matter. If it's your penance, I'll take it. I'm not too proud. Not anymore. Hell," he laughed darkly. "I don't even feel selfish. I did warn you that I might have gotten what I deserve. You actually chose to stay."

"Taylor, please," I pleaded. "What's wrong? Did something happen?"

"Just not forever though, right?" he said. "Penance is temporary."

His right leg shook, forcing him to pause.

"And that's the difference, isn't it?" he asked as he pulled his right foot up to the next step. "You are the penitent and I am punished."

"It's not like that," I said defensively. "God is good, Taylor."

"If that's the case, it would seem I have used up my portion. And if He's as fair as you claim, I'm out of luck."

Near the top of the stairs, another spasm, this time more severe, caused his right leg to tremble violently. Taylor let go of the crutches and they slid away from him down the stairs, as he dropped to his left knee. I waited. Resting his head on his arm, facedown on the staircase, Taylor also waited, forced to let the spasm pass. Only Herman moved, going up to him and licking his hand. After some time, Taylor reached up for the banister again, but then his hand fell away. And still I waited. Sometimes the most important thing to do was *the waitin'*.

"Esther," he spoke at last. "Help me...please."

Instantly I was beside him, and putting my arms around him, I helped him to his feet.

"You think He struck me down for that?" he asked desolately.

Poor *Saul* had to be made blind before he could see. Although he must have deserved it, for all the persecutions, for *Stephen* stoned to death on the ground. But what could Taylor have possibly done? How was this his harvest? Now that he was standing again and holding onto the railing, I started to move away from him to retrieve the crutches.

"No!" sudden panic rose in his voice. "Don't leave me."

Don't leave me.

His dark eyes were stormy, pooling with unshed tears. I slipped my arm back around his waist.

"I won't, Taylor," I repeated the promise. "I won't."

Leaving the crutches I helped him to his room and then into his bed. Jimmy had not sown bad seeds either, and he had not had a harvest at all. Must God always be a mystery? "That's it," Taylor said grimly as I lifted his legs onto the bed. "Work with your willing hands, Esther. The virtuous woman stretches out her hand to the poor, and reaches for the needy. Perhaps there's enough virtue in you to save me too."

A man'll never have her whole heart.

I supposed Jimmy had been right all along. Even back then I didn't have a *whole* heart to give. It belonged to him, and to Grampa, and some portion of it had to be Mama's. The Lord had His share of it, as did the rest of my family, Mandy too. Yet there had always been enough of it to go around. It must be that love could be *abundant* too, in *good measure, pressed down, and shaken together, running over*. Even if it was unspoken. Like the flowers on Sister Callie's grave, love was of its own volition, offering itself up, a burning sacrifice.

And tonight Taylor yielded to it again, to what it made of my hands and my labor. I tossed the strips of wool into the dishpan next to the bed. They seemed to have helped. I knelt on the bed at Taylor's feet and rested his left ankle on my shoulder in order to fully stretch out the calf and hamstring, as he lay silently watching me. We had done this so many times. His legs and my hands knew what to do almost automatically. I moved to his right leg. When I raised it to place his ankle on my shoulder, he briefly gripped the bed sheet and his lips disappeared into a tight thin line. It hurt him. I hurt him. But I continued, forcing the limb through the exercise.

"I suppose you remember it now," he said.

I met his eyes. The secret was so safe that he had no idea what his body meant to me, how I treasured it, and loved it. I made it work hard because I wanted to return it to him in a way that he could love again too. I wished I could give him relief now, put down his leg and give him rest, but I could not fail him. He relied on me. One of us had to keep our eyes on the prize. Somebody had to hold on.

Surely God could have used a kinder way to call Taylor to salvation. But there was no point in pondering that now. The answers wouldn't undo any of it. We just had to wait for the *by and by*. When the morning came. *When all the saints of God were gathered at home.* I wanted Taylor to be there too. In Heaven. Where things had always been done *differently*.

When the last exercise was executed, I gently lowered his trembling leg back down to the bed and then moved to sit beside him.

"You're merciless, Sister Sergeant," he charged, but his expression had relaxed and there was no mockery in his voice.

I was his sister, in the name of the Lord. And I didn't mind being his drill sergeant in everything else.

"The prize is worthy," I told him smiling softly, as I guided him to roll over onto his stomach so that I could complete our routine by massaging his back and shoulders.

He was wearing only his cotton drawers, and my hands glided over his warm supple skin, which was damp with perspiration and liniment. I squeezed and released the strong smooth muscles. The liniment smelled of menthol and was in its way refreshing even though it was always the bergamot that I missed. For a time I lingered on his shoulders, then moved to his neck and back. Did he recall talking about the *prize*? We had struggled together for so long the time investment alone made it worthy. Never mind that it was his life too. And my love. Surely I was massaging him now as much for myself as for him. The therapy was my justification, my permission to touch him. He needed me so I was approved, no matter what anyone else thought about it.

And in a way it was like polishing the church pews at Sweet Water. No matter what Sister Wright said about me and my singing, the pews had always given me my place, and people had seldom seen me doing that work too. They probably never thought about how it was that the church was always clean and bright. No matter. I didn't require accolades.

But I did have pearls. And glimpses of what it might be like to be cherished.

I would do anything for you, Esther.

He valued me. Sometimes it confused us both. But he did value me. He understood what I had done for him. And I yearned to tell him what he had done for me in return. I longed to tell him all the things that he made me feel.

Grampa was right. It had been inevitable. Another old story, this one of the patient and his nurse. A Hemingway tale of a brave man and a devoted woman. Her constancy attracts him. His trust seduces her. But it was temporary, and conditional. Hemingway stories were not fairytales.

...Somethin' gon' start to happen 'tween you.

The *something* had a name. And yes, sometimes I did *forget* myself. Along with the crutches, and his position, his whiteness. And Grampa's past. And what everybody from Sister Wright to Laura Spalding thought of me. I forgot about everything but his smile, and the way his lips felt on my hand, and the way his dark eyes could see me.

So when I felt him find respite in my touch tonight, and I kissed him softly on the shoulder, the act really only startled him. I had known all along that I would do this someday. I had planned to wait until I was leaving, to make it a part of the good-bye. But tonight the *someday* had come. Taylor stiffened slightly, briefly. Thinking for myself and of myself, I placed the side of my face against the broadness of Taylor's back. *A man ain't nothin' but a man.*

"I'm not remembering it now," I said, breathing the words upon his skin. "I don't remember anything."

The scent of the liniment filled my head, making me dizzy and undermining what was left of my last respectable, realistic reserves. I caressed the back of his shoulders and neck with my lips, wandering at last along the line of his spine. For a while Taylor lay still, passively accepting my passion. Eventually he moved to turn over onto his back again, looking up at me, regarding me intently, as I positioned his legs for him, gazing back, wanting in this moment for all that I had ever felt for him to be apparent and clear. Even though I would give it no voice, there should be no secrets between us. Nothing should be left unknown.

My deepest parts warmed and dressed to meet him. He sat up. I stayed in the dark brownness of his eyes, feeling as though I were finally ascending, a full moon rising among the stars. When I kissed his mouth his lips were welcoming to me, intense and engaging; and our tongues mingled smoothly as the chocolate frosting had creamed in the mixing bowl. We might have really been in Eden, in those very first days of desire and promise. In the days before we had found the Tree of Knowledge and learned how to be afraid.

But then it was only for a moment, and when our lips parted finally, I lowered my eyes from his, as if suddenly I only desired to cover myself with a futile fig leaf. His bare shoulders were square as they had been the first time I saw him, the muscles of his arms were redefined again and more powerful now because he had to depend too much upon them. Idle on the bed on either side of him were his hands, large and strong. His *deskman's hands* were now as tough as Grampa's. The blisters created by the crutches had left behind resilient callused skin. I yearned for Taylor to touch me as he had before, boldly, tenderly. This time I would not withdraw. I would cling to these hands and let them go wherever they would. Swollen against the soft white cotton of his drawers was the outline of Taylor's arousal, his penis hard and prominent. My own hands grew damp with longing to touch it. Other parts of me grew damper too. To receive it. I trembled. My breath came quickly, racing with my heart. Back on the edge of some height again, I barely kept my balance. I was ready to fall, to fly, to float. Whatever it was it did not seem to matter. I did not care. I only wanted him. At last he touched me, raising my face to meet his eyes again. His countenance was calm. "But I want you to remember, Esther," he said quietly. "To see me as I am."

A *white* man. Abruptly I saw him again through Grampa's eyes. And I remembered myself and the way the rest of the world would look back at us. Moving away from the touch of his hand on my face, I rose to my feet, retreating to *my* place again. To the safe, familiar rules and rituals that forbid all of this: what I felt, what I had seen in his eyes, what had stirred against the cotton fabric for me, what had warmed and wetted and prepared for him.

Every quarter, every colored community, offered up the evidence. Proved that it had happened no matter how many laws were written. Usually for lust. But sometimes for love. The cream-colored faces, sometimes actually white, revealed the shame. Matilda's shame. To be raised by Jacob. If the Alberts were lucky. And yet I wanted him. An ancestor's memory, preserved as it was, could not make me not want him. But it was enough to bring me back to my senses. I picked up the dishpan of cold, damp strips of wool.

"I can't afford romantic illusions, Esther," Taylor said. "We have to be honest with ourselves."

And I wasn't enough to make him risk his name, his status. My name already had a mark upon it. And all I had was my name.

"Yes," I heard my voice say but I would not look at him.

Both of us understood, and we had watched out for each other, no matter how close we might have come to it. I moved around the room quickly, gathering things, including my self-control.

"We have to be honest with each other," he said to me.

The prize was *very nice* just not *worthy* enough.

A man can count on you, Esther. Even the foolish ones know that.

And Jimmy had said I was good to talk to. Grampa said I was strong. Affirmations that forgave me my lack of beauty, and said I was desirable despite the edicts of Aunt Betty's fashion magazines. A man could choose me for what I could do with him, and for him. The Bible never said that the virtuous woman was beautiful.

"Yes," I said again calmly, looking at him at last before leaving the room. "Good night, Taylor."

VII

In the second bathroom I bathed and dressed for bed while my body ached for him. By the time I returned to the buttercup room, the house was dark but for the light coming from the lamp next to the walnut sleigh bed. Kneeling on the floor beside the bed I said my prayers, reciting the *Lord's Prayer* first, as Grampa had taught me to do when I was a child, and then moving on to ask for blessings for everyone I loved. I remembered Grampa now, seated on the side of the bed supervising my appeals to God, never allowing me to ask for trivial or selfish things like a new doll or good school marks, or for Mama not to whip me. Finishing with an *amen* I rose and crawled into the bed and turned off the light.

Without the electric light the moon could illuminate the room, filtering in through the lace curtains. It was full tonight, a pale gold sphere rising that I watched through the window. As the night passed, the moon climbed higher and faded to a silver blue. Sleep did not come, but it wasn't really because my heart was troubled. I completely accepted the prudence of Taylor's rejection. We were surely friends. There was goodness in that. Physical desire would fade without fulfillment. Without fulfillment it might even be forgotten, so that in some other man's bed, at some other time, I would not inadvertently call out his name. You could not relive what never was.

Danny would never know because no one would. Danny had made me feel pretty and cherished too. Hopefully I had kept his spirits up on the battlefield. I had desired him once. I could again. He wanted Thanksgiving and forever. Perhaps I could manage the *forever*. I just needed for it not to be now. My purpose was as clear as the silver moon in the black sky. *Those that thou gavest me I have kept, and none of them is lost.*

Nothing had happened tonight. Nothing had changed. When the work was done, then like the moon in the daylight, the purpose would simply fade into invisibleness, into memory.

"Esther," I heard Taylor speak my name.

Sitting up I quickly switched on the lamp. He was standing in the open door.

"Are you all right?" I asked alarmed that he was up. "Do you need something?"

"May I come in?" he replied.

"Yes," I said, flinging back the covers to get out of bed.

"No," he said, "Don't get up."

I stopped and waited for him to reach the bed. His gray silk dressing gown hung open and he was now wearing pajamas. I felt immodest dressed only in a cotton nightgown. My own robe was across the room on the chair.

"May I sit down?" he again asked my permission, like this was not his house, his room, his bed.

I nodded my consent and he sat down. He was, after all, a gentleman and he had always treated me like a lady. He almost never entered this room, usually settling for the doorway, speaking to me from the threshold. It was quaint, respectful. A gentleman politely not entering a lady's chamber, despite the chamber being his and the lady being a maid. Grampa did not know him. Taylor could never shame me.

He was quiet, and I sat next him beginning to feel cold and shivering a little, and dreading too that he had come to talk about what had happened earlier. Apparently he was intent on making too much of it, when it was my intent to forget about it, to behave as though it had never happened. Because it had not happened.

"What I said before," Taylor began finally, absently tapping one of his crutches on the floor and not looking at me. "About being honest with each other--"

It wasn't his fault. It wasn't even mine. Connie said no one was to blame.

"Taylor," I anxiously interrupted. "You don't have to... I mean, I understand--"

"No, Esther," he stopped me. "You don't. You can't understand what you don't know. And I--"

"But I do know," I insisted. "I know that what happened...I...I shouldn't--"

"Esther," he said, at last looking at me. "It's customary to let opposing counsel present without interruption."

"I'm not opposing you, Taylor," I contended.

And I wasn't, but he merely smiled, patiently, as if I might have been Spencer.

"Of course you are," he replied. "Or you will."

I sighed but kept silent. So he would make this, my foolishness, my *forgettin' myself* as Grampa would say, some kind of legally analyzed matter. Very well. Maybe he could chill it cold with one of his rational reviews.

"It is to be admired in you," Taylor continued. "This enormous sense of duty that drives you. I, myself, have benefitted from it as you must know. I think sometimes I would have died without it. But I also wonder if sometimes you don't ask too much of yourself. Isn't there something in your Bible about too much sacrifice? Something about it being futile?"

"'In burnt offerings and sacrifices for sin thou hast had no pleasure,'" I recited for him.

He smiled again, but almost sadly

"Yes," he said. "No pleasure. The Bible's not a big fan of pleasure, is it?"

"It depends," I replied.

"On how you define pleasure, I suppose. But then I didn't intend for this be another discussion of dogma."

"What did you intend?" I asked impatiently. "I mean if this is about what—what happened before, I just got carried away that's all. It won't happen again."

He placed his crutches against the side of the bed between us.

"Too *pleasurable?*" he asked, smiling crookedly.

"Taylor--"

"It wasn't for me," he said before I could continue.

I didn't even flinch because how could it be? He had only been kind to me, perhaps appreciative for my faithful service, bestowing a little bit of himself in recognition of my value to him. I was after all his friend.

"Whatever *carried* you away, as you say," he continued. "Brought you to the place I'd longed for. Only once you were there, I realized it wasn't enough."

Because I wasn't a *Laura Spalding*. I couldn't make him *forget* Sylvia, or himself. The lamp light cast a half-shadow across his face as he looked straight ahead again. His black hair was tousled; dark beard was already visible on his cheek. In the beginning, after the fever broke, with his hands so unsteady, Doctor Mitchell had shaved him and taken care of all of his grooming. Once Taylor could tolerate the exertion, Doctor Mitchell had helped him into the bathtub and bathed him. Ultimately helping him with his baths had become my charge. None of it had ever been easy for him, but Taylor had resigned himself to it. Many times I had washed him where I would have touched him tonight. Washed him and felt only the *attachment*. *Separate but equal* applied to feelings too. I nodded now.

"Yes," I said quietly.

He had come in here to ensure that by tomorrow's light of day what had happened tonight would be no more substantive than a cloud, disappearing on a breeze.

"I understand," I told him.

"I'm sure that you don't," he replied, meeting my eyes again. "You have a way about you, Esther, that can undo a man if he's not on his guard."

"But you are."

"Most of the time."

"Just not tonight."

"No."

"It won't happen again."

"I can't be sure."

A man ain't nothin' but a man.

"I promise," I said.

"It's not you I'm worried about," he replied.

"But I--"

"No. *We* did. And I know better."

"Then *we* will be more careful," I resolved.

Smiling softly he lifted my chin, instantly stirring the waiting embers inside me, turning them bright orange and hot.

"So this is your grandmother's face," he said.

"How would you know that?" I asked, pulling back.

He couldn't know her. Grampa had never allowed Ernestine to work in a private home.

"Your grandfather told me," answered Taylor. "She was quite--"

"My grandfather?!" I exclaimed. "You don't know my grandfather."

"Yes," Taylor said. "I do. Mr. Isaac Green. A very impressive man, I must say." I stared at him.

"I don't believe you!" I said. "How? How could you….when did you ever meet him?"

"A doubting Thomas, Esther?" he teased. "I thought you were a woman of faith."

"Taylor," I said confused now and exasperated.

"All right," he smiled again as if I amused him. "It is what I came in here to discuss with you. What your grandfather thinks about all of this. And why he's right."

"Did Nathaniel tell you something?" I demanded. "That's it," I decided. "He did, didn't he? He had no right. My grandfather's not a mean man, Taylor. It's just that--"

"I believe Mr. Green is very capable of making his own case."

"But you don't know him."

"Yes," he said again. "I do. I think I know him very well now. You see, a few Sundays back he came to see me. Of course, it was not what you might call a *social* call. Seems your birthday present, the necklace, was a bit much for his tastes, but I suspect you do know that much."

"That's where he was?" I murmured. "Here?"

"Yes. He wanted me to know that you come from a respectable, Christian family, and while he is very sorry for my sickness and the trouble I find myself in, this uh...as he put it, *situation* has gone on long enough. He never approved of you working here, but he has been willing to give me time to get myself *straightened out*, as he said. And now that I have--"

"You never told me," I said incredulous.

"He explained that you will not leave me because you're faithful that way. *To the Lord.*" Taylor smiled crookedly. "And you think your Lord is leading you to take pity on me, in my *condition*. So that being the case, it's now left up to him, and to a certain extent me, to do what's best for you. To protect you from your charity as it were. But instead I dressed you up like a *Jezebel*. A reference to the pearl necklace, which he apologized for breaking in his anger. He said he paid to have it repaired and he will make sure that you give it back to me, as it is neither a necessary or proper gift for a *domestic*."

"He told you?" I asked still stunned.

"The truth?" questioned Taylor. "Yes."

"So you knew what happened? To the necklace? You knew all along."

"Yes."

"But you didn't you say anything. You-you just let us—I mean me—go on with--"

"A lie?"

"Taylor, I–I didn't know how to–how to--"

"Tell me the truth?"

"To explain why he would do it," I said in defense of Grampa, and in defense of myself. "He has his reasons. If you knew him, if you knew about our family--"

"I do know," Taylor said. "Now."

"What did he tell you?" I asked more uneasily. "Not about Albert and…and Matilda?"

"I had a history lesson that day," confirmed Taylor. "Tell me does he always talk that way?"

"You must understand, Taylor. He grew up differently. Things were harder for him back then."

"They're harder for him right now, Esther. I'm not blind you know. I'm not stupid. I know you think I ignore what goes on, but I don't. I just want to change it that's all. You have to believe that."

I looked down at my hands as I fumbled with the front of my gown.

"He doesn't blame you for it, Taylor," I pleaded. "For what happened to his grandmother. Not really." I met his eyes again. "He knows it's not your fault. He just can't forget it."

"And he shouldn't," said Taylor. "None of us should. That's all a part of it, of being honest with ourselves. And with each other."

"Well you didn't tell me that he came here," I charged.

"And I should have," he replied honestly. "But I reasoned that he came here to see me, not you. The matter was between us."

"I knew something was wrong," I said recalling the Sunday afternoon I had returned to find him so sullen. "I thought Doctor Mitchell had said something or...or Laura Spalding."

"Laura Spalding?" asked Taylor. "What could she possibly have to say?"

"She-she is your friend. You two were...I mean...are... an item."

Now he seemed genuinely surprised.

"Whatever gave you that idea?" he asked.

"I've seen you two together, Taylor. That day in Woolworths. The dinner party last December. When she came to visit you."

He laughed briefly.

"To visit *us* you mean," he corrected.

"That was just a stunt," I replied.

"No, Esther, it wasn't. I was making a point. And she got it, even if you didn't. Your grandfather also gets it. He said you've discussed it."

"Taylor--"

"Seeing me, he said, he could understand how you could be so compassionate. It's hard to see a man crippled, he told me." Taylor's smile was brief and mirthless. "And you've always been such a comfort to everyone. Coming back here to care for your mother for example. Although, he believes as you do, it is what families are supposed to do. What my own sister should have done. Maybe you Greens do have it over all the rest of us when it comes to family. But in any case, yours is a soft heart. So Mr. Green wasn't all that surprised by your decision to stay with me. But really, Esther, telling off the preacher and his wife like that," Taylor smiled wryly again. "That must have been amazing even for you."

"He told you about that too?" I asked.

"My own personal cherub," observed Taylor. "A tongue for a sword. Except that it isn't much of a garden, now is it?"

Still in disbelief, I shook my head. He smiled.

"I suppose you are honest," said Taylor. "*Most* of the time."

"What?" I asked, realizing what was implied by the gesture. "No. That's not what I mean--"

"It's all right," he replied, the sardonic smile still tugging at one corner of his mouth. "You'll get no argument from me. I'm not easy to get along with, I know. I didn't tell you about it, Esther because I suppose I never thought you'd go so long without seeing your grandfather, so he could tell you about the agreement himself." Taylor sighed. "And I guess I also didn't want to speed things along. I'm not too good with goodbyes, remember."

"What goodbyes?" I asked. "I'm not leaving."

"Yes, you are. You have to. We came to an agreement."

"*Agreement?* What are you talking about?"

"A gentlemen's agreement, they used to call it. We agreed that I would look out for you as you have done for me. In other words, in your words, take care of you like you've taken care of me. Mr. Green said that he'd allow you to stay here until I could manage on my own, as long as I gave him my word to respect you in all things. As a white man, he said, I have certain privileges, so I can afford to be reckless, but you can't take such chances. You stand to lose too much. And I gave him my word, Esther." A new ironic smile filled his face, though it did not reach his eyes. "Besides, I told him, his granddaughter is too formidable in her own right, even if I were to try to do otherwise, to let anything happen. So tonight, when I saw you being so reckless, I...I was obligated to caution you, because I gave your grandfather my word that I would. And I--"

"I never asked anything of you," I said.

"I think that's precisely the point. And if you'll let me finish...I also cautioned you because despite having all these *privileges* you both seem to believe I have, I really can't afford to take chances either. Not anymore. If you ask nothing of me then it means I can ask nothing of you, and that doesn't work for me. That's what's not enough, Esther. Yes, I know all too well, commitments are broken all the time... but at least I have to start out with one. I don't do so well with this faith stuff. Never have, and especially now."

You tryin' to play it safe, Esther... But you know what, you playin' one of them too.

"Well," he finished, taking up his crutches. "That's probably more than what I'd intended to tell you. I should let you get some sleep."

"Wait," I said, catching his arm before he could come to his feet. "You called me opposing counsel before. Why?"

"Your grandfather wants you to come home, Esther," he answered. "You have to want that too. So that puts us on opposing sides."

"You don't know that."

"You have to decide between us, and your grandfather and I don't want the same things."

"It's my decision, Taylor. Not his."

"It's settled, Esther. Today in fact. And none too soon as it turns out."

"Today?"

"Yes. He came to see me again. At the office."

My eyes were wide with amazement.

"I was shocked to see him there too," said Taylor. "Although in retrospect neither of us should be. He is a man to be reckoned with, and you are dear to him...We have an agreement. He reasons, and rightly so, that if I can work, drive my car, I can manage on my own. At least I no longer need a nurse. It's time for me to let you go. I'm lame, but I'm still better off than a lot of men, he reminded me. I can hire somebody else to keep my house. He's right. And whatever the case, I did agree to the terms."

"Do you want me to stay?" I asked, letting pass the incomprehensible image of Grampa in Taylor's office in defense of my honor.

"I want what's best for you, Esther," Taylor answered.

"Do you want me to stay?" I asked again.

"I understand there's someone else to consider," he said. "A soldier. He wants to marry you."

"He told you about Danny too?" I asked.

"He plans to take you away from here," Taylor continued. "Get you out of this little hamlet. You deserve that, Esther. The world deserves you. You might like California. You've been waiting a long time for your chance. It's time. I've disrupted your plans long enough."

"I never said I was going to California."

"He sounds like a great guy," Taylor replied thoughtfully, gazing into the darkness. "You've known each other a long time."

Then that meant that I had known Taylor a *long time* too. Only I knew him more deeply. And myself better because of him.

"You've been writing to each other," Taylor told me. "He has expectations. So does your grandfather, and he's worried about gossip. The wrong things getting back to your beau. A man must be able to believe in the woman he marries, Esther. Your grandfather doesn't want to risk that. He wants what's best for you, and he won't have me standing in your way." Again he laughed tersely. "Not that I ever could. Not anymore. Not for very long anyway."

He came to his feet.

"So that's it then?" I asked to his back. "Everybody just does what's best for Esther? Never mind that she can think for herself. You all just have it figured out for me."

"Your grandfather wants you to be happy," replied Taylor. "So do I."

"But I don't get a say in that? Even your precious Constitution eventually got around to giving women the vote. Of course I know I'm just a colored woman, and this is McConnell County after all."

He turned and looked down at me.

"And your house," I continued. "Where I'm just your maid, my grandfather tells me. A hireling."

"Don't," said Taylor.

"Don't what?" I asked derisively. "Have an opinion? Know my own mind?"

"Esther, please--"

"Well now how gracious of you, Mr. Payne," I said in a syrupy-sweet southern voice straight out of his *central casting*. "You're just so concerned for my happiness and all. I humbly thank you, sir."

"Don't," he said again.

"Why I'm just thanking you for your kind considerations," I mocked. "For the way you and my grandfather are so chivalrously protecting me from my foolish self."

"You think I want to let you go?" he asked desperately. "You think I wouldn't fight for you if I could? But look at me. I can't fight for anything anymore. I'm a casualty, Esther. You can't give up your future for me, or your past. I won't let you." The knuckles of his hands whitened as he gripped the handles of the crutches.

But it wasn't his decision alone. And it wasn't Grampa's either. I sprang off the bed and stood in front of him, looking up into his troubled eyes. No, he didn't want me to go. Maybe I could even stay *forever*. But I would settle—gratefully—for *longer*.

"Taylor," I was ready to admit it. "You--"

"It's late," he interrupted me. "I'm exhausted. Good-night, Esther."

I put my arms around him, pressing myself against him.

"Please, Esther," he sighed wearily. "I'm not wearing the brace, and I can't stand on this leg without it. You think the paralysis isn't real. That everything's going to be just fine with time. A little more work, and Sister Kenny's wraps. At least your grandfather sees me for what I am."

But of course Grampa didn't. He couldn't. Not with eyes clouded by a history of grievances. He didn't know Taylor Andrew Payne like I did. Perhaps no one did. Not even Taylor himself. He must not, not if he would measure himself by the yardstick of a crutch. I held on more tightly.

"I'm tired," he said to me again. "My leg hurts."

"Then stay here," I told him. "Rest in my arms," I said holding fast to his hardened frame.

"Esther, you've done enough," he said. "Kinder to me than anyone. But I don't want your Christian charity. I need what you aren't prepared to give me. My uncle is who he is. Perhaps not so different from your grandfather. So maybe Felicia couldn't help it either. But I'm a proud man. I've always had my pride. And now…now it may be all I have left. I can't risk something like that happening to me again. Being deserted. I'm better off on my own."

"I'm your friend, Taylor," I said listening to the quickened beat of his heart.

"Esther, if we--"

"We don't have to," I cut him off. "We won't."

I could feel tears balling up tightly in my throat.

"You'll just hold me," I squeezed out the words. "And I'll hold you."

"And the rest?" he asked sadly. "What about that?"

"We don't think about that," I answered. "Not tonight. Tonight we just hold onto each other."

According to *Scarlett O'Hara* tomorrow was another day. Tonight could be ours.

"Taylor," I pleaded. "Friends hold onto each other all the time."

"Friends," he repeated the word, grimly chuckling.

"Yes," I said more earnestly now searching his dark brown eyes. "Friends. Long and deep."

A broad concept. More so than I could have known. But yes, he was my friend. I locked my hands together against the rigidity of his back and refused to let go. I wanted to have it, the *something* that we had made here in this house. It had its own worth, this prize between us. I wanted it and he wanted it too. Maybe we could have it. If only for a little while. It deserved that much. We deserved that much.

I felt him give. Then letting go of the left crutch, he crushed me against him, fiercely covering my mouth with his own. Suddenly I tasted his passion as his tongue hunted mine and captured it. *His mouth is most sweet: yea, he is altogether lovely. This is my beloved, and this is my friend, O daughters of Jerusalem.* And I clung to him as he traveled down to my throat, passing the ruffled bodice of my nightgown, stopping my heart and taking my breath away as he went.

"Taylor," I murmured, reveling, delighting in every place he touched me. "See, what harm can it be? You've held me before."

"Yes," I heard him say as I danced on the Egyptian beach, my back to the sea and the *Promise Land*. "But you will pull away from me."

PART SIX

I

Tonight I wouldn't. And every gesture passed from the impulsive to the deliberate, as words dissolved into whispers, until they went unsaid altogether, unneeded. I slipped the robe off his shoulders and arms, and it dropped to the floor in a soft gray heap. When he sat down on the side of the bed again he kept his left arm around me keeping me close in front of him. Desire blazed brilliantly between us. He put aside the right crutch and with both hands grasped me around the waist, pressing the side of his face against my belly while I rapturously stroked his dark head, gazing down at him blissfully.

The long-practiced denial and restraint were put aside too, along with the *gentlemen's agreement* that for the moment seemed as inconsequential as Taylor's remaining pajamas and my cotton nightgown. Nothing was between us, and at last we made love. I beamed at Taylor as he moved his hands gently along my sturdy but trembling frame, his face serious and contemplative, as if I were someone that he must study to understand; as if I could be someone that he only now was beginning to know. But how could he be uncertain of me? How could he think I would *pull away*?

When Taylor's hands reached the round cheeks of my bottom, I briefly regretted my strong, straight form. I lacked Mandy's sensual curves which turned fitted skirts into magic wands and placed men under her spell whenever she walked by. Before I could muster words to acknowledge this feminine failing, Taylor had scooted back on the bed, lifting his legs upon the mattress; and then reaching for me, he pulled me onto the bed as well, so that my knees were on either side of him as he lay back with me in his arms. As we kissed our straight hips came together, and I felt the firmness of his manhood against my body. The touch of it, the prospects it suggested, flamed through me so that it was as if I had melted and no longer had a form of my own at all.

It was only after our lips parted that I recovered enough to raise myself up off of him.

"I'm-I'm too heavy," I protested as I moved to lie beside him.

A faint smile lifted one corner of his mouth.

"I won't break, you know," he said, holding me against him.

"I know," I said still moving to nestle next to him.

Sighing deeply Taylor turned on his side and propped himself up on one arm, looking down at me. I breathed the fading scent of the liniment. My hands yearned to touch his skin again, but I settled for toying with one of the buttons on his pajama shirt.

"So friends do this all the time, do they?" he asked skeptically after a time.

"Sometimes," I replied, daringly undoing one of his buttons.

A soft chuckle rumbled in his chest.

"I believe you may have redefined the concept," he said.

"Why not?" I asked, undoing another button. "In this house we do things differently."

I smiled at my own wit.

"Yes, Esther," he said suddenly grave. "Yes, we do."

He brought my hand to his face and kissed the palm. I smiled again and continued opening the remaining shirt buttons. Once the pajama shirt hung open, revealing his bare chest, I reached up to timidly trace my finger along the dark line of hair which ran down the center of his torso, stopping at his navel. Inches away his arousal waited to meet mine. I could touch it now. Perhaps I might even receive it. The darkest parts of me thickened and throbbed eagerly.

But there was the *gentlemen's agreement*. He had given his word to my grandfather. I could not ask him to break it. I must not want more. He should go. I should make him. Their terms should have been my own. The *agreement* had been made for my benefit, for my protection. Grampa was looking out for me. I wasn't wise and colored women needed to be. In this world even God had to be cautious.

Taylor caught my hand again, this time kissing my fingers. I stroked his cheek, caressing the line of his jaw. When tomorrow morning came and he was shaving himself before his bathroom mirror what would he think of this time that we were sharing? As if answering my unuttered question he lowered his head to cover my mouth again with his, and afterwards he stroked my face and neck, and until ultimately he was tenderly tracing the cleavage between my breasts.

"Is this all right?" he asked as his hand disappeared inside the bodice of my nightgown.

I nodded as I reached up to smooth a furrow from his brow.

"I am a woman, Taylor," I said, recalling the night I had told Grampa the same thing.

Had Grampa told him about that too?

"I'm very much aware of that every day of my life," replied Taylor. "However, that doesn't mean--"

"I want you to touch me," I interrupted him with a smile. "I've always wanted you to touch me. *Every day of my life.*"

His left brow arched quizzically, and he grinned mutedly.

"I don't believe you," he said while softly drawing a tiny circle around the hardened nipple of my left breast.

When his warm hand closed around the breast it was not so easy for me to breathe.

"That's-that's because…" I whispered. "I'm-I'm a mistress of dis-disguise."

"A woman of great mystery," he concurred, now fondling my right breast.

"Yes," I heard myself sighing.

"Until tonight," he said huskily.

I nodded, gazing up at him.

"Then let me see you," he said.

Of course, I thought looking into his eyes. I had seen him naked so many times, laid bare in so many ways. Yet I had always kept myself concealed. In Mama's black dresses and behind a domestic's apron. With the rules and the rituals. Beneath Mandy's lace cap. I sat up.

"I'm sorry," Taylor apologized, doubting the wisdom of his request. "I didn't mean to embarrass you."

But I was thinking that I might never have this chance again as I came to my knees on the bed and began pulling the nightgown over my head. Danny was waiting for me in California; and Grampa, with all of his bitter memories, waited for me too. There might never be another time like this. He deserved to see me. I was *entitled* to show him.

As I pulled the gown over my head, Taylor lay back watching me. In the walnut sleigh bed, in the buttercup room that I had made ready for his sister, I was finally near naked, my ample bosom and soft belly presented to him as if I could be pretty, as if I could be his. After a moment instinctive modesty compelled me to place my arms across my chest to cover myself.

"No," he said gently pulling my arms down. "I want to look at you."

In Eden it might have been this way, in the sweet beginning when there had not been enough knowledge to create shame. Now forever after, even though nothing could be perfect again, something might still be sacred. Banished from paradise we might still have a glimpse of heaven, in a lover's face.

Taylor sat up and drew me closer to him again, gently lingering over my uncovered breasts with his lips. I pushed his pajama shirt off his shoulders and ran my hands along the muscles of his arms, caressing the firm flesh of his chest, his *pectoralis major*, according to Doctor Mitchell's anatomy book. Eventually we lay back against the pillows together, looking at each other, my naked breasts against his bare chest.

"Who can find a virtuous woman?" he recited again, this time breathing the words across my lips. "For her price is far above rubies."

"Now who's redefining words?" I teased softly.

"You taught me the meaning," he replied.

In each other's arms it was as if it really could be this way between us. It seemed right. It felt inevitable. Grampa was wrong and right at the same time. A man was just a man, and a woman was just a woman. Nothing else needed to matter, but everything else did.

"I should go," Taylor said after awhile, although he didn't move.

The *gentlemen's agreement* was in jeopardy, I thought bleakly. Our bodies burned with a primeval fire, but I should let him go. Grampa was here, like cherubic guard whom God had stationed at Eden's gate to forbid our entering in.

"Don't leave me," I heard myself say.

Taylor studied my face. If the *gentlemen's agreement* meant that much to him, then he'd have to honor it in spite of me. I would have no part in it. If he chose to leave me tonight it would be his decision alone. When my turn came to go, and it would, then I would, but for now I would hold on for dear life. And for sweet love. Sweet love that had broken me down in the hard places and remade me too—*differently*. I was somebody else. Somebody open. Somebody more. Somebody brave. And yes, somebody beautiful.

I want to look at you.

We had always blamed Eve for it anyway, for *The Fall,* as if the agreement with God had been with her too, when it wasn't. Not in the first place. The terms had never been hers. She had never been hers.

"Do you know what you're asking me, Esther?" asked Taylor.

I would do anything for you, Esther.

"Virtuous doesn't necessarily mean virginal," I answered.

"I know that," he said.

I dared to smile at the furrow that had returned to his brow. This couldn't be forever, but it could be this one night.

"I'm not a damsel in distress," I said lightly. "You don't have to protect my honor. No matter what my grandfather said."

Breathing deeply, Taylor turned away from me and lay on his back, staring up at the ceiling.

"That isn't it," he said.

What then, I wondered and then realized the reason. Of course. He was afraid that we would make a baby; and apart from him now I felt chilled. It was ironic. Grampa's pale stern face was not sufficient to keep us from consummation, but the risk of one just as pale only with Taylor's dark eyes was. I couldn't blame him. It would ruin both our lives and seal us together forever even if, like Matilda, I ran away with the child and raised the child by myself or gave it another's man name.

So the *gentlemen's agreement* would remain, mostly intact. I lay very still waiting for Taylor to get up and leave. I pictured Grampa in Taylor's study and then at his office, Grampa carrying himself like a warrior chief, proud and unbroken, absolutely unconquerable, even if his granddaughter would sleep in the bed of the enemy. In this lovely walnut sleigh bed with its dark brown wood and simple elegant lines. Aunt Betty would have had a canopy bed in this room, a bed all covered in pink ruffles, a bed fit for a princess. For Felicia. But I might be a princess too. I could be of unknown noble birth. I could be a royal daughter and the mother of proud warrior sons.

No wonder they had reached a *gentlemen's agreement*. They were both principled men. Taylor had seen that in my grandfather. I hoped that Grampa had seen that in him too. I was the guilty one, guiltier than Eve because after all I had known and she had not. Everyone had warned me, and I had seen it coming. This *fall* was my fault. Taylor had been vulnerable. His life had not been easy, even before the polio. He tried to ignore the hurts, making light of them, brushing them aside but also hiding them away, even from himself. Then I had come along with my conversation and comfort, looking after his home and seducing him, just as Laura Spalding had said.

You good to talk to, Esther. That's better than dancin'.

Perhaps Eve had bewitched Adam too, suddenly appearing one day to end his loneliness. But then God had come and forced Adam to be mindful of the consequences, of the price he must pay for companionship. Taylor was right. Being alone was simpler. Connections put you at risk and complicated your life. Adam had blamed Eve. And Eve had had no argument. I might have made my deal with the serpent but Taylor had made his with my grandfather. I had faltered and prepared to fail, but Taylor was going to remain steadfast. If only Adam had been so careful, we might have still been there, in Eden; ignorant, innocent, and content.

Long silent minutes went by. Taylor had been kind to me tonight. He had always been kind to me. I would remember it like this always, and never with regret.

"I understand, Taylor," I said after a time. "You gave your word." I pulled the sheet up over my naked bosom and sat up. "I don't blame --"

"I don't think you do understand," he said, looking up at me now.

"I might get pregnant," I offered frankly.

"What?" he asked as if I did not make sense.

"If we did anything...anything more. It's too--"

"Esther," he sighed. "I don't know if I...how I can do *anything more*."

"You're right," I hastily agreed. "We shouldn't. It would only make matters--"

"Esther!" he said abruptly grabbing me by the arm. "Listen to me. What I'm saying is that I...that I don't know if I can... physically I mean...I don't know... how...how I can."

I stared at him.

"You mean...because...because your legs are weak?" I asked.

"Because I'm crippled, Esther." He sighed, letting go of my arm. "You really must learn to say it. I need you to accept me as I am. Otherwise this...this can't--"

"But I do," I insisted earnestly. "I do accept you."

It was bewildering that he could think that I didn't; after all we had gone through together. And now tonight... I was willing to reveal everything.

"No, Esther," he smiled crookedly and looked up at the ceiling again. "You believe in miracles." He exhaled deeply, looking at me once more. "But it's sweet. And it's good. It's who you are. Besides who knows where I'd be without it." He touched my cheek. "Do you recall the first time you touched me?"

"We shook hands. The first day I came here," I said.

"No," he shook his head. "I consider that more my touching you." He smiled. "And actually against your will as I recall."

"That morning then, when you came up behind me and scared me."

"No. Still me."

"Then I don't know what you mean."

"The first time you touched me, Esther," Taylor said, raising my right hand to his lips. "You weren't looking at a man. I was your patient."

You're not my nurse.

Or so he thought. I had tried to think it too. But Doctor Mitchell had recognized the truth, making good use of it. The *attachment* had always been to the man.

"I believe in you, Taylor" I said.

He smiled again.

"I know," he said cupping my cheek affectionately. "Which puts me in very good company."

He pulled me down to him and kissed me.

"Don't change, Esther," he said when I sat up again. "I must have somewhere to put what little faith I do have."

How could I be a safe place for him? When there was the *gentlemen's agreement*. And all the laws in his books. And history and heritage, and proprietors of restaurants who would never let us sit together at their tables. But maybe in this moment we really were alone in this room. None of them had to be here unless we brought them. In this moment there was only us.

Letting the sheet fall away, I slipped my hand beyond the waist of his pajamas until I was stroking his member which stirred and hardened in my damp palm. His breathing changed. I gazed into his eyes.

"The spirit is very willing," he said. "It's the flesh that's weak."

"Not so weak," I countered, smiling at him, as the caresses I gave him further inflamed me.

An uncertain smile pulled at the corners of his mouth.

"I am not your nurse, Taylor," I reminded him.

Could I really be this woman reflected back to me in his eyes?

"I never was," I whispered, gently massaging his thickening shaft. "You said so yourself."

"What if... I," he began tentatively, "If I'm not able to...?"

"Shhh," I interrupted him, bending down to kiss him again. "We're together."

As the final reservations yielded, the last vestiges of clothing separating us went away too. Taylor guided me to straddle him once more so that my knees were on either side of him. This time, however, our bodies were naked. As he moved his strong hips beneath me, his hardened organ brushed against the course black hair between my legs, sending bolts of lightning through my being. I guided it to the place where it disappeared smoothly into my fervently waiting wet walls. Gasping with pleasure, I closed my eyes. When I opened them again, he was smiling up at me. Feeling him deep inside of me, myself all around him, our bodies seemed to seize control, so that our movements were primal, in rhythms as ancient as ocean waves. I called his name, murmuring it half-greedily, half-gratefully, as if I wanted more of him and yet could not bear it. Taylor lifted his hips pushing them upwards as we undulated together. Sliding his hands down my arms, he grasped my hands in his, raising them up, our fingers entwined, black and white and beautiful.

I was hardly conscious, seemingly suspended in time and place, adrift and floating, tethered to the bed, to the earth, only by his dazzling dark eyes which watched me as his manhood probed me. Suddenly, totally consumed by a marvelous fire I heard a woman's frenzied voice crying out, and then a man's comforting voice speaking soft and low. When it was quiet again I found myself lying on top of him, the side of my face pressed against his chest, his arms around me, and I was weeping serenely.

"Sweet darling," he said in dulcet tones. "My sweet darling."

Gently he stroked my back, as I breathed deeply, trying to recover so that I could rise up off of him, but somehow I was too sated and spent. *His left hand is under my head, and his right hand doth embrace me.*

"Taylor," I said his name again.

"Yes, my love?"

Only I had nothing else to say. There was nothing more wonderful than his name. Silently I listened to his heart beating. When it was all said and done, I suspected Eve had not been sorry for eating the apple either. The memory must have been sweet to her no matter how terrible the consequences. Because now she knew. No one could take that away from her. Some prizes were indeed *worthy* enough.

I turned my head and began caressing Taylor's chest with my lips, reverently tasting the line of dark hair on his torso with my tongue. Still buried inside of me, his penis stirred again vigorously, and his heartbeat quickened. With me still in his arms, he turned on his side, moving me with him. Beads of perspiration glistened on his brow but his eyes shone luminously. His breath was warm in my face. Reaching down I pulled his right leg across me, the weight of it fixing me closer to him. *A bundle of myrrh is my well-beloved unto me; he shall lie all night betwixt my breasts.*

When Taylor pushed his pelvis against mine, my own arousal surged anew. Inside I closed tightly around his manhood again. As our mouths mingled, I shut my eyes and imagined us not only of one world, one flock, but also of one body, our glorious groans of passion making only one sound in the otherwise still house. *I am the rose of Sharon, and the lily of the valleys.* As the splendid fire was consuming me again, I felt Taylor thrust his penis fiercely, and I collapsed around it. He shuddered and was still. We lay peacefully in each other's arms. *I charge you, O ye daughters of Jerusalem, by the roes, and by the hinds of the field, that ye stir not up, nor awake my love till he please.*

II

I opened my eyes to the morning's light, and discovering the side of my face resting comfortably against Taylor's chest, my arm draped across his waist, my first thought was that I must be dreaming. But of course I wasn't. We had spent the night together. We were lovers. Now, outside the bright shiny day had come again and real life waited, expecting its reckoning. The end of Eden had only been the beginning. There had still been a whole world to make and dwell in. Time could not stop.

I did not stir, even though I still had the same things to do, the same person to be. As I lay there I inventoried my old and new identities. Fundamentally I wasn't different and neither was he. The *something* between us was the same too. All we had done was fulfill it. But how should I manage now, how should I carry myself? What did we call this place at the edge of Eden?

Taylor's breaths came evenly, so I assumed that he must still be sleeping. He was an early riser but passion had kept us awake most of the night. I didn't remember when we had fallen asleep but we must have done so together. Even now as I lay next to him, with his arm resting around my shoulders, excited if uncertain butterflies beat their wings in my belly. It had been a divine night. Whatever else happened, however else this turned out, I would have last night.

I tried to ease out of bed without disturbing him, but as soon as I moved his arm around my shoulders held me closer.

"Good morning, sweetheart," he spoke tenderly.

Oh yes, it felt like a dream. I rose up to meet his eyes. His amorous smile greeted me.

"Good morning," I returned, shyly pulling up the sheet to cover myself. "Have you been awake all this time?" I asked.

"No," he answered playfully. "Not *all* this time."

Bringing my face closer to his, he kissed me deeply. The secret part of me, which was no longer secret from him, responded to the soft, warm heat of his mouth.

"I should make coffee," I announced modestly, as I tried to surreptitiously look around for my discarded nightgown.

"It's on the floor there," Taylor astutely indicated.

Seeing the pile of crumpled white fabric that was my gown, I wondered how I would take the sheet with me to retrieve it, and worse yet how I would put it back on in front of him, with the morning light coming in through the lace panels I had hung last fall, while his hands had been around my waist.

"No," Taylor confirmed. "I will not cover my eyes, Esther."

The amorous smile had moved from his lips to twinkle in his eyes, gently crinkling the lines reaching toward his temples. My cheeks burned.

"There they are," he observed. "My beautiful roses."

Now I smiled too.

"They are mine, you know," he added, pulling me back to him. "I have claimed them."

He covered my mouth with his once more and my arms went around his neck as I surrendered into his embrace.

"Don't you want your breakfast?" I feigned protest as he laid me back against the pillows.

"Yes," he murmured, nibbling at my earlobe.

By the time I made it to the kitchen to prepare an actual breakfast, it was late in the morning, but it was Saturday so there were no fixed appointments for places to be. As the coffee brewed and the sausage sizzled, my mind day-dreamed hazy, ethereal images. I recalled myself with Taylor as we had been in these most recent hours and imagined us as we could be in the days to come—if only the world was a better place, the place that Jimmy had day-dreamed of it being. I wanted to resist the temptation of hopefulness, and I kept reminding myself that I was not a heroine in a romance novel that would end triumphantly. What I was was the grand-daughter of a Negro Pullman Car porter; a descendant of slaves and sharecroppers; the southern woman who was never mistaken for a belle. If I really could have my own *Song of Solomon*, it could not be a long song, and it was bound to be the Blues.

What were we going to do with ourselves in the land between the Red Sea and the pyramids? Moses required me to come back to where I belonged. Maybe Danny, never knowing all of this, would be willing to wait until April, but Grampa already knew, and he was not willing to wait. If he came to this house again, it would be to get me, and I would have to go. If I hoped to have any more time at all then I would have to go to him first. And probably I would have to lie outright, which I was willing to do. I wanted until Christmas. I wanted my own *agreement*.

Mixed in with the images of now were also memories of the past, as had been taught to me. Matilda was with me, and I thought of Ernestine and Mama too. My aunts could not approve. Yet all of them had had a hand in making me the woman that I was today. They had raised me to be capable of believing that a dark-skinned Cinderella might also have a prince. Even if it were only for a little while. Some things boldly were even though they couldn't be.

Jimmy had told me to think for myself. "You gotta do what you wanna do," he would say, confident in his manhood, even his colored manhood. Urging me to follow his lead, he had perhaps loved me too much to counsel me wisely. I wondered what my brother would say about this curious little East Texas fairytale involving a lord of the manor and a virtuous woman, who lived in an enchanted castle ringed by rose bushes?

They are mine, you know. I have claimed them.

Would he think that we were *changing the world,* that things would be different once this was over?

Because it would be over. I could have no illusions about that. My love was not enough. Our being together last night had happened many times before. Across broader divides than this people had dared to love each other, but by law we remained separate. Last night Taylor and I had liberated ourselves from the bonds of man's edicts and the yokes of religious canon. Meeting in a tiny, tiny place to be sure, where it was unallowable to stay, we had made our moments to remember, to be hopeful from. We might have even made it more possible. We just couldn't make it last.

We had not talked very much as we had gone through the morning exercises. I decided that discussing it, defining it, could only make it more complicated. Besides I didn't want to douse it with cold reality. Words might only break the spell of it. We carried out what was our normal routine, my hands, his legs, just like nothing had happened last night. It was only in his eyes, when I dared to look into them, that I felt treasured and desirable, that I felt once more *worthy* enough. No, I was not his nurse.

As I tended the sausage I thought of a way to tell him that I was going to see Grampa today, a way that wouldn't seem overly dramatic or far too significant. Only there was no way of putting it casually. I had let too much time pass. Too much truth had had to find its own way to the light, and I needed to cover it up again. Time was rushing away from us.

People were not very good with miracles. We didn't know what to make of them, how to explain them. They frightened us. Even if they were our own, we were hesitant in the midst of them. We could dream of the Garden of Eden and look forward to

Heaven, but most of us wondered what we would do there. Where was the catch? The trick? The trap? Oh—beware of joy.

Yet, as Taylor had said, I did believe in them, in miracles. More so perhaps, for my time in this house, because I had seen them here. I had lived them here too, like Mr. Leon had said. I was a Christian with a testimony. I was a witness of Him who had sent me. And He had sent me. Taylor relied on my strength. He had to put his faith somewhere. For now that could be in me. I was his Ananias. I had a reason for being here. I was certain of it.

But I owed Grampa something too, an accounting, and so much more than I could ever repay. I had hurt him; in as much as I had helped Taylor. And I had done it deliberately because I knew how he grieved over it. That was the hardest part of it, knowing that I had done it on purpose. For a purpose. Grampa believed that I had betrayed him and myself for a man who could never be mine, which was worse than giving up my virginity to a colored soldier on leave in the backseat of a Ford. At least the colored soldier seemed to want to give me his name.

And yet none of this made me any more ready to *pull away*. Ambivalence had frozen me in place. I wanted until April. I needed time. Taylor needed time. And as I had been carefully helping him to do his exercises, watching him labor to push his right foot against the slight pressure of my hand, I had concentrated on that, on how we needed time. Every minute was valuable, and too short. Time was winding down. Passion in every way was melting the ice. It could not hold.

As I beat the eggs in a bowl, I reflected on Doctor Mitchell's theories of attachment, and the twelve-year-old Taylor that Mr. Leon had talked about. I remembered Taylor telling Nathaniel that he couldn't manage without me. And how Nathaniel had said that nobody could block it. I thought about what Connie said about somebody having to be in the middle, and while I toasted the bread I made up my plan for how I was going to get more time. April was hopeless. I wouldn't even ask for that. I would settle for *not now*, and pray for Christmas. If we could just have until Christmas. Then Taylor could have New York again. Maybe even his own family in Cambridge.

Taylor said a good lawyer considered the judge and evaluated the jury as he prepared his case. "If you understand them you can appeal to them more effectively, and that's what it's about, Esther," he had said. "Getting them to see it your way so that they give you what you want." The good lawyer had to know not only what he wanted but what he could settle for too. He understood those terms by opening statements so that he deployed his tactics successfully. "You plot it, Esther," he had shared. "Carefully, point by point. And if there's an odd turn of events, something that surprises you, you incorporate it into your plan but you don't deviate."

Taylor often sounded like Grampa. His *But you don't deviate* was Grampa's *Know yo' own mind*. And of course what my mind wanted was to stay with Taylor. I would be settling for April, but I could tolerate Christmas. Just as long as it was longer. As long as it was *not now*. I had to get Grampa to see it my way. I had to get him to *deviate* despite his *own mind*. He might have a plan with Taylor, an *agreement*, but I had a plan of my own.

Taylor and I had our breakfast at the kitchen table, as if it was any other normal day in this house, even though my breasts remembered his touch, and when he was seated at the table, he had caught me in his arms again, pressing the side of his face against my mother's black dress. I had stroked his hair adoringly and wondered if I was carrying his child, and why there could be no place for us. We did not require very much space. We were like angels dancing on the head of a pin. We were a miracle.

And all Grampa wanted to do was protect me. He had enlisted Taylor out of desperation. Poor Grampa. He trusted in the Lord and knew without a doubt that a mustard seed of faith could move a mountain. What he couldn't know though was whether or not the Lord could do anything with a headstrong and foolish woman who was in love. Mr. Leon could tell him that mountains were moved one shovel-full at a time. Grampa was patient. He would prevail.

Even though I was in love. Sitting at the table with Taylor that morning I let myself think the words over and over in my head. I felt them reverberating through my spirit, their rhythms jazzing up the Blues in my heart. Breakfast had started out almost silently, as it sometimes did on other mornings, when Taylor might be preoccupied with the newspaper or some other matter he didn't choose to discuss with me. This morning the paper remained folded and unread next to his plate. With no best way to tell him that I was going to see Grampa, I finally simply informed him directly.

"All right," he replied as I refilled his coffee cup.

"I have to," I told him.

"Of course," he said.

I refilled my own coffee cup and took the pot back to the stove.

"I just think I should, Taylor," I said sitting at the table again. "He should have been talking to me about this, not you."

"Maybe," he replied.

I looked at him.

"It isn't so far removed from custom, Esther, if you think about it," he said.

It was what fathers did with respect to their daughters' suitors. With respect to *gentlemen callers*. I stared down at my plate.

"So what exactly are your objections, Esther?" asked Taylor after a time.

I looked up at him again.

"My objections to what?" I asked.

"To the terms of the agreement," he answered. "If I'm correct in assuming that this is what you want to talk to him about."

Partly, I thought. Maybe mostly. But also I just missed him too. In that instant I realized again how much I missed him. What was my *own mind?*

"The agreement is between the two of you, Taylor," I replied. "I don't really know what the terms are. Except that you would send me away."

He smiled wryly.

"Then I believe it's null and void," he said and sipped his coffee. "Since it appears I'm incapable of keeping it."

It was Eve who had brought ruination to the world. It was all a woman's fault. But maybe I could make a compromise. Being in the middle, I could see all the sides. I could do what was best for all. And maybe only hurt everybody a little bit.

"At my request," I reminded him.

The corners of his mouth lifted more sincerely as he returned his cup to its saucer.

"My mother would be proud of you," he replied.

"Mine wouldn't," I said honestly.

"No," he sighed. "Probably not."

"But I'm not sorry, Taylor."

"Good. Neither am I."

I washed the dishes after breakfast and the morning was almost the afternoon before I was ready to go. Spencer would be coming soon. I went to the study to tell Taylor that I was going to catch the bus. Then I went to the closet in foyer to get my sweater and pocketbook. Taylor followed me. For an instant I fretted about the well-waxed floor and the dangers it posed for him. As soon as I came back I would strip it completely, strip all the hardwood floors until they were dull and safe.

And I would be back. Regardless of where it had begun, and how much time it had left, this was as yet unfinished. And I would not run away anymore. Not from anyone or anything.

I put on my sweater and checked my wristwatch. It had been a long time since I had had to concern myself with a bus schedule. As if reading my thoughts, Taylor told me to take his car.

"A car's too big to borrow," I responded prudently declining his offer.

Grampa would not be pleased to see me driving his car as if I had a right to do so.

"I want you to," Taylor insisted.

"I might be gone awhile," I discouraged him.

"Humor me," said Taylor, nodding in the direction of the keys on the credenza.

Reluctantly I relented. It would be easier to take the car, whatever Grampa felt about it.

"I can stop by the A&P," I offered walking over to the credenza to pick up the keys. "You want me to bring you anything special?"

His characteristic crooked smile reappeared.

"Yes," he said.

Could he think that I might not come back? Last night had blurred my relationship to him, with him. Who was I in this house now? What had I become? How could he keep paying me wages? How could I keep accepting them? Yet that was why I was working here, wasn't it? For wages and the college tuition and books that the wages would buy. Or at least the trousseau I was going to need. For Danny. There was still Danny. Danny whom I was asking to wait for me while I finished all of this—whatever *this* was.

"I have to go see him," I repeated myself. "I've put it off too long."

Taylor nodded.

"It doesn't make sense, him coming to see you, Taylor," I went on unnecessarily. "When it's me and him who should be talking."

"I understand, Esther," said Taylor. "But I'd feel the same way if you were my daughter."

His daughter would be beautiful. And Grampa would love her anyway. Grampa always did what he understood to be right. The past was all we had to judge the present by. It was all we had with which to predict the future. Nevertheless he would cherish any great-granddaughter I placed in his arms. She would belong to him just like all of us did.

"It's just hard for him that's all," I told Taylor.

"Somehow I think he's up to it," he said.

We smiled at each other.

"He's a very good man," I continued.

"Yes, I know."

"But you see he just has all these memories. And they are fresh for him, Taylor. Like it was yesterday."

"I understand."

But how could he? And if he did, how could he think that it was fair? He wasn't why any of it had happened. He had done nothing wrong. Mandy was right. It was wrong to blame him. How was I going to get Grampa to see that? I suddenly felt weary already. I was the *incapable* one. No wonder so few of us ever tried to change the world. It was exhausting.

"You don't have to defend him," Taylor assured me. "He's not the one on trial."

"No one is," I said hastily.

His smile moved closer to his eyes.

"All right," he agreed.

"I better get going," I said and covered his right hand with mine.

Releasing the handle of the crutch, he squeezed my hand. How was he going to treat me, I asked myself, as I dwelled in his eyes. What was going to happen to me for this? Had a single prince of Egypt ever built a palace for his Hebrew maidservant? Did such miracles also happen in the Bible?

"There's cold ham in the icebox," I started. "Uh...I mean in the--the refrigerator." My body was drawing closer to him. "I'll be back in time to fix supper, I mean din--"

Taylor smothered the word by kissing me, longingly, like he was kissing me goodbye. Or maybe it was the way he kissed hello. The end at the beginning. The beginning at the end. And all I wanted to do was hold fast and cling to this moment, to this place, and yes, oh yes, to this man.

III

I drove across town cautiously, in an automobile that seemed much too conspicuous, like I was driving Pharaoh's finest chariot. Taylor was particular about the condition of his car, inside and out. If I did wax the floors too much, the same could be said about him when it came to his car. In that much he reminded me of Nathaniel again, and watching him and Spencer together around the car, I would imagine the way Nathaniel would be with Baby Nate someday. Maybe Mandy would let Spencer come live with me and Danny in California. Maybe Danny could find Willie Gaines.

Convinced that eyes were watching me, mostly I stared straight ahead, my hands gripping the steering wheel tightly. Operating around the hand controls, I longed for the familiar rough ride of Nathaniel's old pick-up truck. I missed the bus. This was after all what I knew, and I craved the familiar, even if that meant contending with a stubborn clutch or the cold blank face of a bus driver. Being in this strange new emotional place, I yearned for what was familiar to me, things as sure as the treetops turning to bright burnt orange with the short autumn season.

Reaching the colored-side of McConnell County brought me the kind of relief that came with arriving at home. I felt safer, even on my way to Grampa's house where his reckoning waited for me. I rolled down the car window to let in the crisp air. It cooled my racing heart. By the time I pulled up in front of Grampa's house, parking Taylor's car along the street, I was glad to be there.

From across the street standing in her yard, Mis' Janey called to me.

"Well how you doin', Esther Fay?" she said.

"Hello Mis' Janey," I returned her greeting. "Doin' fine. How are you?"

"Just fine, baby. God is good. That sho' is a pretty car, you drivin'. That b'long to Nathaniel?"

"No ma'am," I answered.

"Tell me somethin'," she nodded approvingly. "He doin' well and everything, but some of these white folks take offense if a colored man be doin' too well."

"Yes ma'am."

Perhaps one day I would be living in some community somewhere, where even Negroes could have nice cars.

"I ain't been seein' you 'round here much lately," chatted Mis' Janey. "You must be keepin' very busy workin' for that crippled man. It true he got the polio?"

You really must learn to say it.

But Taylor was not crippled. I was not going to let him be.

"Yes ma'am," I replied.

"They had a big scare of it up in Cleveland this summer too. I always said them big cities too crowded. Folks all piled up on top of one another." She shook her head. "My son-in-law, Frank, you 'member Frank, don't you, my Wilma Louise's husband? Well he got him a good fac'try job up there. He a foreman. Ain't that somethin'? A colored man tellin' white men what to do. Guess you have to take the good with the bad sometimes."

"Yes ma'am."

"It's a shame 'fo' God, a sickness like that." The old lady shook her head again. "Leavin' all them crippled babies."

"Yes ma'am."

"Ain't no tellin' how yo' boss-man got it. A crippled chile is a pitiful thing to see. But I guess we get used to seein' men folks that way, what with all these wars and trouble."

"Yes ma'am."

Mercifully another car came towards the place where I was standing in the street, and seizing the opportunity I quickly backed away from Mis' Janey's conversation.

"See you, Mis' Janey," I called hurrying towards Grampa's gate.

"See you, baby," she called back. "You tell that ol' Isaac Green I don't care if he never sits down to another cup of coffee with me. I ain't got no time for his foolishness no way."

Grampa's fence gate creaked opened and closed, and I was safe in his front yard. The plain dirt yard was fine with Grampa given that Albert had been born in a cabin with a plain dirt floor; and in the years immediately after Reconstruction, when the restored Union failed the newly freed Negroes, leaving them to fend for themselves in what was still a slave culture, dirt floors had been common. So much for the eloquent promises, for the fine words of Mr. Lincoln, and Taylor's sacred Constitution. Yet things were better. Nathaniel could have a very nice car if he wanted to, and Grampa could have a nice lawn. At least there could be some flowers.

I respectfully knocked on the screen door before pulling it open and going inside the house. "Grampa," I called, setting my pocketbook down in the front room and taking off my sweater. "It's me, Grampa. Esther Fay." There was no answer.

The house smelled of tobacco smoke and pan sausage spiced with sage. On the front room wall were the faces of my people. In the middle of them was Ernestine's dark and formal image, wearing a fancy church hat with an elegant feather, and next to her was Jimmy in his uniform. Little Evie and Baby Nate already had their own portraits hanging on the wall. There they were, the future, all dressed up in baby clothes and bows. Mama had brought Daddy to this wall the same way that Uncle Perry had brought Aunt Betty. Aunt Grace and Uncle Eddie, perhaps flaunting their northern success a little, had even supplied their own picture frame. It was a glossy golden thing that was too ornate for Grampa's humble wallpaper which was smoked-up from the wood heater. I was on the wall too, wearing my high school graduation dress, and next to my picture was one of Nathaniel and Connie on their wedding day. A rainbow of black colors, where Danny could fit in easily, perhaps wearing his uniform too. Maybe I would even have a wedding dress.

Grampa's pipe lay in the ashtray on the table next to his rocking chair. Touching the rocking chair as I walked by it, I left it going back and forth as I moved on to the kitchen. Had Grampa and Taylor smoked their pipes as they had been resolving the terms and conditions of their agreement and settling my situation, planning how I would leave them both?

In the kitchen Grampa's cold coffee cup sat on the table without a saucer. Poor Mis' Janey. She wanted to set out her best for him, and she had nursed her own *something* for him for so many years. She didn't stand a chance. Some of us wanted to encourage it, but we didn't dare. Grampa was Ernestine's husband and always would be. Some things even death couldn't part.

The rest of Grampa's breakfast dishes were in the sink. I looked out the kitchen window and saw him tending his garden. I had spent too much time in another man's house, I reminded myself. This was my place. I took the time to wash Grampa's dishes. I was wrong to treat him this way.

When I finished putting the dishes away, I wiped down the counter, as well as the fronts of the cupboards. I wiped the table too and refilled the sugar bowl and the salt shaker. I rinsed out the coffee pot and checked in the icebox to make sure there was evaporated milk for Grampa's coffee and pondered what I could cook for his supper.

With nothing else to do in the house, there was nothing left to do but go out to the garden. Gethsemane had also been a garden, and Jesus had been obedient to the end.

He was the standard by which we measured ourselves. Obedience was the only sacrifice that God wanted.

Grampa didn't look up as I approached him, as the saying went, if I had been a snake I could have bitten him. Grampa was like that, deep inside of himself most of the time, unless someone or something drew him—or forced him—out. It must have come from all those days of close, cramped quarters working for the railroad. He had taught himself how to find his separate place, one that was of his own making, no matter what else was going on around him.

Mama used to complain about his moodiness and how hard it was to get along with him. "Papa ain't gon' be bothered," she would grumble. He could seem impenetrable, but nobody ever said that Ernestine had had a hard time with him. I believed that she must have known, as I did, that much more *bothered* him than he ever wanted to show. If a proud man must live a life filled with a multitude of insults, in order to preserve his dignity then he had to seem unaffected. It might be all he had against the world, willful indifference.

Yet protective or not, understandable or not, Grampa did make it difficult to talk things over with him, especially when there was disagreement. Rarely questioning his rightness about anything, he didn't take it well when others did. So most of the time we didn't. Not to his face anyway. Except for Aunt Betty, who was constantly reminding us that Grampa was not her father. He was mine, however. He had raised me. He loved me. I was his.

And I had forced him to go to Taylor, me, his own granddaughter, his ram in the bush, to ask for me back, because I had willfully wandered away. He had had to come after his disobedient child, his prodigal daughter twice, and still all I wanted to do was stay out there, in the wilderness, when a *Promise Land* waited. What was the matter with me? *Nothing*, I resolved to myself. I loved Taylor. And a woman could leave her father and *cleave unto* a man too, even if they could only be *one flesh* for a moment.

That was the part that both Grampa and Taylor had missed in the fashioning of their *gentlemen's agreement.* They thought I was soft-hearted and weak. They thought I was acting out of beguiled compassion and misguided Christian charity. They thought I was naive enough to believe, or even hope, that it could last. It was almost funny really, the two of them having their *man-to-man* talks, so sensibly taking care of me and so completely getting it wrong.

But it was a *moot point,* as Taylor would say. In the end, I would be coming home. Grampa would win. He could be confident in his rightness about things, because usually he was. Maybe Jimmy had not died totally in vain, but he had not accomplished the dream either. It wasn't yet time for the *us* that Taylor and I could make.

"Hello Grampa," I said from the other side of the garden fence that he had built to protect his vegetables, startling him.

Yes, it was me I wanted to say, not the birds or the cicadas that chirped in the trees. And not a snake either.

"Well," he responded dryly. "Where'd you come from?"

"How are you, Grampa?" I asked, opening the gate and entering the garden.

"Doin' fine," he informed me. "Yo'self?"

"I'm fine," I tried to say cheerfully. "I'm good."

I moved closer to the end of the row where he was standing. I was smiling, genuinely glad to see him even if I was a little afraid. It had been a long time since the terrible Sunday after my birthday, and longer still since we had really talked. The distance had been of my making, and ever since that day outside of Taylor's room, when I had first chosen desire over obedience. No, I had never been a nurse.

"The garden looks good," I complimented my grandfather's work.

"That it does, by the help of the Lord," he agreed, passing the credit to God.

He was hoeing weeds from around the turnips. With my preference for planting flowers, I had never been enough help to him in the garden that really mattered, the one that kept our bellies full season to season. Dismissive of both Mama's and my kind of horticulture, Grampa would fuss, "You need to be raisin' us some veg'tables, somethin' we can put in the pantry 'ginst hard times." Mama would usually ignore him, and come the springtime, Grampa would remark that the pretty blooms reminded him of Ernestine. And the *hard times*? I couldn't remember ever having seen hungry ones. Even during the Depression there had been food on our table. And Jimmy's cake at Christmas time.

Grampa resumed chopping at the tenacious green encroachers that tried to violate his valuable produce. I waited. You didn't rush things with Grampa. You waited. It was the best way to get him come around to your position, or at least come to accept it. He had to do it in his own way and in his own time. Perhaps that was Mis' Janey's mistake. She was too pushy with him.

"Guess you don't raise a green garden over yond'a," he said after awhile as he worked his way down the row away from me.

"No-sir," I replied to his back.

But there are roses, I wanted to say. And in my cheeks too. Sister Callie used to say that there was more to life than corn and collards, but Grampa would have dismissed such wisdom as more women's foolishness. A long time passed while I let the silence be.

"He must-a told you I come to see 'im yestiddy," said Grampa finally.

Here it was at last, the *ought* between us, out here with the birds and cicadas, in the bright early afternoon sunshine.

"Yes-sir," I answered him. "And about you coming to the house too," I added.

"I'll say this fo' 'im," Grampa said moving farther down the row, chopping his way to the end. "He didn't put that dog on me."

The silence fell again like a heavy curtain. It was a false charge and he knew it.

"The turnips are pretty," I said pulling it back a little. "And the collards too. You must be proud. Folks'll be glad to come by and take their pick."

"The more you give the more you get," Grampa grunted.

You reaped what you sowed. Good for good. Bad for bad. It was Grampa's custom to share with his neighbors whenever his garden harvest was bountiful. Once the family was taken care of, he gave the rest away. "It ain't ours in the first place," he had taught us. Even if money was tight in the house, he would refuse to sell the harvest from his garden. Grampa was a generous man.

"I didn't put the dog on you, Grampa," I said. "And I begged you to come to the house for a visit. But when you finally did, it was to see Taylor, not me. Why didn't you come to see me about—I mean if you were so worried."

"That what you call 'im when y'all by yo'self, *Taylor*?" asked Grampa.

"He wants me to," I replied. "All of us."

Grampa continued down the row away from me.

"Mighty gracious of 'im," he replied derisively. "His kind ever hear you call 'im that?"

No, I thought, but that was more my doing than his. Spencer had never even heard me use his first name.

"I figgered as much," said Grampa assuming he had his confirmation when I failed to answer.

"Why would you talk to him and not me?" I repeated the question.

Grampa stopped chopping and rested the wooden handle of the hoe against his body. I made my way down a row so that I could see his face. Removing his straw hat, he pulled out a white handkerchief from one of the hip pockets of his faded and patched denim overalls and wiped his balding head. Then he looked directly at me.

"He ain't sick no mo', Esther Fay," he said. "It's time fo' you to come home. He needs to know that even if you don't."

Returning the hat to his head and the handkerchief to his pocket, Grampa went back to work with the hoe. The light-skinned hands that gripped the hoe handle were a sun-burnt brown, as Grampa preferred them to be, sun-burnt until they were brown because they were busy providing for us. He had once confessed to me that he thought his days of being a porter had diminished his strength. The railroad had paid good Negro wages, especially if you added in the tips, he had said, but it was *inside work* according to Grampa, and that kind of work made a man soft. "Get you a pair of desk-man hands," he had complained.

I often wondered when he talked about his porter days, if all the ironing and cooking, and making-up beds had not been harder on Grampa's heart than on his hands.

He had always believed that Jimmy was suited to *inside work* as he called it, a *desk-man's* life, and Grampa had wanted the best for Jimmy. I wondered if he had shaken Taylor's hand when they had met. Taylor would have offered his. If Grampa had accepted it, it might t have changed his mind about the effects of *inside work*. Taylor had always had strong hands, even before the crutches, and now they were that much stronger. Maybe he could even swing an axe again, and without gloves.

"And does he?" I asked, knowing that the answer Taylor had given yesterday had been changed by last night. We had made the agreement *null and void* together. "Does he think I should come home?"

"You know the answer to that better 'an me," Grampa said chopping the weeds.

In the pre-dawn hours reality had transformed and done away with reason. It was more determined now, the *something* between us, having had a taste of victory as we had surrendered to it and each other. It just couldn't last.

"He still needs me, Grampa," I said.

The weeds were no match for the sharp blade of Grampa's hoe. They lay down, without protest, to die and to dry-up in the autumn sun.

"A man reaps what he sows, Esther Fay," Grampa replied.

He meant sickness for sin. That was what the Bible said. Plagues as punishment. Penalty meted out against the flesh. For yielding to temptation. Even though Mama had been a praying woman. And Jimmy, Jimmy who was so beautiful and good, had died anyway. And what about kindness? What about love?

"Sometimes it's not so simple, Grampa," I said.

"It's black and white," he replied. "Don't get no mo' simpler 'an that."

Black and white together rendered gray, the color of fog, of mist, of ambiguity. But I did not want to argue with Grampa, and I was resolved not to rush him. There was time. The bright sun was hot on my back through the black cotton dress. The good garden dirt dusted my black work shoes, threatening the tops of my white socks. If I could not make Grampa understand this day, there would be other days. My mind was made up and in an alliance with my heart. All I wanted was until Christmas. When the plagues had been put upon Egypt, some good Egyptian sons must have died too, and surely some Hebrew mothers had wept with their Egyptian neighbors over the tragedy of collective justice. God could exact a heavy price for our follies and our sins.

Grampa turned and started working his way back down a new row. I walked along side of him. Grampa loved the land, loved planting things, tending them, watching them grow, and worked in the garden every day that he could. In part he measured himself by what he raised and that included me too, and he believed that he had shared enough with a man who could not be his neighbor.

"It's not wrong to help somebody," I said.

"I thought you was s'pose to be workin' fo' 'im," Grampa said without looking at me. "Fo' wages."

I was—except it wasn't work anymore, and I no longer knew what the wages meant.

"He's a good man, Grampa."

"And you a good woman, Esther Fay," he paused for an instant. "Least wise you was. Unless you come to tell me different."

I was still a good woman, as good as I ever was, maybe even better, but I swallowed any confession that would make him doubt it. As Nathaniel and Connie had said, if I wasn't repentant there was no point in subjecting him to it.

"I'm not doing anything wrong, Grampa," I said.

Because I wasn't. The love made it right.

"Be ye sep'rate says the Lord," replied Grampa digging deep holes in the good earth. "Folks is talkin', Esther Fay," he warned me. "Puttin' yo' name in the streets. You think that don't hurt you, don't hurt this family?"

Why would anyone care so much, I wanted to ask him. Why was it anybody's business? I couldn't stay in McConnell County anyway. Even Grampa would send me away. Soon this place would not be my home. Like Aunt Grace and Uncle Eddie, and Willie Gaines, and Jimmy too, I had to go elsewhere for my Promise Land.

"He needs me," I repeated. "But he's better, Grampa, and soon he won't need me anymore, and I'll come home. I'll go back to New York just like you want. Things'll be fine. You'll see."

Abruptly Grampa stopped chopping and trudged off towards the garden gate. Docilely, I followed him. When we reached the back porch, he slipped the hoe into its place underneath the porch where he kept the rest of his garden tools. Then he took a seat in one of the old cane-bottom chairs we kept on the back porch. Taking off his hat again he set it down on the weather-beaten porch rail. Eagerly I hurried into the house to bring him a glass of cold water. When I returned he accepted it from me with an appreciative nod. It did my heart good to do for him, even this little thing. I sat down on the porch steps, not far from his feet and looked up at him. It was as if I was a child, but I wasn't. I hadn't been one for a long time.

"I asked 'im 'bout his family," Grampa said once he finished the water. "Why none of them come to see after 'im."

"He only has the one sister," I explained. "She has three little boys. There's an uncle, but he's very old--"

"He told me his people don't care about 'im," Grampa interrupted my polite explanation.

I fell silent for a moment, staring at him. Surely Taylor had not said it like that, even if he believed it, he would not have said such a thing about his sister.

"There-there was a misunderstanding," I stammered. "It's-it's hard to--"

"I seen plenty men like him in my day, ones that's cut off from they families. Goin' to and fro, can't settle down. They what you call loners. They can't b'long to nobody. A man like that, colored or white, he'll break a woman's heart. He can't understand a woman like you, Esther Fay. How you b'long to us. To yo' people."

I'm better off on my own.

Perhaps Taylor was a *loner* as Grampa called him, but he had come home, to the only home he knew and settled here; and he had understood me well enough to send me to my home on Sundays, to my family and to my church. There was the enduring attachment to Doctor Mitchell, and a growing one to Spencer. Taylor didn't want to be alone, and I silently denied the harshness of Grampa's assessment, feeling a little smile on my lips at how wrong Grampa had gotten this.

Taylor envied me my family ties. I wished I could bring him here to meet them. Nathaniel already liked him. Uncle Perry probably did too. He would impress Aunt Betty, and Connie was always open. In time Grampa might even be able to see him differently. Then when I was gone, Taylor would have these connections. My family would be his friends.

In the chicken yard, the old white rooster, Red Comb, crowed. He was long-passed his prime, and by now too tough even for dumplings, but he still strutted around the yard. The hens might be looking to the younger male birds, but old Red Comb walked around like he didn't know it or didn't care. He ruled; if no longer by might then by right. Another time I might have gone into the house to get Grampa's pipe and tobacco too. We might have enjoyed each other's company, sitting there on the back porch on such a nice day.

"He was wrong fo' askin' you to nurse 'im," said Grampa as Red Comb crowed.

You're not my nurse.

Secret parts of me recalled last night, how I had not been Taylor's nurse, how I had never been.

"It wasn't his choice, Grampa," I replied. "There was nothin' else to do."

The out-house needed a new coat of paint. If Grampa would only consent to bathroom plumbing we could just tear the whole thing down and be done with it, smooth it over and let the grass grow in, as Uncle Perry and Aunt Betty had done. What was the sense of keeping a privy when you could have better? Change could be a good thing.

"And you was the only one?" demanded Grampa. "Wasn't nobody else? It was just left up to you? A man like that, with money, standin' with his people, and wasn't nobody willin' to come to his aid but the hired help?" Grampa rubbed his chin. "Lord, I knowed they was a mean people, but--"

"Doctor Mitchell was there," I quickly interjected.

"Humph," grunted Grampa. "Mitchell. He would-a called the law on you if you'd-a left."

"He was right, Grampa. He was right to ask me to stay."

"You stayed 'cause Mitchell asked you to?"

"Yes," I lied in part. "He's always done right by us, Grampa. I couldn't refuse him."

"But you ain't no nurse," said Grampa. "You his maid. Mitchell knowed that."

"I'm good with the sick, Grampa. You've said that yourself. The doctor showed me what to do for him. How to make the hot-packs and help him with the exercises. And it's working. Sister Kenny's therapy. It is. We can't stop now."

"I'm not in the habit of fattenin' up frogs fo' snakes," said Grampa.

"You can't always judge things by the past, Grampa," I returned.

"How else you gon' judge 'em?"

"Maybe the thing is not to judge at all. "The Bible says--"

"He shall sep'rate them one from another, as a shepherd divideth his sheep from goats," Grampa quoted the Book of Matthew.

The sentiments are nice, Esther. Until somebody misuses them.

"He needs my help, Grampa," I said. "That's all I know."

"And what about you?" asked Grampa. "What you need?"

A little more time was what I wanted to tell him, but I was quiet again.

"What about you finishin' school?" Grampa pressed. "You ain't gettin' no younger, you know. What you think you gon' look like goin' back to that college this late in life? That's if'n you ever do go."

"Hopefully I'll look determined," I said. "Because I will go back, Grampa. I want to teach. I know that now. It's something I'm good at."

"Yo' boss-man tell you that?"

"He didn't need to."

I might have been tutoring my Marxist classmates by now, teaching them the King's English over cups of coffee too creamy and sweet for Taylor's tastes.

"Ain't no man gon' wait 'round on you fo'evah," warned Grampa. "Simmons wants to marry you. What you plan on tellin' 'im? That you makin' him wait on account-a some white man *needin'* you? That boy ain't crazy, Esther Fay. Fact about it, he ain't no boy at-all. And a man don't want his woman livin' in the house with another man. You ain't told 'im who you workin' fo', is you? Why you hidin' it from him if you don't see nothin' wrong with it?"

"He knows where I am," I said. "He called me there."

"He had a right to," Grampa said.

"Yes-sir," I replied looking at him. "I guess he did."

"I know he did."

"It was good to hear from him."

"But you ain't told yo' boss-man 'bout it, did you? How come?"

"I-I didn't see a reason--"

"Humph. Bet Simmons could see a reason, as you say. Fact about it, Payne did too. He didn't even know you was courtin'."

"Grampa, please. I'm not--"

"I know," he put up his hand as if to stop me. "You grown. That's what you keep tellin' me. Well you may got the years, and some book knowledge too, but you missin' common sense."

"I'm not ashamed of anything, Grampa," I settled for saying.

"What Mandy Gaines say 'bout it?" demanded Grampa. "She know somethin' 'bout men. They can't make a fool out of her. Not no mo' anyway. Not since Willie Gaines come through here and left her with all them babies. She ain't all dreamy-eyed. What she say 'bout it?"

You playin' one of them too. And sooner or later you gon' have to do what's right.

"Nothing," I said.

"*Nothin'?*" Grampa shot back. "If it was one of my kinfolks I'd--"

"Me and Danny are fine, Grampa."

"How long you think that's gon' be true? Folks ain't thinkin' you doin' the Lord's work hemmed up in that house, don't care what you say 'bout it."

"What folks, Grampa?" I asked wearily. "You mean Reverend Wright and Sister Wright? Are you talkin' about them? They don't know Danny. He wouldn't be *decent* enough for them."

"I sent them over there to help you. You should-a listened."

"There's no place in *my* Bible that tells us to abandon a person in need, Grampa."

"Plenty-a places that warn you 'bout 'sociating yo'self with strangers."

"He's not a stranger. Not to me."

"Naw, I guess not. You call yo'self havin' feelin's fo' 'im. And yeah, he got some feelin's fo' you too. I'm ol' but I ain't fo'got what it look like. But you just 'member this, Esther Fay, a cripple man can still make a baby. Then where you be? Livin' in shame with his yella bastard. That what you want?"

"I'm not Matilda, Grampa."

Grampa's face hardened and he stood up, towering over me.

"That's right," he spat. "What they used to have to take from our women folk, you givin' up free."

I rose to my feet.

"I guess I been wrong about you," he continued scornfully. "You ain't no Jezebel. She had some sense. You just a fool."

Grampa went into the house, the screen door banging closed behind him. I remained on the porch alone reeling, in a no man's land of my own making. Between the Red Sea and the pyramids. Between everything that I was and all that I wanted to be. When I followed him into the house, Grampa was at the kitchen counter washing his hands.

"I'm not a fool," I disputed my grandfather in a trembling but clear voice. "I've got nothing to be ashamed of, and you can't make me feel like I do."

He turned to face me, drying his hands on a cup-towel.

"How long you been here?" he asked me as if I had said nothing. "You wash these dishes?"

"If he was colored you wouldn't be sayin' these things," I dismissed him too. "You'd be telling me it's what a Christian is supposed to do. All right, he's not colored. He's white," my voice broke. "But he is also my friend."

Grampa stared back at me, his face impenetrable.

"Yo' *friend*," he sneered. "Don't that beat all? His own kind, his own people, got no use fo' 'im, but he done found hisself a friend in you. You got a whole man that wants you, wants to give you his name. But you want the broken one. Why? What fo', Esther Fay? 'Cause he reads them fancy books and gets dressed up in a suit and tie to go to work? 'Cause he got that big fine house you clean up for 'im? Maybe it's just that pretty white skin? That what you like? You like him bein' white?"

"He needs me," I spoke through a ball of righteous hurt.

"He *needs* you? You shackin'-up with a white man, gal, puttin' yo' name in the streets cause he *needs* you." Grampa shook his head. "You done los' yo' mind."

"Is it?" I demanded. "Is my name in the streets?"

Tears spilled from my eyes.

"What you think?" Grampa rejoined. "You all out in the public with it. Goin' to Ray's. It ain't nothin' but a juke-joint, but even they got some respect about theyselves. Folks'll listen to a jick-head when it comes to some things. How come he didn't take you to one of his fancy places? You ever ask yo'self that? How come he didn't take you downtown, and show you off, since he s'pose to be yo' *friend*?"

"Because I wouldn't let him," I replied bitterly. "Because of people like you."

"*You* wouldn't let him? Don't fool yo'self. That man ain't crazy. He ain't riskin' his name fo' you. This world's full of people like me, as you say. White ones and colored ones. You might-a fo'got that but he ain't. He's the Law, Esther Fay. He'll treat you just fine as long as you in them quarters with 'im, in his kitchen. But there ain't no place fo' you in his world, just in his bed."

"You don't know him," I said, wiping my tears.

"Look at me," Grampa said. "Look at what that skin looks like when it gets mixed up with yours. This gon' be the face of yo' chirren, Esther Fay. They gon' be yella niggas. Not black enough. And sholey God not white enough."

In his hazel eyes a grim history smoldered, turning his lips into a cynical thin line, rushing blood into his yellow cheeks, darkening them menacingly. He was right.

Taylor's world could never be *ours*. And Grampa hated Taylor and all the rest of *them* for it, because he belonged to them in a way that he could never overcome. Not even with Ernestine. But I wasn't asking for Taylor's world. I only wanted time.

Grampa narrowed his eyes, examining me.

"He done put his hands on you, ain't he? You carryin' his bastard? You give away your womanhood for a pearl necklace?"

The tears began again, but I quickly wiped them away. Not for pearls, I wanted to tell him, but for love.

"If that's what you want to believe about me," I said unsteadily, "Then I can't help it. I can't change your mind."

It felt as though I were choking.

"But you don't have to worry about it," I went on. "I'm not staying here."

"Danny Simmons ain't gon' want you," said Grampa.

"I don't care," I replied. "I don't need him."

"Where you plannin' on goin' then?" Grampa's voice changed. "Back to Harlem?"

"Wherever it is, you won't have to be ashamed of me anymore."

I found my breath again. There was always California. The land of make believe. With or without Danny. I could make my own life somewhere where no one knew me. And like Matilda, never look back. I could be a *loner* too.

Grampa didn't say anything for a long time. The tears on my face dried up. Eventually he crossed the kitchen and stood next to the table.

"Sit down, Esther Fay," he said pulling out a chair for himself and doing as he had instructed me.

I didn't obey.

"I said sit down, gal," he repeated more firmly. "You didn't come here to clean up this here kitchen. Or to tell me that you was leavin' town fo' that matter. You come to talk. Well let's talk. I ain't never intended fo' that man to come 'tween you and yo' kin. You ain't got to go nowhere. This yo' home. Nothin' you gon' ever do can change that. You sit down and get hold of yo'self."

I reached out a shaky hand to pull out a chair and sat stiffly across from him, steeling myself while Grampa considered me.

"Humph," he began after a time. "You sho' put me in mind of yo' grandmama." He almost smiled. "I wish you'd-a knowed her. I swear she put her mark on you. I seen the time when you couldn't tell her shit stank and she was standin' knee deep in it," he shook his head but the little smile grew stronger. "And even if she did know it, she might not care one way or the other. I loved that 'bout her, Esther Fay. The way she was stubborn as me. You could count on her standin' her ground. She wasn't weak. Up until the day she died. But that didn't mean she was always right. She made plenty-a mistakes 'cause she wouldn't listen. I seen her own papa take a club to her fo' that. I felt like killin' 'im fo' it too. But yo' grandmamma, she took it and didn't even cry. You like that. You stand up fo' things." He shook his head again. "I ain't surprised that man out yond'a got feelin's fo' you. He b'lieves you saved his life 'cause you wouldn't give up on him. Maybe you did. But sometimes, Esther Fay, sometimes bein' stubborn is bein' foolish. Sometimes you just have to listen to somebody.

"I seen fo' myself what life can be like fo' a ruint woman," Grampa continued. "What people'll look over in a man they'll tear a woman down for. I don't want that to happen to you. You better wake up from these dreams you havin' 'bout this man, and see the danger you in."

"I'm wide awake, Grampa," I replied more calmly. "A man needs my help and I'm giving it to him."

"I b'lieve you done give 'im more 'an that."

I was quiet.

"I'm speakin' 'bout yo' heart, baby," Grampa said. "It's yo' heart that's done got away from you. You can't think straight. That's why I went to see 'im. 'Cause it don't do no good to talk to you."

"I am thinking straight, Grampa. I'm thinking for myself. I know what I'm doing. And how long I have to do it. He's getting stronger all the time, and when he's strong enough I'm going to leave."

"How strong you 'spect him to be?" asked Grampa. "He done gone back to work. You can let somebody else do his washin' and ironin' now. You got somethin' better to do."

"He's a good man, Grampa," I answered running away from the question of *when* like I always did.

"He's a white man, Esther Fay."

"He can be both."

"Who you think you is? One of these here movie stars? Some kind-a Lena Horne with a flower stuck off in yo' hair? She bet' not come down here with that mess. They be done reminded her right quick just what she is, don't care who she married to. You call yo'self havin' feelin's for 'im. Like it's just some kind-a everyday thing. You ain't got no right to those feelin's."

"I'm not forgetting myself, Grampa, if that's what you mean. I never have."

"Then what you call it?"

"Friendship," I answered.

"How you gon' be his friend?" demanded Grampa. "You his maid. That's *all* you is. All you ever will be. I don't care what he tell you, or what you do for 'im, how he treat you. You the maid. He'll tell you anything to keep you 'round 'im as long as he--"

"Is that what he said?" I asked. "When you came to see him about me? Did he tell you that? Did he say I'm just his maid?"

Grampa sighed and rubbed his hand across his face.

"See, Grampa, those are your words, aren't they?" I pressed. "It's what you think. Maybe it's what everybody thinks. Except for us. It's not what he said. Taylor is different, Grampa. He's always been different. From the very beginning. He treats all of us differently. Me. Nathaniel. Spencer. Everybody. You too. You know that. That's how come you went to see him. Because you knew you could talk to him, man to man.

"I used to think like you, Grampa. I started out blaming him for being white. Yes, for what happened to Matilda and Albert. And everything else. All of it. Jimmy too. But that's not fair. We can tell ourselves that it is, but it's not. Grampa, don't you see? It's the same thing they say about us. And it's wrong. It wasn't Taylor's fault. He didn't hurt Matilda or send Jimmy off to die. And he wouldn't let me get away with it. Maybe that's the lawyer in him. He won't accept injustice. From anybody. He is a good man, Grampa. You must have seen that. The same as Jimmy and Nathaniel. He's the same as you."

"He ain't the same as me!" Grampa shot back. "He ain't nothin' like me."

"When he got sick," I persisted. "I saw how frightened he was, how alone, and I just couldn't leave him there, not like that. And last night I saw him crawl, Grampa. It's hard to see a man crawl, any man. I thank the Lord I was there to help him. Because I do help him. You can't ask me to turn my back on him. And even if you do, I won't do it. He'll give up if I leave now. And he can get well, I mean really well. But if I go he'll stop trying. No one else will make him work for it the way I do. It's like you said, I'm stubborn. I make a difference in his life. I don't know why it happened like this. All I know is that it's right for me to help him. I have to do it. And, Grampa, I will do it, until it's done."

"I told you takin' care of 'im like that was goin' to give you notions," Grampa said sadly. "I knew you was gon' fo'get yo'self. And, all right, he done fo'got hisself too. He thinks he can't see his way 'thout you bein' there. Yeah, that's what he said. But don't let that fool you. He grateful to you now. He claims you saved him, that you helped him, and all the rest. But he just scared, that's all. What man wouldn't be? Wake up one mornin' so lame you can't even get out of yo' own bed. Any man be grateful to Satan hisself fo' handin' him a glass of water. Anything is better than bein' alone.

"But I done seen a man crawl too, Esther Fay. And it wasn't from no fever neither, 'less you wanna call it a hate fever. It was a colored man I seen crawlin' 'cause-a white men, because they shot 'im in his knees. And you know why? 'Cause he was gettin' 'bove hisself, just like you tryin' to do. He was signin' up colored folks to vote, talkin' 'bout we's all equal 'fo' the Law. Well they showed him just how *equal* he was all right. First they made him crawl and then they killed 'im dead. And you know what, the Law didn't do nothin' fo' 'im. Not for 'im or fo' his people. Nobody could *help* 'im. All we could do was bury 'im.

"Yeah, it's hard to see a grown man crawl. Yo' *friend,* as you call him, might even need you. But that's fo' right now. He'll get better, and if he don't, then he'll get used to it. Then you see what happens to you. You the maid, and that house gon' have a mistress one day. Then where you gon' be? Walkin' 'round with yo' heart busted so bad you totin' it in a paper sack."

"When he's stronger I'm going to leave," I said again. "I know what can happen. But I made up my mind to be his friend through this. We just need 'til Christmas, Grampa. Sometimes the stranger stops being strange. Sometimes in order to help somebody you have to have a feeling for them. They have to have some kind of feeling for you. Doctor Mitchell called it having an attachment. He meant that you have to care about each other. The Bible says, that if you don't have charity--"

"It profit nothin'," Grampa finished for me.

"That's right."

"What you feelin' is nature, Esther Fay," he said. "Not charity."

It was nature, natural. It was the flesh, but the spirit lived in it. And it was the spirit that had come first.

"Maybe sometimes the difference doesn't matter," I said.

"You gon' see what I mean one day," Grampa replied. "If you was a man, I'd-a been done had to cut yo' dead body down from a tree limb somewhere. You ain't never seen a lynchin', Esther Fay. I pray to God you never do. But it's what they do to us when they think we done fo'got our place. I don't care what we done for 'em. How we raised 'em, or nursed 'em, or give 'em comfort. We wasn't meant to live together."

"Taylor's not that way," I repeated.

I wished that I could make Grampa see that, see beyond the Confederate soldier and the night-riders, see Taylor through my eyes. I wasn't a very good advocate. I had lost my direction early and forgotten my prepared speeches. Yet maybe my goal was still achievable. Grampa must be relenting a little. The Christmas date had gone right by. Maybe the ghost of Ernestine had come to my aid. Was I really so much like her, I wondered. I hoped I was. I liked the idea of her still living for Grampa in me. If only I could also show him Taylor. But I would settle for Christmas.

"Nothing like that's going to happen, Grampa. I promise you. Please don't worry."

"The Bible teach us each to his own kind," he reminded me.

"Maybe we're all one kind."

"What book you read that in?"

"Surely Jesus must have said it."

"The Lord ain't the author of confusion, Esther Fay. That much I do know."

"What if we make all the confusion?"

"Ain't no ifs about it. We do."

"But maybe we wouldn't if we just remembered that a man ain't nothin' but a man like you always say."

"'Thou shalt not let thy cattle be with a different kind,' Esther Fay," Grampa recited more Scripture. "'Thou shalt not sow thy field with mingled seed, neither shall you make a garment of mingle linen and wool.'"

"There are no good white people in the world, Grampa? Are they all evil to you?"

"They's all white to me, Esther Fay. That's enough to make me wary."

IV

The wringer washing machine agitator stirred the white sheets and pillow cases around in the warm sudsy water. It was only a truce, and it wasn't fully spelled-out, but I had won until Christmas from Grampa.

"By the first of the year, you gon' be out of that house," he had made me vow.

"Yes-sir," I had agreed as I surrendered any hope for April.

It was a compromise, a *stay*, but it was more time.

And with that accomplished, I concentrated on it being good to be home again, going through the rest of Grampa's house in search of chores to do, looking for ways to take care of him as I had not done in a very long time. *He* was the man in my life. Everyone else was *just passing through*.

I had stripped the sheets off Grampa's bed to wash. Grampa came out on the back porch after awhile, a fresh cup of coffee in his hand.

"Don't you think you best be takin' that man's car back to 'im?" asked Grampa.

"It's all right," I replied as I measured out the bleach to put in the wash water. "He doesn't expect me back right away."

I was cooking Grampa's supper and baking him a pound cake too. I had borrowed butter from Mis' Janey.

"Got no right to be '*spectin'* you at'-all," Grampa fumed.

It was only a *stay* after all, a mere modification of the *gentlemen's agreement*, granting a few more precious weeks for recovery and restoration, to get things *back right*, as Spencer might say.

"He'll be fine," I told Grampa. "Spencer's there."

"Spencer? Mandy Gaines' boy?"

"Yes-sir."

"Seems like ol' Massa Payne done near 'bout hired all of colored McConnell to sit with 'im."

"I'm not his sitter, Grampa."

"That's right, you his friend."

The smell of bleach floated on the air as the laundry soap bubbles formed and burst on the surface of washing machine water. Bleach purified and whitened, but it also stained and ruined colored clothes like Mama's black dress.

"Spencer does odd jobs around the house," I steered the discussion away from me and my status. "Taylor pays him very well. It helps Mandy out. And he's good to Spencer. A boy needs a man in his life."

"Humph," grunted Grampa. "Didn't know we was so short of men folks of our own," he said.

I let the comment pass and moved away from the washing machine and the scent of bleach.

"And I don't care for that that car sittin' out front-a my house," Grampa returned to the subject of Taylor's automobile.

"It's just a car, Grampa," I said.

"That's what you think," he said going back into the house.

After I finished making Grampa's bed, I cleaned the dresser mirror. So this was Ernestine's face looking back at me I thought as I wiped down the glass that was spotted with age. A browner version of it anyway, modified by my own father's family and what Grampa had unwillingly brought to it. Did I remind Taylor of someone? Had he ever been with a Negro woman before?

Maybe he had made love with a foreign woman in the Philippines. Nathaniel had told me about the prostitutes, almost as dark as some of us, on the islands where he had fought in the Pacific. He had described their desperation, how they had been starving. "Willin 'to sell they bodies for little-a nothin'," he had said. Was that how Taylor could make love to me; because I reminded him of one of those exotic women? Colored McConnell County, Negro America, was a world away from him too. It might as well have been dotted with palm trees and choked with jungle vines.

It's not as though the entire world subscribes to Plessey v. Ferguson.

Whatever his reasons, we had come together. And somehow he even thought his mother could have been proud of me. If I reminded him of returning to the Philippines with MacArthur, then so be it. It was a time when he had felt powerful and triumphant. I liked the idea of giving that back to him. In the same way that I liked reminding Grampa of a time when he had been in love.

"Esther!" Connie's voice sang through the house. "Where you at girl?"

"In here!" I called back.

"Mis' Janey said you was here!" she exclaimed, standing in the doorway hands on her hips.

"Word travels fast I see," I replied. "Where are the children?"

"I got 'em with me. They out on the front porch with they great grand-daddy. He can see after 'em for awhile. What's smells so good? You cookin' somethin' sweet?"

"I'm baking Grampa a pound cake."

"Cookin' cakes, cleanin' house, I'll say. Mama Betty sent me to pick-up his washin' but Grampa Isaac say you doin' that too. Guess y'all finally made up, thank the Lord."

"He came to see Taylor on account of me," I said, giving the bureau a final wipe. "What sense did that make?"

"What?" asked Connie, her face serious as she came all the way into the room, shutting the door behind her.

"Oh, Connie, you know it," I replied, irritated by her feigned ignorance. "He's been to see him twice now. But it was left up to Taylor to tell me about it. Since nobody in this family would."

"Lord," said Connie dolefully.

She sat down on the side of Grampa's freshly made bed. I frowned and collected the straw broom and dust-pan.

"I was the only one kept in the dark," I charged.

Connie looked dejected, but I was not impressed.

"Nathaniel said Grampa Isaac said it was 'tween him and Mr. Payne," she explained. "But honest to God, Esther, I didn't think he'd go through with it. I promise you."

"Grampa might still think I'm a child, but at least I thought it was different with you and Nathaniel," I replied coldly.

"Esther--"

"It doesn't matter," I said cutting her off. "It's all straightened out now."

"You mean you come home?"

"No," I said, opening the bedroom door. "I'm staying until he's well."

"Grampa Isaac gon' let you?" Connie asked incredulously.

"He understands that he needs me," I told her, my back to her.

"But he gone back to work, Esther. He must be doin' all right now."

"He needs more time."

"But if he's well..."

"He's just better that's all. He's not well yet."

"May-maybe it's goin' to be like Roosevelt, Esther," ventured Connie. "You know--"

I shut the door.

"He's needs more time that's all!" I insisted fiercely, now facing her.

454

Connie got up from the bed uneasily.

"Sometimes, Esther, even if we do all we can--"

"No!" I repeated. "Taylor is a strong man. He's not going to be crippled."

The juries would feel sorry for him. He would always doubt himself.

"All right, Esther," Connie relented. "I'm not tryin' to argue with you. But it's not right for you to be mad at Grampa Isaac either. Or the rest of us for that matter. It's hard to accept all this."

"Nobody asked you to," I rejoined.

Connie blinked anxiously.

"You do," she said. "You part of this family. What happens to you happens to us too. Colored and white don't be mixin'. It's against the law. Ask 'im, ask Mr. Taylor. I know you's educated and everything. I can see how it happened. You and him a lot alike. I bet you even read the same kind of books. And besides Aunt Grace and Uncle Eddie, I don't know of no other colored folks that be goin' to those fancy music shows, you talk about. He probably like that kind of music too. But--"

"He likes the Blues," I said.

"Huh?"

"He likes the Blues," I said again. "He used to go to Harlem when he lived in New York."

Maybe that was where he had encountered the *exotic* women, women dressed in silks and satins, glittering with jewels and smelling of perfume. The women Jimmy would have known.

"That's what I'm talkin' about, Esther. You might can do that kind of thing in New York or somewhere else up north, but this is McConnell County."

Wearily I leaned against the door. Maybe Connie was right, I was asking them to accept what I was doing, forcing this on them, the same way I made Taylor do the therapy. I believed in my rightness too.

"It's not against the law for us to like the same things, Connie," I said despondently.

"It is for you to like each other," she replied.

I sighed.

"I know it happens," she went on. "It happens all the time. More than folks want to admit, colored or white. All these high-yellow faces must be comin' from somewhere. And it ain't all rape neither. It never was. But it was for this family. It's just not somethin' we can forget that's all."

"Nobody's asking you to, Connie," I repeated forlornly.

"Taylor Payne's a decent man, Esther. Nathaniel says so. And I b'lieve to my soul that he is. And if y'all care for one another, well that can be decent too. But even if he was colored, you still just can't be livin' with him like you do, 'thout some folks talkin'. Shackin'-up is a sin, Esther. It don't matter who it's with. But if it's with a white man...

well-well that makes it dangerous too. Yo' grand-daddy knows that. We all do. Maybe if y'all was to get married, then maybe...but like I said, you can't do that here. He would have to take you away from us. I guess maybe to New York or somewhere like that. You could live in New York. That might be better. I don't know. But what I do know is it can't be here. That's why Grampa Isaac so upset. He thinks that man might take you away from us. He don't say it, prob'ly never will, but he shows it. That ol' man dotes on you, Esther Fay Allen. Always has. It would kill 'im if somethin' was to happen to you. Ain't he been through enough? Sholey God, Esther, you can understand how he feels."

"I do, Connie," I admitted drearily. "But I can't leave him now. I just can't."

"Did he get mad about it?" Connie asked. "Taylor Payne, I mean, 'bout Grampa comin' to see 'im that way?"

"No," I said. "He didn't get mad. They've been having very nice talks it seems. It was all quite *decent* I'm sure. They have a gentlemen's agreement."

"A what?"

"A gentlemen's agreement."

"What's that?"

"They have agreed on how to protect me from myself."

Connie looked at me.

"What?" I asked. "They can't have a gentlemen's agreement? They can you know. They are both gentlemen. Do you realize that, Connie? They have something in common too."

"Yeah," she replied. "You."

"Taylor's not a selfish man, Connie. None of you believe that, but he's not. He's a better man than you know."

"Don't get worked up," consoled Connie. "I see that 'bout 'im. We all do. But--"

"He's white."

"It's the truth, Esther. You can't ignore it."

"Why would I want to? He is who he is, and God made him. Just like you and me."

"Look Esther, I told you before, ain't none of this anybody's fault. But you can't just act like it don't matter. Maybe it don't in his house. But everywhere else it does."

"It's not like that between us, Connie," I resorted to the lie. "I just work for him. I'm taking care of him because he's been a friend to us, to our family. And he needs me. That's all."

"Esther, you don't have to--"

"That's all there is to it, Connie. Why can't people just be friends? What makes it so impossible for men and women to be friends? Why can't it happen between coloreds and whites?"

"Do you love 'im, Esther?" Connie asked.

"Not the way you mean it," I lied.

Connie was silent.

"I'm just trying to be a friend to him, that's all. A Christian friend. Like you said, Connie, maybe I am like Ananias in the Bible, appointed by the Lord to be a help to him."

Connie's face was gloomy, and I was ashamed of trying to deceive her.

"Lovin' somebody's never wrong, Esther," she said. "It's what we do with it, what we do 'bout it, that's what can be wrong sometimes."

Connie reached into her pocket and handed me a letter.

"This come for you on Thursday," she continued. "I was gon' give it to you at church tomorrow, that is if you was comin'."

I unfolded the white unopened envelope. The return address read *Sergeant Daniel Simmons*. I looked up from the envelope meeting Connie's eyes.

"I s'pose he's yo' friend too," she said.

Desperately I wanted to tell her the truth. I wanted her to know that even if it was only for a little while I loved and was cared for, that I very nearly had what she had with Nathaniel, that her kind of happiness was almost possible for me too. But without a word I slipped Danny's letter, unopened, into my dress pocket.

"We better go see about your cake," warned Connie. "'Fo' it be done burned."

I followed her into Grampa's kitchen, where she took the cake out of the oven and tested it for doneness. Deciding it was ready, she placed it on the table to cool. I stirred the pot of oxtails and onions cooking in a covered Dutch oven on top of the stove. We remained quiet; and the letter was like a brick in my pocket, weighing me down with impending realities. *Christmas.* If Danny could just wait until Christmas.

I started to peel potatoes for the stew, and Connie came over to the sink to help me. We stood beside each other, filling a dishpan with muddy-brown skins. Little Evie's laughter drifted in from the front porch. How lucky Connie's children were to have all this love around them. They would always have us. Our family would always be together. Nothing could tear us apart.

He told me his people don't care about 'im.

"What would you think if I invited Taylor to have Thanksgiving dinner with us?" I asked Connie.

She hesitated for only an instant before continuing to peel the potato in her hand.

"Reckon he'd actually come?" she returned.

"I don't know," I replied. "But it's for sure that he won't be visiting his sister."

"How come?"

"It would be a long trip for him," I said.

"Because he's not well."

"That's right."

But he would be well by Christmas. And in the meantime he had me, and I came with a family. And maybe being with us, all of us together, would make him want to see his own people again.

"Then they ought to come here," Connie said. "Families ought to be together for the holidays."

"They're not close," I explained.

Connie stopped peeling a potato to look at me, a frown wrinkling her brow.

"You didn't ask 'im already, did you?" Her tone was a little panicked.

"No," I was able to tell her.

She relaxed a little.

"What about Grampa Isaac? What you think he gon' say? Did you ask him?"

"No," I replied. "I guess I'm tryin' the idea out on you first."

She was shaking her head.

"If the Indians had been like that," I scoffed, "We wouldn't even be havin' Thanksgivin'."

"And they might still have they land," replied Connie, peeling the potato in her hand again. "You can't be sittin' every stranger down to yo' table, Esther. Some of them'll eat you up too."

"He's not a stranger, Connie."

"Not to you maybe," she said.

"And not to you either," I said. "Once upon a time you welcomed him in your home."

"That ain't the same thing."

"What's the difference? You wouldn't welcome him again?" I pressed. "Didn't you mean it then? When he came to your house with a present for Nate? You were nice to him that night. It wasn't all that long ago."

"It ain't the same," she repeated.

"But it could be," I said actually brightened by my idea and the wheels turning slowly behind Connie' uncertain expression. "We could have the dinner at your house. Then it wouldn't be like Grampa had to have him here at all. Nathaniel wouldn't mind, I know it. What do you think?"

"I think you wanna push too hard, Esther Fay," said Connie. "Folks ain't ready for this. Friend or no friend. Or that agreement-thing you was talkin' about in yond'a either."

"That feels wrong to me, Connie," I charged.

"Prob'ly is. But there's a lot wrong in this world. I don't see how one woman all by herself can change it."

We're changing the world. Things will be different once this is over...

"But we have to try, don't we?" I asked thinking of Jimmy, and thinking for myself. "If nobody ever tries then it's all just hopeless. That's all I'm doin', tryin'. If people just got to know each other they'd find out we're really all the same. It's like what you said about bein' in the middle, Connie. Somebody's got to be, if we're ever goin' to come together."

"I guess you figger it's time for us to come together, huh?" she asked sighing, but she was giving in.

"It's got to start somewhere, right? Maybe…maybe it already has. In the war. Jimmy thought that they were changing the world. Who knows? What if all we have to do is recognize it?"

Although that had been Paris, I thought, recalling all the joyous French faces in the newsreels when the Americans were marching in to liberate their city. Faces that had gazed gratefully upon Jimmy too. His letters had said so. They had proclaimed his victory without a single thought about his complexion. No wonder Lena Horne had gone there for her honeymoon.

"I guess if Mama Betty could have the family over to her house last year," Connie said pensively, as her hands stripped another potato. "We could do it this year…If we put the leaf in the table it's s'pose to fit eight," she went on, getting herself used to the idea of it. "I guess we could get seven 'round it."

I smiled thankfully.

"Unless you plannin' on invitin' some mo' of yo' friends," she added dryly.

"What y'all needin' to get seven 'round the table for?" Grampa wanted to know, coming into the kitchen with the children.

Connie and I turned together from the sink. Nate was riding on Grampa's hip while Little Evie was clinging to his leg.

"The family gettin' together for supper tonight?" Grampa asked. "That why you doin' all this cookin' and cleanin', Esther Fay?"

Connie looked to me and waited.

"We were just talkin' about Thanksgiving dinner, Grampa," I answered him.

"Ain't it kind-a early to be thinkin' 'bout that? Tomorrow not promised to us, you know."

But there it was, *tomorrow* riding on his hip, holding to his leg. Full of promise. And we owed them a changed world. Surely it was what their own father had fought for too. And all I wanted was until Christmas.

"It ain't but a month away, Grampa Isaac," Connie helped me. "And with three women cookin', we need to be thinkin' 'bout it right now, if we gon' get it all straightened out."

"What you got to straighten out?" asked Grampa. "I 'member a time when folks didn't even now know if they would have food on the table from one day to the next.

Now we got to be figgerin' out feasts like rich folks. Seem to me, every day ought to be Thanksgivin'."

Unless maybe you were an Indian.

"You ain't got to worry 'bout a thing, Grampa Isaac," Connie said. "Just leave it to us."

"I see I ain't got no say in the matter," he grumbled. "Guess this family done got too good to sit at my table."

Aunt Betty's act of defiance still mattered to him nearly a year later. Perhaps Connie was right, I pushed too hard. Like Mis' Janey.

"Not too good, you grouchy ol' man," Connie teased him. "Just too big. And you might as well get yo'self used to it, we gon' have this year's dinner at our house. It's high time for Nathaniel to sit at the head of a family table too."

Gratefully I looked at her. She winked at me. But then again Grampa wasn't her father either.

"And what you come in here for anyway?" Connie demanded in her spirited way. "Botherin' women folk when they tryin' to cook."

"This baby girl wants somethin' to eat," explained Grampa glumly.

Deftly Connie sliced a piece off an apple and gave it to Nate.

"What he gon' do with that?" asked Grampa.

"He'll gnaw on it for awhile," replied Connie, handing the rest of the apple to Little Evie. "It'll keep 'im busy. Now y'all go on. Get out the way."

Little Evie was biting into her share of the apple, grinning happily, juice running down her chin.

"Got this house smellin' so, folks can't help but to be hungry," complained Grampa. "What y'all cookin' up anyway?"

"Yo' supper," I said, smiling too, reminded again of how good it felt to be home.

"Mean to tell me you don't get enough of doin' this kind of work out yond'a on Webster Road?" asked Grampa, abruptly ending my revelry.

"You let her do for you, ol' man," Connie told him as she rinsed the peeled potatoes in the sink.

I retreated to the safety beside her.

"She ain't got to be no servant 'round here," he told Connie.

"My Lord Jesus was a servant," my "sister-in-law" replied proudly. "Me myself, I don't see no shame in it."

Grampa huffed and left the kitchen with the children, and I thanked Connie for her aid and rescue, but she turned very serious.

"Promise me that you gon' talk this Thanksgivin' thing over with Grampa Isaac first, you hear me?" she said. "I'll do the talkin' to Nathaniel. But it's up to you get it straight with yo' grand-daddy." She shook her head again. "'Course, I don't care what we do, we gon' be in for a uproar. That is if Payne even comes. Visitin' babies is one thing. Sittin' down to eat with a bunch-a us is somethin' else."

"He's not like that, Connie," I said about Taylor.

"How you know? He ever done it before?"

"He wants me to invite you and Nathaniel to dinner at his house."

"Say what?" she asked incredulous again.

"That's right, Connie. And we went to Ray's."

"Yet and still," she replied.

"He's different, Connie."

"Well, we'll sho' see, now won't we?"

"Yes, we will. I'll ask him this evening, and tell you what he says tomorrow at church. And Connie, thank you," I added.

"For what?"

"For bein' Connie."

"We can't help who we is, remember?"

But she smiled.

"He really is a good man," I said.

"And you really do care for him," she replied.

"I'm his friend, Connie."

"All right," she said. "I'm not arguin' with you. We sayin' the same thing."

> "...I'll just get things settled here. But it sure will be hard not to see you. I want to be with you. Guess I'll just have to wait, but come Christmas time, I'm coming for you, girl. It's time for us to get on with our lives together..."

Confidently Danny was *settling* our lives, busily preparing a place for me, for the *us* he was certain we were. Men had the choices. Women waited to be chosen. Unless they chose to be alone. Danny had never really asked me to marry him. He had just decided it, and my only objection thus far was to tell him not to come this Thanksgiving, making my lone decision in the affair not to decide. Was I choosing to be alone then? Was I forfeiting a lifetime of security for a few weeks of love?

I had pulled off the road, parking between the two worlds that I lived in. Maybe it was all right to marry for gratitude and propriety, for position and protection. In the olden days fathers used to choose the spouses for their children. Daughters were bartered for what was best for the family, sons too. Practicality came first. Passion was left to come later—if it came at all. Families were organized by the head and not guided by the heart; all of them the results of *gentlemen's agreements* conceived in the best interest of everyone—well everyone that mattered. And yet life had gone on. People had been happy. People had made love, made children. I folded up Danny's letter and buried it in the bottom of my pocketbook and started Taylor's car. It was getting late.

I could do a lot worse than Sergeant Daniel Simmons. *Esther Fay Simmons* was a good name. It had a kind of easy rhythm to it. Our children could be extraordinary, our home very fine. Our time together had been exciting. Other women had been envious of me, the way he had held me when we had danced, and flattered me when we had talked. Those few days and nights, made all the more urgent by his impending departure to the battlefield, were some of the best times of my life. That night in Mandy's father's Ford had been intoxicating and sweet, and even now was completely without regret.

But for me it had all been without expectations. I had only given him the few summer days and nights, not myself. And yet he was in California *settling* our lives. How could he be so sure of me, when I hardly knew him and barely myself?

The sky over McConnell County was turning as orange as the treetops. I hurried into the A&P. I could learn to love Danny. I wanted him to be happy. At least I was sure about that. Undoubtedly he would be bringing a past to the marriage too. Gossip could die and dry up like the chopped weeds in Grampa's vegetable garden. "Who you pinin' for, Miss Esther?" Danny had asked me once. I would make certain that he never knew.

It had come to this, hiding my mail, hiding my heart. But from whom? It seemed everybody knew everything anyway, or at least thought they did. I kept denying things but no one believed me. They didn't even get mad at me for the lies.

Surely the *something* would finally crumble and give way. The winter winds would inevitably blow down across the plains and snuff out my light. Soon enough it would be Christmas. But until then there was now, and everybody could wait. There might even be a nice Thanksgiving dinner with Taylor at *our* table. Connie would work things out with Nathaniel, and Grampa would resign to it once Nathaniel agreed. Nathaniel had a way with Grampa.

At the A&P I didn't charge the grocery purchase to Taylor's account but paid for the things myself instead, using my own money because it was after all *my* dinner too. And if the world was right then I was going to be cooking it for *my* man. This thought sent the blood rushing up to my face, and my hands shook a little as I counted out the dollars and coins to the clerk. Since she wouldn't be able to imagine why, did she think I was a thief who had stolen the money I was handing to her? My head held up, I left the store with my paper sack of groceries. Why shouldn't Negroes drive nice automobiles, I thought as I drove Taylor's car. Uncle Eddie had a nice car. Danny probably would buy one too. Why should we have to hide *our* prosperity? Why shouldn't I be happy?

By the time I returned Taylor's car to his garage, I tried not to be anything but happy for as long as the little while gave us. One day at a time. And the nights too. Tomorrow had never been promised to us. It was best to live for today today. In case the tomorrows did not come.

But despite my determination, a feeling of being cheated crept after me anyway as I walked towards the house, my arms filled with the paper sack of groceries. Billie

Holiday was singing disconsolately out of the radio through the open kitchen window. I had no right to feel this way. I had known these *terms and conditions* from the start, the inherent risk of brief reward. The risk of only wanting it more. The peril of making an impossible promise. I had no right to feel sorry for myself.

When I came into the kitchen, I discovered Taylor on the floor, his head and torso underneath the kitchen sink.

"Taylor?" I said alarmed. "What are you doing?"

"Hello!" he greeted me cheerfully from under the sink.

"Is everything all right?" I asked, quickly setting the groceries down on the kitchen table. "What's wrong?"

Spencer had already gone home. It was late, I scolded myself again.

"Everything's fine, Esther," Taylor answered me. "Just taking care of this leaky drainpipe."

Herman was nuzzling me insistently for his dose of affection. I rubbed his head obligingly and squatted down on the floor next to Taylor.

"Why are *you* fixin' it?" I asked.

"Why not?" he asked back.

"I don't know," I said. "Maybe because you're not a plumber."

He laughed.

"All you need for this is strong hands and a good wrench."

Strong hands. A *desk-man's hands.* I peeped under the sink. He had propped a flashlight on a box of dish soap to illuminate the work space. He grinned at me.

"So I'm up to it," he assured me.

The flashlight's beam shone on the gold wire frame of his glasses and the smile lines that reached out to his black hair.

"I think capitalism is based on everybody doing their *own* job," I reminded him. "Not somebody else's."

He laughed again.

"Sister Allen, the *only* reason you're not a Marxist is because of a certain Jesus of Nazareth, who by the way might have been the first socialist. So I wouldn't exactly describe you as a *laissez-faire capitalist.* Now turn on the tap, so I can see if this thing is still leaking."

"Guess I'd better not count on you for a character reference then," I said smugly, rising to open the faucet. Cold water began flowing down the drain. "That kind of talk will surely get me black-listed."

"You'll be in fine company I'm sure," Taylor said from under the sink.

"And yours'll be the first name I give up," I replied. "Especially for that last remark about the Lord."

"I'm a veteran," he chuckled. "War heroes are true blue. Not red, madam. Nope," he said about the pipe. "Not quite. You can turn it off."

"Hero?" I teased. "I've never seen any medals, sir."

"Remind me to show you later. You'll be impressed."

I looked out the window for a moment. I was already impressed. I had Mr. Leon's word for it, and Spencer's devotion. I had this year. And last night.

"Esther," Taylor was speaking to me. "Try the tap again."

I turned on the faucet.

"All the way," he instructed.

I opened it more.

"You're not much of a plumber's helper, are you?" he chided.

"How can I hear you with the radio so loud?" I asked. "It sounds like a juke-joint in here."

"You got something against juke-joints, Sister? Okay. You can shut it off again. This ought to do it." I heard the wrench turning against the pipe. "There," he declared.

It was like old times, Taylor fixing things, looking after his house. Except everything really was different.

"Esther," he was calling my name again. "Try it again."

While another Negro male singer was painfully describing the heartbreak of loving a beautiful woman, I turned on the cold water again. At least I was not beautiful, merely *handsome*.

Don't change, Esther.

Even though I was a cracked vessel, a clay jar, he would put his faith in me. Perhaps I was safe. I could not break his heart, not like Sylvia, or Laura Spalding. Whatever investment he had made in me he had already gained back in great dividends. I was the kind of woman who was always thankful for affection and glad to be loved. Perhaps Danny thought he was being generous to me by offering me an *always*.

"Okay," I heard Taylor say, satisfied with his work. "I think that does it. You can turn it off now."

Slipping his left foot under the weaker right ankle to bring the right leg forward, Taylor scooted from underneath the sink. I squatted down again this time to help him, but he waved aside my offer.

"I can manage," he said, turning off the flashlight and handing it to me.

"How'd you get yourself down here anyway?" I asked.

"You mean without the aid of a polished hardwood floor?" he answered dryly. "Took a little planning, but I'm pretty resourceful."

"I'm going to strip off the wax, Taylor," I told him seriously. "I'll do it tomorrow. Tonight if you want me to."

"Don't pout," he laughed merrily. "You deserved that. For being so smug about a working man and his music."

His music? Perhaps it was. I stood up. He closed the tool box and handed that up to me too. I set it on the counter.

"That wasn't fair," I said.

"Ah but there's nothing like a contrite woman," he kidded me. "Go put the tools away."

"Look at you, you're a mess," I smiled down on him. "What have you been doing while I was gone?"

"An honest day's work," he answered me easily.

In the faded dungarees and grimy t-shirt he reminded me of the day we met, when I had mistaken him for a laborer.

"You say that like you're braggin'," I noted.

"I am," he grinned. "Spence and I accomplished a lot today."

"Oh? There are child labor laws, you know."

And laws against loving you, I thought sadly.

"Now who's impugning whose character?" he asked.

"Well now, Mr. Payne, why on earth would I want to do that?"

"I don't know," he said, turning to pull the curtain closed, hiding the kitchen drain. "You were gone so long I was beginning to think my reviews weren't too good."

"But you had to know," I played along. "That I would defend your name with my last breath."

"And how would I know that?" he asked looking up at me again.

Because I love you, I thought desperately.

"Well I would," I replied.

"Why?" he asked.

"Why?" I repeated, laughing a little nervously.

"Yes," he said. "Why? Why would you defend my name?"

Because it was a good name, I thought, as his hand ventured softly up and down my bare leg, his fingers disappearing just under the hem of my mother's dress.

"Be-because it would be the right thing to do," I answered.

"You always do the right thing, don't you?" he asked.

"I try to," I said self-consciously.

He reached up and caught my hand.

"And no one tries harder," he said pulling me down to the floor beside him.

"Are you making fun of me, Taylor Payne?" I asked feeling embarrassed and awkward, and excited all at the same time.

"A little," he confessed, guiding me into his lap.

"That's not nice," I scolded him.

"I have never claimed to be nice," he smiled again, but it was already a different expression, reminiscent of roses.

I was the one who made that claim for him, to anyone who would listen. Our faces were close.

Lovin' somebody's never wrong, Esther.

What was was. And maybe the *something* would still be, long afterwards, when I was far away from here. Taylor stroked my back as I touched his cheek adoringly. I loved his eyes. His brilliant eyes, so dark and warm, and compelling. I removed his glasses and put them into my dress pocket.

I want to look at you.

My beautiful roses. They are mine, you know. I have claimed them.

Tenderly our lips met, our mouths blended, while someone else sang about the pain of love. But the *Song of Solomon* was Scripture too. After a little time, I gently I pulled away.

"Taylor," I whispered.

"What is it?" he asked in a husky voice, as he kissed my throat. "Afraid I'm getting you dirty?"

He done put his hands on you, ain't he?

There was nothing but honor in the way Taylor touched me. Nothing but virtue. Common threads attached us. Why shouldn't we be together?

"No," I said, looking down modestly. "Your legs. Am I hurting you?"

"No," he said, closing his arms around me again and once more taking my mouth with his.

The Blues were almost always about loves that were incapable of casting out fear, loves that could not last. But Blues' love was no less real for its despair. It was no less passionate.

…There ain't no place fo' you in his world, just in his bed.

I put my arms around Taylor's neck and buried my face against his shoulder. I loved that he was wearing an undershirt, that it was dirty, and that he smelled of work. I felt safe in his arms, and happy.

"I missed you," I whispered.

He held me tighter.

"I'm glad," he whispered back.

"Why would that make you glad?"

"Because I can fix that too."

I stayed in his arms a little while longer, wishing that he could.

When I was standing again at the counter, I offered to help him up from the floor. Once more he declined my assistance; and by first kneeling on his hands and knees, he pushed his bottom upwards, and leaning down on his left arm, he secured the right leg brace and stood upright.

"I decided I'd better learn how to manage this floor business on my own," he smiled wryly, holding onto the counter, catching his breath. "Pretty good, huh?" he added and reached for the crutches.

I nodded, smiling, thankful that he would never have to crawl again.

"Spencer's a pretty good coach as it turns out," Taylor explained. "Must take after you."

And he would still have Spencer with him even after I was gone.

"I was thinking, Taylor," I said. "That maybe we stopped using the hot-packs too soon. I mean...shouldn't we be applying them every night? They really do help. And the old washing machine works fine--"

"Sounds like a lot of work," interjected Taylor.

"I don't mind."

"You do realize, Esther, that no matter how hard you work, this could be as good as it gets."

"You don't want to give up, Taylor," I insisted. "You can't."

Despondent music continued from the radio, and I had had enough melancholy for now. I turned down the sound and then started taking the groceries out of the bag.

"No," he said after a time. "I suppose I can't."

Snatching up this bit of affirmation, I turned back to him smiling brightly.

"Good! Is spaghetti and meatballs okay for dinner?" I asked.

"Sounds fine," he replied.

"Okay."

I carried the tool box to the back porch.

"The butcher ground the meat fresh," I chattered when I returned to the kitchen. "Oh and he told me to tell you hello too." I tied on an apron. "The tomatoes are really nice this week. You think they come from California? It's amazing to be able to get fresh tomatoes this late in the season. It's almost like you can have anything you want these days." At the kitchen sink I washed my hands. I set a skillet on top of the stove and went to the pantry for an onion.

"Esther," Taylor said.

"Yes?" I answered as I diced an onion.

"What happened with your grandfather?"

The question prickled the back my neck, and I didn't turn to face him.

"We had a nice visit," I said and kept chopping the onion. "I'm sorry I was so late getting back. But I fixed his supper. Oxtails. And a cake. He fussed about that, but he loves it of course. And then Connie came with the children. I lost track of time," I was prattling, piling up words like the pieces of onion. "I did tell you that I might be gone a while. I don't think he eats right, Taylor. I mean with me being here—I mean...It really was good to see the children. You know if Grampa would just let Mis' Janey look after him. And she would too. She's been carryin'--"

"When are you leaving?" asked Taylor.

My eyes had started to sting and water from the onion scent.

"What?" I needlessly asked, my hands still. "No. No, I'm not leaving."

"Esther--"

"Nathaniel will come for me tomorrow just like always, but I promise to come straight home—I mean right back after church."

"Esther, you have to tell me."

"I'll make you a big Sunday dinner tomorrow. Now you really ought to get yourself cleaned up for dinner. This'll be done before you know it. And I can't imagine that you'd want to come to the table looking like that. Honest day's work or not."

Moving to the stove I scraped the onion into the waiting skillet.

"You playin' Mr. Handy-man around here," I continued. "What am I goin' to do with you?"

"Your grandfather was clear, Esther," Taylor said. "He doesn't want you here. Our little arrangement is unacceptable."

Our little arrangement.

Is that what he called it? Is that how they had referred to it in their *gentlemen's agreement*? As a *little arrangement*? How polite. *Attachment, agreement, arrangement.* Anything but *affair.* I took a cooking spoon out of a drawer. That was what it was now. An *affair.* That was what it had been for a long time. We had just finally consummated it. And in any case the *gentlemen's agreement* had been renegotiated by the woman who was at the center of it. I had made it the awful forbidden *amalgamation* that no one was supposed to want.

"I'm staying," I told him.

"Esther--"

"Everything's all right now, Taylor. My grandfather is fine."

"How can he be?"

I turned to face him.

"Because it's not up to him, is it?" I asked.

"We were wrong, Esther," replied Taylor. "Your grandfather and I, to decide for you. I've admitted as much. But be that as it may, I want to know where things stand today."

I didn't recall him *admitting as much,* not until this moment, and Grampa certainly had not. Both of them were too convinced that they were acting in my best interest; and neither of them could be *contrite,* as it was not in their natures. Taylor's new admission perhaps served the letter of the law but it was not in its spirit, and he had taught me the difference. I smiled.

"I'm staying," I repeated. "That's where things stand."

"That's not what your grandfather wants," he argued. "And he and I--"

"Need to let me run my own life," I finished for him. Then I added more softly, "Please."

"It's my life too," he said.

It was. It involved all of us. I was merely the link, the ties of the *attachment*, the genesis of the *arrangement*, and the necessity for the *agreement*. And I was trying to do the best that I could for all of us.

"Yes, Taylor," I agreed. "And his too, I guess. But since you two have had your say in the matter, wouldn't you agree it's my turn now?"

"That's what I'm asking you," he insisted. "What is your say?"

"No you're not," I replied. "You asked me when I'm going to leave. As if I have no say at all."

"I don't want to wake up one morning and find you've gone, Esther."

Like a dream, I thought, dreading the same thing, that one morning I was going to wake up on the other side of the Red Sea.

"You won't," I said not wanting Christmas to come.

"For Christ's sake, Esther," he sighed.

I ran my hands down the front of my apron and went to him. Putting my arms around his waist, I pressed the side of my face against his chest. We were lovers I thought almost giddily. Whatever happened tomorrow, tonight this was true.

"I came back today, Taylor," I said. "Like I told you I would. I went to the A&P and bought tomatoes and ground meat, and now I am cooking your dinner. Like I always do. Like I will do tomorrow. Because I'll be right here."

His left arm went around me, holding me closely against him.

I ain't never intended fo' that man to come 'tween you and yo' kin.

I wanted them both, and for a little while I was resolved to have them, whatever it took I would have them both for this little while. Taylor kissed the top of my head.

"I think there's a bottle of Chianti in the pantry," he said.

I looked up at him, smiling.

"You better go get cleaned up," I replied. "Somebody might mistake you for the hired help."

"Somebody did," he said.

I laughed lightly at the shared memory.

"Oh," I reached into my pocket for his glasses. "You don't want to forget these."

I slipped the frames over his ears, tenderly stroking the black hair laced with occasional strands of gray at his temples. Now he smiled too.

"Oxtails, huh?" he said. "You've never made them for me."

"The recipe is not in your mother's cookbooks," I told him.

"I'm open to new things, Esther."

Yes. Yes, he was. And so was I.

Later as I set the table for dinner I tried to picture myself in California, tried to make myself be *open* to this other new thing. But all I could think of was how Danny was making a mistake and how I owed it to him to correct it with something at least close to the truth. Perhaps I might have fallen in love with him if only I had not seen my reflection in the pair of brilliant dark brown eyes. Now there would always be another empty space in me. Another memory to haunt me. Like with Jimmy, there would always be some reason to feel a little sad no matter how happy the times were.

I placed the bottle of Chianti on the table near Taylor's place. He said that northern California was wine country. In the southern part was where they made the movies with the happy endings, and where Danny wanted me to live with him. It must be legal to buy and drink alcohol in every California county, not like in Texas. The good citizens of McConnell County, colored and white prided themselves on their abstention; even though it was a law conspicuously not kept. There were country clubs and juke-joints where you could buy it. There were private wine collections for the affluent, and stills hidden in the woods for those with less. Prohibitions never worked.

I swirled the spaghetti around in the hot water, until it softened and folded into the pot. I had changed the radio dial to the station that played orchestra music. Glenn Miller's Band was playing. Miller, himself, had been lost in the war somewhere in France too. But the world was free—almost. I supposed I should be happy just to have it be better.

Why did Taylor like the Blues so much anyway? What did he know about cotton fields and lonesome trains, and greens without meat on your plate? Glenn Miller made more sense for him, and if he would insist on maintaining his mother's Bohemian traditions then all right I could grant him Count Basie, Duke Ellington, and Cab Calloway, maybe Louis Armstrong. After all Aunt Grace loved symphony music.

I added vinegar to olive oil to pour over a green salad. In the bowl the bright red chunks of tomato looked pretty among the green leaves of lettuce. Before coming here there had been few salads in my life. In Grampa's house mostly you cooked the vegetables. "I ain't no rabbit," he would say. "Don't bring me nothin' raw." I wondered if Connie would make a salad for Thanksgiving. Taylor would like that. How should I bring it up? How should I ask him?

I carried the salad out to the dining room. The kitchen was cozier, but there was something to be said for the ritual of formal dining, for lace tablecloths and crystal glasses. If I did marry Danny perhaps he would see to it that I had a house as elegant as Aunt Grace's and Uncle Eddie's. Everyone would visit us. Grampa too. I could talk him into getting on a train again; if for no other reason than to see a great-grandchild born of me. Danny's baby, the cinnamon color of Jimmy, perhaps. A beautiful child.

California must be a nice place. Warm, flourishing, inviting. The west had always been enticing. Everybody was always going there. On foot, part of wagon trains, in caravans of pitiful cars, on buses and trains. Having reached the eastern American shores by ship, people made their way further west, regardless of the ship, from first class, to steerage, to cargo hole. We wanted what was out there with the golden sunset. And yet I liked the prairie. The way the horizon stretched out farther than the eye could see. The way blue northers rolled in with thunder.

Opening the Chianti I wondered about Italy too. Someday I wanted to visit the Sistine Chapel and see for myself Michelangelo's vision of God. His old white man, with piercing eyes and powerful arms reaching out to Adam at Creation. I did not begrudge Michelangelo his interpretation. We put our own image on God, as if we were the ones who had created Him. According to some philosophers, and probably to Taylor too, perhaps we had. But just needing Him enough to make Him up was adequate proof to me that God had come first. In order to miss something, you must have had it once, even if it were only for a short time. Let Michelangelo have his white-faced God. After all I had my own. God was big enough, broad enough, and supreme enough to accommodate and be like us all. I wondered if Taylor would be uncomfortable with us giving thanks to Him at our Thanksgiving dinner. There would be praying around our table for sure.

The tomato-based sauce simmered on low heat around the meatballs. I closed Taylor's mother's cookbook and tucked it away on a corner shelf in the kitchen. *Oxtails.* Scrap-meat on his privileged plate. But I smiled at the thought of it, and I could picture it. No doubt Aunt Grace had put chitlins on her fine china at least once. She loved Uncle Eddie.

By the time Taylor returned to the open kitchen doorway all he saw on my face was the pleasantness of the present, accompanied this time by the music of Gershwin.

"I hope you don't mind that I switched the station," I said efficiently ladling the red tomato sauce with meatballs over the cooked pasta on the china dinner plates.

"No, I don't mind," he replied.

So he was still a little somber. Balancing the plates of food, I squeezed by him through the doorway to take them to the table. The faint scent of his aftershave floated on the air around him. I was tempted to kiss his pursed lips as I passed. Connie would have kissed Nathaniel. I probably would have pecked Grampa on the cheek. But in this situation, in this *arrangement* maybe such an act was still too forward.

We were quiet at first as we ate. The radio stayed on, the melodies of trombones and saxophones coming to us from the kitchen. I kept time silently with the downbeats and the piano bridges, and imagined New York nightlife. Negroes in California must have night-lives too. Lena Horne must go somewhere to dance with her white husband. I had always wanted to go to Paris. Maybe I could take myself there. I had told Grampa that I did not need Danny. Did that make him just security for me?

Immediately I put away the thought, and moved instead to a glimpse myself sitting at some sweet little sidewalk café, a chilled bottle of wine and a small spray of bright flowers on the table. And Taylor. With me. As he was now. Like I was Lena Horne. In Paris. Where in the whole country you might do things *differently*.

"What is it?" the man of my dreams interrupted my fantasies.

"Pardon?" I stumbled in a rush to get back to McConnell County.

"Your smile," he said. "Am I missing something?"

"Oh," I smiled again. "No. I was just thinking of something funny that's all."

"And?"

"Hmm? Oh, uh-Little Evie today," I quickly lied. "She was so cute. She gave me a flower. You should have seen her. All pomp and circumstance."

"I'd like to meet Little Evie someday," Taylor said.

"Oh that's right," I replied, thinking about last January and remembering Mis' Inez. "You only got to meet her little brother."

"Who must be quite the big boy by now."

"Oh yes. Walking and everything."

"Not to mention being falsely accused," added Taylor.

I looked at him. Now he smiled, crookedly.

"Of course we have cleared his good name," he continued. "Thanks to an eleventh-hour confession."

"You know, Taylor, like I said before, you were keeping secrets too."

"Secrets, Esther. Not deceptions."

"I was trying to keep the peace."

"You mustn't lie to me, Esther," he said suddenly grave. "I trust you. Never do harm to that."

This was what made me *worthy* to him. What made me *virtuous*. But what if virtue was worn like a masque? Like it was Aunt Grace's face powder. Or Laura Spalding's rouge. Tomato-based sauces had a strong flavor. Seasoned with the right herbs and spices, the flavor was robust enough to sit long on the tongue. Even now that it was cooling on my plate, I was glad for the food's taste in my mouth. It was diverting. I chewed and swallowed. Human beings failed each other. We failed each other all the time. Call no man good but God, the Bible advised.

"I'd like to see the baby again," Taylor said after a while. "We've talked about it before but I really would like to have Nathaniel and his family over for dinner sometime."

This was the opportunity I needed.

"You mean that, Taylor?" I asked as I reached to refill his wine glass.

"Esther, I would welcome your family in my home," said Taylor.

"What about you going to theirs?"

"As I recall I have. To Nathaniel's house anyway."

"Well would you like to go to Nathaniel's house for Thanksgiving?"

It proved easier to say it than I had expected, and because he had given me the opening, it seemed less extraordinary.

"Am I invited?" he asked.

"Yes!" I answered a little too eagerly.

He looked amused.

"By whom?" he followed.

"Nathaniel and Connie would love to have you," I assured him.

"And I suppose they asked you to ask me."

"Yes."

It wasn't completely a lie, and being *open to new things,* Taylor even smiled. Just how far might he be willing to carry his social experiment? Connie said that someone had to be in the middle, between what was and what could be, for change to come. Maybe Connie would want to invite Mis' Inez to Thanksgiving dinner too. The *middle* she talked about could end up being a very cramped and miserable place. I still had to talk to Grampa about it. The thought of Grampa in concert with Mis' Inez was nearly enough to make me withdraw the invitation altogether. Maybe I wasn't ready for this either. I looked down at my plate.

"That is if you would like to," I said much less enthusiastically.

Now that he was back at work Taylor must be restored to his own society, his own place. He could handle himself much better thus making it more comfortable for everyone. He should go his way and I mine. Why make life any harder than it had to be?

"I mean if you don't have other plans or anything," I labored on. "Of course I'm sure that you--"

"I'd be honored," Taylor said.

I looked up at him, and he was still smiling, and warmly, as if the whole idea was merely nice. For a second or two I let myself appreciate his acceptance before I reminded myself that he just liked to do things differently. It wouldn't be this easy with Grampa for sure. What if my grandfather refused to sit at the table with him? It was his right. All of his life Grampa had worked so hard to have his own, his own house, his own table, his own food. His own dark-skinned family. Why must he share it with a guest that he himself would never invite? It was Nathaniel's house, but *we* belonged to him. And if he forced us to choose, then *we* would have to choose him over Taylor, which would mean that I couldn't be at the table either. It wasn't right to take back an invitation. To fail a commitment.

"Will you make your famous sweet potato pie?" asked Taylor as I privately agonized.

"Yes," I replied, meeting his query with a more cheerful face. "It's a tradition."

"Good," he said sipping the Chianti. "Perhaps some of them are worth keeping."

VI

I waited until Nathaniel was bringing me home after church the next day before I told him that Taylor had accepted the Thanksgiving dinner invitation. Not surprisingly, Nathaniel actually seemed pleased too.

"I guess never figgered you for one of them radicals," he chuckled as he drove us across town. "Next thing I know you gon' be marchin' with A. Philip Randolph hisself and goin' to them NAACP meetin's."

"Attending NAACP meetings is not radical, Nathaniel," I said. "And it's just Thanksgiving dinner."

"It's more 'an that, baby cuz," Nathaniel cheerfully disagreed. "Ol' McConnell County don't know what's done hit 'em 'tween you and Mr. Taylor Payne."

"*Taylor.* You don't have to say mister."

"'Course it ain't the first time for somethin' like this," he carried on still tickled. "Be frank about it, Esther, I'm kind-a proud of you. For the way you standin' up for yo'self and him. Maybe it's *Miss* Esther from now on for you too."

Miss Esther stared out the window at *ol' McConnell County* as we rode through it, knowing that she still had to tell Grampa about this revolution.

"I'm glad somebody is," I said solemnly.

"Taylor's proud of you," Nathaniel replied.

I looked at him.

"That's right," he said as if he really knew this. "He got some powerful feelin's for you, mis' lady. But the way you be actin' sometimes, I be wonderin' how you feel about him. It wouldn't be right to hurt 'im, Esther. Wouldn't be right at-all."

I don't want to wake up one morning and find you've gone, Esther.

When Taylor awakened in the mornings I was now lying next to him. My feelings were *powerful* too.

"You gon' have to help Grampa understand," I told Nathaniel. "I have to tell him first, but it's your house, Nathaniel. You have to let him know that Taylor is welcomed."

Nathaniel smiled as he slowed the pick-up and turned onto the Taylor's long driveway.

"It ain't easy for no man to give up bein' the cock of the walk, Esther," he said. "I ain't gon' like it very well when it comes Little Evie's time neither. That's how daddies do. So tell you what," he offered. "I'll tell 'im about it myself. Might make it easier comin' from me, you know, talkin' man to man."

By the time we were back at church the following Sunday, Nathaniel had kept his word and informed Grampa that Taylor would be with us for Thanksgiving. When I went to greet him after service, Grampa's face was unreadable. He barely had a word for me before walking away. I was forced to hurry after him.

"Don't you think it's nice of Nathaniel, invitin' Taylor to dinner with us?" I asked as I kept pace with Grampa's stride. "They have that nice big dining room, and Connie said that they can put the leaf in the table--"

"Be room enough for Danny Simmons too, I 'spect," Grampa cut me off.

I stopped.

"But he ain't welcomed, is he?" Grampa added as he kept walking.

I watched him leave the church yard.

"He'll be all right," said Connie, who had come over to stand beside me.

"I hope so," I replied dismally.

"Just give 'im time to work his mad out." She hooked her arm with mine and steered me towards Nathaniel's car. "My mama and daddy gon' be spendin' Thanksgivin' in Houston with Calvin," Connie explained. "You 'member my, brother, Calvin, don't you? Him and yo' brother Jimmy used to be friends until Jimmy moved to New York. Calvin moved to Houston. Guess birds do gotta fly. I want you to make yo'--"

"Connie," I interrupted her pleasant prattle once we stood by their car.

She stopped talking.

"Thank-you," I said.

"For what?" she asked. "I ain't done nothin' yet. And I'm expectin' you to help me cook anyhow. I know, I know, you can't come early. But you can cook stuff ahead-a time and put it in the icebox. It'll keep. I'm not gon' be too tired to enjoy my holiday."

Now I smiled a little.

"I can make sweet potato pies," I offered.

"We gon' need a cake or two too. Between Daddy Perry and Nathaniel, and yo' grand-daddy, they can sho' 'nough run through some sweets. And Little Evie takin' right after 'em. What about Mr. Taylor, he like sweets?"

I nodded.

"And for people to call him Taylor," I reminded her.

She nodded too.

"It'll take some gettin' used to, but we'll all be all-right."

Everyone just needed time it seemed, to get used to it, to the bond between us, even those who had suspected it all along, and used it. A few days later when Doctor Mitchell learned that Taylor would be having Thanksgiving dinner with us he reacted apprehensively too. Doctor Mitchell and Grampa shared not only a perspective, they also shared a culture and neither saw no reason to change.

I interrupted Taylor telling him about it when I brought a tray of coffee into the study. "Esther's promised to bake her sweet potato pie," Taylor was saying as he was trying out his new walking cane. "Isn't that right, Esther?" he asked me when I came into the study. "I tell you, Mitch, she's bewitching in the kitchen. I'm completely under her spell." I glanced at Doctor Mitchell, embarrassed by the praise. The older man cleared his throat and looked at me soberly.

"So what do you think?" Taylor wanted to hear from me about the cane.

He moved unsteadily, but he was obviously very pleased with himself and I didn't dare dampen his spirit.

"Sister Kenny would be proud, Mr. Payne," I declared.

His kind ever hear you call 'im that?

"And you?" Taylor asked. "Are you proud of me?"

Taylor's proud of you.

"Absolutely!" I told him brightly, placing the coffee tray on the table in front of the leather couch.

As Taylor made his way across the room his right leg trembled suddenly. He stopped, waiting for the spasm to pass. It wasn't time to put away the crutches yet, but he was continuing to make progress, getting ready for the courtroom, and for Christmas. Maybe even New York. When he reached the couch, he quickly released the right leg brace at the knee and dropped down heavily. The right leg shook again.

"Does Isaac know about this?" Doctor Mitchell asked me.

I looked at him.

"Yes," Taylor answered him. "Naturally."

Naturally. A man was just a man and woman just a woman, but this was more *attachment* than Doctor Mitchell had ever intended, even if Taylor could now walk with a cane. The doctor sat down across from the sofa, and I poured a cup of coffee for him like the dutiful servant I was supposed to be.

"I see," replied Doctor Mitchell accepting the coffee from me.

I poured another cup and handed it to Taylor.

"Thank you, Esther," he said taking it. "Will you join us?"

The astonishment he saw on my face must have amused him because a smile played around his mouth. I should have been used to this by now, remembering Laura Spalding.

"Uh...uh, no," I managed. "I-I best leave you men folk to your business."

"Better things to do, eh?" Taylor replied pleasantly drinking his coffee.

I glanced at Doctor Mitchell. It must be the prosecutor in Taylor, this delight in the ambush, whether it be of adversaries or advocates. At any moment any one of us might be standing one of his trials. But he was my lawyer and I loved him for it. Slowly Doctor Mitchell stirred sugar into his coffee and kept silent. Did he not know that his friend was indifferent to custom and social order? We had been to Ray's Café. Had Taylor informed him about that too, in his usual nonchalant way?

"Can I get you anything else?" I asked.

"Just the favor of your company," replied Taylor. "Which you have declined to give us."

Our eyes met again. It was new and old this relationship between us. A relationship made up of a maid's apron and a *gentlemen's agreement*, and enchanting nights wrapped in each other's arms.

"Do you think it's wise, Esther?" Doctor Mitchell finally asked.

The direct inquiry caught me off guard and I looked at the older man dumbly.

"Is what wise, Mitch?" asked Taylor.

Doctor Mitchell put down his cup and reached into his suit coat for his cigarettes.

"This kind of thing's just not done here, Taylor," Doctor Mitchell said, but he was looking at me. He lit his cigarette. "We're all very fond of Esther. And of course she's been exceptional, but--"

"It's time for things to be done differently," Taylor interrupted him and continued sipping his coffee.

At least in this house. Here he had ruled and here he was judge. As for the rest of the world, we were expected to accept it. The Law was what men made of it. Doctor Mitchell drew in the tobacco smoke deeply. The room was quiet.

"Well I suppose Mrs. Mitchell will survive her disappointment," the older man conceded.

"I very much appreciate the invitation, Mitch," replied Taylor. "You will tell her that for me, won't you?"

I couldn't help but smile at Taylor. He was lord of the manor, and I had found favor in his court. I went over to his desk for his pipe and tobacco and brought them back to him.

"You read my mind," he said beaming at me as our hands touched when he took the items.

"And there's always next year," mused Doctor Mitchell, apart from us.

"Yes, absolutely," Taylor agreed, his eyes still meeting mine. "Who knows, maybe next year I'll be extending the invitations."

Next year. When I wouldn't be here, I thought on my way back to the kitchen, where I was *bewitching*. Next year he'd be eating someone else's sweet potato pie. But I forced it out of my mind for now. For the sake of now, and love, and hope, and change, I refused to think about the tomorrows on the other side of Christmas. Besides he might be inviting Nathaniel and his family to his table. Things could still be *different*.

Giving myself permission to live day by day brought me a little peace. After all I had done this when Mama was sick, out of necessity, taking the doses of misery in daily measures, not knowing what the next day held and not trying to know. Why not live like that for happiness? Why not take happiness in daily doses, without wondering and worrying what tomorrow held?

The weather was mild leading up to Thanksgiving. On one particularly warm night Herman came into the kitchen and parked himself right in front of the backdoor expectantly, signaling that he wanted to go out. "Okay, boy," I chuckled as I opened the door for him. "But you hurry up and do your business," I told him as he trotted down the back porch steps. Such nights as this the dog was as likely to be in the mood for exploration as he was in need of elimination. Sometimes he was just a big, living, panting teddy bear, but in his nature there was still the predator too, even if it was only for sport. I didn't envy the nocturnal creatures that might per chance get in his way when he was out surveying his territory. They would not find him so cuddly.

In the mood for cocoa I put on a small pan of milk to heat. Soon I'd be settling myself into a cozy corner of the couch in the study to read a book, while Taylor continued to work at his desk.

I want you near me.

How comfortable we were together. I wanted to be near him too, and there were those moments when it truly felt I belonged here, *near* him.

The sudden beating on the front door was alarming. I shut off the flame under the milk. The beating continued, and I hurried to the front door. People didn't come to see Taylor this late in the evening, and they certainly didn't beat on the front door. What if it was Cordelia Collier again? Flipping on the porch light I opened the door without asking who it was first. A white man, whom I had never seen before, stood in the porch light, his suit wrinkled, his irate face red and ominous.

"Where's Payne?!" the stranger demanded ruthlessly shoving both the door and me aside as he burst into the foyer. "Where is he?! I want to see him!"

The man smelled of alcohol and he frightened me, yet I stepped back in front of him, asserting myself.

"Yes-sir," I tried to reassert my place. "May I tell him--"

"Get out of my way!" he man raged, splattering my face with spittle and flinging me against the wall. "Payne!" he yelled, looking around wildly. "Taylor Payne, I got business with you!"

"Esther," Taylor's voice spoke evenly in the foyer. "You may leave us."

Scrambling to my feet I rushed to Taylor's side. He didn't look at me, keeping his eyes focused on the stranger.

"You stay the hell away from my family!" the stranger barked, pointing his finger at Taylor like it was a weapon.

Taylor's demeanor seemed completely composed, as if it were a very normal thing to have a drunken belligerent man bellowing at him in his own house.

"Leave us, Esther," Taylor repeated his instruction to me, still only looking at the man.

"You want me to call the sheriff?" I asked frantically, standing my ground.

"I don't know who you think you are," the man railed. "Turning my wife against me. We don't put up with yo' kind in these parts."

"Do as I say, Esther," Taylor said.

What was the man talking about? Was he going to hurt Taylor?

"What's the matter?" sneered the stranger. "You can't control yo' nigger-bitch? Is that why you making trouble in my house?"

Taylor's face darkened.

"Now, Esther," he ordered, still watching the man.

What did this man know about us? Was Taylor ashamed of me? Bewildered, I stepped back, although only as far as behind the stairs.

"We know what to do with men like you," the man continued menacingly.

Who was his *we*? Was it because Taylor had taken me to Ray's? I would not leave him to face this terrible man alone. He wouldn't be able to defend himself if he were attacked, but I could fight. My hands balled into fists. I would fight.

"Mr. Collier," Taylor now spoke to the man, and in the same even voice he had used with me. "You've been indicted."

Mr. Collier? Cordelia Collier's husband? Cordelia Collier with the bruises around her neck underneath the white silk scarf? Was she dead?

"You should not be speaking with me without your counsel present," Taylor continued as if the two of them were standing on the courthouse steps.

"*Counsel?*" Collier laughed maliciously, advancing towards Taylor. "I'll show you fucking counsel."

Taylor did not move. I looked at the telephone on the credenza.

"Don't make matters worse for yourself, Mr. Collier," Taylor said.

"I'm warning you, Payne," raged Collier. "You leave my family alone! You think you can put me in jail? Do you know who I am?"

"I know what you are, Mr. Collier," Taylor told him simply. "And you will get a fair trial."

"*Trial?*" Collier's ominous laugh reverberated in the foyer. "There's not going to be a goddamn trial! You think you such a big-shot lawyer, but you ain't no better than yo' po'-ass daddy. My daddy says he didn't know his place either. Lucky for him he turned that old jalopy of his over in the rain before they had a chance to ride him out of this town on a rail."

"You've had too much to drink, Mr. Collier," replied Taylor in a voice that never changed. "You have no business in my home. I am, however, willing to meet with you and your attorney in my office tomorrow."

"I didn't come here for no goddamn meeting! I came here to kick yo' ass!"

I came from behind the stairs.

"Don't make matters worse for yourself, Mr. Collier, by threatening an officer of the court."

"You believe I won't take you on?!" shouted Collier. "Right here, right now. That crutch don't mean nothing to me. You come after my wife, my family, I got a right to defend my home."

"I'm well aware of your rights, Mr. Collier," replied Taylor. "But among them is not the right to beat your wife."

"Why you--" Collier lunged at him.

There was a metal click, and Collier seemed to freeze in the air like a dancer, locked in a bizarre pose, suspended on the balls of his feet, his arms reaching forward, his hands clenched in fists. He was staring into the barrel of a gun, and Taylor's right hand was steady. Collier dropped back on his heels.

"Get out of my house," Taylor said quietly.

For a time the foyer was silent. I could hear the radio from the kitchen as Collier's fury shrunk into fear. I had never seen a gun in Taylor's house, but here it was in his right hand now, aimed. He had been a soldier. He knew how to kill. As drunk as Collier might be, as enraged at whatever it was he believed Taylor had done to him, he must be sober enough to realize this, and he began to back up, moving towards the front door. The revolver remained pointed. Collier might have a gun too but what he did not have anymore was the advantage.

"I'm warning you, Payne," Collier repeated himself vainly as he stumbled over the threshold, keeping his eye on the gun. "You keep away from my wife."

The screen-door slammed loudly behind him as Collier fled, only then did Taylor lower the pistol. I returned to his side, standing by him as the engine in Collier's car raced and the tires threw gravel.

"Why did he come here?" I asked urgently. "Is Mrs. Collier all right?"

Taylor, his face still unreadable, moved to the credenza and laid the gun down on it before sitting down in the chair. I went to him but he did not look at me.

"Taylor --" I started.

"Close the door," he said.

I did as I was told, locking it too, and came back to him.

"He came here to hurt you!" I said, my voice shrill, still panicked. "Did he kill her? Is Mrs. Collier dead?"

"No," replied Taylor.

"You have to call the sheriff. Oh, Taylor--" a sob broke through my words. "He-he might have--"

"This is a court matter, Esther," he said cutting me off, his tone as neutral as before. "You'll have to excuse me. You should go call Herman in."

I stared at him, but he turned to the telephone and lifted the receiver.

"Taylor--"

"Everything's fine now, Esther," he said, before dialing the operator and asking for Sherriff Boden.

Taylor did not discuss legal matters with me. It was the way he was about court business. Overtime, as I had come to know him and perhaps more importantly learned to respect him, I had stopped prowling through his desk as I cleaned it. It had never been right, and eventually treating him right had come to matter to me very much. What I knew about the Collier case, had come from Cordelia Collier herself, until tonight. I had wondered about what had happened to her, but as there was nothing in the newspapers I had had no way of finding out. Client confidentiality was like religious canon to Taylor, and in a place the size of McConnell County, the smallest comment could potentially breech it. Cordelia Collier was his client, and she deserved protecting. Her husband, however, was a criminal, and he didn't.

But to not even look at me, and then dismiss me hurt me. Was it Collier's open confrontation about me, about us, that had chilled him towards me?

Taylor's proud of you, Esther.

Yet tonight he had seen me as his peers saw me. As Grampa had always warned that he would. *Nigga-maid* and *nigger-bitch*, the epithets were the same.

The sheriff came quickly, and once again I answered the door, although this time I was careful to ask who it was before I unlocked it and Herman was with me.

"Esther," the sheriff nodded a stern greeting to me when I let him in.

"Sheriff," I nodded back, offering to take his hat. "Mr. Payne is in his study."

His kind ever hear you call 'im that?

Sherriff Boden went to the study while I hung his hat in the closet, then following him I stood at the doorway to the study and asked if I could bring them some coffee. Taylor looked to the sheriff.

"Nothin' for me," Sheriff Boden said.

"That'll be all, Esther," Taylor dismissed me again. "Pull the doors closed."

"Yes-sir."

What had happened here tonight had happened to me too. I might be the *nigger-bitch* but I still trembled at the realization that Taylor could have been hurt, even killed. Collier could have come here with a gun himself. I might have lost him tonight. As suddenly as Jimmy, Taylor could have been gone, his blood red on the dull wood of the foyer floor.

Upstairs in the buttercup room, sitting on the edge of the bed, I shivered contemplating it. Taylor's blood, spilling like Jimmy's, vainly. Only this time I would have seen it, seen him leaving me, even as I held onto him. Hot terrified tears filled my eyes, but because they were furious too, I refused to let them fall. All he had had to say to me was that it was a *court matter,* when it felt as if Collier had put his violent hands around my own throat. Taylor had dismissed me like the domestic that I really was, and not the woman who loved him.

I heard the sheriff leave, but Taylor remained downstairs. It was late. He wouldn't want to do his exercises tonight. In the buttercup room I dressed for bed and then went to his room, but I hesitated standing next to his bed. I wasn't sure I wanted to get in. I wasn't sure I was welcomed. I could not feel entitled. Yet when he did come to bed he would be expecting to find me waiting for him; and I might have lost him tonight, and the time for that loss was coming soon enough. Maybe it had actually come tonight anyway. And if so I might as well face it. I might as well make him say it to me. I turned back the covers and crawled into bed. Since we had become lovers I said my nightly prayers silently as Taylor held me in his arms. Tonight he wasn't here, and I got back out of bed and knelt beside it. Taylor was safe. I was thankful. When I got back into bed, I turned my back to the open bedroom door and finally permitted myself to cry. I wasn't exactly sure over what.

It was hours later when Taylor came to bed. The bedroom was dark and cold. He switched on the lamp next to the bed, but I didn't move, letting him think I was sound asleep in the tight little knot I had tied myself into. I listened to him get ready for bed as he changed into his pajamas and brushed his teeth. Eventually he lay down next to me and without a word pulled me into his arms. The knot simply unraveled as my body cuddled against him and my heart began to beat welcomingly. Stubbornly I defied my own instinct and refused to let my arms go around his neck.

"So I guess you're finished with your court matters," I tried to say with Taylor's own kind of detachment.

In the lamplight I saw a smile softly fill his face.

"Yes," he replied. "For tonight."

"What's going to happen to Collier?" I asked. "Is his wife going to be all right? Is the sheriff going to arrest him?"

"Everything's fine, Esther," Taylor replied, telling me nothing.

I struggled to push away from him but he held me fast.

"Are you all right?" he at last asked me.

"Yes," I replied frostily. *"Everything's fine."*

He smiled again.

"I don't see what's so funny," I said turning my head away from him at least as my voice broke and new unshed tears began stinging my eyes.

"Esther," he said gently, "Do you recall the terms of our agreement?"

Which one, I thought hotly. And Danny was somewhere believing that he could simply *settle* everything for us all by himself, when living required a relentless tangle of agreements and arrangements.

"Let me remind you," Taylor offered because I answered him with silence. "I take care of you," he recited my own words back to me. "You take care of me, and everything else we let take care of itself."

What did that have to do with what happened tonight I demanded inside of my head and sullenly waited.

"Tonight, Esther," he said, turning my face back to his. "It was my turn."

"I don't know what you mean," I replied.

"You run this house, Esther," he explained patiently. "I believe you have from the first day you came here--"

"No I don't," I interrupted.

"Yes," he said. "You do. You make this house a home. But darling, Collier was right about one thing, it is the man's place to defend the home. Tonight, I told you to leave and you disobeyed me. You might have been hurt."

"Me?" I protested righteously. "Taylor, I was afraid for you! He was going to attack you."

"It was not your place to defend me, Esther. It was my place to protect you."

"But I--"

"And I can, you know," he continued. "I can protect you. And take care of you too. Do you understand that?"

I nodded.

"Good," Taylor sighed and smiled again, the warmth of it reaching out from the lines around his eyes.

At last my arms went around his neck, and he held me close. For a moment I was a little girl again in Grampa's lap; only I wasn't a child anymore and Taylor was not mine.

"I was frightened," I confessed in the haven of his arms. "I-I didn't know what--"

"Shhh," said Taylor before kissing my lips. "It's settled," he told me. "Everything's fine."

PART SEVEN

I

Awakening before dawn Thanksgiving morning I lay still, close beside Taylor, my body warmed and shielded by his, his arm across me, his hand resting on top of mine. I seemed to feel his easy heart beat against my back. His quiet breathing was like music in my ear. It was fitting that we should make our love in his room, in his bed. It was after all the place where I had loved him the deepest, where my love and his trust had been tried and proven *worthy*. Contentedly I slept with him. Peacefully. As if I should be here like this. I slept next to him as if I had a right to, with no shame whatsoever; and waking up next to him made the mornings especially good. As if I were somebody else or we were somewhere else.

But of course we weren't. We were here. In McConnell County. In the house, the room, where his parents had made love, and perhaps even made him. In the darkness I pictured their young blissful faces over the fireplace. It must be that wedding pictures were always full of joy and promise. In the beginning love must always seem perfect and invincible. And if we were lucky—blessed—then time proved it true. If we were not, then it ended, or faded, or turned into a memory, or a hope, or a longing. As it had done for Mama. Like it must be now for Mandy. Maybe even Cordelia Collier. Endings came. Hopefully later but all too often sooner.

For now Jessica's beloved son held me as beloved. I could only imagine what Taylor's people would have to say about his choices. I wondered if his parents' Bohemian ways could have made our *us* acceptable to them. "Would he have accepted me?" Taylor had asked me about Jimmy. The answer to that was yes, I was sure, because I loved him. And that was the way Jimmy was. As bold and free as the man whose downy breaths I counted lovingly. Mothers and fathers were different, however. And after all Taylor was an only son. A woman like me in Jimmy's life, in his bed, would have made Mama and Grampa frantic for his future.

But there was no future for us to ruin. There was only now, each tiny, little moment of now. Sometimes Taylor would wear one of those rubber prophylactics, but frequently he didn't. It didn't matter to me. A baby, his baby, would be mine alone, and beautiful.

Shackin'-up is a sin, Esther.

Connie must be right, but I could not be repentant because the happy moments covered over the gloomy guilty ones. This could not be *happily ever after* but it was miraculously wonderful right now. Taylor was my lover and I was simply grateful for every single precious, fleeting minute. Tennyson said it was better to have loved and lost than never to have loved at all; so in this time, even as I was losing, I was glad for it. Solomon was wise. *To everything there is a season, and a time to every purpose under the heaven.* It was not in my bed, or even in my *place*, but this was my time to love and I drifted back to sleep. Peacefully.

After a time I awakened again but this time because I felt Taylor moving to get up from bed. Outside the day was barely breaking. I rolled over on my back, smiling up at him drowsily.

"Sorry," he spoke softly. "Nature calls. Go back to sleep."

I sighed lazily and nodded turning on my side to face the empty space he was leaving.

"I can make coffee," I obligingly if disingenuously offered.

"Let's at least wait for the roosters," he replied.

I smiled thinking of old Red Comb.

When he was in bed with me again, I nestled closely once more, and Taylor put his arm around me.

"Happy Thanksgiving," I said quietly.

"That it is," he returned as if I was describing the day rather than wishing him a good time of it.

Last year on Thanksgiving morning he had been in Cambridge. And I had been in Jimmy's bed in Grampa's house. How did a whole lifetime squeeze into one year?

"Felicia must have been disappointed that you didn't come home this year," I said after awhile.

Their letters were so intermittent that I could only guess when he might have informed her about his plans.

"I am home, Esther," replied Taylor.

You make this house a home.

"I mean with them," I explained.

"It's fine," he said. "All the way around."

It was so easy for him to dismiss his family's care and concern, as if he didn't belong to them at all. Could he really believe they didn't care about him? I wanted to understand him, how he could be this way to his people. Because he was not a *loner*, not a willing one anyway. Maybe I would be the same way when I was in California. Maybe having your own home adjusted your focus, and changed your *vantage point*. Only I didn't want to go to California. I didn't want that home or that vantage point.

"Surely you can understand the situation I'm in," I had written back to Danny. "I just can't walk away from someone who needs me." It sounded very good. I sounded very good. And it was a lie. I was stalling. Praying for time. And asking God to forgive me. I couldn't be the only woman Danny had ever wanted. He would bring a past to a marriage too. Why burden each other with the stories that couldn't matter anymore anyway? I wouldn't want to know.

"This year will be different," I told Taylor thinking of the family dinner to come later today.

"I'm counting on it," he replied.

"I've never met anybody like you, Taylor Andrew Payne," I said.

A brief chuckled rumbled in his chest.

"Hmm. Should I be flattered or concerned?" he asked.

"I don't think you can be either," I replied.

"Ah Esther," he said kissing the top of my head affectionately. "You underestimate the sway of a handsome woman."

I rose up to meet his eyes. He was smiling.

"You don't like that word," I charged.

"You redefined it," he said glibly.

"Like I did virtuous?" I dared to ask even while I was naked in his bed.

"That," he answered. "You merely confirmed."

"You are very kind," I said gratefully, laying the side of my face against his chest again.

"No," he corrected me. "What I am is fortunate. Very fortunate."

And I was blessed, but I didn't say that to him because for Taylor fate ruled the universe and being *fortunate* was the best you could ask for.

"You really think your mother would have been proud of me?" I asked after a time.

"Yes," he affirmed.

"And I suppose your father also," I followed, the skepticism leaking into my voice.

"I believe he would have understood," replied Taylor.

"So he was a Bohemian too?"

"No."

"I guess being from McConnell County he would have more traditional ways."

...You ain't no better than yo' po'-ass daddy.

The Law was indeed the *family trade,* as Taylor had described it to me, but Andrew Payne had been in private practice and had been an attorney most often allied with defendants as opposed to the State. Nevertheless he would have honored the Law as much as his son now claimed to love it. How could his father have understood us, being like this, perhaps not exactly breaking the law, but certainly subverting it? And besides that, Andrew Payne would have been Doctor Mitchell's age if he had lived.

This kind of thing's just not done here, Taylor.

The two of them were men of Uncle Perry's generation, with Uncle Perry's understanding about the way the world should be, Grampa's understanding.

Taylor's father would have seen me as a fallen woman, and worst still because I had *fallen* so far out of my place. And with the weekly wages still accumulating in my savings account at the McConnell County National Bank, as Grampa did, Andrew Payne would have also seen me as a harlot. And like Grampa he would have pleaded with his son to come to his senses, so that if we had dared to be together anyway we would have been forced to steal desperate moments in bleak places where secretive embarrassed men took their concubines, their *nigger-bitches.*

"Yes, that's probably true," agreed Taylor. "Between the two of them, my father was certainly the more conservative."

I moved away from Taylor's embrace and lay on my back gazing up at the ceiling. Turning my head towards the window I could see that the sky was lighter. In a few hours we would be at Nathaniel's house, where Grampa would be also, Grampa who was the most *conservative* of them all. I was asking too much of him I told myself. Of everyone else too.

Taylor sat up and switched on his beside lamp before leaning back against the headboard.

"Esther," he said.

I looked at him.

"Remember what I told you about this not being the first time that I've been guilty of disrupting a woman's plans?" he asked.

"Yes," I replied.

"Well it's a long story, but one I think you should probably know."

A man can talk about himself with you.

So at last he was going to really tell me about Sylvia, about what had happened between them, about why she would break their engagement and marry his friend. Maybe he had been too hard on her. He was capable of capturing hearts easily but then he also tried them routinely. As it was with Grampa, to love Taylor required strength and independence, and a growing understanding. Neither of them made it easy. However, Sylvia could have been more patient, she could have been more like Ernestine.

After all Taylor had been fighting a war, and Nathaniel said it wasn't right to worry a man facing combat, and I even shielded Danny.

Holding the bed sheet in front of me I sat up now, preparing to learn what had happened between this man that I loved and his former fiancée. In the *long story* there would probably be clues to what was coming for me, intimations about the way we would also end. The prospect made me nervous because I didn't want to know too much yet. If I learned about the end today I would have to hide it somewhere inside of me while I tried to eat Connie's specially prepared Thanksgiving dinner.

I shivered a little. The bedroom was chilly. I should get up and light the Dearborn heater, but when Taylor pulled me back to him, I just lay my head on his shoulder, and let him draw the rest of the bed covers around us both. A sense of sanctuary calmed me and I couldn't understand how with such moments as this hers by right and fortune, Sylvia could have ever let him go.

"My mother was unconventional from birth," Taylor began. "She even came late for my grandparents, when my grandmother was over forty years old. Uncle Jason was almost twenty years her senior. People said she was a miracle."

"Like Sarah and Isaac," I added.

"Well, perhaps shy of Biblical proportions," mused Taylor. "But miraculous enough all the same to make little Jessica the crown jewel in the Morgan family. By the time she was fourteen both my grandparents were dead and Uncle Jason was her legal guardian, and determined to be father, mother, champion, and treasurer."

"He must have loved her very much," I said, thinking of me and Jimmy.

"Yes, he did," agreed Taylor.

"Brothers love their sisters that way," I reminded him. "And sisters love their brothers."

"Love is usually a good thing, Esther, but my mother wasn't a precious stone for safe-keeping. She was a living being. She wasn't suited for a velvet box. Or a gilded cage." He paused, then continued. "She was a bit of a child prodigy. She could sing, dance, play the piano. There wasn't a school year when she wasn't the star of some school production or another. She loved it. Thrived on it." He laughed lightly. "Unfortunately I didn't inherit her talents. Felicia did. But she lacks her boldness, her *joie de vivre* as they say. She used to have it once...we all did... when we were here together. This was a happy house."

"A good nature runs in a family," I said echoing Mr. Leon from last Christmas.

"Perhaps," replied Taylor. "Maybe Felicia just lost her mother too young. She wasn't ready to be on her own."

"She had you," I reminded him.

His brief chuckle was now a dry, hard, little sound.

"I'm not so sure I was ready either," said Taylor.

He was twelve years old, Esther. He was strong, even then.

To this day, I just think he had to work out his terrible grief.

"Did-did Sylvia have that?" I asked timidly, even as my heart ached for the sad little boy he had been. Talking about Sylvia had to be easier for both of us. "Did she remind you of your mother?"

"She's a fabulous dancer," Taylor reported matter-of-factly.

You good to talk to, Esther. That's better than dancin'.

Sylvia would have been beautiful enough for Stork Club and the Savoy too. And if he had taken her to Ray's, they would have had a table on the inside. I sighed.

"Esther," Taylor said, lifting my chin to look in my eyes. "This is not about Sylvia." He kissed me gently. "Besides," he said when our eyes met again. "You dance *and* sing."

A smile, following his lips, came to my face.

"You've never heard me sing," I replied, as another forlorn moment was pushed aside sweetly. "And that time in the kitchen, when I was baking a cake, you can't count that for dancin'."

"I believe I was telling a story," he grinned softly.

If it wasn't about Sylvia and her plans, then it must be about Felicia. He was finally going to really explain why they were not close. Grampa said that a man like him couldn't understand a woman like me. But Grampa was wrong.

"Yes, Taylor," I yielded readily and returned my head to his shoulder as I slipped my arm around his waist.

I can protect you...

I belonged to him too. He had *claimed* me and my *roses*.

"My mother and father met at one of those society coming-out dances," Taylor continued.

"A debutante ball?" I asked, picturing his father, as he must have been then, this handsome self-assured man evidenced in the portrait over the fireplace downstairs. He would have already been a distinguished southern gentleman even if he was only from McConnell County, no matter what a drunken Robert Collier said. I imagined his father one of the genteel poor, like in an English novel.

"Yes," said Taylor.

I imagined Jessica at the ball, in some fine fashionable gown, as pretty as a porcelain doll. There would have been orchestra music all around them. And Jessica would have never mistaken Andrew for the hired help the first time she saw him.

"He saw her across the crowded dance floor," I supplied romantically. "Like Rhett Butler in *Gone With the Wind* although your mother wouldn't have been like Scarlett. But did she give him some subtle signal."

"What?" laughed Taylor. "Is that how you imagine it?"

"All right then," I sulked a little, offended that he didn't like my southern imagery. "Like Cinderella at the ball."

"Esther," he said, turning my face up to him again. "Sweetheart, my father was the help, as they say. He was on the dance floor all right, but he was working along the edges of it, and if she had signaled to him, as you are picturing it, across the crowded floor, he would have been obliged to bring her a glass of punch."

I was staring at him and he chuckled heartily.

"I thought your father was in law school," I said trying to make sense of Andrew Payne's servitude.

"He was," replied Taylor. "But he didn't come from money, sweetheart. He had to work his way through school. Like you."

"Like me?" I asked.

"Like you," he said tweaking my nose playfully. Anyway, my mother was bored at the ball. So she went outside for a walk in the garden. My father was out there taking a break, smoking a cigarette. She asked him if he had an extra one, but he didn't want to give her one, because he didn't think women should smoke. Mother demanded to know if he was also against women having the vote, and Pop was pretty offended by the charge, since if he was anything Andrew Emerson Payne was a progressive, despite his East Texas upbringing. They argued but Mother got her a cigarette. And although she had smoked before, his cigarettes were cheap and this one made her really sick. My father ended up having to find her a private place to lie down and he stayed with her until she felt better. By the end of this first encounter, according to my mother, she was in love. I suppose Pop did have a certain amount of your southern charm. Kind of a cross between your *Rhett Butler* and *Ashley Wilkes,* assuming either one of them ever waited tables. And that was a large part of the problem for my uncle. Jason Morgan could never approve of his precious little sister marrying a pauper. Even if that pauper did happen to have some promise."

"What did they do?" I asked, nestling against Taylor again, a new picture of his father in my head, one of him washing crystal glasses in a kitchen.

"They were forced to hide their feelings," answered Taylor. "Meet secretly. Whatever they had to. My uncle would have had my father expelled if he had discovered them." Taylor sighed. "He could have ruined him."

And another generation later, an affair of the heart might still ruin a Payne man, if men like Robert Collier had their way. Maybe Mr. Spalding would seek to ruin him too, for the sake of his daughter's wounded pride. But maybe Taylor's father would have been able to understand.

"But everything worked out," I reminded Taylor. "They got married."

"Yes, and that's the point of this story."

"I don't understand."

"Mother wanted to be an actress, Esther. She wanted that more than anything. My father told her she was being naïve. That she had no idea how hard such a life could be. It seems somebody in our family is always being advised that our advantages have made us foolish."

"Taylor--" I started as I tried to pull away from him to sit up and defend my previous words.

"Let me finish," he said firmly holding me against him until I was still. "About a year later," he continued, "She ran away from home."

"From your uncle?" I asked.

"From my uncle," replied Taylor. "My father too. The whole life she saw in front of her. She went to New York, took a new name, and pursued her dreams."

"You mean she just left?" I was incredulous. "Disappeared?"

"Yes, Esther," answered Taylor. "And she did well too. Fell in with a good crowd. She had some good friends. She got decent parts. And even went on tour. She was very happy."

"But your uncle, your father, they must have been out of their minds with worry."

"Ironically it almost brought them together, although not quite."

As I had done to him and Grampa.

"Uncle Jason blamed my father for corrupting his young sister," Taylor recounted. "I suppose if he could have made the charges stick my father would have been expelled. But as it turns out my mother had made for herself quite the reputation. There were some who wondered who had corrupted whom."

Like Mandy said, it was always the woman who got the blame. Even when she was a *jewel in the family crown*.

"For my father's part," Taylor was saying, "He blamed my uncle for imprisoning my mother until she was so desperate that she had to run away. I think what neither of them could understand was that she was her own person. She had her own mind. Her own reasons. Her own will. That's why she'd be proud of you, Esther. She would admire the way you set your mind to a thing and stand fast."

Think for yo'self, Baby Sister. Every tub's gotta sit on its own bottom.

"But your father found her," I said quietly.

"He did," agreed Taylor. "He would get these post-cards signed with various famous female character names: *Bianca, Juliette, Audrey, Cassandra*, but never with a return address. I found them after they died. Pop had saved them. I think she just wanted him to know that she was fine, and a success."

"She didn't want to give him up," I said almost sadly.

"Maybe you're right," replied Taylor thoughtfully. "Those post-cards weren't the only clue, in case he went searching for her. Her stage name was Emilia Emerson."

"She used his middle name." I smiled, impressed.

"Yes. After he graduated and he went looking for her full-time, and that little clue must have helped him find her."

"And they got married, which she must have wanted all along," I concluded. "All the post-cards. She didn't want to lose him, Taylor."

"And they all lived happily ever after, right?"

"Yes," I said emphatically.

"For a dozen years or so at least," he reminded me.

My smile faded. I imagined their car wrecked in the rain.

"Yes," I concurred. "They were together."

I imagined Doctor Mitchell, another Mr. Sommers, bringing the terrible news.

"But you see, Esther," Taylor interrupted my thoughts to continue the story. "That was not what my mother had planned."

"That's the way accidents are, Taylor," I consoled him. "They aren't planned. Sometimes they are just these...these very bad things that happen to us."

"Like polio," he said in the matter-of-fact tone that covered over feelings.

"Yes," I replied soberly. "And mines that explode in the snow."

Taylor again squeezed me against him tightly. At least he was going to recover. Jimmy would never come home.

"Or a pregnancy," he said.

Now I did sit up.

"I know," I said quickly.

But as bad as that might seem it would be life not death. Our baby would know happiness. I would see to it. My family would. Grampa too.

"We should be more careful," I told him. "But you need to know, Taylor, that if...if I should...I mean I can manage on my own."

"What?" he asked, confused. "What are you talking about?"

"None of it will involve you," I explained. "It's my responsibility. I understand that. It's like you said, it's my decision. I made up my mind--"

"Wait," he said frowning. "Are you--"

"I mean, he'll, or she, will know when they're older," I admitted. "They have a right to, and I would want them to, they should know who you are, but--"

"Esther, I'm talking about me," Taylor said sharply. "I was the *accident*...as you call it. I disrupted my mother's plans. The very day my father found her they succumbed to their passions. I was conceived in a cheap little garret apartment in Greenwich Village. And that was that for Emilia Emerson's stage career. My father did the right thing, as I would also do let me assure you, and married her. He brought her back to McConnell County where I was born about six months later. I suppose no one was to be the wiser. But Uncle Jason knew the truth. I'm a bastard, Esther. My uncle, and eventually Felicia, have never let me forget it."

"A *bastard?*" I asked, shocked and bewildered.

"Yes," he said.

But he was his father's son, the man in the wedding portrait downstairs, whatever life his mother might have lived. I had studied both of them enough to pinpoint every likeness. The way their dark hairlines swept back from their high foreheads, the long angles of their noses that rounded off at the tips, the square lines that shaped their jaws. The way their suit coats snuggly hugged their broad shoulders and hung looser at their waists. The long legs that gave them their height.

"No you're not," I argued. "You weren't born out of wedlock."

He even had his father's hands, long strong fingers, with knuckles that were almost too big in proportion. *Desk-man hands.* Only his father's hands had carried silver trays of champagne and punch.

"Technically perhaps," replied Taylor. "They did remedy the situation, but in the spirit of the law--"

"The *spirit?*" I snapped.

His right brow arched dramatically.

"Taylor," I continued amending my voice. "Surely the spirit of the law is to honor family, and--"

"I took away my mother's choices, Esther," he said dryly as if he were presenting indisputable facts in another court case. "Yes, she loved him but she married him because of me. Arguably it was the right thing to do, but it cost her dearly," Taylor added. "She gave up her dreams for me."

For him? It was the most absurd and outrageous thing I had ever heard, but it was clear that Taylor believed it, and just behind his calm and stoic veneer there was a resigned regret. As briefly visible and mercurial as Nathaniel's war clouds, it was nonetheless there, because he had kept it, held on to it these many years. Maybe all his life.

Don't you think it's about time somebody took care of him?

It was how he understood himself, and I was afraid to tell him that it was ridiculous. I didn't have the right to. It was not my place. He didn't like me protecting him. Maybe I could ask Mr. Leon to talk to him about it. Or maybe Nathaniel. He respected them both. He would listen to them.

"I changed the course of their lives," he was telling me.

"*You* did?" I asked abruptly, the incredulity bursting back into my voice.

"Yes," he replied with his certainty unfazed.

"So that's what you mean when you say you disrupted her plans?" I asked. "That she got pregnant with you?"

"Yes. If--"

"If-if," I interrupted him exasperated. "'If the dog hadn't stopped to shit, he'd-a caught the rabbit.'"

"What?" asked Taylor, throwing his head back laughing merrily.

Herman raised up and looked at us.

"What does that mean?" his master wanted to know.

I felt silly and frustrated.

"Oh I don't know what it means," I shot back, my hands flailing. "All I know is that you don't make sense. Disruptin' your mother's plans. Messin' up her dreams. Changin' the course of their lives. For god's sake, how do you know you weren't her dream come true? Your father's? They wanted to be together. She used his name, sent him those post-cards, and what did he do but come lookin' for her as soon as he could. What if the Lord just used you to bless them? You ever think about that? I know, I know, probably not. You don't believe in the Lord. But you will believe that a baby even before it's born can have enough power to change the lives of everybody around him. Well let me tell you one thing, Taylor Andrew Payne, ain't no baby had that kind of power but the Baby Jesus. And as far as your Uncle Jason is concerned, he's just some angry old man who's bitter because a country bumpkin out of East Texas took his little sister's heart. And if he can't get over it, and thank the Lord for what that love gave to this world, namely you and your sister, then I'm sorry for him and you ought to be too. Not to mention for Felicia, who ought to be old enough to know better by now. But bein' pitiful don't make him or her right. My Lord—to let you or your uncle tell it, if it weren't for you, then Felicia wouldn't even be here in the first place. He wouldn't have his *apple* of his eye. Did Jason Morgan ever think about that while he was calling you a bastard and convincing you that you had ruined your mother's life?"

There. I had spoken my piece, and now I paused and breathed deeply, pulling the sheet up to my chin to cover myself. Taylor was quiet. He had every right to order me out of his bed and even out of his house, but I had an obligation to tell him the truth, whether he had asked me to or not. Men could be such foolish creatures. No wonder Adam had eaten the apple. Even the most brilliant among them could get the most important things so hopelessly wrong. I met his gaze steadily. The Bible said that the truth set you free. It was long passed time for someone to come along and bang on Taylor's jail-cell door, and tell him to open the door, because the keys were on the inside. He was prepared to defend his home, and me. Well it was high time for him to do the same for himself.

"I'd like to request a continuance," Taylor finally spoke.

"What does that mean?" I asked.

"It usually means the requesting counsel is having some difficulty with the case."

"So I'm right, then?" I wanted him to admit.

He only smiled crookedly.

"And it also means there isn't a verdict," he answered.

"Yet," I replied, imagining the sound of keys jangling.

He nodded.

"Yet," he agreed.

"All right then," I said almost confidently. "I'll agree to it," I said about the continuance. "Rome wasn't built in a day."

We don't have the same vantage point, do we?

I knew from experience—and with him—that it wasn't that easy to adjust your perspective after a lifetime, not so easy to see things, including yourself, *differently*. To see clearly through a glass.

"I'm cold," I said, sliding down under the bed covers again.

"Hardly," Taylor replied as he reached to turn off the light before lying down again too.

Once more he draped my body with his and instantly I felt warmed and content. Looking out the window I could see the morning coming. Red Comb and his younger brethren would be crowing by now, as the docile hens and pullets clucked and stretched their flightless wings. Grampa would be getting up to have his coffee alone, and preparing to have his Thanksgiving dinner with a stranger at his grandson's table. As this stranger reached to cover my hand with his I was thinking to myself how much I loved them both.

The *long story* had been revealing, just not about Sylvia or Felicia; although maybe it was, because it was about him, and how he was towards all of us. As with Grampa, I imagined that there were few people who told Taylor Payne that he was wrong about anything, and particularly about himself, and fewer still that he would believe, but the *continuance* showed a crack in his strong wall of self-assured detachment. Yes, maybe his mother would have been proud of me. Her beloved son held me close enough to let me love him.

"Your grandfather raised you, didn't he?" asked Taylor after a time.

"Yes," I replied although the question seemed strange to me. "We moved in with him when I was eight."

"Felicia was eight when we went to live with our uncle," he said.

Did he think I was like Felicia?

"And you were twelve," I said. "The same age as Spencer is now."

"Yes," he replied.

"And here we are, a man and a woman," I added bringing his hand to my heart.

"Mother would have been proud," he decided again, holding me more tightly against him.

"Jimmy too," I whispered.

II

Connie had loaned me two of her deep dish pie plates for the sweet potato pies. Taylor's kitchen was adequately supplied, but it was these kinds of extra trappings that reminded you that his house had no legitimate mistress.

You run this house, Esther. I believe you have from the day you came here.

But one day this house would have a wife, and there would be a proper set of pie pans, and cake plates, and children. And by then I could have my own kitchen too. My own husband. My own life. Apart from him and his. As it should be.

I was pleased once again with my perfect bright orange pie custards set in their buttery brown crusts. Taking great pains not to break the crusts or damage the centers, I wrapped the pies in waxed paper and carefully stacked them into the straw-basket on top of the carefully wrapped butter-cream cake. Taylor had a sweet tooth too, like all of the men in my life, and now he would also have some part of Jimmy's cake.

I collected the straw-basket and the gift box of chocolates and carried them outside to put in the backseat of the car. The box of chocolates was Taylor's idea, a suitable substitute for the Chardonnay he had planned to bring to Nathaniel and Connie, until I reminded him that we were Baptists.

"You mean I've corrupted you in that way too?" he had jested.

"Woman tempted man, Mr. Payne," I had returned. "Maybe I've corrupted you."

"Eve was railroaded, Esther. She just needed a good lawyer."

Was that all it took, I asked myself now as I secured the basket on the floor behind the front passenger seat. A *good lawyer*. Taylor was a good lawyer.

But he's the only one who believes me.

Taylor would help Cordelia Collier. He could protect us both.

It was going to be a cloudy day and I fretted about my curled hair. The first time he had seen me using curling irons heated in a bright blue flame on top of the stove, Taylor had been intrigued. I had been embarrassed.

"Amazing," he had commented. "What women will do to themselves."

"Colored women, you mean," I had replied self-consciously.

"All women, Esther. Cooking the hair is actually not unique to Negroes."

Now standing in front of mirror over the credenza I admired the way my hair laid softly against the back of my neck, its soft luster a result of the prudently applied Royal Crown dressing. For those of us without the benefit of infamous ancestry or Indian blood, we had Madame C.J. Walker to thank for giving us long flowing locks; and we had made her a millionaire for it, for pressing our hair into American submission.

I went into the study where Taylor was waiting. Sitting at his desk, wearing a gray tweed jacket and black slacks, he looked the part of an English gentleman, and I wondered if I should ask him to leave off the black silk tie and wear his starched white shirt open at the collar. I had persuaded him not to wear a suit, but still he might look too formal. Nathaniel would probably not be wearing a coat or a tie, although knowing Aunt Betty she would make sure that Uncle Perry did. My uncle would no doubt have to be in his Sunday best, given the guest at Nathaniel's table. Grampa would probably be wearing his pressed khakis and a tie too. It was what he always wore for special occasions in our houses. His suits were for church. I still couldn't be sure that he would be there, but it was too late for the dinner not to happen. If he didn't come we would get through it anyway, relying on Connie's excellent cooking to sustain our bellies and the mood.

I smiled cheerfully at Taylor, and I said nothing about his tie, appreciative that he wanted to dress well for my family.

"Ready?" I asked him.

"Yes," he replied. "You?"

He asked me as if he sensed my anxiety, even though I was trying hard not to let it show. It was going to be a good day, I told myself. It was the right thing to do. We had had friends to our family gatherings before. We were a friendly family.

"Everything's in the car," I said, which didn't answer his question.

"All right," he let it go and began stacking papers neatly before putting them away in the desk drawer.

I went to the closet to get my coat. When Taylor joined me in the foyer, I went to him and lightly stroked the sleeve of his jacket.

"Will this be warm enough?" I asked.

"I think so," he said.

It might rain, I reminded him, but he said he would be fine. I closed the closet door, leaving behind one of his crutches along with his winter coat. I wasn't convinced that he was ready to rely on just the one crutch, but he had been practicing faithfully with the cane when he was in the house, and going to a single crutch was a compromise, an improvement over the need for two but not so ambitious as the cane alone.

At Nathaniel's house, Uncle Perry had parked his car along the street. Nathaniel must have thought of even this little detail and I was grateful for his effort.

"You can park in the driveway," I told Taylor.

He did and shut off the engine.

"Well, here we are!" I said gaily. "It'll be fine. You'll see. Everyone's looking forward to seeing you. Nathaniel and Uncle Perry will be here."

"You don't have to encourage me, Esther," replied Taylor.

"I wasn't trying…I mean…I-I just want you to be relaxed that's all," I offered awkwardly.

"I think it's customary for the man to be nervous in these situations. And I do have a few added disadvantages, we'll call them."

He smiled at me reached over and squeezed my hand.

"Stop worrying," he continued. "I promise not to embarrass you. If anything, I know how to carry myself in a courtroom."

"No one's on trial here, Taylor," I said smiling through my anxiety.

"That's what you think," he said, raising my hand to his lips before letting it go.

I opened my hand briefly against his smooth cheek and its warmth was soothing to my clammy palm. If Eve had had him as her advocate it might have all turned out *differently* from the start.

"Hello!" Nathaniel called to us from the front porch. "Happy Thanksgivin'!"

"Hello Nathaniel!" I called back quickly getting out of the car and retrieving the basket of pies, cake, and candy from the back.

I hurried around to the other side to wait for Taylor to get out.

"Y'all come on in!" Nathaniel was saying.

"Thank you," replied Taylor, pausing next to the car for a moment. "Happy Thanksgiving!"

Aunt Betty was peering out the window at us from around Connie's pretty blue curtains, recalling for me Mis' Inez the night Taylor had come to see Baby Nate. Was that really only last January? At the porch steps, Taylor hesitated. There were only three steps, but he must concentrate to manage the right leg, especially the foot. Nathaniel moved forward to help, but I looked at him and surreptitiously shook my head, handing the straw-basket up to him instead.

"The chocolates are from Taylor," I explained brightly.

"Much obliged, Taylor," said Nathaniel enthusiastically. "Thank you."

"You know this is a very special occasion, Taylor," I said casually hooking my arm through his right one firmly before he could reach for the porch step railing. "This is the first time Nathaniel gets to host a family dinner."

"Really?" Taylor replied as he threaded his fingers through mine and gripped my hand.

We began to climb the steps together.

"Yeah," Nathaniel said, waiting for us. "Sure is. The ol' folks ain't over it yet neither."

"They think the young people are takin' over," I prattled.

"'Bout time you ask me," added Nathaniel.

There was one more step to go.

"Yes," I agreed. "Everything changes."

When the three of us stood on the porch, I let go of Taylor's arm, and he shook Nathaniel's outstretched hand. Using only one crutch made it easier for him to manage the numerous greetings to come, and there would be no more stairs to deal with.

"We glad you gon' be with us today, Taylor," Nathaniel said, passing the straw basket back to me.

"It was kind of you to invite me, Nathaniel," replied Taylor.

"This dinner been all my Connie talked about for days."

I beamed at Nathaniel. His natural ease was a gift to anyone at any time.

"Y'all come on in," he repeated. "It's gettin' kind-a air-ish out here."

In the living room Aunt Betty and Uncle Perry were waiting. Grampa, Connie, and the children were missing. Taylor removed his hat and I took it from him and quickly hung it on the coat rack before returning to his side. Uncle Perry came to him and shook his hand.

"It's good to see you again, Mr. Payne," Uncle Perry said as if he had practiced. "You lookin' very well. We glad to have you to Thanksgivin' with us."

"Thank you, Perry. It's good to see you too. But please, call me Taylor."

"Yes-sir. Mr. Taylor it is. This here's my wife, Betty."

"Mr. Taylor, it's very nice to finally get to meet you," declared Aunt Betty coming forward to also shake his hand. "I don't hear nothin' but good about you. We was so sorry to hear about your sickness, but you take courage. Every step you make, the Lord'll make two."

Such information had never impressed Taylor, but he was smiling warmly at my aunt.

"He wants you to call him Taylor, Muh'dear," Nathaniel attempted to correct Aunt Betty.

"Hello, Mrs. Green," Taylor was saying. "I'm delighted to meet you too."

"I did, son," Aunt Betty said out of the side of her mouth, while she endeavored to maintain her graciousness for our guest.

"Not *Mister* Taylor, y'all," said Nathaniel. "Just Taylor."

Aunt Betty looked flustered and withdrew her hand. Uncle Perry stood next to her also looking uncomfortable.

"Don't worry we'll get it all straightened out," I volunteered as I took off my coat. "Where's Connie and the children?"

I heard myself not ask about Grampa, because I was afraid that someone was going to say that he would not be coming, and then I wouldn't know how to make it up to any of them. Three hundred years of history was a great deal to get *straightened out* in a single afternoon. Even for *radicals* like me. Still it was Thanksgiving and a time for celebrating human perseverance and God's grace. Today was all about different peoples coming together to share a common feast. It could all be very fitting and with a better outcome for everyone too. There were such things as miracles. Pocahontas had saved John Smith, even if she had married another man.

"In the kitchen, where else?" replied Nathaniel to my question about Connie. He grinned. "And done chased Muh'dear right on out of there too."

"Didn't she?" snorted Aunt Betty, having recovered her usual regal bearing.

"Let's us sit down. Here, Mr. Payne—I mean Mr. Taylor—uh-uh—Taylor," stumbled Uncle Perry. "You take this here chair," he said, directing Taylor to take Nathaniel's big easy chair.

It was with every good intention, but Nathaniel's chair was too low for Taylor. It would be like climbing out of hole for him when he had to stand up again.

"Thank you, Perry," replied Taylor. "But why don't you take that one. I'll sit here on the couch."

Again Uncle Perry was unsettled and confused. By his reckoning Nathaniel's chair was the best seat in the house. He couldn't understand why Taylor wouldn't want it.

"You know how it is when your rheumatism acts up, Daddy," Nathaniel intervened. "You don't like a chair that sits low. It's the same for Taylor."

"I can see he got a bad leg, Nathaniel," replied Uncle Perry a little annoyed. "That's why I thought he'd want to prop his foot up and the easy chair got the stool. 'Course it won't be no trouble to move the stool I guess. We can set it in front of the davenport for him."

Was it like this for Taylor at the courthouse, with everyone too concerned and helpful, constantly reminding him of his limitations?

"Please don't go to any trouble," said Taylor.

"The stool's not necessary, Uncle Perry," I added.

"Yeah, Daddy," said Nathaniel. "You take my chair, like you always do."

"Well I'm just tryin' to make sure he's comfortable," my uncle mumbled dejectedly.

By now everyone looked awkward. The Dearborn heater was turned down low, the small flames dancing bright blue at the bottom of the blackened grates, but it felt hot in the room.

"The sofa's fine, Perry," Taylor attempted to assure Uncle Perry. "Thank you."

"Well all right then," my uncle sought to regain his authority. "What we all standin' 'round for?" he asked impatiently and sat down in Nathaniel's chair.

"I'd better go see what I can do to help Connie," I announced, picking up the basket again.

It wasn't meant to be an escape; I was simply trying to move us through the moment as I had seen Taylor do so many times, Nathaniel too. I was trying to make things normal. But then how could they be, in the middle of McConnell County's grand social experiment? I wished that Aunt Grace and Uncle Eddie would call, but it was already after twelve, and so after one o'clock their time. They would be having their dinner by now. Who sat at their table? Might this all have been easier in New York I wondered. Would Taylor ever visit me there? But Danny wanted to live in California.

Once Uncle Perry sat down then Aunt Betty did too, and after she did, then Taylor sat down. Of course. His manners would not let him sit until she had done so first. We had been together so long, with so much of that time being when he couldn't stand up at all, that I had forgotten his gallantry. My Aunt Betty was a lady to him, no less than Laura Spalding's mother, or his own, and due the same courtesy. His right leg spasmed, and Taylor quickly held it still, but everyone saw it, and Aunt Betty and Uncle Perry exchanged worried glances. He was broken to them, crippled. They felt sorry for him, and anxious for me. I was determined that by the end of the day, they would know him better, and they would admire him, and even understand me.

I had been right about Nathaniel not wearing a tie, and already Uncle Perry's shirt was open at the collar although he was still wearing the suit coat. How was Grampa dressed? And where was he? He was the most important judge among them.

"You think *Mrs. Green* will let you?" Aunt Betty was asking me still in a huff over how Connie had allegedly treated her.

"She'll take help," Nathaniel defended his wife, still wearing his good-natured expression. "It's the bossiness she can do without."

"Mrs. Green," said Taylor, "I've never had a chance to thank you for your decorating suggestions."

We all turned our attention back to him at this remark, each of us being surprised for our own reasons. In passing once, he had asked me about the original decorating ideas, obtaining from me a minimal confession of the conspiracy, by which he had only seemed amused. "They were a great help," he went on now. "I hope you'll come by sometime and see what we've done with the house."

You make this house a home.

Aunt Betty instantly blossomed. I felt a little embarrassed for her and for myself, for the flattery she was believing, and the *we* that Taylor was using.

"Well, Mr. Payne—uh, Taylor, it's very nice of you to say so," gushed Aunt Betty. "I was glad to help."

He was charming her, as smoothly as I had ever seen him do it. No wonder I was in love with him. As Aunt Betty reveled in Taylor's attentions, she lit up as if he had given her a present, apparently forgetting the irritation with her offending daughter-in-law. Taylor and Nathaniel sat on opposite ends of the couch, and for a mind's moment I thought I saw Jimmy between them, sharing the satisfaction of the delighted dimples in Aunt Betty's flawlessly powdered, pink-painted cheeks.

"Well now Muh'dear," contributed Nathaniel, "You 'bout the only somebody I know that can do a good deed just by readin' them glamour magazines of yours."

I left them that way, pleasant all around.

In the kitchen, Connie had everything under control. She had probably been cooking for days, preparing individual dishes and storing them in her new Frigidaire. She kindly fawned over the pies and butter-cream cake and gleefully appreciated the chocolates.

"Tell the truth now, Esther," she wanted to know. "Did he give you a box of chocolates for Valentine's Day?"

"No," I said emphatically. "Of course not."

"He will. You'll get flowers too."

"It's not like that between us, Connie, I told you."

"Say what you want," she replied undeterred and turning back to the stove. "He gave you pearls on your birthday. I know that."

And we were lovers. But she could only *suspect* that.

The turkey was cooked to a golden brown and now sat on the back of the stove keeping warm. The kitchen smelled of the celery, sage, and onions all of which was baking together in the cornbread dressing. It was the perfect holiday kitchen. Pots and pans here and there. Stacks of clean dishes ready to be set on the table. A few dirty ones waiting to be washed in a sink of soapy water.

"If you want to go speak to Taylor, Connie, I can look after things and give you a break," I changed the subject as I rolled up my sleeves.

"Do I look like I need a break?" she demanded.

"Well, no," I answered chastened for having made the suggestion.

"Good," she said. "Then let me do my business. Your gentleman caller be that much gladder to see me if this food is right."

Your gentleman caller.

Tonight, I'm both.

In fact I had brought him home to meet my people. For their approval. Just minus those kinds of expectations. All I wanted was for us all to be friends. Friends and neighbors. It seemed perfectly reasonable and doable. The pearls, which I would never wear in front of Grampa again notwithstanding.

"Just what did you say to your mother-in-law that got her so riled up anyway?" I ventured to ask, efficiently washing my hands at the kitchen sink in order to be ready for any assignment Connie might make.

"Not as much as I had a right to," replied Connie.

"Uh-oh."

I dried my hands on a cup-towel and tied one of Connie's aprons around my waist.

"You known her longer than me," Connie said. "So you know how she is. I just let her know that this is *my* kitchen, and I'm havin' my say."

"Rest assured," I quickly stressed. "I'm only here to help. Not to boss anybody."

"Good. Then I might let *you* stay."

We laughed and Connie seemed to feel better. I wanted to say again how much I appreciated that she had arranged for all this, but she had dismissed my gratitude so many times before that I knew she would just scold me for being silly if I said something about it again. Connie and I had grown up in the same county, gone to the same school, and attended the same picnics; however, for all my education and Harlem sophistication, it was Connie who sallied forth into everything confidently. Just like Mandy. Sometimes her faith put me and mine to shame.

"Where are the children?" I asked first, and then finally added. "And Grampa?" Connie stopped stirring in one of her pots and put down the spoon. Taking me by the hand, she led me to the backdoor. From here I could see Grampa standing alone in the backyard with his hands in his pockets.

"The *other* chirren are in Evie's room playin'," she said.

"What's he doin' out there?" I asked haplessly.

"Bein' yo' grandpa seem like to me. You known him longer too." She went back to the stove and lifted another pot lid to look in on what was cooking there. "You Greens can be a mulish bunch," she decided. "We could actually do with some new blood in this family to water y'all down a little."

"What's the matter?" I asked. "Did he say anything to you? I thought he was going to be okay."

"When y'all drove up, he went out the back door," replied Connie. "That says plenty. He's not *okay* with it as you put it. Nathaniel tried to talk to him again 'fo y'all got here, but I guess he just ain't ready to see you two together." She replaced the pot lid and looked into another. "'Course now he did come this far, I'll say that much. He's here even if he is outside." She turned back to me. "So since the Lord Jesus got to have better things to do, seem like to me it's up to you to bring that ol' man the rest of the way."

"Couldn't Nathaniel make him see?" I asked plaintively, looking out the backdoor again.

"See what, Esther?" asked Connie. "See you with a white man? He been seein' it. That's the problem."

"We're just friends," I said again.

"That's what you say."

I sighed.

"We're just bein' neighborly that's all," I muttered. "Why can't he understand that?"

Connie had the oven door open and was stirring the dressing. She paused long enough to taste a bit of it with the tip of her finger from the spoon.

"Maybe 'cause nobody ever told him that his neighbors could live over on Webster Road." She closed the oven door. "Or that his grand-daughter could live out there too."

"I don't live there," I denied hollowly.

"All right, Esther," said Connie. "We ain't got time to argue 'bout it today. You just gone out there and say somethin' to soften 'im up, before he catch the pneumonia. I ain't havin' no hard hearts vexin' the Holy Spirit at my table today."

She went to the sink and ran the water over her hands, then dried them with the cup-towel.

"Or any other spirits for that matter," I said.

Connie smoothed her hair in place.

"That's right," she agreed, untying her apron. "This family's got plenty to be thankful for and that's all this day's about, you hear me. Us being thankful. Now. I'm goin' in here and speak to our company, and you goin' out there and get yo' grampa to come in this house and do the same. You want to be in the middle of it, then be in the middle and bring yo' two men together."

Yo' two men.

Draping one of Nathaniel's old work jackets around my shoulders, I went out the back door. If loving somebody gave you any rights at all, then perhaps they were indeed my two men. How long could Grampa stand around out here with his back to Nathaniel's house? I walk towards him. He was wearing the dark red cardigan that I had given him for *Father's Day*. He had fussed about it being too extravagant, but I had wanted him to have it. He should have nice things. He should have what he wanted. Sometimes.

"Grampa," I said once I reached him. "Connie's says that dinner's almost ready."

He did not respond.

"Grampa," I tried again, placing my hand on his arm. "Don't you think you better come inside? It's gettin' kind-a cold out here."

The red wool of the cardigan was soft to my fingers. Taking his hands out of his pockets, Grampa folded his arms across his chest.

"Grampa?" I repeated myself.

"I heard you, Esther Fay," he finally replied.

I shivered suddenly and pulled together the collar of Nathaniel's jacket.

"Aren't you gettin' chilly?" I asked. "I believe the wind's pickin' up."

At last he looked at me.

"Where yo' coat at?" he asked sternly.

"Inside." I hesitated, and then tried again, "Connie says dinner's almost ready."

"You done said that," he told me looking away.

I looked down at the ground. The grass was dry and brown. Nathaniel took care of his lawn like white folks did, even in the back, for the children's sake. It was their place to play. There were no chicken coops here, and Connie didn't seem interested in gardening, buying her produce from Mr. Moses, the neighborhood fruit man, who sold fruits and vegetables from his truck.

"Grampa, please come inside," I implored.

"When I worked for the railroad," he said. "I served in the dinin' car. We had this colored man on the line that did all the cookin'. Boy, that man could cook. Beat any woman in the kitchen. He'd fix all them fancy dishes. They'd be lookin' so pretty and smellin' so good, make yo' mouth water. But that food wasn't for none-a us. Yeah, you might could sneak a taste sometime, maybe eat what one of 'em left on his plate, and b'lieve you me I done my share of that."

In my mind's eye and in Grampa's grim almost-white face, I could see the dining cars of his railroad days. The crisp white linens, the gay, the indifferent thoroughly white faces. I could see the good food on the good china, as it was being served by the neatly pressed porters, who smiled their apparent subservience.

"Sometimes," Grampa continued. "Us porters wouldn't get to eat 'til late over in the night, when they done gone to bed. You 'bout be done starved to death. Lips turned white, dry. Head swimmin'. That time a'night the kitchen be closed down. What you could get, be cold. Maybe spoiled. Scraps. But you ate it anyhow. If you hungry enough, Esther Fay, you eat anything you can find. You make do."

"I'm sorry, Grampa," I said.

"Don't need yo' sorry. That's just the way it was. And it ain't changed. I never 'spected it to," he continued. "They got they world, we got ours. Long as you in they world you can't 'spect to be sittin' down at some fine table all laid out with good food. Least I never did. That's for when we 'mongst our own." He looked at me. "That's why a colored man works so hard, Esther Fay. So he can have as good as them and provide it to his own. It ain't right. Never was. But I didn't let it bother me to be servin' 'em in them dinin' cars. 'Cause I knowed I had mine."

Grampa took off his hat and examined the brim before returning it to his head. A sharp breeze rose up and stung my cheeks.

"Yo' grandmama and me used to dream 'bout y'all havin' better," he said. "Better than us. That's what we wanted. To each his own, like the Bible says, but better."

Taylor's father had been a server too, perhaps also eating scraps in a kitchen, and dreaming of a better life for his son, but it wouldn't help to tell Grampa that. Regardless of the similarity of their dreams it wasn't the same. Grampa had not been working his way through Harvard Law School, and Robert Collier's kind would have lynched him. Yet I had to try. Back in the house everyone was waiting.

"There's only the one world, Grampa," I said gently. "That's how God made it even if that's not how we left it. Please come inside. Connie's been cookin' all day. You don't want to disappoint her. Sometimes things can be different."

"Colored folks been lookin' for a change to come since we been callin' on Jesus," Grampa replied. "Hopin' and waitin'. Well I ain't lookin' for no change. Not in this life. It ain't gon' be right down here, Esther Fay, 'til the Lord comes back. It ain't in us. None of us. People can't do right."

"Grampa--" I tried again.

"I don't want to sit at the table with 'im, Esther Fay. I don't want to be amongst his kind." He looked at me. "I done had my fill-a white folks."

"Holding him responsible for being born white," I quietly quoted Mandy, "Is the same as holding us back for being born colored, Grampa. "Please try to see him for himself," I pleaded, while the autumn winds blew around us. "He wasn't one of those people on the train, Grampa. Taylor's different. And he's a guest in Nathaniel's house. Jesus sat down with everybody, Grampa. That's all we're saying. If the Lord was willing to die for us—all of us—then there must be something in all of us that's worthy enough. I want to believe that Grampa, I have to, otherwise what's the use? What did Jesus die for in the first place? And Jimmy? We got Little Evie and Baby Nate, Grampa. Don't we want a better world for them? It can start here. You just can't be that hopeless about it."

"Esther Fay--"

"Try, Grampa," I begged, clutching his arm. "Please try. That's all I'm asking. I know you can try. Just for today. Please."

Connie was busily turning boiled sweet potatoes into candied ones when Grampa followed me through her kitchen door. A relieved smile filled her damp, shiny face. "Well, thank the Lord," she said. Maybe it was a victory of sorts, as small as it was, although for whom I did not know for sure. Was it Connie's victory or mine? Maybe it was Taylor's and some little sign that Jimmy had not died believing vainly. Maybe it was for Little Evie and Baby Nate, and all the Spencers in the world who trusted kindness wherever it came from. Or did it belong to all those colored folks who had been *hopin' and waitin'* all those years. To whomever it belonged, Grampa had yielded. He would sit at Nathaniel's table with Taylor. But maybe it was only another *continuance.*

I followed Grampa into Nathaniel's front room. Seeing us, Taylor reached for his crutch and rose to his feet. Uncle Perry, still unsure of how to handle the whole situation, stood up too, looking anxious again, as if once more he didn't know what should be done. Nathaniel, however, now with Little Evie in his lap, kept his seat.

"Hello, Mr. Green," Taylor greeted my grandfather.

Grampa crossed the room to him and extended his right hand.

"My chirren made you welcome?" Grampa asked.

And the strangers shall be joined with them, and they shall cleave to the house of Jacob. Grampa was the head of our family, Jacob's family, welcoming Taylor, the stranger, who, for this day, would join with us. And my life, if only for a little while, was no longer in *separate* parts.

Grampa and Taylor were practically the same height and had almost the same build: broad backs, square shoulders, strong arms, long legs. The hands that brought together the red wool and the gray tweed were almost the same size, almost the same color, and both were experienced with swinging an axe. Symmetry came to mind as the two parts of my life decorously reencountered themselves, now for the third time. My two singular gentlemen of the *agreement.* They may have settled it, but I had unsettled it, to resettle it again, making it to our own purpose and against his. I remembered standing between them outside Taylor's room that day, trying to shield them from each other.

...It is the man's place to defend the home.

But it was a woman's place to make it. And I had ultimately brought them together, the equal parts of my heart. Symmetrical. Were it not for one's age and the other's crutch. One's *place* and the other's *privilege.* I was at home with them both.

"Yes, thank you," said Taylor to Grampa.

"Sit down, Mr. Payne," Grampa told him as he took Uncle Perry's seat by sitting down in Nathaniel's easy chair. I moved towards the Dearborn, backing up to its warmth.

"Mr. Green, I wish you'd use my first name," Taylor said.

"Wasn't raised to," Grampa told him.

Everyone, except Little Evie and Nate, glanced around at each other. The room was quiet enough to hear the metal click as Taylor unlocked the leg brace in order to resume his seat. Grampa casually crossed his legs. Uncle Perry dragged the foot stool he had wanted to offer Taylor closer to Aunt Betty's chair and stiffly lowered himself onto it.

"Looks like yo' legs gettin' stronger," Grampa observed.

"Yes," agreed Taylor. "I still have a little trouble with the right one, but I'm better."

"Thank the Lord," declared Grampa.

"And Esther," added Taylor, looking over at me.

I smiled at him.

"That's right," Grampa replied, the trace of a furrow briefly wrinkling his brow. "You don't put much store in the Lord, do you?"

"I believe in giving credit where it's due," answered Taylor.

My stomach fluttered. As if *I* weren't enough, did they need to have a *gentlemen's agreement* about God too? The peace was too fragile. Don't talk about the Law, Taylor, I wanted to say, not to Grampa. Aunt Betty transferred Nate to her other knee. Uncle Perry looked ready to stand up again.

"Well," Grampa said loosening his tie. "The Lord's merciful. He let it rain on everybody's garden, whether they thank Him fo' it or not."

This disaster seemingly averted, I relaxed a little.

"I suppose that's grace, isn't it?" asked Taylor.

Again I caught my breath. Grampa regarded Taylor. It was my fault. I had misled Taylor to think that he could have this kind of conversation with any believer. Uncle Perry cleared his throat. One of us should say something to change the subject. This was not his kitchen, I wanted to remind Taylor. He was guilty until proven innocent and debates about religion would not make his case. Meanwhile Nathaniel was playfully tugging at one of Little Evie's glossy plaits, and she, exulting in her father's attention, giggled happily.

"That's what the preachers tell me," replied Grampa. "But you not a church-goin' man neither."

Aunt Betty smoothed the bodice of her dress. This wasn't Harvard. This was the South, a Baptist home, and a Baptist family. God, Himself, spoke King James' English and had had little else to say to us collectively since *The Book of Revelation*. To us the Bible wasn't just some anthology of inspirational stories and philosophical essays from ancient, learned men. Whatever they had taught Taylor in Presbyterian Sunday school it had not been reverent enough.

"I've been a few times," answered Taylor affably.

And he read his father's Bible, I wanted to add. Mr. Leon had pronounced him to be a good man.

"Do you some good to go more often," Grampa replied.

"Are you inviting me, sir?" asked Taylor.

I cringed again. He wasn't deliberately seeking to provoke him, was he? I watched Grampa watching him, taking his measure. Surely Taylor realized it. He must know that Grampa was a hard judge, with the proof of history as his evidence. I could say something in Taylor's defense, but it would be better for it to come from Nathaniel.

Maybe even Aunt Betty. My mouth was dry. The heat from the Dearborn was burning the back of my legs.

"The doors of the church is always open," answered Grampa. "By one Spirit we's all baptized whether we be Jews or Gentiles, bond or free. That's the Bible."

"Amen," said Nathaniel.

"Esther, I think it's 'bout time we feed these people," announced Connie, who had returned from the kitchen.

"Yes, let's do that," I answered, finding my voice again.

"Nathaniel," Connie said, "You gon' have to put Evie down. Evie, you talk to Mr. Taylor for a while. Daddy needs to help Mama."

"Humph," interjected Aunt Betty, "I didn't think you needed any help at-all."

"Mama Betty, I would be much obliged if you'd get Nate in his high chair for me," Connie pleasantly instructed her mother-in-law. "Daddy Perry, the foot-tub we use to boost up Evie is on the back porch. You mind fixin' that up for us? Fold up a towel and lay it on the bottom for her rump to sit on. Come on, Esther, let's get this dinner on the table. Folks get tempra'mental when they hungry."

Nathaniel set Little Evie down onto the space between himself and Taylor. The child looked disappointed at first, until Taylor spoke to her and pinched her cheek. Soon she was smiling shyly up at him. Connie was clever. She had not only saved us, she was leaving her little angel to disperse any demons that intended to linger.

I looked at Taylor, and reading the anxiety in my expression, he winked and smiled. He might have been pinching my cheek, for the way I was helplessly smiling back at him, charmed as much as Little Evie. Maybe he really did know how to *carry* himself in a courtroom.

"Esther Fay," Grampa called my name bluntly. "Go help Connie."

I nodded obediently and started towards the kitchen.

"I'll see after yo' patient," he added.

You were not looking at a man. I was your patient.

I stopped, turning around. I'm not his nurse, I said in my head.

"Esther!" Connie was calling. "You comin'?"

But it was a trap. If I denied that he was my *patient* then why was I still there?

"It's Esther's day off, Mr. Green," intervened Taylor, with Little Evie now sitting in his lap. "I'm quite prepared to be on my own. I think I can manage," he continued, as he played patty-cake with the child. "What do you think, Evie?" he asked her, smiling. "You think I'll be okay?" Little Evie was concentrating on patting the palms of her hands in the centers of his, but she looked up at him and nodded affirmatively. "There you have it," said Taylor meeting my eyes now. "Out the mouth of babes."

"Esther!" Connie called to me again.

"Comin'!" I answered and hurried into the kitchen.

Connie had prepared a splendid Thanksgiving table. Absent were Aunt Betty's cosmopolitan recipes and pretty place settings, but they were not missed. In their stead was home, perfection without the pretension of almonds in the green beans and ceramic napkin rings. The golden brown turkey was Connie's centerpiece. The assorted vegetables and side dishes colored her table. Floral bouquets were not required. There were no silver candlesticks to shine over the meal, just the bright smiles of the people gathered.

Nathaniel sat at the head of the table, and Connie was on his immediate right, with little Nate in his high-chair between them. Next to Connie was Taylor's seat and next to his was mine. Grampa was at the opposite end of the table from Nathaniel. Uncle Perry was across from me and Aunt Betty was next to him. Little Evie was across from Connie, but closer to Nathaniel's left.

When Taylor held my chair for me to sit down, Aunt Betty, casting an admonishing glance at Uncle Perry, who had not done the same for her, declared, "It sho' is nice to see good manners."

"Thank-you, Taylor," I said modestly as I quickly sat down.

"Ain't seen a woman yet that couldn't pull out her own chair," Grampa reminded all of us.

"It ain't–uh—*not* about that, Papa Isaac," said Aunt Betty undaunted. "It's just bein' polite. You hold the door for a lady, don't you?"

To this Grampa only grunted and Nathaniel chuckled, although he had not remembered to attend to Connie's chair either. Taylor, smiling, took his seat next to me and placed his crutch under the table out of sight.

"Grampa, why don't you give the blessin'," suggested Nathaniel.

"This yo' table son," Grampa told him. "You the man of the house."

"Aw, come on Grampa," Nathaniel insisted, beaming beautifully. "Bless us with a word of prayer. Somethin' real special for all the work my sweet wife done gone to."

Now he looked at Connie, and they beamed at each other. Connie was blessed with more than good manners, the good man was hers.

"It's a beautiful table, Connie," said Taylor. "My compliments to the chef."

"Thank-you, Taylor," she replied turning her attention to him. "And don't you worry. We always manage to eat befo' the food gets cold. If all else fails, Evie can say her Bible verse, can't you baby?"

"Je-sus wep," Little Evie responded proudly as if on cue.

"Amen, baby!" praised Aunt Betty, chuckling.

Connie laughed too. The rest of us, except for Grampa, were smiling.

"The Lord ain't to be played with," Grampa reproved us. "Let's us bow our heads."

We did, and Grampa began by first giving honor to God, and remembering family members now dead. Was he speaking of Albert and Matilda? Or did he only mean for us to think of Ernestine, Daddy, Mama, and Jimmy? I remembered them all, sacred ghosts hovering about us, amazed, but maybe pleased too. After all there was all that *hopin' and waitin'*. He's a decent man, Matilda, I thought. And Jimmy, you always said a change would come.

"…We thank You, Lord, for family and friends, near and far," prayed Grampa. "For health and strength, and that it is well with us, Lord…"

As the voices of my family echoed Grampa's solemn gratitude, I thought of Felicia Richmond. Of her dining room table and the empty space Taylor's presence here was leaving there. Maybe next year, when he was fully recovered, and there was no crutch to put under the table, he would want to go back to Cambridge and work things out with his own family again. Maybe even by Christmas. He was getting stronger all the time and his family was too small for him not to try. His mother would want him to. Hurts could be healed. You had to remain hopeful.

"…We thank you, Heavenly Father, for these gifts that we 'bout to receive," Grampa continued. "For the increase that made it possible, and for the cooks that prepared it for us. May it be for the nourishment of our bodies, and help us be faithful in doin' yo' will, and not our own…"

I raised my head slightly to glance at Taylor, wondering what he was thinking while the rest of us gave our thanks to a God he mostly considered an abstract idea. To my surprise his dark head was bowed solemnly too, and it occurred to me that I had never seen it so. I had never seen him humbled. Broken yes, and even beaten, but never as a supplicant. I had read that during the 1936 Olympics in Berlin, Adolf Hitler had been offended by the Americans because they would not dip the United States flag to salute him as they had paraded by his grandstand. Other countries had, out of courtesy to the Germans, but not the bold, brazen Americans. To make matters worse Jesse Owens had gone on to show the Germans just what an authentic *master race* looked like.

Did Robert Collier really think that he was capable of putting such a man in his *place?* He might have tried that night. He might have killed Taylor trying, but men like Taylor, and Jimmy, and Grampa, and Nathaniel, my uncles too, and Taylor's father, they *placed* themselves in the world. Make whatever rules against them, write laws, even do them bodily harm, the world did not define them so much as they defined the world.

But here was Taylor Andrew Payne bowing his head now. In deference to my faith, and my grandfather, and my family. Sitting next to me at Nathaniel's table, as the grace went on and on and the collard greens cooled. I supposed everybody could do things *differently;* when the prize was *worthy* enough. I lowered my head again before anyone saw that I had looked up.

"…We ask all this in Jesus' name," finished Grampa finally. "Amen."

"Amen," the rest of us, including Taylor, echoed.

When I looked at Taylor again, my eyes met his. The happy smile filled his face. Under the table he found my hand and squeezed it warmly, entwining his fingers with mine. My eyes lingered so long in his that Grampa's voice sounded abrupt to me, when he told me to pass the dressing.

III

"It's goin' all right, don't you think, Aunt Betty?" I asked eagerly, when Aunt Betty and I were in the kitchen getting ready to bring out the coffee, pie, and cake. We had made it through most of the meal, and the conversation had been relatively pleasant most of the time. Aunt Betty nodded, as she focused on counting the scoops of coffee she was putting into her gleaming new electric coffee percolator which she had brought with her for the day. Grampa was right she did always have another new reason to be in Uncle Perry's *britches' pocket*. But why not? *We* deserved fine things too. Maybe I would suggest that Taylor buy a coffee percolator.

You run this house, Esther.

Maybe I did. Until I left to Mandy to do it. And then perhaps ultimately one day Laura Spalding.

"Five, six, seven, eight," Aunt Betty counted her measured spoons. "Yeah chile, everything's fine," she said. "You act like it wouldn't be."

"Aunt Betty," I replied. "It's not everyday--"

"That we sit down to the table with a white man?" she finished for me. "People is people, Esther Fay. After while the world gon' be too little for us not to."

I smiled gratefully at her as I wiped Connie's good cups and saucers with a towel before organizing them on a tray.

"Maybe," I said hopefully.

"For somebody that's the cause-a all this, you don't sound too sure," my aunt remarked. "It's a first time for everything, chile, but even still, I can't believe this the first time for somethin' like this to happen. Sholey God it ain't always been evil 'tween our people."

"One thing I can say," Connie announced, returning to the kitchen carrying two empty serving bowls. "I sho' can cook."

"You not s'pose to be givin' yo' own self compliments, daughter," Aunt Betty admonished her, taking the dirty dishes from her and setting them on the counter next to the sink.

"Why not?" Connie shrugged. "The truth is the truth regardless of who tells it. Ain't that right, Esther?"

"Yes, Connie," I chuckled meekly and kept wiping and counting the cups and saucers.

Aunt Betty shook her head.

"We might-a got off to a rough start," Connie went on, "With everybody actin' so formal and all. But everythin's good now."

By the time the coffee was ready Nathaniel had changed Nate's diaper, and the two children were contentedly occupied with a variety toys and each other on a quilt spread out in one corner of the dining room. The adults remained around the table to have their coffee and dessert.

"You care for football…Mister-uh—uh-Taylor?" inquired Uncle Perry.

"I enjoy it very much," replied Taylor.

"You played some when you went to school, didn't you?" Nathaniel recalled.

"I did," said Taylor and took a bite of sweet potato pie. Looking at me he smiled warmly. "Superb," he said, sending roses to my cheeks.

"Well reason I asked," Uncle Perry was saying. "Is 'cause we kind-a like to listen to the game on the radio when we get through eatin'."

"Ain't no kind-a to it," corrected Connie. "It's a tradition with us. Well at least with the men folks anyway. Me, I can't see nothin' in it. You, Esther?"

"Uh no, not really," I shook my head.

"This time next year, we plan on havin' us a television," Aunt Betty joined in. "That way these men folk can see the games. You got a television, Taylor?"

"You must think they gon' show colored boys on television," Grampa said irritably.

"They just might," replied Aunt Betty.

"Some of these here colored schools got real good teams, Grampa," said Nathaniel.

"That's right," agreed Uncle Perry.

"I'm a fan of Morgan State," said Taylor surprising us. "Kentucky too."

"So do you, Taylor?" asked Aunt Betty.

Taylor swallowed another fork-full of pie.

"I'm sorry?" he replied.

"Do you have a television?" Aunt Betty wanted to know, stirring her coffee.

"You know somethin' 'bout colored ball?" Uncle Perry asked incredulous.

"No, ma'am, I don't," Taylor replied.

"Well I guess they is kind of expensive," Aunt Betty observed.

"Ed Hurt's one of the best coaches in the game," answered Taylor. "And I saw 'The Tank' Conrad play once. Very impressive."

"Fact about it, a game's prob'ly on right now," announced Nathaniel.

"He got enough money to buy what he want to," said Grampa.

"It'd be just the thing in that nice livin' room of yours," Aunt Betty went on. "Pastor Wright bought them one."

"Them's Morgan State men, but what about Herbert Trawick?" Uncle Perry challenged, showing his allegiance to Kentucky State.

"An amazing guard," conceded Taylor. "I'd watch him on television any day. All-American, wasn't he?"

"Colored newspapers said so anyway," said Grampa.

"He's got my vote," Taylor replied.

"Mine too," proclaimed Nathaniel.

"Well you sho' int'rested in our people, ain't you?" Grampa remarked. "How long we been so important to you?"

"Taylor reads so many newspapers," I hastily put in. "From all over the place."

The smooth rich texture of the pie had suddenly lost its sweetness in my mouth.

"I like football, Mr. Green," Taylor said. "And talent is talent, wouldn't you agree?"

"You think my granddaughter got talent?" asked Grampa.

Uncle Perry's fork was suspended in mid-air, until he remembered to place it back on the plate, the portion of cake it carried left uneaten. Aunt Betty and I looked at each other.

"I think she's brilliant," Taylor said.

I turned to him smiling faintly.

"Then you must b'lieve she ought to be finishin' her schoolin' too," replied Grampa.

"I believe that strongly," answered Taylor.

"Instead of keepin' yo' house?" Grampa pressed.

"Grampa, please," I said softly, looking down at my plate.

"Absolutely," Taylor replied and continued eating his slice of pie.

"You hear that, Esther Fay?" Grampa spoke to me. "Even now yo' boss-man wants you get on with yo' life. Maybe you be in Harlem by the first of the year, you reckon?"

Or California. But I didn't look up. A revived sadness washed over me at the thought of it, the thought of leaving.

"Perry if y'all men gon' listen to that game, y'all better gon' on and do it," Aunt Betty interceded.

Under the table, Taylor briefly squeezed my hand again. Our time together was measured in days. And nights. I couldn't look at him.

"You right, Muh'dear," agreed Nathaniel, rising from the table. "I tell you, Taylor, if I was a gamblin' man, I'd make you put some money on the game."

"Good thing you're not then," laughed Taylor as he reached down to get his crutch.

"I don't know, Nathaniel," Uncle Perry was saying, his mouth full of a last bite of cake. "I b'lieve Taylor knows what he's talkin' 'bout."

Uncle Perry got up too, leaving Aunt Betty, Connie, Grampa and me at the table.

"Taylor, I didn't know you played ball," Uncle Perry chatted as the three men left the dining room. "What'd you play?"

"Tight-end," replied Taylor.

"You comin,' Grampa?" Nathaniel asked.

Grampa's face was a dark beige and opaque.

"I can see that," nodded Uncle Perry looking at Taylor. "You got the build for it."

"That was a long time ago, I'm afraid," Taylor said.

"You better gone on with 'em, Papa Isaac," clucked Aunt Betty as she refilled her cup. "Sholey God, you not wantin' to sit in here with the women and chirren."

The rest of the afternoon passed with Nathaniel's house traditionally divided, the women in one part and the men in the other. Little Evie, old enough to decide on her own where she wanted to be and able to get there on her own too, kept wandering back and forth between us. For a while Nate tried to do the same thing, toddling more and crawling less, until he reached the comfortable conclusion that his mother's lap was the best place of all. Eventually he was napping in Connie's arms, as we three women nibbled at smaller slices of pie and cake, and sipped coffee made creamy with Carnation evaporated milk. Aunt Betty's percolator was seeing heavy duty today with the seven adults being serious coffee drinkers, and Aunt Betty and I taking turns making sure that the men had plenty, as well as cake and pie.

Smoke from Uncle Perry's Pall Malls floated through the house, along with the excited voices of the radio announcers and the living room fans. I should have remembered to bring Taylor's pipe and tobacco. I worried about what else Grampa might say to him. Nathaniel and maybe Uncle Perry would not let things get out of hand. Besides, having been the beam in his own uncle's eye all this time had prepared Taylor well to be the camel in Grampa's throat.

It was kind of pleasant to think of them all in there, even Grampa, with ordinary things in common. Uncle Perry seemed to genuinely like Taylor. This was a glimpse of the world that Jimmy had hoped and died for. Connie and I were of the same mind when it came to football, but if it were powerful enough to bring about such a *cease-fire*, I could certainly learn to appreciate it. They could all just be men, leaving the offense and the defense for a grassy field somewhere else far off.

In the dining room I refilled all of our coffee cups again, adding in Connie's cream and sugar for her too.

"Thank you, Esther," she said, tenderly rocking a sleeping Nate. "So you think you really will go back to college?"

"Why wouldn't she?" Aunt Betty asked.

"I'll go back," I said. "But I've been thinkin' about somewhere closer to home."

"I guess you could do that," Connie said thoughtfully. "Folks talk about Wiley College in Marshall."

"That preacher from Dallas, Reverend Carson went to Bishop," added Aunt Betty. "But won't they make you start over?"

"Not from the beginning," I explained. "I can transfer. People do it all the time."

"Goin' back to New York be better," pronounced Aunt Betty. "That way yo' young man could go with you."

Remembering Danny jarred the timid coziness I was beginning to feel in the dining room.

"Danny wants to live in California," I clarified weakly.

"Danny?" Aunt Betty frowned. "What he got to do with it?"

"He wants me to come to California," I said.

He was *settling* things for us there, fixing my *place*, while I was talking about Marshall and New York. Was there even an *us* to *settle* for?

"I don't know if yo' young man be willin' to wait, what another two years?" Aunt Betty considered.

"I guess it's somethin' we'll have to talk about," I replied emptily.

"Either way you might have to end up choosin' one over the other," said Connie.

"Connie right," Aunt Betty agreed as she sliced another very narrow sliver of the sweet potato pie. "And you gon' have to be quick about it too, seem to me. Ain't no sense in waitin' forever fo' you start a family."

I did have to wait until I had a husband, I thought.

"Maybe I'm just destined to be everybody's favorite auntie," I offered, smiling at Nate who was snuggled securely in his mother's arms. "That wouldn't be so bad."

"An ol' maid school teacher," Connie said soberly.

"Better than bein' just an old maid," I tried to be funny. "At least I can pay my own way."

"In the meantime what you gon' do with that man in yond'a?" Aunt Betty queried.

I looked at my aunt dumbly.

"Which one of 'em?" Connie asked.

"I was talkin' 'bout Papa Isaac," Aunt Betty said. "But you right, could be either one. They both love you to distraction."

They spoke of it so easily. As if it were nobody's scandal. Just a simple statement of the obvious. A natural thing and nobody's news. As if I wasn't a *nigga-maid* or a *nigger-bitch*.

"Aunt Betty, Taylor is my friend," I declared yet again.

"Ain't nothin' to be 'shamed of,'" said Aunt Betty. "He done claimed you. It's all over him when he look at you. All over you too for that matter."

What was? The roses that had now rushed back into my cheeks? Had she seen Taylor squeeze my hand? Did I once again have the *smell of a man* on me? No wonder Grampa was so unforgiving. Perhaps bringing Taylor to Nathaniel's table was worse than wearing his pearls.

"We're just friends," I insisted lamely. "That's all."

Aunt Betty stirred her coffee and shook her head. Connie looked at me, as she smoothed her hand over Nate's little back lovingly.

"She don't trust it, Mama Betty," she said. "You can't blame her. It'll be hard. Folks'll talk, maybe worse. I guess they'll just have to get over it."

"Danny wants to come to see me," I announced feebly. "Maybe he can come for Christmas. He's back from Korea. Did I tell you that the Army got him stationed in California? That's why he wants me to move out there. California's a nice place to live. All those oranges and movie stars. Can you imagine me going for walks on the beach?"

Great beaches.

Separate ones.

Were they separate in California too?

"He wants me," I said, my voice chiming strangely in the dining room, as the background of male voices erupted at various points from the living room. "He wants to marry me," my desperation trailed off into silence.

"Yeah," Aunt Betty eventually said after a time. "I got a cousin that lives in Los Angeles. It's real nice she say." But then Aunt Betty shook her head again. "You not wantin' to go to California, Esther Fay."

"She know it, Mama Betty," said Connie. "In her heart she do anyway."

Aunt Betty sipped her coffee. Nathaniel's voice suddenly boomed a cheer over something that had happened in the game. Baby Nate slumbered on peacefully.

"It would be easier to finish school in New York," I admitted. "The dean wanted me to be a tutor."

"What's that?" asked Aunt Betty.

"It's like being a teacher," I explained. "But to one person at a time."

"That's good, right?" asked Connie. "Askin' you to teach already?"

I nodded.

"Then that settles it," declared Aunt Betty. "You goin' back to New York. They pay you to do—what you call it—tuder, right?"

"Tutoring," I supplied. "Yes ma'am."

"Well it's best for everybody. Me and yo' uncle been worried 'bout you. It used to trouble me somethin' terrible thinkin' of you livin' with that man like that. And we would-a come and got you too, but you so hard-headed. You sho' 'nough is yo' granddaddy's chile, just as sho' is you James Allen's, I tell you the truth. When that man give you them pearls it 'bout give me a stroke. We expectin' big things out of you, Esther Fay, and shackin' ain't got no part in it."

Shackin'-up is a sin, Esther.

"But Nathaniel told us it wasn't like that 'tween y'all," continued Aunt Betty. "He said that man thinks the world of you, and wouldn't do nothin' to hurt you. How if he could, he'd-a been done married you. I heard tell of it bein' like that sometimes 'tween colored and whites. And today I seen it for myself the way he feels about you."

"We're friends, Aunt Betty," I recited.

"Ain't no shame in it, Esther Fay," Aunt Betty said. "Don't care what people say. Sister Wright and her kind gon' do they talkin'. They ain't nothin' but gossips no how. But my boy's right. The Lord put you together for a reason." Aunt Betty looked at Connie. "You said it wasn't no confusion 'til other folks got in it. I b'lieve you right too. Real love is bound and determined. Can't nobody block it."

What's s'pose to be will be.

"You don't want to lie on love, Esther," Connie now warned. "You ought not to say it's not real when it is. You might as well be blasphemin' the Holy Spirit, and you can't get forgiveness for that."

Late in the day it started to rain. The room darkened and Aunt Betty turned on a light.

"How long that football game gon' last anyhow?" she inquired of no one in particular.

"Should be 'bout over," Connie answered her. "Wake up, Nate," she disturbed the baby's nap and he started to cry.

"What you go and do that for?" demanded Aunt Betty.

"If he sleeps all day, Muh'dear," Connie told her, "What you think the night'll be like?"

She passed the wailing child over to me.

"Here, go to yo' Aunt Esther, and let me go see what Evie's up to in there this long. You know how men are. That chile could be in the heater and they prob'ly wouldn't even notice."

Nate was very annoyed and showed it loudly. He squirmed in my arms and I stood up to bounce him around better, hoping that this would comfort or at least distract him.

"Lord, Nate," even his benevolent grandmother had to say. "Where's his pacifier?"

"Connie doesn't like to use it," I replied.

"Well, Good Lord," complained Aunt Betty. "Stick his finger in his mouth or somethin'."

I walked around the dining room and ultimately wandered into the living room after Connie.

"What you do to 'im?" Nathaniel asked when I came into the room with the bawling baby.

Taylor grinned.

"We woke him up," answered Connie. "And he gets up grouchy just like his daddy. Come on, Evie. I think you done worried Mr. Taylor long enough for one day."

Little Evie, happily sitting in Taylor's lap again, looked up at her mother, but put her little arms tightly around Taylor.

"She's fine," Taylor said.

"No-sir, I better take her," replied Connie.

Reluctantly Little Evie went to the arms of her mother. As soon as she did, I saw him rub his right thigh and knee. He must be tired, and I thought that we should go home. *Home.* His home of course. I was already at home. Oh well. Nate was enough to grapple with for now.

"Have mercy, Evie, what's this 'round yo' neck?" Connie asked.

It was Taylor's silk tie.

"She took a fancy to it," explained Taylor.

"Nathaniel, how you gon' sit up here and let the child play with Taylor's good tie?" Connie demanded with Little Evie sitting on her hip. She was attempting to remove the tie, but Little Evie struggled against her to keep it on.

"Huh?" replied Nathaniel absently. "Oh, that's 'tween them."

"I suppose it makes about as much sense around her neck as it does around mine," Taylor said, still smiling but now at the mother and daughter engaged in their own battle.

"Good clothes is not for playin' with," Connie chided everyone involved. "Let it go, Evie."

When she pulled it out the child's hand, Little Evie's face curdled too.

"He give it to her," said Grampa.

"Esther, I wish to God, you'd take that hollin' boy back in yond'a somewhere," complained Uncle Perry, hunching over closer to the radio. "We's at the end and I can't hear nothin' but that boy's mouth."

"Come on Esther, let's go find these chirren somethin' to hush 'em up," Connie said.

"Lord please, do!" pleaded Uncle Perry.

In the kitchen again, Connie gave Nate and Little Evie apple slices. This assuaged Little Evie's frustrations and gave Nate a reason to be quiet. I admired that about Connie. I admired her for many reasons.

"We ought to get goin'," I said. "I think Taylor's tired. It's been a long day."

"He don't look ready to go to me," Connie replied.

"His leg's bothering him. You know how men are."

"Yeah maybe, but I know you too."

"What does that mean?"

"It means you not his nurse anymore, Esther," Connie said. "Let the man be a man."

The way I touched him now, the way I had always touched him. Connie sliced off another piece of apple and handed it to Little Evie. Nate looked bothered by this despite the fact that he was still clutching an apple slice in his hand. Connie sliced another piece and gave him a second one too.

"And you be a woman," she finished.

I wanted to confess how much we were man and woman, in spite of the *gentlemen's agreement* and Matilda's memory. I wanted to tell Connie about all the secret moments when boundaries blurred or simply disappeared. When the rules and rituals of engagement submitted to a natural law. I wanted to say how Taylor's hands felt on me, what his breath was like in my face. I was ready to tell her how hard and strong his body was against me, how the woman that I was warmed and primed for the man that he was. I wanted to admit to everything. But I said nothing. Because it was still a secret, even if everybody seemed to know the truth.

It was easy for Connie to tell me how to be with Taylor because she was with Nathaniel, and they had everybody's blessings. I had legacies and debts, and a love for the wrong man. I got up from the table, went to the sink, and started rinsing out our coffee cups.

"You make it sound so simple, Connie," I settled for saying as the water flowed over my hands and into the cups.

"If I do," she said. "I don't mean to. But just how long you think you can sit straddle a fence? Sooner or later you gotta come down on one side or the other. If nothin' else the wind'll blow you over. I do feel sorry for you, Esther. It can't be easy bein' pushed and pulled in all directions. But it's left up to you to stop it. Sometimes you just have to do right by yo'self. It'll work out. You'll see."

Think for yo'self, Baby Sister. Every tub's gotta sit on its own bottom.

"I'm scared," the two words stunned even me bursting from between my lips.

"Of what?" Connie asked after a time as the children chewed their apple slices.

"I don't know," I said honestly.

Was I afraid of hurting Grampa or myself? Was I afraid of losing what I was not entitled to in the first place? I wasn't Laura Spalding or Sylvia. I didn't have Mandy's courage. Or Connie's confidence. It was only an *attachment*, something convenient and expedient, until Taylor recovered. It was only an *arrangement*.

That house gon' have a mistress one day.

"Job feared a fear and it came upon him," Connie said.

"I need a continuance," I said.

"It's left up to you to continue or not," replied Connie. "You and Taylor."

I smiled wanly. She didn't understand the legal term, or maybe she did. Aunt Betty came into the kitchen.

"Well, it's over finally," she said. "I think we gon' be goin', Connie."

"Us too," I echoed.

"Ain't no need of y'all hurryin'," Connie mildly protested. "I can heat somethin' up. Y'all welcome to stay and have supper with us."

"Chile, I don't want to see no mo' food 'til next week!" exclaimed Aunt Betty. "I'm still full as a tick. Besides, we got to get Papa Isaac on to the house."

"Well just loosen yo' girdle," kidded Connie.

Connie giggled, drawing me in.

"I done told you about that hot mouth of yours, Constance Green," Aunt Betty retorted. "You wait, Lil' Evie gon' sass you one day, and I'll get to tell you 'bout it."

But it was all in fun, and the day had been good, and when we were all gathered in Nathaniel' front room again, I suggested to Taylor that we should be going too. Whatever Connie thought about it, I could tell that Taylor was tired, even though he smiled pleasantly covering it. He would have stayed as long as I liked, and he would have liked it too, but I needed to get him home. I went to retrieve his tweed jacket from the coat rack by the front door and held it for him as he slipped his arms through the sleeves.

"Connie, Nathaniel, thank-you again for a wonderful dinner," he said.

I was putting on my own coat.

"We was glad to have you," Connie told him brightly.

"You're a fantastic cook," Taylor complimented her once more. "I see now how your husband keeps so robust."

"You ain't got too much room to talk, Taylor," replied Nathaniel. "Esther done put some meat on yo' bones too."

Everyone laughed—well, almost everyone.

"We enjoyed you," said Uncle Perry, and he even patted Taylor lightly on the back, as if he were one of the young brethren at Sweet Water.

"We sho' did," Aunt Betty chimed in.

"It's a pleasure to meet you, Mrs. Green," Taylor replied. "I hope to see you again. You must come to the house. I think you'd be pleased."

"The pleasure's ours," enthused Aunt Betty. "The chirren speak real highly of you, and I see what they mean."

We were getting no closer to the front door, and I wanted to get Taylor home where he could rest.

"Well, we better say goodnight," I urged. "Night-night, sweetie," I said kissing Little Evie.

Then quickly I moved to peck everyone else on the cheek—well, almost everyone. Grampa hung back, standing next to the heater.

"Goodnight, Grampa," I said going to him and kissing him last.

I hugged his stiffened form, and after I stepped back he nodded slightly. I supposed it couldn't be a good night to him. I was leaving with Taylor. But we had an *agreement*. I had until Christmas.

"Goodnight, Mr. Green," said Taylor, who waited for me at the front door.

Grampa nodded again.

When we were at last on the front porch, Nathaniel, taking note of the rain, decided that Taylor and I needed an umbrella and went back into the house to get us one.

"Thanks," I said taking it and opening it up over our heads.

"You should go on ahead, Esther," Taylor advised, but I hooked my arm through his. "You're going to get wet," he warned.

"So?" I replied lightly. "We'll dry."

We were smiling at each other as we carefully started down the porch steps. Taylor's right shoe scraped along the wet red brick path to the driveway. The umbrella helped, but there was enough wind to blow the cold rain into our faces. As we were nearing the car, Grampa called after us. "What you hear from that Simmons boy?" he asked. "Wasn't he comin' to town for Thanksgivin'?" Taylor stopped.

"Come on," I said to him. "We're going to get wet."

"Answer him," he replied.

I looked at him.

"It doesn't matter, Taylor."

"Answer him," he repeated, his expression blank.

"I-I haven't heard from him, Grampa," I lied loudly.

When we reached the car I offered to drive. "I can manage," Taylor said. I opened the car door and tried to keep the umbrella over both of us while Taylor lifted his legs into the car. Once he was in I shut the door and hurried back up to the house, where Grampa still stood with Nathaniel on the porch. As I was closing the umbrella to give it back to Nathaniel, he said that I should keep it, but I shook my head.

"You better," Grampa told me. "Be done drowned settin' yo' pace to that man."

"Why'd you bring up Danny like that, Grampa?" I demanded angrily, standing in the rain. "You got no right--"

"You watch yo' mouth, gal," he cut me off. "I say what I want when I want."

"You said it to hurt him. Never in my life did I take you for mean, Grampa. Never."

"Esther Fay," cautioned Nathaniel.

"If speakin' the truth is mean then I'm gon' be mean. 'Cause I'm not gon' stand 'round here and watch you throw yo' life away behind a man you can't have."

"If I am throwing my life away, it's mine to throw away. Not yours."

I ran back to the car, where Taylor waited.

"Did I take his place today?" he asked me once I was in the car.

Grampa had known just what to say to ruin an otherwise encouraging day, finding the weakness between us and gouging at it.

"I don't understand," I lied.

Taylor did not look at me.

"Did I take his place, Esther?" he repeated the question. "Tell me the truth."

"No," I said.

And it was the truth. Because the *place* was his, his alone.

"Taylor, Grampa didn't mean...I mean we wanted--"

"I understand," he said and started the car.

But how could he, when I didn't? Although perhaps I really did, and just didn't like it, didn't want it, and felt hopeless about it. The drive back to Webster Road was silent, except for the rhythmic beat of the wiper blades. Taylor focused on the road. His left foot was much stronger than the right one but it wasn't completely reliable and he still used the hand controls. I thought of his mother and father, how the roads had been wet the night they had died. I looked over at him. The *place* was his. I just couldn't figure out how to be there with him.

When we arrived at the house Taylor pulled the car into the garage and at last spoke to me again.

"Do you mind bringing me the other crutch?" he asked sounding weary.

"I can help you," I offered.

Still he looked straight ahead, his hands gripping the steering wheel.

"Just get me the other crutch, please."

"Taylor--"

"Dammit, Esther!" he swore throwing open the car door. "Can you never do what I ask you?"

Lurching out of the car, he slammed the door behind him, and hobbled towards the house.

...Just how long you think you can sit straddle a fence?

I got out of the car too. The end was coming. Just not today.

Men were foolish creatures. All men. Colored and white. Old and young. So foolish that they made everything that much harder, when you were desperately trying to make it all work out for the best. They wanted to make your decisions. To push you and pull you by their own sense of direction. No, you need never *borrow* trouble. It was indeed the one thing that everybody gladly gave you for free.

I hurried after Taylor. It had almost been a good day. Almost. Why was the best so often only an *almost?* Brothers dying in late winter taking mothers with them. Leaving daughters behind with unfinished educations. To love forbidden men until they married the right ones. And moved to California, to the land of wine and make believe.

When I caught up with Taylor, I once again hooked my left arm firmly with his right.

"I can manage," he said grimly.

"I know," I replied, holding onto him, refusing to let go. "I just want to be with you."

He stopped, meeting my eyes. He was tired and wounded. The rain was cold, and we were both soaked.

"Esther, I can't--"

"Please, Taylor," I interrupted him. "Let me be with you."

IV

Like last year, Mr. Leon would be delivering the Christmas tree to the house on Webster Road. I wanted it by the first day of December, but Taylor said in his family the custom was to decorate the tree on Christmas Eve, so he wanted to wait until later in the month, and that way the tree would last until Epiphany. "Which is six weeks away," he explained as he was straightening his tie standing before the mirror over the credenza.

I had learned all about Epiphany living with Aunt Grace and Uncle Eddie, and while I liked the idea of extending Christmas into the new year, I was also eager to see the house on Webster Road decorated and anxious for this last holiday with its master to be special, sacred, and something I could remember always. "It can last," I countered, going to the foyer closet for his hat and overcoat. "You just have to keep it watered."

I had already purchased his present. It had been difficult to decide on what to buy for him, since it had to be special, something that he did not already have, and something that he would be able to keep. It would be the first and last gift I would ever give him, and I wanted it to be something that he could have even after there was a real mistress to truly make his house a home.

I had decided to buy him a Bible. His father's was much worn, and if for no other reason than its intellectual value, Taylor should have one of his own. He could use it for a reference. People often quoted the Bible in their secular speeches. Holy Scripture had inspired some of the world's greatest literature, as well as some of the world's greatest lives. I imagined Taylor using it to prepare some closing argument for a case. He was excellent at choosing the right passages. I had sent away for the Bible weeks ago. It was bound in a fine grade of black leather and had the customary gold lettering on the cover. Even the edges of its pages were gilded.

I had also had it inscribed at the booksellers where I had ordered it. The inscription read:

> It is written, "I can do all things through Him that strengthens me."
> Always remember that He loves you too.

Any way that he read it, wherever he placed the emphasis, the words would be true. Yet it would also never be unseemly in his house. I had not signed my name in it just to make sure. I wanted him to be able to have it always. He would never forget who had given it to him.

"Oh let's not wait, Taylor," I wheedled. "I already have your present," I attempted to bribe him. "I want to put it under the tree."

"My present, hmm," he mused.

I held his overcoat for him and he slipped his arms into the sleeves.

"Yes," I said eagerly. "That's the best part of Christmas, the presents under the tree."

Relying mostly on the *Sears Roebuck Christmas Wish Book*, I had already purchased an assortment of toys for Little Evie, Nate, and all of Mandy's children. It was luxurious to have so much of my own money to spend on the children who were so dear to me. I delighted in being called *Aunt Esther*. In addition to the gifts I was personally giving, Taylor had also assigned me the task of shopping for presents from him for all of the children as well, although he had reserved the shopping for Spencer for himself.

"Bearing your name I suppose," Taylor now replied.

I moved in front of him, dotingly buttoning his overcoat against the December chill.

"Not necessarily," I said.

"Why am I not surprised," he smiled, yielding. "All right. I'll let Leon know he can bring the tree this week. Is that soon enough?"

"Thank-you!" I grinned up at him happily.

"Don't look so jubilant," he said. "You used bribery, you know. And it's not like I could ever refuse you anything."

"The tree was here before Christmas Eve last year," I reminded him, moving quickly beyond the thought of having what—who—I wanted always. "And you were already in New York by then. So it's not like it *always* has to be delivered on Christmas Eve."

"A lot was different about last year," he reminded me.

That was true. Last year had been normal. This year was *different*.

"You went to New York last year," I said tentatively. "Do you think you might want—"

"I think I was trying to get away," he admitted.

"From what?" I dared to ask.

From who, I was thinking. Taylor smiled crookedly.

"I don't remember," he replied.

"Well," I said impishly. "It was very nice to have two paid vacations in the same year."

"Little did you know it was to be your last," he said seriously.

I kissed him quickly on the lips.

"I don't think I'm any worse for the wear," I pronounced gaily.

"And certainly I'm the better for it," he returned.

He lowered his dark head, kissing me again, lingering tenderly.

"So we can just count it all joy, just like the Bible says," I concluded once we stood apart again.

"With a minor caveat or two," Taylor corrected me, wearing the sardonic smile again.

Caveats. Yes. And qualifiers. Thanksgiving was over and done with, and not a wholly unhappy memory really. What I had hoped for, for my family to know Taylor, had been accomplished. "He's real decent, Esther Fay," Uncle Perry had said to me the Sunday after Thanksgiving at church, but with his positive assessment had come the *caveat*, the qualifier, "You be careful." So yes, he was a good man, but no, he was not *my* man. And Danny was settling things for us in California, but it was not the life I wanted.

When Mr. Leon brought the tree, we set it up exactly where we had placed it last year, where Jessica Payne would have placed it; Jessica, the woman who had followed both her dreams and her heart, and made her son in a garret apartment without benefit of a marriage license or family approval. Now I really did feel almost close to her.

"Y'all ought to have a mighty fine holiday this year," said Mr. Leon as we stood admiring the tree, a

a lush pine, full and green, and fragrant.

"Yes-sir, Mr. Leon," I said fingering the pine needles on one of the branches. "It's a very nice tree. Mr. Payne will be pleased."

Suddenly tears filled my eyes, spilling down my face. Embarrassed, I hastily wiped them away. Mr. Leon waited.

"You just make sure you make it a happy Christmas this year, miss lady," he said. "That's all you gotta do. Everything else gon' be fine."

...Everything else we let take care of itself.

"I won't be here next year, Mr. Leon," I confessed forlornly.

"Say you won't?" he asked.

I shook my head.

"Where you gon' be?" he wanted to know.

"New York," I replied without hesitation, and in that moment I knew that the matter was finally, truly *settled*.

Mr. Leon nodded approvingly. But this was not the way that Danny was *settling* it.

"I 'spect it's 'bout time," Mr. Leon said.

"Did Tay—I mean Mr. Payne tell you about me going back to school?" I asked, taken aback.

Mr. Leon smiled as he collected the burlap fabric that he had used to wrap the tree in to keep it from dropping needles on the floor as he carried it into the house.

"One thing 'bout goin' from house to house the way I do," he said. "I hear things. People liked to talk. They tell me New York City a fine place to live," he added, bundling up the burlap. "You must-a liked it up there."

"I want to come back though, Mr. Leon. This is home."

You make this house a home.

"That it is," he agreed and started towards the front door. "You'll be back," he asserted confidently as I followed him. "Time not as long as it has been."

When we were standing on the front porch, Mr. Leon stopped and pulled off his work gloves, stuffing them into his pockets.

"Don't rightly know if the Good Lord was born in December," he said thoughtfully looking out over the front yard. "But it seem to me that He could-a been. That way come January when everybody's thinkin' 'bout a fresh start, He be right there with us. 'Course now He with us all the time, but 'tween Christmas and New Year's we just seem to take note of it more." He turned back to me offering me his right hand with a warm smile. "Now you do like I say," he repeated himself with my hand in his. "You make this a happy Christmas."

"Yes-sir," I replied solemnly, and I felt a smile from somewhere deep inside me coming to my face. "Merry Christmas, Mr. Leon."

He tipped his hat to me and strode down the porch steps. I watched him climb up into his truck. I didn't even feel cold standing outside without a coat or a sweater.

That night Taylor made a fire in the living room fireplace. Soon it was crackling and cozy. After dinner he reposed indolently on the sofa reading his newspaper, while I sat cross-legged on the floor in front of the fire making popcorn garlands with a needle and red thread. Next to me lay a dozing Herman. Like last year Spencer had helped me string the lights and place most of the ornaments on the tree in the afternoon, and tonight I was adding the finishing touches. It was the season of Advent, as I had also learned living with Aunt Grace and Uncle Eddie, and the radio shows were already playing Christmas music. Cheerfully I kept singing along with the carols.

"You used to sing in the choir, didn't you?" Taylor asked as I sang *Hark! The Herald Angels Sing* with a radio choir.

"Is my voice too bad to sing?" I sang, putting my words to the tune.

"Did I say that?" he replied crossly.

"I'm sorry," I apologized, giggling because I thought I was funny.

"You have a lovely voice, Esther," he said glumly from behind his newspaper.

When I smiled up at him he didn't see it.

"Sister Wright thinks it's too deep for a woman," I said. "She always made me sing with the men."

"Lucky them."

"You're very kind."

I took a garland over to the tree, deliberating a moment before placing it exactly in the right spot. With his parents smiling blissfully over us, the lights on the tree twinkling, the fire in fireplace bright, we might have made the face of a greeting card—except for our faces. Tomorrow I would begin putting the gifts under the tree. Spencer would undoubtedly try to secretly investigate the names on the packages, and I supposed he did have a vested interest. He would be pleased with what he found. Santa Clause was going to be good to him and to his brother and sisters too.

You make this a happy Christmas.

Next year of course, I would not be able to shop for them like this. As a student again, I would be much poorer and have greater expenses. Taylor would be on his own. Next year I would have to be more creative and resourceful than a Sears Roebuck catalog. However, New York was a big and vibrant city, with hundreds of little neighborhood stores and shops, and I could probably find some kind of part-time job to earn a little money while I finished my studies. Christmas in New York might not be so bad, and Grampa would probably prefer it if I didn't come home, believing that I would be safer away from temptation.

It's a wonder our paths never crossed, Esther.

Taylor had been thinking about museums while Laura Spalding had been thinking about murder, or some other terrible thing. Yet the madness could never have been more than temporary. She, like all the rest, would have her chance with him again. Next year. I would be out of the way. Next year I would have to shop early enough to mail packages back to McConnell County. Mandy would help Taylor buy for the children. I returned to my place in front of the fire and resumed threading the popcorn.

A man had my whole heart, and my whole life was changed, irrevocably changed. And Danny needed to know. He didn't have to know why, but he had a right to know. And soon.

From the radio came the music from *The Nutcracker* ballet. The *Waltz of the Flowers* began, and I remembered going to the ballet matinees with Aunt Grace and her friends, the way we would get all dressed up, Aunt Grace and her friends in their fur stoles and fine jewels, and me, the grateful but plain protégé, basking in their elegant company and expensive perfume. Now because of Taylor I would have my own pearls to wear. I swayed easily to the music. I had enjoyed the ballet even though there had rarely been a colored ballerina for us to see, and in my experience a small hammer was a nutcracker, not some enchanted wooden soldier that magically turned into a prince.

"You like that, do you?" asked Taylor.

"What?" I asked looking up at him.

Herman sighed and stretched lazily.

"The music," Taylor answered. "The look on your face says you're a thousand miles away."

Was that the distance between McConnell County and New York City? I laughed lightly.

"It's a waltz, right?" I asked him about the music playing.

"That's right," he said.

"One-two-three. One-two-three," I counted thoughtfully, nodding my head in time. "One-two-three. One-two-three. It seems easy," I decided. "Someday I'm going to learn."

In the bright orange and gold flames, I saw myself whirling around gracefully, as I had seen the beautiful women do on the stages in New York. The magic prince was a lord of the manor, with black hair and very dark brown eyes.

"Too bad I can't teach you," the magic prince spoke into my fantasy.

I looked away from the flames and back to his face. Taylor was getting better with the cane, and soon I was certain it would replace the crutch all together. Before very much longer there would be no sign of the polio at all. He had already left the worst of it behind him. He did not need me anymore.

"You can," I said encouragingly.

"I think I'd have a little trouble moving in time," he said in his usual matter-of-fact way and resumed reading the newspaper.

"You might be surprised," I told him.

"I know, Esther," he replied, still reading. "Keep the faith."

"Yes," I said emphatically.

"Well, for you, my dear," he declared. "Anything."

I would do anything for you.

Would he at least write to me? Would he send me one of his succinct little notes to show that he treasured the memory of this little time together too? Perhaps he would send his regards through Mandy; or maybe even Nathaniel, with whom I was sure he would stay friends. Or Spencer. I could picture him helping Spencer write to me. After all, if a little child could lead us, then perhaps one could keep us connected.

Tomorrow, along with the gifts for the children, I would put Taylor's Bible under the tree. I had wrapped it in a bright red foil and tied it with a gold ribbon. It looked regal, befitting a prince. Maybe he would let me invite Mandy and her children over so we could give them their gifts together. It would be a very *different* party from the one last year with the Mitchells and the Spaldings, but Taylor would enjoy it and perhaps more so. He could get to know the rest of Mandy's family. She should be giving her notice soon. The thought of children's laughter filling the house actually made me happy.

You make this a happy Christmas.

It would be my only one with him, but it would be mine to keep always.

Tchaikovsky's flowers waltzed alone and the sugar plum fairy finished her dance. The Christmas concert concluded and a new radio program began, featuring more of the classics: Bach, Beethoven, and Mozart. I had purposely set the dial away from the Blues tonight. Soon it would be time for the Blues all the time, and I didn't want to be gloomy before I had to be. I was glad for Aunt Grace's pretentious lessons in music appreciation. All those New York concerts and parlor-room and church-dinner recitals had made me comfortable with what Grampa referred to as *white folks' music*. From Aunt Grace and her friends I had learned that *colored folks* possessed and played the classics too. W.E.B. DuBois would have been proud of the standards my aunt and uncle's social circle set. I wondered if Taylor had ever met him, and guessing that he would have mentioned it if he had, I didn't ask him now. Instead I just enjoyed *our* music, satisfied to let myself relax and float in the *air on a G String*.

Meeting the warm glow of the room, the cold of the night condensed and covered the window panes. The lamp light turned the pane-glass into a mirror, capturing our reflections. Taylor was again engrossed in his treasured *New York Times*. The stories made his face thoughtful, occasionally wrinkling his brow. What could those distant reporters possibly have to say to the life he lived here in McConnell County? I smiled looking at his reflection. Maybe the *New York Times* was to him what the Bible was to me, distant and yet relevant, and so revered. His own kind of good news from his own kind of heavenly home. Once I was back in Harlem, reading the *Times* every day would let me feel still linked to him. I would be able to imagine him reading the same stories. Maybe he would eventually move back to New York one day too. He belonged there. In one of those towering office buildings, busy Manhattan below, and Broadway and Central Park available to him. We might really run into each other someday. Perhaps in a museum, in front a Winslow Homer painting, *our paths* might cross.

I turned back to watching the fire dance and threading the popcorn.

"A penny for your thoughts," Taylor said after a while.

"Oh," I looked up at him and smiled. "I was remembering going to the theater."

"With your aunt and uncle?"

"My aunt and her friends mostly," I replied watching the fire. "Uncle Eddie isn't really the theater-type. On special occasions my aunt makes him get dressed up so he can take her to something big, but he never looks very comfortable. I guess he's a country boy at heart."

"But they're happy there?" asked Taylor. "In New York?"

"Harlem," I clarified. "But, yes. They've done well for themselves."

"Did you like it there? I don't think you've ever said."

I looked up at him again.

"Yes," I replied and smiled. "It was *different*."

"Would you go back?" he asked.

"Yes," I said. "If I got the chance."

But without him I would be *settling* for New York too. Perhaps I had become the *wayfaring soul*. The newspaper rustled as Taylor turned its pages. The fire was warm to my face. Herman, too, must be basking in it radiance. It wasn't Grampa's beloved wood heater, but it had become familiar to me. I knew it. Like I knew this house. And this man. And this dog curled up next to me as if he were my own. I would miss this and them, but I was thankful that I had had it all even for a little while.

"You must have seen plenty of white Christmases," I said later on.

"Yes," replied Taylor.

"I've never seen one."

"What about when you were in New York?"

"I always came home for Christmas."

"I suppose it's a fleeting pleasure at best," said Taylor. "The snow melts and then it's not so beautiful."

Between us we had shared a montage of *fleeting pleasures*, of tiny instances of triumph and tenderness, the memories of which would always be beautiful.

"My grandfather always insisted that I be home for Christmas," I explained. "But I really would like to see snow on Christmas some day, like on Christmas cards."

"Does your Aunt Grace come home for Christmas?" asked Taylor.

Aunt Grace rarely came home at all, except for weddings and funerals. And now that it was going to be over between Danny and me, who knew when the family would see Aunt Grace and Uncle Eddie again. To see me graduate from college, we'd have to persuade Grampa to travel north. Nathaniel had a nice car. The drive wouldn't be so bad. Then Grampa should see how well Uncle Eddie had provided for his baby daughter.

"She's married," I explained. "Her home is with Uncle Eddie. Fathers rule until husbands do."

"It's a man's world, I suppose," said Taylor.

"Without a doubt," I agreed.

"Not too many opportunities for a white Christmas in Los Angeles either," he added.

The reference was simple, composed, and it jarred my tranquility. Vigilantly I kept the subject away from us, like the end that was coming. Besides there was nothing to discuss. I was going back to Harlem. I focused on the popcorn garland lengthening in my lap.

You just make sure you make it a happy Christmas this year, miss lady. That's all you gotta do.

"That's true," I replied.

"It's an arid land," Taylor observed.

And there was nothing there for me. Taylor was wrong too if he thought I would be spending my holidays in the land of make-believe and sunsets. The newspaper rustled behind me again. I breathed deeply. It was calming to finally know the truth. I could be at peace.

"It must have been convenient going to college where you grew up," I said changing the subject, as I pulled the red thread through a fluffy kernel.

"For Uncle Jason," Taylor granted, letting go the reference to Los Angeles.

The newspaper rustled.

"He kept a close eye on Felicia," he continued. "There'd be no more star-crossed lovers on his watch."

Shakespeare, I thought. Jessica would have made the perfect *Juliette*, with her Andrew as *Romeo*. But they had had a happy ending for a little while anyway. Perhaps happiness just couldn't last forever. Perhaps the sooner you accepted that the better. What rebellious trait had Jessica imparted to her son that she had not given to her daughter? What made them both so determined to be *different*? A million caveats and qualifiers had not kept Andrew and Jessica apart. In the end it had been like Grampa always said, nobody could block it. What was supposed to be was, and here was their son, the blessed proof of it. But color was more than a caveat. Race didn't just qualify, it disqualified. But still, we were happy now.

"Is that what he tried to do with you?" I asked Taylor about his uncle as I returned to the Christmas tree to hang another garland. "Keep an eye on you to keep you out of trouble?"

"Maybe," replied Taylor indifferently. "Probably."

"Until you eventually moved away. He must have been disappointed when you moved to New York."

"You might say in our case low expectations left little room for disappointment," he said.

When I was satisfied with the latest garland's placement I went back to my spot in front of the fire to make more.

"At least you can say you're Harvard man," I said. "That must have pleased your uncle."

"Not completely. My law degree's from Columbia."

"Columbia University?" I asked, looking up from my garland-making. "In New York City?"

"I believe there's only the one," replied Taylor from behind the newspaper.

"Not Harvard Law School?" I persisted.

He lowered the newspaper, and smiled at me in his indulgent way.

"No, not Harvard, Esther. Don't look so disappointed. Columbia's a fine institution in its own right. And it's where Roosevelt studied the Law. You liked Roosevelt, right?"

"But I thought...I mean... your father, and your grandfather, your uncle...they-they all went to Harvard."

"Not every tradition has to be kept exactly, Esther," Taylor said. "There's nothing wrong with putting your own spin on it sometimes. Not to mention starting your own."

"Doing things differently, as it were," I smiled at him.

"Yes."

I went back to my needle, thread, and popcorn. He was his mother's son.

The radio orchestra began Beethoven's Piano Sonata in C-Sharp Minor, the *Moonlight Sonata*. There was no moonlight tonight. The clouds had been thick and gray all day with winter's coming. Listening for a moment longer to be sure that we could dance to it, I left the popcorn and red thread and went to Taylor, holding out my hand.

"What is it?" he asked looking up from his newspaper.

"Dance with me," I said.

His face changed, becoming blank.

"Please Esther, don't," he said.

"Don't you want to?" I asked.

According to Mrs. Shaw, it was the male voice in the movement that pressed his passion upon his beloved, and it was the female voice that protested the indiscretion of it. I hoped I could be forgiven for being a tenor.

You have a lovely voice, Esther.

In any case I had a strong voice. Taylor didn't move, but I stayed standing in front of him with my hand offered. Silently he studied it, brown and steady before him, as the lovers in the piece inevitably began to come together.

"As much as I've ever wanted anything in my life," answered Taylor, and the sudden sadness I heard was unsettling.

You make this a happy Christmas.

"Then don't refuse me," I insisted. "Besides, I thought you were a gentleman," I gently teased him. "You wouldn't tell me no if I were Laura Spalding, now would you?"

He finally smiled again, crookedly.

"Esther--"

"I know I don't know how to waltz like she probably does, but I can dance, Taylor. It'll just be different. And you like different."

He sat up straight and folded the newspaper.

"I can't dance anymore, Esther," he said. "I wish I could."

I can't.

Do it. I've got you. I won't let you fall.

"Yes you can," I replied. "Dance with me, Taylor. Like we agreed a long time ago. Now, please, before this music stops."

He removed his glasses.

"Do you mean to make a fool of me?" he asked calmly.

I nearly laughed out loud at the absurdity of such a question, when I only admired him, adored him even, and loved him completely.

"No," I said. "I mean to have what you promised me. It could be your Christmas present to me. Or you can just let it be practice for when you go back to your country club parties."

The female voice was beginning her surrender in urgent high piano notes.

He smiled darkly.

"I see," Taylor said. "More practice. Your way of raising the bar. You're a very demanding woman, Sergeant."

The male voice comforted his beloved as he enveloped her.

"How else do I get what I want?" I asked smiling softly.

"And what do you want, Esther?" he asked.

To be with you forever. Except there was no use in telling him that. This he could not give to me. But I could have this moment, this time.

You make this a happy Christmas.

Maybe it was different in New York City. Maybe in a land of so very many others, maybe otherness ceased to be so important. Maybe in a city big enough for there to be miracles on 34th Street and a Statue of Liberty, no one bothered to care. Maybe people could be left alone to make up whatever worlds they wanted to for themselves. Maybe they could live like they wanted to. And go to the same beaches. Maybe it was the Promise Land, just like Harriet Tubman had promised. Maybe it was like California. Like Paris. But McConnell County was his home. Taylor was a son of the South, and I was its bastard daughter. McConnell County belonged to him, to both of us. It would always claim us. Could we give up who we were, what we were, for each other?

"I want you dance with me, Mr. Payne." I told him now. "Here in this house where we do things differently."

He glanced down at his legs as if they were not a part of him and then looked up at me again.

"This is not a waltz, Esther," he said. "Maybe next time."

But our *next times* were running out. The work of it practically done, our curious little imperative idyll must end. The two piano voices were singing almost as one now. The surrender was sublime but soft, fading into silence. Quickly I went into the study and looking through his record collection, I found a recording of the piece. I turned off the radio and placed the record on the phonograph and came back to Taylor.

"Now it's the next time," I said, waiting in front of him once more.

He smiled again as if my determination amused him.

"So it is," he replied.

When I took hold of his right ankle, he objected.

"Esther," he said. "Please. I can't."

My placing his right foot on the floor compelled him to do the same with the left.

"Dance with me, Taylor," I said again as he sat looking up at me.

Another long moment passed. Finally he reached for the cane.

"This is folly," he protested but he was getting up. "Surely you'd want a more capable partner."

Surely I only wanted him. Looking up into his eyes I took his hand.

"Wait," I let it go abruptly. "I want to start the record over. Don't sit back down."

In the study I repositioned the needle to a point just before the *Moonlight Sonata* began and hurried back to him. Taking away the cane and leaning it against the sofa, I took both of Taylor's hands into mine.

"You intend to hold me up too?" he asked.

"I mean to hold you," I replied leading him towards the middle of the floor.

I placed his hands around my waist.

"At least that's an inviting proposition," he said obliquely.

I smiled.

The fine rug on which we stood was a long way from the floor boards worn down smooth by the feet of my friends and neighbors, jumping and jostling to rhythms much older and more modern than Beethoven's. Yet I was at ease with Mrs. Shaw's lovers, who were once more in the throes of their timeless affair. If only she could see what I had arranged for her *Moonlight Sonata*.

"I'll lead at first until you get it," I said, slipping my arms around him.

"Are you so instructive with all of your partners?" asked Taylor.

"Shhh," I said, carefully attending to the rhythm of the music, keeping the circle around which we moved very small and close. "Concentrate."

His right leg was like an anchor, we couldn't move very far or very fast; and if I did dream of Paris, this place, this house, was the safest of harbors to me, and exactly where I wanted to be.

"It is customary for the man to lead, madam," Taylor protested, although he was finally really smiling too, even in his eyes.

"I thought you didn't care about breaking traditions, Mr. Payne," I reminded him, as I acquiesced to his lead now that our steps were matched.

"Some are worth keeping," he returned.

I beamed at him.

"And you'll be the judge of that, I suppose."

"Fathers rule until husbands do, you said so yourself."

"And you are neither," I laughed as I watched our feet. "See!" I declared excitedly. "You're doing it!"

"Determined to make me a believer, aren't you?" he asked.

"In yourself, yes."

There was no soft rustle of a taffeta gown. I was wearing one of my mother's black dresses as usual, and he wore a plain white shirt, with the sleeves rolled up to the elbow and open at the collar. The orchestra was a record, and even the pearl necklace was upstairs in its case. Still I was in Taylor's arms and it felt like being in the clouds. I let go of him again and quickly removed my cardigan sweater, tossing it onto the sofa. It landed near the abandoned cane.

"Did I do that with enough flair?" I asked.

He laughed.

"If you are trying to seduce me, Miss Allen, you'll get no fight from me," he replied.

I slipped my arms around his neck.

"I'm just trying to be sophisticated enough for you, sir," I giggled. "You know, have the right style."

"Style?" he smiled. "You're bewitching."

"In the kitchen, as I recall."

His smiled changed into a frown.

"It is what you said," I reminded him.

"When?" he wanted to know. "When did I say that?"

Now I laughed, because I was the one under a spell. I pressed myself against him more closely, and he closed his arms around me more tightly.

"You're beautiful, Esther," he murmured into my ear.

"You're very kind," I whispered back.

He held me away from him for a moment to look into my face.

"It's not flattery," he said firmly. "You must trust me about that. And believe in yourself too, while you're at it."

I did. At times my heart broke into pieces because I did, but tonight I was just happy.

You make this a happy Christmas.

"I do," I replied.

"Say it then," said Taylor.

"What?"

"That you trust me."

"I trust you."

He held me against him again and for some time neither of us spoke.

"Just what dance are we doing anyway?" he asked eventually. "Since it's certainly not a waltz."

"Down at Ray's they call it a slow drag," I told him.

"Perfect," he observed ironically.

"It is perfect," I agreed, but for different reasons.

When I pressed my pelvis against his, he gazed down at me with eyes as bright as the flames playing around Mr. Leon's logs in the fireplace, and I could feel his passion.

"Is this something akin to dancing in the spirit, my dearest?" he whispered huskily.

"Um-hmm," I replied dreamily, the side of my face against his broad chest, breathing in a faint scent of bergamot and pipe tobacco.

Taylor's halting steps were transformed in the security of our tiny circle, and the angels were dancing very gracefully on the head of a pin to Beethoven's very beautiful composition, Beethoven who had been deaf but still able to hear with his heart. Raising my face, Taylor looked into my eyes again.

"What is it?" I asked.

"I just want to look at you," he said before kissing me.

"Hear how she submits to him?" I asked as the music swelled.

"Who are you talking about?" Taylor asked.

"The lovers," I explained. "In the music. She tries to resist him but she can't. He's too strong, and she wants him too much."

"Is that what you hear?" asked Taylor. "Surrender?"

"Yes."

"An unusual interpretation."

"Perhaps it's just my vantage point."

A low chuckle rumbled in his chest as we rocked gently in place, moving in time with the music.

"Will my words always come back to haunt me with you?" he asked.

The feminine protest was fading. We kissed again, the way I had always imagined the lovers would do had they ever been more than just perfect notes played on a piano. I consoled myself with the knowledge that these *fleeting pleasures* would never be forgotten.

Perhaps there were really such things as Christmas miracles. I drifted on the music, feeling as though I were gliding slowly, across a quiet country prairie on a fair-weather night. We were traveling back through thousands of years before there was segregation and slavery, or even the ambitious Constitution. Before there were continents and cultures. Before anyone had eaten of the fruit and sentenced themselves to reason. We were in a time when there was only Adam and Eve, male and female. And paradise. I blessed Mrs. Shaw for giving me this anthem to remember Taylor by.

"Do you think she loses?" he asked in my ear. "By surrendering?"

"No," I replied. "It's what she wants."

Like his mother, I thought.

You make this a happy Christmas.

Mrs. Shaw had said that although in the end it was only the male voice that you heard, it was gentler for her influence, for what she had brought to his deep resonant chords. She was gone, but it was only to deeply inside of him. The two of them were one in the end. Just like the Bible said. *For this cause shall a man leave his father and mother, and cleave to his wife.* That was the hopeful way to understand it, I thought, although maybe it was only that she had had to finally go far away, leaving him alone.

PART EIGHT

I

The next morning, once I had seen Taylor off to his office, I went to his desk in the study and took out three sheets of his writing paper. I wouldn't need three pages for the length of the message I intended to write. There must not be a lot of words. The extra paper was for the anticipated false starts and necessary practice. Few words meant that they had to be perfect ones.

It was wasteful to use such nice paper for drafting but at least it was getting some use. I caressed the embossed **TAP** in the center-top of the page, as if the initials were the man himself. He rarely wrote a personal letter. At least not to his family. Recalling the note he had included with my wages last year before leaving for Cambridge, I envied him his succinct, clear way with words.

Last night had been too lovely; dancing together in front of the Christmas tree until we had ended the night *dancing* together in his bed. How very *capable* he was everywhere. I smiled and sighed at the same time. Soon I would be gone, and I had no right to feel sorry for myself. I had known all along that it must turn out this way. Surely Taylor knew too. We had simply *agreed* to live day by day, like the birds and flowers in the Bible, with little thought about the tomorrows. But seasons changed. Birds flew away. Flowers faded. I smiled again stroking the raised letters. I would always love him, and he would have the Bible to remind him.

I wished that I had fallen in love with Danny the summer we had met, but there had been so little time. I hardly knew him. I had cared about him, and being Danny's lover had been right to me for all the right reasons. I had been eager for something of life, of nature, and excitement. I just wished that he had somehow sealed me to him, so that

I would have spent all this time longing for him, dreaming of him. Such a love might have kept me away from Taylor far more effectively than Grampa's resentments and a segregated society. I might have still liked him, and been a good servant, even his nurse, but I would not have loved him. Not in this way. I would have reserved myself for a fine Negro man, in accordance with everything that was right and proper. Was that how Taylor had lost Sylvia? Because he had not sealed her to him? But he had given her a ring, and even a pearl necklace could be a very potent thing.

It wasn't human nature to be satisfied. Mama used to say that no matter what God gave us, people were always, *wishin' for meat and wantin' for bread*. Even the Hebrew children rescued from Egypt and slavery had railed against their exodus. *For ye have brought us forth into this wilderness, to kill this whole assembly with hunger.* God made us. He must have known that we would eat the forbidden fruit and crave it endlessly. The desire for that which was not ours always seemed to be more attractive than what we actually had.

Herman had followed me into the kitchen and was loudly lapping up a drink from his water bowl.

I sat down at the kitchen table with the writing paper and a pencil not knowing how to begin. Staring at the blank page I thought about Sylvia and what it must have been like for her to write her *Dear John* letter. How had she told Taylor that she didn't love him anymore or maybe that she had not loved him in the first place? Had she told him in that letter that she was marrying one of his friends instead? How did you take yourself away from somebody? How did you say goodbye when it was forever and you were without the resolution of death? It was one thing to do it when you had no choice, when it was not your decision. A door closing before you was not the same thing as you closing it yourself.

I imagined Taylor's face as he had read Sylvia's letter, how it would have emptied and turned hard, the way Grampa's did when something hurt him or made him angry. It must be pride that dropped the granite curtain to cover a man's face. Feelings that showed vulnerability could not be allowed. I thought about Taylor's face in the foyer with Robert Collier that night, how it had revealed nothing, even though he had been prepared to kill him, and even after it was over.

Negroes weren't the only ones who could wear *the mask*. With Sylvia's letter, Taylor would have veiled the churning emotions of betrayal and grief and anger with his characteristic facade of indifference. He probably hadn't even bothered to tear up the letter as that would have shown too much regard for it. I pictured it now, somewhere decaying into the sand, pieces of it being carried out to sea, a memory washed away just never forgotten, the *better offer* summing up Sylvia's reasons for leaving him. I was leaving him for myself, which was not *better* just *different*.

There were times when the very act of concealing feelings revealed them and attested to their intensity. I knew when Grampa suffered mightily from some word or deed. The very blankness of his expression the day the War Department telegram came, the hours sitting beside Mama's bed, and even on Thanksgiving Day. To me he was as readable as a page in a book. It was the years of living with him and loving him. I had just learned to silently conspire with his impassive expressions, granting him his privacy. Mama had said it was best. "Leave 'im alone, Esther Fay," she used to say. "Everything don't have to be talked about." Like the war-memory clouds crossing Nathaniel's face. Jimmy had said that there were times when a man needed to talk about himself with someone, that it could be *better than dancing*. And both of them were right.

I didn't know what it felt like to be betrayed. Everything—everyone—I had ever believed in had been true. God. Grampa. Jimmy. Nathaniel. Even Mama, and the rest of my family, none of them had ever betrayed me. Not Danny. And not Taylor. Some of them had left me, dying away from me when I needed them, but that wasn't betrayal. There was no lie in dying, no deception. If anything I was the deceitful one. But I had my reasons. My purpose was good. And to everything there was a season and a purpose under Heaven. It was just that any given season ended when its purpose was fulfilled. And so it had come to this, this ending of things, as I had always known it would.

I didn't even feel betrayed by the Constitution, or the dream of America that had persuaded my brother to die for it. How could you be betrayed by what you didn't believe in in the first place? People said that children believed in fairytales, and that women wanted them to come true. In fairytales of glass slippers or ruby ones, everything always turned out perfect like porridge in a bear's bowl so that everybody lived *happily-ever-after*. Like the Constitution, such stories must have been written by men too. They were the true believers. Women knew the truth. Cordelia Collier did. I supposed so did Sylvia. And Jessica, and Mama. And Mandy. You could not make life perfect in this world, no matter how pretty the promises.

You make this a happy Christmas.

I would miss Mr. Leon. I believed in him. Maybe I could make friends with Aunt Grace's milk man. But maybe now I was only being silly, stalling and distracting myself from the task at hand. The blank page waited for me, and the pencil was idle. I wanted—needed—to be concise with my words. They needed to be *beyond a reasonable doubt*. Living in this house I had picked up many legal words and phrases. And I had *lived* here. And learned too. And Taylor had learned from me. We had been each other's teacher, and we had learned together. We were changed. Both of us were.

This was a happy house.

It was a happy house. This house had known joy and triumph. It was a place of books and music, and a boy's laughter; a home to attachments, and commitments, and friendship; to kindness, and courage and faith; to twinkling Christmas trees and lustrous pearls. Jessica's Taj Mahal.

You make this house a home.

Mandy would take very good care of it.

Even ending it with him, Sylvia must have realized how lucky she had been to have Taylor's love. I didn't even believe that Danny loved me and I felt fortunate to have had his regard. I wondered if Taylor had actually asked Sylvia to marry him, or had he just assumed that she would, while he *settled* things for them. Her engagement ring must have been beautiful. Maybe he had knelt down on one knee, like in the movies. I couldn't recall if *Mr. Rhett* had done so for *Miss Scarlett*, and in any case *Mammie* would have been relegated to looking on from her place of invisibility.

I'm invisible to him.

No you're not, Esther. You never were.

But I would be forgotten. Neither man need remember me. I was not the kind of woman that starred in the lyrics of Blues songs, but Sylvia was. Maybe she was why Taylor preferred the Blues as if they were his own. They were. Sylvia had confirmed his doubts about human affections, so that Muddy Waters and Billie Holiday spoke for him too, even if he was an educated white man who believed he ruled the world.

Is that what you think of me?

Yes, I thought this about him, but now it was just one part of the picture. I understood his tendency to be apart. It was his armor, and mostly he lived his life girded for battle. But there could also be times when he wore softer robes, robes silky enough to drop easily away, leaving him naked and tender. I caressed the monogrammed letters again. There could be times when he erased all the distance, when he could be all around you, and within you.

If the war had not taken him away from her, Taylor and Sylvia might have been together still. He might not have come back to McConnell County. I might never have known him.

What's s'pose to be gon' be. Can't nobody block it.

You couldn't make sense of life. The Bible said to count it all joy. The wars, diseases, and broken hearts too. Grampa said our extremities were God's opportunities. Taylor thought it was all just chance.

Somebody wins. Somebody loses. You always know that going in.

Sometimes it turns out perfectly. I'm glad your mother did what was right for herself. Otherwise we wouldn't be here, now would we?

And out in California Danny waited in vain to build a life with me. I wondered what he would make of my new *vantage point*. It was certainly *different* now. I wanted to walk in the law of the Lord, and in Grampa's law too. It was just that in Egypt-land I had sat by the *flesh pots* and ate *bread to the full*.

Herman stood at the back door and barked once indicating that he wanted to go out. I got up from the table and let him out. Standing on the back porch rubbing my arms against the December chill, I watched him go about his business, sniffing at this and that. Like the ravens and the lilies in Luke's Gospel, Herman didn't have to work or worry. He merely had to be. He asked for what he wanted and usually got it. I had worked all my life and worried a good part of it, intent upon earning my place in this world, as limited as it was, yet I was seldom asked what I wanted. On the few occasions when someone did ask I often didn't have an answer. I didn't know how to answer. I wasn't practiced at it. I didn't feel entitled. The world rarely asked you what you wanted when you were a colored woman. You were lucky to get whatever it gave you. I went back in the house and sat down at the kitchen table again.

Perhaps Grampa had not asked Ernestine to marry him either. Perhaps he had also just assumed that she would. A good-looking man like that, ambitious and determined, maybe she couldn't help but to be grateful. No wonder Danny thought all he had to do was make a place for me in his life. I was supposed to be grateful, Grampa had said so. According to Mama all young women were eager for a man's attention, and Grampa had said that he had never seen a woman who couldn't have her head *turned*. Decisive men settled things and thankful women accepted it. But maybe not every time. Sometimes, inadvertently perhaps, such men could raise decisive daughters to be women who could think for themselves, setting their tubs down where they may.

At least Danny was safe and sound in California and not still fighting a war. He was a teacher of soldiers now. It was ironic, me preparing young people to live and him training them to kill. But his wasn't a bad living. The Bible said that there would always be wars. And Danny wasn't just teaching men how to kill, he was also teaching them how to survive. If he was good at what he did, and I was sure that he was, then there would be less Jimmys lost to mothers and sisters, and more Nathaniels coming home to father the next generation.

For a merely handsome woman I seemed to be making a lot of trouble for extraordinary men.

You underestimate the sway of a handsome woman.

It was odd seeing myself in Sylvia's league, or Mandy's for that matter, being desired by exceptional men. Jimmy had been right all along about me *keeping company*, but I couldn't help but to be a little astonished that there was this much bother over someone like me. Beautiful women, with their grace and charms, were entitled to and granted privileges that plain women rarely earned or expected. Yet, amazingly I had become almost as they, esteemed and wanted, and now like Sylvia, preparing to tell a wonderful man that I was choosing not to be with him.

Perhaps I had *redefined* what it meant to be handsome too. Or maybe it was simply that I had come to understand that you didn't have to be a beautiful woman to be valuable, to be worthy. That you didn't have to be married or someone's mother. You didn't even have to be *trained*. You just had to be true. I wasn't giving up Danny for Taylor. I was giving up Danny for myself. Because worse than living alone was living a lie.

You make this a happy Christmas.

The morning was growing late, and I wanted to send Danny the telegram today. There wasn't time for a letter. Danny might be on his way right now to claim what was not his. I had tarried too long. Now I wanted to be sure that the words were right and clear, and already written down before I got to the telegraph office. Now that I was at last doing what needed to be done, saying what needed to be said, I hoped to get it over with as quickly as possible. Like one of St. Luke's ravens I was ready to take flight. With a resolute hand I put the pencil to the paper. "To: Sergeant Daniel Simmons," I began.

Connie had said that to lie on love was to blaspheme the Holy Spirit; and a lie could be to pretend it as much as it could be to deny it. Today, when Danny got this telegram it would be a declaration of the truth, and we would be free.

II

As the bus made its way through town, we passed by the courthouse. I wondered what Taylor was doing. Was he in the courtroom? He must be an imposing figure. The cane—if it came to that permanently—would not take away from his authority. He would always be impressive, and Mandy would make sure that his suits were immaculate, his white shirts starched to perfection.

Spencer would get to see him at trial some day. The boy really wanted to be a lawyer like his most benevolent benefactor. He dreamed of following in the footsteps of the man who could almost be a father to him, in a way that Willie Gains had forfeited in exchange for his own pursuit of the American dream. As Jimmy had done. It was their right, deciding for themselves, and leaving us behind. I hoped that it turned out to be worth it somehow.

There was a good chance that Taylor might see me in town this morning. If he did then I would have to explain myself, which I would of course lie about, because I didn't want him to know what I was doing, because I didn't want him to think that my decision regarding Danny in any way involved him. We had no obligations to each other. With the purpose for our coming together finishing, it was simply time to move on, to return to the lives that were ours in the first place—in the right places, *separately*.

For me this meant going back to Harlem, to my Uncle Eddie and Aunt Grace's house, and City College, and someday a job teaching school; preferably in a new place where no one knew me, not here in McConnell County, where too many people did, or in California, where no one really did. Taylor could stay. Soon enough people would forgive him for his transgressions with his *nigger-maid*. Even Laura Spalding would. It was mostly all my fault anyway. Eve had willfully listened to the serpent, but poor Adam had been tricked. Mandy was right, we were always blamed. We blamed ourselves. The eternal lesson was that you should not trust a woman.

I must have somewhere to put what little faith I do have.

Women were disobedient and deceitful. I had merely proved the point. At least Danny would think so. But I was correcting everything now. *Settling things* in my own way. And if I couldn't make it a *happy Christmas*, like Mr. Leon wanted, at least I would make it a resolved one. Danny would soon get over the disappointment of never knowing me. The bus approached the Western Union office and I reached up to pull the bell cord. Taylor would find somewhere else to place his faith. He was after all most comfortable with the Law.

When I got off the bus, the cold wind blew into my face. Head down, I walked swiftly to the telegraph office. A bell above the door clanged loudly announcing me, and the operator looked up. Thankfully there was no one else in the office. Sending the telegram could go quickly.

"What can I do for you?" the operator, a white man in rolled-up shirt sleeves and a green eye-shade visor, asked.

"Yes-sir," I replied deferentially as I approached the counter, pulling off my gloves. "I want to send a wire."

Keeping my eyes down, I opened my pocketbook and took out the meticulously prepared message.

I unfolded the half-sheet of stationery and presented it to the operator by placing it on the counter. I had cut off the top half of the page with Taylor's initials although I had saved the blank portion of the paper like it was some kind of totem.

"I see you got it wrote down," observed operator picking up the message.

"Yes-sir," I said.

"Good," he pronounced. "Your mistress must be a smart woman. I'm here to tell you, y'all can get things pretty mixed-up. You people don't have too good-a memory."

There were some things that *we* would never forget; but I kept quiet and focused instead on the scarred and worn wood of the counter. It was in need of a good cleaning and linseed oil. The operator read the message.

"And something like this," he continued. "Y'all sure could make a mess of things."

Even without the monogram, the telegraph operator had decided that the paper was too good for me. I was just a *girl* doing an errand for my mistress. He was right about the paper. It wasn't mine.

"This is going to Fort Irwin, huh?" the operator considered.

"Yes-sir," I nodded.

"She's got a lot of words here," he added. "It'll take me a minute. Hope she give you enough money." He shook his head. "Poor sap, and right at Christmastime too.

Well I guess it's quicker than a letter. You can wait over there by the heater, if you want to," he offered. "It's pretty cold out there today."

Obediently I walked over to stand by the gas heater and the operator left the counter to go to his telegraph machine.

Poor sap, and right at Christmastime too.

Danny was nobody's *sap*. Any woman could count herself blessed to be his wife. Surely he would be a good husband and a loving father. By now the operator was typing in the words from the half-sheet of stationery. It was too late not to say them now. The gas stove had made the telegraph office too hot and stuffy. No wonder the operator had rolled up his shirt sleeves. I unbuttoned the top button on my coat and stepped away from the heater, keeping a proper distance from the counter. Danny would meet someone soon. He seemed ready to be married and start a family. At least he would not have traveled all this way to be told that I was going back to New York instead of with him. It was the right thing to do, sending the wire.

I stood perfectly still, gripping the straps of my pocketbook. Once I got to New York the past would be behind me. When classes started again my head would be filled with science and literature, and maybe even political debate. There would be concerts and plays with Aunt Grace and baseball games with Uncle Eddie. The sense of dying would fade into the living of a real life. This would all become something to remember. This was the right thing to do. My future was not in California, and it was not here either.

The telegraph office was decorated for the holidays. A jolly bright-faced Santa Claus beamed at me from amongst an assortment of signs and notices on one of the dingy walls. On a small table in a corner there was a little plastic Christmas tree with a few colored balls dangling from its scrawny branches. Mr. Leon would not have been pleased. Jessica either. Next year Mandy would be decorating Taylor's Christmas tree. Spencer would be helping her, or perhaps some other proper and beautiful creature entitled to share the monogram on Taylor's stationery.

That house gon' have a mistress one day. Then where you gon' be?

In Harlem. Or maybe in Dallas. But some place where I would not see her.

Hopefully, she would still put presents under the tree for Mandy and the children. Taylor would not want an unkind wife. I could understand why Laura Spalding despised me. Any woman would. Proximity had made it too easy for his affections to be distracted. And I had been too willing. That first night, I had asked him to stay when he would have done the proper thing by returning to his bed. I had violated the *gentlemen's agreement*. But maybe we could still have a little party with Mandy and children this year. If I was able to establish the tradition established, at least for the sake of Spencer, Taylor would be sure to maintain it. I wasn't sorry for what had gone on between us. It had become necessary. It had found a purpose. Some traditions could be worth keeping. "You make this a happy Christmas," Mr. Leon had instructed. Sometimes it was easy to do, especially when happiness was accustomed to a place.

When he finished sending the wire, the operator returned to the counter and beckoned for me come back to it too. I noticed that he had laid the handwritten message aside on the counter, and while he was turned away to put the money I had paid him into the register, I hastily picked up the note and crammed it into my coat pocket. The operator came back and put down the change that I was due. I scooped up the coins and put them in my other coat pocket.

As I was pulling on my gloves the bell above the door clanged again. I moved away from the counter, preparing to wait for the new customer, a white woman, to pass before I went out.

"Esther?" the woman spoke my name, bringing my eyes to her face.

It was Cordelia Collier.

"It is you!" she exclaimed pleasantly.

She was smiling. I had never seen her smile, having seen her only once and that was the night that Robert Collier had left bruises around her neck.

"How are you?" she inquired warmly.

I was almost speechless to see that she was even alive, let alone looking happy.

"Fine, thank-you ma'am," I managed to mumble. "How are you?"

"I couldn't be better!" she declared.

I stared at her, wondering how that could be.

"I guess Mr. Payne didn't tell you," she laughed lightly reading the confusion in my face.

"Ma'am?" I replied more confused than ever.

"Do you mind waiting just a minute for me?" she asked. "We'll walk out together. I want to talk to you."

Dutifully, I waited by the door while Mrs. Collier finished her business with the telegraph operator. What did she want to talk to me about? Her husband coming to the house that night? Taylor didn't want me involved. We had never spoken about it since.

I looked up at her for a moment. The telegraph operator was all friendly smiles and agreeable *yes ma'ams* with her. You couldn't blame him. She was pretty and stylish, dressed in a dark red wool coat with a black fur collar, matching hat, leather gloves, shoes, and bag. She looked so smart and fashionable that I admired her too. Once I was back in Harlem under Aunt Grace's watchful eye, my wardrobe would improve. It wasn't a lack of money that kept me plain and nondescript. My weekly wages had been steadily accumulating, practically untouched for months. It was propriety. Maids did not dress themselves in the clothes of mistresses. We weren't even expected to have fine writing paper. But once I was back on the other side of the Red Sea I wouldn't be a maid anymore and Mama's black dresses would be back in the cedar chest at the foot of her empty, undisturbed bed.

"Shall we go?" asked Mrs. Collier cheerfully once she returned to where I was standing.

"Yes ma'am," I replied, increasingly anxious about what it was she wanted to discuss.

"My car is over there," she pointed indicating that we should walk to it together. "I won't keep you long, I promise," she added. "I'm just so glad I ran into you."

"It's no problem, Mis' Collier," I assured her, which was not true.

No matter. Most of *us* had spent lifetimes lying to *them*. Sometimes you didn't even think of it as lying at all. It was just how *we* got along in *their* world. Now, afraid that Taylor would discover me in town, I just wanted Mrs. Collier to hurry up so I could go.

"It's such a nice surprise to see you this morning," she commented as we walked to her car. "Are you on an errand for Tay—I mean Mr. Payne?"

So she called him by his first name too. Naturally. It was her place since they must be more than professional acquaintances. I wondered what she would say if she knew that I did.

His kind ever hear you call 'im that?

"No ma'am," I replied to her question.

In New York I could use his first name. We would just be two old friends, having cappuccinos in a smoky Greenwich Village coffee house. I could introduce him to my Marxist classmates whose first names I had used all the time.

When we reached her car, Mrs. Collier stopped and her face became serious. I steeled myself for some admission, confession, or admonishment, none of which could be good to hear. Maybe she was about to be a kinder Laura Spalding, or a woman version of Doctor Mitchell, perhaps a white version of Sister Wright. Did she speculate too about what went on in the house on Webster Road? Maybe she did have designs on being its next mistress. Robert Collier had been so enraged that night. She would certainly be safe there; and even if he wasn't as rich as the Colliers, Taylor could without a doubt provide for her and her children very well. Now that would be something to drive Robert Collier completely crazy. His wife marrying Andrew Payne's son.

The cold wind gusted, chilling me through my cloth coat and troubling the loose strands of dark hair that framed Cordelia Collier's face. I stuck my hands into the pockets of my coat, and in the right one felt the note to Danny. I wondered when he would get his telegram. I dreaded that he would call me again at Taylor's house, but everything was set in motion now. It couldn't be stopped. It had to be finished.

"Esther," began Mrs. Collier. "I've always wanted to thank you for your kindness that night last spring."

When I thought she was an adulteress, I thought guiltily. I owed her an apology too, although there was no way she'd ever know it. She was a mother herself. She would be nice to Spencer.

"I'm glad you're all right, Mrs. Collier," I said meeting her eyes directly.

"I'm sure I wouldn't be if it weren't for Tay—Mr. Payne." She glanced around quickly. "I got my divorce, Esther, *and* my children." She smiled a little. "He won the case for me. And with the settlement, we'll be just fine. Mr. Payne's a wonderful lawyer, Esther, and a good friend. I know about my husband coming to the house. I'm just glad you were there. If Robert had-had hurt him...well I'd never be able to forgive myself."

I can protect you. And take care of you. Do you understand that?

Most likely Taylor had not told her everything about that night or perhaps much at all. And perhaps he had even used Robert Collier's drunken threats to her very advantage. In her *settlement* there might be a substantial sum of hush money to make the various criminal charges go away. He had freed Cordelia Collier from her *true Southern gentleman* of a husband, and with her children too, and nobody had gone to jail, or died.

"I know I should have visited him when he was sick," Mrs. Collier was suddenly confessing. "But I was afraid to. My husband was so jealous. And you know...the children. I-I couldn't risk it. If one of them were to catch it, or-or me...I-I don't know what I would have done...I just can't imagine...But you, you were so brave, Esther. You stayed with him and nursed him back to health. I admire you so much."

You're not my nurse.

I looked down at our feet. Hers were so small and elegantly enclosed in the silk nylons and black high heels. She must have a matching pair for every outfit, but I doubted that she owned a pair of work shoes, and she probably hadn't worn cotton stockings since she was a child. Yet I had pearls. And they were *perfect* against my skin. I felt a few drops of wetness carried on the wind. Rain was coming.

"I wanted to thank you for that too," Mrs. Collier continued. "For being such a friend. I did worry about him you know. Honestly. With no family to speak of, and practically a stranger in this town. If it weren't for Doctor Mitchell and-and you...I used to ask Doctor Mitchell about him all the time. He would always tell me, 'He's in good hands.'"

Work with willin' hands, Esther.

There's an attachment between you, Esther. He trusts you.

Again I felt the note to Danny in my coat pocket. It might have all turned out differently had Taylor not insisted on us doing things *differently*.

"He was right," Cordelia Collier said.

I looked up at her again. Doctor Mitchell had never intended for my *willing hands* to make love to him.

"I don't mean to embarrass you, Esther," Mrs. Collier said. "But this is something that I want you to know. You helped bring him back to us."

To us.

To the *us* that was separate again. And not equal.

"To everything there is a purpose under heaven, Mrs. Collier," I replied. "I'm glad everything turned out fine."

I was glad. Or I would be. In a hundred years, when I didn't know that I loved him anymore because I would be dead somewhere, waiting on the Resurrection.

"We just have to pray and ask God, right?" Mrs. Collier smiled warmly.

"Yes-yes ma'am," I said, taken aback that she had remembered my advice.

You don't think I know anything about sound doctrine?

"You'll never know how much you helped me too, Esther," she said. "That night and afterwards."

The occasional droplets had developed into sprinkles. I didn't have an umbrella.

"Oh," observed Mrs. Collier. "It's starting to rain and I've kept you. Where're you on your way to?"

"I can catch the bus," I answered her.

"Nonsense! At least let me drive you home."

Home. There were times when I didn't know where that was anymore.

"Please, Mis' Collier, I don't want to put you out," I said.

"It's my pleasure, Esther," she insisted. "Now get in the car. We can have a little visit."

Esther doesn't accept rides from strangers, Mitch.

Maybe I was the one who had become the *stranger*. Most years of your life went along uneventfully, unremarkably. You barely remembered anything about them. But this year, these fifteen months really, I could remember almost every single day. Every single word. Every single touch. How long was it going to take me to forget, to not have it be the most important time of my life?

Soon we were out of the center of town, and I could relax a little. Mrs. Collier turned on the windshield wipers to beat back the rain that had begun falling more heavily.

"I'm moving to Tyler," her voice knocked at the door of my mind. "I think it would be better, now that the divorce is settled and everything. The children and I need a fresh start. We could have that in Tyler. And that way the children could still visit their grandparents...and their father too, I guess. I never wanted to take them away from him, you know...I mean just because it didn't work out between us. You probably don't believe it, but there's a lot of good in Robert Collier. And I know he loves his children. Maybe I just wasn't good for him. You know what I mean," she sighed deeply. "Even if you have everything," she went on. "Love doesn't always work out."

So what chance did you have if you had almost nothing? I thought of Mandy. I thought of me.

"Yes ma'am," I replied politely, staring at the road ahead.

"What do you think, Esther?" Mrs. Collier's topic and tone changed abruptly again. "Would you ever consider leaving McConnell County?"

"I lived in New York for a little a while," I said.

"Oh that's right. You did, didn't you? That must have been very exciting. I'm sure this little place just can't compare. It stands to reason that Mr. Payne won't be staying here. He must miss the big city. I thought about moving us to Dallas. That's not too big. But I like Tyler better. What do you think? You get to Tyler much?"

I couldn't think at all.

"Mr. Payne is leaving?" I heard myself asking.

Mrs. Collier glanced over at me alarmed.

"Oh," she said. "You didn't know, did you? I just thought...I'm-I'm sorry, Esther. It wasn't my place--"

"He's leaving?" I asked again.

"Well-well yes," she said blinking nervously. "When we, uh, met this morning. For me to sign some papers, he-he mentioned it to me, that he had given his notice, you know, resigned. I just assumed that he was going back to New York. But I could be wrong of course. Maybe he's just going into private practice. Like-like his father. He's such a wonderful lawyer. He would certainly be in demand. He would have clients from all around. And that-that little limp wouldn't mean a thing to people. What with the war and everything, I'm sure there are lots of men with limps these days."

"I didn't know," I said to myself.

"Oh dear," lamented Mrs. Collier. "Now you're worried about losing your job, and right here at Christmastime too. Well, really Esther, that is what I hoped to talk to you about too. You see--"

"They fired him," I murmured still talking to myself.

"Fired?" replied Mrs. Collier. "No. No, he resigned. He must just be homesick that's all. And if he is moving away, well, what I wanted to ask you is if you would consider coming to work for me. I'm going to need somebody to help me with the children. The baby's only two, and with three small children, they-they can be quite a handful. I would want you to live with us too. You'd have your own room. I've already picked out a very nice house--"

"Mis' Collier, please stop the car," I said urgently, seeing a bus stop coming up.

"What?" she asked. "Why?"

"I have-I have to go...I-I forgot I was supposed to go see my grandfather. I'll just get out here."

She pulled the car over and stopped. I had already opened the car door.

"Esther, please--" Mrs. Collier tried.

"Thank-you, Mis' Collier," I said one foot on the wet pavement.

"I don't mind driving you to your grandfather's--"

"No ma'am," I cut her off, getting out of the car. "That's all right."

"I'm so sorry, Esther, I never meant to upset you," she apologized. "Will you at least think about it? About my offer. I mean if Taylor really is letting you go. You could start after the holidays. I know he thinks the world of you, and I just told you how I feel. I can pay you very well. Please, just think about it."

"Thank-you," I said, slamming the car door and running to the bus stop.

III

By the time I passed through the Grampa's gate and came into his muddy yard, I was soaked and shivering. I trudged up the worn brick path, and Grampa met me on the porch. "What you doin' here?" he asked, his pale brow furrowed deeply. I didn't know, except that this was where I had told Cordelia Collier I was going, and I needed to go somewhere.

Our *attachment* had become a scandal and it had caught up with him. Taylor was giving up the work he loved and his home because of me, his *nigger-bitch*, who could be nothing more than his *nigga-maid*. Yet he had never said a word to me, making it another one of his *court matters* that I had no right to know about. But Cordelia Collier had revealed the truth, used by the hand of the Lord to remind me, to show me, that every season must truly come to an end.

"Can I come in?" I asked Grampa now, standing in front of him in wet work shoes and mud-splattered cotton stockings.

"This yo' home ain't it?" he sternly replied, stepping aside and holding the door open for me.

Once inside the house the warmth instantly wrapped around me and I ceased to shiver. The smell of burning wood was like a friend, and I went straight to the wood heater, pulling off my wet gloves to warm my hands over the black cast iron.

"You better get out them wet clothes 'fo' you catch the pneumonia," warned Grampa.

As I took off my soaked head scarf and coat, Grampa went to his bedroom, returning with coat hangers.

"Give 'em to me," he said taking the coat and scarf to place them on the hangers. "They'll dry quick enough. Go change." He hung the hangers where the clothes would benefit best from the warm air from the heater. "Betty brung the washin' yestiddy, so there's plenty-a towels in the cupboard."

Obediently I did as I was told, taking a clean bath towel with me to Jimmy's room where I switched on a lamp. I would always come back to this room. I was thankful for it. I belonged here. In the place of my brother.

In the weak light, I studied my reflection in the dresser mirror.

I want to look at you.

My hair, confined to the severe knot at the back of my head as usual, had gone back to its tightly coiled curls around the edges. I wiped my face. Aunt Betty had used too much bleach in her wash water. I removed Mama's dress and my shoes and stockings. Clad in only a brassiere and cotton slip I accepted my *handsome* form.

A man can count on you, Esther. Even the foolish ones know that.

But he hadn't trusted me enough to tell me the truth.

When I pulled back the curtain that served as Jimmy's closet door to get two more hangers for the damp dress and stockings, I saw the set of matching luggage that Grampa had bought for me. The brown leather was fine, the brass buckles shiny. They would mostly be empty, but Grampa would be sending me back to New York in style. He had never stopped believing in me.

New York City had been big enough that I had never seen Taylor before. It must be bigger now.

I still had a few garments stored in one of Jimmy's dresser drawers, and I found an old dress to put on. Going to Mama's room I opened her top dresser drawer where I had stored her combs and brushes after she died. In front of her mirror I used one of the combs to put my hair back into place, restoring the tight knot. It didn't make sense to borrow Mama's old straightening comb to repair the rain damage, since I would have to go back out into it before too long. Most of her life Mama had worn her soft black hair in long thick plaits bundled at the back of her head with a plain comb. Only on Sunday mornings would she press and curl it for church, and even then she had covered it with a hat. The Bible said that long hair was a woman's glory, and Mama's had been envied by many, including me. I hoped that she had appreciated it at least a little but I didn't know. Sometimes it seemed I had barely known her at all. She must have been happy once, but I couldn't remember the sound of her laughter.

I brought the work dress and stockings back into the front room to dry too, since I wanted to wear them when I went back. And I would go back. I had to. If for no other reason than to get my things and say goodbye. But it wasn't a betrayal. And it wasn't like I was running away. I had always been planning to leave after Christmas anyway. I hung up the dress and stockings on a wooden peg. Maybe it would even be easier this way, an absolute end to our time together, and then the house would be closed-up and dark, like it was a theater at the end of a show.

I trust you. Never do harm to that.

And he had taught me to trust him. But in the end our lives were separate.

Grampa gave me one of his old sweaters to wear. I put my arms into the sleeves and closed it snugly around me. It smelled of him, of his pipe tobacco and the wood heater, and it felt like he was hugging me. A woman now, I was too big to crawl into Grampa's lap, but nothing could separate me from him. Nothing. No one. I would always belong to him.

He had set a cup of coffee, smooth and beige with Carnation canned milk, on the small table next to the old sofa for me. The full cup warmed my hands. Grampa sat down in his rocking chair and lit his pipe. I took a seat in the corner of the sofa, tucking my bare feet up under me.

"Better put on a pair of my socks," Grampa said while he watched me sip the hot coffee.

Grampa had never approved of me going barefoot in the winter, and Aunt Grace and Aunt Betty didn't approve of it at any time. In Taylor's house I almost never went without shoes.

"I'm all right," I said to Grampa as the warmth from the wood heater and the hot coffee made its way down to my toes.

This was my home. In the end prodigal children came home to the fathers who received them. All the faces of my people welcomed me from their pictures on the smoky walls. I was richly blessed. I just wished that there was more evidence of Christmas in Grampa's house. If only Grampa was more like Mr. Leon. Perhaps Mama had come by her disposition naturally, since Grampa was solemn too. Perhaps a sober nature ran through our family, yet Ernestine's Taj Mahal was safe and secure, and enduring. I understood everything about this house. I understood my place in it.

"You gon' tell me what he did to you?" asked Grampa after a time.

I looked at him, knowing who he meant.

"Taylor didn't do anything to me, Grampa," I said.

"He must-a said somethin' then," he replied, rocking back and forth easily.

"No-sir," I said.

Not to me, I thought. He had said it to Cordelia Collier. Was Taylor afraid to tell me that he was leaving? Did he think I would become hysterical, like some distraught, love-sick, discarded mistress? Then he didn't know me either. I had never asked him for anything. If they had fired him because of me, then I deserved to know it. It was my name that would suffer, my family who would be made ashamed by the scandal. Maybe *they* would even come after us, hurt Nathaniel and Uncle Perry's business. Taylor's family would never even know, and they didn't matter to him anyway.

We had almost made it to the end. We had almost had a time together mostly preserved from disgrace. I had always been going to leave after Christmas. I had sent a telegram to Danny telling him that I was going back to New York. We had almost gotten away with it.

"I sent a telegram to Danny today," I now told Grampa.

The rocking chair stopped.

"What you do that for?" Grampa asked.

For myself, I thought.

"What it say?" Grampa followed when I didn't answer his question.

"I told him I was going back to New York," I reported, studying the remaining coffee in my cup.

"He takin' you back to New York?"

"Danny wanted me to move to California not New York," I reminded Grampa. "I want to go back and finish school."

"So you goin' by yo'self then?"

I put down the cup and closed Grampa's sweater more tightly around me.

"I'll live with Aunt Grace and Uncle Eddie if they'll still have me until I finish school."

Grampa sighed.

"I b'lieve that's best," Grampa decided. "That soldier cared 'bout you more than I thought, but if you don't him, then you done the right thing. It ain't right to live a lie, Esther Fay. Make yo' life hard."

I looked at him.

You don't want to lie on love, Esther.

"And yo' bed cold," he added.

I didn't say anything.

"What?" Grampa asked meeting my astounded gaze. "You think I don't know 'bout feelin's no mo'? I ain't forgot. What me and yo' grandmama had was good, Esther Fay. It was good, and true, and right. A man don't forget that kind of love. And that's all I ever wanted for you, for all my chirren. What's right. Love can be real, Esther Fay, but that don't always make it good. It can be wrong sometimes. King David was a man after the Lord's own heart, but he killed a man so he could have his wife. He loved her but that didn't make it right."

I knew the story of *Bathsheba*, how from her, from that wrong love, Solomon had been born, ...And the Lord loved him. Yet he had not been spared the Blues either. The entire time I had known her, Sister Callie had been alone. And Mandy's hope for Willie was merely defiant, because like Cordelia Collier she wanted her children to love their father. *Vanity of vanities, saith the preacher; all is vanity.*

"We don't know nobody out in California no-how," Grampa said. "Somebody was to take sick, they be dead 'fo we could get to each other. Bad enough I let Eddie, take yo' anie off to Harlem."

But he was sending me there, and I wanted to go. I had to. Only it seemed that Taylor and I were escaping to the same place. But would he really sell his house? The one his father had built for his mother? How could he? He loved it.

You make this house a home.

Even owned by somebody else, the house on Webster Road would always keep my memories so fresh that the taste of them would choke me.

"I don't doubt you have some feelin's for Taylor Payne," Grampa went on, as if he were reading my mind. "It's na'tral. Like I told you, he got feelin's for you too. A man know a good woman when he see her, who he can trust to stand by him. Payne was sweet on you a good long time, even 'fo' he took sick. I seen it affectin' you, the way you'd light up talkin' 'bout 'im. I seen the way he was lookin' at you Thanksgivin'. Like you was his. Nathaniel been done said it and can't see nothin' wrong with it. And I 'spect Payne's a good man. But he's a white man, Esther Fay, and you's colored. You can't b'long in his world. Sooner or later it had to come to that."

And so it had, sooner than later. Taylor was taking his world away.

I think I was trying to get away.

From me.

"He can't offer you nothin' but secrets and shame," said Grampa. "You raisin' his bastard babies. He may want you, but I don't want it for you. You don't want it for yo'self."

You must have better. You deserve it.

And the *better* could not be with him.

"You gon' meet the right man someday," asserted Grampa. "What's s'pose to be will be. Can't nobody block it."

"Yes-sir," I said.

Grampa breathed deeply.

"So that's what you come to tell me?" he asked. "Out in all this weather? That you turned that Simmons boy down?"

"Yes-sir," I repeated.

It was partly true.

"What yo' boss-man say 'bout it?"

"I don't talk about Danny with him."

Because he was my employer. Now Cordelia Collier wanted to employ me. She wanted become my *mis' lady*, as Mandy called hers. She wanted me to raise Robert Collier's children. She'd never asked me to use her first name, even if she had to trust me with her life.

"I'm speakin' of you goin' back to Harlem," clarified Grampa.

I hid my hands in the sleeves of his sweater.

"We don't talk about that either," I said.

"But he knowed you would," replied Grampa. "Sat right there at Nathaniel's table and said he wanted you to."

Until you reached your *agreement*, I thought, and made him think that I was going to marry Danny.

"When you gon' give 'im his notice?" Grampa asked.

I didn't need to anymore, I wanted to say. He had given me mine. It was a day of resolutions. But it was time.

"I'll quit before Christmas," I answered Grampa, who nodded approvingly as he lit his pipe.

"That's good," he agreed. "Be good to make a fresh start in the new year."

The start would be fresh, but the memories would be too.

"I'm gonna get some more coffee," I said getting up. "You want some?"

"After while maybe," he replied.

In the kitchen I refilled my cup with the remaining coffee in Grampa's ancient pot and shut off the low flame that had been keeping it hot. A wind gust rattled the panes of the window over the sink. I needed to be getting back. Perhaps I could borrow Grampa's umbrella. I was still employed and there was his *supper* to cook.

At least Spencer wasn't supposed to come on days like this. The boy was probably somewhere hating the rain for keeping him away. He would be devastated when Taylor left, and it was my fault, because I had allowed it to turn into something impossible. In thinking for myself it seemed I had been only been thinking of myself, and now Spencer would suffer for it. And Mandy wouldn't have a better job.

Why didn't Taylor tell me? I could have stopped all of this. But he had only made me believe in the impossible.

...Goodbyes don't suit me, and I have been known to postpone them as long as I can.

Perhaps he had only been thinking of himself too.

Judging by the open brown paper sack of pinto beans on the kitchen counter Grampa was planning to cook a pot of red beans. I gathered the sack of beans and a clean cup-towel and took them to the kitchen table. Sitting down with my coffee I unfolded the towel and poured out some of the beans. Spreading them out, I began picking out the tiny gravel and clods of black dirt that inevitably got mixed up with the dry beans and soon I had made a decent pile.

Grampa generally cooked in amounts that said he kept company in mind. He liked to be sure that he had enough food to share with a neighbor, or with one of the kinfolks who might happen by. As if proof of this possibility, there was a knock at the front door. Having emptied the coffee pot, I got up to correct my selfishness. Dreary days like this were especially right for hot coffee.

"Esther Faye," Grampa said in the kitchen door.

"Yes-sir," I replied, striking a match to light the stove burner under the pot. "I'm puttin' on some fresh right this minute."

"Yo' boss-man in yond 'a."

The stove flame burned blue. I turned to look at Grampa, not believing him. Still in my hand, the match burned down enough to remind me to blow it out.

"Taylor?" I asked dumbly.

"B'lieve that's what you call 'im. Say he wants to talk to you."

How did he know I was here? He didn't know where our house was.

"But why?" I asked. "How…I mean… he doesn't know I'm here."

"You can ask 'im fo' yo'self," replied Grampa. "'Stead of standin' there with yo' mouth open."

Taylor stood in Grampa's front room, tall and straight, and white, completely incompatible with the modest furnishings and stained wallpaper. "I went to the house," he said as soon as he saw me. "You weren't there." My mind seemed almost incapable of making sense of what my eyes were seeing. The ceiling was too low, the walls were too close. In all of my fantasies I had never pictured him here. Yet now here he was, at the end. Now his memory would be everywhere, even among the hallowed family faces.

He wasn't wearing his top coat. The felt of the fedora in his hand was wet, as was the wool of his suit, but his countenance was calm. His dark eyes held mine, his expression impenetrable, unrevealing. He was simply here. In my grandfather's house. I didn't know what to do. Everything was changed.

"I came to see my grandfather," I replied evenly.

"So I see," he said.

"Is something wrong?" I asked, finding a stronger voice.

"I don't know," he replied.

I pulled Grampa's sweater around me more snugly. Everything was finally right. The way it was supposed to be. The way it was done. And if some part of me had thought—hoped—that he would not accept the ending that we had to come to, then I would learn to let go of that hope. There was his world and my world, and very little room on the head of a pin, where only angels could dance. It was just that nobody should have known about his leaving before I did.

"Cordelia came to see me, Esther," he explained. "She said she ran into you at the telegraph office."

She must have gone back to his office to confess her indiscretion after leaving me at the bus stop. I felt sorry for her. She had been embarrassed. But she had done me a favor. It was good that I knew. I had never believed that we could be together forever, or even for long. She had only confirmed what we had all known, that it could not last.

"Who did you wire?" Taylor asked.

I wasn't expecting the question, and I didn't answer him.

"Tell me, Esther," he said. "I want to know."

"Mis' Collier offered me a job," I replied coolly. "Seems I come highly recommended."

"You don't understand," he said.

"What's not to understand?" I returned. "You're just lookin' after me, right? Much obliged for the good reference, Mr. Payne."

Closing his eyes momentarily, he sighed. Even he realized this was no way to treat a friend, and I had at least been that to him. He had given me pearls.

"Esther," he began again, coming forward. "I resigned because--"

"Of me," I finished for him.

"No," he said immediately. Then correcting himself, "I mean yes. I suppose it is because of you, but not like you think—"

"I'm sorry, Taylor," I cut him off. "It didn't need to come to this. I was going to tell you--"

"Tell me what?" he interrupted me.

I ached to go to him, to be in his arms, but there was a time for everything including *a time to refrain from embracing*.

"I'm sorry, Taylor," I said, sadness seeping into my voice. "You shouldn't have--"

"What are you sorry for?" he asked. "What were you going to tell me?"

"I never thought they'd fire you over it. You're so good, and--"

"I wasn't fired."

"All right," I conceded drearily. "They made you resign then. But it didn't need to come to this. I was going--"

"Esther, why were you sending a wire this morning?"

I still didn't answer him. He would think it was because of him, and it was but it wasn't.

"I want to know, Esther," he pressed. "Who was it to? Simmons? Tell me."

What difference did it make? It didn't change anything.

"It ain't none of yo' business," interjected Grampa, who was standing in the kitchen doorway listening. "She don't have to tell you nothin'."

Taylor looked passed me and at my grandfather, who came forward to stand next to me. The Red Sea waves were washing back into place, and the Egyptian prince was alone on the opposite shore. The sea swelled and tossed, preparing to drown my love for him like Pharaoh's army.

♪*Oh Mary, don't you weep...*

This was the way it was supposed to be.

You can't b'long in his world.

"Mr. Green," Taylor replied. "With all due respect, this matter is between Esther and myself."

"I say she don't have to tell you," repeated Grampa. "And you in my house."

There was no Nathaniel to intervene, no Connie, or sweet children to calm the troubled waters, no Doctor Mitchell to invoke the authority of the Law.

"You cannot speak for her, Mr. Green," said Taylor, meeting my eyes again.

Don't leave me.

I won't.

It had been a conditional promise. What was supposed to be was going to be. Nobody could block it.

"She my chile--" began Grampa.

"She is not a child," Taylor corrected him, still looking at me. "I need to know, Esther. I have a right to know."

"You got no more rights than me!" I snapped at last. "I had a right to know about you leaving. But Cordelia Collier had to tell me."

Taylor started towards me, but the toe of his right shoe caught on the frayed end of Grampa's carpet, and he was forced to stop to maintain his balance. I withdrew, standing closer to Grampa. It was finished now. We shouldn't expect perfection in this life. That was for Heaven. Where there were many mansions, and cabins.

"You don't understand, Esther," Taylor said standing straight again. "I was going to tell you. I was only waiting for the right time."

"I guess today is as good as any," I replied coldly.

I felt Grampa's hand on my back. I would always have him. At least until we had to send him on to Ernestine, and the Lord, and Mama. And Jimmy. Then they would all be gone, and I would be like Sister Callie, virtuous and alone, seeing after the wild birds.

"I knowed somethin' happen," Grampa said. "He disrespected you. It was bound--"

"You're right," agreed Taylor, still holding my eyes with his. "I'm sorry it came from a stranger. But I want to tell you the part she didn't know. But first," he paused. "First, Esther, you must tell me...what was in the wire?"

In his dark eyes I had seen myself *differently*, and I wanted to look away now but I might never get to see myself like this again.

"What did it say?" he asked again.

"This ain't slavey-times," Grampa defended me. "He don't own you."

My beautiful roses. They are mine, you know. I have claimed them.

And I wasn't Matilda either.

"I have to know," said Taylor. "I deserve to know."

I felt it, the *something*, unfinished, swelling up in me, inflamed and tender. Did Taylor's eyes now see Sylvia? Felicia, perhaps? Cars turning over in the rain. The Bible said *open rebuke was better than secret love.*

"Grampa," I said, turning to him briefly, before wading back into the sea. "Please…could you leave us alone for a minute."

Certainly Grampa's eyes saw Matilda. And Albert's whiteness that shamed his blackness. For a moment I was afraid that Grampa would not give us this last bit of time. There was no reason that he should. This was his house, and I was his too. So with my own eyes I pleaded with Grampa. He had won. The *agreement* was in place. Finally he left us, returning to the kitchen.

Silently I went to my coat hanging near the wood heater. For the sake of all that had been between us, I could not leave Taylor thinking that I had taken a *better offer*. There was no one better. Maybe I would have to know that forever, but I could live with it. Like Mama, and Sister Callie, and Mandy, and Ernestine who had always had to wait for the brief visits from her Isaac, and like Jessica for a time, who had run away from Andrew with only the hope that he would come after her; I could miss him for the rest of my life but I could live. Love was entitled to last forever regardless. I would not blaspheme it by hiding it in a proud silence. I would not make Taylor pay such a price for having cared for me. I reached into the pocket of the coat and pulled out the crumpled message, smoothing it out in my hands.

"You can read it for yourself," I said bringing it to him.

He looked tentative, almost bewildered, and I almost enjoyed it.

"You-you didn't send it?" he asked, his face finally betraying an actual crack in its unfailing composure.

"Yes," I replied, smiling a little as I took the wet hat from his hand. "I just wrote it down first. At least I put that fancy writing paper of yours to use."

He stared at me and I waited.

"Read it to me," he said.

He was a lawyer after all, a prosecutor, trained to listen to suspects and witnesses, able to use their own words, even the inflection of their voices as they spoke to expose the truth. But I was also good with words, and from him and Grampa I had learned to be concise and clear. Still holding his hat, I began to read:

"To Sergeant, First Class, Daniel Simmons: I cannot marry you, because I do not love you. I am sorry for any hurt I may have caused you. I did not mean to. Circumstances changed. I want to do things differently. Forgive me. God bless you. Esther."

When I finished I stuck the message in the pocket of Grampa's old sweater and looked up at Taylor. His face had regained its usual equanimity, but his eyes were softer. "Do you mind if we sit down," he said. I nodded, and he grasped my arm. We sat down together on the sofa. Taylor's right leg trembled briefly. Flecks of mud were on his shoes and on the cuffs of his trousers.

He was quiet for a time, and I honored that. Was he thinking of Danny and remembering how Sylvia's letter had made him feel? People always thought men fought over women, but the actions of women often caused men to ally themselves, to take each other's part, see each other's side; as Taylor's uncle and father had done about Jessica, and Taylor and Grampa contriving their *agreement* about me, even Nathaniel had taken Taylor's part.

"Your suit coat is damp," I said eventually, toying with the brim of his hat in my lap. "Where's your overcoat?"

He smiled wryly.

"From the looks of things," he said pointing towards the various pieces of clothing on hangers around the wood heater. "I wasn't the only one caught out in the rain."

"The storm came suddenly," I explained.

"So it did. Cordelia said she offered to drive you, but you jumped out of the car before she could even stop."

"She exaggerated a little."

"In any case," Taylor said, taking back his hat and setting it aside, behind him on the arm of the sofa. "I want to be clear, Esther, resigning was my choice. I was not fired. There is no scandal."

"Then why?" I asked. "Why would you resign? You love the Law."

"Humph, that sounds fairly sanctimonious," he observed. "Please tell me I don't talk like that."

"Sometimes," I smiled a little again. "When you're arguing a case."

"I suppose it has its utility."

"That's what I mean, Taylor. You're a lawyer. Why would you quit the work you love? And-and leave your home? You never said a word to me about it."

"It isn't for a lack of trying, Esther."

"You never--"

"You never let me," he interrupted. "Every time I...I try to talk about the future... for us, I run into a wall with you, like it's forbidden."

It was, but I kept quiet this time.

"At least with your grandfather," he continued. "I could discuss it, although not with much agreement to be sure. Nathaniel is more supportive--"

"You-you talked to Nathaniel about us?" I asked. "I mean..."

Now Taylor was the one who was amused.

"He has his own reservations of course. We won't have it easy. The brace makes Nathaniel nervous about my abilities to protect you. And there's the matter of the laws against it. In point of fact, your grandfather shares similar concerns, not to mention his profound opposition to having another white relation in the family. However, I do like to think I'm a bit more deserving of that place than your Confederate ancestor was. Like my mother, Esther, you're the jewel of the Green family, and they're not too sure I'm worthy of you. I suppose that makes me like my father. Another brazen upstart, who--"

"You-you talked to Grampa about me... I mean about us?"

"Yes, Esther," Taylor answered patiently. "The agreement, remember?"

"But that was about me leaving you."

The crooked smile tugged at one corner of his mouth again.

"It was also about you staying," he replied. "I told you I was opposing counsel."

Staying? I stared at him dumbly.

"So yes, to answer your question," Taylor continued. "I talked to your grandfather. Nathaniel. Mitch. Just not you. And no, not Cordelia either. Not really. I suppose for her part she may have wondered about things. Others too perhaps, but they didn't hear it from me. You obviously didn't want anybody to know and I tried to respect that. So you see, you couldn't understand what Cordelia was telling you, because she didn't understand it herself."

I was confused, dazed by what he was saying.

"She-she told me you are leaving," I mumbled.

"I can practice law anywhere, Esther. But my home is with you."

...Home is a feeling. Not an address, not an event. It's the feeling we have for a place, for a person.

My eyes welled.

"That's right," he told me. "With you. I resigned because I'm going to New York with you. Or *after* you, if need be. Nathaniel told me about your plans after Thanksgiving, so I made a few of my own. Yes, I know you're not too keen on people deciding things for you, but it's not just you, Esther, it's us...and since my plans at least complement yours..." He smiled warmly. "Besides, you weren't leaving me much time. I had to move rather quickly."

"I-I don't understand," I said faintly.

He smiled again. It was the one I liked best, the one that reached to his eyes and out from them with the little lines.

"Ah, a concession," he replied. "But what's not to understand, as you said? You know how Payne men are. We chase after our women. We have to. They're generally not easily captured. Although as it turns out they will leave clues. You told Connie and she told Nathaniel. Husbands and wives do that. They tell each other things. The lucky ones anyway. Something to do with that two becoming one thing in the Bible somewhere."

"'For this cause shall a man leave his father and mother,'" I recited. "'And cleave to his wife and they twain shall be one flesh.'"

"I see you know the passage," said Taylor puckishly.

One flesh. One flock. I couldn't breathe.

"I have a good friend whose father is a senior partner in a law firm in Manhattan," he continued. "You'll like him. Zach Rueben. We went to law school together, at Columbia, you know, that sub-standard institution." Again he smiled wryly. "He's been after me since the war to join their firm, but at the time I badly needed to get out of New York. Now that circumstances have *changed*, so to speak, I contacted him, and long story short, I can start with them in January.

"Zach helped with the apartment lease. Fortunately I still have some connections with some of my mother's old theater friends. Turns out aiding and abetting Emilia Emerson's son to fulfill his forbidden love has a certain Shakespearean appeal. Lucky for me, given the housing shortage. So I've been thinking that I could go first and settle things. You could come later—just not too much later." He smiled again. "You could resume your classes during the summer term, and perhaps spend the springtime doing a little interior decorating. And this time we could shop together."

He grinned. I was without words.

"Our apartment is in the Village," he continued. "Greenwich Village."

Our apartment.

How was that even possible?

"But I can't--" I finally started, shaking my head.

"Yes," Taylor said. "You can. *We* can. It's the Village, Esther. Bohemians, remember? Leonid Brodsky, our landlord, is your basic romantic socialist, and he likes our little love story. I suppose that means I'll have to get used to your Marxist friends. But please no revolutions," he took the opportunity to tease me. "And it's only a walk-up, no elevator, and we'll be on the third floor." He patted his right knee and smiled again. "But I've been through worse paces. We have a three year lease. That should give you plenty of time to complete your studies, then we can decide—together— where we go from there. If you like New York, you really should consider Columbia. They have a very fine teachers' college. We could start our own family tradition."

"But...but" I stammered. "I-I don't know what to say."

"I had it all worked out, Esther" Taylor said more seriously. "Mostly. I was waiting for the right time to tell you. To *ask* you. I wanted to make it special. You like to hide behind that veil of sensibility and common sense, but you're not above roses and chocolates, Sister Sergeant, and a little champagne. When Cordelia told me what happened this morning, I knew I couldn't wait any longer. But the telegram," he continued. "I didn't know what to make of it, Esther. I thought that maybe I had gotten it all wrong again. And I couldn't face it. Not this time. It means—you mean—too much to me.

"You said it a long time ago, I live in my head too much. Maybe you were right. It's been my best defense, but it maybe it's cost me something too. War is hell, right?" he smiled dryly, then in his face the irony softened and disappeared. "And in any case, my head was no match for your heart. I thought I was drawing you out, opening you up, but all along it was you making me *different*. You got the best of me, Esther… and I want you to keep it."

Reaching into his inside coat pocket, Taylor brought out a small velvet box. Opening it, he revealed a simple gold band.

"This belonged to my mother," he told me. "I suppose I've been saving it."

I looked up at him.

"It never occurred to me to give it to anyone else," he continued. "Not even Sylvia. I'm glad she left me. It makes perfect sense. I wasn't really suited to her, Esther, but I am to you."

Tears spilled down my cheeks. I looked down at the ring again.

"It's not the traditional diamond, I know," I heard him saying as my head spun. "Pop was too broke when they got married and by the time he could afford it, Mother didn't see the use of it. I suppose she was sensible too. However, if you'd like one--"

"It's beautiful," I whispered.

"Really? I was thinking more along the lines of handsome," he teased me again.

I returned my eyes to his, where mirth sparkled in the dark brown. I laughed a little, nervously, as I wiped at my tears.

"And I know it's also traditional for the man to get down on one knee when asking the woman he loves to marry him," Taylor said as he was taking the ring out of the box. "But given that I only have the one reliable one, I was hoping you'd give me a pass on that too." He took my left hand into his. "Will you marry me, Esther?"

I stared at him, brushing away more tears.

"It-it's against the law for us to marry," I reminded him.

"Not in the state of New York," he replied. "We can have our love and our license. Say yes to me, darling. And as you also once said, everything else we'll let take care of itself."

I nodded quickly.

"What do you say, Esther?" he asked again. "I want to hear you say it."

"Yes," I told him.

He slipped his mother's ring on my finger.

"It fits!" I exclaimed.

"Of course it does," he replied.

"But your mother…she was so small and delicate," I said looking up at him.

"All right," he confessed, laughing softly. "I had it sized."

I returned my eyes to the gold ring shining on my brown finger.

"But when..how-how did you…how would you know my size?"

Taylor took both of my hands into his.

"I know these hands, my love, almost better than I know my own."

He pressed them to his lips.

...*She will do him good and not evil all the days of her life. She seeketh wool, and flax, and worketh willingly with her hands.*

In Ernestine's Taj Mahal, with generations of beloved black faces, in an assortment of shades, watching us, I surrendered into Taylor's arms as if we were in the first days of paradise and I had been made for him by God Himself because it was not right that Taylor should be alone. I felt the damp wool of his suit coat against my cheek, and breathed in the faint scent of his aftershave as it combined with the smoky smells of the wood heater and pipe tobacco. Grampa's and his. I might actually have them both. Bringing Taylor's hand to my lips I kissed the place where I had nursed raw blisters in the early days of his recovery. The palm was hard but smooth now, and I tasted the saltiness of his skin.

Don't leave me.

I won't.

I closed my eyes, recalling his courage, and my own, marveling at the miracle of a lifetime with him.

You make this a happy Christmas.

Mr. Leon would be pleased. *And ye shall know the truth, and the truth shall make you free.* But you had to do more than *know* it, you must also confess it. It had to be heard, said aloud like the names of loved ones who had been lost. Jimmy's solemn soldier picture looked out at us from its frame on Grampa's wall. Things were *different*. For me. For Taylor. For others. For us. I hoped that Jimmy knew this somehow. Would Grampa hang our wedding portrait on the wall too? What would Matilda and Albert make of it, of their descendents being whitened again?

"I can't believe Nathaniel and Connie didn't say anything," I said blissfully cradled in Taylor's arms, as we sat on Grampa's old couch, warmed by the wood heater and happiness. "If as you say, husbands and wives tell each other everything."

"I tend to be careful about creating too many witnesses," Taylor replied easily. "I kept the details to myself."

"Even the ring," I said, gazing at my left hand again.

Aunt Grace would make me get a manicure for the wedding.

"It means a lot to me that you like it," said Taylor tenderly.

"I'll never take it off," I told him.

"You might have to for the ceremony. But we'll figure it out." He chuckled softly. "To tell you the truth, I'm a little surprised you didn't discover it. It was in my desk all the time and you are a bit of a snoop."

Although it was true, I gasped, feigning outrage and pulled away. Laughing merrily he pulled me back into his arms.

"The apartment only has two bedrooms," he continued contentedly. "Zach says one's smaller. We could turn the second bedroom into a study until such time that we needed it for say somebody else, some *little* somebody else."

I smiled at the thought of our baby wrapped up in some very soft, very expensive blanket that Aunt Grace would insist on buying from Bloomingdales.

"I'd like to keep my desk," Taylor added. "You can decide about what else we take."

"The sleigh bed in the buttercup room," I announced immediately, fondly.

"Absolutely," he agreed, kissing my forehead tenderly. "I don't want to sell the house though. I can arrange to lease it again. The bank will handle it."

"Of course," I said. "It's your home."

"*Our* home," he corrected me.

You make this house a home.

"Our home," I repeated.

…My home is with you.

And mine was with him. For a time we were quiet again. A chunk of wood tumbled inside the heater, sending up a small waft of smoke.

"Don't you think it's time we tell your grandfather," suggested Taylor. "I want us to have his blessing."

I sighed, and he kissed my forehead again.

"It may not go as bad as all that," he assured me quietly. "And we will face worse."

You can't b'long in his world.

"You don't know him," I replied.

"Actually I think I know him pretty well," said Taylor. "He just wants what's best for you. We have to show him that that's me."

"Yes, you are," I said kissing his lips softly.

Grampa was a passionate man. Ernestine must have been very happy when he was home. But how he must have missed her too, his dark African queen, raising their children mostly alone, relying on letters to soothe their desires. Then at long last when he could be home again, with her, she had died. In the midst of my own joy I felt Grampa's deprivation keenly. No wonder he expected less out of love. Negro life in America was short on *happy endings*, so you learned to count on the Resurrection. That was when we could have our happy endings. And *ever after*.

I stood up to go to the kitchen, but Taylor, catching my hand in his, held me in front of him.

"I won't say this is the only promise I'll ask of you," he said with a mischievous grin. "But I'll start with this one." He pointed to the dress drying on the hanger. "In the future promise me your black dresses will be made of silk or satin, and for gods-sake a little more flattering. No more widows' weeds."

"Those are my mother's dresses," I informed him, bristling a little.

"That's my point."

The bristle quickly melted into another smile.

"Would you buy me a trousseau then, sir?" I asked primly.

"With pleasure," he smiled broadly.

"I can buy my own trousseau!" I snapped playfully, snatching my hand away. "Consider it my dowry."

"That, my dear," he replied, "Is your family. Now go. Your grandfather's waiting."

Grampa was seated at the kitchen table, a cup of coffee in front of him, the pile of picked pinto beans the same size as I had left it. I tried to hide the happiness in my face when I met his inexpressive hazel eyes.

"Grampa," I began. "Taylor would like...we-we have something to tell you."

"He takin' you to New York," Grampa said.

He must have been listening.

"Yes...uh, yes-sir," I answered.

"He gon' do right by you?"

"He's asked me to marry him, Grampa."

"In a church?"

I nodded. We hadn't talked about it yet but I was confident that Taylor would agree to it. Perhaps Aunt Grace and Uncle Eddie's pastor would marry us.

"You heard everything then?" I asked.

"I wasn't eavesdroppin' if that what you mean," Grampa rejoined sharply. "I been knowin' what he wanted. Just didn't b'lieve he'd do it, that's all. It ain't ev'ry man that's able to handle a woman who's his equal, and face down his own kind to do it. So, he gon' give you his name?"

I nodded and showed Grampa the wedding ring on my finger.

"It belonged to his mother," I said. "He'll buy me a diamond if I want, but this is better. He was very close to his mother."

"You know you gon' have it hard, don't you?" Grampa prophesized. "Look at Lena Horne. And she a movie star."

"And beautiful," I added quietly.

"Folks ain't never gon' take kindly to races mixin'. And you know what yo' babies gon' be."

Yes, they would be like Albert, I thought. And like Grampa. And like Taylor.

"They ain't never gon' be white," Grampa told me.

"They don't need to be," I said. "They'll be ours. Yours too. He wants to be a part of our family, Grampa. We love each other."

Grampa exhaled deeply.

"Guess you old enough to know what that is," he said soberly.

"He wants to ask for your blessing," I added. "It's important to him, Grampa. Me too."

"It ain't gon' make a difference," said Grampa resentfully. "You wearin' his ring. Look like to me it's settled. You always was yo' grandmama's chile."

"It does matter, Grampa," I said earnestly. "How you feel about it, it does matter. To us both. We want your blessing."

"When I think about my own grandmama," he began. "What she--"

"Don't think about her, Grampa," I stopped him. "Remember her. I always do. But don't think about what happened to her. Don't hold her against him. I'm not Matilda, and Taylor's not that man. He will love our children. You know that. He's a good man, Grampa. Please." I came around the table and placed my hand on his hard shoulder. "Please, come talk to him."

Grampa took a drink from coffee cup.

"He's my gentleman caller, Grampa," I continued. "Come to ask you for my hand. Please be happy for me."

I loved them both so much. And I deserved to have them both. I was indeed very worthy.

"Please," I said again.

Beneath my hand Grampa's shoulder relaxed.

"Can't nobody love you more than me," he said. "That man in yond'a, he might love you as much as I do, but he can't love you more."

Looking up into my eyes, Grampa roughly grabbed my hand, squeezing it tightly in his.

"You can give yo'self to 'im, Esther Fay," he continued. "But you gon' always b'long to me."

My hand in his, I realized once again how much alike Grampa and Taylor really were. I belonged to them both, and they both belonged to me. The chair scrapped against the kitchen floor as Grampa, still holding my hand, rose from the table. Without another word he led me by the hand back into the front room.

When Taylor saw us he reached for his cane and came to his feet. "Mr. Green," he said. "You'll always be welcomed in our home. I hope we have your blessing." Grampa was quiet, crushing my hand in his, as the two of them looked at each other. I didn't know what Grampa would say, but I knew it was *settled*. Taylor and I were supposed to be. He would not block it.

"There come a time in a man's life," Grampa finally spoke. "When he got to let go of his babies. There's times the good Lord calls 'em home befo' 'im, but most times they get took away by nature. I done it myself. I took a man's chile. A wise man wants a wife. A good woman needs a husband. That's the way it's s'pose to be. But yet and still when it comes to yo' own babies leavin' you, it ain't easy to let 'em. You'll know what I mean one day when they yours, and somebody you ain't never heard of befo' show up to take 'em away from you. Won't be nothin' you can do 'bout it neither. You might as well know that right now. 'Cause what's s'pose to be gon' be. Can't nobody block it."

Grampa looked at me.

"I raised this chile," he continued. "Her daddy died when she was just a lil' thing. In a lot of ways, I'm closer to her than I was to her mother. I know she love you." He returned his eyes to Taylor. "And I b'lieve you love her. But there's bad blood 'tween our people, and plenty of it. Her great-grandmama ain't had no choice. Nobody give her a pearl necklace. But since this our land too, and we ain't goin' nowhere, seem like we gon' have to live together. Even though yo' people done done our people wrong, and still doin' it.

"I tell you the truth. I don't want you fo' her, but she says you different. Judgin' by what you done here today, maybe you is. And either way, her mind's made up. Yours too. Can't nobody block it. So I'm gon' let her go to you without no mo' fightin' from me. And I'm gon' give you my blessin', for her sake." He looked at me again then back at Taylor. "And 'cause you respected me enough to ask for it. But I give you my word, Taylor Payne, as sho' as I'm standin' here on this day, I will come after you, if you ever do wrong by her."

Grampa crossed the room to Taylor, bringing me with him, and standing before him, he guided me to Taylor's side and let go of my hand.

"You her man, true enough," Grampa told Taylor. "But she still my chile. That ain't never gon' change."

Taylor extended his right hand to Grampa, who accepted it.

"On my honor, Mr. Green," Taylor said with their hands together. "I will cherish her as you do."

The porter hand and the *desk-man* hand joined again, sealing another agreement between gentlemen. *Hatred stirreth up strifes: but love covereth all sins.* It tore down walls. And built bridges. And families.

Grampa nodded, and letting go of Taylor's hand, he went over to the heater and put in another piece of wood. Taylor slipped his arm around my waist, pulling me closer to him. Grampa sat down in his rocking chair, and I gestured to Taylor that we should sit down too, and we returned to the sofa.

"Esther Fay," Grampa instructed me as he lit his pipe. "Send me a weddin' picture soon as you take it. I'll buy the frame for it myself."

Taylor's face would be on Grampa's wall, among the beloved. Europe and Africa had come to this land together. We tried to be apart, but we were inseparable. I thought of Jessica and Andrew over the fireplace. Along with the debonair Jimmy, they would come with us to New York. Jessica would be back in Greenwich Village, and I would be wearing her ring, and raising her grandchildren. I wondered if she had ever played *Aida*.

"We'd be honored if you'd come to the wedding," Taylor said. "You could come with Esther."

"I don't travel no mo', son," replied Grampa. "Done seen enough of segregated train cars in my life. Grace and Eddie'll represent the family just fine," Grampa decided. "Fact 'bout this kind of thing be right up Grace's alley. Hope you got plenty-a money. Esther Fay's anie's got some 'spensive tastes. We didn't raise her that way, but I guess most women just like nice things. 'Course now Esther Fay take after her grandmama, so long as you keep her away from Grace, you'll be all right."

"I was thinking she takes after you," Taylor said.

"My mark is on her," agreed Grampa. "But she got my Ernestine in her blood."

"She must have been a remarkable woman."

"That she was," said Grampa wistfully. "Prettiest smile you ever wanted to see."

I looked up at Ernestine's portrait in the center of the collection.

"But she was hard-headed too," Grampa added. "You wasn't gon' make her do nothin' unless she wanted to."

"Yes," Taylor smiled. "I think I've seen that trait."

"Right sho' you have. This world makes it hard for a colored woman. We got to raise 'em to be strong. You understandin' me?"

"I do," Taylor nodded.

"We don't want anything lavish, Grampa," I said changing the subject back to the wedding. "We'd like it to be simple. More intimate."

"And we want it to be right away," Taylor supplied, winking at me.

"You ain't in the family way, is you?" asked Grampa.

"Grampa!" I cried, embarrassed.

"Wouldn't be the first time somethin' like that happened," said Grampa casually. "And there's worse things."

Taylor chuckled.

"You're absolutely right," he agreed. "On both counts."

"Esther Fay's built like her grandmama too, so I 'spect you gon' have a lot of babies. 'Course y'all is startin' out kind-a late. If I could-a been home more we'd-a had us a flock."

"Grampa, please," I begged mortified by the new turn of the conversation, although I was happy too, and still barely able to believe it.

"I'm lookin' forward to it," Taylor said easily. "I want a big family."

Now Grampa laughed lightly.

"Well-well, Esther Fay, don't look like you gon' be havin' a lot of time to be teachin' other folks chirren if you raisin' a bunch of yo' own."

"Please can we talk about something else," I pleaded.

"You know you gon' have to bring my great-grand babies back to Dixie for me to see 'em."

"We will do that, Mr. Green," replied Taylor. "Rest assured."

"Esther Fay, what yo' Uncle Eddie call me?"

"Oh...uh-uh, Papa Isaac, I think," I answered.

"That all right with you, Taylor?" Grampa asked.

Taylor and I glanced at each other.

"Yes, yes-sir," he replied.

"Hmm," Grampa said reflectively. "'Yes-sir' from a white man...Well, once you give Esther Fay yo' name, you be entitled to call me Papa Isaac too. We don't stand on formality in this family."

V

The weather was fair on Christmas Eve. I woke up to bright morning sunshine pouring through the window, as Taylor slept soundly next to me. It would be like this always I reminded myself again, his strong form beside me every morning for a lifetime. Perhaps there was a baby inside of me right now, conceived like its father, in love, and just ahead of the wedding.

...*She got my Ernestine in her blood.*

And Grampa's *mark* was on me. Yet the ring fit, and a tiny castle in a big city awaited us. The dark-skinned Cinderella had her prince. The lord of the manor had made the maid his lady. And perhaps I was a princess in the first place, a revised version of Pocahontas, because my grandfather was indeed a warrior king. And I would spend my life with John Smith.

You her man, true enough. But she still my chile.

There was much left to do and Taylor was leaving for New York by the end of the week, taking Herman with him. He had arranged for the movers to come the Friday after Christmas, the day he was to leave. Although I was staying behind until the end of January to spend time with Grampa and the rest of the family, and to help Doctor Mitchell settle things with the house, Taylor had already purchased my train ticket too. With so many miles to cover in the wilderness that was the South, it was just easier to travel separately by plan because it was required by law anyway. Such awkward, difficult situations would come often enough for us, and even in the Promise Land, so why plunge into them immediately?   In Taylor's study there were packing crates everywhere, but in the living room Christmas still reigned supreme. We would pack-up the living room and the kitchen last. Because it was too hard to gauge what would fit in the apartment sight unseen, we had decided to leave much of the furniture behind in the house. Some new tenant would be very pleased. Once I arrived in New York, then we would be shopping for new furnishings. Aunt Grace couldn't imagine that Taylor would even be interested in doing such a task himself with me. Perhaps she had been living in New York so long that she had forgotten what McConnell County was like, why Grampa and Mama had sent Jimmy to them in the first place, and why Taylor and I would want to relish every moment together.

I stirred finally, doing my best to ease out of bed.

"Why so early?" my fiancé asked, encircling my waist with his arm to pull me back to him.

Smiling, I kissed him good morning.

"We're giving a party, remember," I answered.

"In the evening," Taylor reminded me.

"Which'll come sooner than you think."

"What I think is that you fret too much."

"You would," I chuckled and got out of the bed.

The room was freezing and I searched quickly for my robe in the bed linens.

"I can't help it if I like to sleep in," said Taylor.

"Seems to me you're always wide awake," I replied.

He stretched and grinned lazily.

"Well there's sleeping together and *sleeping* together," he admitted.

I laughed again.

"Come on Herman," I called to the dog. "I'll give you a treat."

"What about me?" asked Taylor.

"I'll be back."

"Promise?"

"For the rest of my life," I smiled at him again.

"I'll hold you to that," I heard him say as I left the room with Herman ahead of me.

Before lighting the gas heaters downstairs, I opened the front door and let Herman go outside. He bounded down the porch steps and raced out onto the brown lawn, where the frost was melting in the sunshine. Herman would surely miss the his wide open spaces to prowl and probe, but there were parks in the city, and we would take him for walks all the time. I supposed I would miss the wide open spaces myself, the horizon that seemed endless when you looked across a field. But there was a lovely vastness in Taylor's dark brown eyes, a wideness in the life that we would make together. So what if our trees were all clumped together in parks, and our potted flowers had to search for sunshine around the shadows of tall buildings? We would be happy, together, and home.

In the living room I plugged in the cord for the Christmas tree lights and paused for a moment to enjoy their twinkling, while I warmed myself backed up to the lit gas heater. I supposed I'd be missing the Dearborn heaters too since New York apartments were usually heated by furnaces or radiators. But there would be Christmas-decorated store windows and snow, and cozy coffee houses and museums, and concerts and plays, and Taylor.

Who would be wondering where I was by now, and so I hurried to the kitchen to make coffee for us. At the sink, while I was filling the percolator with water, I looked out the window and saw Mr. Leon standing near the wood pile. Herman was with him. I was surprised that Mr. Leon would be here at this hour, and I hadn't heard his truck or Herman barking. I set the pot on the counter and hurried out on the back porch. Grabbing Taylor's work jacket I slipped it on and went outside to say hello.

"Mr. Leon," I called to him happily. "Good morning! I didn't know you were coming today."

"Good morning yo' self, miss lady!" he returned. "How you doin'?"

"Very well. You?"

"It's a good mornin', just like you say."

"And you're sure up and at 'em awfully early."

"Well," he chuckled pleasantly. "I was in the neighborhood and thought I'd stop by and see how you folks was fixed for wood. See you got plenty."

Which we would be leaving behind for the new tenants too.

"We're moving—I mean...Taylor—Mr. Payne is moving back to New York."

And my name was going to be *Mrs. Payne*.

"Say you is," replied Mr. Leon. "When y'all leavin'?"

"Very soon. He leaves the Friday after Christmas."

Mr. Leon nodded his head as if he approved of the news.

"We're getting married, Mr. Leon," I said.

The old man smiled broadly.

"He gave me his mother's ring," I added, holding out my hand for him to see.

Mr. Leon nodded his head again, and his eyes twinkled like the lights on the tree in the living room.

"A good nature runs in a family," he said.

"Yes it does," I agreed.

"Well," declared Mr. Leon. "Guess y'all got plenty-a wood then."

"Don't you want to come in?" I asked almost urgently. "I-I was about to make coffee. And I know Taylor would be glad to see you."

"Naw," replied Mr. Leon. "I best be gettin' on. Them's that's wakin' up in cold houses be lookin' for me."

Unexpectedly my eyes brimmed with tears.

"You don't want to say goodbye to him, Mr. Leon?" I asked, more for myself because I didn't want him to go.

"Goodbyes don't really suit me," replied Mr. Leon, and then he smiled. "Him neither."

No, they didn't. And now we had a lifetime of not needing them between us. Only this meant others had to be said, even though I was the happiest I had ever been. Emotions of all kinds jumbled and tumbled inside of me.

"I'll miss you," I said to Mr. Leon.

Another smiled filled his face.

"You better get on back in the house and make yo' man his coffee," he advised. "If he like me, he wants it first thing."

I nodded obediently but didn't move. Mr. Leon climbed into his truck, and Herman came to me and sat quietly.

"Go on now," said Mr. Leon as the engine in the truck turned over. "It's cold out here and you ain't got no shoes on."

"Merry Christmas, Mr. Leon," I said.

"You make it a happy one," he said as he drove away.

Early in the afternoon, Spencer, who was out of school for the holidays arrived, and Taylor put him to work helping him pack up the library. Taylor was assured of a decent office at *Reuben, Fellows & Goldman*, so most of his law books could go there, but still we would have to find space for the other collections that would undoubtedly grow with time. Maybe I could persuade him to donate some of the books to the colored school. These were the kinds of issues that newlyweds had to face all the time, I imagined, the merging of possessions and lives. How very normal it was.

It was also normal for Spencer to be sad to see his friend move away, and Taylor was his friend. I was too. And we were all a little sad. Leaving wasn't easy, even when you were leaving together. Still, I was looking forward to the party tonight, and I wanted Spencer to do so too. Santa Claus was going to be good to them all this year. Nathaniel and Connie and their children were coming. Santa Claus was going to be good to all of us.

Mandy hadn't heard anything from Danny, not that she was expecting to, and not that I had a right to know if she did. I wanted him to be happy. I just wasn't *suited* to him.

"He's a good man," I had told Mandy about her cousin as I had recounted for her the day of Taylor's proposal at Grampa's house.

"Taylor too," she had replied not missing a beat.

She had always been Taylor's champion and now that he was going to marry me, it was as if she had been vindicated. She was frankly proud.

"You had to do the right thing, Esther Fay," she had said. "For yo'self and the both of them too."

"Grampa always says what's supposed to be will be," I had replied. "Can't nobody block it."

"You almost did," my friend had charged.

What a foolish man Willie Gains was. Mandy was the *virtuous woman*.

After lunch, and with the Christmas cookies all baked and cooling on the counter, for a treat I made hot cocoa for Spencer and Taylor and carried it on a tray to the study.

"How come you can't stay here?" I heard Spencer asking Taylor.

Neither of them was aware of me standing in the doorway. Standing on the step ladder to reach the higher shelves, Spencer was handing down books to Taylor, who seated in a chair, was placing them in a crate.

"It's complicated," Taylor tentatively answered Spencer.

I nearly intervened, or at the least announced myself, but then I stopped and kept silent. One day Taylor would have to explain to our own children this *why*. He might as well get used to it. He would be raising Negro children.

"Remember what we talked about when you were writing the essay about Thurgood Marshall?" Taylor continued, looking up at Spencer."

Spencer nodded.

"It has something to do with that," Taylor said.

"'Cause they won't let Aunt Esther teach in a white school?" the boy asked.

"Because they made laws that keep people apart, Spencer," explained Taylor. "The laws in Texas won't let your Aunt Esther and I marry."

"'Cause she colored?"

"Because I'm white."

"But it's all right in New York?"

"Yes. It's legal."

"But how come it ain't legal here then? Ain't this all one country?"

"It is, Spence," Taylor told him. "You're right. They're bad laws, like we talked about. They're wrong. We have to change them."

"And you can do that?" Spencer wanted to know. "From all the way in New York City?"

"I can try," Taylor told him. "I will try."

Spencer shook his head.

"It's ain't—I mean not fair, Mr. Payne," he said and took down another book to hand to Taylor. "You ought to be able to live in yo' own house, you and Aunt Esther. What po' Herman gon' do? He won't have no place to play."

"No, it's not fair," agreed Taylor taking the book.

The cocoa was getting cold. I came into the room.

"You'll come to see us, Spencer," Taylor said. "Every summer if you like. We'll take Herman to the park. And we'll go see the Dodgers play."

"Jackie Robinson?" Spencer now asked more brightly.

"Jackie Robinson," replied Taylor.

"What's all this about the Dodgers?" I asked finally drawing their attention to me.

"Aunt Esther," answered Spencer excitedly. "Mr. Payne say he'll take me to see Jackie Robinson if I come see you this summer."

"I see," I said, passing one cup of cocoa to Taylor while Spencer climbed down from the ladder to get his. "Just so long as Aunt Grace and I get to take you to the theater too."

"The movies?!" exclaimed Spencer. "With John Wayne? And we can get popcorn?"

Amused, Taylor sipped his cocoa.

"That too," he said, knowing that that was not what I had meant at all.

But yes, I thought, *that too*. Jackie Robinson and John Wayne, all of it was America, and Spencer was an American boy. It was good to be able to know it. Jimmy would have been proud.

"Mr. Payne, you think Jackie Robinson would sign my baseball card?" asked Spencer.

"I don't see why not," Taylor assured him. "We'll make it our mission."

"This summer?" Spencer demanded eagerly.

Taylor and I smiled at each other realizing that we were now planning for our first house guest, assuming Mandy gave her approval.

"You bet," said Taylor. "With your mother's permission of course."

"Oh boy!" exclaimed Spencer. "Jackie Robinson!"

I wondered what he was most thrilled about: spending time with Taylor or getting Jackie Robinson's autograph. Perhaps it was just a wonderful combination of both. I pictured the two of them together, and maybe Uncle Eddie with them. Relishing the idea of it, I touched my left thumb to the gold band on my ring finger that proved again it wasn't a dream.

"Aunt Esther, you'll ask Mama for me, won't you?" Spencer was pressing. "She'll say yes if you ask her."

"Okay," I agreed. "But it all depends now, on you keepin' your grades up. I don't want to hear any bad reports."

"Yes ma'am, I will," vowed Spencer. "I promise."

"I've been thinking, Spence," said Taylor. "If Esther's your *Aunt* Esther then by right I should be your *Uncle* Taylor."

"I can call you Uncle Taylor?" asked Spencer, his eyes wide.

"Yes," replied Taylor. "I'd like that very much. If it's okay with you."

For the second time today my eyes filled.

"John Henry and my sisters too?" Spencer wanted to know.

Taylor smiled.

"Everybody," he replied, winking at me. "We don't stand on formality in this family."

By dusk Jessica and Andrew were looking down upon a room full of faces mostly unlike their own except that they were happy. Laughter reverberated around the room. Colorful wrapping paper and toys were scattered around the floor. Mr. Leon's Christmas tree sparkled, and the radio broadcast competed with the children singing Christmas carols led by Connie. Perched on the arm of the Queen Anne chair where Taylor was sitting, I clapped to time as the children and Connie were merrily singing *Rudolph The Red-Nosed Reindeer*, drowning out the radio. Even Little Evie was trying to sing along.

"Come on, Esther," Nathaniel said. "You sing too."

"Yes, sweetheart, sing," Taylor urged.

"I can't sing that high," I demurred.

"It's Gene Autry," countered Nathaniel. "You mean to tell me you can't sing with a cowboy?"

"Yes, Esther, I think it's in your range," teased Taylor.

"Come on, Esther," Mandy came to my rescue. "Let's show 'em what we can do."

Soon we were all singing uproariously, including Nathaniel and Taylor in their base voices, and Herman was even barking, so that the radio couldn't be heard at all.

You make this a happy Christmas.

When the song was over, Mandy told the children to collect the discarded wrapping paper off the floor.

"Look like a tornado come through here," she fussed.

"They's still some mo' presents under the tree!" Mildred announced.

Nancy, stuffing paper under one arm, hurried to see whose they were.

"They don't b'long to y'all, sholey God," said Mandy. "Let 'em alone."

"This one here got Aunt Esther's name on it," Nancy said reading the label on a small wrapped box tucked in the Christmas tree branches. "It's from Mister—I mean Uncle Taylor."

Mildred handed her sister another box from under the tree, and Nancy dropped the paper to take it.

"And this one says Uncle Taylor's name, and it's from Aunt Esther," she informed us.

Spencer came over and took the presents from his sister.

"They savin' 'em for tomorrow mornin'," he spoke with authority as he returned the boxes to their respective places. "Now leave 'em alone."

The adults smiled at each other. Spencer was such a big brother. His sisters were in awe of him and a little afraid of him too. I pictured lots of summers with all of Mandy's children with us, perhaps even Mandy herself.

"That's right," agreed Nathaniel chuckling. "Even grown folk like to have a little Sandi-Clause on Christmas mornin'."

And I could sign the inscription in Taylor's Bible. He would record our wedding date there. And it would be almost like Jimmy was walking me down the aisle, because after all in a real way he had brought me to him in the first place.

...*We're changing the world*...

When Mandy and I were in the kitchen later heating up more apple cider, she admonished me for spending so much money on her children.

"All them presents for the chirren," she fussed. "It's too much."

"We were buying separately this year," I reminded her with a grin. "Next year'll be different."

The warm aroma of cinnamon and cloves began to fill the kitchen.

"Y'all ain't been *sep'rate* for a long time," Mandy laughed.

"I guess not," I confessed. "I'm glad you're gonna let Spencer visit us," I added almost changing the subject. "It means a lot to them both."

"What choice do I have 'tween the three of you?" demanded Mandy her hands on her hips. "That boy-a mine crazy 'bout his Mister—I mean *Uncle* Taylor."

"I guess I just didn't realize how close they'd become."

"I knowed all along," declared Mandy. "Yo' mister is a very lovable man, Esther Fay."

"He is, isn't he?" I smiled.

"'Course you not so bad yo'self."

"The Bible calls that being equally yoked," said Connie who had appeared in the kitchen with a tray of empty cups.

"Nobody else would," I said.

"Nobody else matters," she reminded me.

How was it that everybody but me seemed to have learned this? They had figured it out all around me, even Grampa, and in spite of me. Replaying their constant conversations, the hosts of words and expressions, I was embarrassed by my own protests and arguments. To every purpose under Heaven there was a season, and sometimes more than one.

Bearing replenished trays of cookies and apple cider, Connie, Mandy, and I returned to the gathering just in time to see Nathaniel ushering Doctor Mitchell and Mrs. Mitchell into the living room. Taylor must have invited them, but I was astounded to see them. But why shouldn't he? Our worlds had to come together, and like Mandy said, we had not been *separate* for a long time.

"Merry Christmas, Mrs. Mitchell, Mitch," said Taylor, standing to greet the Mitchells as they came in.

"Merry Christmas, Taylor," replied Mrs. Mitchell walking up to him and offering her hand.

"Merry Christmas," added her husband, nodding somewhat stiffly to the rest of us.

"Merry Christmas," returned a chorus of voices, some now a little less certain of the *merry* than others.

"Mrs. Mitchell," Taylor said holding out his hand to me indicating that I should come to him. "You remember Esther."

Setting down the plate of cookies I moved to stand beside him.

"Yes-yes of course," Mrs. Mitchell said, mustering a smile that grew warmer as we were shaking hands. "Charles tells me that congratulations are in order. We-we hope you'll be very happy."

"Thank-you, Mrs. Mitchell," I replied, feeling Taylor's arm lightly around my waist.

"Uhm... we brought you... a little gift," Mrs. Mitchell continued, looking around awkwardly before Doctor Mitchell handed her a package wrapped in white paper with a gold bow. She passed it to me. "It-it's a...Christmas... wedding present."

"Thank-you, ma'am," I replied.

"I hope you like it," she said more calmly. "I-I know it's probably not as fancy as what you'll find in-in New York City, but maybe it-it'll remind you of home."

"Go ahead, darling," Taylor said. "Open it."

My cheeks flushed hotly at the word *darling* with all the eyes watching me.

"Uhn-uhn!" protested Mildred. "You gotta wait 'til in the mornin' fo'--"

Mandy, in a mother's flash had reached her youngest daughter and clamped her hand over her mouth. The room filled with laughter.

"It's a wedding present, sweetie," Taylor assured Mildred. "It's okay if Aunt Esther opens it now."

The package contained a fine damask tablecloth. I looked up at Mrs. Mitchell. Her smile was finally more confident and she was looking pleased.

"You like it?" she asked.

"Yes ma'am," I said. "Thank-you."

She placed her hand on my arm, holding me fast in her blue eyes.

"Taylor is like a son to us," she told me. "If he's happy, that's all that really matters."

We were a long way from the dinner party last December, and yet maybe we weren't. A year ago the rules and rituals had seemed an indisputable reality, but now what was also real was this room full of Christmas spirit and smiling faces that came in multiple shades of life, young and old, and colored and white.

"You're a lucky man, Taylor," Doctor Mitchell said. "They don't come any finer than Esther."

"I know that, Mitch," replied Taylor. "I appreciate you saying it."

"Esther," Doctor Mitchell turned to me. "I expect to get some personal use out of that tablecloth."

He grinned at me.

"That's right," chimed in Mrs. Mitchell. "He's promised to take me to New York. You'll have to show me how to make those stuffed mushrooms of yours."

I smiled. Still more guests. Our home would be inviting, *a happy house.*

"I look forward to it, Mrs. Mitchell," I replied.

"Connie," said Nathaniel. "Pass around that cider 'fo' it get cold!"

Quickly Connie stepped forward offering full cups to the Mitchells and Nathaniel, before turning to Taylor and me, and then to everyone else.

"Esther made this up too, Mis' Mitchell," bragged Nathaniel. "It'll warm you up, and it's even now fit for a good Baptist."

"And chirren too," added Mandy.

Everyone laughed again. Nathaniel raised his cup.

"Seem like to me we ought-a say somethin' to the happy couple," he suggested.

"Hear-hear!" agreed Doctor Mitchell.

"Allow me," said Taylor meeting my eyes with his and raising his cup.

He was fond of making toasts, I remembered, and I beamed at him, wondering what nice thing he would decide to say.

"'Thou hast ravished my heart, my sister, my spouse,'" he began reciting a verse from the *Song of Solomon.* "'Thou hast ravished my heart with one of thine eyes, with one chain of thy neck. How fair is thy love, my sister, my spouse. How much better is thy love than wine, and the smell of thine ointments, than all the spices.'"

My eyes seeing only him filled and spilled tears. The room was quiet, except for Pearl Bailey's voice on the radio singing about how she really couldn't stay even though it was cold outside.

"I love you," I said.

"That's the Bible," Nathaniel declared.

"Amen," said Connie.

Comment from the Author...

The author would enjoying hearing from you. Please contact her at jgarner869@gmail.com.

Made in the USA
San Bernardino, CA
10 June 2016